And When Forever Comes

And When Forever Comes

a novel

James Edison

ISBN: 978-1-7338463-1-8

www.andwhenforevercomes.com

james@andwhenforevercomes.com

For Chris

Part 1

Part 2

Part 3

Note to the Reader

The story that follows is a work of fiction. It is not a memoir. It is not autobiographical in any way. Nothing I write about here has actually occurred and no character is intended to portray, wholly or in part, any real person, living or deceased. Newton Falls is not a real town and is not intended to refer to the town of Newton, New Jersey. However, with a little research and a lot of forgiveness for artistic license, you might be able to find Nick and Jeremy's rock.

This is a story about child abuse. If you've suffered abuse in your past, please proceed with caution and be aware certain incidents may trigger memories or strong emotions. I am in no way suggesting in these pages that the abuse of a child, whether physical, sexual, or emotional, is in any way acceptable. If you feel you are in danger of abusing a child in any way, please seek help. When you read, I'm asking you to keep an open mind, avoiding simple black and white interpretations of complicated situations and emotions.

Each chapter takes place within a single day. The dates for each chapter are important to understand time and place as well as how much time has passed since a previous chapter – so please take note. They will help point the way if you find yourself lost.

If you care for a child, whether your own or someone else's, love him or her without limits until forever comes.

J. E.

Part 1

Chapter 1

August 11, 2006

I drove into the parking deck and pulled into my very own personal spot. For some unfathomable reason, the architect had placed two concrete walls in the far corner of the roof just far enough apart to park a car and just tall enough to hide it. I couldn't hazard a guess as to his original intention, but I could certainly appreciate the result: a private, secret space that suited me perfectly. As far as I knew, no one else was aware of its existence, because I never arrived to find some asshole disturbing the rightful order of things. After two years of parking there every day, squatter's rights and natural law dictated it belonged to me. I considered making a sign like the executives had on their personal spots right outside the building entrance, threatening death and dismemberment to anyone who dared trespass.

The sun shone in a bright and friendly way like it was smiling inanely in a child's painting, and the air was clean and fresh without a hint of the oppressive humidity that defined northern Virginia summers. The elevator beeped cheerfully the instant I pressed the button, waiting patiently just for me and taking me straight to the ground floor without bothering to stop for anyone else. I even got to make some egotistical dickhead in a Beamer slam on his brakes when I crossed the street. I would've been convinced the universe approved of my plan for the day if I still believed in that sort of crap.

A blast of frigid air greeted me when I entered the office – probably unnecessary on such a perfect day, but still welcome. The short trip from the parking deck left me overheated and sweaty like it always did.

I went straight across the empty lobby to the restroom no one ever used. Anyone looking would assume I was taking a minute to freshen up. After yanking out half the contents of the paper towel dispenser to wipe my face dry, I turned my back to the mirror and fished out two cans of soda and four assorted king-sized candy bars from my briefcase. A dry paper towel became an impromptu bib, because chocolate and soda stains on my shirt would be a dead giveaway. Lately, I never made it all the way through a day without dribbling something on myself. The buttons on my shirt bulged and the waistband of my pants chafed as I struggled to find a comfortable position leaning against the counter. If I dared step on a scale, it'd probably reveal I left three hundred pounds behind a long time ago. I forced a flavorless candy bar down with swigs from the soda can, the combination summoning images of moldy socks. Didn't stop me from polishing it off and immediately tearing open the second. Enjoyment had nothing to do with this. Somewhere in my head, I knew I was no different than a common alcoholic stealing drinks from cleverly stashed bottles. Knowing didn't ease my compulsion to eat and my need for secrecy while I did. If no one saw me, it never happened. No one to witness big fat Nick stuffing his big fat face, whisper behind his back, or flash him looks of recrimination.

The junk devoured and the evidence artfully buried under mounds of damp paper towels, I resigned myself to starting my work day. 11:43 by the clock in the lobby, but I wasn't concerned. No one would begrudge me being later than my usual lateness today. Anyone of importance would be leaving right after lunch. Making my appearance would evoke just the right kind of sympathy – poor, hard-working Nick stuck in the office on the only glorious Friday afternoon summer had to offer.

The elevator opened on the sixth floor into a small foyer. The door to the left was my best choice for slipping in and out without being seen, only a few steps from my home sweet cube. Instead, I chose the main entrance, giving me an excuse to walk a nearly complete circuit of the floor. My pace quickened to a purposeful stride oozing the impression I was a person with important things to do. Can't stop, too busy, only time for a hello and a wave.

"Hey Welles, how do I get your job drifting in here at noon?"

Nobody liked Dave, so I wasn't worried he'd attract the wrong kind of attention. I backed up and spoke louder than necessary. "Take a guess which self-important moron scheduled a client call for eight o'clock tonight?"

"Sucks to be you," he said without a shred of real sympathy. He was too wrapped up in his own world to worry about mine, but I felt the same way about his. "Got a minute? I want to run some ideas by you."

Under normal circumstances, I would've jumped at the opportunity. Dave was an easy way to waste an hour or two. All I had to do was nod my head occasionally while he spouted random nonsense. His idea four years ago launched the most successful product the company had ever seen, but since then everything he touched ended in disaster. Some people might be mystified why he still had a job, but I learned a long time ago that keeping a job had nothing to do with competence. The drawback to humoring him was that he deluded himself into thinking I was his friend, which meant regular unwanted lunch and after-work drink invitations. No time for Dave today. I intended to be in the office for an hour, tops.

"Wish I could, but I'm slammed," I said. "Estimates are due next week. How about Monday? We can have lunch."

"Monday works," he said, visibly disappointed. "Let me know if you free up later. It'll only take a minute."

"Will do." I faked a warm smile and waved as I left. Onto my next stop, the executive hallway. "Good morning, Lucy. How are you today?" My pace didn't slow and I kept my distance from her desk. The idea of exchanging a few words with her was distasteful at best, but she was a necessary evil. Swinging by Lucy's desk helped establish my presence for the day. Everything she saw and heard was reported directly to Fearless Leader Crenshaw (I'd never heard his first name and suspected he didn't have one), a man widely known as a cruel and heartless tyrant. He'd only spoken to me twice in the last two years, which I considered to be an achievement worthy of top ratings on my performance review and a plaque at the all-hands meeting.

She looked up from her gossip magazine, temporarily stunned. "Mr. Welles," she called after me. "Mr. Crenshaw was looking for you earlier."

5

I stopped in my tracks, hiding my uncomfortable surprise. "I'm sorry, I was on a call. There's nothing on my calendar. Was there some kind of mix-up?"

"No, nothing like that." Her tone of voice made my skin crawl. "He'll be free in ten minutes."

"Of course," I said with a crisp nod. She went back to her magazine, and I went back to my walk. Unexpected, but I told myself I had no reason to be concerned. No matter what he wanted to know, I was well prepared with all my facts and figures in nice neat rows.

My cube was exactly the way I left it: jacket over my chair, an extra briefcase stuffed with trade magazines on the desk, laptop open to a screensaver that never went blank, and the desk lamp burning. Anyone who walked by would assume I'd stepped out for a minute to get coffee or use the restroom. I logged in, my master spreadsheet appearing on the screen. It featured endless rows and columns of data, comments artistically strewn throughout, splashes of color, and clever little macros. All who saw it fell hopelessly under its spell, utterly convinced its creator brought limitless depth and dedication to his job.

The truth? It was utter nonsense. Pure fiction.

In the fourteen years since I'd graduated college, I'd been employed at eight different companies in twelve different roles. This place was far and away my favorite. I was hired to rein in a remote development team and turn their barely functional junk into a workable product. At first, the team wanted nothing to do with me, leaving me alone in an empty office for three days when I tried to visit. But I was persistent, and before long we came to a mutually beneficial arrangement. Their job was to sing my praises to management, and my job was to leave them alone. I'd built an entire career by faking my way through jobs, skills honed to perfection by years of tireless practice. People never noticed the details, they only noticed how they added up to a predictable whole. The purposeful stride, a few late nights, well-placed off-handed comments about work-life balance and off-hours conference calls – all precisely engineered to create the illusion I was a weary workaholic. Not that it was very challenging to maintain appearances at this place – no one even pretended to pay attention. My boss was so busy elsewhere he'd expertly

managed to avoid learning my name. I couldn't imagine a job that suited me better.

Five minutes later, Lucy was waving me into Crenshaw's unapologetically ostentatious office, outfitted with expensive furniture, a huge flat-screen TV always tuned to ESPN, and a large conference table where my boss was shifting uncomfortably in his seat. Still no cause for alarm. I'd heard Crenshaw was trying to soften his image, so it was probably my turn. I sat next to my boss, confidently opening my portfolio and clicking the top of my pen. Crenshaw didn't join us, comfortable behind his desk and monitor. He didn't even bother to look up when he spoke.

"I've decided to terminate the Vidbase project. The company is going through a lean period so we don't have any openings for the team in other groups. Your position has been eliminated."

I clicked the top of my pen again. No need to pretend to take notes.

"You'll receive the standard two-week severance package when you complete your exit agreement. Any questions?"

I made a face as though I was considering my response carefully. "No, I'm ok."

"Good luck in your future endeavors," Crenshaw said mechanically, already typing his next email. I glanced at my boss, who tried to summon up a rehearsed look of sympathy. He was so bad at it I nearly laughed out loud.

"Thank you," I said in a businesslike manner.

I walked past Lucy, the look on her face making it obvious she already knew why I'd been summoned. An empty box had already been placed on my desk by the time I got back. I should've known I'd lingered here too long. I'd always been smart enough to see it coming early enough to jump ship, but I'd let myself become complacent, drunk on a job too good to be true. I never brought any personal things to the office, so it only took a minute to pack. My master spreadsheet glowed on the screen. I wondered how long it would take them to figure out it was a fake, but I already knew no one would bother to give it a second glance. By this afternoon, the laptop would be wiped out and given to the next person, just like the cube. And that's the way it should be — every trace I was here obliterated without hesitation or remorse. As

though the last two years had never happened. I left without a word to anyone, skipping my exit interview. My approach to the workplace: leave no impression behind and let none be left on me.

By half past twelve I was in my car headed for home, feeling absolutely nothing.

I slammed on the brakes and horn simultaneously. "Open your fucking eyes!" I screamed.

Yet another spoiled rich bitch in her overpriced luxury car, probably on her way to get her nails done for the third time this week. I swerved in front of her, taking my revenge by forcing her to slam on her brakes. "Learn how to drive!" I hollered, glaring at her through the rear-view mirror. Rush hour was hard to tolerate, but at least people *wanted* to get home. Traffic like this reminded me of marshmallow fluff – it never went where you wanted and refused to budge when it got stuck. Frustration threatened to send me over the edge into real psychosis, giving into the belief these women were actively coordinating their efforts by cell phone. *Let's drive side by side ten miles under the limit and come to a screeching halt at the yellow light just to annoy that guy.* My knuckles were white from trying to rip the steering wheel clean out of the dashboard.

I let my phone ring three times before answering, for appearances. "Hello?" I barked, letting too much annoyance show.

"It's me," Julia said. "I'm still at the conference."

I softened my tone. "Not again. I thought you were already on your way home."

"They needed me to run a presentation this afternoon and attend a client dinner tonight. I won't be able to catch a flight until tomorrow morning." My wife never managed to catch her Friday afternoon flights. The conference ran over, the client needed her, or a crisis demanded her attention. Her time at home each weekend was counted in hours. She'd never learned how to stand up for herself, so naturally her boss walked all over her.

"Whatever you need to do," I said, letting her off the hook.

"I was supposed to take Jake for new school clothes tomorrow. Why don't you take him instead? He's eager to go. I think he's finally starting to care about what he wears. I'm sure you guys will have fun getting in some father-son time."

"I don't know anything about clothes," I said. "I'd be in his way. Besides, I'm not feeling well."

She didn't skip a beat. "Don't worry about it, I'll take him next weekend. I'm already late for my presentation. Love you."

"Bye." I hung up the phone. Better she wasn't coming home. I'd be free to have an exciting evening of mindless television and endless snack foods all by myself. I called the house to make sure Jake wasn't around, the answering machine telling me what I wanted to hear. I had no idea where he was or when he'd be back, but it didn't bother me enough to check in with him. After all, he was twelve, old enough to take care of himself.

I was putting bags of grocery store loot on the kitchen counter when the dog barked urgently. *Upstairs.* Baxter never went upstairs anymore. He was a trooper, but like so many golden retrievers of an advanced age, hip problems left him barely able to walk. Soon he wouldn't be able to stand. I knew I should spend some time with him before it was too late. Just not today. Maybe tomorrow. I got a bone-shaped cookie from the doghouse shaped jar and took it to the foot of the stairs. Baxter stood at the top, panting. "Yummy cookie," I offered. He barked directly at me, loud and insistent. I almost thought he looked vicious, even though he was incapable of harming anyone. We stared at each other, neither willing to endure the stairs.

Until a muffled bang reverberated throughout the house. The cookie joined my stomach on the floor. Baxter turned in place, agitated. The banging became as regular as a drum beat. He limped down the hall, barking incessantly. I frowned, shaking my head at being so easily startled. Jake was home after all, doing whatever kids did when they were home alone. Probably jumping on the bed.

"Jake! Whatever the hell you're doing, cut it out!"

The banging noise continued and Baxter kept barking. "For crying out loud," I muttered, trudging up the stairs. The banging sped up to match my pounding heartbeat. Something shattered with a loud crash.

Baxter's barking became even more urgent. I threw Jake's door open. "So help me, I'm going to ground you for a. . ."

The rest of my threat crawled back into my mouth, the image in front of me beyond my ability to comprehend. I could only process it by breaking it into small pieces.

The banging noise came from the headboard slamming rhythmically into the wall.

Drywall dust billowed out of cavernous holes that grew bigger each time the headboard crashed.

A heap of blankets and pillows were on the floor.

The lamp from the nightstand was in fragments on top of the blankets.

Jake was lying on the bed face down, flailing wildly.

His hands were tied with rope to each side of the headboard.

His feet were tied with more rope to the other end of the bed.

His head was wrapped in duct tape.

He was naked.

I felt dizzy, trying to catch my balance as the room spun like one of those striped tubes in a fun house (which seemed strange because I had no idea how it was possible for a room to spin like that). The banging became dull and hollow, echoing from a great distance. I wondered how Baxter could be right next to me and sound like he was somewhere in Maryland. It also occurred to me I had no idea how to fix drywall holes that big.

A single bark rang through loud and clear, and just like that I was sucked back into myself, sweaty and shaky, heart pounding, clutching the door frame. Jake's thrashing became even more violent. I realized he was having trouble breathing.

Something inside me snapped into action without the need to think it through first. I grabbed the convenient scissors on his nightstand. "Hold still," I ordered, holding his head, looking for a place to cut through the tape fused to his face. He desperately tried to suck air through his stuffed nose, the only part of his face still visible. I shoved the scissors behind his ear, worried I'd cut part of it off, but there was no time to be careful. The scissors gnawed through the tape until it split apart. I ripped it brutally from his skin. It must've hurt, but he didn't

flinch. He wheezed, some kind of fabric jammed in his mouth. I yanked it out. A dirty sock soaked with spit. He gulped deep breaths while I held his head up.

"Hand," he croaked.

At least a dozen loops of rope were wrapped snugly but comfortably around his left wrist, but his right hand was another story – the rope so tight his hand was purple and swollen from lack of circulation. I leaned over him to saw the rope free from the bed, unwinding it from his icy hand.

"Can you feel anything?" I asked.

"Tingly," he gasped. "Sore." I hoped the rope hadn't done any permanent damage, but I had no idea how to tell. I rubbed his hand hard enough to peel the skin off, fighting off visions of amputations.

"Please let me out," he asked, shaking. I was going to tell him I needed to get his blood flowing first, but I let my eyes wander away from his hand for a tiny moment. I started shaking as well, acutely aware of his nude body obscenely on display. Covering every inch of him with the blanket had to be my immediate priority. It didn't help, the image burned into my mind. The need to flee his room was overwhelming. It took every shred of willpower I had to cut the rest of the ropes loose. I shoved the scissors into his hand.

"You take it from here," I muttered.

"I thought I was going to die!" he moaned. "Some guy broke into the house when I was in the shower. He made me lie down on the bed and tied me up and the tape and I thought. . ."

"Everything's fine now," I interrupted, sounding as unconvincing as his story. He pulled at the tape covering his eyes, rope dangling from his wrist. Frayed and well-used.

The closed door behind me wasn't enough of a barrier. Locking myself in my room wasn't enough either. Flying halfway around the world wouldn't be enough. The universe refused to come into focus, the noise inside my head like the roar of a hundred jet engines. *This is not happening, this is not happening, this is not happening. . .* But repeating such a trite mantra over and over again wouldn't make it true. I knew all too well what was true. The rope had been used many times for the same purpose. The scissors on the nightstand were supposed to

11

be his emergency escape route. His right hand is where it went wrong, the knot accidentally pulled so tight he couldn't wriggle out.

I had no idea how much time had passed when he knocked on my door. "My hand's better," he said. "Everything looks normal. I don't think he stole anything." I didn't answer. "You're home early."

"It's a good thing I took the afternoon off, don't you think?" I said.

"I'm going to ride my bike for a while." He pounded down the stairs.

I knew sarcasm wasn't what he needed right now. I should be drawing him out. I should be open and honest. I should acknowledge his embarrassment. I should tell him I was terrified he nearly died. I should let him know it's safe to share with me. Most of all, I should tell him he's not alone.

But "should" is very different from "can." Some things can never be discussed. Some things are too dangerous to remember. The conversation he needed right now would dredge up memories that needed to remain buried.

My thoughts ran in circles as I tried to convince myself he was fine. He has friends at school and out in the neighborhood, at least a dozen different boys. He's smart and a talented artist, getting himself accepted into a hyper-competitive private school with little help from Julia or myself. He's on a baseball team and he's got skills. He's happy and well adjusted, rarely mopey or crying. I knew what it was like to have terrible parents. I'm not that terrible a father.

But that was a lie. A big one. I was the most terrible kind there was. I curled into a ball on the bed. No matter how many facts stared me in the face, the terrifying truth was undeniable. The effort I'd spent protecting him all those years was for nothing. He hates himself enough to hurt himself.

Just like me.

Chapter 2

November 14, 1981

I read somewhere that Eskimos have hundreds of different words for snow.

I wondered what the Eskimo word was for the kind of snow falling today. Big, wet flakes made a noise like the hiss in a pair of headphones before the tape started to play music. A thick kind of snow that hid everything under a sparkling blanket. I imagined I could pull it back and crawl underneath, warm and snug. It made the world seem clean and fresh, at least for a little while.

When I was little, snow meant fun, so lots of snow meant lots of fun. It meant snow forts, mounds of snowballs to throw, and sledding down the steepest hill I could find. But I wasn't little anymore. I was eleven, too old to care as much about snow forts and sledding. I had more important things to care about.

I never remembered a big snowstorm this early in the year. Sometimes there were flurries in November when I lived in colder places than New Jersey, but not a real snow. The difference between flurries and a real snow is that a real snow gets deep enough to cover the grass. Since the grass was covered except for a few blades sticking up, it meant this was officially a real snow. My nose was cold from pressing up against my bedroom window. When I breathed, it left rings of fog on the glass. My fingers got wet when I wiped them away. I imagined I was one of those English guards with the big furry hats that looked like the bride of Frankenstein without the lightning streaks. If I moved, looked away, or even blinked, the snow might stop. I needed

it to keep falling. More than enough to cover the grass. Two feet, maybe three. Nothing was better than a snow day stolen from school – getting to stay home alone in my room, safe from homework and teasing and chores and responsibilities. But I was stupid to hope. I already knew I wasn't going to get a snow day.

I wondered if Eskimo kids had a special word for "heavy snow that falls on Saturday so school doesn't get closed."

Mom never knocked before coming in. My door was the only one in the house that didn't lock. The latch didn't line up right. I tried to fix it, but I couldn't figure out how. One time I asked Mom to get it fixed, but she told me she saw no reason why I'd need to lock my door. When I heard her coming in, I yanked the blanket over myself because I wasn't dressed yet. She frowned. I was in trouble. I was always in trouble for something.

"It's nearly eight-thirty," she said. "I will not allow you to spend the day moping around your room. You're too old to be behaving like this. Take some responsibility for yourself. You may get dressed and be at the table for breakfast in ten minutes, do you understand?" She closed the door without waiting for me to answer. I wanted to tell her to knock next time. If I was old enough to take responsibility, I was old enough to have privacy.

A Lego hidden under a dirty sock bit my foot when I got off the bed. I kicked it, not caring where it wound up as long as it was out of my way. Getting to the closet was like playing a weird game of hopscotch, finding safe spots in-between the piles of dirty clothes, crumpled school papers, Legos, and who knows what else. I didn't know why I bothered because the closet was empty, just like the dresser. All my clothes were on the floor, except for two socks that didn't match hanging out from an open drawer. They looked like they were trying to keep each other company, but it wasn't working because they weren't friends.

The red flannel shirt was my favorite because it was soft and still big on me. I found it under the pile of books I pulled off the shelf because I wanted to organize them. It got boring so I stopped. Mom hated when I wore red clothes because she said they clashed with my hair. People said I had red hair, but really, it was orange. Glow-in-the-dark,

radioactive orange. Jeans were harder to find. The first pair had a huge stain down the side. I had no idea from what. The second one smelled like pee. I found a pair that wasn't too smelly or dirty and put the other two back on the floor. My underwear was dirty too, but no one could see them so it didn't matter. When I was sitting on the bed putting on my socks, I saw some dirty dishes stuck in the space between my desk and the wall. I didn't remember putting them there, so it must've been a while ago. They were probably gross, so I pretended I didn't see them.

Mom said ten minutes and I still had one more minute, so I stared at the Atari magazine on my desk. Every time I got a new issue, I read the whole thing the same day. I liked knowing secrets no one else did, like how to find the dot in Adventure. But this one was special because it had a picture of the most amazing thing I ever saw — a real sword encrusted with gold and gems worth fifty thousand dollars that I could win as part of a contest. I liked imagining myself doing anything and everything that could be done with that sword. I was sure there was nothing else I ever wanted or would ever want as much.

But like the snow day, it was hopeless. To win, you had to solve the riddles in *four* new games. I'd never be able to convince my parents to buy the cartridges. I wasn't sure if I'd ever get to play Atari again. I stared at the spot on the ceiling, the outline of the giant hole easy to see because the new and old paint were slightly different colors. I didn't want to think about how the hole got there. It hurt too much to remember what I did.

"Nicholas!" Mom shouted from downstairs.

I looked at the sword one last time before putting the magazine carefully into the top drawer of my desk to keep it safe. Downstairs smelled like coffee and burnt toast. Dad sat at the table writing something on a pad of paper. Mom was doing dishes. She frowned again. I was still in trouble.

"Is this what you call getting dressed? Your hair is a mess, your clothes look like you slept in them, I doubt you brushed your teeth, and I have no idea when you last took a shower."

I had no idea either.

She kept going. "After breakfast, you may take some responsibility for yourself and get dressed properly. And maybe you'll choose to have

that pig sty of a room cleaned before I get home. Do we understand each other?"

I shrugged and nodded.

"Answer your mother," Dad growled without looking up.

"I said I understand," I mumbled.

"You may fix yourself some breakfast," she said. I hated how she ordered me to do something but made it sound like she was giving me permission to do something I actually wanted to do. You may take out the trash, you may do the laundry, you may clean that pig sty of a room. The bright green plastic floor felt cold through my socks as I slid across it. Something hot for breakfast sounded better than cereal, but it would probably make her mad if I started cooking eggs or pancakes. I stood on my toes to get the bowl used for serving things out of the top cabinet. I had to push the Corn Flakes out of the way so I could get the Sugar Pops from the back. It took almost half the box to fill up the bowl. I wanted to take the cereal back to my room, but that would get me in even bigger trouble, so I sat at the table and tried to be invisible.

All I had to do was wait. In a few minutes, they'd leave for work like they always did. Snow didn't matter. Saturday didn't matter. Nuclear war didn't matter. I made sure to chew with my mouth closed and I didn't let the spoon clank on the bowl. So far it was working – they weren't paying any attention to me. Like I really was invisible to them. I should've waited until they left, but I wanted some juice. I only glanced at the yellow piece of paper under the New York magnet on the fridge for a second, but she noticed. She could burrow straight into my brain like a mind-reading space worm.

"Your Atari account remains empty," she said from behind me. "You know the terms of our contract. Ten dollars towards the game of your choice every week you lose weight." She pulled the paper off the fridge and examined it carefully. "From what I see here, you've *gained* weight since we signed our agreement, so there will be no new games."

"I should throw the damned thing in the trash," my father muttered. "Video games are a colossal waste of time."

"If you were serious about getting what you wanted, you'd be concentrating on staying active and eating properly, instead of pouring

yourself oversized bowls of sugar cereal and spending your days rotting in front of the television," Mom said.

I wasn't hungry anymore. I wanted to go back to my room and be alone.

"Dammit, get back here and finish that food!" my father yelled. I froze in the hallway. "I don't work ninety hours a week so you can throw money away! You never think about how hard I work to put a roof over our heads and food on the table. I spent a fortune fixing the hole in your ceiling, and all you care about is blowing the rest on video games. If you want something, why don't you get off your lazy butt and earn the money yourself? Now sit down and finish that cereal or I really will take that damned video game and put it in the trash once and for all."

"How hard *we* work to put a roof over our heads," my mother said in a voice that made me think of sharp, pointy icicles. The way they stared at each other scared me.

I slouched into my chair, studying the yellow bits of cereal like they were the most interesting thing in the world. Sometimes I swirled the milk to make them think I was eating. A few minutes later, my mother put on her coat and went out the garage door without saying goodbye. My father left two minutes after her. He didn't say goodbye either. When I was sure they were gone, I went to my room. I took the Atari magazine out of the desk drawer and put it in the trash since I didn't need it anymore. A messy kid with ridiculous radioactive glowing orange hair stared at me in the mirror.

"You're stupid," I said to him. "And fat. And lazy."

"If you want something, why don't you get off your lazy butt and earn the money for yourself?" he said back to me.

He smiled at the same time I did. It was so simple, I should've thought of it hours ago. A whole day to myself and a whole neighborhood of driveways covered with snow. All I had to do was a shovel a few and I'd have enough money to buy the cartridge myself. In secret. I took the magazine out of the trash and put it back in my desk, smoothing out a small wrinkle in the corner before I closed the drawer. A minute later I had my boots and coat and scarf and gloves on

and got the shovel from the garage. I was sure I'd be back before lunchtime.

My neighborhood was set up in a giant oval with spikes coming off like the spokes on a bicycle wheel, except the spokes ended in round dead-end streets with houses. Between the houses on the main oval road and the ones on the spokes, there had to be at least a hundred driveways, maybe even two hundred. The best part was no one could see the neighborhood from the main road. There was only one way in and out, and the whole neighborhood was completely surrounded by woods. Nobody from the outside would think to come in. It was perfect.

It was so perfect I should've known it was just another one of my stupid ideas.

By the time I was on the other side of the neighborhood, the shovel felt like it weighed a ton, the inside of my coat was soaked from sweating, my legs were wobbly from walking through so much snow, and my stomach was rumbling. Only one guy said I could shovel. He told me he'd give me a whole two dollars if I did the driveway, walkway, and all the sidewalks. I didn't know what to do, so I said yes. As soon as he went inside, I ran down the road until I was around the corner.

On my side of the neighborhood, the woods around the houses didn't go very far. A short path led to a different neighborhood and my school. On the other side, the woods kept on going for miles. When I wanted to be alone, I went down a path to a little clearing where teenagers left beer bottles and cigarette butts. The path kept going, but I always stopped there, too afraid someone was watching. The woods would be quiet. No one would be out in the snow. I really felt like being alone.

The road down to the path was steep, so I had to be careful not to slip on the ice. The dead-end street at the bottom only had three houses that were more like mansions. Two of the houses already had their long C-shaped driveways shoveled, but the third was covered with fresh, undisturbed snow. It looked like nobody was home, and besides, shoveling driveways turned out to be a stupid idea. I didn't know why I went all the way up to the front door. Maybe I liked having people say no and laughing at me after they slammed the door in my face.

The doorbell didn't make the usual ding-dong sound. It sounded like bell chimes that made me think of Westminster Abbey even though I didn't know what Westminster Abbey was. A man opened the door. He wore a sweatshirt from somewhere called Rochester and round glasses that reminded me of John Lennon.

"Are you shoveling driveways?" he asked before I could say anything. "I'd almost lost hope someone would come around. I did *not* want to do it myself. How much?"

I had no idea what to say. Ten dollars seemed like a good amount for a normal driveway, but this one was so huge it was like shoveling two. But I couldn't ask for twenty. That was a gigantic amount of money.

"Umm, fifteen?" I asked.

He frowned. "Fifteen doesn't seem like an appropriate amount."

My stomach sank. "Ten?"

"Tell you what," he said. "If you do the driveway and all the walkways, I'll give you fifty."

I kicked a little pile of snow off the porch. He was even worse than the guy who offered me two dollars. I'd do the same thing – wait until he went inside and disappear into the woods. I studied the laces on my boots. "I guess fifty cents is ok."

"Hey," the man said in a soft voice like he was sad. "Not fifty cents. Fifty dollars."

Wait. Did he just? Fifty *dollars*?

The man smiled at me. It didn't look like the fake kind of smile most grown-ups gave kids. I was positive he meant it. He would really give me fifty dollars.

"Ok," I said, trying not to seem too excited.

"I'm Jeremy." Not mister so and so – he said his first name. I couldn't remember a grown-up doing that to me before. He held out his hand. I was so distracted, I stared at him looking dumb before I realized I was supposed to shake. Like a reflex, I grabbed his hand, squeezed hard, and shook three times. Not two, not four – three times and three times only. I still remembered how much my hand hurt after my father made me practice for two hours. "What's your name?" he asked.

My mom always reminded me that she named me Nicholas, so I was supposed to ask people to call me Nicholas. She thought Nick sounded vulgar.

"Nick," I said.

"It's nice to meet you," he said. He meant it. I could tell. "I see you've brought your own equipment. Is there anything else you need?" I shook my head. "I'll leave the door open in case you do. Just come on in."

I nodded. He watched from the doorway while I started. Magically, the shovel went from weighing a ton to light as a feather. Fifty dollars! I sunk my shovel into the snow and pushed through it like it was cotton candy instead of wet cement. Fifty dollars was enough to buy two cartridges! After a few minutes, he went back inside. I guessed he thought I was doing a good job. I *was* doing a good job. I didn't leave a single bit behind as I pushed the snow across the driveway in nice neat rows, kicking the shovel up when I hit the grass to make a wall. That way, I never had to lift the snow, so it was a lot easier. It was my own invention.

I was concentrating so hard on shoveling, I didn't notice he was standing behind me. "You look like you could use something to drink. I made some cocoa."

Taking food from strangers was strictly forbidden by my mom. One time for Halloween, someone handed out hot pretzels instead of candy. All the other kids were eating them, so I thought it was ok even though the rule was that I could only eat things in a sealed wrapper and only after it got checked by my parents. My mom found the wax paper when she did her inspection. My punishment was to lose all my candy, every single piece. She even took it to her work so I couldn't sneak any. Jeremy opened a thermos and poured some hot chocolate into the little cup that fit on top. I studied it carefully. It smelled amazing. When he smiled again, I knew a person like him would never poison me, so I took a small taste.

Right up to that moment I thought I was a hot chocolate expert. Quik was good. Swiss Miss was better, but only if it was made with milk and had the little marshmallows in the packet. Ovaltine had a funny taste and smell that reminded me of wet paint. Restaurant hot chocolate

was the best, super-sweet with powder stuck on the side of the cup and tons of whipped cream. I was never allowed to order it. Everything changed after I tasted Jeremy's hot chocolate. It didn't have little marshmallows or whipped cream, but it didn't need them. It was thick like glue, sweet in the right way, and tasted like real melted chocolate.

"This is really good," I blurted out.

"Thank you," he said. "Homemade from a secret family recipe on the back of the Hershey's cocoa container." I didn't know there was a way to make hot chocolate besides putting powder into milk. "I'll leave the thermos. There's more inside if you run out. I'm making a late lunch if you're hungry. Soup, maybe some grilled cheese?" I nodded and he went back inside. I drank cocoa until I got worried that he might get mad because I wasn't working hard enough.

I didn't stop shoveling even when I got sore and tired. I only let myself take more cocoa when I did five full lines, and I made sure to lick the cup clean each time. When he came out to tell me lunch was ready, I was almost done with the whole driveway. He whistled. I wished I knew how to whistle like that.

"You're doing a fantastic job!" he said. "I can't believe you've only been at it for a couple of hours. Hiring you was the right decision. Come on in."

I tried not to stare when I went inside. The entry area had a floor made of that shiny kind of fancy white stone with black lines in it. The ceiling was open all the way to the roof, about a hundred feet high. A huge gold and glass chandelier hung above the curved staircase. In front of me was an enormous open room that looked like the lobby of a fancy hotel. It had big, comfy looking brown couches, the same kind of chairs, a giant black piano, and thick white carpet. The entire back wall was windows, so I could see the whole long hill in his backyard and the woods past that. The sun was out, making the snow sparkle like stars.

"Back here," he called. I followed his voice through the hallway, past a dining room with a table made of a giant slab of stone that reminded me of Narnia. The kitchen had to be four times the size of mine. It smelled like burnt butter. He set up a plate for me with a grilled cheese sandwich and tomato soup in the kind of bowl restaurants use for French onion soup. I carried it carefully over to his kitchen table,

afraid I would drop something. He walked past me to the next room, a huge den with an L-shaped couch, big screen TV, and a real pool table. The floor was covered with the same thick white carpet as the lobby. "Let's eat by the fireplace so you can warm up a bit."

He had a huge fire burning in the fireplace. The den smelled like a campfire. Mom never let me light a fire at home because she thought it would make the whole house smell like smoke forever. I thought that was the point. Smoke smells good. He sat on the floor in front of the fire and looked at me. I took the two steps down to the den one at a time, watching the soup to make sure it didn't spill and watching my feet to make sure I didn't trip. It took me a long time to get to the fireplace. I felt better when I put down my plate without spilling anything. If Mom saw me, with or without an invitation, I'd be in big trouble. But she couldn't see me right now.

"How old are you?" he asked with his mouth full of food.

"Eleven," I said. Butter from the grilled cheese dripped down my chin. I wiped it off with my hand.

"That's sixth grade, right?"

"Yeah," I said.

"Sixth grade is nice."

I decided not to tell him it wasn't. I watched the flames flicker and listened to the wood pop and hiss.

"Where do you live?" he asked.

"On Beechwood. It's on the other side of the neighborhood."

"How long have you lived there?"

"Since August," I said.

"So, you're new to the neighborhood," he said. "I've been here a few years. Where did you move from?"

"Columbus."

"Ohio," he said and nodded without saying anything else. I felt the same way about Ohio. There was nothing to say about it. I ate my food and he ate his food, but the silence kept getting bigger. I knew I should say something, but the only question I could think of was how old he was. It seemed rude to ask a grown-up about his age.

"I'm probably going to get in trouble feeding you this close to dinnertime," he said. Not because I was going to tell on him. "You

should probably finish up and head home before your parents wonder where you are. Should you call them?"

"They're not home," I said.

"Before I forget," he said, taking out a thick wallet from his pocket. He picked through the money and took out a fifty-dollar bill, handing it to me. I never saw a real one before. I couldn't tell if I was excited or scared.

"I didn't finish yet," I said.

"I trust you," he said. I folded it carefully and stashed it all the way at the bottom of my pocket, reminding myself not to leave it there in case I decided to wash my pants.

"Think you have time for a game of pool before you go back out?"

"I'm not very good," I mumbled. I loved hitting the balls around whenever I got a chance to play, which was almost never.

"Me neither," he said. He arranged the balls in the triangle. I knew I messed up as soon as I hit the white ball. Only a few colored balls got knocked out of place. He quickly put one into the hole like an expert. "Your turn."

"But you got one in," I said. I knew the rules. Still, I took the stick from him. I knew I wouldn't be able to get it in, but I shot at the orange ball anyway. It rolled in the right direction, but then it bounced on the edge of the hole and came back out.

"That always happens," I muttered.

"Give it another try, not so hard this time." He put the balls back where they were before.

I hated when grown-ups did this. Now he'd expect me to do better, but I knew I was only going to mess up worse. Then he'd get mad, and then he'd give up because it was obvious I was too dumb to learn how. I missed the orange ball completely. He put the white ball back again.

"Aim for the middle of the ball," he said. I tried, I really did. I lined it up like a hundred times, but when I went to hit it, the stick scraped the top of the white ball. He put it back *again*. "Your hand is too far away from the tip."

He stood right behind me. I felt like my hair was standing up on end. The room got cold. His hand touched mine, sliding it down the stick. I couldn't move. I didn't like when people touched me. It always felt

like I was about to get into a fight. It didn't matter if I knew a person was trying to be nice. My head couldn't tell my body what to feel.

"One more try," he said.

I closed my eyes and hit it. I could tell by the sound it went in.

"You got it!" he shouted, excited. I saw him reaching toward me. Maybe to mess my hair, or maybe to choke me. I couldn't tell. I leaned over to get away from him. He pulled his hand back quickly.

"Sorry," he said. It made me feel better when he took a step backwards. And worse at the same time. "How about some more cocoa?"

"I'll get it," I said, trying to make up for being such a jerk. I didn't want him to be mad at me. He was being so nice. I filled both mugs with cocoa. It looked like mud. Mud is what I deserved. Not cocoa and grilled cheese and playing pool and fifty dollars. I was so busy being mad at myself, I forgot about the stairs. One second I was walking, and then the floor rushed up at me. I wound up face down. My thumb got jammed and I banged my knee.

I realized he was kneeling next to me. "Are you alright?" I rolled onto my side. All I could see was clean white carpet stained by a trail of ugly brown splotches. Both mugs were on their sides, empty. I felt like I wanted to throw up.

"I ruined your carpet," I said out loud.

"Carpet? You took a nasty fall. Are you ok?"

I pulled myself up and dug the fifty-dollar bill out of my pocket. "Here," I said, pushing it toward him. "Maybe this will pay for your carpet. I promise I'll never bother you again."

He stared at the money without taking it. "I don't give a shit about the carpet," he said in a soft voice. "The only thing I care about is that you didn't get hurt. Are you ok?"

All I could do was nod because my brain was kind of stuck on him saying shit.

"You keep that money, you earned it," he said. "It was an accident. The carpet isn't important. Things aren't important. People are important. You're important. Don't ever forget that."

I knew better.

"It's getting late and you should probably be on your way home. You can finish shoveling tomorrow. When you come back, I have another job you can do for me, if you're interested."

"What?" I mumbled.

"I bought a sled – well, sled is a generous word for it because it's just a cheap hunk of plastic – and I have absolutely no idea how to use it. If you show me how to sled down the hill behind my house, we'll call it even for the carpet. What do you say?" The image of a grown-up sledding was just too funny to hold in. "Hey," he said in the same sad voice he used when he explained about the fifty dollars. "I think that's the first time I saw you smile all day. Promise you'll come back tomorrow to show me how to sled?"

"I promise," I said. He let me get up on my own and walked with me to the front door. I put on my coat and boots. He got on his knees next to me.

"I enjoyed having you over, and you're welcome to come by anytime you want to play pool or have hot chocolate or whatever." He held out his hand. "Deal?"

"Thanks," I said automatically as I shook his hand. After I said it, I realized I actually meant it instead of just being polite. He watched from the doorway as I walked up the hill. I looked back and waved a few times. He was still watching when I got too far away to see him.

Even though the streetlights were already on, I thought I had time before my parents got home. I was wrong. Dad's car was in the driveway. He was banging around in the garage, yelling at no one. Something crashed. I hid behind a bush. He spotted me anyway. "Get the hell over here this instant!" he screamed. I was in trouble. Big trouble. I walked slowly but he didn't wait, meeting me in the middle of the street. "I can't believe you!" I was sure they could hear him in Ohio.

"What did I do?" I mumbled.

"What did you do?" He looked like he expected me to tell him something. I had no idea what he wanted me to say. "I work my ass off seven days a week so I can come home to find my lazy kid hasn't done a damned thing?"

"You didn't say. . ."

"I didn't say?" he interrupted. "Do I have to order you to do the most basic things around here? Your room looks like it was hit by a hurricane, dishes are in the sink, your bowl of cereal from this morning is rotting on the table, and you left the front door unlocked. But that's not the best part. I just spent the last fifteen minutes looking for my shovel. Do you want to explain what in the hell you were doing with my shovel?"

"I went to shovel driveways."

"You went to shovel driveways?" I thought his head was going to pop. "Let me get this straight. You shoveled other people's driveways?"

"Uh huh," I nodded, studying the snow.

I didn't think he could scream louder, but he could. "And it never occurred to you to shovel ours first? Look at me! I'm waiting for some kind of explanation!" There was nothing I could say. "What the hell is the matter with you? Do you do these things because you like to make me furious, or are you brain damaged? Get the hell out of my sight!"

"Do you want. . ."

"I said get the hell out of my sight!" he screamed.

I dropped the shovel in the road and ran into the house. I didn't stop running until I was safe in my room, the windows rattling from slamming my bedroom door so hard. He was right. There was something wrong with me. I should know to shovel the driveway and clean up and lock the front door. I was stupid. And fat. And lazy.

And brain damaged.

I stared at the place where the hole used to be in the ceiling, wondering if I should make another one. I knew my mother came home because I heard her arguing with dad downstairs. After a while, I smelled food. I heard footsteps in the hall and saw the light under my door go out. No one knocked. No one cared.

I didn't start until I was sure they went to bed, finding the secret shoelaces I kept hidden under the mattress. I took off all my clothes and threw them on the floor. One shoelace was for tying my feet up, as tight as I could, so it would leave a red mark. The other shoelace got tied to the headboard to make a loop. I put my hands into the loop and started rolling over. Each time I rolled over, the loop shrank and the shoelace tightened. I kept going until it got so tight I was sure it would break my

wrists if I did it again. My hands got dark red and tingly. It hurt. I wanted it to hurt.

Thoughts flashed through my head while I rubbed myself on the bed. Thoughts of being the kidnapped boy everyone read about in the newspaper. The one who was kept tied up all the time. The one who got hurt in ways I couldn't imagine. The one who would never come home.

It didn't take long for me to finish. I wanted to make myself stay tied up all night, maybe all day tomorrow too, but it always hurt too much after I was done. And I knew if I didn't get my hands out soon, they might fall asleep and never wake up. I untied myself and curled into a ball under the blanket, sucking my thumb like a baby. I didn't understand why I did the things I did. I wished I could change into a different person, someone normal. But I knew it was hopeless. Brain damage was permanent. It never got better.

I stared at the ceiling until the sun came back up.

James Edison

Chapter 3

November 27, 1981

Mom told me she's a good lawyer because she pays attention to details. Her job is to notice all the little things no one else can see and connect them together. If she does it well, she can always find out the truth. One time, I asked her if lawyers used longer paper because they needed to remember so many details. She said yes. I thought I was paying attention to details when I asked if there were longer pencils to go with the longer paper. She laughed at me and said those weren't the kind of details she meant.

I was terrible at paying attention to details. She *always* noticed.

"I can scarcely believe you were going to leave this house so unprepared," she said. The contents of my backpack were spread all over the entryway. My plan to sneak out failed. "You remembered your book, but you forgot socks, underwear, pajamas, and your toothbrush. If your head wasn't attached you'd probably forget it too. You're an intelligent young man. I don't understand how such basic things escape you." She was wrong, because I didn't forget anything. To forget something, you had to remember it in the first place. I went back upstairs to get the stuff I never thought about.

"You're sure Jeremy's parents said it was ok for you to spend the night?" she called up the stairs.

"Uh huh," I answered. She'd never *actually* asked me how old Jeremy was, so technically I never *actually* lied to her. Maybe I lied a little about his parents, but he probably had parents somewhere. I knew she'd find out eventually, but she wasn't going to find out tonight so I

had time to figure out what to tell her. I was sure I wouldn't be allowed to be friends with him because he was more like my parents age instead of mine. I just wasn't sure why.

"Can I go now?" I asked when I came back downstairs.

"Make sure Jeremy's parents call me tonight. Is that understood?"

"Yeah," I said.

"Then you may go." She watched me open the door. "Goodbye, Nicholas." Another detail I never remembered to think about.

"Bye," I mumbled. She locked the door behind me with a loud click, like she didn't want me to come back. Not that I wanted to go back, but still. It was a nice kind of cold outside – crispy, like Eggo waffles when they were toasted just right. I felt more awake than I did all day. I walked fast even though it made me sweat. Tonight was going to be the first time I'd ever slept over at a friend's house. I tried once, but it didn't count because I went home before we went to bed. This time felt like a chance to make up for everything I did wrong the last time. The front lights at Jeremy's house turned on automatically when I walked up, like they were saying hi.

I was about to ring the doorbell but stopped when I heard music coming from inside. I looked through the window on the side of the door. It took a few seconds for me to realize the music I heard wasn't coming from a record or the TV. Jeremy's hands were going up and down the notes and his foot was pressing the thing underneath, so it had to be him playing the piano. I wasn't dumb – I knew what a piano was for. But I always thought Jeremy's piano took up half the lobby because it was a nice-looking piece of furniture, not because he actually knew how to play music on it. I was afraid to interrupt him, so I didn't ring the doorbell.

Normally, I didn't think much about music. In music class at school I usually mouthed the words to boring songs (like the chicken soup with rice one) because I wasn't good at singing. Music was the noise my alarm clock made to wake me up. Music filled the empty parts of movies and cartoons. Music was something that belonged in the background. Nothing important.

But this music was different. I'd never heard anything like it. Listening to it gave me a clear picture in my head, as clear as if I was

watching TV. Even better than TV, because it made me *feel*. The music told me to picture myself alone, staring out the window at a gray, wet afternoon. A storm came, rain falling like a waterfall, the wind blowing against the glass, lightning and thunder crashing. Then the sun peeked out, just a little bit, like it was coming up in the morning. The gray day tried to come back but then the sun fought back and won, pushing all the clouds away by shining as bright as it could. The whole world went out to play as if it was the only sunny day all year. But the gray day won in the end, the storm chasing everyone back inside. Even after he played the last note the feeling stayed with me. This wasn't music. This was *music*. Maybe I'd heard *music* before, but I hadn't really listened. Or maybe Jeremy had a way of turning music into *music*.

He played song after song. Circles of water spreading out from throwing a rock into the pond, a butterfly fluttering along, a crazy wild dance, or a demon march – it didn't matter what he played. I got lost in the music like I got lost whenever I was reading a good book, the real world melting away until I could almost feel like I was actually in one of those fantastic places. I didn't realize it got colder out or that my leg fell asleep until the music died out.

"What on earth are you doing?" Jeremy said when he opened the door. I tried to get up, but my numb leg didn't want to cooperate.

"I dropped something," I stammered. My leg tingled painfully when I stood on it.

"How long have you been out here? You look frozen."

I stomped my leg a few times which only made it worse. "I didn't want to bother you."

"I'm pretty sure the couch is lot more comfortable than the porch, unless you know something I don't," he said. I followed him inside, still stomping. "And I keep telling you that you never bother me." I liked hearing him say that. Maybe I kept saying I didn't want to bother him just so I could hear him tell me that I never did. "We're going out to eat so don't take your coat off. You know that new place by the mall?"

Did I *know* it? There were rumors about it all over school. They had gourmet food like fried cheese sticks and hollowed out potato skins with cheese and bacon. They even refilled sodas without having to pay

31

extra. *Free* soda. He was taking me to the most amazing restaurant in town. I managed to nod. He disappeared upstairs.

The piano looked like a piece of furniture again. The cover over the notes was still open. I wondered if he had to leave the cover open because the notes got warm after being played like that. I looked over my shoulder to make sure Jeremy was still upstairs, and then pushed down a white one very softly. It didn't make a sound, so I pushed it a little harder. A low note filled the room, way louder than I wanted. I yanked my hand back like I got burned and dashed out of the lobby before I got caught.

When he came back downstairs, I followed him to the garage. Today was the first time we were going to do something besides stay at his house. The idea we could get in a car and go somewhere whenever we wanted was exciting, like getting permission to ride my bicycle out of the neighborhood only much better. He had two cars in the garage. One was a normal kind of car, a big van. The other was a long way from normal. I thought I was imagining it. Cars like that only existed on posters, in movies, and in the kind of magazines kids passed around at school to everyone except me.

A real, genuine, *actual* Porsche.

At best, I thought I'd be lucky enough to look inside the windshield or touch it when I walked by. There was no way I'd get to ride in it. But he got in the driver's side. "They don't deliver to the garage steps," he said when I didn't move.

I stumbled down the steps. I thought I'd be excited to ride in it. Instead, I was worried I'd scratch or rip or scuff something. It took three tries before I closed the door hard enough to make it stay closed.

"You like it?" he asked.

"It's nice," I said, trying not to touch anything.

He backed out. I stared at all the dials and controls, the dashboard more like a spaceship than a car. For a second we sat in the road, and then the tires squealed and I got pushed back in my seat as we took off up the hill. I thought we were going to keep going up and fly into outer space.

"I still haven't heard from your parents," he said.

"They're really busy," I answered.

"I'd feel a lot better if I talked to them. I want to make sure they're comfortable with you spending time with me. Let's call them when we get back from dinner."

I nodded. I already had a plan. Dial the wrong number and say they weren't home.

"Did you have a good Thanksgiving?" he asked.

"It was ok," I said. "We went to a hotel and had a buffet."

"That sounds nice." It wasn't nice. I wanted a real Thanksgiving with a gigantic turkey and a happy family laughing around a table, like on TV. Instead, I got a bored waiter scooping out dry mashed potatoes while Dad complained to everyone. "It was just me and Mr. Swanson this year, but I do love that little apple pie in the middle. But Thanksgiving's just the warm-up. Are you getting excited for Christmas?"

I wasn't paying attention, or I wouldn't have said it. "Not really."

"What do you mean?"

I hated when I had to explain it to anyone. "We don't celebrate Christmas. My mom is Jewish but my dad isn't. He wants to have Christmas, but she says the tree and stuff offends her. So, he gets mad and says she can't have her candles either. We don't do anything."

"What about presents?" he asked in his soft voice.

"I get a few, after Christmas. When everything goes on sale." I realized I was pressing my nose against the window. I hoped it wouldn't leave a mark.

"I see," he said. We were both quiet after that.

The mall was on the complete opposite side of Newton Falls from where we lived, as far away as a place could be and still be in the same town. Out by us, there was nothing but a bunch of homes, a small lake near my school, and a few farms where I could see horses and cows if I cared about that kind of thing. *Boring.* To get to the mall, we had to drive through the middle of town, which had to be hundreds of years old. My mom called it charming, but that was a grown-up word which translated to boring. It had a statue, lots of brick buildings, and pointless stores with peeling paint and wavy glass windows. It was like the town never found out the Revolutionary War ended a long time ago. The mall was the only ok thing about Newton Falls. They put it out near

the highway, probably since it wasn't made of brick and wavy glass windows. It was a regular mall, with regular stores, a regular arcade with the regular games, the regular restaurants, and a regular movie theater.

Since the mall was the only interesting place in Newton Falls, the whole world had the same idea as us. I wanted to give up, but Jeremy was stubborn. We drove around for twenty minutes until we finally found a parking spot on the other side of the mall from the restaurant. We had to push our way through the crowd in the waiting area to a messy-haired woman wearing a red and white striped shirt standing at the front desk. I could barely hear her say it was over a two hour wait.

"I guess we should go somewhere else," I said.

"Not a chance," he said, winking at me. He leaned over the desk, shaking hands with the woman and talking too soft for me to hear. When he let go, I saw the corners of a bunch of twenty-dollar bills sticking out of her hand. What was that called? Bribery? Wasn't bribery illegal? I was sure we were going to get arrested. Instead of cops coming out from everywhere to take us to jail, the woman took us to a little table in the back of the restaurant. No wait at all. I asked her for a coke and she brought it right away too.

I studied the menu to find the cheapest thing they had. "Look at this, they have cool appetizers like potato skins and mozzarella sticks and tortilla chips with everything on them," Jeremy said. "Let's get all the appetizers. If we're still hungry we can order more afterwards. Oooh, ice cream drinks. Let's get those too."

I thought he was joking, but when the waitress came he ordered every single appetizer on the menu and all five kinds of ice cream drinks. She looked at me like I was the grown-up who was supposed to say no and be responsible. I didn't say anything. My dad hated appetizers. Too much money and not enough food. Bad value, whatever that meant. He went crazy in restaurants about how much things cost. I ordered an adult dinner when we went out for my eleventh birthday. He screamed how it was two dollars more than the kid's meal for the same thing. He didn't understand that I ordered it because I was old enough for the adult meal. There wasn't enough room on the table for all the plates, but the waitress kept bringing more. We had more food than we could ever eat. Dad's head would've exploded.

"I've got another one," Jeremy said with his mouth full of potato. "These two Eskimos were watching a lighthouse being built, skeptical that the thing would work. When it was finished, a thick fog rolled in. The bell rang, the horn blew, and the light went around and around. One Eskimo turned to the other and said 'See, it no work. Fog come rolling in just the same.'" I tried to keep the food in my mouth while I was laughing. His eyes went wide. "Oh no, your brains are leaking!"

It seemed like I laughed the entire time we were at dinner. Jeremy kept eating more and more gross-out combinations (fried cheese dipped in ice cream drink with nacho beans, ketchup, and a whole bunch of pepper on top was the worst). We heaped the leftover food in the center of the table while he told me about the mangled corpses of tortilla chips drowning in tomato sauce mixed with melted ice cream (the aftermath of Food War III). Whether we were racing sleds down the hill trying to avoid hitting trees, playing a crazy game of pool where the balls flew off the table, or eating too many appetizers and leaving a huge mess on the table, being friends with Jeremy was non-stop fun. If my parents saw me having this kind of fun, they'd probably throw me into the bottomless pit of eternal trouble. But they couldn't see me. I smiled whenever I thought about that.

"What's next?" Jeremy asked when we went outside. "We can go to a late movie if you promise not to tell your parents. Before that, there's something I wanted to ask you. How long were you sitting on the porch listening to me play piano?"

"I don't know," I mumbled.

"It must've been a long time. Your foot was asleep when you got up."

"I didn't want to interrupt you."

"At first, I thought you were being polite to the point of silliness. Then I saw you jump like a mouse after pressing a key when you thought I wasn't looking. It seems like you really enjoyed the music."

"You're really good," I mumbled.

"Playing piano is important to me," he said. "Do you play an instrument?"

"I started playing violin in third grade, but we moved away after a few months. I never really learned how."

"I know a lot more music. Would you like to hear me play some?"

Then he used his soft voice. "Would you like me to show you how to play?"

Somehow, I managed to nod.

"You're getting better," he said.

He had to be crazy, because I was definitely getting worse. My fingers fought with me as hard as they could. No matter how many times I tried, the notes in my right hand and my left hand never happened together. I either pushed the wrong key or an extra one I didn't mean to play. When I played, it sounded uneven, clunky, and messy. I wanted it to sound smooth and perfect. Like when Jeremy played.

"Curl your fingers a little more."

I started over again, trying to remember to curl my fingers, but I had too many other things to think about. Like making my fingers go in the right order. A big part of me wanted to give up, but a bigger part decided I wasn't going to quit. I wanted to make music like Jeremy did.

"Not bad," he said.

"It doesn't sound right," I said.

"Playing well takes years of practice. You're not going to master the piano in a single night, even if you've been trying for . . .three hours? Holy shit, it's one in the morning."

"One more try," I muttered.

He let me do it once more and then closed the cover on the keys before I could try again. "If I have to hear those same five notes again I'm going to go crazy." He yawned and stretched. "Come on, I'll escort you to your suite."

I hadn't been upstairs in his house before. "That's my room," he said, pointing to double doors at one end of the hall. "Pound on them if the house starts burning down. Your room is down here." He opened the door into a bedroom that was bigger than my mom and dad's. It had a massive bed with four big poles at the corners, blankets piled up

so high I'd have to climb up to get on, and a stack of fluffy pillows taller than I was.

"You already know how to work the satellite TV and you have your own bathroom through there." I climbed onto the bed, the blankets rolling around me like I was a hot dog in a bun. They were softer than my favorite pajamas. "You might not think so, but you really are getting better. I'm impressed how you refused to quit. You're a pretty amazing kid."

I shrugged.

"Try not to stay up too late," he said.

"I won't," I answered.

An hour later, the lights were still on, my pajamas were still in my backpack, I had no idea where my toothbrush was, and I was propped up on the pillows watching the Twilight Zone.

<hr />

The room was huge, stretching out forever in all directions, full of tables from restaurants, huge beds, and pianos. Thick curtains hanging from the invisible ceiling made it impossible to find my way. I clawed through, searching, but nothing was right. I had to go, worse than I ever remembered. No hope until I saw the garbage can next to a bed. It was wrong but it was the only choice. The endless stream instantly filled it up and sloshed over the sides.

My eyes opened.

The details were different, but the dream was always the same. Needing to go and nowhere to do it. The feeling afterward was always the same, too. A few seconds of comfortable warmth followed by freezing, clingy clothes. But that yucky feeling was nothing compared to what was going on inside my head. Nothing could be a more embarrassing example of just how brain damaged I was – the only eleven-year-old in the history of the universe who still wet the bed.

Wet was a stupid word for it. More like flooded. I jumped off, but it was way too late. The pillows, blankets, sheets, and even the thick feather pad I found underneath were soaked. A round, wet spot on the mattress was spreading fast. When it happened at home, I concentrated

on what I needed to do so I didn't have to think about what I did. Throw everything in the washer, take a shower, put on new sheets, and go back to bed. Like Mom said, if I couldn't control myself, it was my responsibility to deal with the consequences. Sometimes I made too much noise and woke her up. She'd come out of her room and watch me with her arms folded. She never helped.

But I wasn't home. I didn't know where Jeremy kept his washer or how it worked. The blankets and the feather pad would never fit anyway. He didn't have a rubber cover on the mattress to keep it dry like I had at home, so I couldn't put new sheets on until it was dry. If I made too much noise, Jeremy would come out of his room. Maybe he'd laugh at me. Maybe he'd watch me with his arms folded. He'd never let me sleep over again. Or come to his house. Or order lots of appetizers and ice cream drinks and leave a huge mess on the table.

So I had to make sure he never found out.

I did everything as quietly as I could. I rolled up the sheets and clothes into a ball and spread the blankets and pad out on the floor to dry. I hoped I wouldn't need to use a hair dryer because it would make a lot of noise. I ran the shower at a trickle to make sure he didn't hear, happy that my mom made me pack pajamas. Every time the stairs creaked I was sure he'd come bursting out from the double doors to his room.

I found the laundry room downstairs near the door to the garage. The washer wasn't hard to figure out, but I had to climb on the dryer to reach the detergent. I went to the kitchen to wait for it to finish, listening for any sign he was awake. The house was quiet. I got some soda from the fridge and sat in the corner on the floor, invisible to everyone. I didn't dare go back upstairs to get my book, so I counted the tiles on the floor, finding patterns and shapes to pass the time. I started to hope I might get away with it. I might be able to have everything put back together before he woke up.

Until a massive crashing sound started echoing through the house.

The glass of soda skidded across the floor when I jumped up. I must've kicked it. It smashed into the cabinets on the other side and shattered. The crashing sound was getting louder. I raced down the hall to the laundry room. The washer was doing a crazy dance, slamming

into the dryer with all the strength it had, jerking its way across the room like it was possessed by a demon. I pushed and pulled everything until it finally calmed down. The hoses behind it were so stretched out I thought they were going to break. I held my breath, praying for the impossible. The door upstairs opened. I heard him walk down the hall.

"Nick, is that you down there?"

"I was looking for a broom. I broke a glass."

"Sounded more like a herd of elephants broke a glass," he muttered. "Is everything ok?"

"Yeah, I'll clean it up. You can go back to bed."

"I'll help," he said. His footsteps were heavy on the stairs. I closed the door to the laundry room behind me, leaning against it. He passed me without staring and got a broom from the garage. I followed him to the kitchen, keeping my distance. "No bare feet." I cringed, but he picked me up even though I weighed a ton and sat me on the counter, my legs dangling. "What happened?"

"I dropped a glass," I said, lying by telling the truth. But I could tell he already knew. Not because he looked angry – because he looked sad. I didn't want to watch him staring at me so I looked at the floor.

"Did you have an accident?"

I hated calling it that. Accident made it sound like it was something out of my control. Wetting the bed wasn't like falling off my bicycle or tripping over a rock. I knew deep down it was completely my fault. Like jumping off a cliff. On purpose.

"I want to go home," I said.

"I'd really like it if you stayed."

"Why?" I whispered.

"You don't need to feel ashamed or embarrassed," he said. "These things happen and it's not your fault. Lots of kids wet the bed. It doesn't change anything. I still want to be your friend." He pushed up my chin until I was looking at his face again. His eyes looked watery, like he was going to cry. It didn't make sense. Why would he cry? I should be the one who was crying. Except I didn't know how anymore. A long time ago I decided I'd already cried enough for one person's lifetime and swore I'd never do it again. Since then, every tear got buried

somewhere inside me where it couldn't escape. All I knew how to do was feel blank, like a snowy channel on television.

"Tell you what. You light a fire in the den, and I'll go find some sleeping bags. We can have a camp out. We could make s'mores if I had any marshmallows. Or graham crackers. Details shmetails." He lifted me back off the counter and put me down far away from the broken glass, heading upstairs to get the stuff.

I was still standing in the same spot when he came back. He brought a guitar too, the case all covered with stickers. I made myself busy putting newspaper between the logs so I didn't have to look at him. I was afraid he'd want to talk about what happened. The fire caught. I slid into one of the sleeping bags he spread out on the floor, facing away from him.

"Piano is more my thing," he said. As soon as he started playing the guitar, I could tell why. As good as he was at the piano, that's how bad he was at guitar. He kept muttering every time he stopped or played the wrong note. He started to sing, but that sounded even more terrible than his guitar playing.

The very day I purchased it, I christened my guitar
As my monophonic symphony, six string orchestrar

He went on like that for a little while. Then he suddenly changed, becoming good at playing and singing. I rolled over, and he winked at me.

And we'd all play together, like fine musicians should
And it would sound like music
And the music would sound good

He went back to sounding horrible. I didn't feel like I was in the mood to laugh, but I couldn't help it. I hoped he'd play another funny one, but the ones after sounded more serious.

Broken glass was all over the kitchen floor. The soda was probably sticky by now. The wet sheets were still in the stopped washer. He

must've forgotten about all of it. There was no way he could think it was more important to be here with me.

> *Winter, spring, summer, or fall*
> *All you've got to do is call*
> *And I'll be there, yes I will*
> *You've got a friend.*

And I did. For the first time ever.

James Edison

Chapter 4

December 6, 1981

I hated when my parents invited business people to our house. They made me spend hours cleaning this and straightening that. I had to get all dressed up just so I could answer the door and take everyone's coat. Then I was imprisoned in my room for the rest of the night. I was sure they were telling embarrassing stories about me whenever I heard their guests laughing. I didn't get dinner until they let me out to clean up after everyone left.

The only part I liked about business dinner nights was making the cheese plate. Some people painted pictures and others made sculptures. I made art out of cheddar cubes and Ritz crackers. Each time I did something different. Tonight, I wanted to make a masterpiece worthy of a Polaroid picture. I imagined a stone pyramid (cheese) with colorful pennants (toothpicks) on an island in the sea (crackers) with trees crawling up the side (grapes). It had to be perfect, because tonight *everything* had to be perfect. That's why I didn't complain when my parents kept giving me orders. That's why I cleaned up some things before they even asked me to.

"Ellie, where did you put my cufflinks?" Dad yelled from upstairs.

"You left them on the nightstand!" she yelled back. "I haven't touched them!"

"They're not there!" he screamed. "Everyone is always moving my things!"

I looked at the small table in the living room where he left his cufflinks ten minutes ago, wondering if I should tell him. I remembered

a time he was looking for his car keys and I told him that I saw him put them in the junk drawer. He screamed at me for an hour how it was my fault. I went back to making the cheese plate, pretending I didn't see the cufflinks.

He stomped down the stairs, his eyes drilling a hole in my skull. "I told you to fix that tie," he growled.

"I tried," I mumbled.

"Not hard enough. And for crying out loud, you're wearing blue socks with a brown suit. Fix that tie, change your socks, and get your jacket on. Now!"

There was no way I could explain without making him angrier. I was still using the same knot in my tie from a year ago because I forgot how to tie it. I didn't have brown socks because they must've been sucked into a black hole. My jacket didn't fit anymore, and not because I got too tall. He grabbed the empty ice bucket from the bar and turned away from me so I didn't have to keep standing there looking stupid. "Do I have to do everything around here?" He stomped off to the kitchen so he could scream at Mom instead.

"Why isn't the silver polished?" he yelled.

"I've had my hands full finishing the meal," she snapped. "It's not as if you've been any help in here."

"It's not as if I haven't been doing anything!" he shouted.

"Either get in here and help, or get your nose out of my business. And so help me, control your temper or I'm calling this whole thing off."

I prayed. Please Mom, don't do that. . .

"Why isn't the table set?" he yelled at me from the dining room.

"I'll do it right now," I said, leaving the cheese tray. I put all the plates and silverware where they belonged, but I got stuck on the wine glasses. Should I put one at my place or not? I needed a book that explained these things because I couldn't ask my parents. They'd get angry at me for being dumb.

"What the hell is this mess?" Dad screamed from the living room. The wine glass fell over, rolling across the table. I caught it right before it fell off. "Get your head out of your ass and fix this!" I poked my head around the corner. He pointed at the cheese plate.

44

"Sorry," I mumbled. I worked quickly and was just finishing when the doorbell rang. "I'll get it!" I ran so fast I slid the last few feet to the door.

"Hey, kiddo! Long time no see!"

For five days, I wasn't allowed to see Jeremy or even talk to him on the phone. Mom found out about him because I took too long to come home from school one day. She called Jeremy's house to see if I was there. I should've given her a fake phone number, but I always thought of those things too late. I knew she knew about him because she asked if I had something to tell her. She always did that when I was in trouble.

I was scared Jeremy was going to forget about me. But when he said hey kiddo, I wasn't scared anymore. He sounded almost as excited to see me as I was to see him. No one else had ever been excited to see me before. It made me feel so warm inside I even let him mess up my hair.

"Hi," I croaked.

My father pushed his way past me. "Jack Welles."

"Jack, it's a pleasure," Jeremy said in a business voice like Dad's, shaking his hand. "Eleanor, it's good to finally meet you in person."

"Please, just Ellie," Mom said. Every time she said that to someone, I wondered if Grandma insisted that everyone call her Eleanor the same way she wanted everyone to call me Nicholas.

Jeremy gave a bottle of wine to Mom. "I know you said not to bring anything, but I couldn't come empty-handed." I was worried Mom would be mad because Jeremy didn't follow her instructions. I had to find a way to warn him how everything had to be perfect or I probably wouldn't be allowed to come over to his house anymore.

"Thank you so much," Mom said, smiling. If she was mad, she didn't show it. "I'll get this open so it can breathe. Jack, why don't you get our guest something to drink?"

"Pick your poison," Dad said in a super-loud voice, hitting Jeremy hard on the shoulder.

"Scotch, rocks," Jeremy said like an expert. I sat down next to Jeremy on the couch in the living room. He looked at me and smiled, but I was too nervous to smile back at him. Dad poured two glasses of

brown stuff and handed one to Jeremy. Mom came in and put the bottle Jeremy brought on the coffee table.

"I'm so glad you accepted our invitation on such short notice," Mom said.

"Not a problem," Jeremy answered. "I thought we should clear the air after all the confusion."

They all looked at me. I shrank into the couch and wished I could be small enough to crawl under the cushions.

"I still feel like I owe you an apology," Mom said. "I didn't mean to be so harsh over the phone."

"There's no need to apologize," Jeremy said, waving his hand. "I was just as caught off guard as you."

"No harm done," Dad interrupted. "Water under the bridge. No need to rehash what's already settled. So, what line of work are you in?"

"Still figuring that out, believe it or not," Jeremy said. "Right now, I'm between careers. I studied classical piano performance at Eastman, but like so many aspiring musicians it never quite worked out for me. Lately, I've been giving serious thought to teaching full time."

"Fascinating," Dad said. "It must've been a treat to go to school in Boston. Such a thriving music scene."

Mom put her hand on Dad's knee. "Isn't Eastman in Rochester?"

"Yes, it is," Jeremy said.

"Oh, *Eastman*," Dad said. "I thought you meant Juilliard. I've never been much for music, apart from being forced to take accordion lessons for a year."

Jeremy laughed. "You and every other kid during that era." He turned to Mom. "Nicholas tells me you're an attorney."

"I am. I started my career as a corporate lawyer writing contracts, but lately I've discovered a taste for litigation and have been spending more of my time in the courtroom."

"Being an attorney as a woman is impressive enough, let alone a litigator. After the way you handled yourself on the phone, I imagine you'll rise right to the top. You must be positively terrifying in a courtroom."

"I can be fierce when I need to be," Mom said. "But it's still a man's world. I've hit the glass ceiling trying to make partner, especially because

I've specialized in real estate development and construction for the last few years. I can't imagine any other industry being stuffed tighter with male chauvinists."

"I'm involved in construction and development as well, so it's been a good partnership," Dad said.

"Nicholas tells me you're very dedicated to your business," Jeremy said to him. "Some kind of consulting if I understood correctly?"

My father leaned forward. "I run a growing management and systems consulting business. I've dabbled in a few areas – hospitals, automotive repair, and fast food franchises – but lately most of my business comes from systems that improve bill estimation and purchasing for large construction projects." I understood all the words he said, but when he put them together into sentences they made no sense. I had no idea what he actually did. Something to do with computers. He had them all over his office. I was never allowed to touch them. "I've always been an entrepreneur. Tried working for other people, but I could never stomach the idea of making someone else rich off my back, know what I mean? I thrive on the challenge and having responsibility over everything – doing the books, writing the systems, or getting out there and selling."

"I have to admire your spirit," Jeremy said. "I've never been much of a businessman." He plucked a piece of cheese from my plate. "This looks like the creative kind of thing you would do," he said to me. I smiled a little.

"Another?" Dad asked. Jeremy handed over his glass.

"I understand you recently moved from Columbus," Jeremy said.

"About four months ago," Mom answered. "I was offered a position too good to pass up, so we relocated yet again. Between Jack's businesses and my career, we've moved so many times I've lost track. But now I think we're finally in a place where we can settle in for the long haul."

I knew how many times we moved.

"Come on, let's eat," Dad said and clapped his hands.

"Sounds great," Jeremy answered. "The smells from the kitchen have been driving me crazy."

"Nicholas, you may serve the food," Mom said to me. I ran into the kitchen. By the time they were sitting, I already had the salad, lamb,

and rice out on the table. I put some salad in Jeremy's bowl and a piece of meat on his plate. I was already sitting down when I realized I was supposed to do the same for Mom and Dad. They started talking about stuff I didn't care about, so I didn't really pay attention.

"Nicholas tells us so little about how he spends his time with you," Mom said. I heard my name so I started paying attention again.

"No great mystery there," Jeremy answered. "Most of the time is taken up with his piano lessons."

"Piano lessons?" Mom said. "Nicholas didn't say anything about learning to play the piano. I had no idea he was interested in music."

"Interested is hardly the word," Jeremy said. "This kid comes in from school and doesn't bother to take off his backpack or jacket before he starts playing. I have to pry him off after a few hours when I can't stand hearing the same few notes over and over again."

"It's wonderful you've found a passion," Mom said to me.

"Anything is better than those damned video games," Dad muttered. "I have no idea what kids see in them. Shoot the alien or chase ghosts around a maze. There's no strategy. I played chess as a kid and it did wonders for me."

"I play chess on the Atari," I mumbled.

"It's not the same," he fired back. "Chew with your mouth closed."

"I didn't know you played chess," Jeremy said. "We should play sometime. You'll probably kick my ass." I cringed. My parents didn't react. Maybe they didn't notice.

"I'm still not clear how the two of you met," Mom said.

"Nicholas offered to shovel my driveway," Jeremy answered. I hoped Dad didn't figure out it was the same day he screamed at me for not shoveling ours. "I was too lazy to do it and there he was. He was very conscientious and made sure to come back the next day to finish. We spent a little time sledding, had a snowball fight, and then he started dropping by occasionally."

"A snowball fight?" Mom looked at me. I was forbidden from snowball fights until I was eighteen. One time a bunch of kids ganged up on me. I went a little crazy and tried to beat one up. His mom called my mom.

"Just a little one," I mumbled.

"Speak up," Dad said.

"And the time Nicholas spent the night?" Mom asked.

"Not much to report. We went to the mall for dinner. I think that was the first time I gave you a piano lesson, wasn't it?" I nodded. "He was in bed by ten."

"Well, I certainly hope Nicholas isn't making a pest of himself," Mom said. "I'm sure the last thing a man your age needs is a child interfering with the other aspects of your life. I assume you have a romantic interest or two, an eligible bachelor like yourself."

Jeremy laughed. "Of course, but I'm between relationships right now. I was involved in a long-term thing that didn't work out and I'm not ready to get out there yet. I'm fairly well off, so I'm sure you understand how challenging it can be to find someone who's interested in more than the money."

"I'm not quite clear on that subject either," Mom said, leaning forward like she was about to pounce. "You mentioned you're not working. How exactly do you support such a well-to-do lifestyle?"

"No mystery there, either. My family's been successful in business and my share keeps me comfortable."

"You wouldn't mean the Stillwell family that owns SHR Development?" Dad asked.

Jeremy finished his glass of wine in one giant gulp. "One and the same. My father is SHR."

"You're Richard Stillwell's son?" Dad sounded surprised. So was I. How would my dad know who Jeremy's dad was? "I didn't know he had a second son."

"I'm not directly involved in the business, so it's hardly surprising." Jeremy leaned back in his chair. "Do you do any work for SHR?"

"Your father is something of a tough nut to crack," Dad said.

"Legendary," Jeremy nodded. "I'm stuffed. Ellie, this meal was exquisite."

"Thank you," Mom said. "Nicholas, you may clear the plates and serve the cake."

"Let me help with that," Jeremy said.

"I'm sure Nicholas can manage on his own," Mom said.

I didn't complain that it took me two trips to gather up all the dishes on my own. I put them in the sink and was about to cut the cake when I thought to ask if I should get the coffee too. I was about to push the swinging door open when I heard they were talking, quietly. I wasn't supposed to hear, so I listened through the door.

". . .can understand our concern, of course," Mom said. "We thought it was important to make sure you weren't the kind of person who might take advantage of a vulnerable boy like Nicholas."

"I think you're perfectly justified," Jeremy answered. "I'd want to know everyone my son spends time with, adult or child. Especially these days with all the drugs and who knows what else going on out there. I want to assure you that Nicholas has been anything but a nuisance. He's impeccably polite, always cleans up after himself, and is a pleasure to be around. My interest in him centers around his music. I'm not exaggerating when I say his progress has been astounding. He's only been playing for a couple of weeks and he's made more progress than most children make in a year. He has a gift, and I'd be honored to help develop it. That is, if you're comfortable with the idea."

"Of course we are," Dad said.

"Nicholas has changed for the better over the last few weeks," Mom said. "I think this last move was very hard on him. I'm pleased he's found something productive to do besides burning his eyes out in front of the television set. He needs to learn to apply himself. Junior high school is right around the corner."

"Then it's settled," Dad said.

I heard enough. I cut four giant sloppy pieces of cake and balanced them on my arms so I didn't have to make two trips. "Cake!" I announced.

"Please be careful," Mom said.

"You're going to make a mess," Dad muttered.

I put them down without dropping a single crumb.

"You may go back and get the coffee," Mom said.

They talked about the usual things that adults talk about, but I wasn't listening anymore. Everything seemed ok now and I was too excited thinking about what we were going to do the next time I went over to

his house. Jeremy finally pushed the half-eaten piece of cake away from him. "Fantastic, but too rich for me. Did you bake this yourself?"

"It comes from a tiny little bakery right on High Street," Mom said.

"You should have gotten their carrot cake instead," Dad said. Mom smiled.

I stood up. "May I please show Jeremy my room now?"

"Yes, you may," Mom said. Jeremy followed me up the stairs.

"This is your room?" he said, looking around. "You leave such a mess around my place. I expected it to be a disaster area."

"I cleaned up," I said. I spent hours on it. All the Legos were in their boxes (not the right boxes, but still), the clothes hung up and folded, the books organized by size and type, and the dishes secretly washed. I even vacuumed. I watched him look around, stopping at my bookshelf. "I think I see a theme here. Heinlein, Moorcock, McCaffrey, LeGuin, and those are just the ones I recognize. Which is your favorite?" I pulled the box set down and handed it to him. "Seriously? I didn't attempt the Lord of the Rings until I was in my twenties."

"I read them seven times. I even memorized some parts."

"I am truly impressed," he said. I could tell he meant it. "What do you like most about it?"

"I like the battles, and wizards, and things like that," I said. Which was true, but it wasn't the real reason. It was hard to talk about. In Middle Earth, things were much easier to understand. All you had to do was pick up a sword and start fighting. It seemed so much easier than figuring out how to make friends and do good in school. In the real world, Frodo and Sam wouldn't be heroes. They'd be teased for being short and get beaten up a lot. In the real world, Sauron always won.

"You already know it's ok for you to come over," he said.

I acted like I was surprised. "My parents said it was ok?"

"I saw you listening at the door," he said with narrowed eyes. The way he did it made me smile. "You're welcome to come by as much as you want."

"What if they change their minds?"

"Leave that to me," he said like Obi-Wan turning off the tractor beam. A secret plan just between us. "I want to invite you for Christmas. Maybe I shouldn't say this, but I don't think it's fair how your parents

fight over the holidays. I want you to have a real Christmas with a tree and cookies and the whole thing. We can go into New York for a show and have a fancy Christmas Eve dinner. Maybe Santa will leave a few presents if you're a good boy. What do you say?" I nodded. It sounded like the greatest thing ever. He patted the bed and I sat down next to him. "Your mother said you moved around a lot before you came here."

"Eight times. At least, I remember eight times. I think there were three more when I was too little to remember."

"Eight times," he said in his soft voice. Then, without any warning, he hugged me. Tight. I felt like I couldn't breathe. His arms were like iron bars. I stayed completely still even though I wanted to run away. After what felt like hours, he let me go. I slid away before he could do it again, but as soon as I was safe I felt bad again. It was the first time he'd ever hugged me. I knew it meant he liked me, more than a little. I wished I could be the kind of kid who was ok with being hugged by people who like them.

"Well," he said. "I guess we should go back downstairs."

My parents were talking to each other softly when we came down. They stopped as soon as they saw us. "Let me get you another drink," Dad said.

Jeremy stretched out his arms. "Thanks, but I'd better be going."

"You're welcome to stay," Mom said.

"Night's still young," Dad added.

"Wish I could, but I have some things I need to do tonight. We should do this again sometime soon."

"Absolutely," Dad agreed.

Jeremy moved so he was standing behind me and put his hands on my shoulders. I wasn't going to let myself flinch. "Getting a meeting with my father is impossible without the right recommendation. Why don't we have lunch in the city with Wendell Schwartz? He's the family lawyer and his word goes a long way. Besides, he owes me a couple of favors. How about this Wednesday at 21?"

Dad looked around for a notepad. "Number 21 on which street?"

"21 is the restaurant, dear," Mom said. "We'd be delighted."

"It's a date then," Jeremy said. He pointed at me. "I'll see you at 3:30 sharp tomorrow for your piano lesson." I nodded. A quick good night and he was gone. The house felt a lot colder without him. I turned around. They both looked mad. I didn't know what I did to get in trouble.

"Go to bed," Dad growled.

"It's only eight o'clock," I pointed out.

"Go to bed!" he screamed. I ran up the stairs. They started arguing before I got to my room. Usually, I didn't want to hear what they were arguing about, but tonight was different. I snuck back to the top of the stairs so I could listen.

". . .interrogating the man like that?" Dad said. I heard dishes crashing together.

"Was I supposed to ignore a grown man secretly allowing our son to spend the night at his house?" Mom yelled. "I had to make sure he was safe!"

"Come off it," he shouted back. "I kept saying you were blowing things out of proportion and tonight proves it!"

"As though you have any ability to read people," Mom fired back. "What's your track record? Two failed businesses because the partners you swore by were robbing you blind behind your back."

"That has nothing to do with this!" he screamed.

"Same old Jack," she said with a mean laugh. "First, you come off as a complete oaf pretending you know something about music. Then you blurt out the question about his family when it was patently obvious he was uncomfortable about the subject. The nasty comment about the carrot cake was just the icing, pun intended. I suppose I can forgive you for not knowing one of the most famous restaurants in New York because you don't know anything about anything."

"I got us the meeting," he growled.

"*I* got us the meeting," she yelled. "I've had it with your putting the roof over our heads and food on the table bullshit. Who earned more this year?"

"Ungrateful bitch," he spat. "I put you through school."

"You can't stand being out of control, can you? I'm through with being pushed around by you. I'm done starting over at a new firm every

time you come up with a harebrained scheme." I heard a loud crash. "So that's how it is? Big caveman, ooga ooga! What's the matter, Jack? Can't stand the truth?" The front door slammed. Dad's tires squealed in the driveway as he drove away.

I couldn't stop shaking. They weren't fighting about me but it didn't matter. It was still my fault. I crept back to my room and sat on the floor until I heard the door to my parent's room slam.

The shoelaces were still in the same place under my mattress.

I knew one thing for sure as I took off my clothes.

No one was as sick and disgusting as me.

Chapter 5

December 24, 1981

Jeremy reached over my shoulders from behind. I watched his hands in the mirror. "Cross it like this, then wrap it around. Put it through here, keep your finger on it so the loop stays open, then pull it through like this." The knot appeared like magic.

"Let me try," I said. I pulled the tie apart and tried to follow his instructions.

"Not there, put it through the other way," he corrected.

"That's what I was doing wrong!" I said. I pulled it through and the magic happened, but this time I cast the spell. I straightened it out, a perfect triangle right in the middle of my collar. I was proud, and when I looked at his eyes in the mirror I could tell he was proud of me too.

"Looking sharp, kiddo," he said.

"Uh huh," I answered. I never liked wearing suits because they weren't comfortable. The ones my mom bought were always a yucky brown color, too big or too small, and felt scratchy. The one Jeremy got me was dark blue like his, fit just right, and felt soft and warm. He left me to finish brushing my hair, which is when I thought of telling him how he looked sharp too.

The sun was just coming up when we left the house. I didn't feel tired at all even though I hardly slept last night. I was excited because this was the first time I was going to New York City. We were going to see everything because we were supposed to walk everywhere instead of staying in a car. I was also scared because I was sure we were going to get mugged. Everyone got mugged in New York. Jeremy told me it

wasn't true, but I was sure a gang or drug addict would attack us because we were all dressed up and looked rich.

"Manhattan is a giant grid," he explained to me. "Avenues run up and down, streets run side to side. The numbers go up if you go north or west and down if you go south or east. So, First Avenue is all the way to the east and First Street is all the way to south. Except that's not true because there's a whole bunch of streets south of First Street and there's more avenues east of First. I guess you're screwed if you go past First either way."

He was good at explaining things.

He put in a tape. The first song was the Chopin Ballade number one, my rainy-day song. "This is the Rubinstein," I said.

"I can't believe you know that after five notes," he said.

"It's different from the Horowitz. I like this one better."

"What makes it better?" he asked.

It wasn't something I could put into words. "It's just more right. More like how you play it."

"Music is about interpretation," he said. "There's no wrong or right. After all, Horowitz is a genius and I'm a nobody. When you learn how, you can play it however you want."

"I'll never be able to play something that hard," I said.

"At the rate you're going? Look what you can do after playing for a month. You're playing four note chords without thinking about it, changing hand positions without looking, and reading music fluently. You'll be playing it next month." I frowned. "Ok, maybe two months from now."

I liked when he said things like that even when they weren't true. I looked out the window and pretended it was a recording of me instead of a famous pianist. Something had changed inside me since I met Jeremy. When I used to daydream, I imagined being a mighty hero slaying the dragon or leading a squadron of space fighters attacking the evil aliens. Now, I dreamed about things that were ordinary. I dreamt about what it'd be like if Jeremy was my father and I lived with him. How we'd have fun all the time instead of just the times I got to visit. How he'd sing and play the guitar when I went to sleep every night. How he'd help me with my homework and tying ties. Except it was

hard to imagine Jeremy as a dad. He looked like a grown-up and could drive and had money, but he acted more like a kid. I didn't know what that made him, but I didn't think about it a lot.

"I'm serious," he said. "Keep it up and you have the potential to be a truly remarkable pianist."

"I like playing," I said.

"No shit," he answered.

"Here we are!" he said with a huge grin.

"What's FAO Schwartz?" I asked.

"What's FAO Schwartz?" he said, his eyes all wide. "I can't believe you've never heard of it. FAO Schwartz is the best, biggest, most amazing, unbelievable, incredible, awesomest toy store in the known universe!" It was funny how he was more excited about a toy store than me. It made me want to be more excited. He grabbed my hand and dragged me through the revolving glass doors, guarded by two guys dressed up like tin soldiers.

The only toy stores I knew were Toys R Us and KB Toys at the mall. They were always a mess and they never had anything I wanted. When we walked into FAO Schwartz, I could tell right away it was nothing like those toy stores. In the middle, there was a giant Christmas tree surrounded by a whole army of robot bears singing a song welcoming us to their world of toys. The store went back further than I could see and had something like five or six different levels.

Jeremy pulled me around like he was the kid and I was the grown-up. They had all the regular toys, but it was the special stuff you couldn't get anywhere else that made the store amazing. Like Monopoly sets carved out of wood with gold covered pieces. Or four-foot long realistic model ships with complicated rope rigging and tiny furniture in the cabin. Or chess sets carved out of real gemstones. Or a replica of Luke's light saber that looked completely real (except it didn't actually have a light blade). I stared at it for ten minutes before I let Jeremy drag me away.

We ended up on a floor that had nothing but stuffed animals. It was like a zoo. Every animal from the real world had a stuffed version, even animals I never heard of. They had a whole section just for the bears — regular teddy bears in all shapes and sizes, more realistic looking bears, and special bears that cost over a hundred dollars in locked cabinets.

"Get a load of this, kiddo," he said. He pulled me around a corner and pointed at the biggest teddy bear I'd ever seen. It was bigger than Jeremy. A lot bigger. "I've always loved teddy bears," he said. "How about you?"

I was too old for stuffed animals. My animals were in a bag in the back of my closet. All except my bear Scruffy. I kept him on a shelf near my bed so I could see him when I went to sleep and if I woke up in the middle of the night. I didn't want him in bed with me anymore, but putting him in a bag in the dark closet would be cruel. He kept me company on too many lonely nights in a new room after the first day at a new school. I felt better knowing he was nearby. Just in case.

"Yeah," I said.

"We've got to get a picture. You sit on the bear and wrap his arms around you. Yeah, like that." He snapped a picture with his camera. The giant bear had soft fur and was all spongy. I liked spongy bears better than stiff ones. Stiff bears didn't seem friendly. Scruffy was very spongy. The giant bear had the same kind of expression on his face as Scruffy. I could tell from the way he looked that he didn't care if I wet the bed or got beaten up or did something stupid. He liked me anyway.

It was hard to get up from sitting on the bear. When I finally rolled off, I looked around for Jeremy. I couldn't find him anywhere. The store was very crowded and there were people all around me. For a minute, I got scared he left me, but then he grabbed me from behind. "Pretty crazy here, huh?" He smiled, and for a second I thought he looked just like Scruffy too.

My feet were getting sore from all the walking. Going twenty blocks was like going twenty miles. "Are we almost there?"

"You tell me," he said. "We're going to 65th between 9th and 10th avenues."

I looked at the street sign. "Three more blocks."

"We'd better pick up the pace or we'll be late," he said. "The show starts in twenty minutes."

"What kind of show?" I asked. He didn't answer because everything today was a secret. I only found out what we were going to do when we started doing it. We were coming from Rockefeller plaza where they had ice skating and what had to be the world's biggest Christmas tree, way bigger than the one at FAO Schwartz. Jeremy wanted to go ice skating, but since I didn't know how and it'd be too hard all dressed up, we watched and had hot dogs from a cart. He made me get sauerkraut on mine. It looked like swamp grass, but I suppose it tasted ok. I wanted another but he told me dinner was going to be big.

"Here we are, Lincoln Center," he said. "Over there is the Metropolitan Opera." I got worried for a second that he was going to make me see an opera, but we went to one of the other buildings. I looked at the poster. This was even worse than the opera.

"We're going to the ballet?" I groaned.

"It's not as bad as you make it sound," he said. "The Nutcracker is a Christmas tradition. I'm sure you're going to like it. You probably know most of the music already."

I looked at him like he was crazy.

Our seats were all the way down by the stage in the middle. I wondered what I was going to do for the next five or six hours or however long the ballet would take to finish. Maybe if I was lucky I'd fall asleep. The lights went out and everyone started clapping for no reason. "It's for the conductor," Jeremy whispered. "He's down in the orchestra pit but we can't see him because we're up close." They stopped clapping and the music started.

"I heard this before," I said to him. "In a cartoon, I think."

"Told you," he said.

The curtain opened to show an old-fashioned town. A bunch of dancers came out and started doing their ballet moves. I couldn't believe what I was seeing. I had to be wrong.

"They're kids," I whispered to Jeremy.

"Yes, kids dance ballet," Jeremy whispered back.

"But. . ." I couldn't say it. The idea was too ridiculous.

"But what?" he whispered.

"They're *boys*."

"So?"

"Only girls do ballet," I said. I couldn't believe he didn't know something that obvious.

"You understand there are men in the ballet, right?" I nodded. "When do you think they learned?"

What he said made sense, but I still couldn't believe it was true. I tried to imagine what life had to be like for a boy who did ballet. They'd get teased and beaten up worse than me. Their dads would wonder why they didn't have normal sons. Maybe they kept it a secret. They'd slouch down in the car when they went to ballet lessons in different towns where no one knew them. I imagined they were all best friends with each other, sticking together, helping each other survive school and parents and bullies. I wondered what it would be like to have friends like that. It almost made me want to take ballet lessons. Not really, but still.

It was hard to understand what was going on because I was daydreaming about the ballet boys through most of the first part. Something about Christmas, a giant mouse, and a battle with a weird looking soldier. A lot of smoke appeared on the stage and the music changed. It started off slow and soft, but soon it got louder and more powerful. I felt it inside, like when I heard the Ballade for the first time. Not exactly the same, because this music didn't make me picture a story. Instead, it made me feel excited and triumphant, like the feeling I got when I read about the victory at Helms Deep or the Pelennor Fields. It kept building, getting stronger until it finally exploded. The soldier had the girl up in the air, spinning around, flying. I thought if I jumped up on stage, I could fly too. The music told me so.

And then without any warning that part of the music ended and moved on to something that wasn't as powerful. I realized I was on the edge of my chair and slid back. I hoped that amazing music would come back, but the first part ended and the lights came on. I got the book from under the chair so I could find out what that piece was called.

"You really got into that, didn't you?" I stared at my program even harder. "Don't be embarrassed – it's a gift to feel music so deeply." The piece was called Scene in the Pine Forest. Like it was just another scene. Like it didn't matter. Something in-between the important parts instead of being the most important part. How could anybody think it didn't count?

I couldn't wait for the second part to start. Now that I was paying more attention it wasn't too bad. I recognized a lot of the music and liked it. Sometimes the dancing was more like gymnastics, which was fun to watch. I was disappointed when the end came because no other pieces made me feel like the pine forest. Still, I meant it when I kept clapping even when my hands got sore.

When we got outside, it was getting dark. Men in red coats were guarding a line that stretched on forever to get a taxi. "This is going to take a while," Jeremy moaned.

I pointed at a line of horse drawn carriages across the street. "Could we take those? It doesn't look like anyone is waiting."

"Great idea," he said. I smiled. "They won't actually take us anywhere, but sometimes it's nice to go nowhere."

I nodded. We climbed in. The dark red velvet seats were soft, just like the blanket Jeremy spread on top of us. He moved over and put his arm around my shoulders. I let him. I even leaned against him, just a little.

"Are you having a merry Christmas?" he asked.

I nodded.

⌒⌒⌒

"Welcome, mess yours," the guy in the tuxedo said. He sounded like Pepe le Pew. "How may ah assist you?"

"Stillwell, party of two," Jeremy said in his business voice.

"Ah yes, ah have ze best table in the house for you." He snapped his fingers and two more guys in tuxedos magically appeared to surround us. I tried to grab Jeremy's hand, but he was out of reach, letting the guy behind him take his coat off. I felt stupid.

"Don't worry, I'll give it back," the guy behind me said. I knew it was a joke, but it made me feel even dumber. There were more guys in tuxedos at the table pulling out chairs, filling water glasses, and putting napkins on our laps. Like each waiter only had one job to do. I wondered what it was like to be the napkin guy. The chair wasn't like a normal restaurant chair – more like one for sitting in front of a fireplace in a castle. I felt like it was swallowing me.

"This is really fancy," I whispered, but Jeremy didn't hear. Fancy wasn't a big enough word. They had chandeliers, carpet on the floor, and candles that made the whole room sparkle. I had six forks next to my plate. Was I supposed to use a different one for each bite? Another soldier in the tuxedo army put a gigantic menu in my hands. I couldn't read anything because it was in French. It felt like everyone was looking at me, the kid who had no idea what to do. The kid who didn't belong. I wished he hadn't brought me here.

"This is my favorite restaurant in the city," Jeremy said. "Christmas Eve dinner is supposed to be special." He looked up from his menu. I was worried he didn't approve of me either. "Are you nervous?"

I started to shake my head, but I changed my mind and nodded. "It's just a restaurant, no different than any other restaurant."

"There's too many forks," I said.

He smiled. "One for each course. Start from the outside and work your way in."

"I'm going to do something wrong."

I thought he was going to tell me I was being stupid. "If you feel confused, pat your mouth with your napkin. I'll show you what to do." He looked down at his menu, so I looked at mine.

"I never had French food before," I said.

"Sure you have. I know you like French onion soup and croissants. And French fries, but those aren't actually French. If you want, I'll pick out things I'm sure you'll like."

"You won't order anything gross?"

"I promise," he said. I had no idea if he was keeping that promise when he talked to the waiter, a stream of words coming out that I couldn't understand. I sipped carefully at my water, scared I would spill it.

"I'm looking forward to Christmas," he said. "If you weren't around, I'd be alone with another TV dinner."

"How come you don't go see your family?" I blurted out.

"We don't get along very well," he said, not angry at me for asking. "I haven't seen them since my mother passed away a few years ago. I don't mind – all they do for Christmas is go out to Connecticut and get drunk. Their liquor bill could probably put you through college for a year." I knew he was joking, but laughing felt wrong with all the fanciness around. "Besides, I'll bet you're a lot more fun when you're drunk." I wished he'd stop joking.

The waiter put a strange plate down in front of me. It had six little indentations. Each one had a small shell in it surrounded by slimy looking liquid with green stuff on top. "What is this?" I said, trying to push myself back into my chair as far as I could.

"Escargot. Otherwise known as snails." He said snails like he was saying peanut butter sandwich. He *promised*. I wanted to push the plate away, but then I'd have to *touch* it. "Snails are nothing more than an excuse to eat garlic butter, and I know you like that. Use the little fork to dig them out." I shook my head, hard. "Try some butter first." He dipped some bread into one of the indentations.

"It's all slimy," I said.

"There's no slime." I shook my head again. "You're going to love them, I promise. I would never lie to you. Trust me." I got a weird feeling inside me. Instead of the bread, I picked up the little fork and dug a gray thing out of one of the shells. I wasn't trying to be brave – I was so scared I was almost shaking. I wasn't trying to impress anyone either, like how some kids do gross or painful things to show off. I was only going to eat the snail because he wanted me to. Before I could change my mind, I shoved it in my mouth. I expected it to wriggle. I expected it to taste even more gross than the snot flavor I imagined. I expected to throw up all over the table. But it wasn't like that. It was chewy and tasted like garlic bread.

"See?" he said as I swallowed and started to dig out another one. I giggled, just a little, but that seemed ok now. It was like I was in a different restaurant, one that didn't feel scary. It felt cozy, friendly, and warm.

Just like Jeremy.

The giant teddy bear from FAO Schwartz sat watching us from the corner. I still couldn't figure out how Jeremy did it. The bear was sitting on the porch with a giant bow around his neck when we got back from New York. The look on his face was like he was asking what took us so long. He was so big I couldn't carry him in. I had to drag him. His black eyes were sparkly from the millions of lights on the Christmas tree. I helped put them on. Jeremy put me on his shoulders to do the top because it was too high for him to reach. I didn't think he'd be strong enough to carry me. He pretended he was going to drop me, which was fun.

I felt cozier than I ever felt before, snuggled in a corner of the couch with my head leaning against Jeremy's shoulder. The bear looked cozy too. The fire was roaring. The new flannel pajamas Jeremy got me with candy canes and Christmas trees on them were soft and comfy. I felt a nice kind of full, but not stuffed like I did when dinner was over. Cookies and cocoa were on the table in case I wanted them. I didn't, but it was nice knowing they were there.

The announcer said it was midnight. Christmas. I pulled his present from the hiding spot behind the pillows and handed it to him. "You didn't have to get me anything," he said. I didn't care if I didn't have to. I wanted to. He didn't notice how bad I was at wrapping as he ripped it open. "Is this what I think it is? It's a pool cue, a nice one. A really nice one. A really, really, really nice one." It cost me everything I had saved up, seventy-two dollars and sixty-nine cents. The pool stick and case were supposed to cost a lot more, but when the guy at the store found out I was buying it for my friend he let me have it anyway. Usually, I got excited about getting presents. I never got excited before about giving one. I could tell he loved my present because he was running his hands all over it and then he got up so he could hit a ball on the table.

"Your turn," he said. I looked at all the boxes under the tree, but I didn't want to open one. I wanted to keep the feeling I already had.

Opening a present would change that feeling. He didn't argue when I shook my head. I watched him stretch the sleeping bags out by the fire, side by side. He set up the bear next to mine so it would be facing me. I climbed in, pushing myself against him, happy when he put his arm over me. I couldn't describe how I felt. All jumbled up but in a good way. I didn't know a lot about what it felt like to have a friend, but I knew what I was feeling was something different. Something bigger.

"Merry Christmas, kiddo," he said. I snuggled closer.

"Merry Christmas," I said back.

And I meant it.

James Edison

Chapter 6

January 18, 1982

A giant bee was trapped inside my head, buzzing and banging against my skull trying to get out. I thought I could squash it if I slapped the right place on my nightstand. That didn't make sense, so I was surprised when it worked. My head didn't stop hurting even though the buzzing stopped. My eyes opened. The clock said 8:47. I couldn't imagine what 8:47 meant. It could mean a lot of things, anything except the time. . .

I jerked up like I was a puppet on strings. 8:47. School started in thirteen minutes. The pounding in my head felt like one of those loud hammers that make holes in roads. I looked at the clock again, hoping I was wrong. 8:48. The one morning Mom trusted me to wake up for school by myself. No way I could make it on time now. She'd never believe me if I said I felt sick. I had no time to get ready, so I put on the same clothes as yesterday and the day before that. I didn't want to tell Mom the new clothes I got a month ago didn't fit anymore. She'd tell me I shouldn't sneak a whole bag of candy into my room and eat it all in one night. I didn't brush my teeth or my hair since there was no one to yell at me.

My head hurt worse than I could ever remember. I crept into my parent's bathroom and got the headache medicine. Usually I took one, but it was so bad I swallowed two of them. I still wasn't sure two would be enough to make it go away, so I wrapped a bunch more pills in a tissue and stuffed them into my pocket. The clock in the kitchen said 8:56. No time for breakfast and no money for lunch. My backpack

hadn't been touched since I got home from school on Friday. My homework was still inside. I hadn't done any of it. I was all the way to the path through the woods before I realized I forgot to lock the door and had to go all the way back.

No matter how hard I tried, I did everything wrong.

When I came home after New Year's, Mom told me that things were going to be different. My Atari was gone from the hiding place in her closet, probably in the trash, and she somehow disconnected the TV so it only showed snow. She told me I had to shape up or my books would get taken away. I didn't know what I did to make her get so strict. I didn't know exactly what I needed to do to "shape up" either. But the Atari, the TV, and the books – none of them really mattered.

I wasn't allowed to be friends with Jeremy anymore.

She made me come straight home after school every day. If I didn't run, I'd miss her phone call. Sometimes, she'd call again later in the afternoon to make sure I didn't sneak out. Christmas felt like a dream instead of something that actually happened. Did we really stay up all night playing that game he bought me, the one with the weird dice and no board but made me really scared when I thought my character was going to die in a battle with some ghost thing that could kill you with one touch? Did we listen to music in our pajamas for a whole day? Did we go out to eat all the time? Did we see an R rated movie? Did we sleep every single night by the fire? She could keep the Atari, the TV could stay disconnected, and she could even have my books. I didn't care as long as she let me see Jeremy again. I couldn't stop thinking terrifying things – like what if he didn't want to see me anymore, or what if he didn't like me anymore, or what if he forgot all about me, or what if he was the one who told my mom not to let me come over.

I had to walk all the way around the school because only the front doors were unlocked. The headache medicine wasn't helping. The black and white flecks in the stone floor looked like they were swirling. The clock said it was 9:22.

"I need a late slip," I mumbled.

"Of course, honey," the secretary said. She was nice. "What's your name?"

"Nicholas Welles," a loud voice said before I could answer. Principal Chessenring came out of her office, hands on her hips. She wasn't nice. "I recall Nicholas being late on a number of other occasions." She got a file out of the cabinet. My permanent record. "Tardy six times within the last three months. Do you have any excuse for your tardiness this morning?"

I shrugged and stared at the floor.

"My school will not tolerate repeated tardiness." The way she kept saying tardiness made it sound like a disease. "A letter will be going home to your parents. You will report to detention after school for the rest of the week." I wanted to explain I'd get in even more trouble if I wasn't home when my mom called. I wanted to explain that it wasn't my fault I was late. I didn't because it *was* my fault. Everything was my fault. "Report to class immediately," she said, pushing the pink slip into my hand.

The class was doing math problems on the board when I went in. My headache was so bad I couldn't concentrate. I messed up every time it was my turn. Everyone laughed at me.

The day kept getting worse. I handed a blank sheet of notebook paper to the girl behind me in science, hoping she'd pretend to grade it like a lot of kids did because the teacher never checked. She raised her hand and told everyone I didn't do my homework. We had a fill-in-the-blank quiz in social studies on the reading I was supposed to do over the weekend. When I handed it in, the only thing I wrote on the paper was my name. I was starving by lunch, but I had no money and no friends to share with. I sat at my desk and tried to read my book while everyone ate and had fun. My headache was still pounding.

When I was younger, I used to hope each new school would be different. But I'd been to enough schools by now to know that every school has one. The kid who knew exactly where to hit to make it hurt the most. The kid who made sure everyone saw just how much it hurt. The kid who never got in trouble for it.

In this school, his name was Tommy Walker.

I didn't notice him sneaking up on me until he snatched the book out of my hands. I stared at him while he walked away without turning around. He tossed the book into the trash can. I tried to get it back out,

but it was spaghetti day so the pages were covered in sauce. It was ruined. I threw it as hard as I could back into the trash can and sat down, putting my head down onto my folded arms. I wished the world would just go away.

I should've stayed by the doors for recess away from the other kids, but there were a bunch of boys gathered around and I got curious because I was stupid. They were taking turns pushing each other onto a patch of ice. It was fun to watch until someone pushed me, hard. I fell over and smacked my head on the ground so hard it made me feel dizzy. "Look, weebles really do fall down!" Tommy yelled. Everyone laughed. I tried to get up, but I slipped and fell on my butt.

"He looks like a beached whale," some other kid shouted. "Push him back out to sea!" I curled up into a little ball and didn't move, hoping they would leave me alone. "Come on, get your fat ass off the ice," one of them yelled.

I couldn't help it. I screamed as loud as I could. I felt like I was still screaming even after I stopped. I had no idea why I screamed. The whole playground went silent.

"You," the teacher said, pointing at me. "You're sitting against the wall for the rest of recess." I followed her away, sitting by the doors and putting my head between my knees. I heard a girl say "he's in trub-ble" in the way only girls knew how. I waited by the wall until everyone else went inside. Kids called me "dork" and "retard" and "mental case" when they walked by. All afternoon I kept hearing whispers about me.

"Progress reports are going home today," the teacher said. "These need to be signed and returned by the end of the week." She put a brown envelope on my desk. I knew I shouldn't open it, but I did anyway. There were a lot of boxes checked. None of them were the good ones. I was going to have to show this to my parents. There was no hope I could ever shape up enough to see Jeremy again. My aching head roared at me.

"Wittle baby gonna cwy now?" Tommy said, standing right by my desk.

Everything went quiet, even though I knew everyone was still talking. My face felt hot. The room melted away until the only thing I could see was the dark hair on the back of Tommy Walker's head. Then

I was standing. I was holding my chair up in the air but I didn't remember picking it up. I watched the chair slam into Tommy's head like it was on TV. It should've made a noise when it hit him, but I couldn't hear anything. In slow motion, he twisted to one side. Then he crumpled up and fell. He didn't move after that. It looked like he was dead. I hoped he was dead. The chair was back over my head. All I wanted to do was to bash him again, and again, and again, and again.

Then the chair was gone. I didn't know how it disappeared. Hands came from everywhere, wrapping around me and dragging me to the floor. The world rushed back into full speed. Someone was screaming. I realized it was me. The noise of the room rushed into my ears, boys yelling and girls shrieking. I pulled, strained, kicked, punched, and bit - anything to get free from the kids holding me down so I could finish what I started. It almost worked, until teachers rushed in from nowhere to take over. They were shouting orders at each other, pinning me face down, one on each of my arms and legs. I kept screaming and struggling, but they were too strong for me. I didn't know how long it was before I ran out of energy. My headache came back as soon as I stopped.

"I think he's finally calming down," one of them said.

"I think he's just exhausted," another one said.

They kept me pinned down even though I stopped struggling. One of them put her hands in my pockets. "Pills," she said like she won a prize.

"Aspirin," I mumbled.

"Sure, *aspirin*," another said.

They eventually let me get up. The whole room was a mess, desks and chairs everywhere. They walked me down to the principal's office, digging their fingers into my arms. Two of the teachers stared at me with their arms crossed in case I decided to do it again. The clock said 3:42. I already missed my mother's phone call. I stared at my hands, trying to pretend they weren't mine. But they were mine. My hands were holding the chair. I was the one who hit Tommy with it.

The principal sat down and didn't say anything for a long time. "I am thoroughly disgusted," she started. "Violence and drugs. Do you have anything to say for yourself? I don't know if you appreciate the

seriousness of the situation you're in right now. You should consider yourself lucky Thomas wasn't more seriously injured."

"Is he ok?" I said. My voice was raspy.

"We hope he will be," she said, making it sound like he might die.

She dialed the phone. "Eleanor Welles, please. I see, when will she be available? Yes, if she calls please have her contact Lake Elementary school regarding her son. There's been an incident. Thank you." She hung up the phone and dialed again. I could hear my father's voice on his answering machine. "Mr. Welles, please contact Lake Elementary. There's been an incident and we can't release your son until a parent comes to pick him up. Thank you." She stared at me as she hung up. "If I'm not able to reach your parents before five o'clock, I'll have to call the police. They can keep you in custody until your parents can be reached."

I started shaking. They were going to arrest me. They were going to handcuff me, fingerprint me, and lock me in jail. No one was going to pick me up. I could imagine my dad telling the police I deserved to be in jail. He'd make me stay there until I learned my lesson. But I never learned my lesson so I'd be in jail forever.

"Is there another adult who can pick you up?"

I didn't know what else to do. I didn't want to go to jail. "Jeremy Stillwell," I mumbled.

"And he is?" she asked.

"My friend." I gave her his phone number.

It took him five minutes to get to the school. He screeched his tires right outside the office. The principal glared at me like it was my fault. I shouldn't have called him. When he found out what I did, he'd probably never want to talk to me again.

"Kiddo, what happened?" he asked. He sounded scared.

"Nicholas assaulted another boy," the principal interrupted. "The other boy was unconscious when the ambulance arrived but has since woken up."

"Oh my god," he said, putting his arm around my shoulder. "Are you alright? Who'd you hit?"

"Thomas Walker," the principal answered.

"Isn't that the kid you were telling me about?" he asked me. I shrugged.

"We also believe Nicholas was under the influence of drugs," she said. "Several of his teachers reported that he was acting strangely today and we found suspicious pills in his pocket."

"Nick isn't the kind of kid who does drugs," Jeremy said. "What kind of pills did you have in your pocket?"

"Aspirin," I mumbled.

"I'd hardly call aspirin a drug," he said to the principal.

"Students are not permitted to have any kind of medications while at school. Regardless, his behavior was clearly indicative of drug use." She scribbled in her folder and handed a bunch of papers to Jeremy. "Please deliver these to Nicholas' parents. They describe the expulsion process and appeal rights. I'm also recommending that Nicholas be remanded to a residential treatment center for evaluation."

"A what?" I mumbled. I started shaking again.

"No one is sending you anywhere," Jeremy said sharply.

"Mr. Stillwell, I hardly. . ."

"Let me see if I understand this correctly," he interrupted. "I've heard all about this Tommy Walker. That punk has been making Nick's life at school a living hell. I'll give you one example out of the dozen Nick shared with me. Last month, he attacked Nick in the woods, threw his school books in the water, and left him covered with mud. Nick told me he complained to his teachers and to you several times and nothing was done about it. So, when this poor kid finally decides he's had enough and fights back, you throw the book at him?"

"I don't think you understand the gravity of this situation," she said.

"I understand just fine," Jeremy answered, leaning forward in his chair. "I'm not going to allow you to punish Nick in order to cover up your incompetence."

"Excuse me?" she said.

"Let me spell it out for you very clearly," he said, like he was a teacher talking to a misbehaving kid. "Up to now, you've allowed Nick to be severely bullied. You were aware what was happening and did nothing. Questions will be asked after an incident like this, and if you blame it all on drugs your negligence will go unnoticed. I'm going to

make this extraordinarily easy for you, much easier than you deserve. You're going to withdraw that expulsion and that ridiculous treatment center recommendation. You're going to make sure this punk never bullies Nick or any other kid ever again. And you're going to personally apologize to Nick for the misery you've forced him to endure."

She stared at Jeremy so hard I imagined fire coming out of her eyes.

Jeremy leaned forward more. "If you choose not to follow my instructions, I'm going to have my attorney tear your career apart. I'll drag every poor decision you've ever made through every newspaper I can find. By the time I'm done with you, no one'll hire you to be the school janitor. I'll sue this school district to the ground for the suffering you've inflicted on Nick, and I'll make sure you're the one who pays for the rest of your life. And in case you were wondering, the answer is yes. I'm one of *those* Stillwells."

"How dare you threaten me," she said with her lips barely moving.

"I haven't even started threatening you," he answered the same way. It felt like they stared at each other without blinking for a long time. I was so scared I forgot to breathe.

"We're leaving," he said sharply. He took the papers from her desk and tore them in half, tossing them into the trash. Then he grabbed my pills and looked at one. "If you bothered to look, you'd notice it says Bayer." He threw it on the desk in front of her.

He got down on his knees in front of me and brushed the hair out of my eyes. "Let's get you home, kiddo," he said in his soft voice. I let him lead me out of the office. He opened the car door for me. I stared out the window until he pulled up in front of my house. "Do you want me to come inside?" he asked.

"I don't want to go here," I said to the window.

"Let's go for a drive," he said. I watched my house disappear. "We can get ice cream if you want." I didn't answer. He kept driving for a while. I knew he wanted to talk to me and he wanted me to talk to him, but I didn't have anything I wanted to say. I felt blank. I knew I should feel scared. This was trouble like I was never in before. They were going to kick me out of school. They were going to send me away to jail or the insane asylum. I realized I didn't know where we were,

but that was a good thing. I wanted to be as far away as I could from my school, my parents, and my life.

I waited until I felt far enough away before I said something. "Am I supposed to talk to you now?"

"Only if you want to," Jeremy said. "I'm happy to listen. If you don't want to talk, I understand. I can see you're hurting and I don't know what to do to help you."

"You can't help me," I said.

"Please let me try," he said.

"I'm crazy," I whispered.

"Tell me what happened."

Even though I didn't want to tell him, it came out anyway. "I woke up with a bad headache and I was late for school and I failed my social studies quiz and Tommy threw my book in the trash and got it covered with spaghetti sauce and I got pushed on the ice and I got a bad progress report and then Tommy made fun of me and I. . ." I couldn't say it. I didn't even want to think it.

"And you hit him," he said instead. "You had a horrible day."

"I'm in a lot of trouble," I muttered, drawing randomly on the glass.

"I'll help," he said. "It won't be as bad as you think."

"It won't matter if you help," I said. "I got a bad progress report. Mom is going to take away my books."

"I'll talk to her," he said. "I can fix this."

"I'm never going back to that school anyway," I said.

"They're not going to expel you. I won't let them."

"They're going to send me to the insane asylum." I pressed my nose against the glass. "I belong there. I'm crazy."

"Because you fought back against a bully? That's not crazy."

"I wanted to kill him," I said.

"Wanting to kill someone is one thing," he said. "It doesn't mean you could've actually done it."

"I could've. I would've. I know I could do it." He wouldn't believe me. But I knew I could. I'd already proved I could. "Can we go to your house now?"

"I don't think that's a good idea," he said.

"I want to go to your house," I said.

He didn't answer, turning the car around in the street. We didn't talk on the way back. Jeremy seemed to understand that I could only let a little bit out at a time and I already let out enough for now. He parked the car in the garage and I got out. The giant bear was sitting in the corner of the lobby. I could tell he knew I was crazy by the way he looked at me. I sat in the corner of the couch and tried to be as small as I could. The bear was still staring. "Stop looking at me," I muttered. He stared even harder. Jeremy sat down beside me.

"You're not crazy," he said. "You're depressed. You were so happy over Christmas, smiling and coming out of your shell. I shouldn't be saying this, but I don't understand why your parents won't let you visit anymore."

"Do you still like me?" I whispered.

"Of course I do," he whispered back.

Feelings rushed into me, the ones from Christmas. Even stronger. They filled me up until there was nothing I could do to hold them inside.

"I don't like you," I said to him.

"Kiddo?" he said.

"No. I love you."

The room felt cold. I shouldn't have said it. It sounded wrong the moment it came out. My stomach tied in knots. My toes twitched. I knew what he was going to say. "You're a good friend, but. . ." or "That's not really appropriate."

He breathed out slowly.

"Nick," he whispered. His eyes looked wet. "I love you too."

I woke up when I felt him lifting my head from his lap, but I pretended to stay asleep. I heard the door opening.

"He had a terrible day," Jeremy said. "We should let him sleep and discuss this in the kitchen."

"There's nothing to discuss," Mom barked. "Get up. Off that couch right now and get your shoes on. We're going home."

I acted like I just woke up, rubbing my eyes. Jeremy put my shoes down in front of me. For a moment, we looked at each other. Please, I tried to tell him with my eyes. Do what you did in the principal's office. Make everything better. Don't let her take me away.

He stood up. "His things are by the door," he said to her and disappeared down the hall.

"I have no words to describe how furious I am with you," she spat at me. "I can't even look at you right now. When we get home, you will go straight to your room and if you come out for anything so help me. . ." Her fingers wrapped around my arm in the same spot where the teachers held me down. I wanted to scream, yell, and beg, but I couldn't. I let her drag me to her car. We drove away. I looked through the back window, but the door to Jeremy's house was already closed.

James Edison

Chapter 7

January 26, 1982

I sat in the corner of my room, wedged between the dresser and the wall. My knees were pulled up to my chest, stretching out my t-shirt as far as it could go. My mouth was dry and my thumb was sore from chewing on it. I was hungry, but I didn't want to leave my room while anyone else was awake. My hair felt sweaty and greasy when I scratched my head. It was going to get dark soon. I liked the dark better because I didn't have to look at anything.

I picked up the cordless phone I'd stolen from the kitchen and pushed the redial button, counting fifteen rings before I hung up. Fifteen was the right number. Long enough for him to get to the phone no matter where he was in the house. The first time I let it ring until it wouldn't ring anymore. I was sure if I hung it up he'd pick up right afterwards. I waited for three minutes before I dialed again. The phone was still warm. I didn't let it get cold until the battery died.

I hit my head against the wall – hard enough to feel it shake but not hard enough to hurt. I wanted to talk to him so badly. I needed to hear his voice. How could he say he loved me back and then disappear? Didn't he know it felt like I was getting stabbed every time he didn't pick up the phone? He didn't lie to me. I knew he was telling me the truth because he had to be. I wanted him to pick up the phone and tell me one more time so I could remind myself it really was true.

Mom knocked. "Nicholas? Please open the door. I'd like to talk to you." I didn't want to talk to her. I had nothing to say after she told me I'd never see or speak to that *man* again. "I'm coming in." I kept

bumping my head against the wall. She picked her way through the mess and stood in front of me, invading my corner. "Honey, we need to talk."

She never called me honey. She never called me anything besides Nicholas.

"Your father and I have been discussing the situation. I think we've worked out a solution you'll appreciate."

"I don't care," I said and kept bumping my head on the wall.

"I should apologize to you. Neither of us realized just how much pressure we were putting on you. You're so bright and talented and we've always had high expectations. We thought you weren't applying yourself and being firm was the answer. We were wrong, and I'm sorry."

I wasn't sure if this really was my mom. Maybe I was dreaming. I hit my head harder to make sure.

"I also want to apologize for my behavior last Monday. I was out of town because I was being offered a partnership in a new firm." I didn't understand what that meant. "This is a huge opportunity for my career. I'll have more responsibility and I'll be making a lot more money. I heard what happened when I was in final negotiations and it caused them to doubt my commitment. But none of that matters. It wasn't your fault, and I had no right to be angry with you."

She held out her hand. It looked like a poisonous snake. "Can we start over?" she asked. I didn't answer. "I'm going to fix some hamburgers. I'd like if you came downstairs so we can talk."

When she left, I dialed the phone and counted the rings again. I didn't want to go down to dinner. I didn't want to leave my room no matter what plan they came up with. Even if she apologized. Which was weird. I couldn't figure that part out. She never apologized. Was it a trick to get me to go along with their plan?

That's what gave me the idea. What if instead of fighting I pretended to go along with their idea? I could even pretend to like it. Then, just before we all agreed, I could say ok – as long as I got to be friends with Jeremy again. They'd be so happy they wouldn't mind. It was so clever I laughed out loud. She'd shake her head and admit I trapped her. I could be a lawyer too.

I got dressed, brushed my teeth, and combed my hair before I went downstairs. She was just finishing the hamburgers. When she looked up at me, she actually smiled. "I appreciate you making the effort to clean up," she said, putting a plate with two hamburgers in front of me. She didn't make one for herself. I didn't want to eat until I found out their plan, but they smelled good and I was hungry so I started.

She let me eat the first hamburger before she said anything. "Your father and I met with your principal and your teachers last week. They're very concerned about you."

I guessed that was a grown-up way to say they hated me.

"Based on our conversation, your father and I are convinced the public school isn't able to provide the kind of structure and environment you need. They were very focused on your poor performance but were unable to formulate any plan to help you improve. I don't think they have any idea how to offer a bright boy like you the intellectual challenge and stimulation you need. Their inability to protect you from that vicious bully also reinforces our opinion that the public school is not equipped to offer you a safe environment. We've decided it's in your best interest for us to reject their offer to withdraw the expulsion." I wasn't sure I understood anything she said. "Would you like to go to a different school?"

"I don't have to go back?"

She shook her head. "Once we decided the public school was no longer an option, our task became locating the right school for you. We searched for one that offers not only a rigorous curriculum allowing you to flourish academically, but even more important, one where you can be happy. A school where you can be with other smart young people like yourself, ones who read the same kinds of books and listen to the same kinds of music. It's so important to find friends your own age, and the right school would afford you the opportunities to find all the friends you could ever want."

A school like that couldn't be real. Could it?

She pushed a booklet across the table to me. It had a picture on the front of old-fashioned buildings on a big lawn with lots of trees. I opened it up, ignoring the words and staring at the pictures. Kids in classrooms learning, eating lunch in a nice cafeteria, doing science

experiments, acting in a show, playing guitars, and hitting baseballs. I stared at one picture of three boys with their arms around each other's shoulders, smiling. I could tell they really liked it there. It seemed impossible, but it was all there in the booklet. I kept flipping through the pages. Maybe I didn't have to fake liking this plan.

"When I spoke to the admissions counselor, I knew it was the perfect choice for you. They have a strong music program and all kinds of clubs. They even have one for that game you were telling me about. The counselor said it was very popular. Doesn't this sound like a much better environment for you?" I nodded.

Then I turned the page.

"Since it's a boarding school, your teachers and counselors will be there for you to make sure you thrive."

The picture said it all. Two desks, two closets, two beds, and two kids.

"Living away from home and boring old mom and dad is going to be a real adventure for you. I know you're going to make good friends being around children like yourself – smart kids who have a hard time with regular school. And since this school operates on a full year calendar, there's no need to worry about what happens over the summer. You can spend it with your friends. Besides, I'm going to be working late nights and traveling regularly for my new firm. I can't rely on your father to be home in the evenings to look after you, so I think this is for the best."

I flipped the book back to the beginning and read what it said.

The Greenbriar School, set amongst the spectacular scenery of southern Vermont, specializes in meeting the needs of young men aged 11 to 18 who have difficulties adjusting to other educational programs. We provide an immersive academic, social, and behavioral environment enabling our students to achieve their full potential, while offering a caring and structured program to develop self-esteem through social and life-coping skills.

"We made arrangements for you to enroll when the next trimester begins in February. Isn't that wonderful? You won't have to sit around the house and mope for very long. In fact, the admissions counselor said you can come up as early as next week to settle in and become

accustomed to the environment before spring classes begin." She looked at me like she was waiting for me to say something. "Are there any questions you'd like to ask? I'm sure the counselor would be happy to talk to you on the phone and tell you all about the program."

She stared at me again when I didn't say anything. "It's a lot to think about. Why don't I let you read through the brochure, and if you have questions we can talk later. Does that sound ok? We love you, Nicholas, and all we want is the best for you."

She got up, straightened out her dress, and went into the living room. I looked down at my plate. The smell of hamburger made me feel sick.

She called it a school, but it wasn't a school. They didn't show the pictures with the padded rooms and the straitjackets. My parents didn't want me around anymore. They were sending me to a place for crazy kids. They were getting rid of me. Like I wasn't their son anymore. There was nothing I could do or say. She made all the arrangements already. They were sending me all the way to Vermont and I'd probably never come back.

I'd never get to see Jeremy ever again. I thought about the day I met him, when I spilled the hot chocolate but all he cared about was if I got hurt. I thought about him playing guitar when I wet the bed the first time I slept over. I thought about him teaching me piano, playing with me, and listening to me. But mostly I just heard him saying it in my head over and over. *I love you too.*

I felt the same as when I wanted to kill Tommy. It was like I was watching myself from the outside even though I knew it was me. I could hear my heart beating in my ears. I got up from the table and went into the garage. My old baseball bat was in the corner. I picked it up and let it drag behind me so it made a thud on each step as I climbed up to my room. I closed the door and jammed my desk chair under the handle like I saw them do in the movies. I looked at the boy in the mirror. He looked stupid. He looked crazy. He looked brain damaged. I wanted to make him disappear.

I swung the bat around as hard as I could. The mirror disintegrated. I knew it made a crash, but I couldn't hear it. I felt sharp pains all over

my face. A cool wave of air washed all over me, making me feel calmer than I ever remembered feeling before.

I swung the bat again. It smashed into the bookshelves above my desk. The shelves crashed down, books spilling onto the floor. Like they were guts. I hit it again and wood splinters went everywhere. The whole thing came crashing down around me. It felt so good.

I pounded on the dresser until the top cracked in half, the drawers hanging open. I smashed the inside and outside window with one swing, letting the cold air in. I bashed the closet doors down and cracked the rod, empty hangers spilling on the floor. The clock radio exploded in a mushroom cloud of plastic and wires. I could hear my mother shouting and pounding at the door, but I didn't care. I wasn't going to stop until I destroyed everything.

The door crashed in. "Nicholas!" Mom screamed. I turned around and smiled. She backed out of the room as I walked towards her with the bat on my shoulder. She had her back to the wall in the hallway. I heard her scream when I swung the bat around. Dust from the wall went everywhere. When it cleared, I saw a huge chunk of the wall missing only an inch from her head. She screamed again.

All at once I came back into myself. If no one was there to stop me, I would've killed Tommy. No one was here to stop me now. No one to keep me from making my mom's head explode in a mushroom cloud of blood and bones and brains when I knocked it off her body. The bat dropped out of my hands. Mom didn't stop me when I ran down the stairs and out the front door. It was cold but I didn't care. I ran as fast as I could even though I couldn't breathe and even though I fell twice and skinned my knee. I ran all the way down the hill to his house. The lights were on.

"Jeremy!" I screamed. I pounded on the door as hard as I could. I kept screaming until the door opened just a little bit.

"Nick, you can't be here," he said. "Please just go home."

I shoved the door open as hard as I could. He fell back into the hallway. "How come you never answer the phone?" I screamed. "How come you won't talk to me?"

He looked scared. "What happened to you? You're covered with blood!"

"I hate you!" I screamed as loud as I could. "You said you loved me but you don't! You lied! You're just like everybody else! You let her take me away and now they're sending me to a special school all the way in Vermont for crazy kids and they're never going to let me see you again!" I started to hit him. "I almost killed her and it's all your fault! I hate you I hate you I hate you I hate you!"

He grabbed my hands and held them. I started fighting to get out but then I saw the sad look on his face. He wrapped his arms around me. I didn't want to scream at him. I didn't mean to say all those things. I didn't hate him. I just couldn't make the words come out that I wanted to say. But the way he was hugging me, I think he already knew how I felt.

The headlights shone on us like they were a spotlight. "Please," I said. "Don't let her take me back home. I might do it again. I might hurt. . ."

"Listen to me," he interrupted. "Go upstairs and shut yourself in my bedroom. Lock the door and don't come out no matter what. I let you go once and I'm never going to let you go again." I ran up the stairs. The car door slammed.

"Nicholas!" I heard her scream from outside. I made it to the top of the stairs but then I tripped. I started to crawl down the hall. "Nicholas!" she screamed again from the entryway.

"It's ok, he's here," Jeremy said.

"I need to see him," she said. "I'm afraid he might hurt himself." she said. Her voice sounded shaky. I lay down flat in the hallway and tried not to move.

"He's safe," Jeremy said. "He looks like he's been to hell and back. What happened?"

"One moment we were talking pleasantly, and the next thing I knew he locked himself in his bedroom and started smashing everything in sight with a baseball bat. His furniture is destroyed, there's broken glass everywhere, and there are holes the size of bowling balls in the walls. He turned the bat on me afterwards, he nearly. . . Nicholas!"

"My god," Jeremy said. "You must be shaken. Please, come in and sit down."

"I don't need to sit down," she said. "I need to see my son."

"He's in distress and might behave unpredictably. I think the best thing right now is for us to keep calm and give him some time."

"He doesn't need time," she snapped. "He needs professional help. This is all your fault."

"My fault?" Jeremy raised his voice. "What the hell is that supposed to mean?"

"I know what men like you want to do to innocent children. I know how you manipulate them with shame and guilt until they acquiesce. There's only one reason why a grown man would spend all his time around a boy his age."

"All I've done is show him a little compassion. Something you don't seem to understand how to do."

"How dare you," she growled.

"Do you have any understanding how worthless you've made him feel?" Jeremy shouted. "All you do is punish him into submission, and you're accusing me of abusing him?"

"I don't have to take this from you," she yelled. "Get out of my way or I swear I'll unleash everything in my power to make sure you never see the light of day ever again!"

"Bring it on," he yelled back. "I'm not going to let you destroy this boy any more than you already have!"

I clamped my hands over my ears. "Stop it!" I screamed. I stood up and looked over the railing at them. They stared at me.

"Get out of my way!" she screamed and pushed Jeremy, hard. He pushed her back. She almost fell over.

I climbed onto the railing and sat with my legs dangling over the edge. "Stop it or I'll jump off!" I screamed.

They both froze. She put her hands over her mouth. All the color went out of Jeremy's face. He looked like a ghost. Nobody moved.

"Nick," Jeremy said quietly. "Please come down." I shook my head as hard as I could. "I promise we'll stop fighting."

"I don't care!" I screamed. "I'm not going!"

"Going where?" he said. He sounded very calm, which seemed strange at a time like this. I didn't want to be calm.

"To the school for crazy kids!" I shouted.

"It's not a school for crazy kids," Mom said.

"You're lying!" I yelled. I kicked out and almost fell off. "It is too a school for crazy kids and I won't go and you can't make me!"

"No one is sending you away," Jeremy said. He went up one step. "Come down from there and we'll talk about it."

"Don't come up or I'm going to jump off!" I shouted. He stopped. Mom started to run past him, but Jeremy caught her and held her back. "I hate you!" I screamed at her. "I hate how mean you are to me! I hate that you always make me move! I hate that you don't care if I don't have any friends and everyone makes fun of me! I hate that all you care about is your stupid lawyer work! Jeremy listens to me! Jeremy does stuff with me! Jeremy cares about how I feel! I wish he was my parent instead of you!"

"Nick, please," Jeremy said. Mom sat down on the floor.

"Stay away or I'm going to jump off and crack my head open and it'll be all your fault!"

"I don't know what to do anymore," she said, like she was talking to herself. She looked up at me. "I thought you'd be so excited. I don't understand."

"I'm scared," Jeremy said, looking straight at me. "Please get down."

"If I do she's going to send me away!" I shouted.

"You're not going anywhere," he said, coming up another stair. "Isn't that right, Ellie?"

"I don't want to hurt you," she said.

Jeremy kept coming up the stairs. I started feeling shaky. "We only want to help," he said. He was almost at the top. "Come down and we'll talk."

"But she's going to send me away," I said. He reached out to wrap his arms around me, but I jerked away. It made me lose my balance. I felt myself slipping off the railing. I wanted to shout but nothing came out. My arms swung around but there was nothing to catch. I was going to fall. I felt sick. I didn't really want to fall. But I *was* falling, and soon it would all be over. I was going to explode in a mushroom cloud of me and I wouldn't have to worry about anything anymore.

Something yanked me back all the way over the railing. Jeremy's arms were wrapped around me. The next thing I knew we were on the floor in the hallway. "Let go of me!" I tried to pull away, but he held

me tight. I hit my head against the railing. He didn't let go. I kicked and punched. I didn't know why I was fighting. I didn't know what I'd do if I got loose. "I'm not going!" I screamed.

"Shh," he said in a very quiet voice while I fought.

Just like the time I hit Tommy, I eventually ran out of energy. He didn't let go even when I stopped fighting. I realized I was making a weird moaning sound, like I was saying no without the N. I looked up and saw mom standing at the top of the stairs, crying.

Jeremy lifted me up and carried me downstairs. I held on tight like a little kid, wrapping my legs around him. I didn't let go when he tried to put me down on the couch. From the corner of my eye I saw mom sneaking up. I pushed Jeremy so he was in between me and her. "Don't let her send me away," I moaned.

She stopped. "I just want what's best for you. That's all I've ever wanted."

"That's what we all want," Jeremy said.

"He's *my* son," she said to him. "It's my responsibility to keep him safe."

"Let's calm down." Jeremy sat down on the couch. Mom thought about it and then sat down too, on the other side. I pushed myself up against him. "Everyone take a breath and we'll figure this out together."

Mom wiped her eyes and started. "I thought you'd be happy going to a school where you could relate to the other boys and make friends. Greenbriar can give you the kind of attention you need."

"I don't need attention," I said.

"You need help," she said.

"I don't!" I yelled back.

"Shh." Jeremy patted my shoulder. "What kind of school is this?"

"It's a boarding school," I muttered. "For crazy kids."

"For boys who need more than the public school provides," she said like she was a teacher correcting me. "It's a structured program that focuses on social and coping skills alongside academics, tailored for children who have a hard time making friends and fitting in. Nothing more than that."

"You don't want to go," Jeremy said to me.

"I want to stay here."

"Why?" Mom asked. "I don't understand. They're not challenging you academically, they're providing you no support structure, and they couldn't even protect you from a bully. At the first sign of trouble they wanted to kick you out. How could you possibly want to stay?" She looked away. "I'm sorry, that didn't come out the way I intended. I just don't understand."

"I don't think this is about school," Jeremy said. "I think this is about moving away again. Nick is starting to get adjusted. Yanking him away again will force him to start over."

"You need to make friends your own age," she said again.

"I'll bet what happened is going to make that a lot easier," Jeremy said. "Boys will have more respect for him now. Besides, I doubt the school will allow that bully to come within fifty feet of Nick."

"Someday, I'd like to know what you said to them," Mom said to Jeremy. "Even if he could go back to the public school, I'll be working late and traveling. Jack certainly won't be around to watch Nicholas. We don't have many choices."

"Nick can stay with me," Jeremy said.

My heart jumped.

"When you're running late or out of town, he can stay here. He has his own bedroom and bathroom, and I'm happy to arrange my schedule to make sure I'm available to keep an eye on him."

"I don't know," Mom said. "It's a lot to ask."

"It's no trouble at all," Jeremy said. "I enjoy having Nick around. Ellie, listen to me. I promise that Nick is perfectly safe with me."

She sighed and it was like all her bones melted. "I guess I believe you," she said. "I don't know why I do. The better part of me insists I should suspect the worst. But after watching you upstairs, I can't imagine you hurting him. I owe you an apology. You've been so kind and helpful for Jack and for Nicholas. You've done nothing that gives me cause to level accusations. I have no right to..."

"It's quite all right," he interrupted. "Every kid should have people who care as much about them as we care about Nick. I think everyone can use a break. From what you said, Nick's room is not in a state where he can stay there tonight. And I hope you'll excuse me for saying this to a woman, but you look like hell." She laughed a little. "Let Nick

spend the night here. In the morning, we'll all sit down fresh and work this out."

She looked at me. "Do you want to stay here tonight?"

I nodded hard.

She looked at me in the eyes for a minute. I didn't look away.

"Ok," she said. "We'll talk more in the morning. Would it be too much to ask for a hug?"

I nodded and let her come over to me. She hugged lightly, not like the big bear hugs Jeremy gave. I didn't hug back very hard either. Jeremy walked her to the door. They talked for a while, too soft for me to hear. I wanted to know what they were saying but I didn't want to get up. She looked over at me when they were done, said goodbye, and she left. Jeremy came back over and held out his hand.

"We need to get you cleaned up," he said. I followed him to the bathroom, holding his hand the whole way. He wet a towel and got down on his knees. It stung a lot when he wiped my face, but I didn't flinch.

"Did you mean it?" I asked. "About staying?"

"Of course I did," he said. "But if you want to stay here, there's something I want you to do." I nodded. "I want you to pick something about yourself, just one thing, that you want to change. Something we can work on together. Something that will make you feel better about yourself."

I pretended to think about it, but I didn't need to. "I don't want to be fat anymore."

He patted my face dry. "Starting tomorrow, I'm going to help you lose weight. I don't think it'll be very hard. If we cut out the junk food and get a little more exercise, I'll bet you'll see results in no time." He brushed a little hair out of my face. "I'll do everything I can to help you."

"Am I crazy?" I whispered.

"You're not crazy," he said.

"I almost. . ."

"No need to talk about that tonight," he said.

"I didn't mean to yell."

"I understand. Everything's going to be ok." He hugged me again. I followed him up to his bedroom. "How about a back rub?" I nodded. I closed my eyes and lay as still as I could on his bed. Even though I was motionless on the outside, everything inside was like I was on the scrambler at the fair. Jeremy knew what I did and what I could do, and he didn't care. I used to tell things to Scruffy when I was little, all the bad things I did and thought. He always loved me no matter what. If Jeremy really was like Scruffy, maybe I could tell him more. Maybe I could share another secret with him, one even more dangerous. I blurted it out before I was ready.

"Could you tie me up?"

He was going to ask me why, and I was going to tell him. I was going to share all the sick, gross things I did at night with the lights off and the door closed. I was going to talk out loud about my secret shoelaces, the way I would roll over until my hands turned purple, and the horrible things that ran through my head while I rubbed myself against the sheets. The weird part was that I didn't feel scared. I *wanted* to tell him.

"I'm sure I have some rope around here somewhere," he said. He got off the bed and left the room. I didn't move. He came back with a pile of rope and some scissors. "Do you want it loose or tight?" he asked.

"Tight," I whispered.

He cut off a length of rope. "I'll do whatever it takes to make you happy," he said.

He wasn't going to ask. He was just going to do it. It was the first time I was going to be tied up for real by someone else in my whole life.

I closed my eyes, put my hands behind my back, and waited for him to start.

James Edison

Part 2

Chapter 8

August 24, 2006

I had to look ridiculous whenever I awkwardly stood up from the edge of the bed. The grunt I made certainly sounded ridiculous enough, but it somehow helped generate the considerable force necessary to move so much bulk. I was always relieved when I managed to do it without ripping the seam of my pants. My clothes were past the point of being too tight. I'd have to visit the big and tall shop again, undergo the ritual of avoiding eye contact with the other morbidly obese guys while trying to convince myself they were obviously a lot fatter than me because I sure as hell didn't look like *that,* thank you very much.

The four ibuprofen pills I took an hour ago had finally kicked in, the roaring headache I woke up with reduced to a tolerable level of agony. My mouth was dry and sticky after downing three glasses of water, and I needed the bathroom even though I went less than an hour ago. Headache, thirst, and excessive urination: I knew what these symptoms meant. I'd read enough to understand the irreversible damage I was doing to my body. Didn't stop me last night. I was in rare form, eating long past the point of being full and forcing food down that I didn't even want to eat. The highlight had to be when I shoveled spoonful after spoonful of sugar straight from the bag. Knowing the signs of diabetes wasn't going to stop me this morning either. I planned to head straight to the diner to stuff myself with every kind of greasy, sticky-sweet breakfast food on the menu.

Jake was sitting at the kitchen table, his headphones blaring something loud and distinctly un-music-like. "You're up early," I said. He didn't hear or maybe pretended not to. I glanced at his plate and froze.

"You made a bullseye," I stammered.

He made a face and took off his headphones, proving he could hear me. "A what? It's an egg in a frame."

I couldn't stop the movie-memory from playing back inside my head – Jeremy patiently showing me how to cut a neat circle out of a slice of bread with a drinking glass, how to fry the bread in the pan first with a lot of butter, and how to crack the egg carefully into the center without breaking the yolk. I remembered thinking how ingenious Jeremy was for inventing it, and how naming it a bullseye was just as ingenious. I was certain I'd never made one for Jake. I wouldn't have done something that reminded me so acutely of my time with him.

"Where did you learn how to make that?" I mumbled.

"Camp," he said. He ended the conversation by putting his headphones back on.

I grabbed my briefcase and ran out the door without another word.

For years, I'd been successfully burying memories of Jeremy, entombing them in concrete and banishing them to the bottom of a deep trench under the ocean. Then I saw Jake doing . . . that thing I didn't want to think about. Ever since that day, the universe conspired to dig up my past and parade it in front of me. Signs and reminders were everywhere. Pianos for sale at Costco of all places. The Chopin ballade playing on the bookstore speakers. I even followed an early eighties Porsche for twenty miles before I convinced myself it couldn't be *him*.

I wouldn't need to keep up the charade of being employed much longer. Summer break would be over in a couple weeks. Jake would be out of the house for school long before I was supposed to leave for work, leaving me free to let the day drift by comfortably at home instead of in some random restaurant or mall. I could've made the excuse I was taking a few days off, but escaping the house was the best way I knew to avoid awkward conversations with my son. Those few words about eggs this morning was the most we'd said to each other in a week. He

made it obvious he was trying just as hard to avoid me, so it was all for the best.

I was pouring the entire carafe of syrup on a double stack of pancakes when my cell phone started it's crazy vibrate dance on the table. Jake, calling from home. Unusual, and unwelcome. My pancakes were getting cold. I ignored it the first two times, but the third time made it clear he wasn't going to give up.

"I'm in a meeting," I muttered, covering the microphone so he couldn't hear the music in the background.

"You need to come home right now," he sputtered.

"I said I'm in a *meeting.*"

"Baxter's crying and he can't stand up and I know something's really wrong." Jake's voice was shaky.

"I'll be there as soon as I can," I snapped and hung up the phone. I took my time wolfing down the pancakes before I left. After all, I was extracting myself from a meeting and driving all the way home from the office. If I got home too quickly, he'd know I wasn't there. Details.

I found Jake on the kitchen floor cradling the dog. "What happened?"

"He can't stand up," Jake said, sniffling. Baxter whimpered for emphasis.

"It's his hips again," I said with authority. "Did you give him the pain pills?"

"I did, but it's a lot worse than before," he said. "I think there's something really wrong with him. We have to go to the vet."

"Jake. . ."

"We have to take him to the vet right now!" Jake snapped.

I groaned. Didn't he understand I was missing a mission critical meeting with a Lumberjack special? Transmitting my annoyance as clearly as I could, I bent down to pick up the dog. Getting myself up with a seventy-pound animal cradled in my arms proved to be another matter entirely. Jake tried to help, but he only succeeded in unbalancing me. "Would you just let me do it?" I snapped. He recoiled. "If you want to help, get the damned door open."

Jake slipped around me, holding the door to the garage so I could squeeze through, and then running down to the car to open the rear

hatch of the SUV. The dog yelped when I couldn't balance myself well enough to put him down gently. Before I could stop him, Jake climbed in the back and made it clear he intended to ride with the dog. I shook my head and closed the door. If anyone asked, I would've told them it was out of compassion for my son and my dog, but the real reason I didn't protest was because I was out of breath. We didn't say anything to each other on the way to the animal hospital, but I could hear him quietly reassuring the dog. When we arrived, Jake jumped out and came back a moment later with two orderlies in light green scrubs.

"Be careful with him," Jake said sharply.

"We'll be as gentle as we can," one of the orderlies said in a calm voice. "Why don't you go check him in and wait in the lobby? The doctor will be out as soon as she looks at him."

"Why can't I go with him?" Jake asked, crossing his arms defiantly.

"Give us a few minutes. I promise we'll take good care of him." The orderly put his hand on Jake's shoulder, who nodded and turned for the lobby entrance. When I was done with the paperwork, I sat down on the opposite side of the room from Jake, the plastic chair buckling under me. He didn't look up and I didn't approach.

I wasn't always like this. When Jake was small, I was obsessed with the idea of being a father to my son. I was awake and alive. I could *feel*. I knew on an intellectual level I was attempting to undo all the wrongs of my own childhood, but like my compulsive eating, knowledge didn't make my need to be super-dad feel any less right or true. I was going to be the perfect father: fun, wise, committed, and caring. For four years, that's exactly what I did. I took hundreds of hours of video of every moment, dreaming about the day I could playfully embarrass him with it. I took him to Gymboree classes and early playdates. I stayed up with him for three days when he caught a bad fever. I read to him every night and played with him every day. I was there to see his first steps and hear his first words. Until one moment of weakness when he was four years old in a bathtub brought it all crashing down around me. In that instant, I realized the danger to both of us. The permanent devastation he would suffer, and the devastation I would suffer from being the cause of his suffering. I should've known better. It's better not to feel. Deadened nerves shield me from anyone who tries to touch me,

and blunted feelings have no power to cut deeply. I had no business being emotionally involved with anyone or anything, especially someone as vulnerable as a young boy. I was right when I'd decided at nineteen to never feel anything ever again, and I transformed myself back into the angry person I used to be.

But as I watched him across the room, I couldn't stop imagining myself doing exactly what I knew I shouldn't be doing. I imagined sitting next to him, my hand on his shoulder, inviting him to lean into me like a shipwreck survivor clinging to a piece of driftwood. I imagined stroking his head and holding his hand, letting him know it was ok to cry. I imagined speaking to him tenderly, reassuring him that Baxter would be fine, maybe telling him little dad jokes to keep him distracted. I imagined being everything a father's supposed to be. I found myself praying desperately that he wouldn't decide to sit next to me or invite me over to him with a helpless glance. If he did, I might give in, and that terrified me. I gripped my seat to hold myself in place when he walked across the room.

"Can I use your phone?" he asked. "I left mine at home."

"Why?" I asked with more suspicion than necessary.

The look of contempt he flashed withered me. "Because you haven't called Mom yet."

I handed him the phone.

We didn't speak again for the hour it took the vet to summon us. We followed her into a large space that reminded me more of a hospital emergency room. The look of carefully practiced sympathy on her face told me all I needed to know. Baxter was still on a stretcher, panting, an IV stuck in his rear leg. His eyes were glassy and he didn't lift his head when we came up to him. Only a single swish of his tail acknowledged that he knew we were there.

"Is he ok?" Jake asked the vet.

"We've made him as comfortable as we can, but I don't think we can take away all the pain. Baxter can't get up because his hip is broken in three places." Jake gasped out loud. "Why don't you talk to him and give him some pets? I'm sure that'll make him feel better." Jake nodded and spoke softly to Baxter, gently scratching behind his ears. I took the vet's cue and moved a safe distance away to talk to her.

"He's had bad hips since he was a puppy," I offered.

"I don't think this is related to his dysplasia," the vet said, her smile wilting. "I'd need to run a few tests to be sure, but based on the way his hip broke I believe Baxter has osteosarcoma, a form of bone cancer. It makes his bones brittle and very susceptible to breaking. It's developed quickly since his last checkup. Given how aggressive it is, it's likely already spread to other organs."

"Is there anything you can do?" I asked blankly.

"I can give him medication to dull the pain, and we could consider treatment or surgery, but I wouldn't recommend either. Truthfully, there's not much we can do for him. I don't think he has more than a few weeks left. It's time to consider what's best for him."

"Put him to sleep," I clarified.

"Take all the time you need and talk it over with your family. There's no rush to decide anything." She put her hand on my arm, the look of sympathy on her face more authentic. "I've taken care of Baxter since he was a puppy. I'm sorry."

I did *not* want to deal with this.

"He's asleep," Jake told me when I came back to the stretcher. "Can we take him home or does he have to stay overnight?"

I gathered what little courage I had. "I'm afraid Baxter is seriously ill."

"I'll take care of him until he can walk again."

"Baxter broke his hip because he has bone cancer," I blurted out.

Jake turned white. "Is he going to die?"

"It's pretty bad," I said.

"Can we take him home?" Jake asked in a small voice.

"It's not that simple," I said. "We won't be able to take care of him. He can't walk so he can't go out to poop and pee, he won't be able to eat or drink easily, and he's in a lot of pain even with the medicine. He shouldn't have to suffer."

"You want to kill him," Jake said.

"Put him to sleep," I corrected.

"It's murder," he growled, protectively standing between me and the dog.

"It's the right thing to do," I said. "He's not going to get any better."

"If I had cancer, would you kill me too?"

"That's different," I said, an edge creeping into my voice.

"It's not different at all," Jake said. "You don't understand anything."

I walked away before it turned into a real fight. Jake let me go without a word.

Julia caught the first flight back but wasn't able to arrive until later in the afternoon. I spent the day sitting on a bench outside the office, enduring the sticky humidity as a form of penance. I watched the parade of pets without emotion – dogs wearing lampshades, howling cats confined to small carriers, and even two horses in the back of a truck. Jake spent them inside with Baxter. When Julia arrived, she went inside without acknowledging my existence.

The decision was made around dinnertime. We gathered around the table with the vet, who stayed long past the end of her shift. Baxter's eyes focused lazily on each of us. "He looks like he understands," Jake said. "He looks like he knows what's going to happen and he's saying it's ok. Doesn't he?" I thought about telling him he was only seeing what he wanted to see, but wisely decided not to say anything. Jake gave the nod, and a needle slipped silently into the IV line. It happened fast. One moment Baxter's eyes were open and alert, and the next they were closed and his body went completely still.

"Bye, Boxy," Jake whispered.

The room fell silent. When Jake was only two or three, Baxter was too much of a mouthful for him to say. The dog became "Boxy" for a few years until Jake decided to correct himself when he was in kindergarten. I forgot we all called him Boxy until that moment. I wondered how he could remember something from when he was so young.

I tried to force my mind to go blank, but as hard as I tried I couldn't stop the memories flooding through me. Julia and I were having coffee at the local bakery on a blustery Sunday in December when she found the ad buried in the classified section: pure-bred golden retriever puppies for only three hundred dollars, complete with papers. The decision was made instantly, without debate or consideration. Never mind that we both knew getting a puppy through a classified ad was the wrong way to go about it. Never mind that neither of us knew anything

about dogs. We were caught up in the Christmas spirit, images of cute little puppies with bows around their necks peeking out of festive boxes pushing away any doubts we might've had. A few hours later, we had a seven-week old ball of fur nestled in my coat while we ran up and down the aisles at PetSmart buying all the wrong things. If we knew we'd have to put his crate next to our bed to keep him from crying all night, or that we'd have to walk him every fifteen minutes to keep our carpet from turning yellow, or that he'd chew through anything that wasn't (or was) nailed down, it probably wouldn't have changed our decision to bring him home. For me, he was a way to convince her we were ready for a child. For her, he was a way to convince herself.

The plan worked, and Jake came along a year later. Any fears we had about Baxter's reaction to the new baby vanished the first night we brought him home from the hospital. The dog wouldn't leave his side, barking if Jake let out the slightest whimper. When Jake was a toddler, Baxter followed him around the house, warning us with a remarkable degree of judgment when Jake was doing something he shouldn't. No matter how many times Jake pulled his tail or tried to climb on his back, Baxter never lost patience or snapped. I remembered the time they romped together in snow so high it nearly swallowed Jake. I remembered the time Jake threw the Frisbee too hard and Baxter chased it right into the Potomac, forcing me to wade in to fish him out. I remembered how he would whine until we let him into Jake's room to sleep at the foot of his bed. They weren't quite as inseparable as Jake grew older, but when I saw him play with Baxter or nuzzle him while watching television, I knew his love went well beyond childhood attachment. The kind of love that led to the devastation of real loss. The kind of loss I knew all too well.

I should never have gotten that damned dog.

Julia took Jake home, and I went out to get pizza for dinner. No one else was interested, so I ate alone. After I finished, I found Julia in our room, her clothes spread out on the bed. "What are you doing?" I asked.

"I'm catching the late flight tonight," she said, all business.

"You're not even staying the night?" I said as an accusation. "What about Jake?"

"He's in his room," she said.

"That's not what I meant."

"I know what you meant," she snapped. "I told him how nice it was that you could stay home with him for the next few days. He had no idea what I was talking about. You didn't tell him about being laid off?" I didn't answer. "For the life of me, I can't figure out why you wouldn't tell him."

"I'll explain it to him tomorrow," I lied. "I'm sure your boss would let you take a couple days off. For Jake."

"He already offered. I turned him down."

"For the life of me, I can't figure out why you'd do that," I fired back.

She didn't answer, busying herself with the routine mechanics of packing. I flipped the television on, deliberately ignoring how she became violent with the clothes until she finally sat down on the side of the bed with her head in her arms.

"What's wrong?" I asked.

"A lot of things," she muttered. "Sometimes you don't know what you've got until it's gone."

"We can get another dog," I offered.

She turned around to glare at me. "How can you say something so callous and insensitive? We just put him to sleep a few hours ago!"

"There you go again," I muttered. "I try to help, and you accuse me of being callous and insensitive. You're always doing that to me."

I was a little disturbed to see the anger in her eyes fade away. "This isn't about Baxter. It's about us."

"I don't understand," I said.

"There is no us, not anymore." She wiped her eyes with the back of her hand. "There hasn't been for a long time, and I think I finally understand there never will be again. I've been fooling myself for years that things will change. Living with you is like living with a brick wall. You shut everyone out and the only emotion you know how to express is anger."

"I'm not like that at all," I snapped. "How is it possible for there to be an 'us' if you're on the road three hundred days a year? That's why there's no us."

"There wasn't an us when I took the job two years ago. I had this ridiculous notion the distance would somehow make things better. I suppose I was really just running away."

"This is completely irrational," I muttered.

"You know what hurts the most? I still love you, but you've made it very clear you don't feel anything for me."

"Of course I love you." I sounded hollow.

"A marriage needs to be more than this. I need more than this. Losing Baxter jolted me back to reality. I can't keep deluding myself that you'll go back to being the passionate, caring person I fell in love with."

My stomach rolled up into a tiny ball. "What are you going to do?"

"I have no idea," she said.

I needed the conversation to continue. I needed to tell her how the idea of her leaving terrified me, even if I couldn't express how much she meant to me. I needed to tell her that it wasn't her fault I couldn't feel anything. I couldn't explain and I couldn't change. Change was too dangerous. I lay silently on the bed, facing away from her.

"Don't do this to Jake," she said. "He needs his father, now more than ever. I don't know if you can see it. I don't know if you even care. I know your father wasn't there for you. Please don't do the same thing to him." Before I could say anything, she locked herself in the bathroom. I knew there was nothing I could do to stop the inevitable. All that was left was to go downstairs, turn on the television, and go to work on the rest of the pizza.

She left for the airport not long afterwards. I only knew because I heard the front door close through the noise of the television. By the time I got up to look through the curtains, her car was already gone.

I became obsessed with being a father during the summer between my junior and senior year in college. It began with a thunderclap of epiphany. I was engaging in my favorite pastime – insulting people passing by without them being able to hear. A young father and his son caught my attention, and while I was thinking of just the right zinger to describe them, the father hoisted the little boy onto his shoulders. He staggered, like the weight was too much, throwing the kid backwards and forwards until the kid was dangling upside down. The kid was

laughing hysterically and demanding more, having the time of his life, but I thought it seemed like the father was having just as much fun. *I wonder if Jeremy had as much fun doing that to me,* I thought absently. When I realized I'd committed the deadly sin of remembering, I didn't get upset at myself like I usually did. That was the moment when I decided I wanted to have fun like that. I *needed* to have fun like that, as badly as breathing or eating. I needed to be the person who made a boy happy. The decision was made that quickly: I was going to become a dad as fast as I could.

If I was going to be father, I needed to find a woman to participate, and I knew exactly the kind of woman I wanted to find. Timid, shy, and submissive, completely lacking in self-confidence. Someone who would surrender control and give me the complete freedom to have the relationship I imagined with my son, unencumbered by the rules and structure women always wanted to impose. Julia fit the bill perfectly. I watched a professor berate her about some answer she thought was correct on an exam, taking his abuse silently and walking away defeated. I stepped up, defended her, got the exam fixed, charmed her off her feet over a cafeteria meal, and one thing led to another. We were married less than a year later, right after we graduated. I took for granted that she'd remain the same submissive person, but somewhere along the line she changed when I wasn't paying attention. She'd learned how to stand up for herself. Somewhere along the line, I'd changed too. I'd come to love her, in my own way.

I stumbled up to bed sometime after midnight, settling into an uncomfortable state somewhere between awake and dreaming. I knew with the certainty of a zealot that everything terrible in my life was *his* fault. *Jeremy's* fault. I was absolved from any and all responsibility for myself, considering the excuse I carried conveniently in my back pocket. My hatred for him was my mantra. A religion I could cling to while the world fell apart around me. My armor, as easy to strap on as ordering Mr. Worf to raise the shields. I adopted the readymade identity of victim, reinforced by thousands of faceless names in online cults who all spoke with the same words and showed the same unshakeable faith when it came to our status of survivor.

In that moment, I was having a very hard time finding my faith.

I snapped out of my reverie when the windows started rattling. Music was exploding out of Jake's room. "Dammit," I muttered. I pounded on his door. "Jake!"

"Go away!" he screamed back.

"Open this door right now or I swear I'll take that computer away once and for all!" I thought I'd have to break the door down, but he finally threw it open. His eyes were red.

"It's one in the morning!" I shouted. "What the hell do you think you're doing blasting your music as loud as it goes?"

"It's not as loud as it goes," he answered with an adolescent smirk, deliberately provoking me.

"That's not the point! Turn it down and go to bed!"

He crossed his arms. "No. I can play my music as loud as I want."

"What makes you think that?" I growled.

"You wouldn't understand. Can you go away now?"

"Look, I know you're upset about Baxter. . ."

"You don't know how I feel," he interrupted. "You don't know anything about me."

"I'm your father," I pointed out.

"Oh yeah? Who's my best friend?"

"I'm not being sucked into this in the middle of the night."

"That's because you don't know," he said. "What's my favorite band? How about my favorite TV shows? Did you know I haven't had a best friend since Danny stole my baseball cards in fourth grade? I don't know why I cared. I hate baseball. I had drawings and paintings all over the walls in my room and you never noticed them. You never ask me how I feel or how my day was. You don't care. You probably don't even care that Baxter is dead because I got him all riled up until he broke his leg from jumping on me."

"Jake. . ."

"Go away. I don't ever want to talk to you again." He slammed the door in my face. "And *this* is how loud the music goes!" The music became deafening, my insides pulsing in rhythm. I leaned against the wall, sliding down to sit on the floor. Hanging on the other side of the hallway was our portrait, the one we took almost ten years ago when

And When Forever Comes

Jake was a toddler. We stood in the Christmastime line at the mall for hours hoping we didn't get booted for taking the dog with us.

Baxter is gone.

Julia's leaving me.

Jake hates me.

In one day, my entire family was wiped away.

"I hate you," I whispered, trying to hold onto the hatred I needed so badly. But it was gone, replaced with a petrifying need I was not permitted to have. To see him. Talk to him. Have him hold me. Call me kiddo. Be there for me the way he used to be. Just one more time.

I snapped. Something inside me broke. My intellect disconnected and something else started driving. I bounded down the stairs with a dexterity I didn't think I had, digging through my desk drawer to find the remnants of a pack of stationery leftover from a world before email. Only a handwritten letter would do. The words flowed out as easily as the ink from my fountain pen.

Jake,

I don't know how to begin. If I try to talk to you, everything will come out wrong. I'll say all the things I don't want to say, just like I always do. I'm sorry. Sorry about Baxter. Sorry about a lot of things. I wouldn't blame you if you didn't believe me, but I am truly sorry.

I know I haven't been much of a father to you for a long time. You might not believe it now, but once upon a time being a father was the most important thing in the world to me. I lost that drive a long time ago, but I know right here, right now, I have to find that feeling again. Even if it's too late and even if it's hopeless. I want to be a different person – a better person. I want to fix things between us.

I didn't tell you yet, but a couple of weeks ago I was fired. Lying to you was a stupid thing to do. Lies have a way of growing bigger until they've taken on a life of their own and suck in every ounce of effort to keep them going. I don't want to lie to you anymore.

I think it was a good thing I was fired, because now I have time. You told me I never listen to you or ask you questions. I want to change that. I promise if you let me, I will find out who you are, what matters to you, and how you feel. I want to hear your successes and troubles, your hopes and fears, and your wishes and dreams. I want to be there for you like a dad should be.

I know it'll be hard, and I'm sure you have your doubts. You told me I don't know anything about you, and you're right – with one exception. While we might have to start at the very beginning everywhere else, we do have some common ground. I'll let my gift speak for itself.

You probably don't remember how I tucked you into bed when you were little. Every night, you used to ask me the same question – how long would I be your daddy. I always told you the same thing – until forever comes. Forever isn't here yet, and I still want to be your daddy. Please let me.

Love,

Dad

The box I needed was carefully hidden behind another box on the top shelf in the basement storage room. I ripped it open, the tape tearing off the label that read "Nick's College Papers." The label was a lie. Sure, on top there were papers and notebooks, but they were nothing but a smokescreen. No one else knew the real contents of this box, not even Julia. I scattered the papers on the ground and tore the lid off the inner box, packing peanuts flying everywhere. I reached in without looking, rummaging around until I found what I was looking for.

They were still intact after all these years. The dark leather was still soft and pliable. Only the network of tiny cracks covering the surface revealed their age. The metal rings were dull but weren't coming loose. I turned the leather cuff over in my hand reverently, treating it like the holy relic that it was, letting the meaning it once had for me wash over my consciousness.

A tiny voice in my head spoke. *Are you sure you know what you're doing?*

Yes, I answered with absolute determination.

Are you sure you're doing this to help and not for some other reason?

It's not like that.

I ended the conversation.

I placed the box and my letter quietly outside Jake's door. The music had gone silent. I considered knocking, but I knew that gifts like this were best received without the giver present.

I went back to sleep, wondering if I would dream about him standing beside my bed, clutching my letter in his hand.

James Edison

Chapter 9

March 21, 1982

Jeremy had a habit of saying things that made me think harder than I ever thought before. "Humanity is cursed," he said while we were riding in the car. "We always want what we don't have. Kids are in a hurry to grow up and adults wish they could be kids again. I think it's better to enjoy what you have instead of pining away for something you don't. Life is too short. Cherish your time spent as a kid, because it'll be over before you know it."

I used to believe I spent a lot of time thinking, but that was more like lazy daydreaming. *Thinking* was hard. When I *thought* about it, he was obviously wrong. Adults could drive, had money, and could do whatever they wanted. Why would any adult want to go back to asking permission, begging for a dollar, and being told no all the time?

It was hard to concentrate on *thinking* because the smell from the bag on my lap was driving me crazy. The rule was absolute – not a nibble until we got home and set the table. Then I could finally tear into croissants dripping with butter, homemade strawberry jam, weird cheese (this week it looked like it had been rolled in the dirt), fancy meat, and extra strong coffee to wash it down. Our Sunday breakfast wasn't a greasy all-you-can-eat buffet where people piled limp bacon and watery eggs a mile high on their plates, or some hokey pancake house where they used two cherries, a half pineapple ring, and a mound of whipped cream to make your meal smile at you. We were *sophisticated*. Every Sunday we drove a half hour to show up at a little German bakery when they opened at 6:30 in the morning. Gunther,

the baker, reminded me of the dad from the Sound of Music (before he got nice later in the movie). His face was like a statue. Sometimes he'd raise one eyebrow which made him even more scary. But he baked the best croissants, even though he wasn't French.

Every week I was allowed one meal where I could eat whatever I wanted. Most kids would probably choose to eat a whole pizza or chocolate cake, but not me. I always picked our Sunday breakfast. This week I was particularly well-behaved. I didn't even have a single bite of the birthday cupcakes someone brought into school. I *earned* those croissants. They'd taste even better because I made the choice to skip the cupcake instead of someone telling me I had to.

Weekends with Jeremy were the best. There wasn't any time on weekdays to do fun stuff. School, homework, making dinner, exercise, and piano practice filled the whole day. By the time we were done, I was so tired I didn't mind going to bed. On weekends, we could do whatever we wanted. Saturdays were for big trips. Last month, Jeremy took me to a concert in New York to hear the winner of a big piano competition in Carnegie Hall. We also went skiing in Vernon Valley, snowmobiling in the Poconos, and toured around Philadelphia. Sundays were the opposite. We usually went to see a movie or shopped at the bookstore, but we never did anything big. This was the fifth weekend out of eight since the arrangement was made that I got to stay with Jeremy. Even though Mom was home. It felt like a snow day.

I ran inside the house before he turned off the car. I had responsibilities. My most important task for Sunday breakfast was the adult job of making coffee. Pour the water, measure the grounds, and turn on the machine. It wasn't complicated – any kid could do it. I still got excited watching the coffee coming out because I was responsible for something that kids were never allowed to do. Best of all, I was not just allowed to drink it, I was *expected.* I even learned to sort of like it without dumping in half the sugar bowl.

The Sunday New York Times made our breakfast truly adult. Jeremy said there was something intimidating about six inches of densely packed intelligence, but we weren't going to let that stop us. We ate slowly to make sure we tasted every single bite, but we devoured the newspaper. If we didn't have black fingers by the end of breakfast we

didn't do it right. Except the crossword. We tried it once. It was embarrassing.

"It says here that people think we're spending too much money on the space shuttle," I said to him. "I don't think we're spending enough. Exploring the solar system is important."

"Doesn't seem like the shuttle is the way to do that," Jeremy answered without looking up. "To me it sounds like a way to get the government to pay for launching commercial satellites."

"We need something like the space shuttle that can be used over and over again. It's like a real spaceship instead of just a rocket. This way we can build a space station and then we can go to other planets."

"You have a point, but it seems a waste to sink all that money into a space truck. Look, here's another way we're throwing away money. El Salvador is a tiny country gripped by poverty and run by brutal assholes who are stealing everything they can and killing anyone who gets in the way. So, what does Reagan do? He gives these crooks hundreds of millions of dollars more to make sure it stays that way, all in the name of containing communism. Vietnam ended less than ten years ago and we're listening to the same tired rhetoric about domino theory and making the same stupid mistakes all over again. Before you know it, we'll send advisors, and then American soldiers will be dying in the jungle."

I nodded even though I didn't understand what he was talking about. I wasn't sure where El Salvador was, what it meant to contain communism, how it was like mistakes in Vietnam, or what the heck any of this had to do with dominoes. Still, I liked it better when I had to figure out what he was talking about without any kind of explanation. My job was to keep up with him as best as I could.

"What happened to this country? People used to care, but now it's like everyone went to sleep. I probably shouldn't tell you this, but when I was fifteen, I snuck out of my house in the middle of the night and took a bus to DC so I could hear Abbie Hoffman speak. Fifty thousand people gathered around the reflecting pool near the Washington monument. The smoke from the marijuana was so thick there was no way to keep from getting high. A bunch of them were so wasted they tried to levitate the Pentagon with their minds." I giggled. "It was

amazing how everyone became brothers and sisters. I went from group to group playing and singing until my fingers bled and my voice was gone. The only sad part is the dope wore off before I got home. I would've argued better with Father if I was high."

I loved his stories. He didn't leave out the parts adults didn't want kids to hear. He trusted me to understand his real message. Sneaking out and doing drugs wasn't the important part. It was ok to get in trouble for something you believed in.

"Your generation is going to have to fix this mess," he said. "Don't be afraid to make yourself heard. Make a difference. Speak truth to power, and don't settle for the scraps. The world is counting on you."

I knew I would help fix things, because that's what he expected of me.

"Remember, hit through the ball," Jeremy said. His voice echoed across the court. I nodded like I understood, but it made no sense to hit *through* a ball. He served an easy one that I hit right into the net, just like the last three times. I watched it dribble off to the side. I wondered if making me run after the ball was his evil exercise plan all along, because we weren't actually playing any tennis.

"You're stopping once you connect instead of following through," he said, getting the ball himself.

"When I do that it flies way up in the air."

"You like to scoop it from underneath. Hit straight but keep on going. Let's try a few more. I'm sure we'll figure out what's wrong with your stroke."

The only thing wrong was me. I liked swimming and long bicycle rides better than sports involving a ball. I didn't learn how to catch a ball until I was ten. My eyes would automatically close when the ball got close and I wound up getting smacked in the face every single time. I wasn't like normal boys who could throw and catch automatically like they were born knowing how. A couple weeks ago Jeremy made me try basketball. I got three baskets after shooting fifty times. "Can we do something else?"

"Here it comes," he said. I swung through the ball. It flew way up in the air like I knew it would. Jeremy caught it in one hand. *Show off.*

"Don't scoop, hit straight."

"I did," I muttered. I thought about letting the balls go past me until he gave up, but that was a stupid idea. Jeremy *never* gave up. If I stopped trying, he'd hit me with the ball until I started trying again. When he served, I decided to hit it way up in the air to teach him a lesson, except like usual the ball didn't do what I wanted it to do. It shot back right over the net. The ball was going way too fast for him to return. He almost fell over trying to slow himself down.

"Where the hell did that come from?" he yelled. He waited a few seconds to catch his breath before coming back to serve. "Whatever you did, keep doing it." Lightning never strikes twice, so I expected the ball to go into orbit when I tried to hit it way up in the air. Like before, it went right over the net. He couldn't even get close to hitting it back.

"I get it," he snarled. "You're hustling me. I'll bet you're a junior tennis pro. That's it, I'm pulling out all the stops."

I knew he was serious and not serious at the same time. Jeremy loved games and he always played to win. It didn't matter if we played chess or Risk or a card game or even guess which number I'm thinking of. I rarely beat him and he never just let me win. The few times I won at something, he called me a cheater and screamed how he was robbed. The way he carried on made winning a lot more fun. Beating an adult trying his best made all the games I lost worth it.

He served harder this time. I didn't have time to think. I ran after it and swung. Maybe that was the secret too, because it went right over the net and past him *again.* "Shit!" he yelled. I giggled. I got better and better each time he served. I even figured out how to make it go in the direction I wanted, hitting it away from him so he had to run from side to side.

"I'm dying," he finally said, dropping his racquet and lying down on his back on the court. He made it seem like he could barely breathe. I didn't feel tired at all. Before the "incident" with the baseball bat, I couldn't run around like this without collapsing. Now, I could go for hours without getting tired. I showed off by running around the court while he groaned in agony.

I guess I lost the weight, but it seemed like Jeremy did all the work. We ripped the kitchen apart the day after the incident: bags of cookies, chips, soda, candy, sugar cereal, and Twinkies all went straight to the trash can. If I wasn't going to eat it, neither was he. When I complained about plates of plain chicken and broccoli (the third most disgusting food ever invented), he made it a game by seeing who could come up with the best complaint. When I was too tired to ride bicycles, he would poke me in the side until it was easier to just give in to him. When I needed a break, just a little one, he always seemed to have a cookie stashed away like it was a big government secret.

Jeremy made everything better. He picked me up and dropped me off from school every single day, just in case Tommy was planning to ambush me in the woods. He explained that kids weren't teasing me as much because they respected me for standing up for myself. He worked on every little bit of homework I had side by side with me. He was there when I wanted him to be and he left me alone when I needed it. He even let me sleep in his bed like a little kid when I didn't want to be alone in my room. Which was every night that I stayed with him. Which was almost every night lately.

"That's it, you're going down," he muttered as he pulled himself up.

Not anymore, I thought.

We had a piano lesson every day after exercise until dinner, even on the weekends. I kept practicing while he made dinner, because I didn't want to stop until each new piece sounded perfect. It was like I'd found a part of me I never knew existed. Even though I only started a few months ago, I felt like I'd been playing all my life.

"Do you think this part here should have a crescendo?" I asked. "They didn't write one but it seems like it should."

"Yes, I think you're right. Try it." I played it through and we both nodded together. "Enough, you've conquered it. A new world record, only thirty minutes."

"Let's do the next one," I said, flipping the page.

He put his hands on top of mine. "Do you realize how quickly you're progressing? Most kids take years to learn as much as you've learned in the last few months. I haven't been pushing you very hard because you do all the pushing yourself." He used his soft voice. "How far do you want to go?"

"I want to play like you," I said.

"Playing at a high level requires dedication. You'll have to do boring things that seem pointless over and over again for years. Stuff like exercises, hand strengthening, and perfection of technique. It really sucks." He made me laugh. "I think you have real talent. If you develop it there's no saying how far you can go. But if you don't really want it, you won't get through all the crap."

"I really want it," I said.

"Are you prepared to dedicate your life to the piano, for richer or poorer, in sickness or health, till death do you part?"

He made me laugh again. "I do."

"Then I pronounce you boy and piano. Don't kiss it. Goodbye, John Thompson Third Grade Book." He threw the book across the room. "We're going to start with scales again, a little bit different than before." He pushed me over and started to play a scale. Two octaves up his hands separated, his right hand going up while his left hand went down. Then they came back in opposite directions before meeting up and going back to the beginning together.

"That's way too hard!" I whined.

"It's called contrary motion, and from now on this is what we're going to do until you've got them perfect in all major, minor, and modal scales. You need to learn how to use your hands independently."

"I want to play pieces," I whined again.

"That depends on how well you learn your scales. Start with these, and then we'll do thirds, sixths, tenths, and arpeggios the same way. You'll be amazed what you can play after that. For now, I will make you suffer for your art. Do you still want it?"

I sighed. "Yeah."

"I want B major by the time dinner is ready. Mush!" He made like he was cracking a whip and got up. I stared at the keyboard and

wondered how in the world I was going to make my hands do the impossible.

Impossible wasn't going to stop me.

B. . .C sharp. . .D sharp. . .

"Say your prayers," he shouted like a pirate, swinging the pillow at my head. Somehow, I pushed it aside with my own pillow before it slammed into me. He was off balance, so I swung as hard as I could into his stomach. The satisfying "oof" told me I got him good.

"You realize this means war," he said like Bugs Bunny.

"You're dethpicable," I said like Daffy Duck.

I tore out of the bedroom before he could swing again, jumping the last four steps into the entryway. "You're so dead!" he yelled as he chased me. I turned around in the lobby to face him. He studied me with narrow eyes, trying to find my weaknesses. I was getting good at this. He tried to hit me high, but I was ready. He always went high first. I ducked and used my chance to hit his legs. He staggered but didn't fall. "Son of a bitch," he muttered.

The big pillows from his bed were the best for pillow fights. They were heavy enough to knock either of us down, especially when all the feathers gathered at the bottom. I had two favorite attacks – his head and behind his knees. We never held back with pillow fights. It usually didn't end until one of us got hurt. The time when I hated being touched seemed like it was from a different life. Now I loved it – both the rowdy games and the quiet times when he let me put my head on his leg while we watched TV. The best part was that he seemed to like it as much as I did.

"I'm ending this," he said, swinging his pillow high. I tried to block it, but since the feathers were at the bottom the empty parts of our pillowcases got tangled. A second later he yanked my pillow out of my hands. Before I could do anything, he hit me in the chest hard enough to knock me backwards onto my butt. I thought the white stuff in front of my eyes was from getting hit so hard, but then I realized they were feathers. His pillow had exploded. We stared at each other, not moving.

"Holy shit," he said. He threw a handful of feathers at me. That turned into a huge feather fight, the little things flying everywhere, getting in our eyes and mouths. Finally, he tackled me, pinning me to the floor, finding all my ticklish spots while I squirmed and struggled to get away.

"Do you yield, sir?" he yelled with an English accent.

"Never!" I screamed through my laughter. He pulled my shirt up and blew raspberries on my stomach. I laughed so hard I couldn't breathe.

"I said, do you yield, sir?" he yelled again.

"Ok, ok, I yield!" I managed to spit out.

"Then you shall be my prisoner," he announced.

He pulled me up to my feet, pinned my hands behind my back, and marched me to the bedroom. I positioned myself on my back in the middle of the bed while he got the rope. He tied my hands and feet to the posts, stretched out and tight the way I liked it. Being tied up this way was much better than hands behind my back with my feet tied to them. I felt more helpless. When he was done, I struggled and tried to reach the knots. Like always, I couldn't get out even if I wanted to. I could barely move. A real prisoner.

He rubbed my head. "Would you like music or the story?"

"Story," I breathed.

He sat next to me on the bed. I was starting to like the book he picked about rabbits even though there were no spaceships or swords involved. I used to worry he'd tickle me until I puked because I couldn't fight back, but he never did. For the first few minutes, it was hard to concentrate on the story because I couldn't stop thinking about *other* stuff. But after a little while, those thoughts went away because I couldn't do anything about it. It should've been boring after that, but thanks to Jeremy it never was.

He kept me tied up for almost two hours. "Time's up, kiddo. You've got school tomorrow." He smacked my butt as I rolled off the bed and went into the bathroom.

I touched the indentations in my skin from the ropes, wishing they didn't go away so fast. My clothes came off. While I did it, I imagined asking him to keep me tied up all night. I imagined telling him how my

clothes got tangled so he should tie me up naked. I imagined asking him to do other things to me. Darker things.

I always felt horrible after I was done. I got dressed quickly so I didn't have to look at myself in the mirror. Like always, I swore I wouldn't let him tie me up again. What if I got up the courage to ask him to actually do the things I imagined? He'd figure out what was really going on. He'd never want to be my friend again. I had to stop before it was too late. I was taking advantage of him. I was abusing him. I had to be stronger. I had to protect him from me.

I went out of the bathroom and climbed onto my side of the bed, pulling the blankets over me and sinking into the feather softness. When he was done in the bathroom, he snuggled up to me and put his hand under my pajamas to rub my back. "Sometimes, I don't know what we are," I said.

"What do you mean?"

"Sometimes it's like you're my dad, sometimes it's like you're my brother, and sometimes it's like you're my friend."

"I'm a little of all three," he said. "Sometimes you make me feel like an adult, when I'm helping and teaching you. Sometimes you make me feel like a kid, like when we have pillow fights."

"I think it's something more, but I don't know the word for it."

"Whatever it is, I love you more than I thought I could love someone. Before I met you, I was drifting through the motions of everyday life without really living. With you, I feel alive again. I have purpose. Being your friend and your dad and whatever else gives my life meaning."

"Me too," I said. He was the first person who truly loved me, and I returned his love by using him in the most horrible way possible. Telling me that I gave him meaning and a purpose only made me feel worse. If I didn't stop, everything good I had would be gone forever.

Chapter 10

April 10, 1982

Of course it had to rain on the first day of spring vacation. Real rain, loud enough to echo off the windows in the lobby. The backyard was flooded and the street looked like a lake. So much for our plan to go to New York. I didn't care that much. I was staying with Jeremy for the whole vacation. I'd be happy even if we did nothing all week.

"Seven," Jeremy said, moving his shoe piece on the board. I didn't understand why he wanted the shoe. No one ever wanted the shoe. Everyone wanted the car or the horse. "Park Place, that's 35 to you." He handed over the money from his messy pile, which I put into my neat stacks of bills. Keeping neat stacks was part of playing the game the right way. Monopoly was the perfect thing to do on a day like today. The game was never going to end – we had the same number of monopolies and so much money that neither of us could go bankrupt. We kept going anyway even though we'd been playing for nine hours. The house was cozy with a big fire burning and a thick, warm blanket wrapped around me. Laziness felt right.

I landed on chance and went to jail, directly to jail. "Are you excited about your birthday, kiddo? Only a few weeks left before you turn twelve. Your last year before becoming a teenager. You're getting old."

"You're turning thirty next year," I pointed out. "That's really old."

"Thanks for reminding me," he muttered. "Stupid electric company." He searched through his pile for the money. His glass of

alcoholic stuff was almost empty so he filled it up again. "I wanted to talk to you about something."

"Sure," I said. St. James Place was mine.

"Well, you know, you're turning twelve and things are going to start changing for you. I wanted you to know that if you had any questions, I'd be happy to answer them."

"Ok," I said. I had no idea what he was talking about.

"I mean, your body will go through some changes and some of them can be confusing. When I was twelve, I didn't have anyone I could talk to, and it was scary for me. I wanted to make sure you knew you could ask about anything."

Oh no. He couldn't want to talk about *that.*

"Kids your age need someone who provides honest information. Most of the things you see on TV or hear on the playground are just plain wrong." He took another sip. "So, any burning questions?"

I couldn't look at him. "Not really," I said. I made myself busy straightening my money piles.

"Are you sure? There must be something you'd like to know."

"I'm in sixth grade," I said, wishing he would just stop. "It's not like I'm some little kid. Besides, we had a class back in fifth grade."

"A class," he said, like he didn't believe me.

"Yup, so I already know everything."

"I see," he said the same way. "Your turn."

I thought he gave up. I landed on Free Parking and scooped up the money. He took the dice but didn't roll them. "It's ok if you don't want to talk to me about sex right now. Having this conversation is just as difficult and embarrassing for me. I don't want you to suffer from guilt the way I did. I was convinced what I was doing was wrong. No one would talk about it, not even my brothers. The first time semen came out of my penis I thought I broke something inside and I was going to die." I stared at my money pile. The twenties weren't perfect. *Anything* to keep me from thinking about how he just said the "p" word. "I felt stupid when I figured it out. I want you to know there's nothing wrong or evil about sex. It's natural and normal, no matter what anyone says."

He looked like he wanted me to say something. I couldn't imagine saying anything. He didn't understand. What I did wasn't natural and normal at all. What I did *was* wrong and evil.

"So. . ." he said. When he didn't say anything else I looked up. "Are you. . .?"

"Am I what?" I said.

"Are you masturbating?"

I froze. *He knows.*

"I have to go to the bathroom," I said and ran off.

"Wait, I'm sorry," he said. I didn't stop until I was in the downstairs bathroom with the door safely locked behind me. I should've stopped asking him to tie me up, but I couldn't and now look what happened. Why did he have to do it this way? Why didn't he just tell me he knew?

He knocked on the door. "I'm sorry if I embarrassed you."

"Go away," I said.

"Why don't you come out? We can forget the whole thing."

"I said go away!"

He didn't answer. I put my head in my hands. Why did I tell him to go away? Why couldn't I just be casual and say I was embarrassed? Now he's going to be even more angry with me. I never knew how to be casual like other kids who were good at getting away with things.

I tried to calm down and think, but it was hard to keep my thoughts straight. He was probably waiting for me to admit it. Mom always wanted me to confess instead of telling me what she knew. Why did adults have to be so difficult? If I didn't tell him the truth, he might not let me stay with him anymore. I'd become big fat Nick all over again and be lonely for the rest of my life. If I promised never to do it again, maybe he'd still be my friend.

I went out to the lobby and stood near the entry area. He was sitting on the couch, drinking his alcoholic stuff. He looked at me. "Kiddo, I'm really sorry. I was just trying to help."

"I know," I said.

"Do you want to keep playing or do you want to do something else?"

I shrugged and looked down.

"Is something bothering you?" He got off the couch and came over to me. "You seem like you're upset, not just embarrassed. Is there something you want to talk about?"

I nodded. That was the best I could do.

He put his arm around my shoulder and walked me back to the couch. "It's ok, you can tell me."

I moved my mouth, but nothing came out.

"Is it something bad?"

I nodded.

"Is someone hurting you?" I didn't understand. "Is someone making you do something you don't want, something sexual?"

I shook my head hard.

"I was a little scared there," he said. He finished his glass of alcohol. "It's hard to play guessing games."

I wanted to tell him, but to do that I'd have to say it out loud. I couldn't imagine saying something that embarrassing. But I knew a better way. Just like the first time I wanted to tell him. It would work this time. I knew how to make sure it would work.

"Can you tie me up?" I said without looking at him. He didn't say anything, so I looked up. He wasn't looking at me. I got scared. "It's ok, you don't have to."

"No, it's fine," he said, but he still wasn't looking at me. "Does being tied up make it easier to talk?"

I nodded.

"Ok," he said.

I followed him upstairs and into the bedroom. "I'm going to take a shower first," I said because I needed some time to find courage. I turned on the water even though I wasn't going to take a shower and faced away from the mirror while I took off my pajamas. If I went into the bedroom naked, he'd have to ask me why. Then he'd ask me other questions so all I had to do was nod or shake my head.

I pulled down my underwear a hundred times and then pulled them back up each time. I was alone and still I was embarrassed. I couldn't imagine him seeing me. *All* of me. Especially with my thing standing up. I wasn't going to be tied up and still it was sticking straight out. Sometimes it could be so difficult.

He knocked. "You ok in there?"

"Just a minute," I yelled. I put my hair in the water in case he noticed. I didn't have the courage to go out without my underwear, so I left them on. A blast of warm air hit me when I opened the door. There were candles everywhere, hundreds of them. It was beautiful. I held my breath. Jeremy was on the bed, finishing his glass of alcoholic stuff.

"I wanted to do something special," he said.

I nodded. He patted the bed next to him. I didn't want him to touch me with my clothes off so I sat far away and scrunched myself up as small as I could.

"I love you so much," he said.

I couldn't say the words back.

"Let's get you tied up."

He pulled gently on my wrist. I didn't stop him. He did all the work, getting me to lie down on my stomach, pulling my hands and legs out to each corner, tying the ropes until I was secure. I didn't understand why he didn't ask me. He didn't even seem to notice I was undressed. I knew I should tell him to stop, but my thing made me all excited about being tied up in my underwear.

He sat down beside me when he was done and rubbed my back. He must've thought I meant I wanted to talk when I was already tied up. Any second now he'd ask me why I took off my clothes.

"I love you, and I know you love me," he said. "Remember, no matter what happens, I'll always love you."

I didn't say anything. Any second now.

"You're so beautiful," he whispered.

I thought that seemed like a weird thing to say.

Then it happened.

He kissed the back of my neck and rubbed my butt.

I froze.

He kept kissing my back, each kiss lower down. His hand squeezed the inside of my thigh. I couldn't move. I was terrified and I didn't know why. I felt dizzy. I closed my eyes tight.

His hand went into my underwear, squeezing my butt.

"I love you," he whispered in my ear. Then he kissed my cheek.

I stayed as still as I could.

His hand stayed in my underwear.

His other hand rubbed me all over.

It was hard to breathe.

He pulled my underwear down.

His hand went between my legs and touched me *there*.

It felt good.

And wrong.

And good.

And wrong.

And good.

"Stop," I whispered.

"I won't hurt you," he whispered back. "I'd never hurt you."

"What are you doing?" I said.

"Everything will be ok," he said back.

"Please stop," I said louder. My voice cracked.

His hands were gone, then he was gone, off the bed. "Oh god, no," he said. He pulled my underwear back up and used scissors to cut the ropes instead of untying me. I rolled over. He pulled the blankets over me to cover me up. He stumbled backwards until he hit the wall, sliding down it to sit on the floor.

"Are you ok?" I asked. I was too afraid to move.

He started crying. I never saw Jeremy cry. It was impossible to imagine. "I ruined everything," he moaned. He buried his face in his hands.

"What's wrong?" I started shaking.

"We can't be friends anymore. You can't stay here. Just get dressed and go home. I'll pack your things and send them over. I'll call your mother to explain. I'll take care of everything." He looked up at the ceiling and screamed.

"Don't you love me anymore?" I said in a tiny voice.

His face looked wild. "Don't you ever think that! I love you so much it's tearing me apart. That's why you have to go. I can't stand to see you get hurt."

I threw the blankets off and jumped off the bed. Words came out without me thinking about them, because if I stopped to think they

wouldn't come out. "Please don't make me leave. I promise I'll never do it again. I swear, please just let me keep being your friend. Please!" I tried to touch his shoulder, but he jerked away. "I promise I'll never ask again. You have to believe me!"

"You'll never ask what again?" he said, looking the other way.

"I'll never ask to be tied up again. I should've told you a long time ago. I wanted you to ask me why and then I was going to tell you. I couldn't tell you and I couldn't stop. I knew it was wrong and I knew I shouldn't be doing it. I didn't want to keep tricking you!"

"Tricking me?" he asked.

"About why I wanted to be tied up," I said.

He stared at me. I could tell he was confused. "You thought I didn't know?"

"I thought you found out and wanted me to admit it," I said.

"Sweetie," he said. "I've always known why you wanted to be tied up, ever since the first time you asked me."

It was like putting a puzzle together and finding out the last piece didn't fit. The only thing to do was tear the whole puzzle apart and start over.

"None of this is your fault," he said. "You never tricked me. If anything, I've been tricking you. I should've stopped it. I should never have even allowed it to start. I know I've been putting you in an impossible position. It's tearing me apart. I hope someday you can forgive me."

"What are you talking about?" I asked.

"I've suspected for a while that you knew about me," he said. "I swore I'd never hurt you, but every time you asked I went along with it anyway. I can't imagine how hurt and confused you must be. When I asked you about sex and you ran off, I knew you were upset with me. Then you asked me to tie you up again and still I couldn't stop myself. Maybe if I hadn't been drinking."

"I don't understand," I said. He started crying again. "You're scaring me."

"Don't be scared," he said, which scared me more. "I've wanted to confess for a long time now. You deserve the truth. If I acted like an

adult for once in my life, none of this would've happened. But I was terrified I'd lose you, and I couldn't bear it. I need you."

"Tell me what?"

He closed his eyes and took a deep breath.

"I'm attracted to you," he whispered.

"Attracted?"

"I'm sexually attracted to you."

I blinked. "You're what?"

"It means I want to have sex with you."

What was he talking about? Something like that wasn't even possible, was it? Then it clicked. He called me beautiful. He kissed me. He pulled down my underwear. He touched me *there*. Was he trying to *do it* with me? I pushed myself back against the bed, wanting to be as far away from him as I could. I realized I was only a pair of underpants away from being naked.

"I'd never do something to you that you didn't want," he said. "I kept tying you up because I was getting off knowing you were turned on by it. I thought when you came out of the bathroom without your clothes that you were inviting me to go further. You have to understand something. These feelings I have for you are wrong. Adults are not supposed to want to have sex with children. It damages kids in horrible ways. I swore a long, long time ago I'd never do anything to hurt a boy. I broke that promise tonight." He put his head in his hands. "I can't imagine how scared you are right now. How disgusted."

He looked so sad. How could I be scared of him? He was Jeremy. The person who saved me. The person who knew me better than anyone else. The person who loved me when no one else would. He had to know I could never really be scared by him.

"You didn't hurt me," I said.

"Yes, I did," he said. "You can't trust me anymore. Nothing will be the same. I'm the adult. I have all the power. Imagine if I started abusing that power."

"You wouldn't do that," I said, not sure what he meant.

"Of course not, but you might think I would," he said. "You might do things you don't want to do just to please me. I can't risk it. I can't

allow it to happen. We can't be friends. You can't stay with me anymore. It's the only way."

"I don't want to leave," I said.

"I feel like I'm ripping out my own heart," he said.

"But I love you," I said.

"How can you still love me? Don't you realize what I did to you? I *molested* you."

"I don't care," I said. "I need to stay with you." He looked at me and shook his head. I jumped over, grabbing on to his shirt. "Please, please, please, you can't kick me out. I need you too."

He pushed me off and stood up. "I need a drink," he said, stumbling out of the room. I felt empty and alone, the way I used to feel before I met Jeremy. I pulled my knees up to my chest and rocked back and forth. It was only a matter of time before he dragged me away, back to my old room and my old life.

I decided not to let him.

I ran down the hallway to the guest bedroom, the one where I used to stay a long time ago. Locking the door wasn't enough, so I slid the big chair over to block it. All my new clothes were in our bedroom, so I dug through my old clothes for something to wear. My red flannel shirt was so big it was like I was wearing one of Jeremy's shirts. I wasn't going to let it get small on me again. Everything good in my life was because of him. I wasn't going to give up. I had to figure out the most important problem in my entire life to save the most important thing in my entire life.

I started shaking because I had no idea how.

Chapter 11

April 11, 1982

I stared at the ceiling, rubbing my itchy eyes. The blankets were messy from all the times I pulled them up and then threw them off. Being alone in bed felt wrong. The pillows were lined up on the other side of the bed to make it feel like Jeremy was sleeping next to me, but it didn't work. I needed to pee but wouldn't go to the bathroom because I was convinced a monster was hiding underneath the bed. I was turning twelve in two weeks. I *knew* monsters weren't real. Still, I was positive this one was very real. It was green and wore a tuxedo that was too small. If I put my foot on the floor, it would grab me and say: "Let me take you to your doom, sir." I wasn't sure if I'd fight back or let it eat me.

The big chair stopped him from knocking on my door. I knew if he knocked on my door it wouldn't be to kick me out. He would say he was sorry and call me sweetie and tell me that everything was ok and I would hug him and never let go. The chair somehow told him I didn't want him to come. I knew it was impossible – he couldn't see the chair through the door. I didn't know why I left the door blocked, I didn't know why I couldn't knock on his door, and I didn't know why I was paralyzed. My thoughts got so mixed up I believed in magic chairs and monsters under the bed again.

At first, I was so sure I wouldn't give up. I was going to keep working on this problem until I figured out a way to fix everything. Bit by bit, that feeling melted away. I tried so hard, but nothing worked. I wasn't smart enough to convince Jeremy no matter what I said or did. The

only I had left to figure out was what I'd do when someone came to take me back to my old life. I could fight back. I could keep the door blocked and starve to death. I could jump out the window and run away. Or I could do something big. Something permanent. Something that couldn't be taken back.

If I waited any longer, I'd wet the bed. I jumped off, landing hard enough to make the windows rattle. I ran in case a tentacle slithered out and caught my ankle. A part of me wished I'd just get eaten. Or swallowed up in an earthquake or melted in a nuclear war or cut into pieces by a guy who escaped from the mental asylum. It'd be easier if something was done to me instead of me having to do something.

I didn't know what I was going to do when I dragged the big chair away and opened the door. I didn't have a plan. Jeremy's door was closed at the other end of the hall. We usually left it open a little when we went to bed. I only wanted to know if he was in there. I tried to open it, but the door was locked. I checked it again to make sure. The handle didn't turn. I couldn't get in. He locked me out of his room. Of *our* room. Of his life. I was suddenly furious.

I stomped downstairs. It was still night, the lobby dark and still, but the sun would probably come up soon. I didn't turn on the lights. There was music open on the piano desk, so I pushed it off and kicked the books halfway across the lobby. I played the loudest, ugliest thing I could imagine. The noise bounced around the room. I looked down at my hands, E flat minor seventh with a sharp fourth and flat ninth in my right hand. I wanted the chords I played to have no name. I started hitting the keys with my whole hand, up and down the piano, my anger building. I played soft notes just so I could drown them out. I let some last so long they died out on their own, and others I played as fast as I could. I don't know how long I banged before I slammed the cover down.

"That was very moving," Jeremy said in his soft voice. I whirled around, furious that he invaded my privacy. He sat on the step between the entry and the lobby. "I've never heard you compose like that. It was raw, intense, and passionate." His eyes looked watery. "It was beautiful."

Calling that noise beautiful like he called me beautiful last night made me even more furious. "It was ugly," I snarled.

"It was brilliant."

"It was stupid," I said louder. "Why do you always say things like that? Why do you say I'm brilliant or smart when I'm not?"

"I didn't mean to upset you," he said.

"You always upset me!" I yelled.

"I just want to talk to you."

"There's nothing to talk about! Leave me alone!"

"I'm sorry about everything," he said. "Can we talk? Please don't push me away."

My anger turned into a raging storm. "You're the one who's pushing *me* away! You're the one who said I had to leave and never come back! You're the one who locked your door!"

"Sweetie, I don't really want you to leave. I can't live without you. I want to figure this out."

"What if *I* want to leave?" I screamed as loud as I could. "Did you think about that? Maybe I don't want to see you ever again!" I stomped past him and picked up my sneakers.

He stood up. "Please, don't go. We don't have to talk. We don't have to do anything."

I put my shoes on, leaving the laces untied. He went around me and blocked the front door. "Get out of the way!" I yelled.

"I'm not letting you go like this," he said.

"Get away from me!" He grabbed my arm, his fingers digging in hard. "Let go!" I screamed. He did and I ran through the lobby to the back door.

"I didn't mean that," he said. "Please come back."

I went into the backyard. The sky was gray. It was cold and the grass was sloshy from the rain. I started to shiver.

He appeared in the doorway a minute later, wearing his shoes and jacket. "It's freezing out here."

"If it was then everything would be frozen," I fired at him.

"You're not wearing a coat. You'll get sick."

I crossed my arms and shook my head. "No I won't."

"Sweetie, please."

"Stop calling me that!"

"I'm sorry, I thought you liked it. I'll do whatever you want, please come back inside."

"Maybe I want to stay out here," I snarled.

"It'd be better if we talked inside."

"Why?" I started yelling again. "Because someone might hear?"

"Because it's cold out," he said. His voice sounded shaky.

"You're afraid someone will hear! You're afraid someone's going to find out! You're afraid I'm going to tell on you!"

He looked like I punched him in the stomach. All at once the anger turned towards myself. What was I doing? How could I say something like that to him? I didn't know what to do so I turned and ran down the hill.

"Come back!" Jeremy shouted. He ran after me, slipping on the wet grass. The lawn got even more soaked as I got closer to the woods. I had to skid to a stop because the little creek had turned into a raging river. It was too wide to jump across. I was trapped.

I turned around and stared at Jeremy. "Come back inside!" he shouted. It was hard to hear because the water was making a lot of noise. I shook my head and took a step back, right into a muddy patch. My foot sank so deep the mud came halfway up my shin. He took a step closer.

"Go away!" I yelled. My foot was trapped like I stepped in cement. I turned around to pull it from a different angle, but I stepped into another muddy patch and got my other foot trapped too.

"Let me help you get out," he said, taking another step closer.

"I said go away!" I screamed, twisting and jerking as hard as I could. I heard a strange sucking sound. One foot came out – without my shoe. The mud kept it as a souvenir. I didn't want to put my bare foot down, but that made balancing too hard. I leaned too far over and at just the right time the mud let go of my other foot so I lost my balance and fell over backwards into the rushing water.

The blast of cold made me numb all over. I tried to get up, but I couldn't feel my feet and my hands were stiff. My teeth started chattering hard. Jeremy was shouting something, but I couldn't hear

him. I felt like I couldn't breathe. He stood at the side of the creek, reaching out his hand so he could pull me out. "No!" I screamed.

He leaned over. I knocked his hand away. He tried to catch mine but lost his balance and slipped. He wound up in the creek on his butt. "Give me your hand!" he yelled.

"Go away!"

He grabbed me and held on tight. I didn't have enough energy to yank away. He stood up, wrapped his arms around me, and lifted me up. Somehow, he managed to climb up the side of the creek without letting go.

"Why won't you just leave me here?" I screamed. "Why won't you just give up on me?"

"I'll never give up on you and I'll never leave you, no matter what happens!" He stared right into my eyes. "No matter what happens!"

All at once, I wasn't angry anymore. I grabbed his shirt, wrapped my arms and legs around him, clinging on as hard as I could. He carried me up the hill, whispering in my ear. "It'll be ok. Everything will be ok." I could tell he was struggling but he didn't put me down. He carried me all the way to the kitchen. I looked over his shoulder at the trail of muddy footprints he left on the carpet in the den.

Like hot chocolate.

He set me down on the countertop in the kitchen. My legs dangled, mud dripping on the cabinets. "Are you hurt anywhere?" he asked.

"I don't think so," I said. "You have mud in your hair."

He smiled. "You've got mud everywhere."

I looked down at my clothes and then looked at him. We both started to giggle at the same time. "We need to get you warmed up before you catch pneumonia," he said. "Take a hot shower and don't come out until you're defrosted. I'll build a fire. Scoot."

I slipped off the counter and ran up the stairs, my legs stiff and teeth chattering from the shivers. I turned the shower on as hot as it went and peeled off my muddy clothes in a heap on the floor. At first, I didn't even feel the water, then I started feeling pins and needles, and then it started to hurt. Steam swirled around me. I stayed in the shower until it ran out of hot water. Jeremy left my Christmas pajamas, robe and

slippers, and a trash bag for my wet clothes outside the bathroom door. He even left a thermos of cocoa.

I felt horrible.

When I came downstairs, he was sitting in front of the fire, holding his hands out to warm them. He patted the floor for me to sit down next to him. I put my hands out like him. The fire was hot and dry.

"Feeling better?" he asked.

I nodded. But I only felt better on the outside. "I'm really sorry," I whispered.

"Sweetie, you have nothing to be sorry for."

"I was being a jerk," I said.

"You had every right. I did a terrible thing."

I found some courage. "Do you still love me?"

"Of course I still love you. Nothing could ever change that." He put his hand on my shoulder. "I meant what I said outside. I'll never give up on you. I want you to stay. I need you to stay. But only if you want to."

"I want to stay," I said.

He smiled and his eyes got watery. "You know what's weird? I'm glad you know. It's hard to lie to someone you love."

"I know," I said. "I was lying to you too."

"Well, now we don't have to lie to each other anymore. We can be who we really are."

"I thought you would hate me."

"Same for me. I guess we have something very special." He stared into the fire for a while. I wanted to snuggle up against him, but something about the way he was sitting told me I shouldn't.

"I don't want to keep secrets from you anymore," he said suddenly. "I want to tell you about another boy I knew named Colin. I think it'll help you understand why I'm so scared of hurting you.

"I met Colin a couple months after I started music school. You would've been just a baby back then. I don't remember the exact date. I'm sure it was a Saturday, and it had to be October because the leaves were changing. I should've been practicing, but I decided I was entitled to a day off to see Rochester.

"You should know that back then, I was a very different person than I am today. I was a complete, grade A, prime asshole." I giggled. "I was so full of myself that there was no room for anyone else. There I was, eighteen years old and attending one of the best conservatories in the country despite Father's efforts to stop me. I had enough money to do whatever I wanted, whenever I wanted. So naturally, I became a conceited pig who never hesitated to rub everyone's nose in the fact I was smarter, more talented, and richer than they were.

"When I was a kid, I loved collecting comic books. I enjoyed reading them, but I liked having the best collection even more. I bought as many as I could with my own money and Mother filled in rare ones for my birthdays and Christmas. When I saw the comic store in Rochester that afternoon, I assumed there was no way a rinky-dink little place like that could have anything I needed for my collection. I went in anyway, shuffling through the boxes and asking for books I knew they wouldn't have. In other words, being a jerk. I dropped a stack of comics on a table to make the guy think I decided not to buy. I turned around to leave, and right behind me was a boy, about twelve or thirteen, just standing there." Jeremy's voice cracked. "He asked in the nicest voice if I was done because he wanted to make sure the books got put back in the right places. I don't remember if I nodded. I watched him patiently slide them into the boxes, being careful not to wrinkle or fold them. He had a beautiful smile while he worked, like his job was the best job in the universe."

He wiped his face on his sleeve. "I was twelve when I realized I was interested in boys. You know. . .sexually. I thought eventually I'd become more interested in men when I got older, but it just never happened. I had to work up the nerve to talk to Colin, but once I did we talked for hours. He was a comic freak, far more knowledgeable than me. He worked at the store on Saturdays just so he could be near them. The owner paid him in comics instead of money. His ripped jeans and oversized t-shirt told me his family didn't have much, so I figured this was his only way to get new books.

"I fell in love with him, the same way I fell in love with you," he said, looking straight at me. "It was his eyes. Even though he was happy as a clam sorting those comics, I could see a sadness behind them. Just

like you. So, I did what any guy would do after falling hopelessly and helplessly in love. I drove home and loaded up my entire comic collection into the car. The following Saturday, I camped out across the street from the comic shop until he showed up, and then I spent a few hours helping him sort the books. When it was time for him to leave, I invited him to my room to see my collection. I thought I was going to explode when he said yes. I suppose things were different back then. He didn't think twice about going with a stranger and I didn't think twice about asking him. When he saw my collection, he was blown away. He kept thanking me for just letting him look at them. I told him I wasn't into comics anymore and I was looking for someone who'd take good care of my collection. I told him if he promised to do so, he could have every single book. I think he almost cried. I spent years assembling that collection, but giving it all to him made me much happier than the comics ever did.

"I drove him home to a dingy little apartment in a run-down neighborhood. It was just him and his mother, so I waited for her while he started carefully cataloging everything. He made me swear not to tell his mother he was working at the comic shop because he was supposed to stay close to home when she was out working. I don't remember what we told her about how we met or exactly why I was giving her son thousands of dollars worth of comic books, but I don't remember her being suspicious in the slightest.

"We became inseparable. His mother never expressed any concern about me. To her, I was a nice rich kid who shared some common interests with her son, and she was more than grateful for the free adult supervision. A social worker of some kind seemed to have it in for them, but with me around that situation improved since Colin spent less time alone. I set up my spring class schedule around him. Instead of practicing in the afternoons, I woke myself up before dawn every day so I could be free to pick him up after school. I got an apartment instead of staying in the dorm so he could spend the night when his mother worked late shifts. I even stayed in Rochester for the summer just so I could be near him.

"I didn't know why it was only Colin and his mother. I didn't want to pry, and Colin never said anything. Not until my birthday, 1973.

Colin celebrated with me. I let him try some beer. God, he made such a face. We were in my apartment watching television, and out of nowhere he started talking about how things were different when his father was around. They didn't have much money since he was a factory worker, but they were happy. His father taught him to love comic books. They played baseball, went camping, and spent time together. And then just like that, a couple years before we met, he didn't come home from work. He wasn't hurt in an accident or murdered. He left. Colin wasn't aware his parents were fighting. His mom told him that his father had a new family and they'd have to get used to him being gone because he was never coming back.

"It broke my heart how someone could abandon such a sweet, kind boy. Colin told me he prayed every night for his father to come home, even though he knew it would never happen. Then he told me his prayers were answered, just not how he thought they would be. His dad didn't come back – I came instead. I melted.

"It just. . .kind of happened. I wanted to show him how much I loved him. I kissed him, one thing led to another, clothes came off, and we. . .had sex. All the way. I molested him. I never forced him and he never fought anything I did, but I took his innocence that night." Jeremy blinked like he wanted to cry. "Afterwards, he fell asleep in my arms and I held him all night. All I could think was how lucky I was to be in love like this.

"I found a way to do it with him every time we were together. My bed, his bed, his mother's bed, the backseat of my car, hotel rooms, on the beach of Lake Erie – it didn't matter. He never complained, and I was absolutely convinced he enjoyed every second of it. I was so emotionally high that I ignored all the warning signs. First his grades went into the toilet, then he started cutting school. He became moody and withdrawn instead of the happy-go-lucky kid I knew. Once, I went to pick him up and found him smoking weed with a bunch of delinquents. I told myself he was going through a teenage phase. I was arrogant enough to think I could snap him out of it by spending even more time with him.

139

"I remember the date – March 2nd, 1974. He was a wild man in bed that night. He woke me up in the middle of the night to tell me that he swallowed a whole bottle of pills."

My eyes went wide. Why would that kid do something like that? I thought I should say something, but nothing seemed right.

"I rushed him to the hospital. They pumped his stomach and kept him for observation, so I stayed with him all night while he slept. When he woke up he seemed happy I was there. The nurses ordered me home so I could get a nap and a shower. I came back as quickly as I could." He put his head in his hands.

"Did he die?" I whispered.

"No, he didn't die. It all came out. The sex. The cops were waiting for me. They read the charges in front of everyone. 'Lewd and lascivious conduct with a minor.' They took me to jail and put me in a common cell with twenty other guys. Scary guys.

"The cops must've tipped off one of them. Other criminals hate child molesters. By the time the cops stopped them, I was half dead on the floor. They dragged me to a solitary cell and left me there. I'm lucky I didn't die. I don't remember much until I woke up a couple days later handcuffed to a hospital bed. I don't know how, but my family found out and took care of everything. Not because they cared about me – the only thing that mattered to them was their precious reputation. They sent a lawyer to post bail and pay everyone off, but nobody came to see me in the hospital. The case was eventually dismissed. No need for me to show up in court and face Colin.

"I ran away from my life. I never went back to school and disappeared from the face of the earth as far as anyone who knew me was concerned. It took a long time for me to face the truth of what I did. He trusted me, and I abused that trust in the most horrific way. I can't imagine the pain he must still feel today. I'd give up everything to make up for what I did. I've wanted to find him so I could apologize, but I'm scared it'd only hurt him more if I did. I told myself I'd never put myself in a position to wreck another boy's life, and then there you were with your shovel and I couldn't help myself. Look what I did all over again." He held my hand. "Do you understand why I'm so scared?"

"How could he do that?" I burst out. He stared at me. "If that kid loved you, how could he tell on you?" My hands were in fists. "If he didn't want you to do it, he should've told you! You didn't know!"

"Sweetie, he never said anything because he was probably afraid I'd stop caring about him."

"That doesn't matter. He shouldn't have lied."

"I don't want to put you in the same position."

I looked at him as hard as I could. "I'll never tell on you. Ever."

He sighed. "I don't want to do anything that would make you need to keep a secret. It's very important to me for you to understand something. No matter what you do or don't do, I'll never stop loving you. Nothing you could ever do or say will change how I feel. If anything, I mean *anything*, makes you uncomfortable you can always tell me and feel safe." He put his hands on my shoulder. "I need you to promise me."

"I promise I'll never tell on you."

"That's not what I wanted you to promise," he said.

"I promise I'll never forget, too," I said. "Can I give you a hug?"

"Of course. I wouldn't want to go through life without hugs." I wrapped my arms around him. "I love you so much."

"I love you too," I said. Right there, just like that, I knew what had to be done. It was my job to fix the damage that other kid did to him. My job to prove I'd never betray him. My job to make him happy. My job to show him how much I loved him. Even if I wasn't exactly sure what gross things I'd need to do.

No matter what I had to do, I was going to do it.

Chapter 12

April 29, 1982

Jeremy told me I could skip school and do anything I wanted for my birthday. He seemed surprised when I asked if we could go fishing. I thought a lot about how he said this was an important birthday. Twelve years old – almost a teenager. When I was little, I thought it'd be forever until I finally grew up. Time went by *soooooo* slowly. Now, I realized my time as a kid was running out. I needed to learn how to do all the things kids were supposed to know, like fishing, camping, and building a fire. If I didn't get started right away, it would be too late for me. I never realized that time can run out. There was always enough time to do everything.

I threw the pole over my shoulder, watching the line fly out into the water. "What's it called when you throw the line out?" I asked Jeremy.

He was holding the sides of our rowboat so tight his fingers were white. "I have no idea," he said through his clenched teeth. I would've chosen something else to do if he'd told me he didn't like boats. I didn't know until I accidentally rocked the boat after we pulled away from the dock. He looked like he wanted to throw up. I asked if he wanted to do something else, but he told me it was my birthday and we were going to do what I wanted. Period.

The bobber did it's bobbing thing on the small waves while I slowly pulled it in. This time, I was going to catch a fish. I was sure of it. I pulled the empty hook from the water. The fish stole my worm. Again.

"Can you put the worm on for me?" I handed my pole to Jeremy.

He took a worm out of the plastic container with one hand because he wouldn't let go of the boat. "Yummy fish food."

"Gross," I said as he speared it through whatever it's middle was called. "How do you do that without barfing?"

"Ancient Chinese secret," he said.

I threw the line back in. "Oh yeah, it's called casting," I said out loud, turning around a little too fast. The boat tipped to one side and Jeremy's face turned as white as his hands. "Sorry," I said. "Are you sure you don't want to go back?"

He growled. "For the millionth time, I need to get over this irrational fear of boats once and for all."

I grinned. "Then maybe I should rock it even more."

"Try it and I swear I'll get even." He didn't let go of the sides. "Later. After we get back."

"Why are you so scared of boats?"

"I'm not scared of boats," he said. "I'm scared of falling off the boat."

"But you know how to swim," I said.

"Doesn't matter. I got thrown out of a boat when I was a kid. Ever since then boats frighten me."

"Why would someone throw you out of a boat?"

"My older brother thought it would be funny. He said, 'Learn to swim, twerp,' and pushed me overboard. I wasn't even wearing a life jacket. They had a hard time pulling me back in because I was thrashing so violently. You don't know how lucky you are to be an only child."

"I always thought having a brother would be fun," I said.

"Hell yeah, all kinds of fun. If you like getting pushed out of boats, having your bathing suit pulled down in front of everyone, being locked in a cabinet for nine hours, and getting beat up twice a day, then having a brother is for you. Maybe some kids have brothers who care. Mine never did."

"How much older is he?"

"Three years. He was always bigger and stronger and always made sure I knew it. He's discovered more sophisticated ways to be a bully now that we're adults. At least he stopped calling me names. I hated when he called me Germy."

"Germy," I said, holding back a laugh. "That's a good one."

"If you call me Germy, even once, I swear I will stuff this entire container of worms in your pants." I giggled, which turned into coughing. He looked concerned. "Are you cold?"

"No, I'm hot and sweaty. Especially with this life jacket on." He frowned. "I'm not sick any more, I promise."

"One sneeze and you're going right back to bed. You know what the doctor said."

"I know, I know," I said. I wound up getting sick the day after I fell in the creek. Not regular sick, or like the time I had pneumonia when I was eight but didn't feel it at all and got to skip school for a month and have a TV in my bedroom. I had a bad fever for three days and felt lousy for three more. Jeremy took me to the emergency room so they could pronounce me officially sick and give us stronger medicine. When I used to get sick, my mom and dad would help a little, but mostly they left me alone because they were too afraid they'd catch it and miss work. Jeremy didn't care. He took care of me the whole time and never left the room except to get soup.

The rod jerked in my hand. "Fish!" I shouted. I yanked the rod like the guy in the bait shop said I should. The line kept pulling, and I started to wind it back in. The fish was fighting hard with me. "It's a big one!"

"Come on, reel it in," Jeremy said, excited.

I could hardly keep myself sitting down I was so excited. By the way it was pulling, I was sure I caught a whale or at least a very large shark.

My whale or very large shark actually turned out to be about six inches long. It looked like something I could catch in a fish tank. I watched it flop around and felt stupid.

"Hey, you got him!" Jeremy shouted. "Get it off the hook and into the basket."

"I don't want to touch it," I said. "It's slimy."

"He's going to suffocate if you don't get him off the line," Jeremy said. I dropped the rod into the boat, watching the fish flopping around. "Come on!"

I tried to grab it, but the fish was even slimier than I thought. Jeremy snatched it and pulled the hook out of its mouth. "Here, into the basket!" he said. He pushed the fish into my hands, but it was so slippery

it squirmed free. Right over the edge of the boat into the water. I watched it swimming away until it disappeared.

Jeremy laughed. "Did you see it stick out it's tongue at you?"

"Stupid fish. It was too small anyway."

"I'll bait the hook for you."

I shook my head. "Nope. I give up."

"Don't give up yet. I'm sure you'll catch another one."

"Why do people go fishing if it's so boring?" I asked.

"I think fishing is a way of avoiding life for a while," he said.

"I could think of better ways," I said. "Like cleaning toilets."

He laughed. "I'm bored out of my skull too. Weigh anchor, batten the hatches, hoist the mainsail, walk the plank, swab the poopdeck, shiver me timbers, and take us to port. I've a mind to pillage and plunder." I stared at him. "Aaargh!" he shouted.

"You can be so weird sometimes," I said.

"Aaargh," he answered.

I liked weird.

"Ready?" Jeremy asked.

I nodded even though my stomach was twisted up in knots. I wasn't supposed to be nervous. This was *my* birthday dinner. We drove for over forty-five minutes to get to the Japanese place where they threw knives around and lit the grill on fire. I wanted to have dinner with Jeremy alone. At the last minute, both my parents were available to come, even though it was a Thursday. Jeremy said we had to invite them.

Mom stood up when we walked into the restaurant. "Look at you! I can't believe it's only been two weeks since I last saw you!"

"I got new clothes," I said. The shirt and pants fit right, not all baggy like my last set of new clothes, so they made me look thinner.

"You slimmed down so much! How much have you lost?"

"Thirty-seven pounds," I said.

"Turn around," she said, twirling her finger. I did. "You look fantastic."

"Thanks," I said. My face felt warm.

Jeremy rescued me. "It's so good to see you again, Ellie." He gave her a little hug. "You're looking great too."

"Thank you," she said. "Nicholas was so excited about having dinner here. I can't wait to see what this place is all about. Our table is ready."

"Shouldn't we wait for Dad?" I said.

"Your father won't be able to make it tonight," she said.

I pretended to study some Japanese writing on the wall so she couldn't see how angry I was. All that nervousness for nothing. He didn't even bother to show up for my birthday dinner. The only times I talked to him were when my mother called his office and handed me the phone. As far as I knew, he never came home from his office anymore. When I found out he was coming for dinner, I practiced for all his questions. If he asked me about my grades, I'd tell him I had all A's. If he said something bad about the Atari, I'd tell him I never played it anymore. I wanted him to watch me order healthy food and water instead of coke. I wanted to tell him how I exercised and played sports. I wanted to tell him how I practiced piano for hours every day. I was going to sit up straight and make sure to chew with my mouth closed. No matter what he tried, I was going to prove to him that I wasn't as stupid or lazy as he thought I was. He wasn't going to give me the chance. He must've known I was ready for him.

They brought us to a big table with a flat grill in the middle. Another family sat across the table from us. They didn't pay any attention to us so I ignored them too, even though it was weird to sit at a table with strangers. I stared at the menu to hide how I was still mad at my father. After we ordered, Jeremy cleared his throat and excused himself from the table. I got up to go with him, but I could tell that he wanted me to stay alone with my mom by the way he looked at me. It didn't seem like a good idea. When she moved over to sit next to me, I was positive it wasn't a good idea.

"How are things between you and Jeremy?' she asked quietly.

"Good," I said.

"He doesn't do anything that makes you uncomfortable?"

I didn't know exactly what she meant by that, but I didn't like the way she sounded like a detective accusing him of a crime. "No, nothing like that," I said, letting myself sound angry.

"If you ever want to talk, you can call my office in Denver any time. I'm not in court very often so you don't have to worry about interrupting me."

"Ok," I said.

"I'd like you to come to Denver during summer vacation. I promise it won't be like the last time you traveled with me." When I was nine, she took me on a business trip because no one else was home to watch me. I had to stay alone in the hotel room while she went to work. She promised every morning to come back early, but she was always late. I was so scared to open the door, I stayed hungry all day and pretended I wasn't there when the maid knocked.

"When you come, I'll take a few days off so we can go up to the mountains," she said. "The Rockies are so inspiring – nothing like the mountains on the east coast. I heard about a town with the biggest alpine slide in the country, like a race track down the mountain. I think you'd really love it up there." She looked at me like she wanted me to say something, but I had no idea what she wanted me to say. I didn't like when she acted nice. It reminded me of the day we had the incident. "We hardly see each other anymore and I miss you. How does it sound?"

I shrugged a little, thinking it might be ok to visit if they had a race track like she said. And then I figured it out. It was just like before. She was being nice for a reason and it wasn't a good one.

"We're going to move again, aren't we?" She didn't answer so I knew it was true. "You got a new job and you're out there all the time. Now you want me to visit, probably so you can get me used to the idea. I'm not dumb."

"I've never thought you were dumb," she said in a soft voice that didn't sound like her at all. "Listen to me. You don't have to go anywhere because I have a new job. You're happier than I've ever seen you, and I wouldn't do anything to jeopardize that. I wish you could understand how important it is to me that you're doing so well. I'm proud of you."

I started to wonder if the person I was talking to wasn't actually my mother. She was replaced by some evil alien, just like one of those old black and white movies on TV in the middle of the night. Invasion of the mom snatchers.

Jeremy came back before I had to think of something to say. They started talking about Mom's work stuff and then the show started. The chef made a volcano out of an onion and threw little balls of rice at people to catch in their mouths. For the first time ever, I managed to catch it without using my hands.

"Are you coming back to the house?" he asked her when they brought the bill. "We have cake and presents to open."

I was worried she'd say yes. "I wish I could, but I have a flight first thing in the morning and I'm staying near the airport tonight. You two go back and celebrate. Light a candle for me." She pulled a card out of her purse. "Happy birthday. I love you, Nicholas." She got up from her chair, we hugged, and she left.

Jeremy and I got in the car. "What did you two talk about?"

I thought about how weird she was acting. "Stuff."

"She didn't ask you anything about me, did she?"

I remembered the uncomfortable thing. "No."

"You'd tell me if she did? It's important."

"I know," I said.

I tried to put my hand on top of his, but he moved it where I couldn't reach.

Jeremy turned out the lights in the lobby and brought out the cake. The candles were bright and flickering, making shadows all over the room. "Happy birthday!" he yelled. "Make a wish and blow them out."

I decided a week ago what my wish would be. I hated our new rules. No touching, no roughhousing, and no sleeping in the same bed. I wanted us to be the way we used to be. I wanted to snuggle on the couch when we watched TV. I wanted to wake up because he was snoring too loud (well, not really, but it *was* fun to kick him until he rolled over). I wanted to wrestle and have pillow fights. He thought he

149

was keeping me safe. I didn't care about safe. But I didn't wish for our new rules to magically just go away. That's what little kids did. I was twelve now. Like Jeremy said, if I wanted a wish to come true then I had to make it happen myself. I blew out the candles and made my wish.

To be brave enough to do what I had to do.

I kept blowing after they all went out, just to make sure.

He clapped and cut me a piece of cake, but it seemed like he could hardly sit still while I ate it. "I can't take it anymore," he said after I took three bites. "I'm dying to watch you open your presents. They're hidden all over the house. Go!" I forgot the cake and ran towards the stairs. "No, the other way!" I turned around and saw the giant poster in the den with an arrow pointing to the back door. "OVER HERE!!!!!!" it said. How did he put that up without me noticing?

"You got me a ten-speed bike!" I yelled.

"No time to try it now!" he yelled back. "You've got a lot more to find."

Presents were hidden everywhere. A real remote-control airplane in the hall closet. A box full of everything they made for Dungeons and Dragons in his office. A gold chain in the bathroom, way thicker than the ones I saw other boys wearing at school. An envelope of tickets for concerts in New York on the kitchen table. A new tennis racket on the dining room table. He made some of them hard to find so it was like playing hide and seek (except presents were much harder to find than people). Wrapped books mixed into my other books. Lego sets hidden in drawers. The pile in the lobby was huge and he kept sending me back for more. I started to think there was such a thing as getting too many presents.

Finally, he counted the boxes and announced I found everything. He got a card from under the couch cushion. A piece of paper inside fluttered to the ground when I opened it. I knew it was a check because my parents always gave me a check for my birthday. I never understood why. It would be so much easier if they just gave me real money instead of making me beg them for a ride to the bank. I tried to ignore the check because it was rude to look before reading the card, but it fell face up so I saw how much it was for. My hand started to shake when I

picked it up. I had to look at it three times before I believed I read it right.

"Happy birthday," he said.

Five *thousand* dollars. With *three* zeroes (not counting the two after the decimal).

"I wish I could give you more," he said.

I dropped it on the table, afraid to hold so much money.

"Think of it as getting a car a few years early along with a year's worth of gas, oil changes, and car washes." He stared at me. "Are you ok? Did I forget something you wanted?"

I couldn't believe he said that. "How could you? You bought the whole store." He looked sad. "I didn't mean it that way. You bought me so much stuff."

"I wanted to show you how important you are to me," he said.

"How am I supposed to buy this much for your birthday?" I asked.

"I don't need any presents," he said. "Just you." He shook his head and slapped his forehead. "I can't believe I said something that sappy." He laughed and I joined in as best as I could. "Don't worry about my birthday. I'm sure you'll think of something special. I have more money than I need, so if I want to spend it on the most important person to me then that's my business. I'll take care of the mess tomorrow. It's getting late and you have school. How about some TV before bed?"

"Can we watch upstairs?" I asked.

"Your place or mine?"

"Yours," I said. "I'll put my pajamas on." He nodded and I ran upstairs. My stomach was tied up in knots even worse than before dinner. I slammed the door to the guest room. I was sleeping there but I didn't want to call it my room because that made it more permanent.

I wondered what I'd have to do. We'd both have to be naked. Gross, but obvious. Even if I closed my eyes, I'd still be embarrassed. Would he put his hand on my thing like he did last time? Was I supposed to put my hand on his? What else was there to do? It made more sense with a girl, because there was a place to put it. At least, that's what I learned. I had no idea exactly where or how. They only showed us pictures of a girl's insides. Even though I heard kids say "suck my dick" to each other a million times a day, they couldn't mean actually *doing*

something that disgusting. Putting someone's thing in my mouth would be like drinking *pee*. Words from the playground banged around in my head. Gay. Homo. Faggot. I wondered how it would feel when the other kids started calling me one. I hoped it wouldn't be very different from being called spaz or dork. Those were just as true.

I put on my pajama pants with no shirt or underwear. He was still downstairs, so I ran for his room before he could see me. I turned on the TV and left the lights off, crawling onto my side of the bed and pulling the covers all the way up so he couldn't see my bare shoulders.

He came up a few minutes later. "You look snug and cozy." I didn't feel snug and cozy. "Give me a few minutes to get ready for bed." He went into the bathroom and closed the door.

Now, I told myself.

I couldn't.

Before he gets back.

I still couldn't.

I would miss my chance if I didn't do it *right now*.

But I still couldn't.

I ordered myself. I yelled at myself. I begged myself. Nothing worked. I was paralyzed until I made myself remember why I was doing this in the first place. I thought about Jeremy taking me fishing even though he hated boats. I thought about all those presents. I thought about how he rescued me after the incident. I thought about how he didn't care when I spilled the hot chocolate. I thought about what my life would be like if he wasn't a part of it.

I closed my eyes and pulled my pajama pants completely off. Then I kicked them away, just in case I changed my mind. I only meant to push them further down under the covers, but they slipped off the side of the bed. I rolled over and looked. They were on the floor, right where he could see them and too far away for me to reach without getting out of bed.

Oh shit. Shit shit shit shit shit.

The bathroom door was still closed. If I moved really quickly, I could get them back on before he came out. I tried to hook them with my foot, but they were too far away. I was sliding out from under the covers when the bathroom door opened. I pulled my leg back under the

blanket before he could see, holding the covers tight. I was trapped. Naked.

He got onto his side of the bed. "Anything on?"

I almost exploded before I realized he meant the TV.

He looked at me. "Why are you sweating?"

"I'm not hot," I said. It felt like I was under an electric blanket turned up all the way.

"You might be getting sick again," he said. "Into the bathroom, let's take your temperature."

"I'm not sick," I said. "I'm sweating because I ran up here. I'll stop sweating soon."

He narrowed his eyes. If he insisted, I was toast.

"One cough and it's the thermometer for you even if I have to put it up your butt."

"Ok," I said, letting out my breath. He found the clicker and changed the channel a few times. I wasn't paying attention to the TV. The whole room seemed blurry. I couldn't wait until he fell asleep because he always kicked me out before he did. And since he already went to the bathroom, he had no reason to get out of bed. No way to get out of this now. No choice.

I guess that's why I found the courage to start.

"I love you," I said. I couldn't look at him.

"I love you too, sweetie," he said back.

"I mean, I really, really love you," I said.

"I really, really love you too," he said.

I couldn't think of what else to say for a while.

"I want to say thank you," I said.

"For the presents?"

"Not for the presents. For everything."

He turned over and looked at me. "You don't have to thank me. Everything I do is because I love you."

"I want to." I took a deep breath and found the words I practiced. "I'm not like him."

"Like who?"

"The other boy. Colin. I'm not like him."

I felt him tense up even though he wasn't touching me. "I don't know what you mean."

"I won't tell on you."

"What are you talking about?"

"I'm naked."

He sat up on the bed.

I pulled the covers down to my stomach.

"Stop," he said in a shaky voice.

"I just want to say thank you," I said. I pulled the covers down a little further.

He jumped off the bed. "Pull the blanket back up."

I pulled it down almost too far.

"Stop!" he yelled. He ran over to my side of the bed and grabbed the covers, pulling them back up to my shoulders. "What do you think you're doing?"

"Did I do something wrong? I don't know what I'm supposed to do."

"You're not supposed to do anything!" he yelled. He sat down on the floor.

"Why are you mad at me?" I asked.

"I'm not mad at you," he said softly. "I'm terrified. I need you to get dressed. I'll go into the hallway. Put your clothes on and open the door when you're done, ok?" I waited until he left to put my pajama pants back on. I used one of his t-shirts since I didn't have any of mine in his room. I opened the door and sat on the bed.

"I'm sorry I made you mad," I said when he came in. "I didn't do it right."

"Promise me you'll never do that again. I care too much about you to see you get hurt. I'm already scared out of my mind I'm going to lose control. Please don't make it any more difficult than it already is."

"I don't like your new rules," I said. "I want everything to be like it used to be. I want to snuggle on the couch and wrestle around and sleep in bed with you."

He brushed some hair from my forehead. "I know how important physical affection is to you. It's hard to believe you're the same kid who hated being touched just a few months ago. But we talked about this.

When I think you're not paying attention I wind up touching you in places I shouldn't."

"I don't care," I said. "And I trust you."

"I don't trust myself," he said. "I have to keep you safe."

"I don't want to be safe. Everyone wants to be safe all the time and it makes them afraid to try new things. You're a different Jeremy. I want the old Jeremy back. Sometimes, I think you're so scared something will happen that you'll think it's better if I left."

"I'm not going to let that happen," he said. He brushed more hair from my face. "You're right. I know you're right. I don't want to be different, but I'm scared of myself. I miss snuggling and roughhousing as much as you do."

He held my hand. "But this isn't about me. I need to do what's right for you. I understand how much you need contact and affection. I have to put my fears aside for you. I'm going to make you a promise that I'll be strong. You have to promise me to say something if you ever feel uncomfortable. This isn't a game. You can't keep quiet. If you can keep that promise, we can go back to the way things were. We can wrestle, snuggle, and you can sleep in my bed. Wearing pajamas, understood?"

"I promise," I said quickly.

"You understand that you never, ever need to do anything you don't want to do just to make me happy, right?"

"I know," I said. I didn't say what I was thinking.

What if I *want* to make you happy?

I got in when he patted the bed. I pressed my body up against his and he put his arm across my chest. I felt warm, like getting into a bath that was just the right temperature. Snug and cozy. I heard his breathing change as he fell asleep. I should've been happy because I got my wish without having to do anything gross. Things were back to normal and it wasn't that hard.

But I wasn't happy. I felt even more horrible. He told me never to do anything I didn't want to do just to make him happy. But it seemed like that was exactly what *he* was doing. Everything was always for me and nothing was for him. I was selfish. I could've kept going. I could've convinced him. I was the one who chickened out. I squeezed his hand. I had to keep trying, no matter what he said. I had to prove to him that

I loved him as much as he loved me by giving him a gift as big as the one he gave me every single day.

Chapter 13

May 8, 1982

My dad hated when I leaned against the car door. He said it could open even if it was locked and I could fall out. I leaned against it anyway, slouched down as far as I could. He hated slouching too. He also hated when I read my book in the car. I had it pressed against my face so close I couldn't read it. I couldn't concentrate anyway. I felt like I had to throw up, which was weird because I'd never been car sick before. I thought people only got car sick when the car was moving. We'd been stopped in traffic for over an hour. Dad *really* hated traffic.

"Dammit!" he screamed, banging on the steering wheel hard enough to beep the horn, but beep was the wrong word because his car didn't beep. It made a loud sound like the horn on a ship – four low notes that didn't fit together so they got people's attention. He told people the horn was the main reason he bought the car. It reminded me of him. A few cars beeped back. People were probably giving us the finger. I stayed slouched down because I didn't want them to know I was with the guy who wouldn't stop honking even though nobody could do anything about the traffic. The radio said there was a truck overturned up ahead and everything was completely blocked.

"If everyone was ready on time, we'd already be there!" he growled.

"Stuff it, Jack," Mom said.

"We would've been ahead of the accident!" he screamed.

"If I have to hear this one more time," Mom muttered. I felt the same way as her. He must've said it a hundred times already.

"We would've already been there!" he screamed even louder.

"That's it. I've had it. Turn the car around and take me home."

"You agreed to go," he muttered.

"I've withdrawn my agreement," she said.

"How exactly do you expect me to turn around?"

"If you pulled your head out of your ass, you would've noticed the hundred other cars that successfully turned around," she said. If I was keeping score, Mom would get a point. I slouched down lower.

"For the god damned last time, I'm not driving over the median!" he spat. "I'm not turning around and I'm not going home. We're going to this wedding even if there's no one there by the time we show up!"

"As if anyone would notice you're missing," Mom said. Another point for her. He didn't answer, breathing very loudly. I made sure they couldn't see me in the rearview mirror. It was better to be invisible when they fought. One time after they had a fight, my father ordered me to do things for him until I complained. He screamed at me so loud I thought he was going to kill me. I was so scared I wound up peeing in my pants. He left me alone when he noticed. Being invisible was a better strategy than wetting my pants.

We went straight to the restaurant instead of the church because we were more than two hours late. I'd been to this place before. It was a maze of different rooms inside, surrounded by a giant park that was part of the restaurant. When Dad said he didn't want anyone to park the car for him, they pointed us to a parking lot a long way from the entrance. I almost hit my head on the back of the front seat when the car stopped short in the space.

"I expect you to behave," he hissed. I was going to tell him I would until I realized he wasn't talking to me.

"My behavior depends entirely on yours," she said.

I slipped out of the car. My plan was to find a quiet corner away from everyone where I could read my book and be left alone until it was time to go home. Dad straightened his tie and Mom smoothed her dress. As though they could hide their fighting under neat clothes. I followed a long way behind them. My father turned around to check if I was still there.

"What the hell are you doing?" he growled.

"Nothing," I said. Which was the truth.

He walked back and put his face right in front of mine. "No way in hell you're going to slink off into a corner and read," he muttered. "You need to learn how to socialize and I'll be damned if you're going to avoid another opportunity. Am I clear?"

"Maybe you should be taking lessons in socialization instead of giving them, Jack," Mom said loud enough for people to hear.

He turned red and pushed his keys into my hand. "Put that book back in the car," he ordered. He didn't notice I lost weight and was doing better in school. He didn't care. He still thought everything I did was wrong. I wasn't going to change my plan. Maybe I could find something else to read. I unlocked the car, put the book in the back seat, and made sure to lock both doors before I slammed them shut.

I realized what I did as soon as the doors were closed. The keys were on the backseat next to my book. I tried the handle, just to make sure, but I really did remember to lock the door. I walked back slowly, shoving my hands in my pockets. "Get your hands out of your pockets, you look ridiculous," he said. He held out his hand. "My keys?"

"They're in the car," I mumbled.

"Go back and get them! Why the hell would you come back without them?"

"I locked them in the car," I mumbled again.

"You locked the keys in the car?' he shouted. *Everyone* could hear him. "What the hell is the matter with you?"

"It was an accident," I said.

"It's always an accident!" The guy who parked the cars was staring as us. "You did this on purpose! You're trying to make me angry!"

"I'll be damned if I'm going in there if this is how you're going to behave," Mom said. She gave me her keys. I knew they were arguing while I walked back to the car, so I made noise kicking gravel to drown them out. He left before I got back. I gave Mom both sets of keys.

"Your father is impossible," she said.

"Uh huh," I nodded.

"Are you going to be ok?" she asked.

"Yeah," I shrugged. "Are you?"

I didn't say it to mean anything, more like a reflex. I watched a tear, stained black from the makeup in her eyelashes, leave a trail through the goop she put on her cheeks. She patted it dry with a tissue.

"Don't worry about me," she said softly. "I'm sorry you had to see all that. I shouldn't have behaved that way in front of you. Your father brings out the worst in me. I act like a child around him, one much more poorly behaved than you. None of this is your fault, please remember that. Try to have fun today, ok? It's a party. Maybe you'll meet someone you like."

I shrugged. I thought I should feel bad, but I wasn't sure why.

I followed her into the restaurant. Even though they tried not to let me see, I could tell that all the guys who parked the cars were staring at us. She went into one of the crowded rooms, but I went down the hall away from the noise until I found a stairway leading to a dark room made of wood and stone. It looked like the inside of a castle. A perfect hiding spot. I found a stack of magazines behind a big leather chair in the corner. All mine.

I had five whole minutes alone when I heard a whole bunch of teenagers coming down the stairs. Not the nice kind either, I could tell. I smelled cigarette smoke before they even came in. "Score!" one of them said when he turned on the rest of the lights. "Think they have any glasses down here?"

"Who the fuck cares?" another one said. "It's an *antiseptic*. We can drink straight from the bottle."

"Eww, someone else is down here," one of the girls said.

Antiseptic looked right at me. "Get lost, dork."

"Look at his hair!" another one said. "I'll bet I could light my cigarette on his head." I tried to get away, but he grabbed me in a headlock and shoved his cigarette in my hair. "We should keep him down here as our lighter." They were blocking the stairs so I couldn't escape. The one with the cigarette tightened the headlock when I tried to squirm away.

"Gary, Mom is looking for you," a girl's voice said from the stairs.

"I told you to fuck off, twerp," Antiseptic – Gary said.

"I'll tell her you're too busy getting drunk from that bottle you stole from the bar," the voice teased.

"I swear, I'll beat the shit out of you. I don't care if you're my sister."

"Mom also wanted me to remind you to take your pills. You know what the therapist said would happen if you didn't take your pills."

They all stared at antiseptic Gary. "Shut up," he muttered.

A girl around my age came the rest of the way down the stairs. She had a mess of frizzy hair that stuck out in all directions, like a clown wig. "Are you coming?" she said to me.

Cigarette let me go. I slipped through the crowd before they could change their minds. "Sorry, my brother is the world's biggest asshole," she said to me when we were halfway up the stairs. One of them said something back that was too soft to hear. "That's the best you can do?" she yelled back at them.

She stared at me when we got to the top. "He doesn't really take pills. I made that up. You look familiar." She looked familiar too. I remembered her frizzy hair from somewhere. She snapped her fingers. "I know. It was at the picnic last fall. Don't you remember? We did the sack race."

I tried to forget about *that* picnic. My dad forced me to play all the games. The only reason I didn't get splatted from the egg toss was because I messed up the first throw. They made me anchor for the tug of war because I was fat, but I fell as soon as the other team tugged. I thought I could win the sack race because most of the kids who lined up were little. I was ahead of everyone else when I tripped and fell flat on my face. I started screaming – the only eleven-year-old in the universe who screamed when he lost a game. Everyone stared, especially the kid that wound up winning. The girl with the frizzy hair.

"Didn't you used to be fat?" she asked.

"I gotta go." I turned to run away.

"No, wait," she said. "I didn't mean to say it that way. It was rude of me. Sometimes I say things I don't mean." She laughed. It sounded like it was coming out her nose instead of her mouth. She snorted when she was finished. "What was your name again?"

"Nick," I mumbled.

"I'm Molly." She held out her hand to shake. It was limp and sweaty. She had braces on her teeth and pink glasses with thick lenses. "I hate weddings."

I shrugged. Girls liked weddings. Everyone knew that.

"Come on, let's find the kitchen," she said. I had to pull my hand away because she didn't let go.

"I need to find my parents." It was a weak lie, but I wanted to get away from this weird girl.

"I'll go with you," she said. I couldn't think of anything else to tell her, so I let her follow me back towards the party. My parents were on the other side of the main room talking to separate people. It wouldn't be a good idea to actually talk to them, so I pretended I didn't see them. She followed me back out of the room. "They weren't there?" she asked.

I shrugged, trying to think of another way to get away from her.

"Do you want to go outside? It's quieter. I don't like loud music very much. They have nice gardens and the flowers are blossoming, although I usually don't like flowers because they make me sneeze." She frowned. "You must think I'm such a dork."

"No, not really," I said. I wasn't sure why, but I felt bad for her. That's why I followed her down some steps to the garden. Also because I didn't have anything else to do. The sun was starting to go down. "I live in Middleford," she said, walking off the path onto the grass. "Where do you live?"

"Newton Falls," I said.

"That's not very far away. My mom likes to go shopping there. She says Newton Falls is cute."

"My mom calls it's charming," I said.

"I'm in seventh grade. What grade are you in?"

"Sixth," I answered.

"I'm supposed to be in sixth grade, but I skipped third grade and went straight to fourth. They didn't want to let me, but my mom kept arguing and eventually they gave up. My mom can really argue."

"My mom can argue too. She's a lawyer."

"That must be hard having a lawyer for a mom. I'll bet you don't get away with anything."

"Pretty much," I said, kicking a rock. "Why did you skip a grade?"

She smelled a flower and wrinkled her nose. "Because I'm smart. I like to read, do you?" I nodded. "What are you reading right now?"

"Just some science fiction book," I mumbled.

"My dad helps me pick out good science fiction. He just gave me a stack of Ray Bradbury short stories. They're engrossing. I like science fiction that focuses on characters, like Vonnegut."

"I don't know Ray Bradbury or Vonnegut, but I read a lot of science fiction. I like fantasy too."

"Like what?" she asked.

"I don't know, like Lord of the Rings stuff," I mumbled.

"I tried to read Tolkien. The poems were so boring that I stopped."

"I skipped most of them," I said. Wait a second. I was talking to a *girl* about Lord of the Rings? And she *knew* what I was talking about? This had to be some kind of weird dream.

It was like she could read my mind. "Girls read fantasy and science fiction too," she said. "Let's walk barefoot in the grass." I wasn't sure why, but I took off my socks and shoes and followed her across the lawn. The grass felt soft and cool. And wet, but I didn't mind. "Kids at school think I'm a nerd. I don't have a lot of friends. Do you have a lot of friends at school?"

"No," I said. "I'm not good at making friends."

"I hate how kids are always teasing each other. I get teased a lot."

"I used to get teased too. One day, I hit one of them over the head with a chair. After that, they stopped bothering me."

"You did?" She sat down on a bench.

"Yeah. I had a bad day and he made me so mad I beamed him in the head. He got a concussion and they had to take him away in an ambulance." Did I say all that out loud? To another person? To a *girl?*

"I should do the same thing. You're a rebel. I like rebels. Like James Dean." I didn't know who James Dean was. "What was the name of the kid you hit?"

"Tommy Walker," I answered.

"The girl who makes fun of me the most is named Mildred Bunweather." I started laughing. "I made that up, but her name should be something like Mildred Bunweather." She looked at me with wide eyes. "Bunweather."

It was something like five minutes before we could stop laughing.

I never met anyone like her before. In some ways, she seemed like me. She liked a lot of the same kind of books, got teased at school, and didn't have a lot of friends. In other ways, she was nothing like me. She had a way of walking around that was more like dancing, spinning around for no reason or putting her arms up in the air. She was able to say whatever was on her mind, anytime she wanted to, and had no problems finding words like I did. She was full of interesting ideas, like walking through the grass barefoot, or sneaking into the kitchen just to sneak in, or emptying all the matchbooks in the bathroom so people couldn't smoke. The kind of ideas that made me feel good about being a little bad. I could actually talk to her, even though she was a girl and therefore impossible to understand.

We went back outside after dinner. "Let's find somewhere without lights so we can see the stars." I followed her down a long hill until we couldn't see the restaurant anymore. There was no path and I could barely see anything. "Watch out!" she yelled suddenly. I froze, my foot sinking into squishy mud, glad I wasn't wearing my shoes. I didn't want to lose another pair of shoes to mud. "There's a pond. Wouldn't it be funny if we fell in?"

"My dad would kill me," I said.

"My mom would too," she said.

"Let's lie down," she said. The grass was a little wet, but I did it anyway because she did. The stars were spread out in the sky above us. Lots of them, more than I ever saw before. Even more appeared as I stared. I never knew stars could be so beautiful. "My dad counts the stars with me when we go camping."

"I've never gone camping," I said. "I want to go sometime."

"My mom hates camping. I'm more like my dad. My mom wants a girl that likes frilly dresses and Barbie dolls. Not a tomboy like me. Which of your parents are you like?"

"Neither of them," I said. "Both my parents wish I was different. They hate me."

She moved a little closer to me. "I don't think parents hate their kids. Sometimes they don't like their kids, I guess. That's different."

"Mine hate me. They fight all the time and yell at me for every little thing. I hardly live with them and they don't care."

"Who do you live with?"

"A neighbor," I said. "My parents work all the time, so he lets me stay with him. He's much nicer."

"It's kind of him to do that," she said.

"I wish I could trade my parents for different ones," I said.

I realized she was holding my hand. "I wish I had hair like yours."

"I hate my hair," I muttered. "Everyone makes fun of it. I want to dye it brown when I get older so it looks normal."

"I think being different is nice. I liked your hair when I saw you at the picnic last year. I recognized you right away when you got here. That's why I followed you."

"You followed me?" I asked.

"I was about to go down to that wine cellar room to talk to you, but my brother and his stupid friends got there first. I heard him being an asshole so I helped you get out." I didn't say anything. "I wanted to tell you I was sorry for tripping you at the sack race."

"You tripped me?" I pulled my hand away and rolled over to stare at her.

"That's why you fell. I stepped on your sack. On purpose."

My face got hot. "Why did you do that?"

"I don't know. I wanted to win. I never win at any of those stupid games. I felt bad when you tripped, but then you started to scream and I felt really horrible. You ran off and I couldn't find you."

"Is that the only reason you're talking to me now?"

"No," she said in a soft voice like the one Jeremy used. "I like talking to you. I think you're funny, kind, and a deep, interesting person. If we went to the same school, I'm sure we'd be good friends. I want to make sure I get your phone number so we can hang out. Maybe when my mom wants to go shopping."

"I think we'd be friends too," I said. I didn't feel angry any more. I pushed her shoulder, just a little. Girls didn't like roughhousing. Everyone knew that. "You cheated."

"Yeah, I cheated," she said, and pushed me back. "I hate wearing dresses. They're so uncomfortable."

"I think you look pretty," I said. I hardly believed I said that out loud. But I meant it. Maybe some people thought that braces, glasses,

and frizzy hair weren't pretty. They were wrong. She was the prettiest girl I ever saw.

"You really think so?" Her hand found mine again. It didn't feel limp and sweaty anymore. My heart was beating hard. We stared at the stars.

She rolled over and kissed my cheek.

I couldn't move.

"I'm hungry," she said, sitting up. "I'll bet they have dessert. Do you want some?"

All I could do was nod.

We walked all the way back holding hands.

She was right, they had a bunch of different desserts spread out on tables. "Let's get some of that." She pointed at what had to be the biggest bowl of chocolate I'd ever seen along with giant strawberries to dip into it. I followed her through the crowd to get in line. I heard my parents in the bar next door even though it was noisy. They were yelling at each other.

"Maybe we should come back later," I said.

She was staring at them too. "Do you hear those two adults?"

"Come on, let's go," I said and tugged at her hand.

"We're almost there," she said, staring at them. "Who do you think they are?"

My mother threw her drink in my father's face and stomped off.

The whole room went quiet. *Everyone* saw.

"Did you see that?" Molly said. "Like a TV show for real."

My father took out a handkerchief and wiped his face. He didn't seem to care that everyone was staring at him. Then he looked straight at me. Any moment the whole world would know he was my father. Including Molly.

I tried to get away, but it was too late. He came right for me, grabbing my arm hard. "We're going home. Now." I tried to yank myself away, off balance because he let go before I thought he would. I stumbled forward and fell on the table. It collapsed and I fell on the floor. Something hit me in the head.

It took me a moment before I understood what was happening. The feeling reminded me of wetting the bed. It poured over my hair, into

my face, and all over my shirt and pants. Thick and gooey. The whole giant bowl of chocolate. All of it. All over me. My father grabbed me, pulling me up by my armpits. I looked around at the room. Everyone was staring at me. *Everyone.* Including Molly.

I ran away, slipping on the chocolate. Everyone got out of my way. I ran through the hallways, past waiters, past the bride and groom, past antiseptic Gary, past the guys who parked the cars, all the way to my dad's car. I hid behind it. Everyone was laughing at me. Molly was probably laughing too.

My father took a few minutes to get there. "Get in," he hissed. I climbed in the back seat, leaving chocolate stains all over everything. The tires spun as he drove out as fast as he could. We were on the highway before I realized it was only the two of us in the car.

"We left Mom at the restaurant," I said.

"She took a cab!" he screamed. "She's staying at a motel tonight! Any more questions?" He swerved the car so hard I fell over. I couldn't stop shaking the whole ride back. The chocolate got crusty on my face. I didn't scrape any off. I couldn't think about anything. When we got home, I went straight to the shower. It took an hour of scrubbing before the water wasn't brown.

I couldn't stop thinking about Molly. I didn't get her phone number. I didn't know her last name. Not that it mattered. After what happened, she'd never want to talk to me again. We couldn't be friends. Even though I really wanted to be her friend.

I got dressed and went downstairs. Dad was sitting on the couch in the living room, doing nothing. I never remembered hating him more. It was all his fault I couldn't be friends with Molly. But I didn't yell.

"I'm going home," I told him.

"You are home," he said like a robot.

"My *real* home," I said.

He didn't look at me. "I guess you'd better get going."

I walked out and slammed the door without saying goodbye. My face felt hot, but the breeze felt good. I walked fast. It didn't take long.

"Hey, kiddo," he said with a smile.

For the first time in my life, I felt like I was *home.*

Chapter 14

May 12, 1982

Today was the first time since I hit Tommy with the chair that Jeremy wouldn't be able to pick me up from school. He had some kind of business in New York. I waited around until all the cars were gone, just in case. The school was abandoned and quiet. I never realized how loud it was at school until no one was there to make noise. I didn't know if I should go all the way around on the roads where it was safe, or through the woods where anything could happen. Bullies didn't pay much attention to me anymore, but still.

The other kid made up my mind for me. I thought I was the only one left, so he surprised me when he came out of the school. I couldn't remember his name because he was new. When he got introduced on his first day, I was happy I wasn't the new kid anymore. He didn't notice me sitting in the corner by the front doors because he was walking fast, straight towards the woods. His backpack was so full it looked like he might fall over backwards and get stuck like a turtle on its shell. He was short, thin, and wore really thick glasses. If he wasn't scared to walk through the woods, I shouldn't be scared either.

Of course, Tommy was there with his friends.

I hid behind the trees when I saw them in the little clearing halfway through the woods. "Aww, is the wittle baby gonna cwy? Maybe we should call him Cryin!"

That's when I remembered the new kid's name was Brian.

I knew I should sneak back out to the road and go the long way around, but I stayed. I was a mixture of too scared and too interested to move. It was weird watching someone getting picked on instead of being the victim. Almost nice. It seemed wrong to think it was nice.

Tommy pulled the glasses off Brian's face. "These things weigh a ton! Are you blind or something?"

"Give them back," Brian said. His voice sounded like his nose was stuffed up all the time. Tommy held Brian's glasses out of reach so he couldn't grab them.

"I can't see, I can't see," Tommy teased, imitating Brian's stuffed up voice. He put the glasses on. "Man, these things give me an instant headache. How can you wear them?"

"I can't see much without them," Brian said.

"Come over here and get them," Tommy said. Brian stretched out his arms and started walking, tripping over his backpack. They all laughed. Tommy put the glasses down on a rock. "All you have to do is come and get them." Brian got up and looked around. "Not that way, moron."

"Give them back," Brian muttered, taking a couple small steps forward.

"You're almost there," Tommy said. He waited for Brian to take a couple more steps, and then used a rock to smash the glasses. They made a loud crunch. "Shit. I'm sorry, man. I think I broke them."

"That was my last pair!" Brian shouted. "Don't you get it? I can't see!"

"It was an accident," Tommy said. "Don't spaz out on me. We'll walk you home. Tell us where you live."

"I can get home by myself," Brian said. He took two more steps and tripped over the rock where Tommy smashed the glasses. They all laughed again.

Tommy took out a cigarette and lit it with a big silver lighter. "You can have a smoke on me because I'm sorry about breaking your glasses."

"I can't smoke," Brian said.

"Sure, you can," Tommy said, holding out the cigarette. The lit end touched Brian's hand, making him jerk away and hiss. "Sorry man, I don't see too good either. Smoke it, you'll feel better."

"I said, I can't." Brian started coughing.

"And I said, have a smoke." He took a big mouthful of smoke and blew it into Brian's face, which made him cough even harder. "I think you should give us something for being nice enough to walk you home. How much money have you got?"

Brian kept coughing. It seemed like he couldn't stop. He sat down on the ground.

"Seriously, man," Tommy said. "How much money have you got?"

"I need my backpack," Brian sputtered and started coughing again.

"After you pay," Tommy said.

Brian rolled over on his back. His coughing got so bad that his face turned red. Tommy blew more smoke at him while the rest of them stared. Brian's coughing turned to a choking sound that scared me.

"I don't think he can breathe," Tommy's friend Jimmy said.

"He's faking," Tommy said, kicking Brian in the side.

"No really, I think he can't breathe!" Jimmy said. Brian made a weird croaking sound. I couldn't move. "What do we do?" Jimmy screamed.

"I don't know!" Tommy yelled. "We'd better get the fuck out of here."

"Maybe we should do something," Tommy's friend Kevin said.

"Like what? Tell the cops we made him smoke and broke his glasses? Let's get out of here!" They ran right towards me. I slipped behind a tree, praying they didn't notice I was there. They weren't looking. I didn't move until they were out of the woods. When I looked, Brian had rolled over onto his side, clawing at the ground. I was scared, but I was the only one there. I had to do something.

I ran up. "Are you ok?" I asked. His eyes were so wide they scared me. "I'll get some help," I said.

"In. . .hale," he spat between croaking.

"I know, you can't breathe. What am I supposed to do?"

He lurched up and grabbed at my shirt but couldn't hold on. He fell back down on his back.

"Help!" I shouted. "Somebody help!" No one answered.

"In. . .hale," he croaked again.

"I know, you can't breathe," I said. He was still trying to grab my shirt. Something clicked in my head. "Wait, I know! You have asthma!

I knew another kid with asthma. He had a thing to put in his mouth!"
Brian looked straight up, his chest heaving up and down. "Where is it?"
I shook his shoulders.

"Back. . ." he managed to whisper before he went limp. His eyes
looked weird, like he couldn't see even though they were open.

"Oh shit, backpack," I said. I tore open the big section – books,
nothing but books. I dug through the small pouches, throwing out
pencils and papers until I found a little metal thing. "That's it!" I yelled.
I scrambled back over to him. He wasn't moving. It didn't look like he
was breathing at all.

"What do I do?" I yelled. I put the metal thing in his mouth. It didn't
do anything. I started poking and pushing until I heard a little hiss. "Was
that it?" He didn't answer. "Come on, wake up!" I shook him. I picked
up his hand and put it on the thing in his mouth. I heard it hiss again.
His eyes rolled up into his head until all I could see was white, which
made me so scared I almost wet my pants.

"Wake up!" I screamed. "You have to tell me what to do!" He lay
there without moving for what felt like ages, and then his eyes popped
open and he sucked in a huge breath. He grabbed the thing in his mouth
and pushed on it again. I stared while he took more huge breaths.

"Are you ok?" I said.

"Gotta. . .catch. . .my. . .breath," he said.

"Do you need to go to a hospital? I'll get some help."

"No. . .don't. . .go," he croaked. He tried to sit up and fell back
down.

"Are you sure you don't need a doctor?" I asked.

"No doctor. . .I'll be. . .ok," he gasped. The thing in his mouth
hissed again. I helped him sit up. He put his head between his knees
and stayed like that until he started breathing normally, which seemed
like it took like ten minutes. I didn't know what to say the whole time.
"Do you know where my glasses are?" he finally said.

"They're smashed," I said. I picked up the pieces from the rock and
put them in his hand. "Tommy crushed them on purpose."

"That was my only pair," he said. "My dad is going to kill me."

"It wasn't your fault," I said.

"Doesn't matter." He wiped his face with his sleeve and stared at me. "Who are you?"

"Nick," I said. "You're in my class."

He squinted. "Red hair. Yeah." He stood up but almost fell back over. I grabbed his arm to keep him from falling.

"You seem like you need a doctor," I said.

"I said no doctors," he snapped. "I have to go home. Where's my backpack?"

"Over there. I had to take a lot of stuff out to find your thingy. I'll put everything back."

"It's called an inhaler."

"I get it. That's why you were saying inhale." I shoved things back into the bag, noticing a book I recognized. "You're reading the Sword of Shannara?" I blurted out.

"I already read it," he said.

"I thought it was good," I said.

"I guess," he said. "I gotta go home. If I'm late, my dad will be mad at me."

"I can help you," I said. "Where do you live?"

"Bluebird lane," he said.

"There's no bird streets around here. All the streets are named after trees."

"I have to go through the woods, across the neighborhood and down the hill, and then through the woods on the other side. It's around two miles. If you take me to the main road I can follow it home, but it's a lot further."

"That'll take forever," I said. "I'll take you to my house and we'll give you a ride from there." He stuck out his hands and walked over to me. "I guess you can't see much without your glasses."

"I can see a little. I can tell you have red hair when I'm up close." He grabbed on to my backpack. "Don't bang me into anything."

"I won't, I promise." I turned around and started walking, slow at first, making sure to walk around rocks and tree roots. It was easier when we got out of the woods.

"Did you really read the Sword of Shannara?" He sounded suspicious.

"Yeah. I got mad at the part where that gnome, what was his name? Oh yeah, Orl Fane. I was mad when I found out he had the sword the whole time."

"I thought you were making fun of me," he said.

"No. I like fantasy books."

"Who's your favorite author?" he asked.

"Tolkien," I said.

"Mine too. Do you read science fiction?"

"Yeah," I said. "You have a lot of books. Maybe we could trade for ones we haven't read before."

"I don't have very many," he said. "Mostly I borrow books from the library."

"You can borrow some of mine." He didn't say anything. "Tommy used to beat up on me too. Tomorrow, you should tell the teachers what he did. If he gets in trouble again he'll probably get kicked out of school."

"I don't want to tell," he said.

"I could tell if you don't want to," I offered.

"No teachers." He let go of my backpack and I turned around. "Swear you won't tell anyone. No teachers, no doctors, no parents, no one." I stared at him. He was completely serious. "Promise."

"Ok, I promise," I said. I turned around and we started walking again. I didn't know what to think about him. Maybe we could be friends because we read the same books. At the same time, there was something scary about him that made it seem like we couldn't.

"You said Tommy used to beat up on you too," he said. "What do you mean by used to?"

"He doesn't anymore," I said.

"How did you make him stop?"

"I got mad at him in class so I hit him over the head with a chair. He got a concussion and had to go to the hospital. It came out that he was picking on me and he got in trouble." Brian didn't say anything.

We walked down the hill. I knew Jeremy was home from New York because the garage door was open. "You can come inside," I said.

"I'll wait here," he said, letting go of my backpack.

I ran inside. Jeremy stuck his head out from the kitchen. "There you are. I was wondering what happened to you."

"I walked home with a friend," I said. "He broke his glasses and can't see well enough to get home on his own. Can we give him a ride?"

"A friend?" Jeremy said like he was surprised. "No problem. I'll give him a ride." He followed me outside. I was about to introduce him to Brian when I realized I had no idea what to call Jeremy. Friend? Dad?

"I'm Jeremy," he said. "Nick's uncle." That was a good idea. I'd have to remember to call Jeremy my uncle from now on.

"I'm Brian Hanley, sir," he said and held out his hand to shake. "It's nice to meet you, sir."

Jeremy shook it. "Nice to meet you too, Brian. You guys were having fun?"

"No, sir. I broke my glasses. Nick helped me walk here."

"You look a little scraped up. Are you ok?"

"Yes, sir," Brian said. Every time he said sir it sounded weird. I never thought of Jeremy as someone who should be called sir. "I fell down a couple times. I can't see well without my glasses, sir."

"Let me look. Maybe we can fix them."

"They're shattered, sir. They can't be fixed and I don't have any spares."

"I see," Jeremy said. He looked at me suspiciously. "Why don't you come inside? You can get cleaned up while I figure out what to do."

"Yes sir, thank you sir," Brian said. He grabbed onto my backpack and followed us inside. I led him to the bathroom. Jeremy did the thing with his finger to tell me to come over to him.

"You going to tell me what's really going on?" Jeremy asked softly.

"Nothing," I said.

"Bullshit," Jeremy said. I shrugged. "If something happened, you can tell me."

"He made me promise not to," I said.

Jeremy frowned but he didn't ask again. Brian came out of the bathroom. "I'm sorry about your glasses," Jeremy said.

"Thank you, sir. I should go home now."

"I'll give you a ride," Jeremy said.

"No thank you, sir. I can walk."

"I had to lead you here," I said. "How are you going to get home?"

"If I leave now, I can get home before dark," Brian said. "If I'm not back before dark I get in trouble."

"I can call your parents to pick you up," Jeremy said.

"No, thank you sir," Brian said. "They can't."

"I can't allow you to walk home without your glasses," Jeremy said. "We have a few hours before it gets dark. Let's go to the mall and see if that one-hour glasses place can make a new pair for you."

"I don't have any money, sir," Brian said. He looked at me like I should do something.

"Don't worry about the money. I'm not going to take no for an answer. We're going to the mall and getting new glasses. Are we clear?" I didn't understand why Jeremy sounded so strict.

"I can't," Brian said. "Sir."

"Why not?" Jeremy asked.

"If my father finds out he's going to be angry. Sir."

"Then he doesn't need to know about it, does he?" Jeremy said. Brian blinked. "Sir?"

"This stays between the three of us, is that understood?" Brian didn't say anything. "We're leaving in five minutes." He went to his office.

"Why is he doing this?" Brian whispered.

"He likes helping people," I explained.

"I won't be able to pay him back," Brian said. He sounded upset.

"He doesn't care about money," I said. "He's pretty stubborn, too. I usually give up when he makes up his mind. Let's just go to the mall. They have a big bookstore with four aisles just for fantasy and science fiction. Maybe we can look while we're waiting."

"Ok," he said. "I've been looking for a story by Asimov, but I can't remember the name. It was about all the energy in the universe running out and this big super computer figures out what to do in the end. It was one of the best stories but the original book is out of print. Maybe it's in a new anthology."

"You have a lot of books in your backpack. Are you reading all of them at the same time?"

"Sort of," he said. "I read a lot."

176

The store that made the glasses wasn't crowded. I got scared when they asked Brian for his prescription, but he had it on a little slip of paper in his backpack. They had a pair almost exactly the same as Brian's old glasses so his dad would never notice he got new ones. It took over two hours to make his glasses because his lenses were so thick, so we had a lot of time at the bookstore. It seemed like Brian knew something about every single book.

Jeremy got us pizza for dinner even though Brian said he wasn't hungry. I swear, I never saw someone eat so much all at once. Brian ate four slices of pizza, almost all the garlic bread, the fries Jeremy got after the pizza was gone, and the large ice cream sundae Jeremy got when the fries were gone. We picked up the glasses and made it back to Brian's house before it was dark, even though we had to start from the school because he didn't know the streets yet.

"Remember, this stays between us," Jeremy said to Brian.

"Yes, sir," Brian answered. He took a book out of his backpack. "Read this," he said to me. "Bring it back to school when you're done." I looked at the worn cover. S is for Space by. . .Ray Bradbury? Wasn't he the writer Molly talked about? Weird. Twelve years of no friends and then I meet two kids in the same week who liked the same author?

"Thank you, sir, for the dinner and the glasses and for driving me home," Brian said to Jeremy. Then he stared at me.

"Thanks for saving my life," he said softly.

I had no idea what I was supposed to say to that.

"See you at school," Brian said and left.

Jeremy was staring at me with his mouth wide open when I turned around. "You can't leave me hanging. Aren't you going to explain?"

"Explain what?"

"Saving his life?"

"He has asthma and couldn't get his inhaler," I said.

He frowned. "You won't tell me what really happened, will you?" I shook my head. "Fine, keep your secrets. I trust you'll tell me if something is seriously wrong. Brian seemed very frightened of his father. I'm a little worried about him." We waited for him to disappear into the backyard before we drove away. "He's a nice kid, but I swear, if he called me sir one more time I was going to completely lose it."

∞x x∞

Jeremy leaned back in his chair. "That was interesting."

"I played it right," I said.

"You always play everything right. Your fingering was right, your technique was right, and as always, your phrasing was right. Still, I don't think Signore Clementi would approve."

"Why?"

"The poor guy was trying his best to make a living as a serious composer. I'll bet he had six kids and a demanding wife who insisted on having the biggest horse drawn buggy on the block. You took his hard work and turned it into a sarcastic joke. Tell me, what did Signore Clementi do to deserve being treated so rudely?"

I rolled my eyes. "It's *boring*. All his music sounds the same and they're too easy."

"I know it's boring," he said. "This is the kind of music you need to play. These pieces teach important lessons in fingering, technique, phrasing, rhythm, you name it. I know how impatient you are to get to the big stuff, but I don't want you making the same mistakes I did. There's an order to this. If you don't follow it, you'll spend years undoing bad habits."

I groaned. "There's got to be something better than Clementi."

"We can go back to the scales," he threatened.

"No. No way. You said I could take a break because I did most of them!"

He thought for a moment, then got a different book from the shelf. "Try this." Octaves in the left hand, repeated arpeggio triads in the right. Easy. I played a few measures and groaned even louder.

"Come on, not this one," I said. "*Anything* but this one. Schroeder always plays this in Charlie Brown. It's even more boring than Clementi. Besides, it's too easy."

"You think the Moonlight Sonata is easy? The notes are deceiving. Making this one sound like music is far more difficult than you think."

"I want to play something fast," I muttered.

He pushed me off the bench. "Maybe something like this?" His hands flew up and down the keyboard, the music furious and stormy. I couldn't hold all my jealousy inside how he could play something like that and I couldn't.

"Yeah. I want to play *that.*"

"Well, *that* is the third movement of the Moonlight sonata. I'll make a deal with you. You learn to play the first two movements well. If you impress the hell out of me, we'll work on the third." No problem, I thought. I could have the first part done in a day at most. "I need a bathroom break." He went off while I stared at the notes. I couldn't wait to get this out of the way so I could move onto that breathless piece of genius.

The phone rang. "You get it!" he shouted from the bathroom. "It's probably your mother!"

I picked up the phone in the lobby. "Hello?" Silence and then a click. I hung it up and went back to the piano. It rang again before I got there. "Hello?" I said again. Silence. "Who is this?" The person hung up. I went back to the piano. The phone rang *again.*

"Who is this?" I said in an annoyed voice without bothering to say hello.

"Who is this?" a man repeated back at me.

"This is Nick. Who are you?"

He said our phone number. "Is that the number I reached?"

"Yeah."

"Then answer my question immediately. Who are you?"

"I said I was Nick. Jer. . .Mr. Stillwell couldn't answer the phone so he asked me to get it. Who are you?" The guy didn't answer. Jeremy came into the room. "It's some guy who keeps calling and hanging up. He won't say who he is."

"Give me the phone," Jeremy said. "Whoever this is, you'd better have a good explanation." He listened for a moment and then his face turned white, like he was covered in chalk dust. "Hold on a second," he said. His voice cracked. "I'm going upstairs. Hang it up when I tell you to." He didn't wait for me to ask what was going on, running up the stairs two at a time. "Hang up!" he screamed. I dropped the phone like it had twelve wiggly legs. He slammed the door to his room.

I sat down at the piano, but I was too scared to practice.

A few minutes later his door flew open so hard it slammed into the wall. He went straight to the kitchen. I watched him from the den. He filled a glass with alcoholic stuff, swallowed the whole thing in one gulp, and poured another one.

"Are you ok?" I asked.

He whirled around. "Don't you *ever* answer the phone in this house again, do you understand?" he screamed. He drank the second glassful down and threw the empty glass into the sink so hard that shards flew everywhere.

I took two steps backwards. I never imagined I could be scared by Jeremy, but he looked crazy. I thought about running away. The real Jeremy came back only a second later. "I'm sorry. I didn't mean to yell at you." He sat down on the floor and leaned against the cabinets.

I ran up to him. "Your hand is bleeding," I said, worried. He looked down and shrugged. I got a paper towel and ran it under water. "You have a cut on your face too. Does it hurt?" He winced when I patted it. "I shouldn't have answered the phone."

"I never thought he would call here," Jeremy muttered to himself.

"Who was it?"

"Don't worry about it," he said. Which made me more worried, like it always did. He looked at me and frowned. "What am I saying? I trust you with my deepest, darkest secret. I don't know what I should do. Is it wrong to protect you from unpleasant things or is it wrong to burden you with the truth?"

"You can tell me," I said.

He took a deep breath. "That was my brother. He never calls me. If he wants to talk to me, he has a secretary make an appointment." He pulled me next to him and wrapped his arms around me. "My family hates me."

"They can't actually hate you," I said, trying to make him feel better.

"They do," he said. "They hate who I am. *What* I am. When my mother was alive, she demanded they tolerate my presence at family events. I haven't been welcome since she passed away." He hugged me tight. "I had a horrible day. I was in New York because my brother wanted a meeting. First time in two years. It was Father's idea, but he

made Robert do the dirty work, and Robert loves nothing more than doing dirty work. They cut me out of the family business completely. They had papers I had to sign. My brother controls everything now. He gives me enough money to keep me comfortable as long as I stay hidden from the rest of the world. No career, no life, and no purpose. My job is to simply exist. There's only one other rule. I'm supposed to stay away from kids."

My stomach sank when I realized. "So when I answered the phone, he. . .I really messed up."

"It's not your fault," he said. "I tried to explain I was teaching and you were one of my students, but he didn't believe me for a second. He threatened to cut me off, leave me on the street with nothing. I don't think he'll do it. He can't take the chance I might do something to create negative publicity. He called me a lot of names. I'm old enough that name calling shouldn't bother me, but it still hurts." Jeremy looked away. "He said I was doing it all over again. That I was going to hurt you the same way I hurt Colin. He's right. I'm a selfish, horrible person."

"You're not a horrible person!" I said. I pushed his arms away and held his head to make him look at me. "You're the nicest, most unselfish, most good person that's ever lived! He's the one who's selfish! He just wants to keep everything for himself! Like today, you bought new glasses for Brian even though you don't know him. You could never hurt me. You're not horrible at all. You're the best person I've ever met. Don't you understand that if I never met you I wouldn't be here? Don't you understand that you saved my life?" I couldn't believe I said that out loud. I never even said that to myself before.

"Sweetie," he said, pulling me back towards him.

"I love you," I said forcefully. "I want to show you how much I love you." My heart was pounding. I didn't want to, not right now and not here like this. But I knew I *had* to. It was my job and I was going to do it. I leaned in and kissed him on the cheek. Like Molly kissed me.

"Nick," he moaned.

"What if I want to? Would it be ok then?"

"No," he said. "It wouldn't. It would never be ok."

"Don't you trust me?" I said.

He closed his eyes. "I can't. I won't. Please don't tempt me." He looked away and sighed. A few times it looked like he wanted to say something, but nothing came out. "I'm sorry. I'm so sorry I put you in this position. I don't deserve a boy as wonderful as you." He gently pulled away from me and stood up, leaving me alone on the floor. I knew I should grab at him, make him sit back down, make him do whatever came next, but when he started cleaning up the glass, I helped him without saying anything.

Neither of us could sleep. We both tried to read, but I couldn't concentrate and it seemed like he was having the same problem. We were both probably thinking about the same thing, but neither of us wanted to talk about it. Jeremy finally turned on the TV at midnight so we could watch Star Trek. I had my head on his chest while he rubbed my back. A part of me thought I should try again, but I liked the way we were right now. He got up at one of the commercials and got another alcoholic drink. As soon as he got back into bed, I snuggled right back the same way we were. I thought I'd be happy to stay like this all night if I didn't get sleepy, and it gave me a warm feeling inside because I knew he'd be just as happy.

"I've been thinking," he said.

"Me too," I said.

"I love you," he said.

"I know," I said.

He burst out laughing. "Into the carbonite with you!" He tickled my sides until I rolled over, and then he put his head on my chest instead of me putting mine on his. I decided to rub his back the way he did for me. Like I was the adult and he was the kid. "You're an amazing person."

"I know," I said again.

He didn't laugh this time. "I want to do something for you."

"Like what?" I asked.

He took a deep breath. "I can't take from you, but what if I gave you what you wanted? Nothing else. Then it wouldn't be about me. Only about you. That would be ok, wouldn't it?"

"I don't understand," I said.

"If you want, and only if you want, I could tie you up. Nothing else."

I shivered a little. It seemed like forever since I was tied up for real. I didn't tie myself up very much like I used to before Jeremy. It just wasn't the same now that I knew what it was like being tied up by someone else. I didn't realize how much I missed it. But if I said yes, I was being selfish. It wouldn't fix anything. I was supposed to do something for him. I had to say no.

But my thing *really* wanted me to say yes.

Just this once, I told myself. Then it would be his turn. I promised.

"Ok," I whispered.

James Edison

Chapter 15

May 28, 1982

I had no idea how I'd survive school today.

Jeremy revved the engine when we pulled up in front of the school. Whenever he did that, the other kids would look and see me getting out of the Porsche. I liked making them jealous.

"Do you have to do that every time?" I muttered.

He looked over at me. "Are you sure you're ok?"

"Would you stop asking me already? I'm fine. I keep telling you I don't want to go to school today."

"We talked about this. I can't sign you out sick because you've taken too much time off. Monday is a holiday, and school will be over in a few weeks. Try to hang in there."

I kicked the door open and climbed out of the car.

"I'll see you after school, ok?"

I slammed the door without answering him and stomped to the door. By the time I turned around to look, he was already gone. He was going to think I was angry at him because of the stuff we were doing. He worried about it all the time. He had no way of knowing that I wasn't angry at him because I didn't explain. I knew I wasn't being fair, but I didn't know what to do about it because I couldn't figure out what to say.

I walked through the halls, dragging my fingers on the baby blue bricks they used to build the school. But I realized they weren't actual bricks – they were just made to *look* like bricks. The wall was solid. I

never noticed before. Was it made of stone? Maybe cement. Whatever it was, it seemed like a strange choice. Schools should be warm and friendly. These walls were hard and cold. Like a prison.

I pictured a small room made of baby blue cement fake-brick walls. Closed in with iron bars.

The noise in the hallway snapped me back. Every single kid probably knew what I just imagined, and more important, why I imagined it. It had to be obvious to anyone who looked in the right place. I knew everyone was looking in the right place because that's what I did to them all the time. Wondering what they looked like inside their underwear. Girls *and* boys – it didn't matter because I was equally curious. I slid my backpack off so I could carry it in front. It was a dorky way to carry my bag, but I didn't have a choice. Once my thing woke up, it stayed awake for a long time. I needed the One Ring, right now, just once.

I used to have a dam inside my head. The river of my dirty thoughts would be held back until they started spilling over the top. Then I'd do something about it, and the thoughts would go away until the river filled up again. But now it was like the dam was completely gone. Ideas poured constantly into my head. Every day it got worse. My brain was in danger of being so flooded that everything else would be washed away.

I stuck to the walls and got into the room early so I could get my books out and sit at my desk without anyone seeing anything. I told myself to relax and think about something else.

The baby blue prison cell popped into my head, this time with torches and chains.

I slid down lower into my seat, but that only made things worse because my thing was pressed against the bottom of the desk. It had to be so obvious. Soon the girls would be pointing and giggling. I had to find something in the room to distract me.

Teacher's desk? I could be tied to that. A couple of different ways.

Coat closet? I could get locked in there.

Pink backpack? I wonder if she has any rope.

Windows? They have wire in them, like a prison.

I opened my math book to a random page. Maybe solving problems would distract me. I couldn't concentrate hard enough to do a single one. It finally happened. Everything else had washed away, even something as easy as fractions. Nothing was left but bondage.

I still couldn't believe there was an official word for it. Jeremy showed me, right there in the dictionary for anyone to see. *Bondage (n): The state or practice of being physically restrained, as by being tied up, chained, or put in handcuffs, for sexual gratification.* I wondered why there wasn't another sentence. *As practiced by a very perverted boy named Nicholas Welles in Newton Falls, New Jersey in the 1980's.* It wasn't possible other people had the same ideas as me. I kept looking at the dictionary to make sure it wasn't my imagination. And because it was exciting to read.

I always thought getting something you wanted would satisfy you. Not being allowed something like ice cream made you want ice cream even worse, but once you got ice cream you wouldn't want it anymore, at least for a little while. I was completely wrong. Getting tied up that first night didn't satisfy me at all. Instead, I wanted it even worse. We weren't playing games anymore. No stories. No tricks. Just me stretched out on the bed in my underwear. That first night, Jeremy whispered in my ear how I was all tied up and couldn't get out. He told me it was ok to do what I wanted to do. Even though it had to be the most embarrassing and scary thing I could think of, I actually did the most private and secret thing I could ever do right in front of him. Now, I wasn't scared or embarrassed anymore. I was used to it.

I had become an official connoisseur of bondage, like it was food or wine. Plain rope was for amateurs. Jeremy went shopping and brought back a pile of new supplies. We had ropes of all shapes and sizes, from thin plastic cord to heavy, rough stuff half as thick as my wrist. We had chains, some thin and light, some so massive they were hard to lift. We had padlocks, duct tape, and sleep masks that made good blindfolds. Jeremy even went to a special store to buy me two real pairs of police handcuffs along with bigger ones for feet that had a longer chain. The handcuffs were my favorites. Rope was more comfortable, but chains and handcuffs were impossible to escape. We had everything mentioned in the dictionary for bondage.

Jeremy made some rules. First, if I wanted to be tied up, I had to ask him. He didn't want me to feel like I was under pressure from him. Second, the moment I said I wanted to get out, he would untie me right away. He didn't want me to feel trapped. Third, I had to keep my underwear on. Just in case. Fourth, he was not allowed to touch me when I was tied up, no backrubs or anything. Also just in case.

The first rule was hard at the beginning. After all, it's not something that comes up in a regular conversation. Want to get some ice cream? Want to play tennis? Want to do some bondage? It got easier the more we did it. Now, it felt normal because he tied me up every day.

I kept promising I'd do something for him and stop being so selfish, but two weeks had gone by and I hadn't done anything. Everything was for me again. Each night, I forgot all about my promise and got the handcuffs from the drawer beside the bed. But I had an even bigger problem. I wanted more. I wanted to break all his rules. I wanted to break rules he never even thought about. Each time he tied me up it got worse. I was getting worried I wouldn't be able to stop myself.

The bell rang, so I automatically started looking for my math homework – until I remembered there was no math homework, the first time all year. What if I didn't do my homework? I would get put in detention. Not detention like having to stay after school for half an hour. Real detention – all night or maybe all weekend if I was especially bad. They would take me to a little detention room that had no windows, make me take off my clothes, chain me to the wall, and leave me alone in the dark. . .

I noticed the room got noisy. Big letters on the board said "Math Relay Race." It was easy to figure out what was going on. The first kid in each row had to run up to the teacher's desk to get a problem, solve it on the board, and then run back for the next kid to go. The problems were easy. The only fun thing we did in math all year and I was missing it.

Then I realized I had a seriously big problem.

I'd have to go up to the board soon. The first kid in my row was almost done. I was fourth. My thing was as hard as it could get. Why did I let myself imagine detention? The second kid ran up. Everyone was yelling and helping solve the problem. I slouched lower. I tried to

relax, tried to think about math, tried to think about *anything* besides detention. It wasn't going to go down. The second kid was done and the third kid ran up. Please, please, please just go down a little before it's my turn. The girl in front of me was almost done. . .

"Nicholas!" the teacher yelled. "You're wanted in the office! Take your things!"

I stared at her. She had the office phone in her hand. Someone shouted how it wasn't fair because my team would have one less person. Everyone was looking straight at me. "Nicholas, office!" she yelled again.

It only took a second for them to stop caring about me because the game was a lot more interesting. I held my books in front of me while I got my backpack from the closet and slipped out of the room as fast as I could. The hallway was deserted – everyone was in their classrooms. I was safe.

It didn't matter anymore, so my thing went down on its own.

Jeremy was talking to the secretary in the office when I got there. He looked annoyed. "What?" I said.

"We're going to be late. What took you so long?"

"Late for what?"

"Your doctor's appointment." He looked at the secretary. "I swear, I don't know how these kids survive. It seems like they can barely remember their own names."

"I don't have a doctor's appointment," I said.

"I told you about it last week. You're twelve years old. Can't you remember some of these things on your own?"

"You never told me," I muttered. Doctor's appointment? That meant coughing with my underwear down. That meant needles and blood. I'd rather stay in school. "I already had my checkup and I'm not sick." He finished writing on the paper and grabbed my arm. "I'd remember if you told me." He yanked me out of the office. "Ow, let go!

He dragged me outside. "Just get in the car," he hissed.

"Fine!" I yelled. I slammed the car door as hard as I could. The tires squealed as he drove away. I crossed my arms and planted my feet. He was *not* going to drag me into the doctor's office.

He burst out laughing.

"What's so funny?" I demanded.

"Don't you get it?" he spat out.

"I don't get why you didn't tell me. . ." I started to realize. "I don't have a doctor's appointment, do I?"

"And the Oscar for best performance in a school rescue goes to. . . Nick Welles!" He burst out laughing again.

"Why didn't you just tell me?" I punched him in the arm. "That was embarrassing."

"Come on, aren't you glad I pulled you out?"

I slammed my head back into the seat. "You didn't have to do it that way! Why'd you make me come to school if you were going to pull me out a few minutes later? I could've stayed home."

"I didn't plan to. I realized you seemed unusually upset this morning, so I decided to come back. I figured if you were there when they took attendance, they wouldn't mark you absent."

"You could've come back sooner. You could've not dropped me off at all."

"Something's wrong," he said seriously. "Do you want to talk?"

"There's nothing to talk about." I watched the roads go by. We were going in the wrong direction, away from home. "Where are we going?"

"I have no idea," he said, ending the conversation.

All the windows were rolled down, the wind tearing through the car as we zipped down the highway. The music was turned up as loud as it would go so the trumpets and timpanis overpowered the noise. Saint-Saens third symphony, one of my favorites. My hand was outside the window, slicing through the wall of air like a knife, rolling and twisting like an X-wing fighter in the middle of a battle.

It was Jeremy's idea to get lost on purpose. It sounded stupid to me at first, so I wouldn't join in when we came to an intersection and had to pick which way to go. We were on the highway because we kept finding roads Jeremy knew when we were closer to home. I thought driving around doing nothing would be boring, but I was getting more

interested the farther we went. I didn't want to stop feeling bad, but my anger had melted away. Maybe it was because of the music or maybe because we were on an adventure.

Without any warning, Jeremy swerved over two lanes and took the next exit. He slowed down so suddenly I had to put my hands on the dashboard to brace myself. "I've never been here, how about you?" he asked. I shook my head. "Looks like a good place to get lost." The road was quiet with only a few cars going in either direction. Nothing to see besides trees and some farms. After a few miles, a yellow sign said we were entering a "Densely Settled Area," which turned out to be a tiny town. Jeremy took a sharp left turn up a hill. On the other side of the road, I saw teenagers running around on a big lawn behind an iron fence, all wearing the same clothes. It looked like some kind of school. I wrinkled my nose.

The school disappeared behind us, and we passed by a few more farms and homes as we left town. Without any warning, the road became narrow, gray, and full of cracks and holes. The trees closed in to the edge of the pavement, growing over the top of the road to make it look like we were in a tunnel. Jeremy slowed down. "Should we turn around?"

"Let's find out where it goes." I felt a little scared, but it was fun to be a little scared. The road curved and twisted. We went over small bridges barely wide enough for one car at a time. The trees blocked out most of the light until it seemed like it was about to get dark outside. I thought of being in Mirkwood, expecting to be attacked by giant spiders at any moment. We didn't see any other cars going in either direction. The road climbed upward, twisting around, the trees getting closer. People didn't belong here. The Sibelius symphony on the tape agreed. It sounded spooky too.

We turned around a bend at the top of a hill. The trees broke apart. The music swelled to a big triumphant sound at exactly the right time. Jeremy slammed on the brakes. My eyes got wide. I think I stopped breathing.

"Would you look at that," Jeremy whistled.

Spread out below us for miles and miles was a huge valley, carpeted with trees. Green fields stretched into the distance past a sparkling river.

The sun was shining on everything until it seemed like it was glowing. I imagined I just crossed through into another world, like I was looking out over the Shire, hobbit holes just out of sight behind the hills. I read in books a lot about how people's hearts swelled, but I never understood what it really meant until that moment.

Jeremy pulled the car off the road so we could stare through the windshield, but I wanted to see better so I got out. Off to the side of the road was a rocky, steep hill with only a few trees on top. From up there, I'd be able to see everything. I ran through the ferns and scrambled up the rocks without worrying about how slippery they were or what would happen if I fell. Jeremy shouted something to me, but I didn't stop. I had to get to the top and see. The hill was calling to me. I was right, the view from the top was amazing. I could see the whole valley in every direction. The wind blew on my face. I stretched out my arms and felt like I could fly. I shouted because it felt good to shout.

Jeremy took a while to climb up. The other side of the hill wasn't as steep, but it was a much longer walk. He put his hands on his knees to catch his breath when he got to the top. I didn't wait for him to be done. I ran up to him as fast as I could and jumped onto him, wrapping my arms around him tightly. He fell over backwards onto his butt. We both laughed.

"It's beautiful, isn't it," he said. I snuggled into him and let him hold me while we stared at the fantastic land below us. Beautiful wasn't a strong enough word for it. I didn't think a big enough word existed in any language. I felt something special here. A kind of real magic. My emotions were short circuiting. Up on this rock, anything seemed possible.

He interrupted the silence first. "Are you upset with me?" he asked. "Please tell me, I'm worried."

"I'm not," I said. "That's not what it is."

"Talk to me," he said.

I didn't think I'd be able to talk about these things. But the magic here made it ok.

"What do you think is down there?" I asked.

"I think that's the Delaware river," he said. "See, there's the I-80 bridge."

"I think there's something secret down there."

"Ah," he said. "You're right. I heard about it on the pirate radio station before it went off the air. There's a secret lab, down past that little rise on the other side of the river. They're doing genetic research to create an army of brain-eating mutant zombie clones. It's part of Pennsylvania's evil plot to subjugate northern New Jersey. They'll be ready to attack soon, maybe even tonight. Our only hope is to join them and become brain-eating mutant zombie clones ourselves." He groaned like a zombie. "On this side of the river, there's an ordinary asylum for the criminally insane, including the infamous mass murderer Aaron Buzzby. I heard he escaped yesterday. Way off over there is a secret Finnish military base. You've got to watch out for Finland, they're sneaky. Everyone underestimates Finland."

"I was thinking something different," I said softly to let him know I was serious. I pulled his arms tighter around me. "There's a little building made of cement with no windows and one metal door. It's hidden so nobody knows it's there. That's just the part you can see because most of it's underground. They have guards and cameras and locks to make sure no one can get in or out."

"What is it?"

"A school," I breathed. "A special kind of school. The kids live there all year long. They never get to leave. They can't escape."

"It makes me want to rescue them," he said quietly.

"You can't. No one can. The kids are chained up all the time. They get chained to their desks when they go to class. When they're not in class they got locked in little prison cells and get chained to their beds or the walls." My heart was beating so hard I could hear it. "The kids aren't allowed to have anything of their own, not even clothes. They're naked all the time. Sometimes they have to stand with their hands chained over their heads in the dark for days. Sometimes they don't even get food or water. If they misbehave they get tortured, like getting whipped, stretched on a rack, or zapped with electricity. They're real prisoners, forever. They'll never be allowed to go home."

"How could anyone do that to a child?" Jeremy asked. His voice was shaky.

"I want to go to that school," I said.

Jeremy hugged me very tight.

"I can't stop thinking about it," I said. "I don't want to get kidnapped and locked up and tortured for real. But sometimes my thing takes over and I think about being a real prisoner. I think about how easy it would be to get kidnapped. I could go hitchhiking or take a bus into New York. It can't be fake or pretend. I want to know I can't get out. I want to know I'm going to be tortured for real. Then I think about how terrible it would be and how I'd never see you again. What if one day I got myself kidnapped and then I couldn't change my mind? I'm worried I really could. I've done bad things to myself before." He didn't say anything. "There's something wrong with me. Do you hate me now?"

"I could never hate you, and I don't think there's anything wrong with you either," he said. "I can't stand the thought of you suffering, not after everything you've already been through. I want you to be happy and healthy, have a normal life, and find love. I'm not going to let anything happen to you. I'll always be here to protect you."

"Until when?" I whispered.

He held me close.

"Until forever comes," he whispered back.

I squirmed in the chair. My arms were getting sore, but that was ok because I wanted them to get sore. I was hungry, but that was ok too. The more uncomfortable, the better.

I heard Jeremy come back from the kitchen. Something clinked when he put it down on the coffee table. I thought it might be a drink, but I wasn't sure because I couldn't see anything except a sliver of light at the bottom of my blindfold. I tried to pull my hands apart to remind myself that I couldn't. The first time he handcuffed me to the chair, I managed to wriggle out by getting my legs under me and standing up. He figured out a way to stop me by cuffing my ankles and locking them to the handcuffs using a short chain under the chair. Escape proof. I wasn't going anywhere.

"Do you want some water?" he asked.

"No," I said. I was thirsty, but I wasn't allowing myself to drink anything. "How much longer?"

"You know I'm not going to tell you," he said. That's what I wanted to hear him say. "Bedtime is hours away so get comfortable. You'll be here for a while."

I got the handcuffs out as soon as we got home. We stayed on the rock for hours, but we didn't talk after I told him about the school. That was enough talking for a little while. I wound up falling asleep with my head on his lap.

I decided I was ready to talk some more.

"Can I ask you a question?" I said.

"You just did," he answered.

I wasn't in the mood for witty fencing with words. "Do you like seeing me in my underwear?" He didn't answer. "Did you hear me?"

"Yes," he said. "I don't want to answer that question."

"Why not?"

"What I want doesn't matter," he said.

"I want to know," I said.

"I'm uncomfortable talking about it."

"Why? I tell you about my stuff."

"Let me ask you a question first. Do you like seeing me in my underwear?" I didn't say anything. "Now you understand."

"No," I said. "I don't like it."

"That's why I'm uncomfortable talking about it."

"You said I could ask you about anything."

"I meant in general," he said. "Not specifically about me."

"If you tell me, I'll stop asking. Come on, I answered your question."

I heard him take a drink. "Yes, I do. But I think you already knew that."

I squirmed a little to make sure I was still secure. "Was the other boy embarrassed about being naked like me?"

"You said you would stop asking questions," he said.

"I really want to know."

I heard him fill his glass. "No. He was something of an exhibitionist."

"What does that mean?" I asked.

"Someone who likes showing off," he said. His voice sounded edgy.

"Being naked," I said.

"Enough questions," he said.

"What kinds of things did you do with him?"

"What's gotten into you?" he said.

"I really want to know, that's all," I said.

"Well, he loved basketball so we used to go to the Y to shoot hoops a lot. We rode bikes, saw movies, talked, and hung out. Pretty much the same as you and me."

"That's not what I meant," I said.

"What exactly did you mean?"

I took a deep breath. "I mean sex stuff."

I heard him take a long drink. "There is no way I'm talking about the intimate details of my sex life. I know you're curious about sex and I'm happy to answer your questions, but I'm not talking about my own experiences."

"Did you suck his dick?"

"Jesus," he said under his breath. I heard him pour another drink even though he just poured one. I could smell the alcoholic stuff across the room. "You need to understand something. The physical act of sex isn't the important part. What matters is what you feel when you do it with someone you love. Despite everything I did to him, I truly loved him just like I truly love you. Sometimes sex was like a game, laughing and tickling without taking anything seriously. Sometimes it was wild and exhausting. But the times that really meant something were the tender ones, when it didn't matter what we did as long as we were together. When I felt his heart beating, I knew he loved me as much as I loved him. We'd lie together in a jumble of arms and legs until it didn't matter which ones were his and which were mine. We were one complete being." I heard him gulp his drink down. "I shouldn't be talking about him this way."

"Do you imagine doing that with me?" I asked.

He sat down next to me. "It doesn't matter if I do or don't."

"But do you?"

"I'd be lying if I said I didn't," he said.

"How do two boys do it?"

"When two men have sex, they can masturbate each other, or as you crudely suggested they can suck each other's dicks. They can also have intercourse. The word you probably know is fucking. One man will penetrate the other."

"I don't understand," I said.

"One man puts his penis in the other man's rear end."

"Rear end?" What the heck was he talking about?

"His butt."

I shook my head. "I still don't get it."

He took a deep breath. "In his butthole."

I blinked under the blindfold. "You're joking with me."

"I'm entirely serious," he said. "With a woman, the man puts his penis in her vagina. Obviously, that's impossible with two men, so they use what they can."

I wanted to say how unbelievably gross it sounded, but I didn't. "What's your favorite sex thing to do?"

"I need you to stop asking questions about me."

"I want to know," I said.

"This is the very last one I'm going to answer, understood?" I didn't say anything. "I like fucking. Now, be quiet or I'll figure out how to gag you."

"Ok," I said. Being gagged sounded exciting. We never did that before. But I didn't say anything.

I couldn't imagine doing any of the things he talked about. Actually sucking dicks was bad enough, but that was nothing compared to whatever that word was. *Fucking.* How could anyone do something so disgusting? So *wrong*? But what I wanted was just as wrong. I wanted him to break all the rules. I wanted him to decide when I got tied up, and I wanted him to keep me tied up even when I wanted to be let out. I wanted him to hurt me. I wanted him to force me to be naked.

That's what I could do. Something for both of us. Something in the middle until I could find my courage.

"Can you pull down my underwear?" I asked. Out loud. My stomach jumped. My thing got harder.

"You know the rules," he said.

"I want you to," I said.

"No, you don't," he said. "I don't want to do it either. End of discussion."

I took a deep breath. "I want you to make me. Even though it's embarrassing. Like the kids in the school."

I sat there in silence for what felt like a long time.

"I think I finally understand," he said. He ran his hand through my hair even though it broke the rules. "This morning, I thought you were upset because I was doing something to you that you didn't want. That's not it. You want me to take responsibility, don't you? You want me to make the decisions."

"Yeah," I said, holding my breath, waiting for him to do it.

Instead, he unlocked the handcuffs.

"Then I'm deciding you've had enough for now. I won't hurt you. I can't. I love you too much."

He untied me the rest of the way and took off the blindfold. His face was red. "I'm not going to take advantage of you. My job is to keep you safe. I'm going to protect you, just like I promised. Maybe one day the time will come when you're ready. For now, I want you to just be a boy. My sweet, wonderful, caring, beautiful boy." He kissed my cheek. "I love you."

"I love you, too," I said.

"You go get dressed. I'll bet you're hungry. I have some dinner left over for you." I nodded. I watched him go to the kitchen and then went upstairs to put on my pajamas.

I knew he meant it. I knew I never had to do anything I didn't want to do. He'd never kick me out or stop loving me, ever. I knew I was safe. Safer than I'd ever been in my entire life.

Which made me even more certain I wanted to let him do it anyway.

Chapter 16

June 7, 1982

I had a *real* plan.

We had it all carefully plotted out like we were committing a huge robbery, complete with contingencies and alternatives. Everything I needed to do and say to make sure we succeeded was carefully written down and rehearsed. Brian stood beside me, pledged to aid my most noble and sacred quest. No knight could ask for a better squire than Brian. After all, he was the one who figured most of it out. I wouldn't even know what contingencies and alternatives meant without him.

I imagined putting the visor of my helmet down. "Ready?" I asked. "Ready," he said.

We set out to conquer the mall.

My duty and obligation was to buy the most special, most amazing, and most awesomest birthday present Jeremy ever got from anyone. Way beyond Christmas. I knew exactly what I wanted to get, where I could get it, and how much it cost. The idea came to me when we were eating our croissants and reading the Sunday newspaper. "This is amazing," Jeremy said. "Imagine listening to music at home without any pops, scratches, or tape hiss, just like at a concert hall. This thing uses a laser to read the music instead of a needle. Even if it gets scratched, they still work perfectly. No more cleaning dust, no more handling records by their sides, and no more skips. They call them compact discs. I've got to get one of these."

Later, I snuck the paper out of the trash. There were plenty of advertisements so I learned they cost about five hundred dollars. I didn't have that much money at home, so I had to get it out of my bank account. That's where it got tricky. It said on the bank book an adult signature was required for withdrawals. If I asked him to sign something, he'd ask why I needed so much money. I'd have to tell him it was for his birthday, and he'd tell me I was spending too much money. We'd argue for an hour and he'd never give in.

I wasn't going to give in either.

A few days ago, Brian helped me figure out the solution to my bank problem while we threw stones into the creek. "It's my money," I told him. "Why can't I take it out when I want it? It's not like I'm some little kid – I'm twelve years old. I won't spend it all on candy. Adults think kids are stupid, but we know how things work."

"They're bigger, stronger, and they make all the rules," Brian said. He threw a big rock that made a very satisfying kerplunk sound. "They think kids are stupid, but that's their weakness. We can trick them. The bank book says you need an adult signature, but it doesn't say you need an adult with you. Sign his name on the form and they have to give you the money."

Brian was smart that way.

"How much does it cost?" he asked.

"About five hundred dollars," I said.

If he was amazed, he didn't show it. "Five hundred and thirty with tax. You should take out extra, just in case. Get six hundred." I didn't know how he figured out the tax. I didn't even know there would be tax. He threw another stone. "That's a lot of money to give a kid without a grown-up around. You have to make up a story why you want to get the money in secret. You could say you hit a baseball through a window and wanted to get it fixed with your own money. I don't think windows cost that much, though. Say you hit it through a window and then it broke a Chinese vase on the table by the window and kept going to smash into a TV set."

"I can't remember all that."

"The more details you have, the more believable it'll be. You have to rehearse, but you should only say it if they ask why you want the money. Can you make yourself cry?" I shook my head. "Practice looking very sad. We have to think of a name for the person's window you broke."

"How about Mr. Brown?"

"That sounds fake. It has to be a harder name or it's not believable. How about Tymczyczyn?"

"Tim. . .what?"

"Tymczyczyn. That was my neighbor's name when we lived in Clifton. Do you know what your dad's signature looks like?"

"I can get a paper from his desk," I said.

"Good. It has to be right in case they have a way to tell."

"You're good at thinking of this stuff," I said. "Can you come to the mall with me? If something goes wrong you could think of a plan."

He threw another big stone in the water. "I don't want to get in trouble."

"You won't get in trouble. I'm the one who'd get in trouble."

"It wouldn't matter. I have to go home to water the lawn." He threw one last rock.

"I'll help you," I said.

"My dad has to work all night. He's not good at sleeping during the day so I'm not allowed to have any friends over."

"I'll be really quiet," I said.

"Doesn't matter," he said sharply.

I decided not to say what I thought about his dad.

"I want to take some money out," I said.

"No, say 'I'd like to make a withdrawal,'" Brian corrected. "Look at your shoes and mumble, it makes you look sadder. Did you practice the signature?"

"About a hundred times. I put all the pieces of paper into a trash can and used a match to burn them like you said."

I thought I was ready after all the times we practiced. The way he kept correcting me made me feel like I wasn't ready at all. "You get the slips," I said.

"Me? I don't know where they are or what they look like."

"They're on the desk with the pens," I said. "I know the white ones are for deposits, but I don't know which color are for withdrawals."

He smiled and nodded. "I get it. If they see you, they'll know your dad isn't with you because you just got the paper. That's pretty smart." I nodded even though I only asked because I was too scared to go myself.

He went around the corner. I sat on the bench, saying my lines to myself, hoping I wouldn't mess up. He came back with a bunch of different colored slips. "I had to wait until they weren't looking. I wasn't sure which one you needed, so I got some of each. Is it checking or savings?"

"Savings," I said. "I think."

"You have to be sure or they're going to know," he hissed.

"It's savings, definitely," I said. I didn't feel so definite. He handed me a bunch of yellow slips. "I only need one."

"I got extra in case you mess up."

The form was simple. Name: Nicholas Welles. Date: June 7, 1982. Account number: copy it from the bank book. Amount: six zero zero dot zero zero. Write it out on the line: six hundred dollars. Signature: the hard part. I smoothed out the paper and took a deep breath.

"Come on, sign it already," Brian whispered.

"Don't rush me," I said. I held my breath while I wrote it, all the moves I'd practiced over and over again. Nope. The squiggle that was supposed to be the J looked wrong, the little bump that stood for "erem" was too big, and the line stood for "tillwell" was too long and pointed the wrong way. I crumbled the paper and got another one. Ok, again. Name: Jeremy Still. . . shoot.

I ruined five slips before I figured out I should do the signature first. Each time I tried, I messed up even worse. Brian was looking around like he expected the cops to arrest us any second. I was almost out of slips. Brian would have to get more if I didn't get it right soon. I traced out the signature one more time and studied it. "Got it!" I yelled.

"Shh!" he said, his eyes wide. He puffed on his inhaler.

I finished filling everything out. "Ready."

"I'll wait here," he whispered.

I took a deep breath. What if they call Jeremy anyway? What if they call my parents? What if they realize I faked his signature? There was a crime for that, wasn't there? What was it called? I turned around the corner, practicing my lines in my head.

The gate in front of the bank was shut and the lights were turned out. Closed. Abandoned. I imagined the sound Pac Man made when the ghost ate him. Beew-weew-weew-weew-womp-womp. Game over.

I stomped back to the bench. "How could they be closed? You were just in there!"

He looked around the corner. "The sign says they're open from nine to four," he said. "They closed five minutes ago." He took another puff of his inhaler.

"Now what am I supposed to do?"

"Maybe they have a cheaper one," Brian said. "How much did you bring?"

"I only had a hundred thirty dollars at home."

"You could get him some of the discs," Brian said.

"What's the point of the discs without the player?" I muttered. I started to crumple up the slip.

"Don't do that," Brian said. "You can come back tomorrow." He was right. I folded it in half and put it in my back pocket.

"Let's go to the bookstore," I said, frowning. Brian followed silently behind me. "Soon it'll be summer. We can go to the bookstore anytime we want."

"I won't be here," he said. "I have to go to Maine and stay with my grandfather."

"All summer?" I asked, disappointed.

"Yeah," he said. "There's no one here to watch me."

"You need someone to watch you?"

"I guess. Look over there, they have all different kinds of paper in that store. Do you think they have any parchment?" I turned around. He was looking at a store that sold things for writing letters and cards. I

never bothered looking in there before. I was sure they wouldn't have real parchment, but they did. Lots of it, in all different colors. "They have ink and pens so we can make it look like whatever we write comes from medieval times. We should make maps. We could even make a book that's filled with spells. Then we could go out in the woods, find branches to carve into staves, and make some robes so we look like real wizards."

I thought I was the only twelve-year-old who still liked to play pretend. One time, I pretended to be a space fighter pilot in the Porsche. The gear shift was my throttle, the stereo was my powerful computer system, and the other controls fired my high-tech weapons. I made all the sound effects for my laser cannons and explosions. "Red leader, this is red seven, I'm making my attack run now, proton torpedoes away." I was very careful to say proton torpedoes instead of photon torpedoes. I knew the difference between Star Wars and Star Trek. Things like that are *important*. I was really embarrassed when Jeremy caught me. Even though he told me it was completely normal, I didn't believe him. I was excited Brian wanted to play pretend too. Making spell books and dressing up like wizards sounded like so much fun.

Brian put the parchment back on the shelf. "Come on, let's go to the bookstore."

"Don't you want to get some paper?"

"I don't have any money," he said.

I grinned. "I do." I grabbed a bunch of paper so we wouldn't run out. Brian found a kit that had ink, pens, and an instruction book on how to make old fashioned letters. He also found some special wax that was used to seal letters and metal things to press into the wax to leave a fancy design. I got one with an N and one with a B for Brian. All together it cost thirty-eight dollars, but I had plenty of money.

"You know what else we should do," he said, excited. "We should learn how to write in Tolkien elvish. Maybe not in real elvish, I don't think there's enough words. They have a chart in the back of the book that shows all the sounds the letters make. We could just spell out the sounds in English words and write them down that way."

"We could use it to pass notes at school," I said, just as excited. "Then, if the teacher read them, she wouldn't know what they said."

He nodded. "I want to find something good at the bookstore, but it's so hard to tell. The books with the pictures of girls wearing metal bikinis always suck. The good ones have a dragon or castle or spaceship on them. It's hard to tell though, because a lot of those are still bad. Even if you read the first thirty pages you can't tell, so I like opening to the middle and reading them even through you don't know what's going on." We went to the back of the bookstore where they had the science fiction and fantasy shelves.

We both saw it at the same time. Right in the middle of the top shelf, all by itself. Red leather with a matching case. Letters in gold. The design of a tree with stars around it. We both knew what it was without reading the title because of the tree.

"The Lord. . . " I started.

". . .of the Rings," he finished.

"Whoa," we both said at the same time.

It was sealed in plastic so we couldn't look inside. Picking it up gave me chills. I knew everything about this story, but somehow holding this version made it new for me again.

Brian shuffled his feet. "You'd better put it back before something happens to it."

I didn't want to put it back. Now that I had it, I didn't want to part with it. It was my own. I found it. It came to me. My precioussss. I turned it over to look at the price. "Fifty dollars," I said out loud. A ton of money for a book.

"So it's fifty dollars. I'm going to buy it." I didn't care about new books anymore. I didn't want to wait. I carried the book up to the register and put it with the price tag up so the guy didn't have to turn it over and maybe bend a corner.

"We got three of these this morning and now they're all gone," the guy said. Jeremy sometimes said how things happen for a reason. If I didn't mess up the signature so many times, the bank would've still been open. I would've gone to the stereo store and bought the disc player. By the time we got to the bookstore someone else would've bought the book and we wouldn't know it even existed.

"Can I see?" Brian asked.

"When we get home. I don't want to unwrap it here." Even though I was dying to see the inside too.

"Can I hold it?"

I handed him the bag. "I'm hungry," I said.

"Let's get some fries," he said, his eyes on the book. "They're only fifty cents."

I still had a lot of money in my pocket. Being bad felt good. "We still have some time before Jeremy picks us up. I want cheese sticks and potato skins. I want ice cream drinks. I want chocolate cake. I want everything we're not supposed to have before dinner because no one can tell us we can't."

Brian smiled. I really liked making him smile.

I imagined how much my present would make Jeremy smile.

I stopped walking right in the middle of the mall. My mouth dropped and my mind started going a mile a minute.

The idea revealed itself to me in a flash, like it was waiting for me to stumble onto it. If I was in a cartoon, there'd be a light bulb floating over my head. I was so stupid. Why didn't I figure it out earlier? Way back on my birthday, he told me he didn't want any presents. I could use the parchment, the ink, and the wax to write him a letter. Even better – a poem. It turned out there was an even bigger reason I didn't get the money. A compact disc player wouldn't be a very special present at all.

"Nick, are you ok?" Brian asked.

"I gotta go back to the paper store," I told him. "Need more stuff."

"Ok," he said.

I could barely keep myself from shouting out loud.

The present wasn't a thing to be bought and wrapped.

The present was *me*.

Chapter 17

June 11, 1982

I tore down the stairs, jumping the last four in a single bound. Jeremy was right behind me, slipping on the marble floor because he wasn't smart enough to take off his socks first. Dishes and glasses rattled in the dining room cabinets. We didn't care. I dashed through the kitchen and into the den. I made the mistake of looking back to see where he was and lost my balance. He charged. I tried to dodge to the right, but he guessed which way I was going. He wrapped his arms around me and threw me to the floor.

"Gotcha!" he yelled. He sat on my back and pinned my arms down. I tried to kick my way out, but he was too heavy. He lifted his entire body and crashed back down, hard.

"You weigh a ton!" I yelled.

He crashed down twice more, and then his fingers slipped under my shirt, tickling my sides. I was laughing so hard I couldn't catch my breath enough to scream. He tickled me for ages before letting up, but instead of letting me go, he rolled me over onto my back and pinned me down again. "We don't do this enough," he said, burying his head into my stomach. It didn't exactly tickle, but it still made me squirm with giggle fits. "Blame the movie, kiddo. I feel like I'm twelve again. When those bicycles took off at the end and the music and wow!"

It was his birthday, so he chose what to do. I thought he'd want a fancy dinner in New York and a concert. Instead, we went for pizza and a movie. He didn't even want to go on his actual birthday – we waited an extra day just so it'd be Friday. The movie *was* amazing. And

I learned a very valuable trick — how to hold a thermometer against a light bulb to fake being sick.

He sat up, his hands loose on my wrists even though he was still holding them down. I caught him looking at me. The same look I saw when I peeked at him while I played the piano, or when we watched TV, or when he was in bed and I was still getting ready. A secret look he didn't want to let me see. As soon as he noticed I saw, he always looked away. I knew without knowing that it was his "love" look. I didn't understand why he didn't want me to see it.

He finally rolled off me, panting to catch his breath. "I need some ice cream," he said, heading for the kitchen. I panicked. Looking in the fridge would spoil my plan.

"Wait, don't!" I yelled after him.

He turned around. "What? It's just ice cream."

"I have to finish getting your present ready first. You can have ice cream afterwards."

He put his hands up in surrender. "Ok, it's your show."

I grabbed his hand and pulled him into the lobby. "Sit right here facing the windows," I said. "And close your eyes. No matter how long it takes you have to keep them closed."

"Don't make me wait too long. I'm dying to see what you got me."

I went to the stairs to make him think I was going up. "Are your eyes still closed?" I yelled.

"I can't see a thing!" he yelled back.

I went as softly as I could into the kitchen. The bottles of champagne were in the same place I left them, hidden behind the milk, so I knew he didn't see them. Jeremy explained this stuff wasn't real champagne when he let me taste it one time, but it was sweet and I liked it a lot more than the other wine he let me taste. I'd swiped two bottles from the liquor cabinet and put them into the fridge before we left for the movie. I didn't think I needed two, but Brian taught me having extra was always a good idea. I untied the string on the pink bakery box. Chocolate with strawberry filling, his favorite. The cake looked like a candle forest when I was done putting in all thirty candles (Jeremy was turning twenty-nine but one for good luck). I had a lot left to do so I didn't light them yet.

I ran upstairs with the bottles, hoping he didn't open his eyes at the wrong time. It took three trips to get all the stuff I hid in the guest bedroom. I had tons of candles, matches, glasses for the champagne, and the biggest gift bow I ever saw from the card store. I set up the candles everywhere and lit them. The room filled with a cozy yellow glow.

Next, the champagne. Jeremy always opened wine when he drank some at home, so I had no idea what to do. I tore off the foil on top first. A metal cap on top held the cork down. It was attached to a wire thing that unscrewed from the bottom, which was easy enough. I thought the cork would come out on its own when I took the metal cap off, but it was still in tight.

Jeremy used a thing to open wine. I couldn't remember what it was called and I didn't know where he kept it. If I asked him for the wine thingy it would give me away. I thought I'd have to go back downstairs and dig through all the drawers until I remembered my Swiss army knife had one. I dug through my drawers, but no knife. How come I could never find something when I needed it? I thought it might be in the nightstand, so I twisted around and stubbed my toe on the bed, hard. "Oww!" I hissed, hopping the rest of the way. The knife was there, right where I should've known it would be. I pulled the twisty thing out, no idea how to use it. Maybe I should jab it in somehow. That's when I thought to look at the label to see if it had any instructions.

"DO NOT USE CORKSCREW," it said.

Which reminded me the wine thingy was called a corkscrew. I felt stupid. My toe throbbed harder because it got hurt for something I didn't need. So, if I wasn't supposed to use the corkscrew, how was I supposed to get it out? Was I just supposed to pull it out or something? I rolled my eyes. Duh. I'd watched Jeremy do it before. Something was wrong with my brain tonight. The bottle was slippery so I couldn't get a good grip. I sat on the bed, put the bottle between my knees, and yanked with both hands. I felt it give a little, almost there. . .

POP!

The cork went flying across the room. I was so surprised I almost let go of the bottle. Before anything else could go wrong, I rushed over to the dresser and poured some into the glass. It foamed over and spilled everywhere.

"Come on!" I said out loud.

I put the bottle down so I could get a towel from the bathroom, but I didn't realize I put it right on the edge. I caught it right before it fell over and spilled all over the floor. It was like the bottle was fighting with me on purpose – like it didn't want me to drink it. I mopped up the mess and filled the glass more carefully this time.

I got the idea from a movie where a guy got a girl drunk to make her want to do it with him. I asked Jeremy if that was real. He said it was so real, there was even a line from Shakespeare. I didn't believe him – Shakespeare would never write about people being drunk. It gives desire but takes away. . .something. I couldn't remember. Desire is what I needed. Besides, I still remembered when Jeremy made a joke back at Christmas about how I'd be a lot more fun than his family if I was drunk. We were going to find out if he was right.

I took a small sip. It bubbled on my tongue and burned a little on the way down. But I didn't have time for sips. Jeremy was probably wondering where I was. It took forever to light all those candles.

So I drank the whole glass in one gulp.

I waited for two minutes, but nothing happened. I felt exactly the same. I didn't know how much I needed to get drunk, but one glass obviously wasn't enough so I poured another one. "Bottoms up, kiddo," I said out loud and drank it down. It burned worse than the first one. I didn't have any more time. Two would have to be enough for now. I ran downstairs, turning off all the lights on my way.

"Are your eyes still closed?" I yelled.

"I'm falling asleep over here!" he yelled back.

"Almost done." It took nine matches to light all the candles on his cake. I carried it into the lobby. "Open your eyes!" I yelled. "Happy birthday to you, you belong in a zoo, you look like a monkey, and you smell like one too!" I put the cake down on the coffee table in front of him.

"You actually put twenty-nine candles on it," he groaned.

"No," I said like he hurt my feelings. "Thirty. One for good luck."

He groaned even louder. I watched him close his eyes like he was making a wish and then he blew all the candles out at once. I clapped. "This looks yummy," he said. "Should we dig in with our hands?"

"Shoot, I forgot plates and forks," I said, jumping off the couch and running to the kitchen for all the stuff I forgot. I wiped my forehead on my sleeve because I was sweating. "You cut the cake, but I want a big piece with an icing flower."

"All yours." He cut me a giant piece of cake. I stuffed a huge forkful in my mouth.

"What did you wish for?" I asked with my mouth full of cake.

"If I told you, it wouldn't come true," he said. He stared at me. "Are you ok?"

I stopped in mid-shovel. "Why?"

"Your face is all red."

"I'm fine. Perfect." I wiped my forehead on my sleeve again. All that running around made me really sweaty. I took one last bite and let my fork fall on the plate. "You finish your cake while I get your present." I ran off before he could say anything. My present was hidden in the dining room because he wouldn't think to look for it in there. I wiped my face and washed my hands first, picking it up carefully to make sure I didn't wrinkle it. I brought it out without dripping any sweat on it. That would've been a disaster.

"What is it?" he asked when I handed it to him.

"It's my very special present for you," I said.

It was probably the hardest thing I'd ever done. For two days, I sat at the desk in the guest bedroom trying to think of something to write. Nothing. No ideas. Then the idea hit me all at once, just like when I was at the mall. Except this time, I was on the toilet. I had to stumble out of the bathroom with my pants around my ankles to find a pen and paper before I forgot it. But that was only half the job, because I still had to figure out how to write it using calligraphy. Half the parchment was in the trash because I kept screwing up. I finished it late last night, folded it neatly, and sealed it with my N stamped in wax.

"Are you sure you're ok? You're sweating up a storm."

"Just open it," I said.

"It's too pretty to open," he said, gently pulling the wax apart. "This is beautiful. I didn't realize you knew calligraphy. It looks like you worked on this for weeks." My plan was to stay while he read it, but I

realized listening to him would be way too embarrassing. I ran for the stairs, unable to stop giggling. "Are we going upstairs now?" he asked.

"You stay and read it," I said, pushing my face through the posts in the stairway. I ran up the stairs and slammed the doors to the bedroom behind me. Why did I sing the silly version of happy birthday? I wanted to do it seriously. More sweat dripped down my face. All that sweating was making me thirsty, so I got some water from the bathroom. And then some more water, and then some more.

I sat down on the bed, got up, and sat down again. I didn't know what else to do, so I figured I might as well get ready. I found his favorite shirt in the closet – a soft, dark-green button down one. My shirt went on the floor. His shirt was so big on me that it looked like I was wearing a dress. I kicked off my jeans and took a deep breath. Just the shirt, that was my plan. I pulled my underwear down before I could change my mind. Even though the shirt was low enough to hide everything, it didn't stop me from feeling naked.

The candles made the bedroom very warm, which was probably why I *still* couldn't stop sweating. I frowned because I didn't feel any different. Two glasses of champagne still wasn't enough so I poured another one. "To happy birthdays." The champagne didn't mix well with the chocolate cake. I let out a massive burp. That had to be one of the funniest things ever. I couldn't stop giggling.

I tried to fill both glasses, but there was only enough in the bottle for half of one. Good thing I swiped the second bottle. Opening it was easier because I knew what to do, and I even managed to hold on to the cork this time. I filled the other glass and used the pillows to prop myself up on the bed. My hands felt tingly. I wondered if that was a part of getting drunk.

I was looking at the glasses of champagne when I realized what I did. Two glasses and two bottles. Shit. I left the empty bottle on the dresser. If Jeremy knew I drank that much he'd kill me. I rolled the empty bottle under the bed so he wouldn't see it in the trash, reminding myself to get it tomorrow. Then I flopped back down on the bed. Then I realized there was too much champagne in the new bottle because half a glass came from the old one. So, I got up and drank some more and filled the glass. Back down on the bed. Then I realized I forgot the bow on

the dresser. I groaned out loud. Up *again*. I peeled the tape on the back and stuck it on my head. "Perfect," I said to the boy in the mirror wearing a bow, a big shirt, and nothing else.

The door to the room opened. Jeremy stood in the doorway. I couldn't tell the expression on his face because it was too dark, even with all the candles. He started reading my poem out loud.

When

When I am happy
 You are there to share it
When I am scared
 You help me to be brave
When I am in trouble
 You protect me
When I am mad
 You calm me down
When I am sad
 You make me smile
When I fall
 You pick me up
When I am lost
 You show me the way
When I am lonely
 You hold my hand
When we are apart
 You are in my mind
When we are together
 I feel like I can fly
And when it hurts more than I can bear
 You are there
 To comfort me
 To hold me in your arms
 To keep me safe
When I say I love you

It means forever

And when forever comes
I will be there
To comfort you
To hold you in my arms
To keep you safe
When you are ready
I am waiting
With all my heart
With all my love
When
Is Now
And Forever

It was hard to listen. His voice cracked and he had to stop a few times. I wanted to run away but I didn't move. Before he got to the end he started to cry. I ran up to him when he finished and hugged him tight. "It's ok," I said. "Everything's ok."

The poem fell on the floor when he hugged me back. "I never. . .I mean. . .I thought I knew. . .I can't think of words. . .I love you so much!" He got on his knees without letting go of me. He couldn't stop crying. I rubbed his back and shushed him until he calmed down. Then I kissed him on the cheek, like I did the last time.

He let me go and put his hands on my shoulders. "No matter what happens, I love you and I'll always love you. I can't imagine how empty my life would be without you." He touched my cheek. "Does this mean what I think it means?"

I nodded.

"Ok," he said gently. "You have to make me a promise, the most solemn promise you will ever make in your life. Swear to me this won't change anything between us. Swear to me you'll still love me when it's over. Swear to me this is something you truly want to do. There's no room for mistakes and no second chances. Promise me."

I could get out of it. Nothing would change.

But I was sick of always taking gifts. I wanted to give one.

"I promise," I said.

He smiled. "I'm scared out of my mind right now."

"Don't be scared," I said. "I'm not scared. I *want* to have sex with you." I realized I just said that out loud. Was being able to say embarrassing things out loud part of getting drunk?

He stood up. "I love what you did with the candles."

"I got the idea from you," I said.

"I remember," he said gently. "Wait. Where the heck did you get bubbly? You little sneak thief." I giggled. He tugged at the bow on my head until it came loose. "You look so cute in my shirt."

"I don't want to look cute," I said. "I want to look sexy." I just said that out loud too.

He got the glasses, handing one to me. "To my sweet boy," he said.

"Bottoms up, kiddo," I said. I started gulping it down.

"Whoa there, tiger," he said, pulling my arm down. "We don't want you getting drunk."

I couldn't help it. I sprayed him with the champagne still in my mouth. Some drooled down my chin. Some felt like it came out my nose. An insane giggle fit took over. "What's gotten into you?" he asked, taking the glass away from me.

"It's so funny when you said drunk," I sputtered.

He put his arm around my shoulder. "It's ok if you're nervous."

"I'm not nervous," I said.

"Your face is as red as your hair." I burst out in another giggle fit. "Are you sure you're ok with this?"

"Stop asking me, I'm fine." He was being *soooo* annoying. "Let's get in bed. You should take off your clothes." I just said that out loud too. Being able to say embarrassing things had to be a part of getting drunk. Maybe it *was* working.

"Plenty of time for that." I lay down and he pressed against me, his hand rubbing my neck.

"That feels good," I said. I wasn't lying. It felt awesome. I let him rub me for a few minutes. "Am I supposed to do something?"

"Whatever feels comfortable," he said softly. "You don't have to do anything if you don't want."

"I want to have sex. Sex sex sex sex sex." I flopped my head back and forth each time I said it and broke out in another giggle fit. I didn't want to giggle so much. It was ruining the mood. I couldn't stop myself.

"It's ok if you're nervous," he said.

"It's taking a long time," I whined.

"I don't want to rush things. First times are special."

I rolled over. "It's special because it's with you." I was getting *really* good at saying things out loud.

"Sweetie," he said, breathing deep. He didn't try to hide the love look from me. He leaned forward and kissed me on the lips. One hand went up my leg, under my shirt. "Hmmm," he said when he figured out I wasn't wearing underwear.

"You *are* sexy," he whispered.

He started sucking on my neck. His hand was on my butt. I closed my eyes, feeling a little dizzy. Somehow, my shirt got unbuttoned. Somehow, he wound up in his underwear. Somehow, we got tangled up with each other, just like he described. And somehow, it felt nice. It felt good. *That* kind of good.

I realized my thing was hard.

My eyes opened. The world rushed in at me. That wasn't supposed to happen. This was *not* supposed to be about me. This was for him, only for him. I wasn't supposed to enjoy it. I was only supposed to get through it. I wasn't supposed to be like *that.*

His hand found my thing, touched it, wrapped around it. It felt good. No, great. No, incredible, awesome, amazing.

And *wrong.* It wasn't supposed to feel good. *Wrong wrong wrong wrong wrong!*

Before I knew what I was doing, I pushed him away from me and rolled in the other direction as hard as I could. I didn't realize how close I was to the edge of the bed until I fell off. I landed on my butt, stunned. He was right next to me a moment later. "Are you ok?" he asked. I looked around the room, dizzy. "Please, say something."

"I didn't mean to push you," I moaned.

"Shh," he said, pulling my shirt closed. "You're not ready."

"I am too ready!" I pulled my shirt back apart. "See, it's ready too. Hiya, hiya, hiya." I started giggling again.

He held my shirt closed. "No, you're not. This isn't right. We should stop."

"No, no, don't stop, I am, I promise, really. I don't know why I did that. I just got scared."

He put his finger on my lips. "Someday, maybe, but not today. Sweetie, it's ok. I'll wait. It doesn't matter how long it takes. A week, a month, a year, or a decade. If it doesn't come naturally, then it's not meant to happen."

Oh no, no no no no no no NO! I was so close!

My mind raced a million miles a minute. I had to do something. I was NOT going to give up. I had to find a way to make this work, no matter what. He'd never believe me again.

Out of nowhere I got an idea. Just all the other ideas, it hit me all at once. A terrifying, exciting, and *extremely* wrong idea. A twist I'd never thought about on the darkest things I'd ever imagined.

"I want you to make me," I blurted out.

"I'd never force you to do anything," he said softly.

"But I *want* you to. Listen to me. You always talk about how you don't want to make me do anything I don't want to do. I want to have sex with you. I really do. I don't know why I got scared. It felt nice, it felt good, and then all of a sudden. . .I don't know why I pushed you." He shook his head. "You told me to do what's comfortable. Being tied up is comfortable for me. I want you to tie me up. Then I want you to do your favorite thing. If you make me do it, I can't mess it up. This is *my* way of doing it."

"You don't know what you're saying," he said gently.

"I do know what I'm saying! I'm telling you to fuck me!"

"Nick!" he said, grabbing my shoulders. "That was never going to happen tonight. It's difficult. It'll hurt. A lot."

"I don't care if it hurts," I said. "I want it to hurt."

"I'm not doing this," he said. He stood up. He drank an entire glass of champagne and poured another.

"Not fair," I moaned. "Everything is always for me. Nothing is for you."

"That's how things are supposed to be," he said. "You're the child and I'm the adult."

217

"I'm not a little kid anymore," I said. "It's my life and my body. If I say I want to do this, why won't you believe me?" He didn't answer. "Didn't my poem mean anything to you?" I yelled.

He looked like I punched him. "How can you say that? It means everything to me! It touched me more deeply than you can imagine! It's the most wonderful gift I've ever received! I'd do anything for you. I'd die for you and I mean that. But please, don't ask me to hurt you."

"Don't you want to have sex with me?"

"Please," he said.

"Don't you?" I shouted.

"Not like this," he said.

"No!" I screamed. "Don't you want to have sex with me?"

He looked at the floor. "Yes," he said in voice that sounded like a little kid.

"Then do it! I'm asking you! I'm telling you! What do I have to do? Just tell me and I'll do it, anything you want, anything! I'm not doing this for you. I'm doing this for *me!* Making you happy makes me happy! Don't lie to me! I know doing it would make you happy! Let me make you happy, just let me!"

"Nick," he whispered.

"Do it for me," I moaned. "For me." He slid down the dresser and sat on the floor. "For *me.*"

"How do I know everything will be ok afterwards?" he asked, his head in his hands. "How do I know one slip won't ruin everything forever?"

"I won't let it. I'd never let anything bad happen."

"For you? Just for you? Not for me?"

"For me," I said.

He held my hand tight. "Ok. For you."

He was right all along. I should've listened to him. I had no idea what I was doing. The bottle was trying to tell me I shouldn't get drunk, but I didn't listen to it either.

I lay very still. I heard running water in the bathroom.

I didn't want to let myself hope it was over.

I wished I could forget. I wished all the champagne I drank could wipe it all away. I wished I'd wake up in the morning like it never happened. My wish wasn't going to come true. Every moment and every sensation was burned into my mind like it was carved in stone, permanent and forever. His hot breath in my ear, panting, moaning, and stinking like alcohol. The touching, licking, kissing, and sucking all over every single part of my body. How he touched and stroked and tugged on my thing until I went all the way. How heavy he felt when he was lying on top of me. How his chest hair felt like sandpaper on my back. How he spread goo on my butt to make it easier. How he poked around my butthole until he found the right place. How it felt like I was being stabbed when he pushed it inside me no matter how careful and gentle he tried to be. How he yelled when he finished.

I did this. I made sure I couldn't escape by telling him to chain me to the bed. I told him to tie a sock in my mouth in case I asked him to stop. I was the one who pleaded, begged, and convinced him to do this to me. There was no going back. No changing what happened. It was done and it would forever be something we did. I looked at the giant teddy bear in the corner. He wasn't friendly anymore. He witnessed everything. His eyes told me what a terrible thing I did. There was nothing I could tell him. I had no explanation.

Jeremy sat beside me. I buried my head in the pillow. He put a cold washcloth on my butt, gently wiping away the goo. Cleaning me up was pointless. I'd never be clean again.

"I'm so selfish," he said. "You're so open and so giving. You told me what you needed, but I was too scared. I failed you. I couldn't take the next step. Not because of what it would do to you, but what I thought it would do to me. I don't want to be selfish any more. I want to be like you. No matter how difficult it is for me, I'm going to do what you need me to do."

I didn't understand. I started to sweat. The handcuffs were biting into my wrists. I mumbled into the sock gag. I pulled at the chains but they didn't let me move.

I heard it first. A swish and a thud.

Then I felt it. A horrible sting on my butt.

Every muscle in my body seized up. My back arched and my head jerked back.

Another thud, another vicious sting.

I screamed.

Another, and another, and another, and another. I thrashed violently. I had to get free, even if I had to rip my arms from their sockets. Faster, and faster they came. I howled. I begged. I prayed. I yelled. On and on and on and on. He'd never stop. The pain would never stop.

Until it did. I realized he wasn't hitting me anymore. I couldn't move and couldn't think, terrified he was about to start again. I felt him unlocking my hands one at a time, then my feet. He put his hand on my head. I curled into a ball as tightly as I could.

"I'm here," he whispered. "Just like you said. 'When it hurts more than I can bear, you are there to comfort me, to hold me in your arms, to keep me safe.'"

I jerked up and threw my arms around him, squeezing, hanging on as hard as I could. I would never let him go. His eyes showed me how much he loved me. I hoped my eyes showed him the same thing.

Then it happened.

I felt one run down my left cheek.

Another one, on the right. I tasted it. Salty.

His mouth was open in amazement. "Sweetie, are you crying?"

It poured out of me. I shook, I moaned, and I wailed. I cried for being teased by other kids. I cried for my mother watching with her arms folded. I cried for my father screaming at me. I cried for being so lonely. I cried for being so weird. I cried for hating who I was. This didn't feel like crying felt a long time ago. It was clean. It made me feel free. Jeremy held me. He didn't shush me.

"Let it out," he said. "Just let it all out."

I put my head on his chest. The tears kept coming. He rocked me back and forth. He sang to me – no words, just humming. When the tears finally stopped and the shaking ended and I was quiet and I let my thumb find its way to my mouth, he still held me. I drifted off to sleep, and still he held me.

I wanted him to keep holding me until forever came.

James Edison

Part 3

James Edison

Chapter 18

October 14, 2006

hat the hell am I doing here?

W I tried to look casual, but my anxiety had to be completely obvious to anyone who glanced my way. I tried to let the steady hum of the idling engine soothe my nerves, but an annoying squeak kept interfering. It took a few moments to realize I was chewing on my thumb – an old habit that always chose the wrong moment to come crawling out of its hole. I buried my hand in my lap, hoping no one saw and then snorted at how self-conscious I was being. I was acting like a child.

This place made me feel like a child, and not in a good way.

Pinehurst was nothing short of breathtaking. Carefully manicured lawns, bronze statues, and red brick buildings with colonial windows – a scene straight out of any movie featuring an exclusive private school. The leaves were changing – the golden, maroon, and plum colors of autumn adorning carefully cultivated, stately hundred-year-old trees, planted in strategic locations around the campus by architects who had the foresight to realize the power of the impression they'd make someday. The campus was far more crowded than I expected on a Saturday night, likely due to the peak leaf weekend attracting hordes of visiting families despite the unseasonably cold weather. Small packs of teenagers deliberately under-dressed for the chilly evening zipped around randomly. Their conversations were so boisterous and grating when they passed that tightly locked doors and rolled up windows offered no protection. I had the distinct feeling they lingered to stare

through the windshield at me, their laughter at my expense. I should know better. I was long past the point of teenagers taking any notice of my existence. A quick glance classified me as "parent" and therefore unworthy of attention. I was also supposed to be long past the age where I felt intimidated at a school.

I looked at the clock, wondering where he was, tapping the gear shift with my fingers. We were going to be late if he didn't hurry. I checked the crudely drawn map for the third time – right turn past the wrought iron gates and around the circle to meet him in front of Decker Hall. Exactly where I was and apparently where he wasn't.

I assumed Jake liked Pinehurst. The best I could get out of him was "it doesn't suck" and a grunt. I would've liked it too, in a different part of my life. The history and tradition here had the power to make students feel they were a part of something important, something bigger than themselves. It would be nice if I felt like I belonged when I wrote the tuition check. A year at Pinehurst cost almost as much as my entire college education. I couldn't help noticing how the kids wore nicer clothes and drove more expensive cars than me. I was intruding on a private club comprised of CEO's and congressmen, security one step away from tossing me out the front gate in the most undignified manner they could muster. I wondered what my life would've become if I chose a fancy prep school when I had the chance. But that opportunity passed me by a long time ago. I pushed the would-have-beens away before they could hurt.

The sharp rapping on my windshield interrupted my daydream, a smiling face and gesticulating hands motioning for me to unlock the door. I fumbled with the controls, eventually finding the right one. He slid gracefully into the front seat.

"Hey, Nick," he said.

"Hey there, kiddo," I answered back. My heart fluttered.

I met Alex a week after school started.

Jake caught me off guard that afternoon. He could've called, but instead chose to spring it on me when he opened the car door during

pickup. No hello – just a phrase that wasn't formed as a question. "I invited a friend to come over and told him you could bring him back tonight." He ensured my compliance by having his friend stand next to him while he delivered my orders, making it awkward for me to counter with excuses why I didn't want to make the trek back.

"The least you could do is introduce me," I said. Jake didn't answer.

The other boy climbed into the car, sliding over to sit behind me. He was thin and gangly, all arms and legs, with a disheveled shock of jet-black hair to match the jet-black clothes. All that black made his face look pale, as though he spent the last month living in a cave. Or maybe it was makeup. Didn't that go with the territory? I decided he wasn't the kind of friend I wanted for Jake. The last thing I needed was for my son to become goth, or emo, or whatever the kids called it these days. Weren't they all suicidal?

"I'm Alex," he said in a husky but unbroken alto voice. He held out a thin, bony hand, his fingers long, delicate, and artistic, each one ending in a fingernail painted the same jet-black.

I took his limp hand and shook briskly. "Nick Welles." I waited for a thanks, or at least an acknowledgment of my existence, but introductions were apparently finished. They whipped out their phones and proceeded to peck away. I looked back at Jake expectantly, but his concentration was completely engaged with the tiny screen. His friend was doing the same. I might as well put on a chauffeur hat.

"Do you need to check out somewhere?" I asked Alex. He handed me an official looking card without looking up. Off campus pass, expiring at the end of September. Seemed good enough. We joined the impossibly long line snaking to the exit.

"Alex, what grade are you in?" I asked, deliberately intruding.

"Eighth," he answered brusquely.

"Is this your first year at Pinehurst?"

"No," he said. He chuckled.

"I missed the joke," I said with slight annoyance.

"It's nothing," Jake said quickly, stifling his own laugh.

"What are you guys doing back there, playing a game?"

"We're texting," Alex said. I glanced in the rearview mirror to see Jake elbowing Alex in the side. He flashed a playful look, then typed

something else. Jake burst into laughter. It was patently obvious the messages were about me. This had to be Alex's influence. I decided to dig a little deeper and see where it went. Maybe I could find some ammunition. A delicate operation, given that my disapproval would probably encourage Jake to become closer friends. I should tell Jake how much I like Alex. That would seal his fate.

"Where are you from?" I asked.

"A little town outside of Gettysburg, Pennsylvania. Central Podunk, USA."

"How do you like being a boarder? Do you miss home?"

"You're asking me seriously if I miss living in the ass crack of Pennsylvania? Definitely not. I love it here. Almost as much as they love their rules. It's the only thing I can't stand. Like being allowed to leave when I want. My parents practically went to war so I could get that off-campus pass. Only juniors and seniors get them."

"That worked?"

"Here I am!" he said dramatically, arms spread wide. "Free as a bird."

"Alex gets to leave school whenever he wants," Jake said, more than implying the expectation he should be able to do the same. When I didn't answer, he went right for the jugular. "His parents *trust* him." As though I didn't trust Jake.

Alex chimed in as though he sensed the conversation was about to escalate. "Suckers."

We all had an uncomfortable laugh. "What's your favorite subject?"

"What's with the third degree?" Jake muttered.

"I'm just making conversation," I said.

"None of them," he answered. A pause and more chuckling. "They don't teach the things a person really needs to know. Like how to roll a joint so the weed doesn't fall out." I looked back at them sharply. "That was a joke. You know, ha ha?"

"You should warn me next time," I grumbled.

"It's more fun when you don't see them coming," Alex said. More giggles. The texting hadn't ceased. "But if you want to know, I'm studying performing arts. Theater, acting, stand-up comedy – that sort of thing. All I want to do is *siiinnnngggg!*" He held the note for ten seconds, his voice strong and clear. The clothes made more sense now.

Drama department kid. That meant something at Pinehurst. The theater program was one of the best in the country.

"Not bad," I commented.

"Except I still can't decide between theater and astrophysics," he said thoughtfully. "You should come to my show. We're doing the Fantasticks for workshop next month."

"Sure," I said without meaning it.

"Next semester I'm going to take a production class and do the backstage work," Jake chimed in. "I volunteered for set construction for the winter musical too."

"You'll like being involved in theater," I said to Jake without considering my words. I caught a glimpse of him in the mirror, his face full of questions I wasn't expecting. I wasn't prepared to explain anything to him right now. I moved the conversation away. "What are you two planning to do today?"

"Hang out," Jake said quickly.

"I see." I nodded like I knew they were up to something. "I guess if you have nothing better to do, we'll have to find you guys a couple of girls."

Alex burst into laughter. Jake looked mortified.

"What did I say?"

"But Mr. Welles," Alex said between giggles, "I'm *gay*."

I barely kept from slamming into the car in front of us.

"Ventiupsidedownquadshothalfcafcaramelmacchiatolightwhip."

As though she understood, the girl behind the counter scratched a couple of notes on a cup and handed it off. Her expectant gaze settled on me. I looked at the menu board with an utter lack of comprehension. I avoided this place whenever I could. It was too complicated. Where was a copy of *Starbucks for Dummies* when I needed one?

"Large coffee," I stammered. They did have plain coffee, didn't they? She had mercy on me and didn't ask any more questions, making notes on another cup. Alex put a package of shortbread cookies on the

counter and took out his wallet. "I'll get this one," I told him, reaching for my own.

"No," he said, handing over a ten-dollar bill. "It's my thank you for taking me to the concert tonight."

"You don't have to do that," I said weakly, but I was too late. The change was returned – and very little of it. The girl thrust the coffee into my hands, her attention already turned to the next customer. I ducked out of the way, certain I'd screwed up an important part of the ritual and annoyed everyone else in line. Alex waited for his drink while I dumped sugar and cream into mine, snagging a pair of overstuffed armchairs in a corner. I watched him at the counter, standing on his toes, elbows folded in front of him. I'd never seen him dressed presentably, wearing an ordinary sweater and neatly pressed khakis. The new green streaks in his hair complemented his outfit well. I found myself staring a bit too long and forced myself to look away.

I wasn't supposed to be chaperoning this concert. Alex was the one who found the ad in the Post for a retrospective for some dead film composer playing at the Kennedy Center, but I was surprised when Jake was equally excited about a concert that didn't involve speakers the size of skyscrapers spewing incomprehensible noise. Swept up in their excitement, I bought them tickets online without bothering to check the calendar. It took a few days before I realized we were scheduled to visit Julia's mother in Raleigh. She didn't give me a hard time about slipping out, but she insisted on taking Jake to see his grandmother. Alex couldn't find anyone else who wanted the other ticket and asked if I'd go. I jumped on the opportunity without hesitation.

I was starving for any time I could get with Alex. Every time he came over the house, Jake always made sure I had no opportunity to ask my question. The question that plagued me from the moment I woke up in the morning to the moment I fell asleep each night. How could a boy whose voice hadn't changed be so sure of himself? I'm thirty-six years old, and I *still* haven't figured out if I'm gay or not. Alex had the answer I needed – the key to finding some resolution to the struggle I'd endured since I was a child myself. Since my time with *him*. Or perhaps I was just making excuses. After all, I was a master of

rationalization. Was understanding myself the real reason I was so desperate to find some time alone with him?

I'm not on a date with a thirteen-year-old boy.

"What is that?" I asked as he put his drink on the table.

"It's sweet," he said, sucking half of it down. "Yum."

I made small talk, unable to find a way to the question I needed to ask. "Any big plans for autumn break?"

"Nope, just hanging out at school."

"I heard the campus is a ghost town that week," I said.

"There's a few international kids, but otherwise it's dead. I've got no way to get home, so I'm stuck here. Not that I want to go home. I'd be bored out of my skull. Besides, my parents are in Africa."

"On safari?" I joked.

"Probably handing out stolen AIDS drugs," he said. "That's what they did last time they went."

"I didn't know your parents are doctors."

"Not even close. They're professional protestors, do-gooders, and revolutionaries. They find something wrong with the world and off they go. Hunger, Iraq, global warming, land mines, the death penalty, rainforests, poverty, injustice, racism – they're into all of it. They missed the memo that the sixties are over, going on about free love and wearing tie-dye shirts. They want me to be a lawyer so I can destroy the system from the inside, but I can't imagine being a lawyer. I want to follow my own dreams, not theirs."

"To be a big star?" I asked.

"I'm not interested in being famous." His voice dropped, making him sound older than he was. "I love to perform. I like singing, acting, telling jokes, juggling, mime – well not mime – but you get the idea. That's why I picked Pinehurst over the other schools that recruited me. Sometimes, I wonder if I should be doing something to directly help the world, like my parents do. Then, I think if I can make people question the injustice around them and make them happy at the same time, all while loving what I'm doing, I'm making the right choice for me and for the world."

"How do you do it?" I blurted out. "How can you be so sure about yourself?"

"What makes you think I'm sure of myself?" he asked.

"You know what you are and what you want. I wish I had as much self-awareness at your age. My life would've been very different. Don't sell yourself short. You're an incredible person, and no matter what you choose to do, I'm sure you'll change the world." He'd probably heard praise like mine a million times before, but his expression said otherwise. I wanted to put my arm around his shoulder, give him a hug, and show him just how special I thought he was.

"We'd better get going," I said abruptly, staring at my watch.

I followed a safe distance behind him as we left.

<p style="text-align:center">❦</p>

Jake said nothing about Alex for a week and a half after our first encounter. I became worried he was a one-hit wonder or a particularly lucid dream. I couldn't ask Jake what happened. He'd think I was prying, and I might betray my intense need to see Alex again.

I knew I was being ridiculous. I'd spent no more than ten minutes talking with the boy. I barely knew anything about him, and still he filled every waking thought. I couldn't concentrate on television, couldn't sleep at night, and couldn't close my eyes without picturing his face. After he announced he was *gay*, I couldn't put together a coherent thought of my own for the rest of the ride home. They vanished into Jake's room when we got home, blaring music to cover up whatever secrets were being shared. They had headphones jammed in their ears for the ride back, shutting down any possibility of conversation. I hadn't felt anything this powerful since I was a teenager myself.

*I am **not** having a crush on a thirteen-year old boy.*

Then, out of nowhere, Jake asked me if Alex could spend the night. Jake was staying late to help with Alex's play and some mom would bring them home afterwards. I nearly jumped up and down after I hung up. I spent the rest of the afternoon cleaning the house top to bottom. By the time they spilled out of the car I was bouncing off the walls with adrenaline.

"Hey, Mr. Welles," he said. His sweet voice was musical even when he wasn't singing.

"Nick," I said. "Mr. Welles is my father." What a stupid thing to say. Why did I imitate the turtle? Jake rolled his eyes. Alex smiled. "You guys hungry?"

"Nope, they brought in dinner," Jake said. So much for my plan to trap them in a restaurant. They went to the kitchen table instead of disappearing upstairs, so I drifted over. The two of them placed white and black glass beads randomly on a folding board.

"What are you playing?" I asked.

"It's called go," Jake said, not looking up.

I couldn't believe he dismissed me like that. "There's no need to be rude," I snapped.

"No, the *game* is called Go," Alex giggled. Jake glared at me. "It's Japanese. At least, I think it's Japanese. Maybe it's Chinese, I don't know. I saw it in an anime. You can watch if you want." I moved in closer. "The idea is to capture more territory. You play on the intersections and form groups, and if you get surrounded your stones become prisoners. The rules are simple, but the strategy is complex. Expert players are skilled at finding patterns and reading moves far ahead. Computers can beat people at chess, but they can't beat an amateur at Go. They could probably beat me, though. I play online and I always get my butt whipped."

That brought up entirely the wrong image.

I didn't care about the game. I pulled up a chair so I could watch Alex. His long fingers were sensitive and graceful when he placed a bead on the board. He had a deadly serious look in his eyes when he concentrated, but the faint smile never evaporated from his face. His movement was a mixture of a trained actor's awareness of his body in space coupled with the lanky awkwardness of a young teenager. It made him adorable. Alex was generous in his game, pointing out mistakes Jake made while accepting his own and magnanimous in his victory when they counted at the end. Jake seemed thoroughly puzzled and frustrated at his loss.

Alex stretched his arms, his t-shirt riding up a little, stifling a yawn. "I'm gonna catch a shower," he said, heading upstairs with his small duffel bag. My eyes were fixed on him until Jake dumped the beads noisily off the board, scattering them over the table and floor. I held my

233

snide comment and helped him gather them up. The last thing I wanted was to start a fight that might impact my ability to see Alex again.

"How did you meet Alex?" I asked. "Is he in your classes?"

"No," he said abruptly. "I met him in the theater when I went to find out about volunteering." When he didn't elaborate, I had the impression there was more to the story. Prying ran the risk of derailing my strategy, so I didn't press. Who was I kidding? I didn't have a coherent strategy. We focused on putting the game away. He was under the table picking up stray beads when he spoke.

"I don't know why he wants to be friends with me."

His vulnerability shocked me. "Why would you say that?"

"He's at Pinehurst on a special scholarship that pays for everything, even his food and clothes. He's the only person in the world ever given that scholarship for middle school. I think he's supposed to graduate two years early and I heard he already has acceptances to some top colleges. He's smart and he's good at everything – games, sports, singing, music, painting – anything he wants to do. He's funny, popular, and everyone likes him." Jake put the pile of beads on the table and swirled his finger through them. "Why would someone like that want to be friends with me?" He avoided looking up.

"I don't think it's a big mystery," I said. "People like Alex are always under pressure because everyone expects them to be smart and funny all the time. It can be overwhelming. Sometimes, the kind of friend they need is someone who can be a friend without putting expectations on them. Maybe he wants to be himself and you let him. True friends like that are hard to find."

He wasn't looking at me, but I could feel his need to open up radiating out. If I nudged him, it would all come pouring out. The real reason he was friends with Alex. Maybe even his thoughts about the box I left outside his door. But I didn't. Couldn't. He closed down quickly, unable to start sharing on his own.

"I'm going to my room," he announced suddenly, leaving the game on the table and taking the steps two at a time. A letter and a box of equipment wasn't going to undo the years of hurt and distance I deliberately created to keep him safe from what I could do. From what

I almost *did*. Opportunities to fix my relationships had a way of getting away from me. I always waited too long.

I had to stop myself with Alex before I left him permanently devastated.

But I couldn't. Wouldn't.

"That was an amazing concert," Alex said as we made our way through the crowds at the theater. "The saxophone concerto was unique. At first, I thought using a sax wasn't the right choice for his harmonic structure. Saxophones are too whiny for classic tonal harmonies. But it grew on me and I liked it by the end. They selected his best film scores. I prefer modern film scores to formal classical music. Orchestral film music is obvious in its emotional manipulation where classical music tends to be subtle and more restrained. Film scores bash you over the head until you get the message."

"I enjoyed it too," I said with complete sincerity. It'd been a long time since I went to a concert of any kind, especially one that featured an orchestra. Music in general was something I tried to avoid, preferring the monotony of talking heads or some modern pop crap I could tune out when I was in the car. Classical music brought back memories and feelings I wanted to forget. I didn't want to be reminded about a time when music meant so much more to me. I expected tonight to be a sacrifice I was willing to make for the chance to spend time with Alex. Unexpectedly, the music didn't dredge up the past. I found myself too enamored with the boy sitting next to me to think about *him*. I was fascinated by how Alex was physically moved by the music, humming quietly along, his body swaying in time to the rhythm. His hand hung by his side as we walked. I had to fight my desire to hold it.

"I'm hungry," he said as we got into the car. "I missed dinner tonight."

"We could get a pizza if you want," I offered. "When is curfew?"

"They lock the doors at midnight."

"Doesn't leave us enough time," I said, looking at my watch. "We're barely going to make it without a stop."

"I'll be ok," he said.

I said it before I could stop myself. "Why don't you spend the night at the house instead?" *What am I doing?*

"I wouldn't want to impose or anything."

"It's no trouble at all. We can swing by school to sign you out, get your stuff, and pick up something to eat."

"That's very nice of you, thanks," he said, genuinely appreciative. "I'll get my guitar since you said you wanted to hear me play. Staying with you guys would be a lot more comfortable. I hate the dorms, especially when no one is around."

"If you like, you're welcome to stay with us for the week," I said, trembling. "I'm sure Jake wouldn't mind having a friend around and we don't have anything planned. We have a spare bedroom where you can camp out."

"You wouldn't mind?"

"Not in the slightest."

"I promise, I won't be a pest," he said.

He could pester me all he wanted. "A pest? Please."

"Don't you have to work?"

"I'm on an extended leave of absence," I explained. *Very* extended. I had no intention of going back to work anytime soon. We weren't in danger of running out of money – between our savings, the vast equity in the house, and Julia's income I didn't need to worry about getting a job until sometime next year. I went through the motions of searching to satisfy the unemployment requirements, sending resumes to jobs where I had no hope of qualifying. I was so stunned when one of them called that I told them I'd already accepted something else. Who'd want to hire me, anyway? "I'm free to shuttle you guys around. King's Dominion is still open on the weekends, and if you like camping, Shenandoah is great this time of year."

"I'll be happy as long as I can avoid the dorm," he said. "They're so strict about everything. I'll never understand why the administration has to impose rules if what I do doesn't bother anyone."

"Did you get in trouble for something?"

"All I did was walk naked from the shower to my room. I'm just being practical – there's nowhere in the bathroom to put clothes so they

stay dry. It's not as though any girls were around. The dean told me it made other kids nervous, but I think the proctors were the only ones who were uncomfortable. They should get over themselves. It's just a body – it's not like I was jumping everyone's bones in the hallway. Being naked is no big deal at home. I used to see my parents, brothers, and sisters all the time and no one cared."

I searched around for a delicate way to ask, but there wasn't one. "Do you think it's because. . ." I couldn't say the word out loud.

"Because I'm gay? Probably. That's why I have a single room. No one gets a room to themselves, ever, not even seniors. No one except the openly gay kids. It makes sense in a perverted way. A straight kid would get weird about it, and two gay kids would fuck like rabbits."

"Seems like an unfair stereotype," I stammered, trying to banish the image from my mind.

"It's completely fair. I'd definitely fuck my roommate five times a day." He smirked. "That was another joke."

"I told you, I needed fair warning before you let those fly."

"And I told you it's more fun this way," he teased.

"Do you take a lot of crap?"

"Not much. Some teachers look at me funny, and every now and then a closet case tries to hide his own insecurities by picking on me. You know, the boy scout types who jerk each other off in their tents. But they're the exception. Being gay is considered cool by most everyone."

"You let another one fly without warning."

"No, seriously. Half the members of Galyap aren't gay. They hang out with us because we're the in crowd."

"Galyap?"

"Our campus club. Gay and Lesbian Youth at Pinehurst. We should change the name because it doesn't include transgender and questioning like most gay straight alliance clubs, but it's been around for so long no one wants to fix it."

I couldn't process the concept. "The school allows you to have an official club?"

"Sure. We have faculty advisors, meeting rooms, and we host a dance every semester. I only considered schools that have clubs or support

groups, but Pinehurst takes it to another level. They don't just welcome openly gay students, they go out of their way to recruit us. That's probably why there are three Summit scholars besides me." He noticed my confused look. "My parents could never afford a place like Pinehurst – they don't have squat in the bank. One of the requirements for Summit scholarships is to be openly gay. The foundation mostly gives out scholarships for college students. They don't publicize that they do the same thing for high school. Political shit."

"Jake mentioned something about you being the only recipient."

"For middle school. I don't talk about it much. I don't like to brag."

I searched for another angle. "How about your parents, are they understanding?"

"Understanding? They're proud." I couldn't help coughing. "I turned twelve the week before I came out to them. They didn't throw me a birthday party, but they put together a huge coming-out shindig. Another cause for them to fight. It wasn't a surprise to them because everyone knew I was gay since I was a little kid. Not that I was playing with Barbie dolls and putting on frilly pink tutus – I'm not that kind of gay. I was the kid who sang along at the top of my lungs to the Sound of Music when I was seven. If that doesn't tell you a kid is gay, nothing will. Every time I talk to my parents they ask if I have a boyfriend and tell me to use condoms."

"I can't believe how much things have changed since I was a kid. From watching the news, I'd never even know it was like this now."

"Things are changing. When I'm an adult, the fight over gay marriage and equal rights will be over. My generation is a lot more tolerant and open. But it won't happen on its own. We have to get out there and fight."

"I'm amazed. Supportive schools, parents, campus clubs, scholarships, it sounds like everything is going perfectly for you."

He was silent for a moment. "That's one way of looking at it."

A chink in his armor. A vulnerability I could latch onto. "What do you mean?"

He took a deep breath. "My family is seriously fucked up. My parents believe that kids should raise themselves. They think we'll become responsible and caring people by finding our own way. I can tell you

from personal experience that their philosophy of child rearing doesn't work. My oldest brother is in jail for stealing stuff and my next oldest grows weed for a living. Both my sisters are strung out on drugs. At least my oldest sister is going to community college now, but the younger one got pregnant at fifteen and is pregnant again. Her first baby is kind of messed up from the drugs. My brother who's only a year older than me ran away from home. No one knows where he is. I worry about him a lot. I'm number six, the baby. I don't want to turn out like the rest of my family. When I go to parties, I'm scared to have a drink because I'm convinced I'll turn into one of them. I feel like I'm fighting all the time."

"You're far too smart to be sucked down that hole," I told him. "Besides, you're away from them now and can follow your own path. You're not doomed to follow in their footsteps."

He smiled. "It's easy to talk to you."

I felt a warm glow inside. "Thanks."

I listened to the sound of water running through the upstairs pipes, waiting for Alex to finish his shower. The remnants of a pizza littered the coffee table. A battered guitar case covered with stickers, like all battered guitar cases were supposed to be, sat across the room from me. I was unable to stop imagining him, water running down his body and bending over to pick up the soap. Hoping he would consider my home no different than his dorm, unafraid to walk naked down the stairs.

I growled out loud, forcing myself up and pacing across the family room again. I had to be nuts. Having any boy alone in the house with me was crazy, dangerous, and insane. Having *this* boy alone in the house with me was far worse. He was irresistible – talking so easily about boy scouts jerking each other off, his parents insisting he use condoms, and getting it on with his roommate. Being gay made him *available*. His openness about sex made him seem *willing*. I plotted a hundred ways to get him into bed and dismissed each one quickly out of fear and disgust. I was such a hypocrite, telling Alex he wasn't doomed to follow in his family's footsteps. I turned out exactly like my father. I turned out

like *him*. Jeremy did this to me. *He* turned me into a pedophile. Chester the Molester.

Alex said it's easy to talk to me. Of course it's easy to talk to me – I learned that skill from a master. I know the things to say, the ways to act, and how to find the path to his heart. I intuitively knew how to manipulate him with such expertise that even a boy as intelligent and aware as him would never see it coming, even if I never consciously devised a plan. I tried to convince myself I was pursuing him because I craved companionship and friendship, or a way to recapture myself at his age to undo the hurts I suffered. But I knew I was lying to myself. My interest in him was nothing more than raw lust under a blanket of excuses. I was weakening. I could feel it with every passing minute. Rationalizations were battering the walls of my mantras. Denial had a way of building up. I kept reminding myself what it would do to him. What it did to me.

I needed a drink.

But I knew exactly what could happen when people started drinking.

I held my breath when he came downstairs, relieved he was wearing a t-shirt and boxers, and disappointed he was wearing a t-shirt and boxers. I pretended to be eager to hear him play. His guitar was as battered as the case. "It used to be my mom's," he explained while he tuned it.

I once saw a movie where a man learned how to travel in time but got yanked back by a penny. It felt that way in reverse when he started to play a tune I hadn't heard since my days with *him*. I was dragged back into memories so vivid I was convinced they happened yesterday. Being nestled in my sleeping bag by the fireplace in the den. The smell of cocoa. Jeremy sitting on the hearth, strumming his guitar and singing. He changed the words for me, singing about my red hair instead of hers.

In my memory, I couldn't see the demon I knew *he* was. I only saw a perfect moment. I remembered how cozy I felt, how happy I was, how much I loved him, and how much I knew he loved me. I couldn't stop myself from singing along to Alex's clean, pure voice.

"Hey, you know it," Alex said as he continued to strum.

"Bob Dylan," I mumbled.

"I didn't know it was Dylan. I heard it on an Indigo Girls album. I guess they did a cover."

Alex kept playing and I sang along with him. My mind muddled until I was unable to distinguish who was the child and who was the adult, or whether this was happening now or was some memory of many years ago. I was lost in the feeling of being *home* in a way I hadn't known since my time with Jeremy. I didn't want it to end. Without choosing to do so, I forgot the sorrow, the guilt, and the pain. The only thing left inside me was a child clinging to a giant teddy bear.

Why did you leave me? I still need you.

"Are you ok?" he asked me when I choked up.

His eyes met mine, and in that moment the battle was over. I didn't have the strength to withstand this onslaught. Maybe not tonight and maybe not next month, but eventually the moment would be right. I wouldn't be able to stop myself. With Alex, it wouldn't be the way I remembered it all these years. Sex would be something beautiful. Something special. Something *right*. Something *true*.

Run, kid. Run away before it's too late.

Chapter 19

June 14, 1982

When I was little, I thought it was called growing up because kids got taller. As I got older, I realized it was about growing in other ways too. Every year, I got stronger, smarter, and faster. Every year, I was allowed to ride my bike farther, stay home alone longer, and do more things on my own. Every time I was given new privileges, I was proud of my achievement and looking forward to getting more. For months, I hated being in elementary school. True, the power that came with being the biggest and oldest was nice. We were sixth graders – the kings of the blacktop and lords of the lunch line. But the hallways were closing in. The artwork hanging outside the rooms seemed childish. The rules were ridiculous. Twelve-year-olds didn't belong at a school where walking silently from room to room was the most important thing ever. We deserved more respect. We'd *earned* more respect. Elementary school held us back, stopped us from growing, and kept us little.

I sat by the corner of the school, the very edge of sixth grade territory. On the other side of the wall, the first and second graders played on their tire playground, threw kickballs, and pumped as hard as they could on the swing to make it wrap around the top bar. They laughed, ran, and didn't seem to care about anything. Watching them reminded me of one of my kindergartens. I used to take naps on my favorite orange mat. We built a fort out of paper towel rolls, wore medals to say where we were playing, and sang songs about blow-up

cartoon characters to teach us the alphabet. I still remembered Mr. M and his munching mouth.

I started counting how long it was until the end of elementary school when 107 days were left. I checked with a calendar to be sure. Every day, I crossed the number out in my notebook and wrote the new one. It seemed like it was going to take forever to get to zero. Now, here I was, on the zeroth day. Instead of celebrating, I wanted to roll back the numbers as far as I could. I felt like I was losing something, which is not what growing up was supposed to be about. I almost ran back into the woods this morning so they'd mark me absent and make me do the year over.

I wiped my forehead on my sleeve, but all that did was spread the sweat around because my sleeve was sopping wet. Jeremy told me the sun would be set on flambé today, but I still wore long sleeves buttoned around my wrists and long pants with my socks pulled up. I had no choice. If anyone saw the deep red marks on my wrists and ankles, they might figure out what they were from and then figure out what I did to get them.

I thought I should be proud. I went all the way. I *fucked*. I should be bragging to anyone who would listen. Instead, I wanted to sing songs about Mr. M and nap on my orange mat. I thought about the time I mixed all my Lego sets together. My plan was to build something big and interesting, but I couldn't think of anything worth building. When I tried to put the sets back together, it took me ten minutes to find the first piece. I wound up pushing all the Legos under the bed, where they stayed until we moved. I felt like the mess under the bed. I'd never be able to sort out all the pieces inside me.

"Are you listening?" Brian said.

I forgot he was sitting next to me. "Uh huh," I said. He was trying to push a wrinkled piece of notebook paper into my hand.

"I was saying that I made some changes, because doing the vowels was too hard the other way. Throw away the old version and learn this one instead." He pointed to the paper. "Here are the Elvish letters and the sounds for each one. Don't copy the letters. You have to sound out the word and then spell how it sounds. Sometimes words will come out with less letters, sometimes with more. Although if we do it by sound

then the vowels might get confusing, so just use the same ones from the English words." He scratched his head. "Except if more than one makes the sound, then just use the sound. I'll have to think about it. Learn it before we leave on Thursday."

"Ok," I said. I didn't understand anything he said.

"I'm glad you're coming," he said.

"Me too." Jeremy had talked Brian's dad into letting us drive Brian to his grandfather's cabin in Maine so I could visit. Jeremy said it was easy because Brian's dad was a cheapskate about the gas and didn't want to take off from work anyway. Brian was even allowed to sleep over the night before.

I hoped I still knew how to do all the things we talked about doing.

I decided to pretend I didn't see Jeremy when he pulled up in front of the school. I had no idea why. I watched his car inch up for ten minutes while wishing the line would go faster, but when he got to the front I waited until he honked before getting in the car. I had to squeeze my feet around the picnic basket.

"I thought we could have a picnic since you're out early," he said.

"I figured that out from the basket," I said, looking out my window.

"Let's go up to that rock we found with the view. That was a nice place."

I glared at him. "I don't want to talk."

"Who said anything about talking?"

"Why else would you want to go all the way up there?"

He didn't say anything, driving away from the school. I managed to avoid talking to him all weekend because I was sick. I woke up on Saturday morning with the worst headache I ever had. I couldn't stop drinking water because I was so thirsty from all the sweating I did. Then I threw up. I felt sick to my stomach most of the day and then I caught a cold after that.

"Don't you think we should talk?" he said quietly.

"All you ever want to do is talk." I kicked the basket. "Every time something happens you want to talk about it. Why can't you leave me alone?"

Jeremy's eyes were on the road. He held the steering wheel tight. "I found the bottle under the bed," he said. I felt like I was going to throw up again. I forgot to throw it away. "I can't believe I didn't notice you were hammered. Maybe I didn't because I was three sheets to the wind myself. Maybe I didn't want to see. The headache, vomiting, guzzling water like you were lost in the Sahara for a week, and your behavior that night – what else could it be? I told myself I only let you have one glass. I told myself it wouldn't be like you to sneak liquor. I should've checked the cabinet. You drank a whole bottle." He slammed the steering wheel and I jumped. "What were you thinking? Don't you realize what could've happened to you? People die from drinking too much! They go to sleep and never wake up!"

"I didn't know," I mumbled.

"You must be upset, scared, angry, and who knows how many other things right now. I can't ignore it anymore. I can't wait for it to happen at your pace. You don't have to say anything. I guess you don't even have to listen. I've got to get some things off my chest before I explode." I thought he was going to start, but he shoved in a tape and turned the radio up loud.

I didn't want to talk because I didn't know what I wanted to say, not because I didn't want to talk to him. The Lego pieces inside me were still mixed up. He would want to talk about what happened, but that would make it more real. I knew it happened, but if we never talked about it out loud it was easier to pretend. I wasn't angry at him. I just wanted to be angry at something and he was the only person around. Maybe drinking all that champagne messed up my brain. Maybe it wasn't done messing me up yet. Maybe my brain was turning to goo. Soon I'd forget my name, then I'd forget how to talk, and then I'd go to sleep and never wake up. I knew I had to say something to save myself, but I felt paralyzed.

I was thinking about what color my coffin would be when he pulled over on the side of the road near the rock. He got out and opened my door when I didn't move. I banged my head on the top of the car on

my way out and almost fell on my face. Proof that I was close to death. He set up the food, just some regular bread and sandwich meat from the grocery store. Like he threw it together without thinking. He always made the best picnics, so it scared me. I didn't feel like eating. He didn't make a sandwich for himself either. Only the ants were hungry.

He pulled up his knees and wrapped his arms around them, looking more like a kid than a grown-up. I pulled grass out of cracks in the rock, feeling bad about it afterwards. The poor grass was trying to find a place to live and I came along and killed it for no reason. I rolled up my sleeves and touched the marks on my wrists. He wasn't looking at me, so I took some bread and made dough balls, throwing them at the back of his head. I wasn't sure why I did that. He ignored me.

"Wow, this is the most fun I've ever had," I said.

"Time of my life too, kiddo," he answered.

"You were the one who wanted to talk before you exploded."

He stared off at the valley. "I don't know where to start."

"You had no problem starting in the car."

He turned around, his eyes red. "Do you hate me?"

"Don't you understand anything?" I muttered.

"Help me understand," he said. "Are you angry, ashamed, or confused? I can't figure out what's going on in your head. I can't figure out why you drank an entire bottle. I'm terrified that I'm losing you. Look at what I did to you. Look at the marks on your wrists. I made you cry. I've never seen you cry before. God, I'm so sorry."

I didn't say anything.

"I made a huge mistake. Maybe if I wasn't so drunk I might've noticed you were drunk. Maybe I could've stopped it. But it's too late and we can't take it back. I don't know about you, but I think pretending it never happened isn't going to work."

I still didn't say anything.

"I'm not making excuses," he said. "I want you to understand how difficult it is being someone like me. No one is more universally hated than. . ." He lowered his voice. "Than a pedophile. There's no one for miles around and I can barely say that word out loud. I wish I knew what I did in a past life to earn such bad karma. This isn't the kind of life anyone should have to lead. I keep everything about me wrapped

in a layer of lies. Gays have their bars, the Castro, and a whole society. What do I have? Revealing what I am would ruin my life. There are freaks who join societies and subscribe to newsletters, but they're painting a target on themselves. It's only a matter of time before they're arrested or attacked by a vigilante. It's turning into a witch hunt. I heard about crazy accusations being made in California – some ridiculous thing about preschool teachers practicing satanic abuse with toddlers. People gobble it up anyway. I wish I had somewhere I could go like a club, a support group, or a twelve-step program. Maybe I wouldn't have screwed up if I had somewhere to talk to other people going through the same thing. Maybe I would've found the strength to keep our relationship pure. Could you imagine if there was a place I. . .no, a place *we* could go to be with other couples knowing they have the same problems? I hate having to keep our relationship a secret. I want to scream out to the whole world how much I love Nick Welles." He looked at me. "Please say something. Don't shut down on me."

"You wouldn't really tell anyone, would you?" I said.

"God, no," he said. "That would be the end of everything. I never want us to end."

"I don't want to break up," I said.

He blinked. "Neither do I."

"So, ok," I said.

"I promise you I'll never, ever cross that line again."

I wanted to tell him he was making me angry taking all the responsibility. I wrote the poem. I put on his shirt and nothing else. I got drunk. I asked to be tied up. I screamed at him until he gave in. Nothing would've happened if I didn't make it happen.

But I couldn't say all that out loud. Saying things was a lot harder when I wasn't drunk. I shrugged.

"I won't let you down again," he said. "My life is in your hands."

I didn't know what he meant about his life being in my hands. "Ok."

"Can I have a hug?"

I got up and gave him one, glad our talk was over.

"Can we go home now?" I asked.

We didn't talk during the car ride back. I wasn't in the mood to talk. I didn't know what I was in the mood to do. There was nothing I wanted to do but I wanted to do something. I wanted to be alone and I wanted to be with Jeremy at the same time. When I felt like being with him, I'd go downstairs and lean against him while he read on the couch. Then I'd feel like being alone a few minutes later and go back upstairs. I wondered what he thought about my behavior, but I didn't want to ask him. I didn't know what I'd say if he asked me. He never did. He put his arm around me when I sat down and let me go when I was ready to leave again.

The idea came to me later, when he was watching TV.

"Let's build a couch fort," I said when I came downstairs. "You know, when you take the pillows off the couch and make a tunnel with the table."

"I know what a couch fort is," he said. "Sounds like fun."

We pulled the coffee table in closer and lined up the pillows. "Did you make couch forts when you were a kid?" I asked.

"Every kid with a couch makes couch forts," he said. "I used to make really elaborate ones with blankets that went between chairs and the couch. My brother would wait until I finished before he destroyed them, always when I was inside."

"I only made one," I said. "My dad got so mad at me I never tried again." We got blankets from upstairs and hung them over the ends for entrances. Jeremy made a gap in the pillows so we could stick our heads up, surrounding it with the small pillows from the couch. He put another blanket over the top so it was like a bunker. I thought that was a pretty cool idea.

Jeremy got the sleeping bags and I dragged the giant bear out of our bedroom. He was too big to fit inside, so he became the guard at the entrance to make sure no one could invade. I turned out the lights and we crawled inside.

"This used to be a lot easier," he said as he squirmed, trying very hard not to mess up the fort. He grunted when he finally got to his sleeping bag. Our pillows were next to each other. I lay on my back,

shining the flashlight around to make sure everything was still intact and secure.

"All clear?" I yelled to the guard bear. I waited for a few seconds. "He said it was all clear," I told Jeremy.

"That's good," Jeremy answered. "The squirrel army has been itching to get a hold of our nuts." I burst out laughing. "No, no, I didn't mean it that way, you know, squirrels like nuts and. . .For crying out loud!"

I made the flashlight dance around the fort, then I pointed it towards him like it was a microphone. "What's your favorite color?"

"I thought you knew I like green."

"What's your favorite piece of music?"

"I thought you knew that too. I don't have one favorite because I like a lot of different pieces in different ways. Why are you asking me?"

"I don't know," I said. "Do you have a girlfriend?"

"Well, not exactly," he said, finally playing along. "I have a boyfriend."

"What's his name?"

"His name is Nick," he said. "He's the most incredible, sweet, loving, smart, and amazing person I've ever known."

"Sounds like a dork," I said.

"If that's what it means to be a dork, I want to be one too."

"What kinds of things do you do with him?"

"We do a lot of things," he said. "I teach him to play piano. Sometimes we go out to concerts and fancy dinners. He likes a game called Dungeons and Dragons but I'm terrible at it. One time he made me take him fishing even though I hate boats." I giggled. "Sometimes we sit on the couch and snuggle."

"That sounds boring," I said.

"Try it sometime, you might like it."

"What are you going to do this summer?" I asked.

"I don't know," he said. "We're going to visit his friend in Maine but after that we haven't made plans."

"I think you guys should have more fun. You have the whole summer so you should do something big. Like going to all the amusement parks in the country and riding the biggest roller coasters

over and over again until you throw up. Or going camping somewhere far away in the mountains where there's snow all year. Or you could go to England to see real castles and eat fish and chips."

"We could get a hotel in New York and live like city rats, going to museums and eating cheesecake at four in the morning," he said. "Or how about California to see the redwoods and Yosemite? Maybe Alaska to see the glaciers. Or Hawaii so we could see the volcanoes erupt. We could even go to Japan and eat raw fish."

"Now you're being gross," I said.

"I think you're right. I should do more fun things with my boyfriend. I think sometimes we get so wrapped up in life that we forget to have fun."

I turned out the flashlight. "Do you love your boyfriend?"

He was quiet for a moment. "So much it hurts."

I wrinkled my nose. "That doesn't sound nice."

"Not true at all. It's the nicest thing in the world."

"I don't know," I said. "I want to learn more about this snuggling thing you talked about. Can you show me how?"

"Might be a little tricky in here," he said.

"Nah, piece of cake," I said. I managed to turn around so my feet were by his head. He pushed himself against the couch and I slid down so my back was against his stomach. He wrapped his arms around me. "This is snuggling? I was right. It seems boring."

"Give it a chance."

Even though we were jammed together, I pressed in as tight as I could go.

"This reminds me of being under my bed when I was little," Jeremy said in a small voice. "It was my favorite place to go when I was scared. I had a special bunny rabbit I kept under there. The poor thing lived its entire life in darkness. I remember thinking that was ok because rabbits lived in holes, so the bed was his hole. For the life of me, I can't remember what he looked like. I don't think I ever saw him in the light. The only thing I remember about him is how he tasted." I giggled. "I liked chewing on him. I couldn't have been more than four or five years old. He had a sweet and salty kind of taste that I've never found anywhere else. Not that I chew on stuffed animals regularly."

"Don't start chewing on me," I said.

"I might. Maybe you taste like bunny."

I held his hand.

"I have a boyfriend too," I said.

"Really? What's his name?"

"His name is Jeremy. His favorite color is green, he doesn't have a favorite piece of music, he hates boats, he stinks at playing Dungeons and Dragons, and he likes to snuggle. And I really, really love him."

"That sounds wonderful," he said softly.

"Can you tell him something for me?"

"Of course."

"Can you tell him I'm not mad at him? Something happened and he thinks I'm angry, but I'm not. I don't want him to think I hate him or I'm scared of him or anything like that. Just tell him his boyfriend is still his boyfriend and will be his boyfriend until forever comes."

"I will," he said.

"I think I like snuggling. Tell him that too."

We stayed there all night.

Chapter 20

June 28, 1982

B rian shouted from the bottom of the stairs. "Are you ready yet?"
"Almost!" I shouted back. I was ready five minutes ago but
I couldn't stop staring in the mirror. I could hardly believe the
person staring back was me. Nicholas Owen Welles, the unremarkable
son of Jack and Eleanor from the puny fiefdom of Newton Falls, was
gone. I was Aragorn, son of Arathorn, Elessar, heir to the throne of
Gondor. I was Legolas. I was Boromir. I was Gimli. I was Samwise
Gamgee. I was everyone I'd ever wanted to be.

I made sure to learn the correct names for the clothes I was wearing.
The pants were called breeches, buttoned just below my knee. I wore
a gambeson on top, which was something like a layered sweatshirt with
padding. I needed the gambeson for the chainmail armor. *Real* armor –
a long shirt called a hauberk that went almost to my knees, made from
riveted steel rings. It weighed a *ton*. A wide belt around my waist held
everything I needed. A real metal sword (not sharp) hung in a leather
scabbard. A dagger (sharp) hung in another scabbard. A pouch to hold
my coins and jewels (D&D dice) on one side. A leather mug to hold
my ale and mead (water and lemonade) on the other side. Knee high
leather boots, studded gauntlets on my arms, and a heavy hooded cloak
with a jeweled brooch made the outfit complete. Everything was too
big because it was meant for adults, but I didn't care.

I mopped my head with a towel and hung it on the back of my belt
under the cloak so it couldn't be seen. It was way too hot to be dressed
up like this, but there was no way I was going to take a single thing off.

253

I grabbed the staff I'd carved from a fallen tree branch with my Swiss Army knife for three days until it was smooth all over. Brian was waiting at the bottom of the stairs, dressed the same way as me. He had both our backpacks, full of iron rations (nuts, raisins, and sunflower seeds), lembas bread (peanut butter sandwiches), canteens full of water, the spell books we made last week, his inhaler, and the bible (Lord of the Rings books). Brian had one thing I didn't – a small golden ring on a chain that he wore under his shirt. Just like Frodo.

"You two look amazing," Jeremy said. He pointed to a spot near the trees and picked up the video camera. "Ok, good, here we go. Do something." I let my staff drop and drew my sword. I'd never get tired of the sound it made. We charged each other, hitting our swords together hard enough to make a clang but not too hard because the vibrations hurt. We shouted about dying orcs until I decided to be the loser, letting Brian slide his sword under my arm. I fell to my death making all the right noises.

"That's great!" Jeremy yelled. "Where are you going today?"

"Moria!" I yelled. I tried to get up, but the armor was so heavy I was having trouble.

"Mount Doom!" Brian yelled.

"Helm's Deep!" I yelled back.

"Cirith Ungol!" he yelled back.

We could've gone on like that for a while.

"Ok, I get it," he said and shut off the camera. "Make sure to drink plenty of water and come back for more when you run out. You guys are going to sweat gallons in that gear." I finally managed to get up. "Be back before six so we can get to dinner before they close." We were already heading up the hill. "I mean it about coming back for more water!" he shouted after us.

I turned around before we disappeared into the woods and waved. He waved back. We were on day eleven of our two-day visit and under no circumstances did I want to leave. I told Jeremy a few days ago that I felt bad about ignoring him. He told me I was nuts because he was enjoying the peace and quiet and to get lost so he could read his book. Even though he said he was fine, I hoped he didn't feel too lonely. At least we spent the whole day with him yesterday. When we came home

the day before, he was so excited about the commercial he saw for a medieval fair in Massachusetts that he drove us four hours each way and spent a *huge* amount of money buying our outfits. I wasn't supposed to know, but I found out the swords cost over three hundred dollars each and the armor was even more. Brian was scared his dad would find out, especially about the swords and daggers, but I told him we would keep his stuff at our house and he could play with it whenever he wanted.

We trudged slowly up the hill behind the cabin, taking time to slay the occasional fern orc and cast spells of protection as we entered Middle Earth. Our adventures in the forest had turned into us playing out scenes from Lord of the Rings in perfect detail. Now that we had these outfits it would be even more realistic. Brian always made sure we did everything *exactly* as it was written in the book. We never skipped a word and we did every little thing that was described. He was much better at it than me. He could memorize the lines after reading them once or twice. I had to practice a lot longer to learn them.

We found a perfect spot for the bridge of Khazad-dûm – a ledge on top of the hill with another one beneath it that made it look like Gandalf really fell. I spoke my lines, proud that I remembered them.

"That was ok," Brian said. I could tell he was disappointed.

"What?" I asked.

"Gandalf wouldn't say it that way. You sound like you're reading it out of the book. Gandalf would be trying to act brave, but he's scared at the same time because he thinks the Balrog is more powerful than he is." He picked up his staff. He made his voice sound different, more powerful. Like he was a real wizard. He started shouting at the end and slammed his staff into rock to break the bridge. The noise echoed for a while. "More like that," he said in his normal stuffy voice.

"I'd be scared if I was a Balrog," I said. "You should do Gandalf."

"You like doing him," he said.

We took turns picking scenes. "Let's do some battle scenes," I said when it was my turn, excited to use our new weapons. I liked the big battles, so I got to play the heroes and he played the orcs. We did all my favorites: Aragorn at Helm's Deep, Théoden's charge on the Pelennor fields, Aragorn leading the army of the dead, Eowyn battling the Lord of the Nazgul (even though she was a girl), and Pippin at the Black

Gate. The clothes and armor made me feel like I was in the story for real.

By lunchtime we were exhausted. We stumbled down the hill to the lake where there was a small boathouse with an old rowboat and a grassy spot. It was fun wearing the clothes, but taking off everything but the breeches and laying on the grass felt fantastic. I drank an entire canteen all at once.

"We should get the camera and film some of our scenes," Brian said. "We can set it up and figure out exactly where the edge of the frame is so that we know what's on screen and what isn't. We can even make separate parts for each scene and cut it together like a real movie. My dad has a film splicer, maybe we can use that. Except video tape is different because I don't think you can see the frames." He ate his lembas bread. "Maybe we need two video tape machines."

"Do you want to go swimming today?" I asked.

"Maybe later, after the Frodo scenes," he said. Brian always wanted to do Frodo scenes, especially the ones later in the books when it was just Frodo, Sam, and sometimes Gollum. Brian was amazing doing Gollum's voice. One time, he did it when we were already in our sleeping bags. I couldn't sleep for hours because he sounded so real.

"Which ones do you want to do?"

He thought about it. "Frodo and Sam leaving the fellowship, Cirith Ungol, and Mount Doom. I chose a new one I want to do." He showed me in the book.

"Nothing happens in this one," I said. "They're talking about what would happen if other people were telling their story."

"I think it's an important scene," he said.

I didn't understand why he picked the scenes he did. For Mount Doom, he didn't want to do the good part where Gollum steals the ring and falls into the lava. He wanted to do the part where Frodo and Sam walked through Mordor. He always let me do the scenes and play the parts that I wanted to play so I let him do the same thing.

I learned my lines and got up. "Come on, Mr. Frodo, to Mordor," I said, trying to sound as much like Sam as I could. I held out my hand to help him up. For some reason that made him smile.

"*Hello ma baby, hello ma honey, hello ma ragtime gal,*" I sang, making the lobster do a dance on my plate. Jeremy spat out his drink from laughing. Brian looked confused. "Bugs Bunny?" I said. "The one with the singing frog?" He shrugged. He wasn't allowed to watch much TV at home.

We had the same dinner every night. It took over thirty minutes to drive to a town on the Passagassawakeag river, telling fart jokes the entire time (the river bubbles when it *passas gassas* was my favorite). Instead of a fancy restaurant we went to a lobster pound, which was the place fishing boats dropped off the lobsters they caught. It looked like a barn with tanks on the sides that could hold thousands of the weird things. The whole place smelled *terrible*. They served our lobsters on Styrofoam plates with plastic forks and we ate them on picnic tables looking over the river. The first time we got one, I swore there was no way I'd eat it. It looked like a giant bug. It stared at me like it wanted to eat me instead. Now, lobster was my new favorite food. Brian liked clams better. I thought it was weird that Brian stayed in Maine all summer for years, but he'd never tried lobster before.

Brian's grandfather was a real-life hermit. Mr. Sevier (pronounced sev-ee-ay, not sev-eer) spent all his time in his workshop fixing old furniture for people or sitting on his porch smoking his pipe. I only talked to him once. His accent was so thick I could hardly understand what he was saying. He never wanted to talk to anyone, so I thought maybe his accent was on purpose. Brian's grandfather didn't make any rules. As long he stayed out of the workshop, Brian could do whatever he wanted whenever he wanted. That also meant Brian also had to make his own food and do his own laundry. If Jeremy wasn't around to be the grown-up, it would've been like having no adults at all. Total freedom.

I was hungry enough to eat a whole three-pound lobster all by myself. I dunked the tail in the butter and tore off a huge piece, letting it hang out of my mouth. Jeremy shook his head. "I assume you two savages will be sleeping out tonight. Again." It didn't make sense to stay in the cabin. The only place to sleep was the floor downstairs since

Jeremy was using the only guest bedroom. "Do me a favor? Take a shower before you go. You guys reek."

"We don't need to because we swim in the lake every day," I pointed out.

"Perhaps you've heard about a couple new inventions called soap and shampoo?"

"Very well," Brian said. "We will take this soap and shampoo of which you speak, whatever it is, and bring it with us to the lake the next time we go swimming." I giggled.

Jeremy threw up his hands. "Don't come crying to me when you develop a horrible skin rash. You two have become completely wild." I howled like a wolf and tore off another piece of lobster tail. He was right. We were wild. I liked being wild.

We got ice cream from the gift shop across the street before they closed and drove back through the darkness. There were no streetlights and no other houses so nighttime here was serious darkness. When there was no moon it was like being in a cave. We decided it might not be a good idea to go up the hill in our adventure clothes (Brian thought of the name) when it was so dark out, so we put on sweatshirts and jeans. And a whole can of bug spray each because of all the mosquitos. We had a long walk to our campsite in a clearing on the other side of the hill. Having our camp far away made it more secret. I still used the flashlight even though I felt like I knew every rock and tree root on the path. We didn't talk much on the way up because it felt wrong to mess up the silence.

Brian got out our sleeping bags and stuff from the garbage bags where we kept them to make sure they stayed dry. He had a system worked out from using the campsite for the last three years. I worked on building a fire in the middle of a stone ring that Brian had made a long time ago. I was getting good at it, setting up birch bark and little twigs in a small teepee, then arranging bigger branches on the outside. I only needed one match to start the fire. Using matches felt like cheating, but I didn't know any other way to light it because I had no idea what flint and tinder was. As soon as the fire was big enough, I turned off my flashlight. Firelight was so much better.

Brian set up the D&D game. We never got to play at home because there wasn't enough time after school. He read the rulebooks when he slept over the night before we went to Maine, and now he knew the rules better than I did. Jeremy used pre-made adventures when we played. They were fun at first, but they got boring quickly because all you did was go through rooms in a dungeon killing monsters. Brian made up his own adventures. He was amazing at it. His stories twisted and turned until you didn't know who was on your side and who was the enemy.

"You're in the catacombs beneath the temple. You just killed the priest and took his skull pendant with the daggers in its eyes." The pendant gave me the chills whenever I thought about it. "There's an altar with a grimoire on top."

"What's a grimoire?" I asked.

"A book. A big, thick, scary book."

"I search for treasure."

He rolled his dice. "You don't find any." I hated when he did that. I never knew if I missed it or if there wasn't any treasure to begin with. He liked to trick me with the dice.

"Ok, I pick up the grimoire."

He rolled the dice again. "Nothing happens." I realized I was holding my breath. "There's an indentation in the altar underneath."

"I push on it."

He rolled. "Nothing happens."

"I push on it again."

He rolled. "Nothing happens again."

I frowned and he rolled his eyes. So, I wasn't supposed to push on it. It took me ten minutes to figure out that I had to push the skull medallion from the priest into the indentation, which made the altar move and reveal a stone stairway going deeper than I could see. I went down, battling demons in an alternate dimension. I had to solve the riddle of the missing magical orb of Gallonia, which sealed the link between this world and the demon world. If I failed, the world would be plunged into darkness forever. I thought I was at the end of the adventure when I finally defeated the high priest and his demon minions, but that turned out to be only the beginning of the quest.

We stopped around three in the morning when I got tired. After I got into my sleeping bag, I put my flashlight under the rolled-up towel I used as a pillow in case I needed to pee. I put a pile of wood on the fire because I wanted to keep it burning all night. It wasn't camping without a fire.

"Is it a good adventure?" Brian asked.

"It's the best," I said. "Much better than the pre-made ones. Yours is like reading a good book. A *great* book. It's better than most actual books I read. You should write it down and send it to the people that make the game. Maybe they'll publish it and you'll be famous."

"Maybe," he said.

I closed my eyes and rolled over.

"Nick?" he asked. "Are you asleep?"

"Not anymore," I said, rolling back over to face him.

"Sorry," he said. "I was thinking it's a nice night. Do you want to go swimming?"

"Right now?"

"It's peaceful by the lake in the middle of the night. Sometimes, I go swimming at night when I'm alone."

I thought that swimming at night might be a little dangerous, but that made it more interesting. Probably forbidden, too. "Yeah. Sounds like fun." I sat up. "Wait, we left our bathing suits back at the cabin. I guess we could sneak in and get them."

"If we wake up my grandfather he'll be furious," he said.

"I'll be quiet."

"I dunno," he said.

"We can't go swimming without bathing suits," I pointed out.

"I usually go skinny dipping," he said.

"Like naked?"

"Yeah," he said. I stared at him. "Nah, forget it. If you don't want to, we don't have to go."

Naked? Actually naked? Naked wasn't allowed, was it? But no one was around to tell us we couldn't. No one was around for miles so no one could see us. And we were both boys, so what was the difference? I read that kids used to go swimming naked in a book that took place a hundred years ago. One time the other kids tied the main character's

clothes in knots and soaked them so he couldn't untie them. He had to walk home naked. I was embarrassed for him even though it was a book. And besides, being naked made me feel even more wild. It seemed so exciting that I didn't care too much about being embarrassed.

"No, I want to go," I said.

He stayed in his sleeping bag. "I want to tell you something, but you're going to think I'm weird."

"I won't," I said.

"When I go down to the lake by myself, I like to make myself feel like I'm a part of the forest." He looked away. "I don't know how to describe what it feels like. I have a certain way of doing it."

"Like you're a tree?"

"No, more like an animal or a spirit. Like I'm a natural part of the forest. If I do it right, the forest lets me in and I become part of it. It's a kind of magic. I know it doesn't make sense."

"No, I know what you mean," I said. The way he described it sounded exactly how I felt up on my rock the first time I went.

"Really? Do you want to try it with me?"

"Yeah," I said. Being a part of the forest felt truly wild.

"Ok," he said, excited. "We can't take anything from the human world with us, otherwise the forest won't let us in."

"So, no flashlights or backpacks or canteens," I said. "I guess the moon is bright enough to see. What about your inhaler?" He shook his head. "Isn't that dangerous?"

"If the forest wants me to die, then I'll die."

That made me shiver, and also made it feel more like a real adventure.

"The most important part is no talking. If you talk then the forest will know you're a human and won't let you in." I nodded. "I've never told anyone about this before. You can't tell anyone."

"Ok," I said.

"I mean it. You have to swear to never tell a living soul as long as you live."

"I swear, cross my heart," I said as seriously as him. He nodded, got out of his sleeping bag, and used some water from the canteen to put

out the fire. Then he pulled off his sweatshirt. "What are you doing?" I asked.

"Clothes are from the human world," he said. "I mean, if you don't want to, I guess, I didn't mean. . ."

I didn't know how to feel. I knew how important it was that he was letting me in on such a big secret. I didn't want him to feel bad. "I was just surprised, that's all. I didn't think about that part, but it makes sense. Wild things don't wear clothes. I want to try it with you." To show him I was serious I pulled off my sweatshirt too. This was getting really exciting.

He didn't say anything. He pulled down his jeans, took off his socks, and then he just pulled down his underwear. He didn't seem to care at all. I stared even though I knew I shouldn't. There was enough light to see that his looked smaller than mine. He took the ring off his neck and put it carefully in his backpack.

I pulled down my jeans and took off my socks. Taking off my underwear in front of him felt weird, but if he could do it then I could do it too. My heart was thumping.

"Remember, no talking," he said.

"What about your glasses?" I asked.

"I can't see without them," he said.

"But they're from the human world," I pointed out.

"They don't count," he said. "I have to wear them. The forest doesn't care. I always wear them and it still lets me in."

"I guess," I said.

He started walking down the path. I followed, but had a hard time keeping up with him. I could hardly see and kept stepping on sharp things. I wouldn't normally notice branches brushing against my skin, but without clothes to protect me they scratched and bit. It made me feel like the forest didn't want me to be there. I had to keep making sure I didn't mutter something every time I tripped or got scraped. Brian was so far ahead of me that I couldn't hear him anymore. I looked around but nothing seemed familiar. I wondered if I wandered off the path and didn't realize. I listened to the leaves and the branches, certain that any moment the trees would close in and swallow me whole. I

started to shiver. I was lost. I'd never find my way back. I would be stuck here forever.

Brian came out of nowhere and put his hand on my arm. The way he looked at me calmed me down. He put his finger to his lips to remind me to be quiet. I nodded. I made sure I could see him, and he looked back to make sure I was still there and slowed down when I couldn't keep up.

It took forever to get down to the lake. I followed Brian straight into the cool water. The mud squished between my toes. We didn't go very far in, just enough to be up to our chests.

"The forest didn't let us in tonight," he said. "Maybe because it doesn't know you."

"I thought it seemed angry," I said. "When I got lost, it felt like the trees wanted to eat me."

"Trees don't eat people," he said. "The forest doesn't get mad, it just doesn't let you in. I can't describe it."

"Do you want to swim out further?"

"It's too dark," he said. "One time I got to the middle and couldn't figure out where the shore was." I nodded. "Can I ask you something?"

"Sure," I said.

"I. . ." He looked away. "I saw yours does it too."

"Does what?"

"You know," he said. "It gets long." I shook my head, no idea what he was talking about. "Kind of stiff."

Now I knew what he was talking about. My face burned. When did I do that? Right in front of him?

"Why does it do that?" he asked.

"You know." I forced myself to giggle a little.

"I don't know," he said seriously.

"Didn't you learn? They taught us about it in sex ed."

"I wasn't allowed to take sex ed. My dad said I was too young. I tried looking in the library, but I couldn't find any books about it."

"Really? You don't know?" He didn't say anything. "I mean, it's called. . .an erection." He still didn't say anything. "A boner."

"I was wondering what that meant," he said.

"We're almost teenagers. We have hormones and stuff."

"So, it's normal?"

"Yeah," I said. "I get them all the time."

"I sometimes get one when I wake up in the morning," he said.

"It's called morning wood," I said. For once I knew more than Brian about something. "Makes it hard to pee."

"Yeah," he said. "Why does it get that way?"

"You know," I said. "For sex." I got strangely curious. "Do you play with it?"

"My dad said I wasn't supposed to touch it except to pee. He said it was wrong."

"Why?" I asked. I mean, I knew there was something wrong with everything having to do with sex, but I couldn't remember anyone actually telling me it was wrong. Somehow, I just learned it. Maybe because everything about sex was so secret.

"He wouldn't explain it to me. He said it was wrong, and I should never touch myself, and if I did I'd get in big trouble." He looked at me. "Do you play with it?" I managed a little nod. He looked confused. "Why?"

I made myself giggle again. "You know, it feels good."

"It does? Like how?"

"It just feels good," I said. "I can't describe it."

He nodded and I hoped that would be enough. I was scared he'd want to know more specifics. Or even worse, a demonstration. I felt bad for him. I knew these things when I was ten. He was about to turn twelve. His dad was so unfair. I felt special that I was the person he chose to ask about sex. I mattered to him.

"I hate my dad," he said.

"I hate mine too," I said.

"I mean, I really hate him. I'm never allowed to do anything or go anywhere. I always have too many chores, and no matter how hard I try I can never get them finished. If I do, he thinks of something else or says I did it wrong and makes me do it over again. He makes up rules so I'm always in trouble for something. My homework is never good enough. He makes me do it over even when I get everything right because I didn't write neatly enough. He never wants to do anything with me except football. He hates me. He tells me that he hates me. He

hates that I don't like sports and I'm not some kind of big football quarterback like him. He hates how I cry too much and calls me a big baby. He threw away all my books because he said I should be doing sports. The books in my backpack are the only ones I have left. I have to hide them in the backyard every day so he doesn't find them."

I didn't know what to say.

"When I was ten, I decided to run away. I packed a bag and left while I thought he was still asleep. He knew what I was doing, but he didn't try to stop me. We lived in Clifton then, which was very different from Newton Falls. I got scared because the neighborhood was dangerous with all the drug dealers, so I went back home after an hour. He wouldn't let me inside. He told me he knew I'd be back because I wasn't man enough to be out on my own. He said he'd make me into a man and locked me out for the whole night when he went to work. I stayed in the backyard of the apartment building. It was so cold I couldn't sleep at all. The next day he put a latch on my door so he could lock it from the outside and screwed my window shut. That's why he never lets me sleep over. He thinks I'm going to run away again. I don't know why he cares. He'd probably be happy if I was gone."

"Would you run away?" I asked in a very small voice.

"No," he said. "I don't want to leave my mom." I didn't realize he had a mom. He never talked about her. "She's sick. She takes pills that make her sleepy, so she stays in bed most of the time. I talk to her, but it's like her body is there while her mind isn't. She goes to the hospital every few months. I don't want to leave her alone with him."

"Couldn't you live with your grandpa instead? He's not strict."

"It's different when I'm alone," he said. "There's no one to talk to and nothing to do. No one who lives nearby has kids. No other grown-ups come by because everyone who lives here knows my grandpa wants to be left alone. He doesn't care that I don't want to be like him. Last summer, I read all my books in a week. I wandered around the woods. I slept out even when it rained. I thought I was going crazy, like mental hospital grade schizophrenic. Like my mom."

I didn't know if I should say anything.

"How long are you going to stay?" he asked.

"I don't know," I said.

"You could stay the whole summer if you wanted."

He looked at me. I said the only thing I could say.

"Ok."

"I've never had a best friend before," he said.

Even though it wasn't the kind of thing that was ok to do with a friend, especially when we were both naked in a lake in the middle of the night, I held his hand. He squeezed back.

"Best friends," I said.

Chapter 21

July 7, 1982

I wasn't sure if the sky was getting lighter or if I was imagining it. I didn't check my watch because I didn't want to find out if it was time for the sun to come up. I hoped the night wasn't over yet. The stars and moon were blocked by thick clouds. It was going to pour today. We were lucky it didn't start raining on us in the middle of the night.

The fire was down to coals. I put on another branch on even though we didn't need the fire for warmth. When we first started sleeping outside, it was freezing at night. We had to wear sweatshirts, pull the sleeping bags tight around us, and stay close to the fire. Then the weather changed, and tonight was the worst night so far. The humidity was like a big wet blanket. I poked the branch until it lit because I wanted to keep smelling smoke.

It was Brian's idea to stay up all night, but he didn't make it. I went to pee on a tree after we got back from swimming, and by the time I was done he was snoring on top of his sleeping bag. He didn't bother to put any clothes on. I stayed up for both of us because I didn't want to miss my last few hours in Maine. I was supposed to go home yesterday, but there were too many things I wanted to do one last time. We had scenes to play until they were perfect, we had lobster to dunk in gallons of butter, we had a D&D game to finish, and we had to take one last silent walk through the woods to the lake. It was hard to believe we did all those things for the last time. I felt like time stretched on

forever during my three-week visit. Now that it was over, it seemed like it happened in the blink of an eye.

When I was little, I was glad I didn't have a summer birthday. Kids with summer birthdays didn't get a celebration in school and no one was around to go to their parties. Brian's birthday was especially bad because it was the day after Independence Day. His parents sent him a card without a gift, and his grandfather either didn't know it was his birthday or didn't care. I wanted him to have the best birthday ever. We drove all the way to Boston to watch fireworks on the river with a million other people on July 4th. For his actual birthday, Jeremy found a water park near Portland that had huge twisty-turny super-fast slides that shot you out like a gun into a big pool. They had real go-carts too. I knew they were real because you had to be at least eleven to drive them. I didn't realize it's harder to drive in real life than in a video game. It was a good thing they put tires on the sides of the track, because otherwise I'd probably have seventeen broken bones from all the times I crashed. We bought a cake for him at the store and I decorated it. More like I *tried* to decorate it. It was supposed to be a Lord of the Rings cake with Mount Doom and elvish writing. I learned that once you put icing on a cake you can't take it off, and I also learned that icing is too goopy to make a mountain. The cake was a mess, but icing tastes good no matter how messy it looks. And big glops of icing made it more fun to shove pieces of cake into each other's face. I probably still had some stuck in my hair.

I didn't know where he found them out here in the middle of nowhere, but Jeremy managed to buy a set of D&D rulebooks for Brian. They were supposed to be from both of us, but I had a better idea for my present. I wanted to give him something special to show him I was his best friend. I gave it to him privately at our campsite. It was wrapped in old newspaper because that was all I could find in his grandfather's cabin.

"You got one for me too?" He handled the book very carefully like he always did.

"Look inside," I said. He opened the red leather cover, looking at the inscription I wrote with the calligraphy pen. I managed to write it without messing up a single time.

Brian didn't need the cheat sheet to read it. "For my best friend Brian on his twelfth birthday from Nick." He paged through it. "This is your copy. It has the little fold on page 57. Why are you giving me your book?"

"Because you're my best friend," I said.

"I don't want it," he said, handing it back to me.

"How come? I wrote in it and everything."

"My dad will throw it out if he finds it."

I handed it back to him. "You can keep it up here for now. When you come home, you can keep it at my house with the adventure clothes." He looked sad. "Don't you like it?"

"It's the best present anyone has ever given me," he said softly. I smiled. He played with the ring under his shirt. He hardly ever took it off. He even wore it when we went swimming and when we went to sleep. Like it was the real ring. "I feel like Frodo. He had to carry the ring all by himself."

"Sam was there to help him," I pointed out.

"Yeah," he said. "Sam was there."

I knew I had to tell him I was going home. I was worried he'd cry or be angry when he found out. I kept putting it off even though I knew we were leaving after his birthday. I didn't have to go home. Leaving was my decision. I talked to Jeremy about it a few days ago.

"Brian wants me to stay all summer," I told Jeremy.

"That's great!" he told me. "You can stay as long as you want."

"Don't you miss me?" I asked him.

"Of course I miss you," he told me. "I'd be lying if I said I didn't. Right now, I think your friendship with Brian is incredibly important for you. When I watch the two of you together, I can't think of another word besides beautiful to describe how close you've become."

"What about all the traveling we were supposed to do?" I asked him.

"There's plenty of time for that later. You'll never have friends again like you do when you're twelve. Take advantage of the time you have with Brian." He looked at me. "I swear, I think you grew a couple of inches." He stood back to back with me. "Nope, same height. But it still feels like you grew."

"I feel different," I told him. "Like I'm changing inside."

"How so?" he asked me.

"I don't know. Just different."

He brushed some hair from my forehead and made a face. "Eww. There's enough grease in your hair to run the car for a hundred miles." I giggled. "You really have to get your butt in the shower."

I stuck my tongue out at him and ran away before he could make me.

I took a deep breath, looking at Brian on the other side of the campfire. "I have to go home," I said.

Brian shrugged. "I knew you couldn't stay the whole summer." Like he was ok with it.

I shrugged too and that was the end of the conversation.

He wanted to do our quiet walk to the lake last night without his glasses – to really leave everything from the human world behind. I let him hold onto my shoulders the whole way down. I thought a lot about how he wanted to walk through the forest naked with me. I wondered at first if it was because he wanted to know about his thing. Maybe it was just a funny way of asking me about it. Then I wondered if it was because he wanted to see me naked. Maybe he was curious or maybe he was interested. I decided it was neither. He really believed in the stuff about the forest, just like he believed he really was Frodo. He wanted me to share the walk because I was his best friend. Nothing more than that.

He cried at the lake last night. Not because I was leaving, even though he was sad about that. He talked to me every night in the lake. He told me about the horrible things his father said to him. He told me about his mom and what she was like before she was too sick to get out of bed. He told me about the mean things kids did to him in his old school. He told me about feeling lonely. Mostly I listened, and I think he liked that. On the way back, I understood what he meant by the forest letting us in. The trees felt peaceful, and when the wind moved through the leaves it felt like the forest was talking in a language I could almost understand. Brian said he felt it too.

When I couldn't pretend it wasn't getting light out anymore, I got dressed quietly. The campsite was a total disaster. We kept bringing things up but never taking them back. I decided I wanted to clean up

the camp before Brian woke up. I didn't have to – I could've left it for Brian to do. I *wanted* to. I dumped the water out of the pots and pans. The soaking didn't help. We tried cooking over the fire a few days ago but wound up burning everything. It was going to take a while to scrape them clean so I figured they were a good place to start.

I was surprised Jeremy was already awake when I got back. "You look exhausted," he said, letting me finish his cup of coffee. "Where's Brian?"

"Still sleeping," I said. "I stayed up all night. I have a lot of stuff to clean up."

"Can I help?"

The camp was secret, so I couldn't take him there to help. "You can wash these while I get the rest of the stuff," I said. I got some extra trash bags to help carry things down.

"What the heck did you do to these?" he growled as he started scraping them. He winked at me, and I smiled back.

It took four trips to bring everything down. Brian didn't move even when I made a lot of noise. I only woke him up after sitting next to him for a while to see if he would wake up by himself. He looked around the camp. I thought he'd be happy that everything was cleaned up, but he looked sad. He got dressed and we started down the hill. I carried his sleeping bag for him. The air felt heavy and thick.

"What are you going to do today?" I asked.

"Read," he said. "It's going to rain. I have to stay inside."

"Yeah." I turned around. "When I get home, I'll mail you some extra books so you have enough to read."

"I don't need them," he said. "I'm going to read Lord of the Rings again and memorize some of the big poems."

"We can do new scenes in the woods behind my house when you get back," I said.

"There won't be any time," he said. "I come home the day before school starts."

"On the weekends," I said.

"I guess." He stopped walking. "Don't you wish we didn't have to go to school?"

"Duh," I said.

"I mean regular public school. What if we could go to a school for smart kids? They have special schools in New York called magnet schools for science and art."

"I don't think there are schools like that anywhere near Newton Falls," I said.

"We could go to a magnet school to learn how to be wizards. Then we'd be able to cast fireballs at Tommy Walker's head and maybe burn a few others in the blast radius."

"Blast radius? Where do you come up with this stuff?"

"It says fireballs have a blast radius in the spell description. Would you go to a special school to be a wizard?"

"Of course. But wizards aren't real."

"Maybe they are. Maybe they exist in secret. Maybe there's wizards all around us and we don't know about them. Maybe I'm supposed to be a wizard but nobody told me yet."

"Sounds like a good story. You think of so many good stories. I think you should try writing your own books."

"Maybe," he said.

It started to drizzle. We ran but didn't make it. Weeks of rain came down all at once. We were soaked by the time we got inside the cabin. I went upstairs to the guest room with him. It was dark, so he lit an oil lamp. The room felt cozy from the flickering light.

"Nick?" Jeremy called up the stairs. "Car's all packed. We'd better get going before the road floods out."

"So," I said. "I gotta go."

"See ya," he said.

I could've changed my mind. I could've told Jeremy I wanted to stay. I knew how much Brian wanted me to stay and I wanted to stay just as much. I wanted to live on a hill, play scenes and D&D, and swim in the lake for the rest of my life. But I made my decision for an important reason. It was time to go home. I had some things I needed to do, and I knew it was time to do them.

I went downstairs. "Where's Brian?" he asked.

"Reading," I said.

"Brian, we're leaving!" he yelled up the stairs.

"Bye!" Brian yelled back.

We ran out through the rain to the van. "Is everything ok? Did you and Brian have a fight?" Jeremy asked when we got in.

"No," I said. "We said goodbye in his room. We're not going to hug and cry like a couple of girls."

"I guess not," he said.

I watched out the back window as we drove away. I couldn't tell if Brian was watching from his window because of the rain, but I hoped he was.

I stayed awake until we crossed the bridge over the Piscatauqua river. Right in the middle of the bridge, a sign showed we were leaving Maine and entering New Hampshire. It didn't feel like we really left until we crossed the border. It took hours to get to the border from the cabin, but it still felt like we could turn around and be back in a few minutes. Once we crossed the bridge, I closed my eyes to rest for a few minutes. The next thing I knew, Jeremy was shaking me awake in the garage at home. I missed the whole ride. We didn't get back until very late because the rain and accidents made the traffic terrible.

"You could've woken me up if you wanted company," I said, feeling bad for him.

"Nothing could've woken you up," he said.

I helped him bring everything inside. The house felt cool, dry, and for some reason, incredibly clean. It felt wrong to be as dirty as I was in such a clean place. "I'm going to take a shower," I said.

"My prayers have been answered!" Jeremy shouted. I made a show of sniffing my armpit, but that was a huge mistake because I seriously stank. I wondered how I never noticed. In Maine, I was a wild thing and wild things were dirty. I wasn't a wild thing anymore now that we were home. Being clean felt nice. I blow dried my hair and brushed my teeth twice because they were yellow.

I put on my pajamas. They still fit, but at the same time they felt too small for me. Or maybe I was too big for them. Underwear and one of Jeremy's t-shirts felt better. I went downstairs. Jeremy patted on the counter in the kitchen and I hopped up.

"Hungry?" he asked, handing me a peanut butter sandwich. I ate it in less than two seconds. He laughed and handed me another. "I gave you the bread with the least amount of mold." I stopped in mid bite and glared at him. "Joke," he said. I slid off the counter and pushed him in the chest. "Hey," he said.

"What are you going to do about it?" I teased. He grabbed my hand, but I twisted free easily. He looked surprised.

"You've gotten a lot stronger," he said. I made a bodybuilder pose. "Is that because of the armor and swords I bought you guys? What have I done?" I backed up into the den and stuck out my tongue, my thumbs in my ears. He charged but I didn't run. I let him come up to me and hugged him.

"I missed you," I said softly.

"I missed you, too," he said.

"What do you want to do?" I asked.

"Now? It's past midnight. I don't know why sitting behind a wheel in traffic is so exhausting. I'm ready for bed."

"Let's camp out tonight," I said.

"How? Everything outside is soaked."

"I meant inside, by the fireplace." I worked on the fire while he got the sleeping bags and pillows. I had it roaring before he got back.

"You've gotten pretty good at that," he said.

"Lots of practice," I said. "I never need more than one match."

"You guys were out every night," he said. "I barely know what you spent your time doing."

"You want to see?" I put one of our video tapes in the machine. "We played out scenes from the Lord of the Rings. This one is Helm's Deep. The Uruk-Hai, that's Brian, are attacking, and I'm Aragorn defending the keep."

"Looks like you worked pretty hard on these," he said.

"We planned everything out and figured out exactly where the edges of the screen would be, like making a real movie." I explained all the scenes, what they meant in the book, and what was happening. The tape changed to a video we made of the campsite. I turned it off as fast as I could.

"What was that?" he asked.

"That's our campsite, but it's secret," I said. "No adults allowed."

"It looks like you had a good time," he said.

"I had a great time. I didn't want it to end."

"Then why did you tell me you wanted to come home? You could've stayed. There was no reason to leave." I didn't answer him. I turned out the lights and lay down on my sleeping bag. The fire was crackling. I gave it another log to make it bigger.

"I wanted to come home because I don't want to be afraid anymore," I said when I gathered all my courage.

"What are you afraid of?" he asked. He sounded scared.

"Turning back into the person I used to be." I rolled on my side and looked at him. "I know you thought I was going to say you, but I'm not scared of you. Did I really cry?"

"For an hour," he said.

"I wasn't sure if I imagined it. I thought I didn't remember how to cry."

"That's not something people forget how to do."

"I did," I said. "I hated how I used to cry every single day. I decided I didn't ever want to cry again and forgot how."

"I think that's more like bottling it up inside," he said softly. I curled into him.

"Maybe. Crying felt different than it used to. It felt like stuff was coming out of me. It felt good." I put his hand on my head so he could run it through my hair. "There's a lot more stuff stuck inside me."

"You have to let it out," he said. "It's not healthy to keep things bottled up inside. You can tell me, tell Brian, or tell the teddy bear, but just tell someone."

"It doesn't work that way," I said. "The only way is to cry. I thought about it a lot when we were in Maine. I tried to make myself cry but I couldn't." He didn't say anything. "I wasn't mad at you when it happened."

"We don't have to talk about this," he said.

"I want to talk about it. I didn't want to talk before we left, but now I do. I wasn't mad. I just needed some time to think about it. I'm glad we did what we did."

"How can you say that?" he said. His voice cracked.

"You made me cry," I said. "I think I need to cry. I think I need to cry a lot more. I don't know how or why, but I think it made me better. I don't want to be afraid. I don't want to be the old Nick anymore."

"What are you saying?"

"I need you to do it to me again."

"You want me to hurt you," he said softly.

"I want you to make me cry," I said.

"Are you testing me? Are you asking me so you can hear me say no? If you are, just tell me. I'll say no and this will be over."

"I don't want you to say no," I said. "I'm sure it'll make me better."

"How can that be? How can hurting you make you better?"

"I don't know. All I know is that's what happened when we did it. You can't tell me I don't know what I'm talking about or that I'm too young to understand."

"I'd never say that," he said.

"I need your help," I said. "Please."

"You told me in Maine that you were changing," he said. "It's true – you've changed. When I look at you, I don't see the little boy who shoveled my driveway. Sometime in the last few weeks you left the little boy behind. I'm proud of you." I snuggled in closer. "We have a lot more talking to do. Not tonight – when our minds are clear. I need to be sure. I need to know there's no other way. And I need to find some strength inside me that I don't think I have."

I snuggled in tight.

I waited until he was snoring before I carefully lifted his arm and slipped away. I wasn't tired. I wasn't sure if I'd ever be tired again. I went upstairs, put on a pair of shorts and t-shirt, and came back down for my sneakers. The night was still but full of familiar noises – leaves, crickets, and animals making their own kind of music. Music I knew well from living outside. The air smelled clean and fresh after all the rain. Everything sparkled in the dim light from the streetlamps.

I walked down the lawn onto the street. I didn't know where I was going and I didn't care. I didn't realize my legs were so twitchy until I

started walking. Then I started going faster until I was jogging. That wasn't enough to make my legs stop twitching. As soon as I got to the top of the hill I broke into a full run. I thought it would only be a few minutes before I got tired, but energy seemed to be exploding inside me. The road was pushing me to run faster and further, power flowing into me from deep inside the earth. I ran past my parents' house. No cars in the driveway and no lights on. I didn't care. I raced with a deer that darted in front of me. I sucked in air, my heart pounding in my ears and my feet like drums on the pavement.

I ran two full loops around the whole neighborhood before I tore back down the hill, diving into the grass on our front lawn. I felt like I wanted to shout a war cry. Sweat was stinging my eyes. The lawn was soaked and so was I. It felt just like the forest last night – the same kind of magic, but even more powerful.

When I caught my breath, I went inside quietly. Jeremy was still asleep and the fire was still burning. I went upstairs and got in the shower for the second time today, running it as cold as it could go. I dried my hair, brushed my teeth, used some of his mouthwash, cut my fingernails and toenails, and used q-tips on my ears until the only thing left was a perfectly clean me. I put on the whitest pair of underwear I could find. It felt like I was glowing. I snuck downstairs and fed the fire before I slipped back underneath his arm. He seemed like he was going to wake up, then started snoring again.

I made his arm into my pillow and his body into my blanket. The way it was supposed to be, and the way I knew it always would be.

Chapter 22

July 14, 1982

I don't remember where I learned that the French celebrate a day called Bastille Day on July 14th. The Bastille was a prison where they kept the important prisoners King Louis didn't like. I wasn't sure which Louis – it seemed like all the French kings must've been named Louis since the beginning of time to get to a number that high. On Bastille Day, the people stormed the prison and set all the prisoners free, starting the French Revolution. July 14th became French Independence Day. I didn't know as many stories about the Bastille like other famous prisons. I knew about the Tower of London, where they locked up and killed two princes who were around my age. I knew about Nazi concentration camps, where they tortured and did medical experiments on kids. But from now on, the Bastille was going to be the prison I thought about the most because I was going to become a prisoner on the same day they set the French prisoners free.

He shook me hard. "Wake up."

I opened one eye. "What time is it?"

"Six in the morning. Get out of bed." I opened the other eye when I remembered why he was waking me up so early. He pulled the blankets off. "Bathroom, now. You have five minutes." I scrambled out of bed, stumbling to the toilet. It was only after I pulled my sweats down and sat that I started to shake all over. This was it. The discussions were over, the plans were complete, and everything was ready. I didn't know if I should ask him to get started right now or if I should climb out the

window and run away as fast as I could. I was positive this was what I wanted, and I felt like I was completely crazy at the same time.

He handed me a big glass of water when I came out of the bathroom. "Drink all of it," he ordered. My hand was so shaky I thought I was going to spill. He was doing his best to look mean, but I knew he was still Jeremy. I could tell him I changed my mind. He'd listen and the whole thing would stop before it even got started. One look was all it would take.

"Face the wall," he ordered. I turned around. He pushed me until my nose was pressed up against it. "Hands behind your back."

I obeyed.

He put the handcuffs on me.

Five days ago. . .

Even though it wasn't a Sunday, Jeremy decided he wanted croissants the day after we got home from Maine. He never broke the tradition before. At first, I thought he was making up for lost time, but then he picked out a bunch of dessert things instead of our usual six plain croissants. Gunther's expression never changed. When Jeremy went to get some other food, Gunther put some plain croissants in a bag and handed them to me without saying anything. I made my face stony like his and did the eyebrow thing. I swear, he almost *smiled.*

I started a conversation with Jeremy in the car on the way back. "I don't remember going upstairs last night."

"You were asleep," he said. "Out cold. I brought you up around four in the morning."

"Did I sleepwalk?" I stuck my arms out and snored as loud as I could.

He didn't smile. "I carried you," he said.

"Did you put me on your shoulders or did you do sack of potatoes?" I loved when slung me over his shoulder with my head halfway down to the floor. He would push me further and further over until he was holding my ankles on his shoulders.

"I carried you in my arms."

"Like a baby," I giggled.

"Like a baby," he repeated, his mind somewhere else.

I wished we could skip this part. He would get upset, we'd talk about it, and then he'd be ok. It always went this way. Seemed like such a waste of time.

We didn't bother setting up the table neatly like we usually did. Jeremy dropped the bags on the table and opened the box of desserts. "Which one do you want?" he asked. I wrinkled my nose. Dessert for breakfast didn't seem right to me. I picked off a small piece of a giant sticky bun and nibbled on it. He slumped back in his chair with a frown.

"What the hell was I thinking? I don't want this stuff. Every time we go, we get the same thing so I wanted to try something different. Break the rules. I thought I might find something I liked even more. But all I really want is a plain croissant." I found the bag Gunther gave me and pushed it to Jeremy. He opened it and smiled. I made my face stony and raised an eyebrow like I did to Gunther. Jeremy burst out laughing. "Oh my god, you look exactly like him."

"I'll make some coffee and set the table," I said.

He grabbed my hand when I went past him. "I liked carrying you up the stairs," he said. "At first, I couldn't find a way to balance. When you're asleep, you're not helping to manage your weight. You slipped when I was halfway up and I thought I was going to fall down the stairs. I never went back to sleep after I tucked you in. I watched you from the chair, fixing the blankets and the pillows every time you turned over. You looked so peaceful, like you didn't have a care in world. You looked like you felt safe. I can't describe how special it makes me feel to be the person you trust to take care of you."

I used double the normal number of scoops for the coffee. While it was brewing, I put the box of desserts into the trash can. I didn't sit down at the table until the coffee was done, the cream was in the pourer, and the croissants were on our plates at just the right angle. Jeremy watched me the entire time. I didn't put any sugar in my coffee at all. When I drank it, I made my eyes pop open. He laughed.

"You're wonderful," he said. He reached across the table and held my hand. "I've been thinking about what you asked me all morning. I need to understand something, and I don't know how else to ask this. Which head are you thinking with?"

"Huh?"

"Are you thinking with your head or with your dick?" I giggled. "I'm serious. Is this a sexual fantasy, or is this something more emotional?"

"Both. I think. I don't really get it. It's hard to explain." I giggled again.

"I think it's my responsibility to help you," he said. My stomach filled with butterflies. That's it? No arguing? No long back and forth? No big speeches? "Think you can look after yourself today? I have to go to New York."

"I want to go too," I said, excited.

"Not this time," he said. "I need to learn more about this stuff. I don't think this is the kind of thing I'm going to find in a library book." I giggled *again*. "I need to find a store that sells bondage equipment. I've never been to one before. Maybe they have some books or I can get some advice. I'm sure these places are strictly eighteen and over, so just me today."

I *really* wanted to see a store like that. "I can wait outside."

He shook his head. "The neighborhoods won't be safe, and we don't want to attract the wrong kind of attention. Besides, there's something I need you to do for me today. I know this might be difficult, but I want you to write down what you want me to do to you." He put his hands on my shoulders. "Don't hold back and be as detailed as you can. The only way I'm going to be able to do a good job is if you tell me everything. When I get back, we'll read through it together." I nodded. "Are you sure you'll be ok on your own today?"

"I can take care of myself. Do you want me to make dinner when you get back? I can make spaghetti."

"I love spaghetti," he said, blinking.

Jeremy put the handcuffs on too tight, but I wasn't going to complain. When he brought me down, he made me stand in the corner with my nose to the wall and told me not to move. That was a while ago. I had no idea why he was messing around for so long. Even though

the basement was cool, I was sweating. It was too tricky to wipe my forehead with my hands behind my back, so I let it run down my face and drip onto my shirt.

The storage room was the only part of the house that wasn't finished. The rest of the basement had carpet and regular walls. In here, two walls were made of gray brick and the other two were wood with the wall sheet on the outside only. The floor was bare cement. The only light came from a single bulb in one of the corners, so it was gloomy inside. Jeremy didn't have any stuff to store, so it was empty. We turned it into a prison. In a way, a prison is still a storage room – for people instead of stuff.

He pulled my arms up so he could unlock the handcuffs. I didn't realize my arms were stiff until I moved them. "Turn around," he ordered. I did. He glared at me.

"Undress," he ordered.

My stomach dropped even though I knew this was coming. I pulled my t-shirt over my head, already uncomfortable about taking off my clothes. It didn't make sense that I was embarrassed. I was naked around Brian all the time and didn't care. I was in my underwear around Jeremy all the time and I didn't care either. Now, I only had my shirt off and I already felt embarrassed. The string on my sweatpants was knotted and I couldn't get it out. He tapped his foot like he was getting impatient. I finally managed to get my sweatpants off, but then I stopped. My thing was hard and it was just too embarrassing. I looked up and tried to ask him with my eyes.

"I told you to undress. Everything off."

"But. . ." I said in a small voice.

"You were not given permission to speak!" he barked. He grabbed the back of my neck and walked me across the room, pushing my face against the notebook paper I nailed up yesterday. "Rule number three, prisoners are not allowed to talk without permission. Rule number seven, prisoners are not allowed to wear clothes. Rule number one, prisoners must do everything they are told. Rule number two, prisoners have no say what happens to them. You've already broken four rules. Now, read rule fourteen out loud."

I didn't need to look. I knew the rules. It was my handwriting on the paper. "Prisoners will be punished if they break the rules," I mumbled.

"I'm not going to ask again," he said. "Strip."

I could run for the door. If I got past him, I could run faster than he could. I could tell him I didn't want to do this anymore. I could beg if I had to. I could stand still doing nothing. He wouldn't be able to force me if I didn't cooperate. I had all the tools I needed. All I had to do was pick one.

I closed my eyes and finished getting undressed.

Three days ago. . .

I was on my stomach on the picnic blanket. Jeremy sat in a lawn chair. He didn't want to have this conversation on the rock, even though no one was anywhere near us. Talking up here was my idea. Something about the rock made it easier for me to say difficult things.

"The prison is a better idea," he said. "The kidnapping idea feels too intimate. A kidnapper would be doing things to his victim because he wanted to. A prison guard is just doing his job. Business instead of personal. I think that would make it easier for me."

I wrote down "prison" in my notebook and underlined it twice.

"Let's make a rule that prisoners have to do everything they are told. That will make it easier for me as well." I nodded and wrote it as rule number one.

"The most important part is that I don't have a choice," I said. "I don't get to decide how long I get locked up or how bad the torture will be. I shouldn't know what's going to happen. Even if I want to be let out or I want you to stop torturing me, you should keep going."

"The moment I think it's going too far, I'm going to stop even if you want me to keep going. Having no choice works both ways. I'm in control, which means I decide when I think you can take more and when you've had enough."

"It has to be real," I said. "It has to be too much or it won't work."

"I understand," he said. "I'll make it as real as I can, but I won't do anything to seriously hurt you physically or psychologically. You'll have to trust me." He pointed to the notebook. "Write down this rule. Prisoners have no say what happens to them."

"Rule two," I said. "I think the storage room will make a good prison. There's lots of room and it gets dark when the lights are out. Having it dark is important."

"Fair enough. I want a rule that says that prisoners are not allowed to talk without permission. That will make it easier for me too."

"That's a good one," I said writing it down. "I have another rule. Prisoners have to be chained up at all times."

"I guess that goes without saying. If I didn't chain you up, you'd just walk out."

"Not just chained around the foot, either. Really chained up."

"Prisoners have no say what happens to them," he pointed out.

"I don't want to be allowed to. . .touch it."

"I understand that part," he said.

"Especially because prisoners aren't allowed to wear clothes."

"I understand that part too," he said. "I know being naked is important to you even though it makes me more than a little uncomfortable. I'm drawing a line when it comes to sex, no matter what you wrote. There's another rule – sex with prisoners is forbidden." I nodded and wrote another rule.

"This has got to be the weirdest conversation I've ever had," he said.

I found that funny.

<hr/>

Being a prisoner is very. . .

Very. . .

Very. . .

Very. . .

Boring.

I imagined being tied up this way many times, but Jeremy never did it to me because we didn't have anywhere we could do it until now. My arms were stretched over my head far enough apart that I couldn't

come close to touching my hands together. My feet were chained to a low wood platform. I helped Jeremy build it because I wasn't really tied up if my feet were free. I imagined I looked like I was the letter Y sponsoring a perverted version of Sesame Street. The prison was pitch black, not even a little bit of light coming in from under the door. We blocked the windows around the entire basement with wood to make sure it was completely dark.

After he left me, I tried to escape. He put everything on tight and used padlocks to make sure I couldn't get out. The bolts in the ceiling didn't budge or twist, same with the bolts in the platform. No slipping out and no pulling free – nothing I could do. Once I was convinced I couldn't escape even if I wanted to, I let my mind run free thinking about all the things I usually did when I was tied up.

Eventually, my thing gave up on me. It was like a little kid – if you didn't play with him, he ran home. It wasn't a surprise because this happened to me all the time when Jeremy tied me up. The difference was that Jeremy was always there playing guitar or reading to me to keep me busy. Down here, there were no distractions. My arms were getting sore. I rested them by letting them hang from the chains until my hands started to fall asleep. Then I'd stretch them back out until they got sore again. Repeat over and over again.

I thought of things to do that would take a long time. I tried to remember the names of all my books. I tried to tap out each note of each piece I memorized on the piano. I tried to count to a million. Nothing worked. Being this bored made it hard to concentrate. I had no way to tell how much time was going by. I already knew that being tied up made time feel like it was on one of those taffy machines, stretching and twisting until you couldn't tell what was going on. I didn't know how much time passed between letting my arms sag and stretching them back out. A minute, five minutes, ten minutes, an hour? Counting to thirty took way longer than thirty seconds. I had no idea how long I'd been chained up like this. I had no idea how much longer I'd have to stay chained up like this. Four more hours? Four more days?

My arms ached worse every time I stretched them out and my feet were starting to hurt. I tried to put my weight on one and then the other. I tried to stand on my toes to stretch my legs out and give my

arms more room, but I couldn't stay like that very long. The darkness felt like it was getting thicker. Soupy. I started saying words out loud to make sure I could still hear. I rocked back and forth. I hummed out loud. I started hearing noises besides the rattle from the chains. Creaks. Drips. I thought I heard a footstep. Was that a shadow in the other corner of the room? I knew no one else was here, but I was sure I saw it move. It had to be a ghost. I felt very cold. Out of the corner of my eye, I saw a flash of light. I twisted to see it, but it moved to the other side. I was getting very frightened. A ghost was in the basement. I was chained up and couldn't get away. I realized I was breathing very fast. I thought I felt something brush up against my shoulder.

"Jeremy!" I screamed. I sounded like a girl.

I heard pounding on the stairs. The door crashed open. I blinked from the light being turned on. "What's wrong? Are you ok?" he asked, sounding as frightened as me.

"I got scared," I said. "And my arms hurt."

"I'll bet they do," he said. He walked in front of me and held my hands. "Not too cold. Do you feel sick to your stomach?"

"No," I said. "Can you let me out? This was a stupid idea. I'm bored and I'm sore."

He smiled. "I was wondering how long it would take." He ruffled my hair and went behind me to get the keys.

"How long was I down here?" I asked, trying to turn around to look at him. He put a hand on my shoulder. I twisted my arm so he could get at the locks.

He grabbed my head without any warning. Something was pushing against my mouth. I tried to twist away, but he pushed a hard ball deep into my mouth. I tried to spit it out, but it wouldn't move because it was attached to something he was holding behind my head. I felt something dig into the back of my neck. It held the ball tightly in place so I couldn't spit it out. I yelled, but the sound came out muffled. He slapped me on the face. I was so surprised and scared that I stopped yelling.

"If you can't keep your mouth shut, you'll stay gagged," he said harshly. "You're a prisoner. You don't have any say what happens to

you." He put his face in mine. "You broke the rules, so you're going to be punished."

I shook my head and grunted. He slapped me in the face again and disappeared behind me. I wasn't ready to be punished, not yet. I yelled and pulled at the chains. He had something in his hands when he came back around.

Something bit my chest. Hard. I looked down. A little metal clip thing was attached to my nipple. It hurt. I groaned. Then it started to *hurt.* There was a little chain attached to it, another little clip at the other end. I tried to twist away from him but I couldn't move very far. He put the other clip on. I screamed. He slapped my face again.

"I'm starting your sentence over from the beginning," he said. "If you pull a stunt like that again, I'll double your time. Understand?" I screamed again. "Those stay on until you learn how to act like a good little prisoner. I'll give you a couple of hours to think about it."

My stomach sank below the floor. He *couldn't,* he *wouldn't. . .*

"Hang in there," he said. He walked away. The lights went out. The door slammed.

I couldn't believe this was happening. No matter how many times I told him what he was supposed to do, I didn't think he'd actually listen to me. But he did. It was real. Really for real. The clip things burned like they were on fire. My arms ached even worse than before. I started shaking. My knees felt weak.

What the heck is wrong with me?

Yesterday...

A special delivery package showed up in the afternoon. Jeremy put a big box wrapped in brown paper on the coffee table. "Remember when I came back from New York and took all those measurements?" I nodded. It was a weird experience. I stood in the bedroom in my underwear while he used a tape measure all over my body — like how big my wrists and ankles were and how far it was from my hands to the floor when I stretched them out. I knew why he was doing it, but I couldn't figure out what most of the measurements were specifically for.

He wrote them down on a notepad and went into the office with the door closed to make a phone call. I tried to listen, but I couldn't hear what he was saying.

He tore the paper off. I leaned forward to see. "Back up. I want some of the things in here to remain secret for a little while." Packing peanuts spilled out while he searched around until he found what he wanted. "Custom made just for you. I had to convince the guy at the shop it was for my very petite girlfriend."

He handed me a rectangular strip of black leather. It had two metal loops attached to it, one big and one smaller, and a whole bunch of slits cut into it. I didn't understand what it was. He wrapped it around my wrist. The small metal loop fit through one of the slits. "The larger ring is for attaching it wherever we want you attached."

"I can just take it off, see?" I pulled the small ring back through the slit.

"Ahh, but wait," he said. "Look what happens when I put a lock on." He snapped a padlock on the smaller loop. I tried to take it off, but the lock was too big to fit through the slit.

"I get it," I said. The leather was snug on my wrist – not tight enough to hurt but not loose enough to slip off. It was a lot wider than the handcuffs. More like old fashioned shackles made of leather instead of metal. I touched it, feeling how smooth the leather was and how tightly the loops were attached. Everything else we used for tying up had a real purpose. Even handcuffs, because they were meant for official police business. The thing around my wrist was specifically made for only one reason. Tying people up. Tying *me* up.

"Leather cuffs are much safer than metal handcuffs," he said. "I was worried you'd break a bone with those things. The guy at the store told me that people who are into bondage rarely use handcuffs." He produced three more cuffs from the box – one for my other hand and two for my feet. He also got a handful of the small padlocks that used the same key to make things easier.

He put his arm on my shoulders. "Now that the cuffs are here, everything is ready." He was right. We spent the day yesterday building a small platform, screwing bolts into the ceiling, and measuring everything out. "All you have to do is tell me when." I looked at the

cuff on my wrist and then looked at him. "Why do I get the feeling you're ready right now?"

"Because I am," I said.

"Promise me two things," he said. "Promise you won't forget how much I love you, and promise you won't forget how much you love me."

"I promise," I said in the most serious way I could.

"I'll be waiting for you downstairs," he said. "You can put those on yourself." He left me alone in the lobby. For the last few days we talked, shopped, built, and planned as if that was all we were ever going to do. I felt like I just got off the merry-go-round and went straight for the biggest upside-down roller coaster in the amusement park.

I looked at myself in the mirror when I was ready. Four wide pieces of leather locked on my hands and feet. Nothing else on but underwear. My thing was driving me crazy. I could barely keep from touching it. The padlocks jingled on the cuffs as I went down the stairs. I decided I liked that sound.

He was waiting in the prison. The chains were already hanging from the bolts. "Everything's all set," he said. "You ready?"

I nodded.

"You're supposed to take off your underwear," he said. I shook my head. "The rule says no clothes."

"I don't want to," I said.

He took a step towards me and I stepped back, afraid he was about to pull them off himself. "It's all right, you can leave them on this time," he said. I nodded and stood on the platform. I let him pull my wrist up to the chain. He used a clasp thing to attach it. I was worried he would stretch my arm out straight, but my hand wound up even with the top of my head. He did the same thing with the other hand, did my feet, and stepped off. I pulled at everything to make sure it was secure.

"How's that, not too uncomfortable? I'll be right outside if you need me."

"I'm not supposed to talk," I said.

"You have permission to talk if you're uncomfortable," he answered. "Do you want me to turn the lights off?"

"Yeah," I said.

The room got dark. "I'll be back in a little bit to check on you." He shut the door.

I was a real prisoner chained up naked in the dark. Well, sort of. The light coming under the door was enough to see. I wasn't exactly naked. The chains were loose enough that I could bring my hands together. I figured out the clasp had a little spring in it. I pulled it back and had my hand free in two seconds. This wasn't the way it was supposed to be. I let myself out the rest of the way.

I threw the door open, letting it slam into the wall. He jumped out of his chair. "What are you doing? You were only in there for three minutes!"

"You did it wrong," I muttered.

"I did it exactly the way we discussed," he said. "What did I do wrong?"

"These are what's wrong," I said, holding up the clasp thing.

"The guy who made your stuff said that's what people used."

"I'm not supposed to be able to get out on my own," I growled. "My hands were so loose I could move all over the place. It wasn't dark because you left the light on out here. You were nice instead of being like a jailer. That's not how you're supposed to do it."

He sighed. "Honey, this is the first time we're doing something like this. I don't think I should be too hard on you. We have no idea where your limits are. The guy at the store said to take it slow, and I think he was right. I know you want me to go straight to the rough stuff but what if you're not ready? I used the clasps so you could get out if it was too frightening." I shook my head. "I told you I wasn't going to do anything that could seriously hurt you. We have plenty of time. We can work up to the rough stuff. Slowly."

"I want to do it over. The right way this time."

He sighed again. "I'll use the locks, but I don't like the idea of leaving you alone. The guy at the store said not to leave someone tied up alone." I frowned at him, but I let him lead me back into the storage room. I stretched my arms out straight. He left them loose anyway, barely any tighter than before. He forgot all about my underwear. "Better?"

"Are you going to punish me?" I asked.

"If that's what you want," he said. I shook my head. "Maybe a little."

"No," I said. I turned around to watch him. He got something out of the box. I knew what it was right away. The handle looked like a checkerboard with a mess of long thin strands coming out of it. "Is that a whip?" My voice shook. He didn't say anything. "You're going to whip me?"

"We'll try a few and see how it goes," he said.

"I'm serious. I don't want to get whipped." I pulled at the cuffs, but they weren't coming loose. Why did I get him to use padlocks?

"Let's start with ten lashes," he said.

"Don't, stop. . ."

I scrunched my eyes closed and clenched my teeth. I was sure that a real whip would hurt a lot more than anything I ever felt before. I tensed up, waiting for the pain.

The strands brushed against my back. It didn't hurt at all.

"One," he said. I opened my eyes.

He did it again, this time on my shoulders. "Two," he said.

"I can't feel it," I said.

"We're taking things slow," he answered. "They'll get harder towards the end." He went all the way to ten. The last one barely stung, like scratching an itch a little too hard. "You did pretty well."

"It didn't hurt at all!" I snapped. "This is stupid. Do it right!"

"What do you want me to do? I don't want to hurt you."

"It's supposed to hurt. I thought you understood. Do it harder, like you did on the bed!"

"Ok," he said. "Try this."

I heard the swish and heard it crack on my skin. I felt the sting right away. I yelled, more out of surprise. It hurt, just not that bad. He did it again. This time it felt like it burned. A little.

"Oww! That really hurts! Let me out!" I yelled.

"You wanted it to hurt," he said in a soft voice.

"It's too much! I'm serious, don't do it again!" I pulled at the chains.

He grabbed my hand and put the key in the padlock. "Sweetie, calm down. I'm letting you out." My arm flopped to my side and he let the other one out. "Are you ok? I'm sorry, I know I did it way too hard. I won't do that again." He let my feet out.

I was furious at him.

"Why'd you let me go!" I screamed.

"You asked me to," he said. He looked scared.

"You're not supposed to do that!" I yelled. I pushed him when I got off the platform. "You're supposed to keep going even if I want you to stop!"

"The whip left marks on your back," he said. "You screamed."

"It didn't hurt that much!" I couldn't believe it. He said he understood what I wanted. He said he would follow the rules. He was planning to mess it up all along. I got so angry I threw one of the locks at him. I missed him by a few inches. He cringed.

"I thought you were going to help me! You said you would! You lied to me! You were never going to do it for real, were you? Never!"

"This is very hard for me," he said in a soft voice. "I can't suddenly transform into the kind of person capable of hurting you."

"Are you going to do it the right way?" I yelled.

"I'm scared," he said. "I'm terrified you'll hate me afterwards. You're asking me to put you through a very traumatic experience. I already hurt you once and I don't want to hurt you again. You might really hate me this time. I want to help you. I really do. I hope you know that."

I breathed hard through my nose. We stared at each other. I realized I wasn't being fair to him. I never thought about what it would be like to torture someone, even if they wanted to be tortured. I wondered what it would be like if he asked me to hurt him. I wondered what it would be like to do the same thing to Brian. I wasn't sure if I could. But I needed his help. There was no one else who could do it for me. I would pay him back. I promised myself.

"It needs to be for real or it won't work," I said softly. "Just one time, for real. If afterwards I say it too much we never have to do it again. Instead of wondering what it's like I'd finally know. How could you think I'd hate you? This whole thing is my idea. If I don't like it, I'd feel stupid for getting you to do it, but I wouldn't hate you. Just one time." I blinked. "Please help me."

"Do you promise you won't hate me?"

"Cross my heart." I made the sign.

"One time," he said.

"When?"

"Tomorrow," he said. "I need more time to get myself ready."

"Tomorrow." I said. "For real."

He sighed.

I wished I could go back and tell myself I was as truly insane as the stereo guy on TV.

There was no point in wondering how much longer it was going to be. Time stopped moving. I was already down here forever and I was going to be down here forever. I was long past hungry. A spot on my elbow itched worse than any mosquito bite I got in Maine because I couldn't do anything about it. Everything hurt. I wished I could go to sleep, but no matter how tired I got I couldn't fall asleep standing up.

He left those clips on me for a long time. The longer they stayed on, the worse they hurt. It seemed like forever before he finally came down to take them off, but he left the gag on until the next time he visited. After he took off the gag, he made me drink some water and asked me if I needed to go to the bathroom. I told him I did because I thought he meant the actual bathroom. I wasn't planning to escape – all I wanted was a few minutes out of the chains to rest my arms. He held a bucket in front of me and expected me to pee while he watched. I couldn't do it. I got the gag and the clips again as punishment for lying. They hurt much worse the second time he put them on.

I yelled and yanked at the chains to let him know I was angry for leaving me like that. He ignored me. Eventually, I realized getting angry wasn't going to help anything. I had no choice. He wasn't going to let me out and he wasn't going to stop. He never gave up once he decided something. If I didn't want to be punished, I needed to behave. I decided to be the best little prisoner ever. When he came back to take off the clips, I kept myself from screaming. I drank all the water he gave me. I even managed to pee in the bucket. When he told me I could talk, I thanked him for the water and asked him very politely if I could have more. At least he didn't put the gag and clips back on that time.

When the door opened and the light came on, I was rocking back and forth even though it didn't help the last ten times I tried. I closed my eyes because it was so bright. He came behind me and rubbed my shoulders. It felt really nice. "You must be sore," he said. I didn't move. "You did it," he said. "You can talk if you want."

"How long?" I croaked.

"Almost eight hours," he said. "Your original sentence of six hours plus the extra time for starting over."

"I thought it was a lot longer," I said.

"I'll bet you did. You wanted me to be hard on you and I was. We're almost done. One last thing to do."

I started shaking. It wasn't going to happen in the way-off future. It was going to happen now. "I don't think I can take it," I said.

He switched back to being the jailer. "You're being whipped whether you can take it or not." He held the gag up. "Open your mouth."

"Please," I whispered.

"Do you need to be punished?" he snarled. "I can leave you down here for another eight hours."

I opened my mouth. He pushed the gag in and buckled it tight.

He held the whip in front of me so I could see it. "I'm not going to hold back. This is going to hurt." I pulled at the chains and shook my head. He went behind me. "Scream as loud as you want. I'm not going to stop."

I heard a loud swish and a louder crack. I felt a thud. I flew forward and the chains yanked me back.

I thought I knew what pain was. I was wrong. Scraping my knees, breaking my leg when I was seven, shots at the doctor's office, the time he hit me with his belt, and even those horrible clip things were nothing compared to the agony I was feeling. My mind went numb. Every muscle in my body locked up.

Another crack. It felt like the skin on my back was torn off. I screamed as loud as I could. I couldn't have stopped myself from screaming if I wanted to. My body was on fire. I thrashed in the chains – not because I was trying to get out, because I couldn't even think straight enough to get myself out. I thrashed just so I could feel

something besides the whip. Over and over again he hit me. I managed to find words between my howls and shrieks, begging and pleading for him to stop. He kept going. Faster and harder. The whole world shrunk around me until pain was the only thing left in the universe. Time became the space between the last time he hit me and the next time he was going to hit me. I hung in the chains, too weak to struggle. He kept hitting me. It went on forever. It would go on forever. My body was torn apart. My skin was shredded. My insides were spilling all over the floor. Still, he kept going.

I only realized he stopped when he was talking to me, saying something I couldn't understand. His hands were under my arms. He was trying to make me stand up. I wanted to hang there forever. He sounded muffled, like he was under water. One of my arms came loose. It fell to my side, aching and stiff. The other one came loose. He held me up.

"Put me down," I croaked. I realized the gag was gone because I could understand what I said.

"I'm taking you upstairs," he said. His voice shook.

"Leave me alone," I moaned. He ignored me. He carried me out into blazing bright light, up the stairs, and put me down on the bed. The sheets felt like ice. I hissed, rolling onto my side, curling into a ball. My thumb was in my mouth. I hissed again when something cold touched my back.

"Shh," he said. "I'm cleaning you up. You're bleeding a little." I jerked and somehow rolled away, standing up. The room spun. "Sweetie, wait," he said, but I couldn't wait. I stumbled into the bathroom, looking over my shoulder into the mirror.

Angry red and purple lines covered my back, butt, and legs.

Little drops of blood were on some of them.

He carried me back to the bed.

"Jeremy?" I whispered.

He held me while I cried.

Chapter 23

July 30, 1982

J eremy interrupted me. "More legato."

I made a face. "I *am* legatoing!"

He laughed. "Legatoing?"

"You know what I mean," I said.

"Your hand is tense again. Shake it out, make it nice and loose. Good, now place your hands. Wrist up a little more, higher on your thumb, arms not so tight to your side. Use your arm to play the notes and touch each key before playing."

"I can't remember that much all at once," I said.

"Yes, you can. Give it another try."

Jeremy was right. The Moonlight Sonata was *impossible*. I'd been playing the same sixteen measures for days without getting any better.

"Keep your hand loose when you play the fifth finger," he said after I tried again. "You're losing the circular motion. Ease up on the pedal, you're getting blurry. And don't forget cut time – you're slipping back into four." He looked at his watch. "It's getting late. That's enough for today."

"One more time," I said.

He let me. "Ok, let's get ready."

"I didn't like it," I said. "The cut time wasn't right. Just one more."

He got up. "Play the whole thing through while I get the mail. Then we need to get dressed or we're going to be late." I concentrated on the music, trying to remember all the things he told me to do. I forgot most of them. Whenever I fixed one thing, something else broke.

Beethoven was a jerk. I imagined him sitting at his desk, angry because every picture showed him looking angry. "Zey vill never be able to play zis one, ha ha ha." I let the last few notes hang in the air.

"Nice job on the final chords, you had beautiful tone."

"I did it with my arm," I explained.

He smiled. "Letter for you." For me? I never got mail. He handed me a big brown envelope, the kind that paper fit into without folding it. I tore it open, already knowing who sent it. Inside was a pile of notebook paper, filled with Brian's neat handwriting. In elvish, of course.

"How's Brian?" he asked. I showed him the paper. He scratched his head.

"I'll translate it later." I looked at him. "Do we have to go out for dinner?"

"I'm going stir crazy," he said. "We've barely left the house for two weeks."

"What if it happens again?" I asked.

He put his arm around my shoulder. "You'll be ok," he said. I looked at him doubtfully. "I promise. Let's get you dressed."

I followed him upstairs. "Should I take a shower?" I asked.

"We'll have to make it a quick one." I followed him into the closet. "What do you want to wear?"

"Can you pick something out for me?"

I took off my clothes while he picked out the new light blue dress shirt and custom-tailored navy pants he bought for me. "My paisley tie would look nice on you," he said. I nodded. He turned around to pick out his clothes, and I wrapped my arms around him.

"Can you help me in the shower?"

"Of course," he said.

I turned on the water and got in. He came in a minute later, wearing a bathing suit like he always did. He rubbed shampoo in my hair and used a washcloth and soap to scrub me down. My job was to stand there while he did all the work – except for the parts normally covered by underwear. He was much more thorough than I ever was, washing under my feet and the part of my back I couldn't reach. It took longer this way, but I didn't mind.

"How does my back look?' I asked.

"Fully healed," he said. "Are you still sore?"

"Not anymore," I said.

I used to think being naked in front of anyone would be the worst humiliation I could ever experience. I was embarrassed just taking off my shirt to go swimming. I changed because of Brian. He didn't care, so I learned not to care. Being naked with him was no big deal. I changed again because of Jeremy. Different from Brian, because I actually *wanted* to be naked around Jeremy. If he didn't tell me to put on clothes, I'd stay naked all day. Sometimes he let me, although he wanted me to wrap a blanket around myself when we snuggled on the couch or had a snack at the table. Wearing clothes around him felt like I was hiding, and I didn't want to hide any more.

I left the bathroom when he was done with me because he liked his privacy. By the time he finished, I was dressed and waiting in the lobby. "Can you help me with the tie?" I asked.

"I thought you knew how to do this," he said.

"I do, but you do it better." I turned around when he was done. "You look very handsome," I said. I could tell he really liked that because he gave me a little kiss on the cheek.

"I was just about to say the same thing to you," he said.

I held his hand as much as I could on the ride to the restaurant. I liked feeling how the bones in the back of his hand connected and moved, tracing my fingernail across the lines in his palm until he complained that it tickled, and pressing my fingers against his wrist until I found his pulse. "Can we hold hands in the restaurant?" I asked.

"That might be a little awkward," he said.

"Under the table, so no one can see."

"Ok," he said.

It took thirty minutes to get to the town by the big lake. The marina where people kept their boats was in the middle, surrounded by stores and restaurants joined by boardwalks along the water. Jeremy paid extra to valet park with the other expensive cars so we didn't have to walk too far. We were lucky we had reservations at the fancy Italian restaurant because I heard people saying all the restaurants were booked. They

gave us a big round booth facing the windows so we could watch the sunset over the water.

"What do you feel like?" he said. "Everything looks good."

"You order for me," I said. I found his hand under the table.

When it got dark, the waiters lit candles at the table and a violinist walked around the restaurant playing songs for people. Some of the songs were soft and romantic. Others were loud because all the waiters sang while they filled wine glasses and carried six plates of food on their arms. Jeremy and I shared our meals. The food was delicious, the best I ever had. I ate very slowly, making sure I tasted every single bite. The violinist came up to us.

"Anything you want to hear, kiddo?" Jeremy asked me.

"You pick," I said.

He looked thoughtful. "Do you know the Meditation? Massenet?"

The violinist smiled. "I don't get that request very often. Are you a musician?"

Jeremy pointed at me. "He is."

I listened carefully to each phrase, noticing all the little things that turned notes into music. I squeezed his hand the whole time. Each note sounded so perfect, so beautiful, the most beautiful music I ever heard. It wrapped itself around my heart and wouldn't let go.

We had to run to the ice cream place on the other side of town before they closed. It was fun because you got to pick things like chocolate chips or candy that they mixed into the ice cream super-fast before it could melt. I didn't want to eat too much, so I got a small scoop on a cone. We found a bench in the park next to the lake where we could see the lights from the town. I closed my eyes and let the breeze from the lake cool my face.

"It's a nice night," Jeremy said.

I licked my ice cream. It was sweet and delicious, the best ice cream I ever tasted. Everything seemed that way tonight, like the whole world was in sharper focus. I could see each blade of grass, each ripple in the water, and every feather on the duck swimming in front of us. Colors were brighter and smells were stronger. When Jeremy held my hand, a jolt ran though me like electricity. The moon was low and large, the light rippling on the water.

"You seem peaceful tonight," he said.

"Everything is so beautiful," I whispered.

I didn't want to do it out here where people could see but I couldn't stop myself. First a blink, then a sniffle, and then it poured out of me. A river of tears ran down my face. I howled and moaned from deep inside. That's how it usually happened, as random as a roll of the dice in D&D. One moment I was fine, and the next moment I was crying as hard as a person could cry. I couldn't stop for fifteen, twenty, sometimes thirty minutes. Some days I didn't cry. Other days I cried every other hour. Jeremy wrapped his arms around me, held me close, and shushed me in a way that told me it was ok to keep going. He loosened my tie and unbuttoned my collar. He gave me his handkerchief to wipe my eyes and blow my nose. He rubbed my back and squeezed my hands. We stayed on the bench until the sniffles ended. He kept his arm on my shoulders for the walk back to get the car. I turned off the music on the way home, opened the window, and listened to the sounds of the world going by.

When we got home, I curled up in a corner of the couch. "Come upstairs when you're ready," he said, understanding without me telling him that I wanted to be alone. I wasn't ready to go upstairs yet, not with all the emotions bubbling inside me. I had no way to describe them with something as weak as words. I looked over at the piano, and right then I needed to play. Not to practice. Practicing is something you do very carefully with your head, slowly, thinking about the shape of each note and how they fit together into a phrase. I needed to *play*. I found the right place for my fingers with my eyes closed, and without thinking the music flowed from my hands. I didn't hear the notes – I felt them. I saw the candles flickering in the restaurant and the moonlight on the water. I heard the notes from the violin twisting around my heart. I felt the breeze on my face and the warmth of Jeremy's hand. I saw the prison, the long lonely hours in the dark, the helplessness, the fear, and the pain. It all poured out through my fingers, the piano translating for me. I let the final notes linger in the air before I released the pedal. When I turned around, Jeremy was standing behind me.

"Was that ok?"

"I've never heard you play like that," he said in his soft voice. "That was art. *Real* art. It didn't matter if you did everything exactly the way Beethoven wrote it. You captured a feeling and put it into your music. It was so expressive, so rich, and so personal that I can't find the words. I'm so proud of you." He sat down next to me on the bench. "I've been putting this off for too long. How would you like to go to a concert in a couple of weeks? Bernstein will be performing Mahler's second and Copland himself will be conducting his third symphony. I know you like that one."

"I don't remember listening to the Mahler," I said.

"I haven't played it for you. Mahler's second is a piece you have to hear live for the first time. The first time I heard it, Bernstein conducted. No one captures the Mahler like Bernstein. It's a gala weekend, but I can still get tickets."

"Where is it, Carnegie Hall or Lincoln Center?"

"It's at Tanglewood," he said, choking up a little. "Tanglewood is out in the hills of western Massachusetts. They have a big outdoor amphitheater that's fantastic for concerts." He took a deep breath. "It's more than a place for concerts. People come from all over the world to study there. You can watch rehearsals, listen in on master classes taught by some of the most accomplished musicians around, and get a taste of the best parts of what it's like to have a life in music."

"I want to go," I said.

He held my hand. "I want you to play the Moonlight for some people. The way you just did."

I sat up a little. "What kind of people?"

"Teachers. Musicians. People who recognize talent."

I shook my head. "I'm not good enough for that."

"Listen to me, kiddo. When I was in the conservatory, a lot of people thought I had a real shot to be the concert pianist who won the big competitions and landed the recording career. They thought it came naturally to me, and I guess it did. I started a lot later than most everyone else and I learned fast."

"You're very talented," I said.

"I think you're more talented than me," he said. I couldn't figure out what to say. "You've been playing for, what, eight months? It took

me years to learn the things you do without trying. You've got such a fierce determination that you're inspiring me to practice more. You have an ability to get underneath the music and let it sing in a way I still don't understand. If you keep progressing at this pace, you have the talent to become someone truly special. The kind of person who leaves a mark on music forever."

He smiled. "Or, maybe I'm hearing what I want to hear because I'm madly in love with you." I giggled. "The people I know will be able to tell. Especially my teacher. I know she'll be there because she teaches at Tanglewood every year. Three bars and she'll be able to tell."

"It'll be neat to meet your teacher," I said.

His face got dark. "This is going to be hard for me. Do you remember why I left the conservatory?" I nodded. He left because that kid betrayed him. "I disappeared. There one day and gone the next. I left everyone behind without a word and haven't spoken to any of them since. I don't want you to worry about me, but I wanted you to know in case anything happens." I nodded. "You play the Moonlight the way you did tonight, and I'd be surprised if she didn't invite you to audition on the spot."

"What if she says I suck?"

"Then she'd be the one who sucked," he said.

"I'm going to practice non-stop until we go."

"And I'm going to buy a six pack of ear plugs," he said. I punched his arm, but he didn't seem interested in roughhousing. "I'm beat. Bedtime."

"I want to practice," I said.

"Tomorrow," he said. "You're a growing boy, you need sleep."

I grumbled but followed him upstairs. We got ready for bed. He read his book while I worked on Brian's letter. I still needed the cheat sheet. It took forever, writing down each letter on a separate sheet of paper. He started by telling me how the lake flooded the boathouse because of the rain and how there was mud everywhere for days afterwards. Then he told me about parts from Lord of the Rings he didn't notice before. I was in the middle of translating a long quote from a poem I never read when I gave up.

"What're you reading?' I asked. His book was so thick it looked like a cube.

"Les Miserables," he said. "It's about a guy who steals a loaf of bread, goes to prison, gets out and becomes a good person. Well, that's what I've heard. So far, I've spent fifty pages reading the life story of a minor character." He folded over the corner of his page and closed it. "Maybe I'll try something else," he said. I rolled over so he could rub my back.

"What's the prison like in the book?" I asked.

"No idea. I'm sure it'll describe how each stone was quarried when I get to that part."

His hands felt warm and soft. I closed my eyes.

"I was thinking about the prison when I was playing the Moonlight."

"I'm sorry," he said. "I went too far."

"You keep saying that, and I keep telling you that you didn't. I remember thinking how horrible it was when it was happening. But when I think about it now, it doesn't seem that bad."

"I don't understand how you can say that," he said. "You were a mess afterwards. You refused to get out of bed for two days. You couldn't stand to be alone for two more. It took over a week for your bruises to heal. You've cried enough to fill the Atlantic Ocean and you still burst into tears for no apparent reason. If I knew what it was going to do you, there's no way I would've done it. Maybe your body has healed, but I'm worried about your mind. Are you really ok in there? I'm terrified I've damaged you permanently."

"It's the opposite," I said. "I'm getting better. I can feel it. I don't know why and I don't know how. You said I seemed peaceful at the lake. I feel more peaceful than I've ever felt. When I was seven, I broke my leg. It hurt more when the doctor set it than when I broke it. If he didn't, I wouldn't have healed. Sometimes it needs to hurt in order to heal. It feels good when I cry. All this stuff is coming out of me. But I'm worried that it's wearing off. Maybe it's like medicine. Maybe I need more than one dose."

"Kiddo. . ."

I interrupted him. "I sneak down to the basement sometimes when you're asleep. I stand on the platform like I was chained up and put the gag and those clip things on. I try to remember what it felt like to be

actually locked up and tortured, but I'm forgetting how it really felt. I think it's wearing off. I'm scared I'll turn into the old Nick again."

"You're going to ask me to do it again," he said, his voice shaky.

"Worse," I said. "Longer. You keep saying you went too far but I think you didn't go far enough."

"Jesus," he whispered. "We're going to the concert in a couple of weeks. Why don't you give yourself more time to think about it? Besides, if you're going to play, I don't want to take any chances you haven't fully recovered by the time we get there."

"When we get back, it'll be almost time for school to start and there won't be any more chances. It'll wear off. I can't let the old Nick ever come back. It's not finished yet and there isn't any more time. We have to do it again tomorrow. You could leave me there all day and all night this time. You could do two whippings. You could leave the clips on longer. You could. . ."

"Stop, please stop," he said, holding his head in his hands.

"Please, you have to believe me."

"Sweetie, of course I believe you," he said. "It was very hard for me to do this the first time. I don't know if I can do it again."

"You're the only one who can help me."

"I know," he whispered.

"I love you so much," I said.

He hugged me while I cried.

Chapter 24

August 14, 1982

Jeremy tried to describe how beautiful the lawns, gardens, and trees at Tanglewood were during the ride to Massachusetts. He explained why the outdoor theater was called the Shed (because some architect told the people who built Tanglewood that he could only build a shed for the amount of money they wanted to spend). The place was pretty, but I thought it was the music that made it beautiful. Music was everywhere: a string quartet rehearsing in a garden, a woman practicing her opera singing in front of a building, or a man playing jazz clarinet under a tree. Instruments and voices coming from open windows mixed together into a symphony as though it was written that way on purpose. People stopped to listen, but the musicians weren't performing. They were making music because they loved to play, surrounded by other people who felt the same way.

"I applied for a fellowship here," Jeremy said quietly. "It's very competitive. Hundreds of students apply to the piano program and only a few are accepted. Fellows live and study here all summer with some of the top performers and conductors. Winning one guarantees a successful career. I left before I found out if I got it. I've always wondered what it would've been like."

I smiled at him. "How's your headache?" I asked.

"Much better," he said. "The pills worked."

"Are you still thirsty? We could get more water. If you still feel like you have to throw up we can go back to the inn."

"I'm fine, don't worry about me."

307

I tried everything. I told him I wasn't ready. I told him I was too nervous to play. I told him we could go a different time. I told him we could ask someone else. He wouldn't give up. A part of me liked that he was here for me even if it was difficult for him, but the other part thought this was a bad idea. Something was going to happen to make him upset.

It was already a hot day, but for some reason my hands felt like I'd been making snowballs all morning. I tried putting them in my pockets, rubbing them together, and breathing on them, but nothing worked. My face felt warm, so I tried putting them on my cheeks. That didn't really help either.

"Your hands are cold, aren't they?" he asked, holding one of my hands in both of his.

"How did you know?" I asked. He dug into our backpack and handed me his winter gloves, the ones I liked with the rabbit fur inside. "Why did you bring gloves in the middle of summer?"

"It's performance anxiety," he said. "Happens to a lot of people, including me. When you get nervous, the blood flow to your hands becomes restricted. The gloves help. I always put gloves into my bag when I was going to perform, so I brought them just in case." It'd look weird for me to wear winter gloves in the middle of summer, but I put them on anyway. They helped. A little.

He took the piece of paper out of his pocket for the fifth time in the last thirty minutes. "Vivian Cole, piano master class, eleven o'clock in room 102," I reminded him.

"I know," he said quietly. "It starts in fifteen minutes. We should get seats." The room was set up like a classroom with chairs that had little folding desks attached, a chalkboard, and a big grand piano in the front. I thought nobody would be interested in a piano class, but the room was already crowded when we got there. We had to sit all the way in the back on the right side, which meant we wouldn't be able to see the keys on the piano. I was surprised there were so many kids in the audience. Other kids couldn't be interested in classical piano like me. Maybe they were being forced to spend a day of their summer in a classroom suffering through "culture." Jeremy put his hand on mine. I realized my fingers were tapping out the Moonlight sonata again.

"Play from your heart," he said. "You're going to do fine."

I put my other hand on top of his to make a sandwich. "Are you nervous?"

"Nah, I'm ok," he said. His smile told me the opposite.

I tried to hold back a yawn. Now that it was important for me to be awake, I finally felt tired. Jeremy thought it would be fun to stay in a house built hundreds of years ago instead of a regular hotel. What that meant was a room with no TV, no clock, and worst of all, no air conditioning. The electric lights were the only sign we didn't get sent back in time to eighteen hundred something. The bed was so small that whenever one of us moved, the other got bumped. Jeremy's snoring made the windows shake, no exaggeration. He always snored when he drank a lot, and last night he drank a huge amount. I had to guide him when we walked back from the restaurant because he wanted to go in circles and I had to convince him to get back up when he felt down in the street. He talked like he had a mouth full of cotton from the dentist. I thought it was funny until he passed out on the bed without taking off his clothes. Jeremy told me what happened to people who drank too much. They went to sleep and never woke up. I kept pushing him until he grunted, just to make sure he wasn't dead. When he started snoring, at least I knew he was alive. I didn't kick him in the back like I did at home to get him to shut up.

I understood why he got drunk last night, so I held his hand tight.

Everyone started clapping. A woman stood in the middle of the room, holding up her hands to get everyone to quiet down. "Is that her?" I whispered. He squeezed my hand. I figured that was a yes. She didn't seem like a teacher to me. She had long brown hair all the way down to her waist and wore a billowy dress that reminded me of the medieval fair.

"I'd like to thank everyone for coming today. It's especially wonderful to see so many young people in the audience. How many of you hope to be professional musicians someday?" I thought I'd be the only one, but almost every kid raised their hands. "Tanglewood is more about developing the future of music than performances. The best way to get insight into what we do here is to watch a master class. You get the opportunity to see how we work with some of the best and brightest

upcoming musical geniuses. Just like all of you." The adults laughed. "A reminder before we begin that this is a working lesson. Please hold your applause and conversation until we've finished out of respect for our performer today. That said, I'd like to introduce you to Anya Kurouvina from Indiana University." A tall thin woman in the front row stood up and bowed. "Anya, please tell us about the piece you'll be playing today."

"Scriabin, piano sonata four, F sharp major, opus thirty," she said in a thick accent.

"You play that one," I whispered to Jeremy.

He didn't answer. I knew the music, but right from the beginning it sounded different from the way Jeremy played it. Not in a good way, but I couldn't figure out why. She didn't miss a single note, even during the hard part at the end. The tempo seemed ok and the phrases seemed right. I just. . .didn't like it.

She finished and everyone clapped even though they weren't supposed to. Jeremy leaned over. "She's a machine," he whispered.

"Yeah, she didn't make a single mistake," I said.

"All technique and no expression. Vivian is going to shred her."

"Is that why I didn't like it?" I asked. He put his finger on his lips.

"Your technique is very accomplished, so I have little to offer you there. Instead, I'd like to focus on your interpretation. In the first movement, what mood are you trying to convey?" the teacher asked.

"Starry night. Scriabin say so."

"I want to feel that starry night. Help me quietly contemplate the beauty of the heavens with your music."

Jeremy was right. The teacher wasn't mean – she was patient and helpful the whole time. She kept explaining how she was looking for more expressiveness through variations in tempo and dynamics. Jeremy told me the same thing all the time. I was working on the same things as someone who could play difficult music? The student didn't get it, playing everything the exact same way each time. Sometimes, the teacher would play an example. When she played, it sounded more like Jeremy. It sounded like how I'd play it, if I could. By the time the class was over, they didn't even get through the first movement.

People clapped when the lesson was done, but the student left before the clapping was even finished because she was frustrated. I was about to get up from my chair, but Jeremy put his hand on my knee to keep me there. We watched everyone leave. The teacher sat in her chair writing notes on a clipboard. I heard a cello somewhere else in the building practicing something I didn't know. She finally looked up and noticed us. Jeremy squeezed my knee so tight it hurt. She smiled.

"Can I help you with something?" Then her eyes went wide. The clipboard fell off the desk and crashed on the floor. I put my hand on top of Jeremy's and squeezed back. "Oh my goodness," she said. "Is that really you?"

"Afraid so," he said very quietly.

"Jeremy Stillwell," she said like she was talking to herself. For a moment she didn't move, and then she rushed up through the desks towards us. Jeremy barely had time to stand up before she hugged him tight. She held on for a long time before letting go. "I can't believe it's you," she said.

"It's really me," he said. "This is my star pupil, Nick."

I didn't want her to hug me the same way, so I held out my hand to shake. "It's wonderful to meet you!" she said, shaking my hand quickly and turning back to him. "You used to say you wanted to teach children." She grabbed his hand and dragged him to the front of the room. "Sit with me. I want to hear all about what you've been doing. I need to hear that you've been playing. Never mind, I need to hear you play."

"That didn't take long," he laughed.

"Did you know your teacher was once my star pupil?" she said to me.

"Come off it, we were all good," he said. They sat across from each other. She never let go of his hand. I sat on the piano bench. "I still play. Not as seriously as when I studied, but I've been inspired to play more lately. Blame that on Nick."

"I was afraid you'd given it up," she said. "Someone with your talent has the obligation to the world to develop and share it." Jeremy told me that all the time. Maybe he learned it from her.

"Nick is the one with real talent," he said.

311

"I'm not that good," I said.

"I'll take that as an encouraging sign," she said. "At least you're not an arrogant ass like most musicians I know." She touched my knee. "Don't worry how well you play. The only thing that matters is to enjoy making music."

I shrugged. "I like playing."

"You *like* playing?" Jeremy said. "This kid doesn't bother to take off his jacket and backpack before he sits down at the instrument. He'd crank out scales for hours if I didn't pry him off." I giggled. "I'm not exaggerating. He has an unshakeable practice ethic that makes me insanely jealous. He patiently works single phrases over and over until I'm ready to pull my hair out."

"You're lucky to have such a dedicated teacher," Vivian said. She pulled my glove off. "You have great hands. What's the farthest range you can play comfortably?"

"A tenth, but I have to line it up first." I turned around and played one. My fingers felt like fish sticks before they were cooked. I put the glove back on.

"Nick shows tremendous promise," Jeremy said. "At least I think he does. Honestly, I don't have the experience to judge. It seems like he was born to play piano. The instrument comes naturally to him."

"So, you've brought him to me," Vivian said with a smile, looking straight at me. I looked down at the floor. "You've no idea how many children I turn away with similar stories. The difference is they're not being brought to me by someone like your teacher. I'd very much like to hear you play. I take it from the gloves you're prepared."

My nervousness jumped to maximum.

"Warm up with some scales," Jeremy suggested.

I put the gloves on the bench. Everything I knew about the piano flew out of my head. I wanted to play a C scale but I couldn't remember where C was. Jeremy and Vivian didn't say anything while I sat doing nothing, which made me even more nervous. I knew I was going to screw up, so of course I did. My fingers got tangled on the first octave. I put my hands in my lap.

"Hands back on the keyboard," she ordered. Now she sounded more like a teacher. "What do you do when you make a mistake?"

"Keep playing," I mumbled.

"Then why aren't you playing?"

Because I forgot how, that's why. It seemed ridiculous. I couldn't forget how to play scales, I've played a million of them. I put my hands back on the keyboard and closed my eyes. This time I got through the first and the second octave without a mistake, even if it didn't sound good. My hands went in opposite directions, left hand down, right hand up. Cross the thumb like so, arms in motion, steady wrists, find the bottom of the key. If I stopped worrying, my fingers knew what to do. They had minds of their own. "Mistakes don't matter," she said as I came down the scale. "It's not about being perfect, it's about being musical." I finished the scale with four octaves of arpeggios the way we always did.

"Try a different key." I played a B scale. Much better this time. "How about D flat?" she said. My fingers didn't feel like ice anymore, just cold. "A flat minor," she said.

Trick question. "Melodic, harmonic, or natural?" I asked.

"Ooh, I *like* him," she said to Jeremy. "You choose."

I was going to do the regular A flat minor harmonic but I decided to try something harder. I knew every scale in every key and mode there was in every possible combination including thirds, sixths, and tenths. I played the scale in sixths, much closer to the way I played it when I was alone at home.

"Watch this," Jeremy said to her. "Mixolydian mode, start on A flat." I nodded and played it.

"You're not kidding," she said to Jeremy. "I don't think any of my beginning conservatory students know their scales like he does. I see my influence at work." He laughed. She turned back to me. "You sound sufficiently warmed up. What would you like to play for us?"

"Umm, Moonlight sonata. . .no, wait, piano sonata number fourteen, opus twenty-seven number two in E minor by Beethoven, first movement."

"Nicely said," she said. I put my hands on the keys. "Take your time. Think about what you're going to play." Jeremy told me the same thing all the time. I put my hands back in my lap and closed my eyes, concentrating on the things I thought about at home. My tempo. The

313

sound of my first notes. Finding the right feeling. Letting the rest of the world disappear until it was only me and the piano. I was worried I would mess up, but the idea I could forget this piece was even more ridiculous than forgetting my scales. I could play it in my sleep. All I had to do was stop worrying.

I found the right feeling inside from the very first note. The room disappeared. Sometimes I controlled the music, sometimes the music controlled me. It was only after the last few chords faded away that I realized the mistake I made. We worked so hard on the details in phrases and the ways to make the notes beautiful. I didn't pay attention to any of them. I simply played. Jeremy told me to play from the heart, but that's not what made music sound great. You had to play from the head too. Both at the same time. She sat down on the bench next to me. Here it comes, I thought. She's going to tell me I suck.

"Tell me about your choice of tempo," she said quietly.

"Beethoven marked cut time," I said. "A lot of pianists play it too slowly. I think it's supposed to sound mysterious, not sad."

"And your use of the sustain pedal?" she said.

"Beethoven says to hold it down through the whole piece, but that's because the pedal didn't work as well on his piano. I tried to hold it down as much as I could without it sounding muddy. Beethoven is better when it sounds clear."

"You're remarkably musical," she said softly.

"Tell Vivian how long you've been playing," Jeremy said.

I did the math in my head. "Nine months."

"Nine months?" She put her hand on mine. "How do you feel about becoming a concert pianist? If that's what you want, I'm confident you have the skill and drive to make it happen. I expect in a couple of years, when your playing has matured and your repertoire has broadened, you'll be seeing me to audition." She turned to Jeremy. "You might have found yourself a prodigy."

I had no idea what a prodigy was, but it sounded good.

"And now, my patience is at an end," she said to Jeremy. "No more distractions. I want to hear you play."

"Oh, no. No way. I'm not prepared."

"Do you think for a moment I'd allow talent like Nick's to be wasted by a teacher lacking skills? I demand an audition." She winked at me. He laughed and shook his head. I thought about joining in, but I was worried it would make him upset. "You didn't really think you could come here and get away without playing?"

"For crying out loud, I knew you wouldn't let me off the hook. You never let any of us off the hook." I switched seats with him. "How about this?" He played the Scriabin sonata like the student did. Vivian groaned and waved her arms.

"Don't get me started. When did everyone decide the only thing that matters is perfect execution? Technique, technique, technique, everything is technique! What happened to interpretation and feeling? It's disgusting. You heard what she said when I talked about using rubato more freely?"

"She pointed to a metronome marking she made on the page," Jeremy said. "Nick, if you ever do that I'll rap your knuckles with a ruler." We laughed. "I've got one," he said in a softer voice.

I recognized it right away because it was one of the songs he played the first time I heard him. The name was in French so I could never remember it. Something about water. The beginning reminded me of the way ripples in a pond spread out until they fade away when you drop a pebble in. I loved the way he made notes sound like they were made of water, how the long runs up and down reminded me of waking up in Maine staring at a spider web covered with dew, and the way it ended with little drops falling off the trees after a rainstorm.

Vivian sighed when he finished. "You know how I love Debussy," she said.

"I remember," he said softly.

"Your playing has matured," she said. "That was one of the freshest interpretations of Reflets Dans L'eau I've heard in a while. A little spit and polish and you could be recording." Jeremy looked away. "At the very least, you should be performing. It's a shame the competition circuit has such strict age limits. You'd stand a real chance. Listen to me – you'd think I was easy to please."

"The way I remember it, you were *impossible* to please."

"I'm not all that bad," she said, laughing.

"You were worse than impossible! Not that it was a bad thing. We learned more because you were such a stickler." He looked at her. "I learned more from you than anyone else." It looked like she was going to say something but the door to the classroom opened.

"Excuse me, sorry for the interruption. Vivian, do you still want to meet for lunch?"

I glanced at Jeremy. His expression didn't change but his body looked stiff. I didn't know what I should do because I didn't know who this guy was.

"Will, look who showed up at my master class," she said. The man looked at me with a strange expression, then back over at Jeremy. It took him a second.

"Hi," Jeremy said like it hurt him.

"I don't believe it," he said. It looked like they weren't sure what to do next, hug or punch each other. They shook hands. "It's been a long time."

"Too long," Jeremy said.

"The one weekend I was able to come, and look what happened," he said. "I suppose you're here for the concert."

Jeremy waved me over. "This is Nick, one of my students. I'm here so Vivian can hear him play. Nick, this is Will Gatton, my best friend from Eastman." I shook Will's hand.

"You always said you wanted to teach children," Will said. Funny, Vivian said the same thing. Jeremy never told me he wanted to be a teacher.

"Why don't we all have lunch together," Vivian said.

"Might be a little tight," Jeremy said. "I promised Nick we'd go to the open rehearsal at two."

"I'm not asking," she said. "Have lunch with us."

"We'd be happy to," Jeremy said in a stiff way. We followed them out of the building. I tried to keep up so I could walk next to Jeremy, but he was walking with Will and Vivian so I wound up following right behind them. It wasn't a good place to be if something went wrong.

"I'm finishing up my doctorate," Will said. "Performing didn't work out for me. I should be able to get a job teaching somewhere."

"Sorry," Jeremy said. "I always thought you played brilliantly."

"You know how it goes," Will said. "I never seemed to catch a break." We had to stop while a bunch of people carrying big instrument cases blocked the path, hurrying to wherever they were going. Jeremy watched them with a sad look on his face.

"Do you miss being a student?" Vivian asked him.

"Not in the slightest," Jeremy said. "Apart from your classes, being a student meant playing only what we were permitted to play and only in the way we were permitted to play it. We were constantly under the thumb of the Dr. Sherman's of the world."

"That coot is still as crotchety as ever," Will said.

"How does a guy who thinks nothing worthwhile has been composed since Mozart get the responsibility to train the next generations of musicians?" Jeremy asked. "I remember him grabbing my book of Chopin nocturnes and berating me in front of the entire class for looking at something besides Bach."

"Sherman always was a curmudgeon," Vivian said.

"How about that time he caught you playing the banjo in the concert hall?" Will said. "'Trash masquerading as music has no place in these halls.'"

"You played the banjo?" I said to Jeremy.

"I went through a folk music phase," he said. "I wasn't very good."

"Not true," Will said to me. "He played a very respectable version of dueling banjos."

"I want to hear you play banjo," I said.

"I burned it and scattered the ashes," Jeremy said. He laughed a little. "The banjo remark pushed me over the edge."

"The stuff of legends," Will said to me.

"Stop," Vivian said. "I'm still pretending I know nothing about this."

"What did you do?" I asked Jeremy.

"Don't tell him," Jeremy moaned. "He'll never let me live it down."

"One day, Dr. Sherman's prized harpsichord magically found its way to the roof of his building," Will said. "Courtesy of your teacher."

"It cost me a fortune to get it up there," Jeremy said. "I had it crated and moved in the middle of the night. I even waited for a day I was sure it wouldn't rain. Out of respect for the instrument, not Sherman.

He nearly burst an artery. I nearly burst one myself from laughing the way he screamed in front of the entire school. What an immature jerk I was."

"Not completely immature," Vivian said. "An anonymous donation for the two thousand dollars it cost the school to move it back down showed up right around the time you found out how much it was." Jeremy winked at me.

"Sherman still pays a security guard out of his own pocket to guard that harpsichord," Will said. "You always had a problem with authority. Like that time we wrote a theme and variations. Everyone chose a theme from a great master, but you picked Hey Jude."

"I was proud of that," Jeremy said. "Especially the jazz variation in the middle. I wonder what happened to that music."

"You know, it took me a moment to recognize you without the hair," Will said.

"The hair?" I asked.

"We're *not* getting into that," Jeremy growled.

"Down past his shoulders," Will said to me. I giggled.

"Everyone had hair back then," Jeremy muttered. "Including you."

"Not like yours. It was luxurious. Went well with that buckskin coat you used to wear, the one with the fringe." I tried to picture Jeremy with long hair and a fringed coat but it was too ridiculous to even imagine. I completely cracked up.

"Now look what you've done," Jeremy complained. "Yes, I had long hair. Yes, I wore those clothes. Yes, I give thanks every day that it's not 1972 anymore." They all laughed. I wasn't sure what they meant.

"I remember the first time I heard you play," Will said. "In that practice jury."

"The Liszt etude," Jeremy said quietly. "I was being a show-off."

"You carried it like you'd been playing it for a lifetime. When I found out you didn't start playing until you were twelve and you'd studied with no one in particular, I wanted you dead." Jeremy didn't start playing until he was my age? I always assumed Jeremy played the piano from the time he was born. He just popped out of his mom and played Beethoven.

318

Jeremy laughed. "Good thing you got over it. I would've failed all my first-year theory classes without you. You had a much deeper formal music education than I did. Call it a parasitic relationship."

The cafeteria wasn't for visitors, only for people who worked at Tanglewood. Will told me it had better food and it was cheaper. We got our lunch and sat down at a table in the corner. I sat next to Jeremy, on guard even though I didn't think I needed to be worried anymore. Everything was going well. Jeremy was laughing and joking around with them while they talked. I was worried someone would say something to make him upset, but no one did. The conversation moved on to things I didn't care about, like Will's brother-in-law becoming a doctor and Vivian's nieces and nephews. I wanted to hear more about Jeremy.

"You remember that reduction we did for the Gottschalk?" Will said. "Tony and Joe recorded it for a small label. I don't think they sold any because there wasn't any money from it. Still, it was something to hear it on vinyl."

"That was the single most boring thing I ever did," Jeremy said. "Especially the piece of counterpoint in the middle of the second movement."

"We won the competition," Will said.

"Another piece of music I wish I had," Jeremy said.

"Oddly enough, I have a copy in my car," Will said. "You can have it. I'll get it for you."

"No wait, you don't. . ." Jeremy said, but it was too late. Will ran off.

Vivian moved in closer to Jeremy. "I missed you," she said, holding his hand.

"Look, there's some things. . ." he started.

"Whatever happened, it's not important," she said. "That's all in the past. The only thing that matters to me is right now. You came back. Things haven't been the same since you left. I've missed your friendship and your company."

"I'm sorry for leaving like I did," he said. "There were reasons."

"None of that matters. I don't want you to disappear again."

"I'm not going to," he said. He was looking at the floor. Their conversation seemed weird to me, not like a teacher and student. The way she was looking at him, the way she held his hand, it seemed like they were friends. Maybe more than friends. I didn't have any way to tell for sure.

"I have two extra box seat tickets for the concert tonight," she said. "Please join me."

"We've already bought our tickets," he said.

"I'm not asking," she said. "We can have some coffee afterwards and talk some more."

"Ok," he said quietly. She held his hand until Will came back into the cafeteria with a stack of papers. He handed them to Jeremy. "I didn't think I'd ever see this again. I was proud of what we did."

"A tape of the album too," Will said, handing it to Jeremy. "They did a good job. You should listen."

"I will," Jeremy said. He gave me the papers so I could put them in the backpack. The pages were covered with handwritten music. It looked like he must've spent days writing it all out.

"You didn't even want to enter the competition," Will said. "I had to talk you into it, but once you were in, you insisted we pick something far more difficult than anyone else. Like usual."

"I was always trying to show off," Jeremy said.

"It came off so well the first time we played it," Will said. "That kid – I forgot his name, the one with the comics – he really loved it. Whatever happened to him? Do you still keep in touch?"

Oh *shit*.

I had a plan in case something like this happened. I made it look like an accident when I knocked the water glass over with my elbow. It spilled all over the table. "Sorry," I said.

"Oops," Will said, backing away from the table before he got wet.

"Look at the time," Jeremy said, standing up. "The open rehearsal starts in ten minutes."

"I'd join you if I wasn't teaching at two-thirty," Vivian said. "Let's meet at five at the music shop near the front entrance. I'll make arrangements for a picnic dinner." She held his hand again. "Promise you'll be there."

"I promise," he said. They hugged.

"I'll take care of this," Will said. "You guys go ahead. I'll find you at the Shed."

"See you in a few minutes," Jeremy said.

I followed Jeremy out of the cafeteria. He was walking so fast it was hard to keep up with him. "Wait up," I said, but he didn't slow down. We passed by the sign for the Shed and went the other way. "We're going the wrong way," I said. He ignored me. I followed him to the front gate. "Where are we going?"

He turned around suddenly. "I want to go home. Right now. I'm sorry about the concert. I'll make it up to you another time."

"But you said that. . ."

"I know what I said," he snapped. "We found out what we needed to know. We're leaving." He turned around and started walking again. I ran after him.

"Everyone was being so nice," I said.

"That's why I want to leave," he said.

"Will shouldn't have said what he said but he didn't know."

"That has nothing to do with it!" he yelled. He turned around. "Please, I want to go home," he said in his soft voice. "We'll swing by the inn, get our things, and be back by dinnertime." He held my hand tight. "Please."

I wanted to see the concert. I wanted to hear more stories about Jeremy. I wanted Jeremy to be happy that his old friends wanted to be his friends again. But what I wanted didn't matter. I decided in bed last night, when he was snoring from being so drunk. This time, it was my job to take care of him. The way he always took care of me.

"Ok," I said.

We drove to the inn without talking. I couldn't think of anything to say to change his mind. "Wait here. It'll only take me a few minutes to pack."

"I'm going in with you," I said.

"I'm fine," he said.

"I'm not leaving you alone," I said, getting out of the van.

I followed him into the room. He started throwing things into the suitcase. I wish I knew what to say. I never knew what to say. He took

the music and tape Will gave us from the backpack and threw them in the trash.

"I wanted to hear that," I said.

"I don't," he said. "Do you need to use the bathroom?" I shook my head and he went in. As soon as the bathroom door shut, I pulled the music out of the trash can. I didn't know where to hide it so I folded the papers in half, pushed them into the back of my pants, and pulled my shirt down so he couldn't see. The tape fit in my pocket.

"I'll take the suitcase down," I said loud enough for him to hear. I took the car keys from desk and dragged the suitcase down the stairs. I wanted to get to the van before he did so I could hide the music somewhere. By the time he came out, I had the van started and the air conditioning running. He didn't say anything. We drove away from the inn onto the main road. I turned the radio on.

"I'd rather not," he said, turning it off.

I put my hand on his and squeezed a little.

"Why won't you talk to me?" I asked. "Is it because I'm a kid?"

"That's not the reason," he said.

"I feel like I don't know you," I said.

"You know me better than anyone," he said.

"When I found out you didn't start piano until you were twelve and all about that stuff when you were at school, I realized I hardly know anything about what you were like before I met you. I know about your thing with boats and the bunny underneath your bed, but that's it. I've never even seen any pictures of you. I want to know more."

"I don't like talking about my past," he said. "Too much pain. I'd rather forget. Besides, you've got enough to deal with. I don't want to lay my troubles on you."

"That's not fair," I said. "I tell you everything." He didn't answer. "Why did we have to leave? They were being so nice. They only wanted to be friends again. It seemed like they care about you."

"That's what hurts the most," he said. "They *were* good friends, and look what I did to them. I was supposed to perform that piece of music Will gave me three days after I disappeared." He sniffled. "Eastman was the happiest time of my life before I met you. I'm not the person they remember. They'd be disappointed in the person I've become."

"I don't understand," I said. "We can go back. There's still time."

"I can't," he said.

We drove for a while without saying anything. Out of nowhere he pulled over on the side of the road. "What are you doing?" I asked.

He stared through the windshield. I held his hand.

"Do you know how important music is to me? Music saved me. I want to forget my childhood because I didn't fit in anywhere. I was quiet, sensitive, and painfully shy. My brother Robert was the only kid who paid any attention to me, and he spent all his time concocting ways to make me miserable. I was invisible to everyone else. My mother was too busy to spend much time with me, always occupied with her charities and luncheons. Father spent all his time with Robert and the business. And with Harry.

"Harry was my oldest brother, seven years older than me. He was Mr. Perfect. Top grades in school, star athlete, popular and good looking. Everyone loved Harry. He seemed nice enough to me, but I hardly knew him. By the time I was old enough to remember, he was away at school. Father was insanely jealous when Kennedy was elected. He became obsessed with setting Harry up for political office. Father also knew what kind of bastard Robert was – the perfect person to take over his business someday. Harry would be President of the United States, Robert would be President of the company, and Jeremy? There was no place for Jeremy. I was the leftover. The mistake. I wasn't smart, I wasn't popular, and I wasn't a soulless bastard.

"When I turned eleven it was off to military school, just like my father, uncles, and brothers. A Stillwell family tradition going back before the Civil War. I was as far from the right kind of kid for military school as it gets. Harry smiled his way to the top of his class, Robert bullied his way up, and I couldn't do anything right. Do you know how it works in military school? When one kid screws up, the entire group gets punished. The other kids hated me. The other cadets would sneak up in the middle of the night and hold down my blanket so I couldn't move. Then they beat me with pillowcases full of clothes. It hurt like hell. I told one of the senior officers after the first one and I got punished for saying something. The upperclassmen hazed us all the time. We had to actually scrub toilets with our toothbrushes. We had to stand with

our noses to the wall in our underwear for hours. Robert made sure I suffered more than any other cadet. And the screaming – everyone screamed so much all the time. I couldn't stand all the screaming." He covered his ears like he could still hear it.

"One morning, I broke. I wouldn't get out of bed. I was bruised from head to toe from being beaten by bags of clothes for the third time. They screamed at me until I couldn't remember who or where I was. I was so terrified, I threw up all over myself." I squeezed his hand. "They sent me home without honor, but I didn't care about honor. Father was furious. I didn't get a chance to unpack before he shipped me off to a different military school. I didn't even know where I was going. I lasted four days before they sent me home the same way.

"Father didn't want his failure of a son around him, so he shipped me off to my mother's sister in San Francisco. I was only supposed to stay there until they came up with another plan for me, but I wound up living with them for three years. I was a mess when I got there, but Aunt Rachel and my cousin Amy pulled me out of it. I don't know what would've happened to me without them. Aunt Rachel turned me on to music by accident. She tried all kinds of things to pull me out of my shell. We went to see Bernstein performing Mahler's second, and I was hooked. I was a lot like you – they couldn't pry me off the piano with a crowbar. My cousin Amy made me her project. She taught me how to take care of myself. By the time I went back to my parents, I was a completely different person. I got myself into the high school of the arts, arranged my own life, and was accepted to Eastman. I had a purpose."

He stopped for a second. "I can't believe I told you all that."

"You never told me you have another brother," I said.

"I don't," he said. "Harry died in Vietnam." I squeezed his hand even harder. "Don't look at me like that. I hardly knew him. He was fresh out of West Point. Father used his influence to arrange a safe posting as a photographer. Keeping him closer to home would've been safer but wouldn't have been ideal for his political career. If Kennedy was a war hero, Harry had to be one as well. He was killed in a helicopter crash two weeks after he got there. An accident, not in combat."

He pulled the van back onto the road. I didn't know what to say. I'd always imagined Jeremy as the kind of kid who was cool, popular, and good at everything. The kind of kid all the other kids liked. Now all I could think of when I looked at Jeremy was a scared kid in bed being screamed at until he threw up. I wanted to save that boy. I wanted to help him out of his bed, clean him up, make him some hot chocolate, and be his friend. I wanted to be Jeremy for him. It sounded like he really needed his own Jeremy.

"Are you ok?" I asked.

"I'm better now," he said. "Sorry for telling you all that."

"I'm glad you told me," I said. "You help me all the time. I like helping you too."

"You're so sweet," he said. "I don't deserve you."

"I want to listen to this," I said, taking the tape out of my pocket. "I think you should listen to it too. They made a record out of your music. I think that's really important."

"You got the tape from the trash," he said.

"I got the music, too."

I put the tape in. We listened. It started off with a quiet theme, then turned stormy after a few minutes until the sun burst through with a big major theme that I fell in love with.

"I can't believe you wrote this!" I shouted over the music.

"Transcribed!" he shouted. "Gottschalk wrote it. We turned it into piano music."

"It sounds like it was meant for pianos!" I yelled back.

It stayed quiet for the rest of the first part, and then went into a lopsided dance. It reminded of something from South America although I wasn't sure why. It kept building, the two pianos tossing big chords back and forth. The main theme was full of complex rhythms and harmonies passed back and forth. It got better and better until I couldn't sit still in my seat. The ending was big and satisfying. I pushed the rewind button so we could listen to it again.

"We have to play this," I said to Jeremy.

"Kiddo. . ."

"No. I *have* to play this with you."

"Ok," he said.

We listened to it the whole way home.

Chapter 25

September 7, 1982

Brian rolled over. "This sucks."

The grass was soft and cool. Every fifteen seconds it rained on us courtesy of the sprinkler. Another record hot day – the fifth in a row over a hundred degrees. The water had already evaporated from my chest by the time the sprinkler came back around. Brian and I didn't want to move very much.

The weather made it impossible to run around in full armor and cloaks like we planned. We tried, but I felt like I was going to throw up after ten minutes. Instead, we went inside and played D&D all dressed up. Then the air conditioner decided it was working too hard and died. Soon it was hotter *inside* the house. Jeremy called every single repairman in the phone book, but they were busy fixing other people's air conditioners. He had to drive to one of their shops to bribe them to fix ours first. The guy was still working on it. Jeremy brought back a bunch of squirt guns and water balloons. At first, I thought Brian wouldn't want to play but he really got into it, planning complex strategies with strategic feints and flanking maneuvers. I had no idea what strategic feints and flanking maneuvers were, but it turned out they were just fancy ways to say faking out the enemy and attacking from the side. We defeated Jeremy and his garden hose of death by sneaking inside and throwing water balloons through the window so he couldn't spray us. He screamed that we were cheating.

"This really sucks," I said. It was close to four-thirty, which meant it was almost time for Brian to go home. Which meant the day was

almost over. Which meant the end of all happiness, the end of life as we knew it, and the end of all things.

School started tomorrow.

Not regular elementary school. *John Witherspoon Junior High School.* I went on a tour last week. The building was huge – four times the size of my elementary school without counting the second floor. I'd heard all the stories about the classes being harder and tons of homework, but the part that bothered me the most was going from being the oldest in the school to being the youngest. Bigger kids meant bigger bullies. I was the kind of kid bullies loved.

Jeremy poked his head out the back door. "Praise the sweet lord Jesus, he has blessed our air conditioner and brought it back from the dead! Hallelujah!"

"Ha ha," I said, rolling my eyes at Brian.

"It's time to take Brian home. You two should get changed."

We didn't move, so he shut the sprinkler off and left us to bake. Brian got up first. We took turns rinsing the grass off in the shower.

I was toweling my hair dry when I realized the kid in the mirror was me. Sure, he still had bright orange hair and was covered in splotches of freckles and sunburn from being out all summer. Otherwise, he didn't look anything like me. He was thin – not like Brian with the sunken hole in his chest and his bones sticking out – like a normal boy, the kind that was good at sports and didn't care about taking off his shirt in front of everyone. He had muscles in his arms and legs, his stomach was flat and tight, and even his butt looked solid. All the tennis, bike riding, and running around in armor and swinging swords must've been what made him that way. And the torture, too. Thrashing around while being chained up took muscles.

I looked at my back in the mirror, disappointed the welts disappeared so fast. They never lasted as long as I wanted. I thought of them like medals a soldier wore proving his bravery in battles. The second time he put me in the prison was a lot worse than the first. I was seriously frightened when he told me he was going to make sure I'd never ask him again. But that was nothing compared to the third time. He locked me up for three whole days after we got back from Tanglewood. He even bought a metal bed frame so I could take naps when I wasn't

chained standing up. He forced me to eat disgusting prison food made from cold oatmeal, spam, canned vegetables, and lots of hot sauce. I asked him to videotape the torture. He thought it was a bad idea to have something permanent that someone could see, but he did it anyway. I hadn't watched it yet, but I wanted to watch it soon. I wanted to make sure I'd always remember what it was like.

I jumped the last few stairs like I always did. Jeremy was carrying a big cooler out to the garage. "What's that?" I asked.

"I swung by Gunther's after I got the guy to fix the air conditioning," he said. "It wouldn't be a real picnic dinner without the best goodies." I nodded. "We're going to be late if we don't leave right now."

We sped over to Brian's house, making it back just before his five o'clock deadline. Brian's dad was very strict about that kind of thing. If Brian was late, he wouldn't be allowed to come over for a while.

"Shit," Brian said softly when we turned onto his street. He never used curse words. "My dad is outside. When he asks, tell him we played football."

"Football?" I wrinkled my nose. "Why?"

"It's the only way I could convince him to let me come over."

Brian's father was sitting on a lawn chair in the driveway, wearing the kind of undershirt that didn't have sleeves. It made him look like a criminal. Brian didn't look like him at all. His dad was short, wide, and bulging with muscles. A small black and white TV was sitting on a folding table with the antenna all the way out. "What the hell is wrong with you bums?" he shouted at the TV. "Now you can't even field a pop fly?" He finished his can of beer, crumpled it up, and threw it at the trash can. It missed, but he didn't care enough to pick it up. He had another one opened before the crumpled can stopped rolling around.

"See you later," Brian whispered, trying to close the door as softly as he opened it.

"Aren't you going to introduce me to your buddy?" Brian's dad said without looking up from the television. I thought he didn't know we were there. It was like he had eyes in the back of his head and wanted to make sure we knew it. Brian sighed and waved at me to get out. "Hey Stillwell, how's it hanging?" Jeremy waved through the window without saying anything.

"This is Nick," Brian said as we walked up. The only reason his dad looked up was because a commercial came on.

"So, this is Nick," he said, looking me up and down like he was deciding if he could beat me in a fight. He held out his hand. "Dick Hanley." It was hard to keep from laughing. He gripped my hand so hard I thought he was going to break it. "You've got chores," he said to Brian. "The hedge needs clipping and there's weeding to do in the backyard. And get your friend some lemonade from the icebox, show some manners." Brian went into the garage. "Pick up those beer cans while you're at it." He turned back to me. "What sports do you play?"

"I like all of them," I said. "Football. I like football best."

"Good, because that kid of mine is going to need a hell of a lot of help if he stands any chance of playing high school ball like his old man. He's so scared of a ball you'd think it had teeth." He turned to Brian, who was busy gathering beer cans. "Isn't that right?"

"He's not that bad," I said. "We played today. He runs pretty fast and can catch the ball most of the time."

His father snorted. "Maybe for kid games, not the real thing. Go move those sandbags I bought for you around the backyard. Put some meat on your bones." Brian shrugged. His dad walked over to the van to talk to Jeremy. "Mets this year have no business playing professional ball. Down six to one in the fourth. It's the same thing every year. Ever since 68 they haven't fielded a team worth a damn."

"Can't say I follow baseball much," Jeremy said.

"Neither do I. It fills the time between football seasons." He laughed at his own joke. "How about a brew?"

"Driving," Jeremy said.

"More for me," Brian's dad said, emptying the whole can. "Not that I can drink so much anymore. Made supervisor last month. Can't afford to be rolling into work with beer on my breath, know what I mean?"

"Yeah," Jeremy said.

"That reminds me, I owe you gas money for taking Brian to his grandfather's." He pulled a thick wallet out his pocket and found a five-dollar bill. "That should cover it, don't you think?"

"Don't worry about it," Jeremy said. Brian's dad nodded and put the bill back in his wallet without arguing. Brian pressed a paper cup into

my hand. He looked like he was sorry. Like I should be embarrassed by his dad instead of him.

"Did the kid behave himself today?" He grabbed Brian in a headlock that didn't look friendly. "You know boys. If you don't keep an eye on them every second they'll raise hell."

"We'd better get going," Jeremy said. "Nick, back in the car. See you around, Hanley." I got into the front seat. Brian waved from the garage and picked up giant scissors that looked bigger than he was.

Brian's father was already looking at the TV. "You too, Stillwell."

We drove away. "I hate that guy," Jeremy said. "He's such a *dick*."

I laughed for ten minutes.

"More pâté," I said.

Jeremy ripped off a piece of bread and spread a bunch of the pinkish goop onto it. I leaned back and nibbled. Jeremy went all out for our end of summer picnic feast on the rock. Gourmet ham and salamis, cheeses, foie gras pâté, fresh bread, and fancy French fizzy water to wash it all down. All my favorite stuff. He bought way more than we could ever eat. The sun was low and red in the sky, close to disappearing behind the hills past the river. A nice breeze made the heat almost bearable. A perfect meal in a perfect place.

"I'm going to miss having you around all day," Jeremy said. "The house is going to be so quiet without you pounding on the piano from breakfast until dinner."

"Don't remind me," I groaned.

"Keep in mind what we talked about, ok?"

I rolled my eyes. "I know what I'm supposed to say. You're my uncle who ties me up naked and whips me." Jeremy's sprayed a mouthful of his drink everywhere. I giggled. "I'm not going to mess up. Trust me."

"Of course I trust you," he said in his soft voice.

I looked at the sky turning slowly from blue to red as the sun disappeared. I was still hungry, but I wasn't interested in eating any more. Jeremy scooted over to the edge of the blanket, leaning back

against our tree while he ate his sandwich. The last time we were here, I used my Swiss Army knife to carve our initials in a heart on the other side. That's what made it our tree. For a while, he watched the sunset while I watched him. A few weeks ago, I would've cried. Not anymore. Everything had been cried out. Almost everything. I had one thing left to be let out and let go. I slid between Jeremy's legs, leaning into him, the sky red as fire. He massaged my shoulders.

"What do you think you'd be doing if we never met?" I asked.

"That's a hard question. I think I'd be sitting at home. Maybe watching television, reading a book, or playing the piano. Waiting for my life to go by."

"Why?"

"That's what I did before I met you," he said. "I never went out. I didn't talk to anyone. I was almost as bad as Brian's grandfather. I didn't want to be around people." His hands stopped rubbing. "I didn't want to be around boys."

"But you like boys," I said.

"I couldn't stand to look at them," he explained. "I couldn't stand being teased by what I couldn't have. When I was in school, I seriously considered marrying Vivian. She was finishing a divorce, and even though I was fifteen years younger than her I knew she was interested in me. I thought about having my own boys with her. But I never did anything about it. I was too involved with. . ." He sighed. "I shouldn't be telling you about this."

"I want to know," I said, snuggling in closer.

"I'm afraid I'm going to scare you off," he said.

"You couldn't even if you wanted to."

He ran his hands through my hair. "After I left school, the marriage idea seemed ridiculous. I couldn't imagine any woman falling in love with someone like me. I wasn't a hermit back then. I went to playgrounds, amusements parks, arcades, malls – anywhere I could see lots of boys. I would watch them until I found one I liked. One who looked lonely or sad, or one holding hands with his father, or one I thought was particularly cute. I'd follow him around for hours, imagining what it would be like to be with him. It was like torture.

"One day I decided if I wasn't going to be allowed to have what I wanted, I was going to take it instead." His hands shook. "I bought the van and I went all the way to Virginia to buy a gun. I had crazy notions that after I kidnapped him, he'd grow to love me more than whoever he was with before."

I kept myself from shivering. "I took long drives hundreds of miles from home, scouting out locations and looking for the right boy. I finally came to my senses in a truck stop halfway across Pennsylvania. I watched a single mother trying to handle her two out of control boys in a diner. They seemed miserable with her, and she seemed miserable with them. It looked like the perfect opportunity. I was seriously thinking about doing something and it hit me. Up until that moment, I never believed I could actually do it. All that planning was nothing more than a fantasy. Now I was seriously considering acting, and it scared the hell out of me. I got out of there, drove home, threw the gun in the Delaware river, and swore to myself that I would never, ever put myself in a situation like that again. I locked myself away from the world to keep it safe from me. That's where I'd be if you never knocked on my door. But I'm not like that anymore. Because of you. You saved me." I snuggled in closer.

"You saved me too," I said softly. "I know where I'd be."

"Where?" he said.

"In a box. Buried underground."

"You don't know that," he said, brushing my cheek.

"Yes, I do." I looked across the valley. "I want to tell you about a day a month before I met you."

"What happened that day?"

There was no way to say it except to say it.

"I tried to kill myself."

His arms wrapped around me tight. "You don't have to tell me about that if you don't want to."

"I had a bad day at school. I can't remember for sure, but I think it was a Friday. We had an assignment to write an autobiography for Language Arts. We could invent whatever we wanted for the future, so I thought it was a stupid idea. Stupid enough that I didn't do it. I was tired because I wet the bed the night before. I wanted to write it sitting

on the blacktop before school started, but Tommy was throwing big dirt clods at me whenever the teachers weren't looking. I couldn't concentrate, so I had nothing done when the bell rang. When I got into class, the teacher called me to her desk and gave me a note to take to the office. It said 'Read me, Nicholas' on the outside. She told me I had dirt in my hair and that I should go to the bathroom to clean up before coming back."

"That was a nice way to tell you," Jeremy said.

"It didn't seem nice. I thought she was picking on me. I went to the bathroom, got all the stuff out of my hair, and washed my face. By the time I went back my social studies class started. I had three sentences done when it was time for Language Arts. I was the last in line outside the classroom because we lined up in alphabetical order. I didn't go in with everyone else. I knew I was going to fail my assignment and they were going to make me do sixth grade over again. Then I wet my pants."

"Sweetie," he said in his soft voice.

"I ran down to the nurse's office. She was nice. She tried to call my parents to pick me up or bring me new clothes. My dad was in a meeting and my mom was in court so they couldn't help. I wound up staying in the nurse's office for the rest of the day. The nurse kept leaving messages. I hoped my mom or dad would call back but they never did. I waited a long time after the last bell rang so I could walk home without anyone seeing me.

"I sat on my bed for a long time. I thought about how my life was terrible and how it was only going to get worse. The other kids would never stop picking on me. My parents didn't care about me. No one would miss me if I wasn't here anymore. I hated myself. Everything hurt all the time. I didn't deserve to be alive anymore." He hugged me tighter.

"I unscrewed a big orange hook my father had in the ceiling of the garage and screwed it into the ceiling in my room. I made sure it was in the wood because I knew it would rip right out if I didn't. I couldn't find any rope, so I used one of my dad's extension cords. I didn't know how to tie a noose, so I tied it around my neck with a bunch of knots and hoped that would be good enough."

"Sweetie." His voice shook. "You don't have to tell me this."

"I decided to write my autobiography. I remember exactly what I wrote. 'I was born in 1970 and moved eight times before I was eleven years old. Then I moved to Newton Falls. I didn't do anything and everyone hated me so I hung myself and died. The end.' I left it on my desk so whoever found me could see it. I stood on my desk chair and tied the other end of the cord to the hook. I used some old toy handcuffs behind my back so I couldn't use my hands to get myself out. When I was ready, I asked myself if I was sure. I didn't have to think about it. I was sure. I did it. I kicked the chair out. It tipped over and I fell a little bit. The cord got tight around my neck. It hurt a lot and I couldn't breathe. I was scared at first, so I kicked around and tried to yell. But then I realized it was working. Soon I was going to pass out and then nothing would hurt anymore. I stopped kicking. I was happy. I was really happy."

Jeremy started to cry.

"I was getting close to passing out when the ceiling collapsed or maybe I was too fat and the wood couldn't hold my weight. Maybe I screwed the hook in the wrong place. I crashed to the floor. Once I fell, the cord loosened and I could breathe. I was angry it didn't work, but I didn't want to try again. Dust, pieces of the ceiling, and wood splinters were everywhere. My dad was furious when he came home. He grounded me for a month and took away my allowance until the repairs were paid off. He never asked me what happened. My parents never noticed how the cord left a deep red mark on my neck.

"I used to think a lot about what I did. I wasn't pretending. I really tried to kill myself. I should've died. The only reason I'm still alive is luck. You said how you realized you couldn't do something bad, but it's different with me. I know I can do bad things because I've done them before. For a long time, I was scared something would happen and I'd try again. Except this time, it would work and I'd die for real. I think about all the good stuff I would've missed if I did. But I'm not scared anymore. The old Nick is gone and he's never coming back. I'm looking forward to things. I know someone cares about me now. All because of you."

"Think about the coincidences that led us to this moment," he said. "I ran away from the truck stop and your ceiling collapsed. We wound up living down the street from each other. We both love the piano. I can't shake the feeling we're meant to be together, that we couldn't have avoided finding each other even if we tried. The universe is always trying to tell us something. All we have to do is listen. With us, it's not whispering. It's screaming." He rubbed my head. "Do you need to cry?"

"No," I said. "I'm done crying."

"I don't want to go alone," I said.

He turned off the van and walked behind me. My parent's house was dark and abandoned. My mother was probably in Denver – she was always out there. My father was probably sleeping at work. They were never around. It didn't matter. I got the spare key from the backyard because I didn't keep one with me anymore. I didn't want to turn on the lights inside. In the dark, the house seemed like someplace unfamiliar. Someplace that had nothing to do with me. It felt haunted. I shivered.

We made our way upstairs. Jeremy turned on the lights in the room that used to be mine. I knew the damage I caused had been repaired, just like I knew the furniture I destroyed was gone. I still pictured the room the way it was before that night. The few things left were covered in a thick layer of dust. This wasn't my room. The old Nick lived here a long time ago in a galaxy far, far away.

"Where is it?" he asked, his voice hushed.

"In one of the boxes in the closet," I answered. "Can you see the outline in the ceiling? That's where it happened." He nodded. I opened the boxes until I found my old school papers. The one I wanted was near the top. I gave it to Jeremy.

"I want to get out of here," I said. "And I never want to come back."

We left the house. Jeremy locked the front door.

"I can't remember the last time you talked to your parents," Jeremy said.

"I don't have any parents," I answered.

He didn't argue with me.

I didn't feel safe until we got back home. He carried the shovel and followed me to the far corner of the yard, down near the woods. I found a nice spot underneath an old tree where I could hear the creek babbling softly. The breeze was getting stronger. According to the news, it would rain later tonight, finally breaking the heat wave. For now, the sky was clear, the stars were shining, and the moon was bright. He dug a small hole.

I looked at the piece of paper clutched in my hand. *My Autobiography, by Nicholas Welles*. I placed it carefully in the hole, words facing up. Jeremy handed me the matchbook. I lit the match, holding it to the corner of the paper until the flames caught. It only took a moment for the entire sheet to turn black, the words vanishing as if they were never there. A moment later it was gone, nothing but ashes. Jeremy handed me the shovel. I scooped the dirt back in, patting it flat on top. I marked the spot with a small twig stuck in the ground, in case I ever wanted to find it again. I was sure I wouldn't.

"Done," I said, looking up at him.

"Bedtime," he said quietly.

I was ready first, teeth brushed and clothes off, snug under the covers. The house was chilly from running the air conditioner full blast. I liked the feeling of being cozy and warm. The blankets weren't the reason I felt that way. He finished a few minutes after me, sitting on the edge of the bed. "You are one tough kid, you know that?"

"I'm not tough," I said.

"Like hell you're not. Look at everything you've been through. You're not just surviving – you're thriving. If that's not tough, I don't know what is." I smiled a little. "Proud isn't strong enough a word for me right now."

Feelings swirled inside me. New ones. Powerful ones. Good ones.

"Would you like a back rub?" I asked.

"I'd love one," he said softly.

He pulled off his t-shirt and lay down on his stomach on top of the covers. I sat beside him, pressing on his back. He sighed and I smiled. I traced the outline of the muscles in his arm, exploring the curves and

ridges, how they met near his shoulder, the way his back moved when he adjusted his arms, the little dark hairs that grew everywhere on him, and the goose bumps that appeared on his skin as my fingernail tickled him lightly. I bent over and kissed the back of his neck.

"Sweetie," he said, rolling over.

"I think I'm ready," was all I said.

I waited until I was sure he was asleep before slipping out of bed. He looked so peaceful. I thought it would be like a crime to disturb him. I didn't bother to get dressed, closing the door silently behind me, stealing down the steps like a burglar. The house was still and dark, but the shadows didn't make it spooky. I opened the back doors, stepped onto the deck, and took in a deep breath of night air. It smelled like rain. I didn't care if someone saw me standing naked out in the open. Let them. I didn't care what other people thought any more.

Jeremy left a part of himself deep inside my body, permanently and forever a part of me now. I decided tonight counted as my first time. We were joined as close as two people could be. Nothing could ever split us apart. I didn't feel ashamed or disgusted. What we did was *right*. It was *true*. It wasn't something I did to him or he did to me. It was something we did together. Sex wasn't the right word. We made love. We were tangled up until we couldn't tell each other apart. We were one person. I decided when I got back into bed I was going to wake him up because I wanted to do it over again. Again, and again, and again, and again for the rest of my life.

I thought about that lonely little boy from so long ago. The only thing left of him was a small twig under a tree in the backyard. He was dead and buried. In his place was someone much better. Deep down, I knew I wasn't dreading school as much as I pretended. I wanted to show off the new Nick Welles to everyone. The promise of a new year as my new self was in front of me and I was ready.

Bring it on.

James Edison

Part 4

Chapter 26

November 10, 2006

I checked my watch – a whole thirty seconds later than the last time I checked. Five minutes after six – they were supposed to be here by now. I looked through the front window. No sign of them coming up the street, so I went downstairs to make sure everything was set up just right. The food was exactly where I left it, arranged on the folding table with the same precision as my childhood cheese plates. Not the normal array of chips, chocolate, and fried appetizers. This crowd required everything to have at least one of the following words on the package (in order of preference): organic, natural, fat free, low fat, vegetarian, vegan, or at the very least, healthy. The table was covered with pita bread, hummus, baba ganouj, tabbouleh, baked tortilla chips with all-natural salsa, low fat seven-layer dip, organic guacamole, fruit salads, and massive trays of raw veggies with dairy-free, fat-free dips. Drinks, on the other hand, were specifically requested to be unnatural and unhealthy. Boxes of Frappuccino stuff from Starbucks and several kinds of energy drinks with enough caffeine to give an elephant a heart attack were piled on another table. And that was just the snacks. Dinner was an Asian theme: mass quantities of udon soup, chicken and veggie teriyaki kabobs, piles of brown rice, and a nearly endless supply of fresh sushi. All courtesy of the very convenient and inconceivably expensive natural foods market in Reston.

The food wasn't the only surprise waiting for them. I checked the new big screen television – excuse me, "home theater" – to make sure it was still turned on. I was afraid to turn it off. The manual for the

343

touchscreen remote read like a graduate level math textbook. I told the guy at the "home theater" shop I wanted the setup that would have the entire neighborhood lined up begging for an invitation to my Super Bowl party. Between the television, sound system, speakers, accessories, fancy couches, electronic recliners, and computerized remote, I was well north of thirty-five thousand dollars poorer.

I was ready for movie night.

I found out about movie night from Jake a couple weeks ago. All I needed to hear was that it was sponsored by the Pinehurst gay and lesbian club, and I volunteered on the spot to host the next one. Jake went on and on about the multi-million-dollar Great Falls estate where they had the last movie night, complete with a real theater in the basement that featured electronic reclining seats. I couldn't compete, but now I was a lot closer. I wouldn't have cared if it cost twice as much money. My plan was to become the host of movie night for the foreseeable future. I wanted these kids in my house.

The money to pay for it was a phone call away.

"Hello?"

"Hi Dad," I said.

"Hi there, son." He was genuinely happy to hear from me. He always was. "How are you doing? Haven't heard from you in a few weeks."

"Truth is, not so good," I said, making myself sound depressed. "Still haven't managed to find another job. Prospects have been slim."

"Are you ok for money? Do you need some help to tide you over?"

I was quiet, like I was thinking it over. "I guess we could use a little help. Things are pretty tight and it would take the edge off, especially with Jake's tuition for next semester due."

"Say no more," he said. "Why don't you come by the house for dinner on Sunday? We'll take care of it."

"Thanks," I said, like I was a little embarrassed. "I think Julia will be out of town but Jake and I should be free."

"I spoke with your mother," he said. "You should call her. She'd like to see Jake sometime."

"I'll call her," I lied. The only way I'd call her was over my fucking dead body.

"Sunday, then, at six like usual."

"See you then."

If I called him once every couple of weeks and stopped by for the occasional dinner, his fat wallet was mine to plunder. I suppose some people would think it was sad how my father threw money at me to get my attention, but it was the only way he knew how. I felt no remorse taking his money whatsoever. Maybe he managed to forget what he was like when I was a kid, but I sure as hell hadn't.

I had one other call to deal with.

Julia sounded panicked. "Nick, there's something wrong with our credit card. Someone charged over thirty thousand dollars at a television store!"

"Didn't Jake tell you I bought a home theater system?"

"He told me about a new television for the basement, not thirty thousand dollars for a home theater system!" I didn't answer. "What are you thinking? You don't have a job and you have no prospects. We have no business buying anything unnecessary now, let alone a television that costs more than a new car!"

"My father gave us the money. What's the problem?"

"That money could've gone towards Jake's education!" She took a deep breath. "I don't want to be angry, but I'm very concerned. What's next, a hundred-thousand-dollar sports car? Are you going through some kind of mid-life crisis?"

"Just the home theater," I said. "If my father wants to give us money to buy a TV and some furniture, let him. I don't understand why you're getting so bent out of shape."

"I need to go," she said. "Check with me first next time."

"Sure thing," I said, hanging up the phone.

It was almost six-thirty when three late model luxury cars turned into our cul-de-sac, parking in front of our house. It looked like a good crowd, thirteen or fourteen of them at least. I made for the office before they came in, typing on the computer as casually as I could muster.

"Dad, are you here?" Jake called from the front door.

"In the office, be there in a minute." I waited until the noise level grew loud enough before coming out. "Hi, everybody," I said, waving. Jake introduced me. I made a conscious effort to remember names, but

I was hopelessly lost after the fourth handshake. I suppose I was distracted by how different this group seemed from my early teenage world, when a single Asian friend stood out as being different in a sea of white faces. Pinehurst was a place of privilege, and they made a conscious effort to build a diverse student population from privileged families all over the world. It seemed as though every culture on the planet was deliberately represented by their group. Alex and Jake stood out as being several years younger than the rest. They were all polite to a fault, thanking me nicely for hosting. "Everything's set up down in the basement, help yourselves," I told them. "Alex, Jake, can you help me bring down dinner?"

The group filtered downstairs. Alex and Jake followed me into the kitchen. "What's the movie for tonight?" I asked.

"Don't know, but it's a long one," Jake said. "Nathaniel said it was going to be a late night."

"It's always a secret until the movie starts," Alex explained. "Like a box of chocolates, you never know what you're going to get. That was a hokey thing to say but movie night's supposed to be hokey. Last time we watched Independence Day and Mars Attacks, a cheesy alien double feature. Doesn't get any hokier than that."

I nodded. "Jake, get the kabobs from the oven." I stacked trays on Alex's outstretched arms.

"Did you buy out the whole store?" Jake said when he opened the oven. "There's got to be a hundred of them in here."

"And a thousand pounds of sushi," Alex said. I put another tray on the stack. "Oof. You know there are starving people in Darfur, right?"

"You guys aren't seriously going to stand there and tell me a dozen teenagers can't plow through all this in one night," I said.

"He has a point," Alex said to Jake.

I helped the boys carry the food down and set it up. The sushi was as big of a hit as Alex said it would be. Nathaniel (I assumed) already had a DVD loaded and paused to hide the title screen.

Alex pulled me out of the crowd into a quiet corner. "Some of the guys wanted to know if you'd be cool with couples pairing up," he asked. "I told them you probably would, but they wanted me to double check."

"What do you mean, pair up? Sit together?"

"Holding hands, necking, exchanging fluids, that kind of thing."

"As long as no one does something that could get me arrested, I'm cool," I said, trying very hard to keep my voice from cracking.

"A lot of parents aren't ok with it," he said. "They don't mind hosting as long as they don't have to see two guys or girls making out in front of their faces." I nodded, the image burning into my brain. "I'll set up a bedroom schedule to make sure no one walks in on anyone. No problem with screwing on your bed, right?"

"Make sure someone washes the sheets afterwards," I said.

"Damn, you see them coming now. I'll have to come up with new material."

"Gotcha," I said. "So, who are you pairing up with?"

"Jake," he said casually. I stared at him. He winked. "Gotcha back."

I glared at him playfully.

"Ok everyone, grab a plate and find a comfortable spot, because it's going to be a long one tonight," Nathaniel (I assumed) said. "It has come to my attention that our newest and youngest victim has been deprived of one of the most important film experiences of the twenty-first century. Seeing that he and his father have seen fit to provide this most excellent and admirable feast. . ." He spread his arms out and the whole group applauded. ". . .it is only fitting that we take the responsibility to fill the gap in Jake's education. And now, we'd better get started or we'll be up all night." He looked at the remote. "If I can figure out how to make this play."

Alex came up behind me as I headed for the stairs with my food. "Aren't you going to stay?"

"I didn't know I was invited," I said. *Please* say I am.

"Of course you are." Alex pointed to a half empty couch. I sat down, balancing my plate on the armrest. He squeezed in next to me, less than an inch away. I stopped breathing.

"Lights!" Nathaniel called out. Someone flipped the switch. The movie started with mysterious music, but I wasn't paying any attention to the television. It took everything I had to avoid gawking at Alex. When the room erupted in a loud cheer, I glanced at the screen in time to see the title.

The Lord of the Rings.

Oh no. No no no no no no no.

I'd worked so hard and for so long to avoid these movies. Five years after they were released I could honestly say I'd never watched a single second of any of them, not even a commercial. Until now. I knew what these movies would do to me. The feelings they'd rake up from the muck inside. The memories they'd stir up that I wanted so desperately to forget.

I had to leave. But I couldn't leave.

If I left, I might never get the chance again. I needed to be a part of what surrounded me. I needed what these kids had, what these kids *knew*. Even if I hosted, I wouldn't be invited. Alex sat so close I could feel his body heat. If I got up now, he might think it was his fault and back off.

The scene changed to depict the first war of the ring. Tens of thousands of orcs filled the screen. Not what I thought orcs looked like, but what I realized they *should* look like. Elves in golden armor lining up, arrows flying inches from their faces. The armies of Gondor marching to Mount Doom, armored with winged helms. Sauron himself on the field, wielding the power of the ring.

Something I thought was long dead and buried woke up. Excitement in a way I hadn't felt in longer than I could remember jolted me upright. Joy. Was that joy I was feeling? We were less than two minutes into the movie and I was completely and utterly transfixed. The dead, fat, thirty something lump of a guy got pushed off the couch. In his place was a twelve-year-old boy watching a story that once meant everything to him, transformed into something far more beautiful than he could've imagined.

And then Frodo was sitting under a tree. Not some actor. My once upon a time friend. My best friend. A best friend like I never had before and never had after. And would never have again.

I'd forgotten the story, but twelve-year old Nick knew every detail. He was the one who spoke after Frodo was stabbed on Weathertop by the Nazgul. An elf appeared to rescue the hobbits.

"Was it Arwen who showed up in the book?" one of the boys asked another.

"No, it was some other elf I think," another one said.

"Glorfindel," I/kid Nick said. They stared at me. "The elf from Rivendell who found them was named Glorfindel. Is that supposed to be Arwen? She was a minor character at best."

"She was added for a romantic lead," a girl explained.

"What happened Tom Bombadil? And the barrow wights? Aragorn didn't hand the hobbits their swords, they earned them. Gandalf riding to Isengard, we're not supposed to know that yet. And what's with Merry and Pippin? They're a lot more than comic relief."

Fourteen sets of eyes were on me.

"I'm not much of an expert," I mumbled.

"You know the name of a minor character off the top of your head, but you don't think you're an expert?" Alex asked. "How many times did you read the books?"

"A few," I stammered. "More. I lost count. I have a good memory for these things."

"You've never seen the movie before?"

I shook my head.

I was a part of the story as it unfolded. I spoke the black speech of Mordor at the council of Elrond. I braved the pass of Caradhras and the dark of Moria. I stood on the bridge of Khazad-dûm, speaking words I'd learned so long ago and couldn't forget if I tried. I pounded my foot to break the bridge, dragged over by the balrog's whip. I ran into the water to chase Frodo as he slipped away. I wasn't going to let him go to Mordor alone.

But I wasn't with him.

Brian went to Mordor without me.

"Are you ok?" Alex whispered.

I looked at him and realized I was holding his hand. Kid Nick did that. He was the one who could reach out and always have a hand to hold. I put my hand back in my lap. "Sorry," I said. "Kind of crowded in here."

"I guess," Alex said, but he kept looking at me.

The first movie ended and a fifteen-minute intermission was announced. Everyone scattered to find bathrooms. Jake wound his way through the crowd from his place on the floor. "What do you think?"

I asked cautiously. I didn't expect much. He never expressed an interest in fantasy or sci-fi, and never showed much enthusiasm for playing with the toy swords, castles, and knights I bought him when he was small.

"It's great!" he said enthusiastically. "I didn't know you read books like this."

"I used to," I said. "Lots of them, but the Lord of the Rings was always my favorite. Anyway, this is nothing. All the best parts are still coming. I don't want to spoil it but there's so much story left."

"Can I order the books on Amazon?"

"I'm sure I have copies somewhere," I said.

"How come you didn't take me to see the movies?"

"Good question," Alex said. "If you were so into these books, why didn't you see the movies?"

"I thought I'd be disappointed by them," I said.

Alex frowned. "Really."

He was too perceptive for a lie. The truth, at least a bit of it, would be necessary to satisfy his curiosity. "Watching these movies brings back a lot of memories. Some of them good, some of them not so good. Sometimes, it's better to forget the happy memories so you don't have to remember the sad ones."

Alex blinked. "Do you really think so?" he said in a soft voice.

I turned away to get another plate of food.

Accidentally grabbing Alex's hand didn't stop him from sitting back down next to me on the couch for the second movie. Jake sat down on Alex's other side, squeezing us all together. Being so close to me or to Jake didn't seem to bother Alex. Maybe he wasn't joking around about pairing up with Jake. Other couples were holding hands, kissing, and pawing each other. As though it was perfectly normal for two sixteen-year old boys or girls to make out in the open. I suppose in their world it *was* perfectly normal. They'd probably be just as comfortable in a movie theater, at the mall, or on a park bench. Things were so different in my time. Coming out in high school was unheard of. These kinds of relationships were so dangerous they had to remain hidden behind a web of lies and locked doors. If my past was like their present, maybe I'd understand what I was. Maybe I would've found kids my own age. Maybe I would've become a normal straight guy. Maybe I wouldn't be

plagued by my curse. But wondering about the what-ifs was a waste of time. What happened to me then would never have happened today. People are far more aware. My relationship with Jeremy would've been stopped before it got started.

But maybe I wouldn't have to wonder what I'd do if Alex and Jake started necking right next to me.

Freak out?
Smile?
Ask to join in?

I was completely wired by the end of the second movie, jabbering on a mile a minute about the little details I remembered, the details that were changed, and the details the films captured so perfectly. I had an audience, a small crowd gathering around me that seemed interested in what I was saying. It was past one in the morning. I was more awake than I'd been in a very long time. Kid Nick took over completely. He was in charge.

Until Mordor.

It started when Frodo and Sam looked out over Mordor for the first time, dressed in oversized orc gear. I had a hard time separating the movie and my memories of two young boys running around the forest in armor too big for us, hacking at ferns with swords too heavy for us to manage, and shouting at legions of orc trees until we were hoarse. And then Sam picked up Frodo to carry him up the mountain.

All at once, it hit me. I was blind to what was right in front of me as a child. In a flash, I understood why Brian chose the scenes he did. I understood why he always played Frodo to my Sam. I understood why he always wore the ring around his neck. I understood what he was trying to tell me. I was breathing too fast, too hard. How could I have been so blind to what he was telling me? Not Frodo and Sam.

Brian and Nick.

What our friendship meant to him. How much he needed me to help him carry his own ring. And I failed him. I wasn't there to carry him up the slopes of Mount Doom. I wasn't with him at the end of all

things. The ring being destroyed and the victory over Sauron on screen felt hollow. I couldn't see the story playing out on the screen. All I could see was my first and only true best friend in times I'd forgotten. I remembered lobster hanging out of our mouths. I remembered practicing our lines. I remembered walking together naked through the woods in silence under the moonlight. I heard those words, those damned words, not spoken by Frodo to Sam, but by Brian to me. *You cannot always be torn in two. You will have to be one and whole, for many years. You have so much to enjoy and to be, and to do. Your part in the story will go on.*

"You're crying," Alex whispered.

I wiped my sleeve across my eyes. "Sorry," I said, launching myself off the couch, shutting myself in the bathroom. My eyes were red, my face streaked. How long had I been crying without realizing it? I splashed cold water on my face, blew my nose, and found some eye drops buried in the back of the medicine cabinet. By the time I came back the movie had ended. I kept myself busy insisting that the drivers get some rest before they leave, spreading out air mattresses and blankets all over the floor. I went looking for Jake and Alex after I had the rest of them settled, finding them in Jakes's bedroom.

"I'm sorry if I embarrassed you," I said to Jake.

"You didn't embarrass me," he said, getting off the bed.

"Did you still want the books?" He nodded. I led them to the basement storage room, making a show out of wondering which box they were in. "I need some help, it's extremely heavy." I somehow pushed it off the shelf, the two of them barely managing to hold on while we struggled to set it down.

The red book was on top, right where I knew it would be. I handed it to Jake. "My paperbacks didn't survive, so you can have my special copy."

He pulled it out of the slipcover. "I'll take good care of it."

"The Lord of the Rings was very important to me when I was growing up. I *lived* this story. I faced the balrog on the bridge of Khazad-dûm. I stood with Aragorn on the walls of Helm's Deep. I rode with Théoden on the Pellenor fields." I smiled. "You must think I was a dork."

"I don't think it's dorky at all," Jake said, paging through the book.

"You guys want to see something?" I pulled the long, thin package out of the box, tugging at the strings holding it together until it unwrapped itself. Two sets of eyes went wide.

"Is that a real sword?" Alex asked.

"It's made of steel, but it's not sharp," I said, offering the sword to Jake. "Careful, the blade is covered with grease to keep it from rusting." Jake handed the book to Alex, taking the sword from me. I smiled when he realized it's weight. "I got that when I was around your age."

"Grandpa let you have a real sword?"

"It's not sharp," I repeated to avoid the question. "Check this out," I said, pulling out a heavy bundle, unwrapping it to reveal the armor. "This stuff weighs a ton." Jake looked at me in wonder. "It should fit you if you want to put it on."

Something fell to the floor with a splat. An old envelope with pictures. Where did those come from? Alex picked them up and laughed. "Is this you?"

He held up a grainy photo from a cheap camera. It was me, fully dressed in the adventure clothes, holding my sword in the air, the cabin in Maine behind us. But I wasn't alone. Brian was standing next to me, equally dressed for battle, grinning as broadly as he could. I felt like I'd been punched in the face.

"Let me see," Jake said. "Whoa, that's so awesome! Your friend has the same stuff as you. Grandpa bought both of you cosplay outfits?"

"You know how he is about buying things," I said.

"You said he was the exact opposite when you were a kid," Jake pointed out.

"There's an inscription in the book," Alex said. "But I can't read it because it's in Lord of the Rings language."

"For my best friend Brian on his twelfth birthday, from Nick," I murmured. "I wrote that myself."

Jake looked through the pictures, handing one to me. "Who's this?"

The moment I looked at it, I realized these pictures came from Brian's cheap 110 cartridge camera. He must've have stuck them in the book. I'd never looked inside after it was returned to me. The picture in my hands had to be taken by Brian, there was no other way it could

exist. My arms were wrapped around Jeremy's waist from the side. The picture was blurry, but it didn't matter. I knew how that boy felt without needing to see his face. I knew he had no idea what was in store for him. The wound that would never fully heal.

"No one, just a family friend," I said, handing the picture back. "This stuff is all yours if you want it. I have both sets in the box in case Alex or anyone else wants to play along."

"I don't understand," Alex said. "If you gave the book to your friend for his birthday, why do you have it?"

I closed my eyes. "He didn't need it anymore." My voice cracked.

"Are you ok?" Jake asked, his tone more caring than I expected.

"I miss my friend," I said. "We used to act out scenes from the stories in incredible detail, memorizing all our lines and choreographing every move. Brian was a stickler for precision. Every line and every motion had to be exactly as written in the book. He was the real expert. I don't think he would've liked the movies, too many details were changed." I took a deep breath. "Those pictures were taken at his grandfather's cabin in Maine. I stayed with him for three weeks the summer I was twelve. We camped out, swam in a lake in the middle of the night, and lived like barbarians. I had one of the best times of my life with him."

"We could look him up if you wanted," Jake said. "There are sites on the internet. Maybe he's on Myspace."

"That's not it," Alex said quietly. "He died, didn't he?"

I looked away.

"I'm sorry," Alex said gently. "It looked like he was a good friend." I nodded. "Come on, Jake," Alex said softly. Jake followed him out of the room, leaving the pictures on top of the box.

I took the pictures upstairs with me. The house was quiet even though there were kids sprawled out on the floor, chairs, and couches. I got my coat and went outside onto the deck. The cold night air slapped me in the face. I flipped through the pictures, only a dozen of them, the color washed out and faded from age. All from that summer. Some I remembered him taking, like the one with my disaster of a birthday cake. Some I didn't remember, like the one of me holding a lobster with its claws around my neck. Some I didn't know existed, like

the one he took of our campsite in all its disheveled glory. And the one with the two of us, swords in the air. Best friends.

But I stared the most at the one with Jeremy. I hadn't seen his face in a long time. All the pictures I had of him were lost or destroyed a long time ago.

"I was wondering what happened to you," Alex said, his teeth chattering. I didn't notice him come outside. "Shit, it's cold out. Icicles are hanging off my balls. I'm not bothering you, am I?"

"No, it's ok." I put the pictures on the table.

"Jake passed out," he said, answering my question before I asked.

"What about you?"

"I had three Red Bulls. I'll be up for days. Besides, someone purloined my bed." He fidgeted a little. "I didn't realize you were an actor."

"I'm not," I said. "What gave you that idea?"

"Those scenes you used to play out with your friend. That's acting."

"Play acting is more like it," I said. "Brian was the real actor. He got into the character's heads and made the lines sound believable. But he didn't do theater, that was my thing."

"You did theater?"

"I played the piano for a couple productions in junior high school. We did Charlie Brown and Snoopy." He started singing.

If just one person believes in you,
Deep enough, and strong enough, believes in you

"Please stop," I said quietly.

"My singing isn't that bad, is it?" Alex said playfully.

"That's not why," I said.

"Memories again," he murmured. "You must have some terrible memories to be so willing to forget the good ones."

I couldn't look at him.

"Does it have something to do with that guy in the picture?" he asked.

I whipped my head around, glaring at him so sharply that he recoiled.

"I'd better go," he said, heading for the door.

"No," I said more harshly than I meant. "Sorry, I didn't mean it that way." I slumped back in my chair. Alex turned back around. "His name was Jeremy. We were close when I was a kid. He bought the swords and armor for us. He taught me how to play the piano." I took a deep breath. "He helped me through a bad patch in my life when no one else was there for me. When I was eleven, I hit a bully over the head with a chair. The school expelled me, but Jeremy threatened the principal until she backed down. He was the kind of guy who took me fishing for my birthday even though he was terrified of boats. He was very special to me."

"You were lucky to have someone like that," Alex said.

"I guess," I said.

He stared for a moment, then smiled a little. "You know, I'm not like my dad at all. I'm more like my mom, but it's not the same thing. My dad and I don't have much in common. Not like you and Jake."

"Jake and I aren't much alike," I said.

"I like Jake," he said. "Not as a boyfriend, in case you were wondering. And before you ask, he hasn't come out to anyone. If I had to guess, I don't think he knows yet, which is perfectly fine. I like him because he's so serious about the things he believes in and he thinks so deeply about them. I call him my pit bull, because when he gets his teeth into something he won't let go. He's very open and honest, at least with his close friends. So, I know you two have a lot in common."

"Like what?"

"He told me about the stuff you gave him," Alex said. The temperature dropped another fifty degrees. "Actually, he told everyone by accident. We were doing a group thing at Galyap where everyone was supposed to tell their dream to the group. The leader said fantasy instead of dream, so it sounded like he meant a sex fantasy. Jake jumped right in and blurted it out. He was so embarrassed when he realized that's not what we meant, but everyone was cool about it. We talked a lot afterwards."

"What did he tell you?" I asked.

"You have to promise me not to tell Jake I told you," he said.

"I can't keep that promise if he's in any trouble."

"Nothing like that," Alex said. "He told me about the time you caught him, and he showed me the equipment you gave him. You know, the bondage stuff." My stomach tied up in knots. "Everything you gave him was pretty old and beat up, so I assumed it belonged to you. I guess you have that in common with each other."

I couldn't look at him.

"Promise you won't tell Jake I told you?"

I was silent.

"I'd better go inside," he said. "I can't feel my ass anymore."

I waited until he was in the doorway. "Why did you tell me this?"

He turned around. "Because it's incredibly sad to forget everything good that ever happened to you. Because I can see you're depressed. When I see people who are depressed, I want to do something about it." He smiled a little and closed the door.

I used to think people who said they learned something about themselves from a dream were full of shit. People should just admit they figured it out. Why disguise what they did by claiming it came from a dream? As though you weren't responsible because the answer just came to you.

I changed my mind that night.

I dreamt I was in the basement of our house in New Jersey. Jeremy's house. I opened the door to the storage room and turned on the light. He/I was standing on the platform, naked with his hands chained above his head. I walked in front of him. He/I looked at me with determined eyes. "Let me out," he/I said.

"I'm not allowed," I said.

"Let me out," he/I said again.

"I can't," I said. I turned around. I wasn't alone. "What should I do?"

Jeremy put his hand on my shoulder. "Let him out."

I turned to Brian, wearing his armor. He nodded. "Let him out."

Others, frozen in time from long ago. Chris, Daniel, Andy, Jonathan, and Parker. Jonas and Kerry. Sean. Jeff. Ana. They all said the same thing. "Let him out."

"I don't have the key."

"Yes, you do," Jeremy said.

The key was in my hand.

I couldn't figure out how to put it in the lock. The key wouldn't turn. I turned around. "Help me," I said.

No one else was there.

I had to do it myself.

I woke up.

I understood.

I was going to figure out how to let him/me out.

Chapter 27

September 8, 1982

Jeremy slammed on the brakes right before he hit a kid on a bicycle. "This is the clusterfuck to end all clusterfucks," he muttered.

At elementary school, everyone knew what they were supposed to do. Things were organized and teachers made sure everyone followed the rules. At junior high school, the rule seemed to be that there were no rules. Cars and school buses pushed their way forward sloppily instead of moving in a neat line. Bicycles weaved through traffic. Kids jumped in front of cars. I looked at the little slip of paper in my hand. My class schedule – the only guide to where I was supposed to go and what I was supposed to do. I was sure I was going to lose it. The computer ink was smudged from me holding onto it so tightly.

"Now we know why everyone pulled over on the main road," Jeremy said. "You'd better get out and walk the rest of the way. It's getting late." I wasn't ready to get out yet. All the bravery I felt in the middle of the night was completely gone. I wanted to hold his hand, but someone might see through the windows. Jeremy did everything for me this morning. He made a big breakfast, packed me a nice lunch, and put notebooks and pencils in my backpack.

I stalled. "What are you doing while I'm at school?"

"I've got a full dance card today," he said. "The car needs an oil change, grocery shopping, cleaning, and laundry. All the fun things in life."

"It's my week for laundry," I said, still stalling.

"We talked about this. You've got school now, that's your only chore. I'm not going off to work, so I've got plenty of time to take care of things. You do the homework, I'll do the housework." I liked how we split up the chores. It made me feel more grown up. Not that I was going to miss doing dishes and cleaning toilets. He zipped into an open space when a car moved. "Alright, time to go. Do you have everything?" I refused to move. "Come on, it's only the first day. Can't be anywhere near as bad as the fifteenth." I groaned. "Love you," he said.

"I love you too," I said back. I had to squeeze out because the car next to us was so close. I was immediately swallowed by a sea of people that were all bigger than me, and unlike me they all seemed to know what to do. I ducked and dodged my way to the front doors until I saw a teacher with a whistle, her arms crossed and a scowl on her face. She made it pretty obvious the front doors were off limits. I backed up into someone.

"Watch it, dweeb," she said.

"Sorry," I mumbled, twisting around. I was scared even though I knew there was nothing to be scared about. Someone put a hand on my shoulder. I whirled around to see a man wearing the kind of suit jacket that had suede patches on the elbows.

"Seventh grade?" he asked.

"Uh, yeah," I mumbled.

He pointed to the other end of the school. "The seventh grade awaits the bell on the corner section of asphalt. You will find your comrades there." I stared at him, no idea what he just said. "That way," he pointed.

"Ok," I said. He already turned away to help someone else. I felt stupid. They told us where to wait at orientation last week. I weaved through the crowd until I got to a fenced off section of the blacktop. It had to be the right place because the kids seemed more my size. They were standing in groups like weeds coming out from the pavement. I didn't recognize most of them. Three different elementary schools came together into the junior high school which meant I didn't know two thirds of the kids here. I couldn't believe I did math before school even

started. Everyone looked unfriendly. So many kids I wouldn't like and who wouldn't like me.

Brian found me before I could find him. "I was waiting for you," he said.

"There was a lot of traffic," I explained.

He pulled me behind another group of kids like we were hiding. "Tommy Walker is looking for you. I don't know why. He told me to tell you."

I shrugged, trying not to look worried. Tommy knew he was supposed stay away from me. He knew how much trouble he'd be in if he picked on me. A loud bell screamed. All at once, the entire crowd moved like a wave towards a pair of open doors in the side of the school. No lining up like in elementary school. Every man for himself. "See you in French!" Brian yelled before the crowd pushed him in a different direction. I wished he had homeroom with me. Brian would know what to do and where to go. I got shoved in every direction, clutching the schedule tight in my hand. Homeroom, 117. All the doors looked the same. How was I supposed to tell which one was 117? I wandered around aimlessly until I figured out the numbers were on top of the doors. 112, 113, almost there. Another bell rang and the entire hallway emptied impossibly fast. I ran, slipping into 117 right before the teacher closed the door behind me.

Junior high didn't work the same way as elementary school. Instead of a desk and coat closet where we kept our things, we had lockers in the hallway. The teacher hovered over us while we tested the combinations. In elementary school my homeroom class stayed together most of the day. Here, homeroom was only for announcements and having attendance taken. No lining up and no quiet in the halls – no more being treated like little kids. Freedom. The price of freedom turned out to be a thirty-page rulebook they told us to learn before the end of the week. The place ran on a point system. Five points for being caught in the hall without a pass, ten points for wearing inappropriate clothes, twenty points for fighting, twenty-five for smoking, and so on. There had to be over a hundred ways to get in trouble. Ten points got you detention and twenty got you suspended. You got extra points for saying you didn't know you were breaking a rule.

After homeroom was French, then math, then history, then English, and then lunch. I had music, gym, and science in the afternoon. I chose French instead of Spanish because of Brian. His family came from northern Maine near Canada, so they spoke French instead of English. The class was impossible. The teacher didn't say a single word in English the entire time. I had no idea what she meant when she kept saying "repetay" and "plufor." Textbooks piled up, bigger and thicker than any I ever had in elementary school. By the end of third period, I had homework in every single class. On the *first day*. By the time I walked into English class, I decided this junior high school thing sucked.

"Ladies and gentlemen!" a man said from behind the teacher's desk. The same man who pointed me to the seventh-grade blacktop this morning. I couldn't figure out why. He couldn't be the teacher. I assumed he was the vice principal or something like that. Teachers were women. Teachers were always women. Everyone knew that.

"Please select your preferred seat and take it without delay. Our time here is short and we have a great deal to accomplish." Every other class assigned seats. Kids scrambled to grab the back row in a mad rush. Brian and I were a second too slow, so the only desks we could get together were in front. "Ladies and gentlemen, thank you for your undivided attention!" He waited until everyone was quiet. "First, let us ascertain if we are all in the correct classroom. I am Mr. Humber, we are in room 224, and this is seventh grade honors level English. If you've arrived here in error, now would be the opportune moment to depart."

It took me a moment to figure out what he said. At least, I think I figured it out. Maybe.

"Excellent. The next item on our agenda is to create placards to identify ourselves. As you will observe, there are two sheets of paper on your desk. On the piece folded lengthwise, please write either Mr. or Ms. as appropriate, followed by your surname and only your surname."

"Mr. Ummm, what's a surname?" some kid asked.

"Your surname is commonly referred to as your last name," the teacher said. "As you can see by the placard on my desk, my name is Mr. Humber. The same as when I announced that information less than a minute ago." I wasn't sure if he was telling a joke. He didn't seem like the kind of teacher who told jokes. I wrote my last name on the sheet

of paper. It looked funny. Mr. Welles. No one ever called me that. "Ladies and gentlemen, if I'm to have the opportunity to learn each of your names, it would be necessary for the placards to face towards me and not yourselves." I turned mine around, embarrassed until I saw everyone else made the same mistake.

"Mr. Humber, why are we writing down our last names?" another kid asked.

"I've asked each of you to write your surnames because it would be extremely inconvenient to call on a student by saying 'Hey you in the second row with the glasses.'" No one laughed. "Very well, our next order of business is to validate that each of you has received a textbook. You will find it located on the wire shelf beneath each of your respective desks. If any of you find it is not present, please respond by raising your hand." I looked under my desk at the thickest book so far today. I groaned out loud.

"As you've all been informed, this class is seventh grade honors level English. During this course, we will focus on one thing and one thing alone. Writing." He stopped and looked around the room with a stern expression. "I can assure each and every one of you that by the end of this course you'll be able to communicate your ideas precisely, succinctly, and eloquently. I have only two expectations of students in my class. First, I expect you to respect me and your fellow students at all times, without exception. I have no patience for those who believe that mistakes made by others are an opportunity to belittle and humiliate. Second, nothing less than your finest work will be tolerated." He looked around the room again with the same stern expression. I decided I didn't like Mr. Humber.

"As this is a course in effective writing, I see no reason to delay. Therefore, I'd like each of you to write an essay on the following thought." He wrote quickly on the blackboard, reading the words out loud. "The pen is mightier than the sword."

"When's it due?" asked some kid. Mr. Epstein.

"At the end of this class."

I slammed back in my chair. He expected us to write an essay by the end of class? That was impossible! The whole class was murmuring. "I suggest you use your time wisely. You'll find the second piece of paper

on your desk suitable for this purpose. Additional paper is available should it be required."

"But how long is it supposed to be?" one of the girls asked. Ms. Ackerman.

"As long as it needs to be to explain your thoughts clearly."

I decided I hated Mr. Humber.

I stared at the paper. I'd heard the expression before and I thought I understood it. But I couldn't take that feeling and turn it into words. No matter how hard I tried, my thoughts wouldn't come together. The minute hand on the clock was moving as fast as the second hand usually did. Who ever heard of writing a whole essay this quickly? The room was filled with the sound of pencils scratching on paper. Everyone had something to write except for me. Brian had already covered one side of the paper in his small handwriting and was flipping it over.

For no reason at all, a group of kids in the far corner started laughing. I looked at them, but they weren't doing anything besides writing. The teacher was busy grading papers and didn't notice. I tried to concentrate, and then the same corner laughed again even louder this time. This was hard enough without them distracting me. The teacher didn't do anything. They cracked up *again*.

"Mr. Humber, tell them to stop," whined Ms. Ackerman.

The teacher looked at the clock above the door. "Ladies and gentlemen, only twenty-seven minutes remain for you to complete your assignments. I suggest you utilize the time that remains wisely." What was with this guy? He makes a big deal about being strict, and then he ignores a bunch of kids cracking up? More kids in the corner laughed again, even louder than last time. I slammed my pencil down on the desk and stared at them.

I finally saw a note being passed. The next kid opened it, read it, and for no reason that side of the class burst out laughing. The girl who read it turned a little red and passed it on. The next kid read it, and this time the girl who passed it on laughed along with the rest of them. It didn't make any sense.

The explosions got louder and lasted longer each time another kid read the note. Half the class was cracking up and the other half, me included, was staring at them wondering what the heck was going on.

364

The teacher ignored the whole thing. He was acting like he was deaf. The note snaked through the rows. I stared as hard as I could when the kid behind me read it, but I swear I couldn't tell what made everyone else laugh. He handed the note to me.

Look at the footprints on the ceiling.
Pass it on.

Footprints on the ceiling? I looked up. I didn't see any footprints on the ceiling. The class exploded again. Duh. I felt stupid. I tossed the note on Brian's desk. He was so busy writing he didn't notice. I had to tap him on the shoulder twice. I didn't understand how he could concentrate on writing. He saw the note, read it, and looked up. I couldn't stop myself from laughing at him.

The note made its way quickly around the rest of the class. I suppose it was unfair to be the last kid who read it because she didn't get to laugh at anyone. The girl at the back of the last row looked around, confused about what to do next. The teacher looked up. He seemed *really* annoyed.

"Am I to assume that whatever it is has finally run its course? Where is the cause of the disruption?" The girl in the back raised her hand. He walked over to her quickly, took the note from her, and stood in front of the whole class like he was going to lecture us. Everyone stared at him. He opened the note. I leaned forward in my chair. Would he really do it?

He looked up. Just for a second.

I swear, I never laughed so hard in my entire life. Real tears were coming down my face. I thought I was going to pass out. We were so loud I thought the teacher next door was going to scream at us. It took five minutes before the laughing died down. The teacher looked even more annoyed.

"I strongly suggest you use the last ten minutes of class to your advantage."

The only thing I'd written on the paper was my name. Ten minutes, how could I write anything that fast? I thought I had no idea what to

write, but I did have one stupid idea. No time left and no other ideas, so stupid it would have to be. I only managed to write one paragraph when the teacher spoke again. "Ladies and gentlemen, as utterly enjoyable as this class period has been, we've now reached its inevitable conclusion. If you would most kindly pass your papers to the front, I will eagerly collect them." He swept the papers from my desk while I put my pencil away. "While it is tempting to keep you in suspense, I've decided to inform those of you who care about such things that this essay will not count towards your grades this quarter. However, I can assure you we will be doing exercises of this nature on a regular basis, and those will count heavily in my evaluation of your performance." The bell rang. I grabbed my books, glad to be the heck out of Mr. Humber's seventh grade honors level English class. I waited for Brian outside the door.

"That was hilarious," he said.

"I couldn't concentrate," I said. "What did you write about?"

"How it's easier to change people's minds if you convince them than if you force them." I felt like I wanted to slap myself on the forehead. He put the feeling I had into words so easily. "What about you?"

"It was stupid," I said. "I wrote about how that footprints note had the power to mess up the whole class."

He stared at me. "That's not stupid at all. I didn't think of that."

"Who do you think started it?" I asked.

"I don't know, but when Mr. Humber finds out, they're going to be in deep trouble. Come on, we'd better go to lunch."

The cafeteria was about as far from our English class as a place could be in the school. We walked as fast as we dared. In elementary school, we sat at our desks with our classes for lunch until they sent us outside no matter how cold or wet it was. Here, it was up to us to find our own table. Rows and rows of them, eight kids per table. My plan was to get to the cafeteria early so we could find an empty table. That way, other kids would have to choose to sit with us. But we were too late – every table already had at least three kids. We were probably going to get stuck with kids we didn't like.

We wandered the rows, but the few tables we might be able to join were already full. The ones with space were the ones where we didn't

belong, full of burnouts, ninth graders, or girls. Tables were already being called to go up to the lunch line. A teacher started walking towards us, forcing us to go the other way. If we didn't figure this out soon the tables would be empty from kids lining up for lunch and there'd be no way to figure it out.

Then I heard it. Two words. Barely loud enough to understand.

". . .saving throw. . ."

I whirled around, spinning in place, trying to find where it came from. Two tables to the left, a D&D rulebook. Three open seats. I dragged Brian over. "Hey," I said. "Can we sit here?"

Five faces I didn't know stared at us. That's must've been why we passed this table before. One of them, a tallish blond kid with freckles spoke first. "Why the fuck should we let you sit here?"

"We play D&D too," I said.

It felt like they all breathed at the same time. "Yeah, all right," the blond kid said. "Weren't you guys in Humber's fourth period class?" I nodded. "That was fucking classic! Whoever thought of that was some kind of genius!"

"Whoever thought of that is going to be in detention for a year," the chubby kid with brown hair said.

"Don't be chicken shit, Parker," the blond kid said. "All I know is that it started near the corner where I was sitting, but no one will fess up." He shoved two blank character sheets at us along with a handful of dice. "If you guys want to play, make some characters. We play by advanced rules and we're already at level eight, so you have to start there. You need to borrow a rulebook?"

"Nah, we know how to make characters," I said. Finding five kids who played D&D had to be some kind of dream. I rolled the dice and scratched out my numbers on the paper. This was going to be awesome.

Some kid, probably a ninth grader by the size of him, grabbed the blond kid from behind in a headlock. "Hey, dork," he said. The blond kid didn't seem scared. He seemed annoyed. *I* was scared.

"Fuck off, Paulie," the blond kid said. "I'm busy."

"Playing again? Don't you guys ever take a break?"

"Why don't you go jerk off your friends?"

"You'd love to watch, wouldn't you?" the ninth grader – Paulie fired back. He let the blond kid go, who turned around and punched Paulie in the arm. Hard. The blond kid had to be completely crazy, that was the only explanation.

"Fucking baby brothers are such a pain in the ass," Paulie said. Brothers? They didn't act like brothers. At least, not like how I thought brothers were supposed to act. "Did you have Humber yet?"

"Yeah, he's almost as big a prick as you," the blond kid said.

"He's not. He's the best teacher I ever had."

"He sucks!" the short kid with black hair said.

"I'll leave you dorks with this one." Paulie leaned in. "Look at the footprints on the ceiling." He laughed and walked off. My mouth was hanging open. So was everyone else's.

"How did he know that already?" the chubby kid – Parker asked.

"Fucking beats me," the blond kid said. "Come on, let's play."

"Nick the prick!" Tommy Walker sat down in the empty chair next to me. "And Cryin' too. Still cryin' about your glasses?" Tommy looked like he grew a foot in every direction. He had a *mustache* on his face. I tried to move away, but he grabbed my hair and yanked me back, hard. "Damn, I think you've got the flames cranked up too high again." Everyone at the table was staring at us. It didn't take a genius to figure out what Tommy Walker was all about.

"I'll call a teacher," I said, trying to keep my voice from shaking.

"New school, new rules," he said. "You think they're going to care? I owe you for putting me in the hospital. The ambulance cost my dad five hundred bucks. Now it's my turn." I thought he was about to beat me up right there. Then out of nowhere, someone grabbed Tommy in a headlock from behind, pulling him out of the chair. Walker jerked around and struggled. Whoever grabbed him didn't let go. I looked up. Paulie.

"If I ever catch you bothering my brother or his friends again, I'm going to kick your ass so hard they'll be pulling it out of your mouth," Paulie hissed. Tommy was big for a seventh grader, but Paulie still made him look puny. "Get the fuck out of here, and make sure I never see your fucking face again." Paulie dropped him on the floor. Tommy struggled to get up and was having a hard time catching his breath. He

didn't look at me before disappearing into the crowd. I wanted to hug Paulie.

"Ok Paulie, you can go now," the blond kid said.

"Chris, you are a *complete* asshole," Paulie said, slapping the blond kid in the back of the head. "Next time I'll let him beat on you." I watched him sit at a table nearby, giving a high five to one of his friends. Everyone looked directly at me.

"What did he mean when he said he owed you for putting him in the hospital?" the blond kid – Chris asked.

I tried to come up with a lie, but Brian opened his big fat mouth. "Nick hit him over the head with a chair and gave him a concussion. They took him away in an ambulance and everything." I elbowed him the ribs. "Oww," he said quietly.

"So, you're like a psycho," Chris said. "Psycho is cool." I let out my breath. Chris pointed at Parker. "See, instead of throwing your notebook at Matt Chadwick when you spazzed out after he called you Porker, you should've been more like Nick." I was instantly curious about what he meant about Parker spazzing out. Between that and the chubbiness he almost reminded me of the old Nick.

The bell rang before I could find out. "We're playing at my house after school, want to come?" Chris asked.

"Definitely," I said.

"I can't," Brian said, grabbing his backpack and disappearing into the crowd. I waved to the guys and ran after him.

"Why can't you come?" I asked him.

"I have extra chores. My dad wants me to paint the house before winter," he said. "And I have to learn to throw a football."

"I can help," I said.

"Just forget it, ok?" Brian stormed off. I knew he wasn't mad at me. He was probably disappointed he couldn't play. I wondered if I could get Jeremy to hire someone to paint Brian's house like he paid a guy to mow my parent's lawn so I didn't have to do it. But I knew it wouldn't work, because Brian's dad cared more about making Brian do it than about getting the house painted. And arguing with Brian's dad only made things worse. I felt bad for him.

Still, I smiled. One friend to six in just a few minutes. And it was so easy.

<center>⌒✖︎✖︎⌒</center>

"Holy shit!" Paulie said when he answered the door. "No, it's cool. I'm not laughing at you. I'm just thinking what Chris is going to say when he sees you." It was Jeremy's idea for me to get my D&D stuff before I went to Chris' house, but it was my idea to wear the adventure clothes. Jeremy waved as he drove away.

"Nice wheels," Paulie said, watching the car disappear down the street. "Come on in. They're down in the basement. Do you need any help with all that stuff?"

"I'm good," I said, dragging in two backpacks full of my D&D books. He pointed me towards an open door in the hallway. Their house seemed nice enough even though it was smaller than my parents' house. I figured they must be religious since there were crosses on every wall. Some plain and some with Jesus nailed to them, blood and all.

"There's soda in the fridge if you want," he said from the other room.

"Hey, Paulie," I said.

He poked his head around the corner. "Just Paul. Chris calls me Paulie to piss me off."

"Sorry." I smiled a little. "Thanks. For lunch."

"I hate bullies," he said. "Let me know if that punk bothers you again. I straightened out that Matt kid last year and I'll do the same to whatever his name if he doesn't leave you alone." I nodded. I went down the narrow stairs to the basement, dragging the backpacks behind me. It wasn't finished like Jeremy's, but there was a rug on the floor and some Star Trek posters on the gray brick walls. The group sat around a table covered with D&D books, papers, dice, maps, and little metal miniatures.

"If that's you Paulie, get lost," Chris said without looking up.

"It's Nick," I said. They all looked up at me.

"Holy shit!" Chris shouted. Just like Paul predicted.

<center>370</center>

I shrugged. "It's more fun to play dressed up." I let the armor jingle as much as I could as I walked to the table.

"Is that real?" the short kid asked, pointing at the sword.

I pulled the cloak back and drew the sword from its sheath. "It's not sharp, but it's hardened steel so you can hack at things without nicking the blade. You want to hold it?"

"Shit, that's heavy," he said as I handed it to him.

We never got around to playing that afternoon. Every single one of them wanted to try the armor and play with the sword. Chris also insisted on making *absolutely* sure I had *absolutely* everything they made for D&D by going through *absolutely* everything in my backpacks. They played every day after school so all I had to do was come over tomorrow for a chance to play for real. At least I found out all their names. Parker's real name was David, but he wanted everyone to call him Parker because he hated his name. I didn't understand why he hated David so much, it didn't seem like a bad name. The Japanese kid (not Chinese like I thought) was named Daniel, not Dan, and definitely never Danny. The short one was Andy. The last one, Jonathan, didn't talk the entire time I was there.

Everyone left at five o'clock. They all lived nearby so they could walk home. "I guess I'd better call my uncle to pick me up." I was proud I remembered to call Jeremy my uncle.

"My mother doesn't get home until late tonight so you can stay as long as you want," Chris said. I shrugged and sat back down. He was scribbling something in his notebook.

"What are you writing?" I asked. He blocked the notebook with his arms.

"An idea for a new adventure. I've got lots of ideas. They pop into my head all the time." He kept writing. "Are you rich?"

"I guess so, a little."

"You seem like you're rich. Your uncle has a seriously fucking cool car and you have all this stuff."

I shrugged. "What's your adventure about?" I asked, trying to change the subject.

"Like I'm going to tell you. Find out when you play it. We can run some old ones separately that everyone else already played." Chris

slammed the notebook shut. "Let's go piss off Paulie." I didn't want to piss off Paul, he seemed like a good guy. Still, I followed him up the stairs. Paul was on the couch, reading a textbook. Chris yelled, jumped over the armrest of the couch, and landed right on top of him.

"Shit, Chris," Paul said, throwing him back on the other side of the couch without looking up. "What do you want for dinner?"

"Macaroni and cheese," Chris said.

"Not four nights in a row. We've got TV dinners in the freezer." Paul looked up at me. "You want to stay for dinner?"

"I don't know," I said. "I have to ask my uncle."

Chris yelled again and launched himself into Paul so hard the couch jerked. It knocked into the table at the end. A picture frame made of glass wobbled and fell to the floor, breaking into a hundred pieces. Paul tossed Chris off again. "What broke?" Paul asked me.

"Picture frame," I said.

"Oh shit," Paul said. "You idiot!"

"It wasn't my fault!" Chris yelled back.

"How is it not your fault?" Paul screamed. "You knocked the table! Mom's going to have a conniption when she sees! That was Grandma's crystal frame!"

"It wasn't my fault!" Chris screamed again. "You're the one who threw me over that way! You broke it!" He tore past me, knocking me hard in the shoulder. I heard pounding on the stairs and a door slamming.

"Shit," Paul said, bending down to pick up the pieces.

"Can I help?" I asked. It felt right to help him, considering what he did at lunch.

"I got it," he muttered. I went down the step into the den and bent down to help Paul pick up the pieces anyway. I watched him carefully brush off an old black and white wedding picture.

"Maybe it can be glued," I said.

Paul shook his head. "Not a chance. I have to vacuum. You should probably go home."

"Yeah. I'll go say bye to Chris."

"Don't," he said. "When Chris gets like that it's better to leave him alone. Don't let it bother you." I nodded and called Jeremy, waiting for

him by the front door. There was no noise from upstairs, just the whine of the vacuum from the den. I felt weird standing around with nothing to do.

"My uncle is here," I yelled to Paul when Jeremy got there. He helped me bring out my stuff and put it in the trunk.

Jeremy rolled down the window and stuck his hand out. "I'm Jeremy."

"Paul," he said, shaking it. "We'll see you tomorrow. Right?" he said to me. Like he wanted me to come back even though I wasn't hanging out with him.

"Yeah," I said.

"Is that one of your friends?" Jeremy asked as we pulled away.

"His brother," I explained.

"Hope you're hungry, I have a prime rib in the oven."

"You made prime rib? Seriously?"

"With Yorkshire pudding, and mashed potatoes," he said. "I wanted to make you something nice for your first day."

"I have a lot of homework and I still have to practice," I said. "It's five-thirty already. How am I supposed to do two hours of homework and then practice for two hours? Maybe I should've come straight home."

"Making new friends is more important," he said. "I'll help with the homework so you can practice. Don't sweat the other stuff."

"Yeah, I guess," I said.

When we got home, Jeremy went straight to the kitchen to check the meat. The house smelled delicious. I watched him getting dinner ready. "Sorry for ditching you today," I said.

"What are you talking about?"

"After school," I said. "You picked me up but all I did was tell you take me to a friend's house. I told you nothing happened when you asked about school, but a lot happened today."

"Kiddo, please. I'm excited you made new friends. If you want to tell me about school, I'm happy to listen."

"Later," I said. I wrapped my arms around him. "Let's go upstairs."

"We haven't had dinner yet," he said.

"Early bird gets the worm," I said.

"What do you mean?" he asked.

I put his hand between my legs so he could feel I was hard. "Ah," he said. "That kind of worm."

He chased me all the way to the bedroom.

Chapter 28

October 1, 1982

I wrote in the biggest letters that fit, holding up the piece of notebook paper when my work of high art was complete. The entire lunch table applauded my brilliance.

Mr. Humber is an Asshole!

The capital A was important, because he wasn't just any old asshole. He was *the* Asshole. I drew a number 3 on its side with a big arrow to the middle to make sure my point was completely clear. Andy took that as a challenge and drew something more. . .anatomically correct. If a teacher saw it, we'd probably be suspended for a week. Chris laughed so hard soda came out of his nose, which of course only made us laugh harder.

Plenty of teachers were assholes with lower case a's. Our math teacher, Mrs. Wojack, handed out ridiculous assignments. The first night of school we had to count all the letters in a long paragraph to figure out the mean and median. It took *hours*. Mrs. Howard, the history teacher, insisted on calling Parker by his first name even after Parker asked her three times not to. She also insisted on using Daniel's Japanese name which sounded like "shcaroo." Daniel hated that name worse than Parker hated David. The science teacher, Miss Lyons, talked so softly no one could hear her. She was such a neat freak that she used a ruler on the board to make sure her writing was straight. She even

marked us down a grade if we didn't cut off the little ends left over from ripping paper out of a spiral notebook.

Mr. Humber was *the* Asshole because he was impossible to please. On the second day of school, he handed back our pen is mightier than the sword impromptu essays (there's a special name for writing an essay without enough time). My single paragraph was covered with corrections marked in that special shade of red ink only teachers used. How could he expect me to worry about things like grammar and punctuation when we had such a short time to write it? At the bottom, he wrote: "How perceptive of you, Mr. Welles. I will be expecting great things from you this year." Everyone else at the lunch table got the same warning how his class was going to be hard. He made us give him back the essays after we looked at them, the same way he did with all our assignments. And it was so annoying how he called us by our last names. One time, it took three "Mr. Welles" before I realized he was talking to me. Mr. Epstein (Scott to the rest of the world) had the nerve to ask him about it once. "Just as it would be inappropriate for you to call me Ken, it would also be inappropriate for me to use your given names. Respect is bidirectional." I hated how he used fancy words when regular ones were good enough. He sounded artificial. I wondered if he planned out everything he said.

No one would confess to starting the footprints note. I heard a rumor it was Jason, but he could prove it wasn't him because his handwriting was different from the note. Paul spilled the secret even though he wasn't supposed to. None of us believed him when he swore Mr. Humber wrote it himself. Teachers did *NOT* do things like that.

"He picks someone who comes into the room early and swears him to secrecy with a free A on an assignment."

"But why?" Chris asked.

"Pen is mightier than the sword," Paul said. "Figure it out for yourself."

We thought Paul was fucking with us. I went back to Jason and asked him if Humber gave him the note. He wouldn't answer, but I could tell from the look on his face that it was true. I wondered if he actually did it to show how one little note could mess up a whole class, like I wrote in my essay. But I couldn't be right. He must've had an evil purpose in

mind. He wanted us to do badly on those essays. He wanted us to screw up so he could give everyone bad grades. He wanted to see us fail. Paul kept saying we were wrong and that he was a great teacher. No way. The truth was too obvious.

Mr. Humber proved Paul was full of shit again today. Our assignment was to write a story with a surprise ending. He assigned it on Monday and it was due on Thursday, so I didn't have much time to write it. Between my other homework and piano and playing D&D every day, I didn't start until late Wednesday night. It was my idea to write an exciting skiing scene, and Jeremy came up with the surprise that it was a movie being filmed. I thought it was a good story. When I got it back today, there was no red ink. *None.* Just a note at the bottom that said: "See me after class." That couldn't be good. I went up to his desk when the bell rang.

"You said to see you," I said.

"Mr. Welles," he said, pointing to the chair beside his desk. "I thought we might take a brief moment to discuss your assignment. It is my assessment that you have an innate talent for writing. The quality of this story is indicative of a nascent and yet formidable skill." If I understood what he was saying (and I wasn't sure that I did), he said I was a good writer. "However, raw talent is only one side of the equation. Developing talent into true skill requires hard work and dedication. You cannot grow as an author when you write your stories the night before they are due."

"But I didn't. . ."

He cut me off. "You've earned a D on this assignment."

He paused to let it sink in. I clenched my hands into fists.

"However," he continued, "I have decided to extend you an opportunity. If you'd like to have your grade revised, you may resubmit your assignment, provided you have it on my desk before class on Monday morning. I trust you understand I'm being generous in this matter, and I can assure you this is the only opportunity I will extend you on any assignment for the remainder of the school year. Whether you choose to accept my offer or not, I highly suggest you do not repeat your act of procrastination on any of your assignments for my class. Would you care to ask any questions?"

Plenty of questions popped into my head, but none that I'd dare ask a teacher.

"I suggest you depart for lunch before it becomes necessary to write a hall pass." He turned away from me, picking a paper off the stack and scribbling on it in red ink. I was so furious it was hard for me not to slam the classroom door on my way out. First, he tells me I'm a good writer (I think, maybe). Then he tells me I got a bad grade and wants me to write it all over again. That's how he earned his capital A.

"Can I have some of your chips?" Parker asked Andy, who gave him a broken one. Parker inhaled it and looked around at the rest of the table. "Can I have a piece of your Twinkie?" he asked Chris.

"No," Chris said, shoving the rest of it in his mouth all at once. "Why don't you bring your own lunch?"

"I did," Parker whined. "I was so hungry, I ate it after second period. My mom won't give me any allowance either so I can't buy anything. I hate this stupid diet."

"Your mom sucks," Andy said.

Brian sat down in the chair next to me. There was so much food on his tray he had to pile things on top of each other. He bought two pizza lunches, a double order of fries, two desserts, and three cartons of milk. He must've used the entire five dollars I gave him. Parker looked like he wanted to kill Brian. I knew how Parker felt. It wasn't fair that Brian could eat so much and still look like he was starving to death.

"Give something to Parker," I said to Brian so no one else could hear.

He sighed and I frowned. It was *my* money after all. "Do you want some fries?" he asked Parker.

"Yeah, please," Parker said. Brian dumped half of them on his tray and handed the container to Parker, who stuffed them in his mouth by the handful. Maybe I shouldn't have done that, because I knew from experience that Parker would feel better after he lost weight. Still, his mother was wrong to force him to diet. Parker had to decide for himself, and obviously he'd decided losing weight wasn't important to him. But I wasn't thinking about Parker's diet when I told Brian to give Parker food. I was getting worried that the other guys thought Brian didn't want to hang out. Giving food to Parker gave them another reason to

like him. Brian was my best friend and I wanted him to have as much fun as I was having.

"Are you still coming tonight?" I asked Brian.

He nodded. "I told him we're playing football."

"Andy, show your picture to Brian," Chris said.

Brian looked at it. "Is that supposed to be Mr. Humber?" Andy snickered. "Why did you draw a picture like that about him?"

"Because he's an asshole," Andy said.

"I don't think he's an asshole," Brian said. "I like him."

"You *like* him?" Parker exploded.

"I think he's nice," Brian said.

"Do you live in the same universe as the rest of us?" Parker was turning red. "I got a C on my story! I've never gotten a C on anything in my life. I used the same idea for a story I wrote last year that the teacher said would make a good book someday. I worked on it for *hours.* It was twelve pages long when I was done. Even my sister said it was good, and she hates my stories. What am I supposed to do, write a whole novel in three days? Humber's a jerk!"

"He's not a jerk," Brian mumbled.

"What did you get on your story?" Parker asked.

Brian looked around the table. "I got an A."

"Nobody got an A!" Parker shouted. "I asked half the kids in the class. Everyone had C's and D's! Everyone!"

"Don't spaz out," Chris said.

"Why not?" Parker looked like a star about to supernova. "It's not fair! Humber gets to hand out bad grades because he feels like it. He's ruining my life! When my parents find out I got a C they're going to kill me. It's going to ruin my grade for the whole year! It's not fair!" He glared at Brian. "How did you get an A? What was your story about?"

Brian pushed his chair back so fast it fell over. "I gotta go to the bathroom," he said as he ran off through the tables. Brian was a smart kid, but sometimes he could be incredibly stupid. Why didn't he just go along with them? Why didn't he lie about his grade? And how the hell did he think Humber was *nice?*

"It's one stupid C," Chris said to Parker. "At least you didn't get an F like me. You get A's on everything else so it'll wash out. Don't spaz out so much. Daniel's going to get fried by his parents worse than you."

"Only if I tell them," Daniel said.

"I'm not spazzing out," Parker muttered.

Brian wasn't back when the bell rang. His books and lunch were still on the table. I gave Parker the rest of the food and picked up Brian's books so I could give them to him in fifth period. He was waiting for me outside the cafeteria. I pushed the stuff at him.

"I never get a chance to have a sleepover," he said. "We could go to your house. I have some new scenes I wanted to try."

"I don't think the other guys want to act out scenes," I said.

"They don't need to come," he said.

"It's fun to play D&D," I said. "You'll see."

He walked next to me. "They don't like me."

"They do. They just don't know you because you usually can't come."

"No, they don't," he said. "I don't fit in. I don't want to go tonight."

"I want you to go," I said. "You're my best friend and I want you to have fun. Why don't you come over on Sunday? We don't play because Chris goes to church and Daniel has Japanese lessons. We can do all the Frodo scenes if you want."

"My dad won't let me," he said. "I have to paint."

"Tell him we're going to a football game."

"He won't believe me," Brian said. "He never believes me."

"Jeremy will convince him," I said. "But only if you come tonight."

He thought about it. "Ok," he finally said.

"Special delivery," Jeremy said. I tried to swipe the brown paper bag from him, but he held it over his head. "Hold your horses, tiger. These are not to be shared with your friends. I don't want them knowing you even have them. These could get me in all the wrong kind of trouble if their parents find out. Do you understand?"

"Come on, no one's parents will find out," I said, rolling my eyes. I tried to grab it again.

"I'm not kidding," he said. "You have to promise me."

"Ok, I promise," I said.

He looked at me suspiciously.

"I promise," I said softly. "I'll keep them hidden and I won't tell any of my friends."

"In that case, I have what every growing twelve-year-old boy needs," he said, handing me the bag. He bought a whole stack even though I only asked him for one. Playboy, Penthouse, and even Hustler, a few of each. I opened one of the Playboys to the middle, letting the long picture fall open. You could see *everything*. I had to fight to keep myself from giggling. I wasn't sure why it was funny, but I *was* sure I didn't want to let Jeremy know I thought it was funny. I knew laughing wasn't the right reaction when looking at naked women. Not that I knew the right reaction. I wished I knew how to whistle like they did on TV.

"Not bad, huh?" he said, ruffling my hair.

"She's ok," I said, playing it cool. "I'm going to put these away." I ran up the stairs. He laughed, probably because he thought I was going to do something that required privacy. That was ridiculous. Why would I bother to jerk myself off when I had Jeremy to do it for me? I didn't argue with him because I needed privacy for a different reason. I slipped the magazines carefully between the books in my D&D bag. If I lined up the books the right way, the magazines were impossible to see. Better than casting an invisibility spell.

The only reason I asked him to buy me naked magazines was to show them to my friends. Naked women were interesting, but they didn't seem that exciting. At least, not to me. I wondered why. Not that I would get excited by seeing a magazine of naked men. Gross. I got used to Jeremy – seeing his bare butt was no different from seeing his bare foot. Sometimes, I felt guilty I wasn't turned on by him, especially the times he whispered in my ear when we were fucking. He kept saying how I was sexy and how my body was perfect. It wasn't fair I didn't feel the same way about him.

I carried my backpack downstairs on one shoulder, because wearing both straps wasn't cool anymore. I tossed it casually next to my sleeping bag as if it didn't have anything special inside. Jeremy sat at his desk sorting through the bills. I massaged his shoulders. "Kiddo, I don't know where you learned how to do that, but it feels fantastic." He sighed.

"Can we get a computer?" I asked.

"What for?" he asked without looking up.

"I could use it for homework. Daniel prints his homework out instead of writing. He uses it for math too, and he said it was good for paying bills. We also played a cool game that was like D&D with time doors from that movie we saw last year."

"Now I see, it's for games," he said. "We could hook up the Atari."

"Computer games are way better than the Atari," I said. "Daniel says the Apple II is better because it has more room to put stuff in it. Memory. More L's or H's or some letter like that. Besides, it'll make me smarter if I use it for homework."

"I doubt that," he said. "Two weeks ago, it was a pinball machine. Last week, a synthesizer. A real one, not one of those stupid little keyboards, to quote your exact language. What's it going to be next week, a yacht? It might seem like I have an unlimited supply of money, but that's not the case. We can't afford all this stuff."

"We could call it an early Christmas present." I put my arms around him and hugged him from the back. He leaned back and sighed.

"All right, all right, but I'm drawing the line. Nothing else until Christmas, understood? Find out from Daniel what we should get since he's the computer expert."

"Thanks," I said, resting my chin on top of his head.

"Why don't you invite your friends to sleep over here next time? I'm sure everyone will have a good time with the pool table, the synthesizer, the pinball machine, and whatever else you'll rope me into buying."

"It's hard for them to come here," I said. "They all live near Chris' house, so parents don't have to drive when we stay there."

"I could pick everyone up," he offered.

"I'll ask tonight," I lied. No way. I didn't want my friends at our house. My life with Jeremy was separate. I was a different person at

home and I wanted to keep it that way. Besides, if they came over, Jeremy would want to join in because he liked boys. My friends would think he was weird.

"I'm going to miss having you around tonight," he said softly.

"I'm here now," I said, kissing the back of his neck the way he liked. He didn't need any other hints.

<center>∼✕ ✕∼</center>

The front door of Chris' house was wide open when we got there. I heard slamming cabinets and banging pots from inside. "Hello?" I called. I didn't want to walk in without being asked. Chris poked his head from the kitchen with a scowl on his face, waving me inside.

"Mom, I can't find the macaroni and cheese!" he yelled up the stairs.

"I bought five boxes earlier this week," his mother yelled back. "They're in the cupboard next to the oven."

"I already ate those, don't we have more?" he screamed back. "I told everyone I would give them dinner so we could start earlier. There's nothing to eat!"

A door slammed upstairs. "Christopher, you have no business promising to feed your friends without asking!" She came down the stairs, noticing Jeremy and I standing near the front door. "Oh, I'm sorry. I didn't realize anyone was here. Katie O'Neill." She shook Jeremy's hand.

"Mom, go buy more macaroni and cheese," Chris interrupted.

"Mind your manners," she snapped. "I will do no such thing. I never agreed to provide dinner for your friends. You'll have to tell them to eat at home first."

"Then we won't be able to start for hours! I'm not calling anyone. It's your fault everyone will be hungry." He crossed his arms.

They stared each other down until his mother sighed. "I'll run to the grocery store."

"How about I pick up a few pizzas for the boys?" Jeremy said smoothly.

"You don't have to go through all that trouble," she said.

"It's no trouble at all. Pizza good for you guys?"

<center>383</center>

"Pizza's good," Chris said. "Get one with all the meats and double extra cheese. Parker only eats mushrooms so we need one of those too with extra cheese, and one with sausage and onions for Andy. With extra cheese."

"You're getting pizza?" Paul said, emerging from the family room.

"You can't have any," Chris said.

"I'll get plenty for everyone," Jeremy said. "Paul, would you mind coming along? I'll need help picking everything up. I assume you guys need drinks and snacks as well."

Paul looked excited at the chance to ride in Jeremy's car. "Sure."

Chris' mother opened up her purse. "This is awfully expensive," she said.

"It's on me," Jeremy said. She looked like she was going to argue with him. "Please, it would be my pleasure. If you could show me to the phone I'll call it in."

"It's very kind of you to offer," she said. "Lord knows it's a challenge keeping up with two growing boys."

"Have you got a football?" I asked Chris.

"Somewhere in the garage, I think," he said, wrinkling his nose. "Why?"

We went outside to wait for everyone else. I kept my eye out for Brian's dad's ancient gold colored pickup truck. When I saw it turn the corner, I tossed the half-deflated football to Chris. He missed and had to chase it halfway down the lawn. Brian opened the door before the truck fully stopped. I waved at his dad while Chris threw the ball back way off to my side. It was one thing to tell Brian's dad we were playing football, but I knew it'd be more convincing if he saw us actually doing it. I prayed he wouldn't get out and start playing with us, but he drove away without saying anything. As soon as the truck disappeared around the corner, I dropped the football. We didn't need it any more.

"That was smart," Brian said, grinning. "He was suspicious."

"Whatever," Chris said. Jeremy and Paul came out the front door. "Get Mountain Dew and six cans of Pringles," Chris shouted after them. Jeremy waved and they drove off. He skidded the tires and gunned the engine to show off. Chris didn't seem impressed. "Let's sword fight."

We were banging the swords together when Andy came down the street on his skateboard. "Guys, check this out," he said, throwing his stuff on the lawn. "I figured out how to pop the curb." He swung back around into the street, gathered up speed, and then smacked into the curb at full speed. Andy went flying and crashed into the grass while the skateboard stayed behind. I giggled, but Chris burst into a full laugh. Brian watched silently from the step on the porch. Andy looked embarrassed as he stood up, brushing grass off his clothes.

"I had it at home," Andy said, picking up the skateboard to try again. This time, the front wheels of the skateboard made it over the curb, but the back wheels got stuck. He fell on his butt in the street.

"You should give up," Chris said. "You suck at skateboarding."

"Fuck off," Andy said, wincing. "It's not like you know how."

"Only because my mom won't let me have a skateboard," Chris fired back. "On guard!" he yelled at me. The swords banged together hard enough to make my hands hurt. He was already swinging the sword around again, straight for my head. If I didn't block him, he would've hit me.

"Watch out!" I yelled, my ears ringing.

"Don't be chicken shit," he said.

Parker's car pulled up in front of the house. "David, don't leave without giving mommy a hug goodbye," his mother said in her thick "new yahwk" accent. He looked like he wanted to die. He put his arms around her for a nanosecond. "Have fun with your friends, honey," she yelled before driving away.

Parker's shoulders sagged. "Don't say anything."

"You live two blocks away," Chris said. "Can't you walk?"

"She wouldn't let me," Parker said. "Is there anything to eat? My mom made me have dinner first."

"Pizza's coming," I said. "Mushroom for you." He smiled.

Jonathan and Daniel showed up together a minute later. "Let me try," Daniel said, pointing at my sword. He held it in both hands with his feet apart, like he knew what he was doing.

"No fair!" Chris whined. "You took sword classes!"

"It's called kendo," Daniel said. He charged Chris with a loud yell. Chris tried to hit him, but Daniel blocked it easily, knocking Chris backward onto his butt when he struck back. "Score!" Andy yelled.

"Come on, Parker, let's fight," Chris said as he got up.

"No way," Parker said. "It looks dangerous."

"You should try," I said to Brian. He shook his head.

"Jonathan then," Chris said. "How about it? You want to get your ass kicked?"

Jonathan shrugged and took the sword from Daniel. Chris charged him with a yell. Jonathan didn't move. At the last moment, he stepped to the side, swinging the sword around so it smacked Chris on the butt as he passed by.

"Who kicked whose ass?" Andy yelled. "You got *spanked!*"

"Put your money where your mouth is," Chris growled. "Or are you chicken shit?"

Andy never, ever refused a dare. Jonathan handed him the sword. Chris charged like he always did. Andy put his sword up to block, but Chris knocked it right out of his hand. "Oww!" Andy yelled.

"Christopher Matthew O'Neill!" his mother screamed from the porch. We all stared at her. "Put that thing down this instant or as God is my witness I will ground you until your eighteenth birthday!" She looked at Andy, who was shaking his hand out. "Andrew, are you hurt?"

"I'm fine, Mrs. O'Neill," he said. "We were just fooling around."

"Where in the name of all that is holy did you boys get real swords?"

All eyes turned to me. "They're mine, but they're not real. The blades aren't sharp."

"They're stage props," Jonathan said.

"Yeah, stage props," I said to Chris' mom. "They look real but they're not."

"They sound real enough," she said, not quite believing me. "I don't like you boys playing with them. God forbid someone gets hurt."

"Aw come on, no one's going to get hurt," Chris whined. "You never want me to have any fun." His mom rubbed her forehead like she had a bad headache and collapsed into the rocking chair on the porch. "Let's go inside," Chris said when it became obvious she wasn't

going to leave. We gathered our stuff and followed him down to the basement, leaving his mother by herself.

"I brought candles," Daniel said. He pulled a pile of them out of his backpack, big fat ones that could stand on their own instead of needing holders. Most of them still had price tags.

"Where did you get those?" Parker asked.

"Not telling," Daniel said. "But I didn't get them from home."

"Did you lift them?" Andy asked in a soft voice. Just in case someone was listening.

"Not telling," he said again, which told us everything.

"I brought my handcuffs," I said to Daniel, digging them out of my bag.

He looked them over, working the ratchet and watching what happened when he turned the key. "The lock mechanism is different from my toy pair, but they basically work the same way," he said. He bent one end of a paperclip from his pocket with a small pair of pliers until it looked like my handcuff key. The handcuffs opened on the first try. "If I get arrested, I can get out of the cuffs no problem. You know those warehouses near the mall? I hear they keep stereos there. I'll bet I can break in."

"You're going to steal stereos?" Parker whispered.

"No, just break in," Daniel said.

Daniel had *everyone* fooled. He wore Izod shirts and khaki pants instead of jeans and t-shirts, was always polite and helpful to adults and teachers, and never got in trouble for anything. In reality, he was the exact opposite. I had no doubt he stole the candles. He said the other day he wanted to blow up Humber's desk in the middle of class. If anyone knew how, it would be Daniel. He knew how to pick locks and hack computers. He told me he'd be able to retire from being a master jewel thief before he was twenty. Daniel was a little scary, but that made it fun to be his friend.

"You have to be able to get out with your hands behind your back," I said.

"I did it with mine," he said. "I just need to practice with yours."

"Pizza!" Jeremy yelled from the top of the basement steps. As if he knew what I was thinking, Daniel shoved the handcuffs deep into his

bag. Jeremy came downstairs with four pizza boxes, Paul carrying a few grocery bags of other stuff.

Daniel switched into full goody two shoes gumdrops mode, taking the pizzas from Jeremy. "Thank you for the pizzas, Mr. Stillwell. It was very kind of you to buy them for us."

"You're welcome. Remind me how to say you're welcome in Japanese."

"Doe itashee moshta," Daniel said. He did one of those stiff Japanese bows. Jeremy bowed back and I fought the urge to giggle.

"I'll leave you guys to it," Jeremy said. "Give me a call in the morning when you want to get picked up."

"See ya," I said. At least Jeremy knew how to say goodbye without embarrassing me. I poured a cup of yellow-green glow-in-the-dark soda. I didn't really drink soda any more, but I didn't want to be left out. Parker had already finished his first piece of pizza before I could take one. Without any warning, he let out a huge burp.

Chris swallowed some air. "Nice one," he burped.

"How do you do that?" I asked, jealous.

"Down low, from the diaphragm." He swallowed more air and burped out the ABC's all the way to H before taking another breath. I tried, but it sounded obviously fake. "Not like that. Down low." I had no idea what down low meant.

"Betcha I can go longer," Andy said. Parker started the clock on his stopwatch as Andy belched. They went back and forth, but Chris won.

"Anyone else want to try and break the world record of four point two seconds?" Parker yelled.

"You should try," I said to Brian. He shook his head.

Jonathan stood up. He looked around and let out the biggest, loudest, longest burp I'd ever heard and would ever hear. It went on forever. Jonathan was good at everything. I heard a rumor he took the SAT test for getting into college and got a 1300, which was better than most high schoolers. Jonathan wouldn't say if it was true or not. He never bragged.

"We have a new world record, seven seconds!" Parker yelled. Andy wrote a ten on a piece of paper and held it up like an Olympic judge. We yelled and clapped.

Having friends couldn't get better than this.

"You climb the black, slippery stone slabs up the tower," Chris said in a dramatic voice. The candles flickered, making everything seem mysterious, dangerous, and scary. It took us five hours of fighting and solving riddles to find our way into the impossibly tall castle tower. We had to be getting to the end. I wouldn't dare tell Brian, but I thought Chris was better at being the dungeon master. Brian came up with better stories, but Chris knew how to make his adventures exciting. Everyone said this adventure was his best one ever. "They wind upward along the sides, so far up you can't see the top." He rolled his dice. I felt my stomach sink. "Be careful not to slip or you'll fall to certain death."

"Maybe we should tie a rope around our waists like mountain climbers," Brian said. We all murmured our approval. Chris looked a little annoyed. We climbed higher and higher. Three hundred, four hundred, five hundred feet up with no end in sight. My hand was clenched around my twenty-sided die so hard it left a mark.

"You finally reach the top," Chris said. "Dead end. It's completely solid."

"I search for secret doors," Daniel said. His thief character had the best chance to find one.

Chris rolled the dice behind his screen. "You find a tiny hole that might be a lock," he said. Daniel's character picked the lock open. "The trap door magically opens. An ancient rope ladder drops in front of you."

"You go first," Parker said to me in a nervous voice.

"Why should I go first?" I asked.

"You're the strongest fighter in the group," he said.

"Your fireball does more damage than my sword," I fired back.

"I'm going," Andy said. His character was a mixed fighter and magic-user called a bard. Andy liked it because it had to do with music. "I have my sword at the ready."

"How do you climb a ladder and have your sword out at the same time?" Chris said in a sly voice.

"Oh shit," Andy said. "It's a trap."

"Maybe Parker can levitate him up," Brian said. "That way he could be ready to fight."

"That's a good idea," Parker said, paging through the rulebook. "It's a second level spell. I can levitate you up twenty feet per round. No wait, ten feet, it's only twenty if I do it on myself. It only goes up and down so once you get up there you have to push yourself in or you'll fall when I lift the spell." Parker always checked every little detail in the rules.

"Just cast it," Andy said impatiently. "We're at the end of the adventure."

"You float into the room," Chris said. "You see a desk on the other side and an ancient skeleton sitting in a chair behind it. On the desk, you see a scroll and a big ring made of solid platinum."

"No monsters," Andy said, letting out his breath. "You guys can come up."

Chris rolled the dice and didn't say anything.

"I read the scroll," Andy said.

"You touch the scroll and. . ." Chris rolled the dice. "The skeleton leaps up and attacks you for sixteen points of damage!" he yelled. "Roll a saving throw against poison."

"Sixteen points? This isn't an ordinary skeleton," Andy muttered, rolling his die. "Twelve, is that good enough?"

"For now," Chris said. "Only one of you can climb up each round, who goes first?"

"I'll go next," I said.

"Hurry up. I only have forty hit points left," Andy said.

"What spells are good against undead?" Parker said, paging through the rulebook again. "Maybe I should cast the fireball."

"You might incinerate the scroll," Brian said.

"I attack the skeleton," Andy said, rolling his die. "Come on, a four."

"You miss by a mile," Chris said, rolling his dice. "The skeleton doesn't. Twenty-two points of damage."

"Shit!" Andy said. "You guys better send Brian up next to heal me or I'm going to die next round." Brian was playing a cleric character, kind of like a priest. He wanted to be the wizard, but Parker was always

the wizard. At least Chris let him be a halfling (like a hobbit) even though the rules said he couldn't. I didn't think Brian would play if he didn't get to be a halfling.

"Ok, Nick, you're up there now. What do you do?"

"I attack," I said, rolling my dice. "Eighteen! With my plus-two sword and my strength bonus that's twenty-three!"

"Crunch!" Chris said. "You break one of his rib bones, but he doesn't seem to care. He attacks Andy again." Chris rolled the dice.

"Don't hit, don't hit, don't hit," Andy prayed.

The lights went on.

"Fuck!" Chris yelled.

"Christopher, I need a word with you," his mom said from the top of the stairs. Chris threw his pencil on the table and stormed towards the stairs. Everyone was quiet so we could hear their conversation.

"What?" Chris said.

"It's midnight," she said. "Time for bed."

"We're right in the middle of the adventure!" Chris whined. "That's not fair! You never said we had to be done by midnight!"

"When will you be finished?" she asked.

"It doesn't matter. I'm too old to have a bedtime and it's the weekend anyway."

"One o'clock, no later," she said.

"Four-thirty," he fired back. "No earlier."

"Christopher," she said in a warning voice. "I gave you my answer."

"You're so unfair," he sneered, walking away from the stairs.

"Don't you walk away from me, young man," she said. "One o'clock."

"Turn the lights off!" he yelled back. They went out.

"Your mom is a pushover," Andy said. "If I argued like that, my mom would make the bedtime even earlier."

"Shut up," Chris said. "Don't talk about my mom. Where were we?"

The skeleton nearly killed Andy, Brian, and me before we defeated it. Its bones turned to dust in front of our eyes. Parker's magic-user, who quivered uselessly at the bottom the ladder while we almost died, came up to read the scroll. My stomach dropped. It wasn't the end of

the adventure. We made everything worse when we touched the scroll. In two days, the end of the world would happen. The only way to stop it was to find the portal hidden inside the other tower. The scroll said it was the mirror to the one we were in.

"Another tower? Where?" Parker said, scratching his head.

"Maybe it's in another castle," I suggested. I knew it was wrong when I said it.

"What if we looked in one of those mirrors in the castle?" Daniel said. "If we see the reflection of the tower, we might figure something out."

Chris leaned back in his chair and put his hands behind his head. "You guys are never going to figure this one out."

We spent five minutes throwing out bad ideas until Brian finally said something. "It's the mirrors," he said quietly. "Everything in the castle has a mirror. We're looking for the reflection of the tower. What if it isn't next to the tower? A mirror shows everything backwards. If the first tower goes up, maybe there's another one going down."

"How does a tower go down?" Parker asked.

"Underground," Brian answered. "The entrance to the tower was at the highest point in the castle, so the entrance to the tower going down might be at the lowest point. We have to go down into the dungeons where the green demons come from."

The idea gave me chills it was so good.

Chris exploded. "How did you figure that out so fast? You looked at my notebook when I was talking to my mom, didn't you?"

Brian shrunk in his chair. "I didn't."

"You're lying," he spat.

"Nobody looked," I said.

"What's your problem?" Daniel asked.

"He's my problem," Chris said, pointing at Brian. Brian ran for the stairs, taking them two at a time.

"What did you do that for?" I muttered.

"He fucked up my game," Chris said, folding his arms.

"Why can't you lay off him?" I said, angry. "He didn't do anything."

"Real nice, asshole," Andy muttered at Chris.

"You guys suck, you know that?" Chris slammed his notebook shut. "Game's over."

"Come on, we were getting to a good part," Parker whined.

"Nobody looked in your stupid notebook," Daniel said.

"You're only being a jerk because he's smarter than you," Jonathan said. Everyone was silent. Chris made a fist. I thought he was going to start a real fight. Then he slumped back in his chair. Jonathan didn't talk much, but when he did, everyone listened. Even Chris.

"I'll get him," I said. "You'd better be cool."

"Yeah," Chris muttered, spinning dice to keep busy.

Paul was eating a cold piece of pizza in the kitchen. "Is this my brother's fault?" he asked. Brian was sitting on the couch in the den with his arms wrapped around his knees.

"Nah," I said. I didn't want to cause more trouble. "Chris said he was sorry," I told Brian. "Everyone wants you to come back."

"Can't we go to your house instead?" he said.

"I thought you were having fun," I said.

"They don't like me."

"Come on, they like you," I said. "Everyone was mad at Chris for being a jerk."

"No, it was before that too," he said. "I told you. I don't fit in."

"That's not true," I said. He shook his head. "Are you coming back downstairs so we can finish the game?"

"No," he said. "I want to leave."

"It's after midnight," I said.

"I'll walk alone if you won't come with me," he said.

I felt like I was being watched. Jonathan was standing on the stair to the den. I elbowed Brian in the side until he looked up. "No one will play without you," he said to Brian. Jonathan went back downstairs without waiting for an answer.

"Holy shit," Paul breathed. "I've known that kid for four years. I swear to God that's the first time I've ever heard him talk."

"See?" I said to Brian.

He was quiet for a long time. "I guess," he said.

We went back down together.

"Give up yet?" I asked.

Daniel grunted and shook his head. He contorted himself in different directions, trying to find a way to get the paper clip into the keyhole. He had no problem getting out of the cuffs when I put them on in front. Now he was handcuffed like the police did: hands behind back, palms facing out, keyhole away from his fingers, and the double lock keeping the ratchet from moving. I knew from experience it was hopeless. I had the feeling that Daniel wouldn't give up even if he had to stay handcuffed all night.

"Check this one out," Andy said. He put his headphones on my ears and pressed the play button on his Walkman. The music was so loud it hurt. I couldn't figure out why Andy liked heavy metal bands like Twisted Sister and Iron Maiden. It sounded more like noise to me. Every single day he wore a black t-shirt with the logo of some metal band. I was relieved when he took the headphones back. "Think you could play the keyboard part when you get your synthesizer?"

"I dunno," I said. "Could you get the sheet music?"

"My dad said yesterday I could get an electric guitar for Christmas but I have to pay for the amp out of my own money. My allowance is squat so I'm going to get a paper route. We gotta find someone that plays drums. Are you sure you don't know anyone?"

I shook my head for the millionth time. Andy was crazy about starting a band. He spent hours drawing his ultra-cool guitar, his costumes, and especially his hair. He knew everything but the name of his band. He showed me his latest idea – a detailed skeleton spider with flames coming out of its mouth, the band name written in black and red letters that looked like bolts of lightning.

"Spider Vomit?" I cracked up.

He scratched his head. "Maybe Spider Puke would be better."

The D&D game finished a while ago but no one was asleep. Chris wanted everyone to stay up all night just because his mother told him he had a bedtime. The ending of the game was better than a movie. We fought our way to the bottom of the tower through hordes of green demons until we reached a gate. Brian figured out all the riddles, like

how to unlock the gate at the bottom of the opposite tower so we could fight the green demon king.

Chris came pounding down the stairs. "Paulie *finally* went to bed," he said. For some reason, Paul was staying up as late as we were, watching old black and white movies in the den. "We can finally find out Nick's big fucking secret."

I dug into my backpack, my fingers touching smooth, glossy pages. Carefully, I pulled one out, holding it up so everyone could see the cover.

"Holy shit," Chris breathed.

"That's a Penthouse," Andy asked, awestruck. "Where did you get that?"

"I swiped it from my uncle's stash," I said, handing the magazine over to Andy. He handled it gingerly, like he was scared of breaking it. I pulled another one out. "Who wants a Hustler?"

"Fuck!" Chris grabbed it out of my hands. "I never saw one before but I heard they were hard core."

"You gotta see this," Andy said, holding his up so we could see the picture.

"Whoa," Parker said. "What if your uncle finds out you took these?"

I handed a Playboy to Parker. "He has tons. He'll never notice if a few are missing for one night." I tossed one each to Jonathan and Brian, who took them off to a corner and huddled with each other.

"Would someone let me out?" Daniel grumbled. Naked women were obviously more important than beating the handcuffs.

"Make him stay like that if he can't get out on his own," Chris said.

"Fuck you," Daniel spat. I unlocked him anyway and let him choose his own magazine.

"Oh man, look at these tits," Chris said, his voice squeaky.

"Let me see," said Parker, craning his neck. Chris pulled his away.

"Why? You can see tits anytime you want. Just check out your sister."

"Come on," Parker whined.

"Seriously, Allison is fucking *hot*. I don't know how you stand living in the same house with her. If it was me, I would drill a hole between

the bedroom wall and the bathroom so I could watch her taking a shower."

"She's my sister," Parker said weakly.

"But she is hot," Daniel agreed.

"I'll bet you jack off thinking about her," Chris said to Parker.

"That's sick!" Parker said.

"Well then, who do you think about when you jack off?"

"None of your business," he said, burying his nose into his magazine.

"You can see her whole pussy," Andy said, holding up another picture.

"Shit," Chris breathed. "I would eat out her pussy if she asked me."

"That's disgusting," Daniel said. "I heard it gets wet and smelly."

"You only think it's gross because you're not man enough," Chris teased. "It's a 69, she sucks my dick while I eat out her pussy." He waggled his tongue like he was doing it right there, making everyone groan in disgust. "Oh baby, oh baby, suck my big fat one!"

"You wish you had a big fat one," Daniel said.

"Cindy Davis thinks so," Chris said.

"In your wet dreams," Andy said.

"I have two words for you. Ricky's. Party." Chris winked in an exaggerated way.

"What happened at Ricky's party?" I asked.

"Nothing happened in the closet, everyone knows that," Andy said.

"Believe whatever you want," Chris said.

"Was that before or after she kicked you in the nuts and called you a perv?" Daniel said, deadpan. Chris gave him the finger.

"Did she really do that?" I asked, eyes wide.

"No," Chris said. "But I'll bet I got further than any of you guys."
Bet you didn't.

"Oh yeah?" Andy challenged.

"I felt her tits," he said. "They were awesome."

"She barely has tits," Andy fired back. "Not like Amy Torricelli." He put his hands on his chest like he was holding up huge ones. "She has cantaloupes. No, watermelons. She had them since fourth grade."

"So what?" Chris said. "It's not like you never touched them."

"In sixth grade gym class," Andy bragged. "I ran into her during a kickball game and copped a feel."

"You told that story a million times and it's still not true," Chris said. "What about you, Nick? What's the farthest you ever got?"

It *was* tempting to brag. *Well, Chris, I got my dick sucked off twice yesterday and then I got fucked.* I tried to imagine the looks on their faces. Awe first. Disgust when they found out who I did it with. I searched around for a story that would be just believable enough. An old memory came back I thought I'd forgotten.

"I made out with this girl named Molly at a wedding," I said.

"What do you mean, made out?" Chris said, sitting forward.

"We were down by a lake at night with no one else around. We held hands, and then you know, we made out. Kissed."

"On the lips?" Parker breathed.

"Frenched," I said.

"Bullshit," Chris said. "You don't even know what that means."

"We stuck our tongues in each other's mouths," I fired back.

"You are so full of it," Chris said.

"Believe whatever you want," I said the same way he did.

"What was it like?" Parker said. He sounded like he was going to start drooling.

"Awesome," I said. "Her teeth were smooth. She tasted like minty strawberries because she was wearing Chapstick and used mouthwash before the wedding."

"Nick is a *real* lady's man," Andy said. I stood up and took a bow. Everyone clapped and cheered.

If they only knew the truth.

The sun was shining through the small basement windows. My watch said it was just after seven in the morning. I was the only one still awake. Lumpy sleeping bags were scattered around the room, looking like snakes that swallowed large animals. Half-naked bodies spilled out of each of them. An arm here, a leg there, a couple bare chests. I was going to sleep in my clothes until they all stripped down to their

underwear, so I did too. Brian was the only one who didn't. It seemed strange to me, because Brian never cared about being undressed before.

I liked my friends even though they could be annoying. Parker was a whiner, Daniel was a little scary, Jonathan seemed unfriendly the way he never talked, and Andy was a twerp. Most of all I liked Chris, even though he was always trying to be better than everyone else and had a short temper. The old Nick would probably have hated Chris as much as Tommy Walker. But I wasn't the old Nick anymore. I didn't care about being teased. I knew how to tease back. Teasing was fun. Jeremy taught me that.

Brian had a good time after the thing with Chris. Everyone was nice to him. He seemed to be making friends with Jonathan, which would help him feel better about being part of the group. I could have all my friends at the same time.

That wasn't why my head was too jumbled up to go to sleep.

It wasn't hard for me to tell they were doing it. A funny movement here and some heavy breathing there gave it away. After all, I was an expert at this stuff. Not that I was surprised. No one snuck off saying they had to go to the bathroom after I handed out the magazines because we would've teased anyone who did for the rest of the night. Mostly, everyone did it quietly to keep it a secret. Except Chris. He *wanted* everyone to know what he was doing. He moaned. He kept saying Cindy Davis. Andy finally yelled at him to shut the fuck up and finish jacking off already, which made everyone giggle for ten minutes. I watched the way his body moved until he obviously finished, rolling over on his side. My hand went into my underwear and I did it by myself for the first time in a month.

It was only afterwards that I realized what happened.

Chris did it thinking about a girl, but I did it thinking about him.

I had no idea what that meant but it scared the shit out of me.

Chapter 29

October 29, 1982

I stopped short in the doorway. 224 was the right room, wasn't it?

"Would you get out of the way?" Jenny Ackerman said in her snooty voice. Listening to her reminded me of nails on a blackboard. She was one of those girls who thought they were superior, bossed everyone around, and made that special girl noise somewhere between "eww" and "ick" a thousand times a day. She sneered as she pushed her way past me, her nose in the air like she owned the whole school.

She screeched when the spider web stuff stretched all over the room got caught in her hair. I watched her do a mad dance around the doorway, scraping her painted fingernails through her hair. A small plastic spider fell to the ground. "EWWW!" she screamed.

"Ms. Ackerman!" Mr. Humber boomed. He had the kind of voice that could boom. "I feel certain there's no need for such theatrics, nor is there any need to destroy the scenery on which I expended several hours of effort this morning. Please show some consideration for your classmates and step outside while you collect yourself." He looked around the classroom. "I also suggest that those of you enjoying yourselves at Ms. Ackerman's expense silence yourselves." The room went quiet. I ducked as I went inside, weaving around massive amounts of web stuff and ignoring the giant rubber tarantula on my desk. Boys didn't scream about things like that.

Some teachers hung up a cheesy cardboard jack-o-lantern or a smiling witch on a broomstick. Others put on a lame costume or said

they were dressed up as a teacher for Halloween. Ha ha ha. Mr. Humber was on a totally different level. The windows were covered with layers of black construction paper so no light came in from outside. A seriously evil looking pumpkin with an actual candle inside sat on his desk. A dark purple light in the corner made everything glow. Another machine churned out smoke covering most of the floor. He was wearing an old-fashioned suit with a top hat that made him look like a funeral director. His face was pale and shadowed from makeup. When the bell rang, he walked stiffly to the door like a ghoul.

"May I request that you all remain *deathly* quiet," he said from the middle of the room. Any other teacher would sound stupid if they said that. Not Mr. Humber. The way he looked around the room made me shiver. "'A house is never still in darkness to those who listen intently; there is a whispering in distant chambers, an unearthly hand presses the snib of the window, the latch rises. Ghosts were created when the first man awoke in the night.'" He went silent for a moment. "J.M. Barrie wrote those words nearly a century ago. Can anyone tell me the play for which he is best remembered? No one? Mr. Schuster, I'm sure you have the answer for us."

"Peter Pan," Jonathan said from the back of the room.

"Thank you," Mr. Humber said. "Perhaps some of you are also familiar with this particular playwright."

Double, double toil and trouble;
Fire burn and cauldron bubble.
Fillet of a fenny snake,
In the cauldron boil and bake;
Eye of newt, and toe of frog,
Wool of bat, and tongue of dog,

"How many of you are familiar with this particular passage?" Everyone's hand in the room went up. It went with witches in every cartoon ever made. "How many of you are familiar with the poet?" All hands went down. "Would it surprise you to learn those words were penned by William Shakespeare? The passage is part of a scene from Macbeth. We've spent some time as a class discussing poetry, so let's

analyze the first line's meter together. Double, double, toil, and trouble. How many feet?"

"Four," the class murmured.

"Iambic or trochaic?" I heard both words being said. He read the poem again with more stress. "DOUB-le, DOUB-le, TOIL and TROU-ble."

"Trochaic," I murmured with everyone else.

"Correct, the accent comes first. What about the inner lines, FILL-et OF a FEN-ny SNAKE? How many feet? It doesn't work out evenly. Who would say three?" Hands went up. "Who would say four?" Other hands went up. "Who doesn't care?" A few giggles and a lot of hands, including mine. "After all, what difference does meter make? Why should it matter that the inner lines were written in regular trochaic tetrameter catalectic?" He handed out a stack of dittos with the Shakespeare poem on them. "Read along with me. Double, double, toil and trouble. . ."

I was trying to hang on to my hatred for Mr. Humber, but each day I felt a little more melt away. I couldn't figure out why. His class was the hardest I'd ever had. Every day, I left with a headache from having to think on my toes. If you let your mind wander for a second, he fired a question like a missile straight at you. I spent hours on his homework assignments, endlessly refining and polishing each word. If I didn't, I was certain he'd see through my lack of effort and punish me with another terrible grade.

At the same time, I had to admit his class could be kind of fun.

"Again, please, with more emphasis this time. Double, double, toil and trouble," he directed, waving his hands like a symphony conductor. "Is the meter creating a sense of time and place? Can you see the witches stirring the pot? Would it work as well if it didn't rhyme or keep a strict rhythm? One more time, louder!" He was pacing in the front of the room, stooped over like he was a witch himself, his voice raspy and high as he recited the words with us. I had to fight to keep myself from smiling.

Mr. Humber's class ran on a rhythm like the poem we were reading. Every Monday we started a new theme. He also gave us our assignment for the week on Monday, always due on Thursday, which was also

impromptu essay day. He never gave tests. Our essays were the only things that counted towards our grades. He didn't teach on Fridays. Instead, he read interesting and funny stories or poems out loud that had something to do with whatever we studied that week. He also assigned a story every Friday to be turned in on Monday. I didn't mind even though I had to work over the weekend, because we could make it about anything we wanted.

"Stop!" he yelled before we started a fourth time. His voice became soft and mysterious. "Now listen to the power of meter and rhyme in this masterpiece, so appropriate for All Hallows Eve."

> *Once upon a midnight dreary, while I pondered, weak and weary,*
> *Over many a quaint and curious volume of forgotten lore,*
> *While I nodded, nearly napping, suddenly there came a tapping,*
> *As of someone gently rapping, rapping at my chamber door.*
> *"'Tis some visitor," I muttered, "tapping at my chamber door –*
> *Only this, and nothing more."*

He had the whole poem memorized, like a lot of the things he read out loud. I found myself leaning forward, not only because the poem was full of suspense, but because of the way he was reading it. I felt like I was going to jump out my chair if that raven said "nevermore" again.

He made me so angry when he gave me a D on my story that I wound up re-doing it. I worked on it non-stop from the time I got home from Chris' house on Saturday afternoon until I handed it in Monday morning. At first, I couldn't find anything wrong with it, but the more I looked, the more I decided to change. A better word here, a little more action there, take out that dull sentence. It was twice as long and way more than twice as good when I was done. I slapped it on Mr. Humber's desk with a scowl before class started. When I got it back the next day, there was no red teacher ink. Just an A+ at the top and a note at the bottom. "You have exceeded my expectations and produced a work of superior quality. I am impressed." That made me feel fantastic. Impressing Mr. Humber meant something.

He trailed off at the end, his last whispered "nevermore" hanging in the air. "The meter is complex but unmistakable. Did you notice how the poet's use of repeated words helped to build suspense? Or perhaps he was merely being lazy, unable to find words to fill the required number of syllables." A few giggles around the room. "Who can enlighten us with the name of the poet?"

"Edgar Allen Poe," someone said.

"Well done," he said. "I have one more poem to share. While it is not as strongly associated with Halloween, I believe you will find it appropriate."

> *'Twas brillig, and the slithy toves*
> *Did gyre and gimble in the wabe:*
> *All mimsy were the borogoves,*
> *And the mome raths outgrabe*

"Everyone still with me?" he said. "Who would care to explain the meaning of that stanza? No one? Perhaps we can start with the definitions of unfamiliar words. Can anyone ascertain the meaning of brillig?" He picked up the dictionary from his desk and paged through it. "Let's see, brillig, brillig. . .It seems that brillig isn't in the dictionary." He scratched his head. "What kind of word isn't in the dictionary?"

"A made-up word?" Scott said, meaning to make a joke.

"Precisely," Mr. Humber answered.

"I was right?" Scott said, shocked.

"Even a stopped clock is correct twice a day," Mr. Humber said with a little wink. Everyone giggled. "In fact, each and every noun and adjective in this stanza are, as Mr. Epstein puts it, made-up words." He threw his hands up in the air. "Why bother coming up with real words to fit the meter if they can simply be invented? How many of you wish you thought of that little trick for your own poems? However, before you go off creating poetry out of nonsense, listen carefully to the words the poet has constructed. Slithy toves gyring and gimbling in the wabe, does that conjure up an image in your mind? Mimsy borogoves, what does that imply? Perhaps the poet had more in mind than attempting to

write his poem the morning it was due in his seventh-grade English class."

He picked up a pile of papers from his desk. "Now, if you will kindly indulge me, I've selected two of your poems to read aloud in front of the class." I groaned. Under no circumstances did I want him to pick my poem. "Rest assured, I have no intention of revealing names, so the poets can remain comfortably anonymous if they so choose." He cleared his throat dramatically and began to read in his booming, serious voice.

> *There once was a man from Nantucket,*
> *Who. . .*

He trailed off, looking puzzled. The whole class started to snicker. We all knew Nantucket was used in limericks for one reason and one reason only. "Perhaps this poem is not appropriate in an educational setting," he said under his breath. He looked down his nose at us when we laughed. I wondered if he was deliberately cracking a joke or if he was serious. I used to think he wasn't the kind of teacher who cracked jokes, but lately I wasn't so sure. "Ahem," he said, clearing his throat the same way.

> *A butterfly spreads his wings*
> *For the first time.*
> *He flutters while the wind blows*
> *This way and that*
> *Sometimes a stormy gale*
> *Demanding he follow, pushing him around*
> *Sometimes a sweet zephyr*
> *Whispering gentle promises in his ear*
> *It's hard to know*
> *Which way to go*
> *When you're just a butterfly*

"Analyzing this poem reveals a clear and creative metrical construction. Two groups of four lines with each alternating line containing the same number of feet. The third set is different but

contains the same number of feet as the first. I call your attention to the poet's powerful use of rhyme in the last set, so unexpected as there is no other rhyming scheme apparent within the poem. Within those boundaries, the poet has expressed a sentiment you might share. I wonder if any of you feel like the butterfly, sometimes pushed around, sometimes having promises whispered in your ears." The class was completely silent. "Something to ponder this weekend."

He handed back our papers so we could see our grades. "I have two announcements to make while your papers are being returned. First, in honor of the holiday this weekend, many of you will be devastated to learn there is no assignment due on Monday." Everyone cheered. "Second, I would like to call your attention to the coupon stapled to your assignment. This coupon entitles you to erase the grade from one and only one assignment for this quarter, whether that is a poor grade or a zero for failing to turn in your homework. Do not lose this coupon as I will not replace it. You may consider this my addition to your trick or treating haul." *Now* he hands out coupons, after I fixed my only bad grade. He placed my poem face down on my desk. I flipped it over, relieved to see the A on the top of the page. Mr. Humber placed Brian's also face down. I turned to him.

"What did you get?" I whispered. He turned his over carefully, trying to keep me from seeing. I caught enough of a peek to know. "You wrote the butterfly poem?"

"Shut up!" he whispered, turning away.

"It was as good as a real poet," I said softly.

"Shut up!" he whispered even more harshly. I scowled.

The bell rang. "Ladies and gentlemen, it has been an honor and a privilege to be your teacher this week. I look forward to seeing each and every one of you at the Halloween dance tonight. Papers in the basket on the way out, if you please. Have a memorable weekend, and I beg of you, do not overindulge your sweet tooth. Monday stomachaches are a common side effect of Sunday Halloweens."

"Let's go to lunch," I said to Brian. He stared straight ahead like he didn't hear me. Half the time he didn't bother eating lunch with the rest of us. I had no idea where he went. A couple times I looked for him, but he wasn't anywhere in the cafeteria. I picked up my stuff.

"Mr. Welles, a moment of your time," Mr. Humber said as I was walking through the door. I had to dodge through the web stuff to get to his desk. "No need to be concerned. I merely wished to compliment your performance on this week's assignment. Your poem was both technically accomplished and inspirational. I particularly appreciated your selection of references from the Lord of the Rings."

"You knew those?" I thought I was picking things he wouldn't know, like T.S. Eliot did in his poems.

"I'm familiar with Tolkien's works, although I must confess I needed to consult my copies to verify several. While I selected another student's poem to read aloud, I wanted to express that yours was also under serious consideration. I couldn't be more pleased with your development as an author, a poet, and a thinker, and I deemed it unnecessary to wait until the end of the quarter to inform you."

I shrugged. "Thanks."

"I have an additional matter to discuss, if you'll indulge me. Due to the absence of a formal drama department, I have taken on the responsibility to produce the annual spring musical. I find myself in a quandary this year as my pianist has moved on to high school. I've searched for a replacement without any success and have no budget to hire a professional musician. Mr. Hanley mentioned you're an accomplished pianist. Perhaps I might be able to persuade you to join us as musical director?"

"You want me to play piano for a show?" I realized Brian was standing right next to me. "I only play classical music."

"I feel certain from Mr. Hanley's recommendation that you have the requisite skills. There's no need to respond immediately. Participation represents a significant commitment. I hope you give my request serious consideration."

"Ok," I said.

"Thank you, and I look forward to seeing you at this evening's dance, assuming you plan to attend."

"Yeah, both of us are coming," I said.

"I can't go to the dance," Brian said. "My dad said I'm grounded."

"He already said you could. We're supposed to pick you up."

"I can't go, ok?" Brian sounded upset.

"Mr. Hanley," Mr. Humber said in his strict voice. "Despite my earlier announcement regarding this weekend's assignment, I believe in your case this decision was made in error. Therefore, I expect you to submit on Monday morning a detailed, first-hand report describing the events at this evening's dance. To meet the requirements of this assignment, you must personally attend tonight's dance and remain for the entire duration. Failure to turn in this assignment with the quality I've come to expect from you shall result in a failing mark and will negatively impact your grade this quarter. To ensure you are able to fulfill my assignment, I shall prepare a note elucidating my expectations to be shared with anyone responsible for your schedule. Are my expectations clear?"

What? Mr. Humber just gave Brian extra homework? Seriously?

Brian smiled and nodded. "I understand. I'll do my best."

"I expect nothing less from you," Mr. Humber said.

Wait. . .no, he didn't. . .really?

"Now, I suggest both of you join your companions at lunch before I'm required to prepare a hall pass," he said. Brian stared at Mr. Humber like he wanted to say something. I thought Mr. Humber wanted to say something too, but neither of them did. It felt awkward.

"Let's go," I said to Brian.

"Yeah," he said quietly.

I was glad the weather turned cold because I could finally wear the adventure clothes without get soaked by sweat. The extra layers and heavy cloak felt comfortable for once. I looked at the bare trees out the car window, realizing I missed the leaves changing. Like they went straight from green to dead, skipping all the reds and purples in between. We were supposed to go to the rock to see the leaves. I forgot about doing that.

"We have tickets next Saturday night," Jeremy said. "Why don't we make a weekend of it in the city? We could head in Friday after school, stay at a nice hotel, eat at fancy restaurants, and get a limo to take us around. Just you and me. What do you think?"

"What about D&D on Friday?" I asked.

"You could skip it this week," he said.

"If I miss a game my character falls behind and I don't know what happened. Besides, Daniel's birthday is next week. He was talking about a party on Sunday afternoon."

"How about the following weekend, or over Thanksgiving break? We could go to Boston. Maybe we could go somewhere further, like California."

"Chris' mom is going to invite us for Thanksgiving since they don't have any other family," I said.

"Ok, how about Christmas?"

"We're going to have a marathon game. Last year they went four days straight." I frowned. "How come you want to go to all these places all of a sudden?"

"I thought it might be nice to get away," he said.

"Things are pretty busy," I said.

"Let's go to Europe," he said. "We could see the old castles and cathedrals. You'd like that, wouldn't you?"

"Yeah, that would be neat. Do you think Brian could come with us?"

"We'll have to see," he said.

Brian was waiting for us on the porch. He yelled that he was leaving and ran for the van before his dad could change his mind. "My dad said I could stay over tonight since he'll be at work when the dance is over, if that's ok."

"Sure," Jeremy said.

"Nice," I said. We got in the back so he could change into the adventure clothes. Jeremy drove slowly so we didn't fall over. He took off his jacket and shirt.

"My dad is really pissed off," he said quietly. "He wanted me to be grounded but he had to let me go because of Mr. Humber's assignment. He's also in a bad mood because he has to work for twelve days straight. I'm probably going to get grounded for a month."

"Maybe you should've stayed home," I said.

"Mr. Humber said I had to go, so I have to go," he said. "So what if he grounds me? I don't care anymore." Brian sounded more certain than he usually did.

"What do you mean?" I asked.

"Nothing," he muttered. The look on his face told me he didn't want to talk about it. I helped him put the rest of the gear on. We pulled up in front of the school.

"I'll see you guys at ten," Jeremy said. "Have fun!" I climbed out and closed the door behind us. Right away, I realized that wearing these costumes to school was a terrible idea. Everyone was walking around wearing normal costumes like cheerleaders and vampires. We were going to get teased all night. Jeremy was gone by the time I remembered to wave goodbye.

"Mr. Welles and Mr. Hanley." Mr. Humber's mouth was actually hanging open. "I am in absolute awe of your costumes this evening. Are those real coats of mail?"

"Riveted steel," Brian said proudly.

"May I?" Mr. Humber took a handful of the chainmail. "You must be akin to Hercules to be wearing something this weighty without difficulty. I am jealous beyond all possible description. You must tell me where you obtained such exotic vestments."

"It was a special kind of fair," Brian said. "Everyone dressed up in costumes from the Renaissance. They had real jousting and entertainment like knife throwing and people swallowing torches."

Mr. Humber took a notebook out of his pocket. "I am dying to know where and when this fair occurs so I may partake of it in the future."

"Somewhere in Massachusetts," I said. "King something or other, I forgot the name. My uncle knows."

"I'd appreciate being provided that information on Monday morning," he said. "Perhaps I shall return with a costume of my own." I had a hard time imagining what he would look like wearing adventure clothes.

"We have swords too," Brian said. He pulled his out and handed it to Mr. Humber.

"I'm relieved you brought this to my attention," Mr. Humber said. "I'm sure you're both aware the school is highly intolerant of weapons on the premises."

"They're not sharp," I explained. I knew if I was caught bringing my dagger, I'd probably get something like a million points.

"Regardless, they are metal and quite heavy, and could therefore be classified as weapons," he said. "If you were to be caught with these inside the school, they'd likely become permanent decorations in the principal's office. I would be honored to be given the responsibility of caring for these fine blades until the dance has concluded. I swear a solemn oath to return them to you despite my fervent desire to keep them for myself."

Brian looked at him seriously. "I accept your oath and entrust you with the grave responsibility of caring for these mighty blades."

Mr. Humber looked just as serious when he took the swords from us.

Parker showed up first because his mom dropped him off. He was wearing a pirate costume with an eyepatch, a hook, a plastic sword, and a big hat with a gigantic feather. It looked authentic. I was jealous.

"I hate this costume," he said. "I wanted to go as Marvin the Paranoid Android. My mom wouldn't let me make my own costume and made me rent this stupid thing from the costume shop. Only little kids dress up like pirates." I nodded my agreement.

The rest of them walked up a few minutes later. I cracked up when I saw Andy. Of course he dressed up like a punk rocker, but his hair was beyond crazy. The sides were all shaved off and he did something that made it stand up in spikes running down the center of his head. Bright, glow-in-the-dark green spikes.

"Yeah, yeah, ha ha," Andy said.

"You'd better hope that green stuff washes out," Chris said.

"The can said it's water based so it'll come right out," Andy said. "You'd better hope that crap you put on your face washes off." Chris' face was covered with white and black makeup to make him look like a ghoul.

"I used special makeup paint, not something from the hardware store," Chris fired back.

"Your mom is still going to kill you when she finds out you shaved the sides of your head," Daniel said. I had a feeling his costume wasn't really a costume. He was wearing a black sweater and black pants, a black stocking cap on his head, and a black pouch attached to his belt with fake jewelry spilling out of it.

"It's my hair so I can do what I want with it," Andy said. "She can say whatever she wants but she can't stop me from cutting it whatever way I like."

"She can't, but she can ground you afterwards," Jonathan said. Andy frowned.

"Gentlemen!" Mr. Humber said. "Please do not loiter outside, as the festivities are all located indoors. Mr. O'Neill, you've done quite the job with the makeup. Mr. Nakamura, I will be guarding my wallet closely this evening. Mr. Parker, the feather in your hat is quite ostentatious. Mr. Schuster, that is a remarkable taxidermy falcon on your arm. Mr. Welles and Mr. Hanley, I can only say once again I am awestruck by your costumes this evening. And finally, Mr. Ciccolini." He paused. "I'd like to offer a compliment but in truth I'm completely baffled."

"It's punk," Andy said.

"It's *green*," Mr. Humber replied. We giggled. Andy punched me in the arm. Big mistake because I was wearing armor. We laughed at him while he shook his hand out.

The tables in the cafeteria were cleared out to make room even though no one was dancing. Parker went straight to the snack table. The rest of us stood to the side in a tight circle facing each other because that's what everyone else was doing. The circles reminded me of bubbles floating around the room. Sometimes they combined to make bigger bubbles and sometimes they popped, forcing some unlucky kids to find new bubbles. When Parker came back, we made just enough space for him.

"I'm going to ask Cindy Davis to dance," Chris said. "She's wearing some kind of fifties outfit and her sweater is tight in all the right places."

"Five bucks says she kicks him in the balls again," Andy said to Daniel.

Daniel sniggered. "No bet, that's a sure thing."

411

"You guys are assholes," Chris said.

The music was blaring annoying songs that were everywhere like the man eater and the one by the guy who called himself Boy George even though he dressed like a girl. Nothing happened for twenty minutes. "You're chickening out," Andy said to Chris. He made chicken noises and flapped his arms to make the point.

"Shut up, I'm waiting for the right song," Chris said. "It's not like you asked anyone. You're the one who's chicken shit."

"Oh yeah? Watch this." Andy broke away from the protection of our bubble, straight to a bunch of girls next to us. "Any of you beautiful ladies want to dance with me?" I held my breath. The girls giggled and gave him their answers.

"No way, dork."

"Get lost, twerp."

"Dweeb."

"Oh man, that was classic," Chris said, cracking up when Andy came back.

"At least I asked," Andy said. "More than you can say. They didn't say yes because I didn't do it right."

"But they dissed you so bad," Chris teased. "Total humiliation."

"Put your money where your mouth is," Andy challenged.

"Fine!" Chris said. He didn't move.

"Then go!" Andy said, crossing his arms.

"When I'm ready!" Chris crossed his arms too. Andy made chicken sounds again. I started making chicken noises too until we were all doing it, even Brian. Chris turned so red he looked purple. He stomped off muttering something about getting punch.

"I'm serious, Cindy Davis kicked him in the balls," Daniel said. "He was rolling on the floor for ten minutes."

"Then why does he want to dance with her?" I asked.

"He's had a crush on her since fifth grade," Daniel said. "Totally hopeless."

Someone tapped me on the shoulder. "What?" I said, turning around.

Two girls I didn't know were staring at me. "Are you Nick?" one said. She looked like she wanted to throw up.

"Yeah," I said, trying to be cool.

"Here." She shoved a piece of paper into my hand. They disappeared, giggling the whole way. I opened the note.

Sharon H wants to dance with you.

"Who's Sharon H?" I asked.

"I know her," Andy said. "She's kind of plain looking with long brown hair and glasses. She played the piano for all the choir stuff in elementary school." Oh, the piano girl. She was in music class with me. We both played for the music teacher to accompany the choir, but I decided not to do it. We'd never talked to each other. Why did she want to dance with me?

"You gotta answer," Daniel said.

"Should I go ask her?" I said.

Andy looked at me like I was insane. "You have to send a note. Does anyone have a pen?" Brian handed him one. I noticed he had a notepad too. Seriously, he was taking notes?

"Nick likes you and wants you to have his baby," Andy said as he wrote.

"Give me that," I muttered. I grabbed the note. It said I liked her and wanted to dance.

"I'll take it to her and see what she says next," Andy said.

"Shouldn't I take it to her?" I asked.

"Don't you know anything about girls? Come on Parker, let's go."

"Why me?" Parker whined.

Andy groaned. "If I go alone, she'll think Nick only has one friend or that she's not important enough for him to send two friends. She sent two friends, so we have to send two friends back. Am I the only one here who gets how girls think?" He grabbed Parker by the arm and dragged him away.

"I don't get it," I said.

"Neither do I," Brian said.

"It's not how you ask, it's *who* you ask," Jonathan said.

"No way," Daniel said. "No girl will dance if you don't ask them the right way."

"So what's the right way?" I asked.

"I don't get this stuff either," he said with a shrug. "All I know is you can't just ask."

Jonathan handed his falcon to Daniel and crossed the room to a table where some girls were sitting. It was too far away to hear, but it looked like he was *talking* to Ann Solomon, a girl from our classes who was smart but a little weird. She stood up, walked with him to the center of the room, and started to dance. I think my mouth was open. Brian scribbled some notes. I glared at him.

"For Mr. Humber's report," he explained.

"Delivered," Andy said, grinning.

"Did you get an answer?" I asked.

He rolled his eyes again. "No, her friends have to send a note back. This stuff is complicated."

"Jonathan asked Ann Solomon and now they're dancing," I pointed out.

"Well, he did it all wrong," Andy said.

"I've been looking all over for you guys," Chris said even though we hadn't moved. "I asked Cindy Davis to dance. She said she couldn't because her boyfriend is in ninth grade and he's the jealous type and he would kick my ass if he saw me dancing with her. Then she said I was cute."

"You're so full of shit," Daniel said.

"Nick has girls asking him to dance," Andy bragged.

"Girls don't ask guys to dance," Chris answered. "*You're* so full of shit."

"She sent a note," Daniel said. "We're waiting for an answer to our note."

The same giggling girls came back a few minutes later to deliver her response, running away when I took the note. "Read it!" Andy said. He was more excited than me.

Do you like fast or slow songs?

"Oooh," said Chris, Daniel, and Andy at the same time.
"What?" I said.

"It's a test," Andy said. "If you say fast dance, it means you want to check her out first because you're not sure. If you say slow dance, it means you already like her. She wants you to pick, but if you pick the wrong one you'll blow it. If you say slow dance but she's not sure about you, she'll think you're coming on too strong. If she wants you to say slow dance but you pick fast dance, then she'll think you don't like her."

"How do I know which one to pick?" I said.

"You don't," Andy said.

"Why do girls make things so complicated?" Brian asked.

"They love mind games," Andy said.

"It doesn't seem worth all this trouble," Brian said.

"Maybe if you're a homo," Chris said.

I'd heard that word a million times before. Just another tease word, no different than calling someone an idiot or an asshole. I knew it shouldn't bug me. But it did. A lot. A moment ago, I felt like I belonged to my group of friends. Now, I felt like they were total strangers. They were going on about getting a girl to dance, getting one to be your girlfriend, then maybe to kiss, then maybe more eventually. It'd probably take them months or years to get anywhere. Me? I woke up this morning and had real, full-blown sex. Home run baby, all the way. And could I brag about it? If they knew I did it with Jeremy, I wouldn't be getting high fives. They wouldn't dare go within fifty feet of me ever again. The whole thing made me furious.

A moment ago, I was just going along with them, not caring if I danced or not. Now, I was going to dance with a girl tonight. Any girl, as long as she was a girl. It was a matter of life or death.

"This is stupid," I said, walking away.

"What are you doing?" Andy said, grabbing my arm.

I pushed him, harder than I meant. He stumbled back. "By the time everything gets figured out, the dance is going to be over," I yelled and stomped off.

"They're starting a slow song!" Andy yelled after me. I ignored him. I kept on ignoring them when they followed me across the room. I found Sharon sitting at a table with the girls who delivered the note. My armor felt heavier than usual. I started to sweat. They whispered to

each other. Maybe Andy was right and I was doing it all wrong. I tried to take a deep breath but forgot how.

"Hi," I croaked. My heart pounded in my ears.

"Hi," she said back.

"Do you want to dance?" I blurted out.

I couldn't hear what she said. She stood up, so I figured she said yes. We walked to the middle of the room into a sea of ninth graders. My friends were whispering to each other like they were a bunch of girls. Everyone was staring at me. Rumors about whether we were dating would be floating around for months. Even worse, I had to dance in front of everyone and I had no idea how to dance. Looking around at other people dancing didn't help. Most of them were dancing *way* closer than I would dare. Should we dance separate? Should we hold hands? Should I put my hands on her waist like Jonathan was doing with Ann? Sharon H was staring at me, like she wanted me to figure it out already.

Molly didn't make me figure everything out on my own.

I stuck my arms out straight so we could be as far away from each other as possible. She put her arms out the same way. We tried to figure out who would hold whose hand. When I held hers, it was nothing like the time I held hands with Molly. I remembered feeling all kinds of somethings. With Sharon, I felt nothing. Just the sense a million eyes were watching, judging, and criticizing everything I did.

"You play piano really well," she said.

"Uh huh," I said. My words splatted on the floor before I realized. "Thanks," I said. "Umm, you do too." Her hands felt sweaty. Or maybe mine were sweaty. It's probably grossing her out. I wanted to wipe them on my pants but I couldn't let go. I rocked back and forth and she copied me. Why did she say that? Did she mean I was better than her? Was she jealous? Or did she want me to know she played better than I did? Did she ask me to dance only because she knew I could play piano? I scowled. She only cared about the piano. I looked her up and down. She wasn't pretty like Molly. No way she read science fiction books. I didn't want her to be my girlfriend. We rocked back and forth until the song was over. A fast, annoying one started.

"I don't like this song," I said.

"Neither do I," she said.

We let go. She went back to her friends and I went back to mine.

"Awesome," Andy said, giving me a high five.

"I'm going to the bathroom," I muttered.

Right outside the bathroom doors, two ninth graders were necking. It happened all the time during school. Public display of affection was only five points. Getting in trouble didn't stop anyone, and usually the teachers didn't bother anyway. I always wondered if they were showing off or just didn't care if anyone saw them. I shoved the bathroom door so hard it slammed into the wall and kicked the door to a stall open. The whole row shook.

Jeremy loved to neck. His tongue went in and out, licking my teeth and tickling the roof of my mouth. I thought having someone else's tongue in my mouth was slimy and gross. The only reason I let him do it was because I loved him. I never told him that I didn't like it. Usually I didn't care when I saw kids necking in the hall, but now I was jealous how those ninth graders could do whatever they wanted. What happened if they kissed in public? Boohoo, a few points, big fucking deal. If Jeremy and I necked in public? Everyone would know I was a homo. I'd lose all my friends and never get new ones. Jeremy would go to jail and I'd never see him again.

I had another terrifying thought. I tried to push it away, but it kept coming back. I hated that I could even think such a horrible thing. Jeremy was the most important person in my life. He saved me. He loved me. I loved him. I needed him. I couldn't imagine living without him.

But it would make some things a lot easier.

Chapter 30

November 15, 1982

I stared at the ceiling, thinking through my schedule. Math test today, but I was ready for it. French test on Wednesday, also easy. Gym clothes were washed and in a plastic bag next to my backpack. The leftover roast beef would make a good lunch. I had to remind Jeremy I was staying for dinner at Chris' house so he should pick me up at seven.

"Are you alive down there?" he murmured.

"Mmmmm," I moaned. I closed my eyes and wished he would hurry up. He shifted his weight and pushed back inside me. When we first started fucking, it hurt. A lot. Now, it was uncomfortable but not really painful. I wondered if I'd gotten used to it or if my butthole was just bigger. Fucking was definitely sex, but it didn't give me a sex feeling. As far as I was concerned, and at this point I was a world class expert, being fucked and taking a shit felt *exactly* the same. Maybe it would be different if I was the one doing the fucking, but no way in hell was I going to find out. I still didn't understand how he could do it without getting scuzzed out. When I was in the right mood, fucking was less about the physical feeling and more about sharing our love. That mood was getting hard to find. Fucking felt like a chore, something I had to do after he was done with me. I told myself it was more than a fair trade for all the things he did for me, sex and otherwise. This morning, all I felt was irritated. I glanced at the clock. Seven fifteen. If he didn't finish soon, I'd be late. That irritated me even more.

I decided to move things along, moaning like I was enjoying it and pressing myself into his body. He didn't speed up, so I gave in and did the thing he liked with my big toe. That did it. A minute later he was done. I tried to squirm away, but he wrapped his arms around me for some after sex snuggling. I looked at the clock again. Two minutes was all I was going to give him.

"You drive me crazy when you do that thing with your toe," he murmured.

"You were taking forever," I said.

"It's nice to savor the feeling," he said, gently tickling my stomach. "Admit it, you love it when I make you wait."

"Not really," I grumbled. I did love it, but that only made me more irritated. I pushed at his arms. "I gotta take a shower. I'm going to be late."

He held me tighter. "So, you'll be late," he said, kissing my neck. "Stay home with me today. I'll make it worth your while." He nibbled on my earlobe. I hated when he did that. "I'll call you in sick. You haven't skipped a single day this year. It's about time you took a day off."

"I have a math test," I said.

"The world won't end if you take it tomorrow. Let's do something. Anything you want. I can think of a few things we haven't done in a while." His hand traced down my back. "Maybe I should tie you to the bed."

I shivered. "I'm serious, I'm going to be late," I said, letting him see how irritated I was. I pushed at his arms until he let me go. "About time," I muttered. I went into the bathroom and closed the door. I was getting in the shower when he came in. "Some privacy, please?"

"Do you need any help?" he asked.

"If you want to help, make my lunch instead," I growled.

"Sorry," he said and left.

I felt bad. I didn't care about my math test. I liked when we showered together. Taking a day off sounded like a great idea. Maybe not tied to the bed because that didn't get me excited like it used to. But I couldn't today. Being absent meant you weren't allowed to participate in after school activities. Mr. Humber had a new club called

Great Books, where we read stories and talked about them. Brian convinced me to come to the first one even though it sounded like another class. I thought we'd be the only ones there, but so many eighth and ninth graders showed up we had to meet in the cafeteria. We read a cool science fiction story about forcing everyone to be equal by having smart people wear devices that made it harder to think so they'd be as dumb as everyone else. Jeremy would understand why I didn't want to skip today if I told him.

Except I couldn't tell him.

I was practicing piano when he got back from open house at school last week. He interrupted me, which he *never* did. "You have to be extremely careful around your English teacher," he said. "Mr. Humber's the kind of guy who could figure out what's going on between us. I think he's already suspicious. He asked who I was, why you were living with me, and how involved your parents are in your life. All the right questions. I was as disarming as I know how to be, but he's too sharp to be easily fooled. I don't want to scare you, but you should avoid him. If he asks any questions about me or your parents, no matter how unimportant they seem, you need to tell me about it right away. Promise me."

He didn't know Mr. Humber like I did. I looked forward to his class because he made me think and laugh out loud. He never got mad and he was always fair. Outside class, he was a nice person. Brian finally explained he was having lunch with Mr. Humber instead of coming to the cafeteria. Mr. Humber even brought him food every day. I had lunch with them once. It was fun even though the idea of having lunch with a teacher seemed horrible. We talked about science fiction and fantasy books the whole time because Mr. Humber had been reading them since he was our age. I wanted to tell Jeremy he was wrong, but that would only scare him more. So, I promised him I would stay away from Mr. Humber. I kept the book club, lunches. and playing piano for the musical a secret. I would need his help with the music eventually, but rehearsals didn't start until January so I had time to figure out what to tell him.

Being forced to keep secrets made me furious. I didn't want to tell Jeremy everything that happened in my life. He didn't need to know

about my friends and normal stuff at school. I was supposed to be able tell him anything I *wanted* him to know, and I wanted him to know about Mr. Humber.

He knocked on the bathroom door. "Lunch is ready." He came in when I didn't answer. "Is everything ok? You seem a little upset this morning."

I didn't want him to get more upset so I came up with something. "I could take a day off next week instead. It's Thanksgiving, so nothing'll be going on in school. We could stay home and do all kinds of fun things." I pressed my butt against the shower door to emphasize what I meant.

"There's no way I'll be able to keep up with you," he said.

"That's because you're old," I said.

"I've created a monster," he teased.

I growled.

We sat on the edge of our seats. "The key turns with a loud click. You hear the sound of machinery buzzing as the locks open. Slowly you push the door open. . ." He rolled the dice a couple of times. Nobody said a word. The candles flickered. "And. . ." Chris loved drawing it out like this for effect. It worked.

"Chris, phone!" Paul called from upstairs.

"I'm busy!" Chris snarled.

"It's Dad!" Paul yelled again.

Chris moved like he had three haste spells cast on him at the same time. He was halfway up the stairs before his chair landed. "Not fair!" Parker said. "I'm dying to know what's in the room." He crossed his arms and sulked. Nobody talked much while we waited for Chris to come back. We played with the dice and candle wax to keep busy. Until we heard shouting upstairs. Everybody stopped so we could listen. I couldn't make out anything Chris or Paul were saying. Something crashed. A door slammed.

"Go find out what's going on," Andy whispered to Daniel.

"I'm not going, you go," Daniel whispered back.

"Nick?" Andy whispered at me.

"No fucking way," I whispered.

Heavy footsteps echoed on the basement stairs. Paul peeked his head around the wall. He looked angry and depressed at the same time. "I think you guys should go home," he said in the most serious voice I could imagine. It made me wonder if he was actually a grown-up in disguise. The look on his face squashed any attempt to bargain for more time. Everyone packed up their things without arguing and left. Jeremy was running errands since he thought I was staying for dinner, so I was stuck there.

"I don't have a ride," I said to Paul. He stared off into space. "What should I do?"

"You can hang out here as long as you stay away from Chris," he said. I had no idea how to do that if Chris came downstairs. He was an expert at putting people in his way. Chris only had one kind of bad mood — angry. I'd never seen him moping or depressed. And when Chris was angry, his mission was to make everyone around him as angry as he was. I thought about going with one of the other guys, but hanging out with them individually didn't really work. Andy was still in trouble for the green hair so he wasn't allowed to have anyone over. Daniel's parents would create homework for us if we didn't have enough. Jonathan never said anything so hanging out with him was awkward. Parker was kind of a baby, and besides, his mother wouldn't leave us alone for two seconds if we were at his house.

If Brian came like he promised, I wouldn't have this problem.

"I can't come today," he told me before lunch.

"Why not? You said you could."

"The usual," he said.

"Tell him we're playing football."

"He doesn't believe me," Brian said. "He threw a pass at me while I was trimming the hedge. I missed it, so I told him he surprised me. He threw another, and another, and another. I couldn't catch a single one."

"Yeah, sure." I didn't believe him. He just didn't want to play and was making up an excuse.

"Maybe I can come over your house on Sunday," he said. "We could act out some scenes in the woods." I shrugged my shoulders. "Whichever ones you want."

"I'm busy on Sunday." I wanted my best friend to be a part of the first group of friends I'd ever had in my entire life. Was that so much to ask for? Why did he have to make things difficult? He wasn't acting like a friend. I did everything for our friendship and he did nothing. It wasn't fair.

"Maybe another time," he said.

"Yeah, maybe," I muttered. I stomped away. We didn't speak to each other for the rest of the day.

I was sitting on the porch wondering what to do when Chris came outside. "Hey," he said in a depressed voice. His eyes were red and puffy. I couldn't imagine Chris crying. Anything that could make Chris cry had to be serious. He sat down next to me. "Want to do something?"

"Sure, I guess," I said. Paul told me to stay away, but I thought I could help Chris feel better.

"Let's go to the doughnut shop," he said. "The Chinese guy who works there goes mental if you don't buy anything."

"Why don't we just buy a doughnut?" I asked.

"My stupid mom cut off my allowance," he said, his usual anger seeping back in. It made things feel normal. "I haven't got a fucking dime."

"I've got money," I said.

He narrowed his eyes. "Enough for McDonalds?"

I narrowed mine too. "Maybe."

"I'm so fucking starving right now I could eat a dozen Big Macs, three chocolate shakes, and fifty large fries. You got enough for all that?"

"Maybe," I said the same way.

He pushed me on the shoulder. "So? Ask Paulie if you can borrow his bike. Don't tell him I'm going too."

I went inside. Paul was still staring off into space. "Is it ok if I borrow your bike?"

"Yeah, sure," he said without looking at me. Whatever happened on that call with their dad, it upset both of them. They never talked about their dad. I'd never met him or even seen a picture.

Chris had a little kid bike, the kind where you pushed the pedals backward to brake. It was way too small for him, so his knees were up to his chest when he pedaled. If I was riding a bike like that, he'd tease me constantly. Teasing him right now didn't seem like a good idea. Sometimes we raced, and sometimes we cut each other off on purpose to see who would fall off first. Chris scared me on the main roads. He weaved in traffic, cut into intersections when the light didn't change, and made cars wait for him at turns. One time he made a car slam on the brakes, tires squealing. We could hear the guy yelling even though the windows were shut. Chris flipped him off. I thought we were going to get murdered.

"You gotta watch out for those stupid drivers," I said.

"They gotta watch out for *me*," he said. "It's the *law*."

Jeremy taught me the law of bicycles. If there was an accident it didn't matter who was right. The person on the bike loses. Chris didn't think of stuff like that. Or maybe he just didn't care.

I didn't want anything from McDonalds. I used to like it, but after eating good food all the time with Jeremy, McDonalds seemed kind of disgusting. I couldn't remember the last time I went. I locked the bicycles to a pole and caught up with him inside. "I'm hungry enough to eat a fucking horse!" he shouted so everyone could hear. A lady in line with two little kids glared at us. He got into the same line as her. "I'm so fucking hungry. Fuck fuck fuckety fuck." The kids looked scared. I thought about telling him to shut up, but I didn't say anything. It'd only make him worse.

We got to the counter. "I'll have a Big Mac with double cheese, extra mayo, no mustard, two tomatoes, and twelve pickles." The girl behind the counter stared at him. "Double cheese, extra mayo. . ." he repeated like he was talking to a baby. She looked annoyed, writing his order on a piece of paper. "With large fries and a large chocolate shake, extra chocolate." He waited until she put the paper in a holder and shouted special order to the back. "Make that fourteen pickles and extra ketchup, no mayo."

Now she looked pissed off. "What do you want?" she snapped at me.

"Small fries," I said. "The normal way, nothing special."

"You didn't change my order," Chris barked. He slapped his hand down on the counter. "I said ketchup and fourteen pickles with no mayo and you didn't change it."

"That'll be three thirty-five," she hissed.

"I'm not going to pay for it," he sneered. "You didn't make it the way I wanted. It's the *law.*"

"Look, kid," she said, leaning over the counter. "Shut up, or I'll call the manager and have you kicked out with nothing. Get it?"

"Fine, call him over," he said, folding his arms.

"Just forget it," I said, poking him in the side. I gave her the money.

"No. I have the right to get my food the way I want it. Go ahead, call the manager. I won't get thrown out. You'll get fired."

"If I get fired, my boyfriend will take your ass apart one piece at a time."

I started shaking. She shoved the change into my hand. We had to wait off to the side for Chris' order. "Punk little shit," she said when she shoved the tray towards us.

"Kids these days use such foul language," he said, pretending to look shocked.

Chris stuffed a whole jelly doughnut in his mouth.

"Nice," I said. Watching him eat a whole box of doughnuts was better than watching him crush doughnuts in the store. He wanted to see how far he could squirt the jelly filling. I had to talk him into leaving the doughnut shop just like I had to talk him into leaving McDonalds after he spread fifty ketchup packets on the seat next to him.

I kept a lookout, certain the cops would catch up with us any minute. We snuck onto the golf course through a hole in the fence. "Don't be chicken shit," he said when I told him it was a bad idea. "No one plays golf at night. Besides, I've been here loads of times to play golf when I was little. I'm entitled. It's the *law.*" I was getting sick of him saying

that. He rode his bicycle across the lawn, picking up speed and slamming on his brakes so that he tore up the grass. The trail of destruction led right to us.

"This looks like a good sledding hill," I said. "You should come to my house when it snows. The whole backyard is one long hill. There's a creek at the bottom, so if you don't ditch you wind up soaked."

"There's one I go to sometimes that's better," he said. "If you don't ditch, you wind up right in the middle of a busy street and get splatted by a car." He demonstrated with his hands, making an appropriate sound. "Are your parents divorced?" he said out of nowhere.

"Huh? No."

"Did they die in a car accident or something?"

"No, they're alive," I said.

"How come you live with your uncle?"

I was prepared. "I don't live with him full time. My parents are always at work because my dad has his own business and my mom is a lawyer. My uncle lives in the same neighborhood, so I stay with him when they're not around."

"What does your uncle do for work?" he asked.

"He doesn't work. His family is rich."

"What do you mean, his family? You're the same family."

"You know, his dad, whatever your uncle's dad is called. His regular family."

"Your uncle's dad is your grandpa," he pointed out. I felt like I was getting a stomachache. I wasn't so prepared after all. "If your family's rich, why does your dad work all the time?"

"It's complicated," I said, trying to sound casual. I had no idea what to say if he asked another question.

"Sounds pretty weird to me," he said. He picked at the grass. "My parents are divorced."

I started breathing again. "How long?" I asked.

"Four years ago," he answered. "It sucks. Some kids make it sound cool because they have two rooms and get extra stuff for Christmas, but that's bullshit. Divorce fucks up everything." He pulled out a fistful of grass. "You know what we should do? Let's get all the flags from the holes and throw them in the lake. It's not deep. I'll bet if we throw

them like spears, they'll stick up in the middle so everyone wonders what happened."

"I dunno," I said.

"Fraidy cat," he fired back. "I love fucking up their precious little course. Golf's the stupidest game ever invented. Only assholes like hitting a little ball into a little hole and driving around in those moron carts."

"Why do you hate it so much?" I asked.

"I don't hate golf. I hate people who play golf." He hawked up a huge glob of snot and smeared it on the grass. "We could use the flags like we were jousting on our bicycles."

"You can't joust without armor and shields," I said.

"Don't be chicken shit," he said.

"Seriously, I saw it at a fair. It doesn't work without a shield." I imagined the flag sticking out of my chest, spurting blood.

"Whatever," he said. "Do you hate your parents?"

It was hard to keep up with him. "I guess so. I don't see them a lot, so I don't think about it."

"I think about it all the time. How come so many parents make it their mission in life to fuck up their kids?"

"I dunno," I said.

"Daniel wants to steal stuff because his parents are too strict. Parker's mom treats him like a baby so he acts like a baby. Your parents are so busy working they sent you to live with someone else. My mom is never around, and when she is, she treats me like a slave. I have to do a million things around the house while she watches TV and smokes. I'm not allowed to be outside after dark or go to the doughnut shop by myself. Paulie gets to do whatever he wants, but I'm the little baby who can't take care of myself. And my dad? He's just a fucking useless prick who never has time to do anything except hit his fucking golf balls." He stretched his arms above his head. "I gotta take a piss."

"Where's the bathroom?" I asked.

"Right there," he said, pointing at one of the flags. "Can you imagine the look on one of those golf fuckers when he figures out that wet stuff in the hole isn't water? If I had some TP, I could leave them a really special gift." I rode down the hill with him to the flag, the grass

short and neat. He made sure to tear up a big chunk. "Do you have to piss too?" I shrugged. "Let's piss in the cup together. Bet I can aim better." He unzipped his fly and turned around to face the hole.

Jeremy talked a lot about thinking with your dick. I knew he meant that a person could do stupid things when he got horny. Right now, my dick was doing all the thinking. I wanted to see him. I *needed* to see him. Curiosity had nothing to do with it. I didn't care if it was bigger or smaller or if he had hair. I was excited. *That* kind of excited. Standing up straight hard as a rock excited. It made no sense. Seeing dicks never turned me on before. I tried not to look at Jeremy's. I saw Brian's a million times and never cared.

"You coming? I can't hold it all night."

My brain told me this was a bad idea. He might see I was hard. I should tell him I didn't have to go. My dick said fuck that, I want to see. It won. Easily. Not even a competition. I stood facing him on the other side of the hole. His hand was in his underwear.

"Not over there you moron! If you miss, you're going to piss all over me. Stand on this side." He stomped his foot. "I'm going to explode!"

I fumbled with my zipper. Getting it through the hole in my underwear when it was hard was almost impossible. I wrapped my hand around it to hide it as much as I could, angling myself so I could see him while hiding mine.

He pulled his out. "Ok. One, two, three!" I intended to take a quick look, but I couldn't stop staring. He was smaller than me. I wanted him to pull down his pants so I could get a better look.

"What's the matter, are you chicken shit?"

"I don't have to go," I mumbled.

He snickered. "Probably because you've got a raging boner."

I felt dizzy as I stumbled away from the hole. I didn't care which direction I went as long as I was going away from him. He *saw*. He knew I was turned on. He knew I got off looking at his dick. By tomorrow, everyone at school would know I was a gaywad homo faggot. I tried to stuff it back into my pants, but it wouldn't cooperate. I was going to lose all my friends. My life was going to become hell. Maybe I could stab him in the stomach with the flag. I could say jousting was his idea.

"Can't you take a fucking joke?" he yelled.

I slipped on a wet patch of grass, sliding down a short hill on my butt. He ran up. "Geez, it's not like I'm a homo or something. I couldn't help seeing, that's all. Sometimes I say stupid things." The worried look on his face confused me. "You're not going to tell anyone I was looking, are you?"

It took a couple of seconds before I figured it out. "I'm not going to tell anyone," I mumbled.

Holy shit, that was close.

"I'm not a homo," he said carefully.

"I know," I said. "Me neither." Just in case.

"I get boners all the time," he said. "I'm so fucking horny. You've got to lend me one of your uncle's Hustlers. You said he had hundreds. He'll never miss one."

"Maybe not hundreds," I said. I tried to stop thinking about him jacking off. "I guess you could borrow one as long as you keep it a secret, especially from your mom."

"Do you think I want my mom to know I have a porno mag? Her head would go nuclear." He made an explosion sound. "She'd lock me in the confessional booth until I did a zillion Hail Mary's. I've got a hiding spot she'll never find."

"Where?"

"Like I'd tell you." He lay down on the grass. "I'd give anything to see a naked woman. I'd sell my fucking *soul* to get a blow job."

My dick had the stupidest, most terrifying, and most exciting idea.

"I'll bet blow jobs feel awesome," I said.

"Yeah," he said.

"But think about it for a second. What difference would it make who did it? It's just a mouth, right?"

"What do you mean?" he said, sitting up.

"Why would it have to be a girl who did it?"

My brain screamed to stop what I was doing *right now*.

My dick told my brain to shut the fuck up.

My brain apologized and went away.

He narrowed his eyes. "You're fucking with me."

"No, I'm serious. If you closed your eyes and pretended, it wouldn't make a difference."

"You mean like some guy?" He made a face. "That is *so* gay."

"It's not gay," I said. "Gay is when you want to do it with guys. If you're thinking about a girl, it's not gay."

"Bullshit," he said. But he didn't sound so sure. I was almost there. "The guy giving the blow job knows he's sucking some other guy's dick. What kind of guy does that if he isn't gay?"

"Maybe he's doing it because he's going to get one in return," I said.

He looked right at me. "Are you saying we should suck each other off?" I held my breath. If I shrugged and nodded casually enough, it might actually happen.

"Because if you said that I'd have to beat the shit out of you. I'm not a homo."

Oh shit. Shit shit shit shit shit.

I made my mouth drop open. "I didn't mean us. What kind of sick fuck are you? I was saying hypothetically. Seriously, you've got a problem if you think I'd do something like that.

"You were fucking scaring me there for a minute," he said, staring at me. "I hate homos. They're disgusting."

"Yeah," I said.

"Yeah," he said back and looked away. "What time is it?"

"Fuck, it's after eight," I said. "My uncle was coming to pick me up at seven. He's going to kill me."

"Then what difference would it make if you stayed out later?" I stared at him. "Let's do some real damage. If you're going to get killed, might as well go all out."

"I dunno," I said.

"Don't be chicken shit."

I knew Jeremy was worried about me. I shouldn't make him wonder where I am. But I was angry. Furious that he almost made me late for school today. Furious about the Mr. Humber stuff. Furious that what just happened with Chris was completely his fault.

"Let's do it," I said.

We peeked around the corner at Chris' house. There were two cars in the driveway, his mom's station wagon and Jeremy's Porsche.

"Fuck," I said under my breath.

"Fuckety fuck fuck," he said. "My mom's home early."

"It's ten-thirty," I said.

"She usually gets back after eleven," he muttered. "You'd better not come inside. It'll be worse if she thinks you were with me. I'll tell them you went home hours ago."

"How?"

"On Paul's bike, fucking duh," he said. "I'll give you a head start so you get home before your uncle."

"What about my stuff?"

"I'll bring it tomorrow," he said. "It was fun. See ya."

"Yeah, see ya," I said back.

I pedaled through the streets. We seriously fucked up that golf course. We filled the holes with sand. We tore up lots of the short grass near the holes. We threw the flags into the lake. They wouldn't stand up, so they disappeared under the water. Chris was right. It was fun.

My plan was to pretend I fell asleep. I figured Jeremy went to Chris' to pick me up and never went back home. Piece of cake, he'd believe it. But another part of me didn't want to lie, and not because I felt bad about lying to Jeremy. I wanted to tell him what I did to the golf course. I wanted to tell him that I didn't give a shit if he was worried. I wanted to get into a fight with him. I wondered if this is how Chris felt all the time.

I beat Jeremy home by a few minutes. He came into the house just as I was lying down on the couch. "Nick!" he shouted.

"Huh?" I said. I sat up and rubbed my eyes.

"What the hell is going on?" he shouted from the hallway. "You've been missing for hours! I looked everywhere for the two of you! We were about to call the police!"

"I came home hours ago," I said. "I guess I fell asleep."

"That isn't going to work," he said, stomping up to me. "Your partner in crime already confessed. What the hell were you thinking?

You bicycled home in the dark? You could've been hit by a car! Someone could have snatched you!"

"Nothing happened," I muttered. "What's the big deal?"

He stared at me and shook his head. "I can't believe you said that."

"Said what? It isn't a big deal. I'm not a little kid. I can take care of myself."

"You're twelve years old!" he shouted. "You have no business bicycling around town in the middle of the night!"

"It's not the middle of the night, it's only eleven," I pointed out. I knew that would make him angrier.

"Did you stop to think how worried I was about you? I drove around everywhere, terrified I'd find you dead on the pavement!" I crossed my arms and smiled. "Chris put you up to this, didn't he? That kid's nothing but trouble. I don't want you being friends with him."

"It was my idea," I said. "And I can be friends with whoever I want."

"I'm still the adult. I'm responsible for you."

"You're not my father. You can't tell me what to do."

I knew I shouldn't have said that. I was going too far. I didn't mean it. But I couldn't stop myself. He collapsed into the chair across from me.

"I guess not," he said quietly. "I'm scared, kiddo. I don't know what's going on with you. You've been moody and distant lately. I'm scared you're drifting away from me. I'm scared I hurt you and I don't know how. Please tell me what's going on."

"Nothing's going on," I muttered.

"Do you know what yesterday was?" he said.

"Sunday, duh," I fired back.

"It was our anniversary. We've known each other for one year."

SHIT!!!

"Why didn't you remind me!" I screamed.

"Remind you?" he said softly. "You couldn't stop teasing me about it. You said you had a special surprise planned. You figured out the date. It mattered more to you than it did to me. Yesterday came, and nothing happened. Not even an acknowledgment it was a special day."

I wanted to make a big deal out of it. I wanted to plan a special surprise. It was important to me. I forgot all about it. I felt horrible.

"Well, I forgot, ok?" I yelled. "You should've reminded me!"

"I don't want to fight," he said.

"You started it."

"I'm relieved you're home safe," he said. "I'm sorry I yelled at you. Please tell me what's wrong."

"The only thing wrong is you," I sneered.

"It's late. We're both tired." He stood up. "We should go to bed and talk more in the morning."

"I'm not tired. Besides, there's nothing else to talk about."

He held out his hand. "Let's go to bed."

I shook my head. "Thanks, but I don't feel like getting fucked in my ass tonight."

I wished I didn't say it. I didn't know why I was so angry at him. I knew he was worried and upset. I knew I was wrong. The anger took over. Like I was a puppet. Like the real me was tied up and helpless inside myself.

"I never want you to do anything you don't want to do," he said. I couldn't say anything. "I've got to get out of here."

"Where are you going?" Terror mixed with my anger.

"I don't know. Out. Stay up, go to bed, go out on your bicycle. Do whatever you want to do. I'll be back later."

"Fine!" I screamed. "Leave! See if I care!"

He left.

I pounded up the stairs and slammed the door to the guest bedroom.

I felt like a piece of shit.

Because I was a piece of shit.

I wished I understood what was wrong with me.

Chapter 31

December 17, 1982

There had to be a million fucking restaurants in New Jersey. Why did they have to pick this one?

The lawns and gardens were lit up with thousands of Christmas lights, sparkling in the pine trees. If I wasn't in such a bad mood, I'd probably think it was beautiful. Instead, I scowled and adjusted my suit. I couldn't get it to feel comfortable like it normally did. It itched, chafed, and pulled in the wrong places.

"Doing ok, kiddo?" he asked, putting his hand on my knee.

"Stop calling me that." I pushed his hand off.

"You've told me the story so many times I feel like I was there," he said. "I guarantee no one remembers what happened. It was an accident. Nobody blames you."

He was full of shit. I'd remember if I was them. I would point and whisper behind his back. *There goes chocolate boy. Wonder if he still has chocolate up his ass.*

The valet opened the door. "Good evening, sir," he said. I could tell he knew exactly who I was. I stomped into the restaurant, Jeremy following. They took our coats and led us into the bar. The restaurant was crowded with people in suits and fancy dresses. A huge Christmas tree took up one corner, fake presents underneath. It would've been nice if it was any other restaurant. Everyone was so loud, I wanted to jam my fingers into my ears. I didn't because I would've looked ridiculous. *Chocolate boy is picking fudge from his ears. I'll bet he eats his own earwax.*

The people who used to be my parents were sitting at the bar, facing away from each other. This stupid dinner was their idea. I only talked to my mother once a week. I couldn't remember the last time I saw her because she was in Denver all the time. My father never called me. Mom told me to call him, but I never did.

"Jack, Ellie. It's good to see you," Jeremy said in his bullshit business voice. Mom turned around.

"Nicholas!" she said with a big smile. I tried not to smile but a little one slipped out. "Look at you! I think you grew six inches since the last time I saw you!" She put her arms out to hug me. In *public*. I let her, hugging back as lightly as I could. Everyone was watching us. "You're looking very sharp, although I don't care for your hair brushed backwards." I backed up before she could touch my hair. Messing up the suit was bad enough, but messing up the hair? Didn't she understand anything? "Jack, are you going to say hello to your son?"

He grunted something I guessed was supposed to be hello. He grabbed the bartender. "Another perfect Manhattan," he growled.

"You've already had two," my mother said. "Don't you think that's enough?"

He pointed a finger at her like it was a knife. "You don't get to tell me when I've had enough. You don't get to tell me what to do anymore." He turned back to the bartender. "Make it a double."

My mother took a deep breath and straightened out her dress. They were going to do it again. They were going to be even worse this time. "I'm going to wait in the hall," I muttered, not caring if they heard me or not. I found a big leather chair near the end of the hall where it was a little quieter. People walked by me, every single one of them staring. Whispering. *Chocolate boy.* I watched them, hoping I'd see her face. I knew the chances were ridiculous, but I couldn't get her out of my mind all day. I wondered if she'd be here. I wondered if she'd taste like minty strawberries if we kissed.

Molly wouldn't laugh at chocolate boy.

Jeremy came to get me. "How are you doing?" he asked.

"Just great," I muttered. "This is *soooooo* much fun."

"I hope you can act like an adult tonight even if your parents can't. I wouldn't want anything to jeopardize our arrangement."

"Nothing's going to happen," I said, rolling my eyes. "They like it better when I'm out of their hair."

He bent down. "Please. If not for me, do it for yourself. We don't want to make things worse than they already are."

I frowned. "What bug crawled up your butt?"

"Nothing. Never mind." He stood back up. "I'll be in the bar."

"What are you talking about?" I asked as he left. "You never tell me anything."

My mother came out a minute later. I stared her down. "I'm sorry about before," she said quietly. "I hope we can have a nice dinner."

"That depends," I said as coldly as I could. "Are you going to behave?"

Her mouth opened and closed a few times as though she wasn't sure what to say. It gave me goosebumps. "I'll come get you when they're ready to seat us," she said.

At least our table was in a small dining room where we could be out of the way. I sat in the corner, hoping to avoid everyone staring at me. It didn't work. I stuck my face in the menu like picking my dinner was a life or death decision.

"So, Nicholas," my mother said finally. "I didn't talk to you last week. How are things going?"

"Fine," I said through the menu.

"How's your schoolwork?"

"Good."

"Your grades last quarter were outstanding. Are you keeping it up?"

"Yeah," I said. I put my menu down because she wasn't going to quit.

"Are you playing anything new on the piano?"

"Not really," I said.

"What are you working on?"

"Nothing." She was questioning me like a witness in court.

"Nothing? What pieces are you playing?"

"The same stuff. Classical."

"Jeremy was telling me you've been spending a lot of time with your friends playing that game you liked about dragons?"

"Dungeons and Dragons," I corrected. It felt good to know a detail she didn't.

"Yes, that one. It sounds very creative."

"I guess."

She ran out of questions. "Anything else new?"

"Nothing."

"Nothing at all?"

"Nothing." I said again.

Jeremy jumped in. "What about you, Ellie? I thought I saw something about your firm in the papers, some big case?"

"I'm not involved in that litigation, but things have been going well." Business conversation, blah blah blah, that's all they knew how to talk about. I ignored them. They stopped talking after a minute, much faster than usual. Everyone stared at each other.

"I suppose there's little point avoiding the discussion," my mother said to my father.

"By all means, go ahead," he said. "Don't let me get in your way."

She glared at him and then looked directly at me. "Sometimes, when two parents aren't getting along, the best solution isn't to work things out." She shifted uncomfortably in her chair. "Your father and I have decided. . ."

"Leave me out of this," Dad interrupted, snorting. "I didn't decide anything." He drank the rest of his drink. "Another one," he yelled at the waiter.

Mom took a deep breath. "We've decided the best choice for everyone is to end our marriage."

"You're getting a divorce," I said.

She looked like she was in pain, like she was taking a crap that was too big to come out easily. I fought to keep myself from cracking up. This wasn't a laughing situation. Why did I think of something like that?

"I want you to know the most difficult part of our decision was the impact on you, but we concluded a divorce is in your best interests," she said.

"Why mine?" I asked. That made no sense.

"I'm sure you're aware that your father and I haven't been getting along."

"Really?" I said as sarcastically as I could. "I *never* noticed."

Jeremy kicked me under the table. I ignored him.

"We've tried to work out our differences, but your father and I are going in different directions with our lives." He snorted again. Like a pig. I made sure he knew I was disgusted from the look I gave him. "It's not fair for us to put you in the middle of all this rancor. We're convinced divorcing will make both of us happier people in the end, which can only have a positive impact on you. Wouldn't it be better if we didn't fight as much?"

"Why should I care if you fight?" I said with a shrug. "It's not like you care about me."

"I'm your mother," she said.

"Some mother," I muttered. Jeremy kicked me again, much harder this time. I kicked him back. He winced and I smiled. She didn't say anything. "Like I said, why should I care?" My father laughed out loud.

"Do you have anything you'd like to add?" she said to Dad.

"I think you're doing fine all by yourself," he said.

"Maybe I should excuse myself," Jeremy said quietly.

"You stay right where you are," my mother snapped.

"Don't talk to him like that," I said.

"You tell her," my father said.

"Shut up," I growled at him.

"Why don't we all take a deep breath and calm down," Jeremy said.

I thought she was going to rip into him with her lawyer claws. "You're right," she said. "I apologize."

"None necessary," he answered.

"This is very difficult for me," she said. My father laughed out loud again. She turned to me. "We need to make some important decisions."

"What kind of decisions?" I asked.

"We need to decide where you'll be living and who will be responsible for you," she said softly. I got the chills.

I slid my chair back, suddenly feeling trapped in the corner. "What are you talking about?"

"I'm moving to Colorado permanently," she said. "It's beautiful out there. The mountains are majestic, the city is clean and new, and the people are so much friendlier than here. You'll enjoy it – skiing and sledding in the winter, hiking and camping in the summer." She took a sip of water. "I met someone out there and I'll be living with him. His name is Allen and he works at the same firm as me. I think you'll like him, he's a very nice man."

My father stood up. "I'll be in the bar."

"Allen has a son close to your age," she said, ignoring him. "I know you'll get along well with him. He's smart like you and I'll bet he'll like the same books and games if you show him. You'd be like brothers. You used to talk a lot about wanting a brother." That was when I was young and stupid. I knew better since Jeremy told me about his brother and watching Chris with Paul. I shivered for real.

"You want me to live in Colorado with you?" I asked.

"Nothing's been decided," she said.

"Don't I get a say where I live?"

"Of course you do, but. . ."

"Then I'm staying here," I interrupted.

"We'll take your preferences into account, but it isn't entirely your decision. We have to do what's best for you."

I folded my arms. "What's best for me is to stay here."

"Your father is in no position to be responsible for your welfare," she said. "With his work schedule, he couldn't possibly take care of you."

"I can take care of myself. I'm not a baby."

"While I understand you feel as though you're grown up, you're only twelve years old. You have a lot of maturing left to do."

That made me furious. "How would you know?"

She leaned inward. "What makes you think you can talk to me this way? I'm not up for any mother of the year awards, but I've still done my best to do the right thing for you. You are still my son and you will treat me with some respect or so help me I will treat you like the snot-nosed kid you sound like right now."

"I think I should leave," Jeremy said, standing up.

"Sit down!" she snapped. "If it wasn't for you interfering we wouldn't be in this situation!"

"Shut up!" I yelled at her.

She looked like she was going to sink her lawyer claws into me. Jeremy looked terrified. I knew I was scaring him. I knew he was right and that I should behave. I didn't want to do anything that could mess things up. But I couldn't stop myself. I kept going too far. I kept saying things I didn't mean to say. I kept seeming angrier than I was.

"This isn't going the way I wanted," she said softly. She put her hand on the table like she wanted me to hold it. I didn't know why I did. "It's selfish to expect you to live with me, but it would mean everything to me if you did. I haven't been a good mother for a long time. I haven't been around for you. I haven't paid attention to you. I've been so wrapped up in my own problems, I was completely blind to yours. I'd love to change everything that's happened. I want to give you a normal life with a normal family and a good mother who's there for you. But I suppose it's too late, isn't it?" She turned to Jeremy. "I'm so sorry. Please accept my apology. You've done so much for Nicholas. I'm not angry with you. I'm grateful. Look at the boy he's become. All because of you."

"I understand," he said, putting his hand on top of mine on top of hers.

"This is the hardest thing I've ever done," she said like she was about to cry.

"Getting divorced?" I asked.

"No," she said. "Leaving you behind."

I went blank. Every feeling drained out of me.

"I already knew the right thing was to let you stay. I don't want to rip you away from school, your friends, and the piano. Not when you're doing so well and becoming such a wonderful young man. I'm proud of you. I hope you know that. I've already written up all the papers granting your father full custody."

I couldn't move.

She turned to Jeremy. "The only way this works is if you're willing to be responsible for Nicholas until he goes to college. I think we all

know Jack isn't cut out to be a parent. I need your commitment. Once I do this, it'll be difficult to undo."

Jeremy looked at me. "I'm honored," he said. "I care deeply about Nicholas. I promise I'll be there for him. I'll sign whatever you need me to sign."

"You can visit me," she said to me. "Anytime you want. For as long as you want."

I still couldn't move.

"Why don't you find your father? Jeremy and I have a lot of things we need to discuss." I stared at her. "I know he's a difficult person, but please believe me when I tell you he loves you underneath all that anger. Talk to him."

For some reason, I stood up. My mind was still a complete blank.

"I love you," she said.

I couldn't answer.

I knew the restaurant was noisy, but everything was silent. It reminded me of the time I hit Tommy Walker with the chair. I found my father in the bar. "Mom told me to talk to you," I heard myself say.

"She did, huh?" His voice sounded slushy. "I'm going to need another drink for this. Bartender! Another double!"

The bartender walked up. "Sir, I think you've had enough."

"Pour the damned drink," he spat. He took his keys out of his pocket and put them in his empty glass. "I'll take a cab to a motel. Satisfied?" The bartender went off to get his drink. "What are we supposed to discuss?"

"I'm not going to live with her," I said.

"You don't want to go live with her fancy new boyfriend in their fancy house with their fancy car in the fancy mountains? What's the matter? They didn't offer a big enough bribe? I'm going to make her pay a fortune in child support." The bartender put a new drink in front of him. He drank half of it in one gulp.

"I'm staying with Jeremy," I said.

"Of course," he said. "Why should anything change?"

I shrugged.

"If you're living here, we should do something sometime," he said. "What do you like to do?"

He didn't know what I liked to do. He didn't know anything about me. He never paid any attention to me. He didn't care about me. The only thing he did was yell at me. He was the biggest hypocrite who ever existed.

"I'm busy," I sneered.

"Yeah, I'm busy too," he said. He finished his drink. "One more for the road."

"I'm leaving," I said. I got off the chair.

"Make sure you behave for Jeremy. Do what he tells you to do."

"Or what?"

He didn't answer.

"It's none of your business," I said. "You don't get to tell me what to do. I'm divorcing you just like mom. Jeremy is a better dad than you could ever be. I never want to see you again."

I expected him to explode about how ungrateful I was and how he worked sixteen hours a day to put a roof over our heads. I expected him to scream the same bullshit I'd heard for twelve years. I expected him to throw his drink in my face. I expected actual steam to come out of his ears. I *wanted* him to explode. I wanted to see him have a real live conniption fit.

"I guess you'd better get going," he said without turning around.

"Goodbye," I muttered. "Forever."

He didn't answer.

The Christmas tree in the corner of the lobby was full of happy colored lights. I wanted to smash them. Jeremy brought the big teddy bear down from our bedroom and set him up next to the tree. The bear didn't want to look at me and I didn't want to look at him. Dozens of wrapped presents were stacked by tree and more were appearing every day. I didn't want them. I was hungry because I skipped dinner at the restaurant. The thought of eating made me sick.

Jeremy sat quietly with me on the couch. I knew he didn't know what to say to me and I knew why. After I left my ex-father in the bar, I found the downstairs cellar room from the last time I was here. If

Molly was here, that's where she'd look for me. Jeremy found me down there after an hour. He was so excited. I was going to be living with him permanently, all legal and official on paper. "Just like you were my son," he said. I shoved him. I told him to shut up and ran away. I felt horrible afterwards. Why didn't I feel as excited as him? I was his son now. He was my father. Nothing should make me happier.

I was terrified.

I told myself I had no reason to be scared. My parents were practically divorced already. It made no difference if they were together or not. I didn't have to change a single thing about my life. Everything would go on being the same.

Except me.

Chris said it. "Divorce fucks everything up."

But that's not what he was *really* saying.

"Divorce fucked me up" is what he meant.

I could pretend I didn't have parents and I could pretend they didn't matter to me, but they did. Mom was leaving me behind. She didn't care about me, no matter what she said. She cared about her lawyer firm and her new husband and her new son. My father didn't fight with me when I told him I was divorcing him. He didn't care about me either. I was an orphan. Their divorce was going to fuck me up just like it fucked up Chris. Not the same way as him, though. I wouldn't get angry and destroy things. I'd become depressed, get fat again, and try to kill myself. The boy in the backyard wasn't as dead and buried as I hoped. He could come back at any time. He could take over. He could end everything.

"I want to go in the prison," I said to Jeremy.

"Sweetie," he said. "I thought we were done with that."

"Put me in there and don't let me out," I said. "Make me stay there for the whole Christmas break. Make it worse than you did before. Punish me the whole time."

"Please stop," he said like he was the one about to be tortured. "You don't need this."

"Yes, I do," I said. "I need it now more than ever."

"You're upset. Talk to me."

"There's nothing to talk about."

"We'll find another way," he said. He tried to put his arm around my shoulder. I pushed it off. "We're going to have a fantastic Christmas. Presents, ice skating, dinner in the city, everything. I'll rent us a suite in Times Square to watch the ball drop on New Year's. I don't care what we do as long as we're together, like it used to be. I don't understand. This is the happiest day of my life. You're living with me for real and I want you to share that happiness. You're hurting. Let me help you. I love you."

"Are you going to do it or not?" I asked.

He didn't answer.

"I thought so," I said. I went upstairs to the guest bedroom alone.

My head was thick with soupy sleep. The bed was soft and warm. I didn't want to wake up. It felt like I was a hooked fish being pulled out of the water. My eyes opened a little even though I tried to keep them closed.

"Wake up," someone said. I didn't know and didn't care who it was. If I pulled the pillow over my head, maybe he would go away. I tried to roll over but my hand was stuck on something.

"Go away," I mumbled while I tried to pull my hand out.

"I said wake up," the voice said again. Someone started shaking me.

"What?" I groaned. I realized both my hands were stuck.

"Get up, right now." The blankets were yanked off me. The comfy warmth disappeared. I groaned again. I tried to sit up, but I couldn't get my balance right. The sleep melted away like cotton candy when I figured out what was going on.

My hands were tied behind my back with the leather cuffs.

"What are you doing?" I yelled. "Let me out of these things. I don't want to do this right now!"

"Get out of that bed," Jeremy ordered. He grabbed my arm and yanked me to the edge.

"Let go!" I said, trying to kick with my feet, but he'd cuffed them too. He pulled me off the bed and let me fall on the floor. "Ow!" I yelled. He sat on me and forced me to flip onto my stomach. "Get off

me!" I yelled. He pulled my feet towards my hands. I tried to squirm away and push him off. He was too strong. A moment later, my hands and feet were clipped together so I was hogtied. "Stop it, I mean it!" He pulled my hair and slapped me in the face. "That hurt!" I yelled.

"That's nothing compared to what you're getting," he said. "You've been a sulky, spoiled, snot-nosed, and impossible brat for weeks. Now, you're going to pay the price. I should've done this a long time ago."

"Fuck you!" I yelled.

He dragged me along the floor. When we got to the stairs, he picked me up by my hands. It hurt like hell. I yelled, I struggled, I kicked, I scratched, I punched, and I fought as hard as I could. In the end, he won. I wound up standing naked on the platform with my hands chained over my head. He stood in front of me with the whip. "You're going to scream now."

"No fucking way," I snarled.

"We'll see about that," he said.

"Fuck you!" I yelled again.

He went behind me. I clenched my teeth.

The whip cracked hard on my back.

I couldn't help it.

I did what he told me to do.

Chapter 32

January 11, 1983

The only sounds were the ones I made. The cold burned my nose when I breathed. Old snow and dead leaves crunched as I walked through the woods. No wind to rattle the branches, all the animals were in their burrows, and the rest of the world was asleep. Nothing between me and the frozen darkness. Technically it was morning, but the sky wouldn't turn winter gray for at least a couple more hours. I zipped up the last few teeth on my coat, wrapped the scarf tighter over my mouth, jammed my gloved hands deeper in my pockets, and tightened my hood until I could barely see. It didn't matter. The cold found ways to seep through four layers of clothing, wrapping icy fingers around my bare skin. I kept walking. No way I was heading back inside to light a fire or take a hot shower.

The woods were the only place I could go to be completely alone. The rock would be even better, but then I'd need Jeremy to take me. I didn't want anyone to know where I was. No crowds. No teachers. No other kids. No parents. No friends. No Jeremy. Just me.

I brushed some snow off a rock so I could sit down. The rock was freezing, so I pulled my coat underneath my butt. I turned off the flashlight and put it inside my coat to make sure I didn't lose it. The blackness was complete. If the light was on, someone could find me. I let the dark swallow me like it swallowed me in the prison.

The need to be alone was as strong as eating or breathing. I couldn't explain why. I couldn't explain to my friends why I skipped the marathon game during break. I couldn't explain to Jeremy why I moved

into the guest bedroom. I couldn't explain to myself why I was walking in the woods at four in the morning. I wished I could reassure them it was temporary. No need to worry because I'd go back to being myself soon. They wouldn't believe me because I didn't believe it either.

I wanted to spend my time alone thinking about important things: Jeremy, my friends, my parents, my future. Holding onto my thoughts was like trying to catch smoke in my hands. My head was filled with stuff that didn't matter at all. The words to Andy's latest favorite punk song. Wondering what would happen if the world filled up because people wouldn't stop having babies. My thoughts would twist and turn until I wondered how in the world I wound up thinking about such weird stuff in the first place.

Jeremy stopped asking me how I was feeling. I never answered because I didn't know how to tell him. I knew he was frightened by the way I was acting. I wanted to tell him not to be scared. I wanted to tell him underneath everything I still loved him and I'd never stop loving him. I couldn't tell him because every time I had the chance my anger pushed everything else out of my head.

The prison didn't work the way it was supposed to. Jeremy did everything the right way. He was harsh but never lost his temper. He punished me the way I thought I needed to be punished. He made sure it was real. He was the same as before, but I was completely different. I refused to be a good little prisoner. I wouldn't follow his orders, fought him when he moved me around, called him names, spit on him, tried to bite him, and even peed on him once. I dared him to punish me worse. I made myself laugh when I wasn't screaming. I felt worse when it was over instead of better. Stuff inside me felt stuck even tighter. The old Nick was closer than ever. Something had changed, something important. By the time I figured out another way to fix myself, it would be too late. The old Nick would return and be completely in control. I couldn't stop thinking about Chris, grounded for a month after we stayed out on the golf course. Last week he was suspended for two days from school because he threw a temper tantrum when a teacher told him to throw his trash away after lunch. *Fucked up by divorce.*

I stayed in the woods until the sky turned gray. If I didn't leave soon, I'd be late for school. Last night I hardly slept because of bad dreams I

couldn't remember. Jeremy let me sleep until I woke up on my own at noon. I knew he'd let me do the same thing today, but for some stupid reason I felt like I shouldn't skip two days in a row. The garage door was still wide open, the way I left it in case someone felt like stealing the car. I stomped in and slammed the door.

"Hey, kiddo," he said, peeking around the corner from the kitchen. "Out for a walk?" I grunted. "I made pancakes and hot coffee."

"I don't want pancakes. I want eggs."

"I could whip up a few if you'd like. Scrambled?"

"I'm not hungry." I dropped my coat on the floor. My stomach rumbled. I walked all the way down the hall to the kitchen and back to the entryway before I took off my wet, muddy boots. The mess didn't make me feel any better.

"I made you lunch from the leftover chicken and pasta, tomato soup, and a fruit salad. Do you want anything else?"

"I'm going to buy my lunch," I grumbled. The lunch he made sounded good.

"No problem, I'll have it myself instead," he said.

"I'm taking a shower," I announced. I undressed on the way up, my clothes littering the stairs. I purposefully left the shower door open as the water warmed up so it would puddle on the bathroom floor. When I was done with the shower, I hung the wet towel on the television. By the time I got back downstairs, my clothes were picked up, towels were laid out over the muddy mess in the hall, and my coat was banging around in the dryer.

"Where'd you put my homework?" I shouted from the dining room.

"In your backpack," he answered.

"If I wanted you to do that, I would've told you!"

"Just making sure you don't forget anything," he said.

"The only way I'll forget something is because you messed it up. Leave my stuff alone from now on!"

"Okey dokey," he said cheerfully.

"Take down the stupid Christmas tree already!" The presents were still wrapped. I wouldn't open them. I didn't want Christmas this year. He wouldn't take it down until I opened the presents.

"I know you're not hungry, but I made you a thermos of coffee to take to school anyway." I dumped the coffee in the sink and slammed the empty thermos on the counter.

"Aren't you going to ask where I was?" I asked.

"I figured you were out for a morning walk," he said.

"I was out all night," I said. "I'm going to do it again tonight."

"Make sure you take some extra blankets. They said it's going to be even colder than last night." He smiled. "We'd better get going or you'll be late. Do you need anything else?"

"Not from you," I muttered. "I want to take the van today."

"Van it is," he said. "Your coat. . ."

"Is in the dryer. I'm not an idiot." I went to get it. He kept smiling that same stupid smile. It made me even more furious. I sat in the back of the van without talking to him on way to school.

"Have a nice day, kiddo," he said.

"Fuck you," I spat after I slammed the car door.

He drove away. I didn't know what was wrong with me. He was trying so hard to be nice, but the nicer he was the angrier I got. I wanted him to yell at me. I wanted him to make me behave. I wanted to get into a full-blown, knock down fight with him. He thought all that fucking cheerfulness was supposed to calm me down. Instead, it made things worse. He was as unsatisfying as punching a pillow. I wanted the thing I hit to react.

I walked into the school feeling like I was going to go thermonuclear.

"Mr. Welles," Mr. Humber boomed. "Would you be so kind as to refresh our memories on the esoteric details regarding the correct way to use the words lay, lie, and laid?"

I looked up from my desk. I didn't remember putting my head down. Not a good idea in Mr. Humber's class. He lived to pounce on kids who weren't paying attention. I stared at him, trying to put the answer together. Even though I knew that I knew it, the words teased me from just out of reach. He looked at me curiously while a couple of

girls sniggered, then turned to one of them. "Ms. Russo, perhaps you'd care to offer some words of enlightenment on the same subject?"

Whatever she said bounced off like I had trampolines blocking my eardrums. He never let go that easily when he caught someone. I couldn't remember what I was thinking about before Mr. Humber fired his question at me. Maybe I wasn't thinking about anything at all. Did I fall asleep? I didn't feel sleepy. I slumped back in my chair and tried to pay attention. My mind wouldn't stop wandering

The bell rang for lunch. "Mr. Welles, a moment of your time," Mr. Humber said before I could escape. I tried to look as goody two shoes gumdrops as I could, but my heart wasn't into pretending. He waited until everyone else left.

"You don't seem yourself today, Mr. Welles," he said.

I shrugged. "Whatever."

He pointed to the chair in front of his desk. I didn't move. "Would you mind doing me the courtesy of a few minutes of your time?"

"Fine," I said. I dropped my books on his desk, slouching down in the chair as low as I could without falling off. He brought his chair around the side and sat backwards in a very un-teacherlike way. "You were absent yesterday, and while you're physically in class today, I have the distinct feeling your mind is still absent. It's not like you to be daydreaming. You're always right with me every day without exception. Is everything ok?"

"I'm fine," I said.

He leaned forward a little. "If something's troubling you. . ."

"Nothing's troubling me," I snapped.

"If something is troubling you, there are people who can help. Perhaps a guidance counselor, the school nurse, or possibly one of your teachers."

"I know," I said. "Nothing's wrong and I don't need any help from anyone. Especially you. It's none of your business anyway."

He cleared his throat. "Mr. Welles, I'm willing to forgive your lack of attention in class today and I'm also willing to tolerate your disrespectful tone. Let this serve as your official notice that I will not tolerate either starting tomorrow. If you continue this behavior it will

reflect negatively on your grades and there will be disciplinary consequences."

I stood up and snapped to attention. "Yes, sir!" I said with a sarcastic salute.

He looked at me for a moment. "I'm writing you a referral to the guidance office," he said in a gentle voice. He scribbled on a piece of paper. I rolled my eyes. "I'm not requiring you to go, but I'm strongly suggesting you do. I'm sure Mr. May will find some time for a discussion." He held out the piece of paper. I refused to take it. "I take a great deal of pride in knowing my students. Something is clearly troubling you deeply. Whatever it is, you don't have to bear it alone."

"Can I go to lunch now?" I said, yanking the paper from his hand.

He nodded. I picked up my books and stomped out of the room. As soon as I was out of sight, I crumpled up the paper. I was about to throw it across the hallway when I stopped myself and leaned against the lockers. Carefully, I unwrapped the paper and smoothed it out. I looked back at the open doorway, but turned and went the other way.

"Shit," I yelled. "I forgot my notebook."

"So?" Chris asked.

"My math homework is in it," I grumbled. "I have to get it."

"Who cares?" Chris spat on the sidewalk. "What's the fucking difference if you don't do it?"

"Wait up for me," I grumbled as I turned around.

"I'm not waiting for you," he yelled. "Meet us at my house."

"Whatever," I said under my breath, walking as fast as I possibly could without running. I didn't know why I agreed to play. I didn't want to be around my friends right now. Chris nagged me until it was easier to say yes. I wanted to go home, lock myself in the guest bedroom until it was dark, and disappear all night in the woods no matter how cold it was.

"Hey, Nick," Brian yelled. "Wait up!"

Not fucking now. I didn't have the patience for him. I shook my head, but I waited up anyway. He ran up to me, wheezing a little. He made me wait while he used his inhaler. "What?" I asked impatiently.

"What're you doing today?" he asked.

"Going to play D&D," I muttered. "The same thing I do every day after school. What's it to you?"

"I was wondering if you wanted to play," he said.

"Play?" I spat. "Little kids *play.*"

"Hang out," he said in a small voice.

"Do you want to play D&D or not?" I asked. He didn't answer. "That's what I thought. I have to go."

"Wait," he said as I pushed past him. "Are you mad at me?"

"Why would I be mad at you?" I said without turning around, walking around the side of the building. He didn't follow me. I stomped all the way to the back, turning the corner, freezing when I saw what was happening.

"I need my money," Walker said. His hands were on a small kid's shoulders, shaking and pushing him up against the wall. I knew the small kid's name was Simon only because I heard Walker picking on him in the cafeteria every now and then. He liked robbing kids of their lunch money. "If I don't get my money, I get pissed off. You *know* what happens when I get pissed off." Tommy twisted Simon's arm behind his back until he cried out, and then shoved Simon's face against the bricks.

"I told you I don't have any," he whimpered. "Please let me go."

All I had to do was back up quietly and disappear. Walker hadn't noticed me yet. But I didn't. My ears burned, my stomach twisted into knots, and my face got hot. My hands balled into fists. I wasn't thinking anything when I let my backpack slip off my shoulder and walked toward them. Walker was too busy pushing the other kid around to see me. "What's the matter, simple Simon? Too complicated for you? You bring the money, I take the money. It's easy to understand, even for you."

"Leave him alone!" I shouted, pushing Walker's shoulder. He stumbled, off balance, but didn't fall.

453

"Nick the prick," he said, grinning. He pushed Simon to the ground. "Stay right there, I'm not done with you."

"I said to leave him alone!" I pushed Walker's shoulder as hard as I could, but he didn't move an inch. He shoved me back so hard I fell on my butt, stunned. He kicked me in the shin. I hissed at the sharp pain.

"When I'm done with you, they'll need a spatula to scrape you off the ground," he growled. "They needed an ambulance for me, but they won't for you because you'll be leaving in a hearse."

I scrambled backwards, trying to get my feet under me. What the fuck was I thinking? The three of us were alone, no other kids or teachers in sight. Tommy had at least twenty pounds of muscle on me. He supposedly carried a switchblade and brass knuckles in his back pocket. I heard a rumor he strangled cats with his bare hands. It wasn't a secret that he wanted me dead. The only explanation is that I was completely crazy. He left Brian to die that day in the woods. He was going to do the same to me if I didn't get the hell out of there.

"Aww, big bwother's not awound to change wittle Nicky-wicky's diaper." I tried to tell my legs to move, but they wouldn't listen. "Too bad. I'm sure he'd like to get his dick sucked by you and your faggot friends one last time."

Images flashed through my head. Walking naked with Brian. Chris on the golf course. Jeremy's face scrunched up when he fucked me. My brain shut down completely. The only thing left was fury. I got up. "What did you call me?"

"I called you a *faggot*," he said with a grin.

I charged him, yelling. I didn't think about what could happen because the only thing that mattered was shutting him up. He was ready for me. Before I could swing, he punched me in the stomach. I gasped, hunched over, the breath knocked out of me. I thought I was going to suffocate to death. While I was trying to catch my breath, his fist slammed into my face. My right cheek felt like it was shattered. I realized I was on the ground again.

"Fucking faggot," he said, hawking a glob of snot at my forehead. I tasted blood. "Get up," he hissed. "Get up so I can kick your fucking gaywad ass so hard you'll never get up again." My face felt like it was swelling up, forcing my eye closed. My leg stabbed when I tried to put

weight on it. There was no way I was going to be able to run fast enough to get away from him. I cringed and pulled into a small ball when he threatened to kick me again. He laughed. I realized this is what panic felt like. This is what it felt like to know you're going to die. Everything hurt so much. . .

Wait a minute.

I was an expert on pain. I survived real torture. My face and my leg hurt, but the pain was nothing compared to what I'd been through before. I realized I was scared only because this was a different type of situation. I didn't need to be frightened by a little pain. The world pulled into focus. Just like that, I became alert. I was in control and I knew exactly what I had to do.

I stumbled to my feet, ignoring the inconvenience of my face and leg, pretending it was a lot worse than it was. "About fucking time," he said. I put up my fists, but it was just for show. I didn't know how to fight like he did. His punch to my shoulder came so fast there was nothing I could do. I ignored the pain, standing my ground. I looked at my shoulder, then looked him right in the eyes.

"You punch like a girl," I taunted.

I heard a loud gasp behind me. We had an audience. Twelve kids, maybe more, standing in a half circle precisely the right distance behind us, like they measured it with a ruler. They made me feel even stronger.

"Fucking flaming faggot," he snarled. He tried to hit me in the face again, but I managed to dodge to the side so it glanced off my cheek. His guard was still up, so I couldn't find a way to do what I wanted to do to him. I had to be patient. The right time would come.

"Is that the best you can do?" I teased again. "I was wrong. You punch like an old woman. You think you're tough but you're nothing but a big fat wimp who still wets the bed." I heard a few chuckles. "Tommy wets the bed, Tommy wets the bed," I chanted. Walker yelled and twisted around, his punch coming from the side. I knew I could turn away to dodge it. Instead, I turned right into his punch. His fist connected with my nose. I ignored the sharp pain. It put me in the right place to do what I wanted to do, and put him in the right place for me to do it.

I grinned and kicked him in the balls as hard as I could.

In slow motion, the look on his face changed from surprise to absolute agony. The only thing that came out of his mouth was a weird squeak. He bent over and rolled onto the ground, holding his crotch. I jumped on top of him, forcing him onto his back, sitting on his stomach. He flailed his arms and tried to kick me off, but I didn't let him. I punched him as hard as I could square in his nose. I heard a crunch. Blood flooded onto his face. I punched his eyes, his neck, his cheeks, and his mouth. His tooth cut my hand. I ignored it.

"You are *never* going to pick on me again!" I growled as my fists pounded his face. I grabbed his hair and slammed his head into the concrete. "You are never going to pick on *anyone* ever again!" He tried to block my punches but I pushed his hands out of my way. He made the same squeak sound when I smashed his nose a second time. "If I ever. . ." I hit him again. "Ever. . ." And again. "Ever. . ." And again. "*Ever* catch you picking on anyone again. . ." I wrapped my hands around his neck, choking him, lifting and banging his head on the ground. "I'll kill you. Do you understand me? I'll fucking kill you!"

"Teacher!" someone yelled. I looked up. My audience scattered. I was distracted long enough for Tommy to push me off. He staggered to his feet and ran off in a crooked line. I licked blood from my face, more running from my nose into my mouth.

"What exactly is going on here?" I looked up at the familiar booming voice and the familiar face, his expression as stern as I'd ever seen. Brian was standing beside him, his eyes looking like they were on fire. Mr. Humber sat down next to me, taking a handkerchief from his back pocket. "Hold this beneath your nose and tilt your head back." I nodded and did what he said.

"It's not Nick's fault," Brian said in a powerful voice, like the one he used for Gandalf at the bridge of Khazad-dûm. "He didn't start the fight."

"It's true," Simon added. "Tommy ganged up on him."

"I have absolutely no idea what either of you boys mean," Mr. Humber said. "A fight requires two participants. I see no evidence anyone else was involved. Mr. Welles is injured and in need of medical attention. Therefore, I intend to escort him to the nurse's office. I see

no reason why anyone should be in trouble. Is there something else either of you would care to add?"

I stared at Mr. Humber, confused.

"No," Brian said with a little smile. "Nothing you should know about."

"Are you able to walk?" Mr. Humber asked. I nodded. He helped me stand up. Whatever gave me all that strength was gone. I felt exhausted. I realized the puddle of blood on the sidewalk was mine. It made me dizzy to think about it. "Steady," he said, holding my arm. He held on to me as I shuffled into the school. I knew Brian and Simon were following us, talking too softly to hear. We went through the office to the nurse's room. "You boys wait here while I tend to Mr. Welles."

I sat down in the chair. "Head back, please," he reminded me and replaced the handkerchief with a wad of damp paper towels. He was quiet while he gathered supplies. I flinched as he placed an ice pack against my eye, but I held it in place. He put a pile of bandages and gauze on the counter next to me.

"Let's take a look," he said, removing the paper towels from my nose. "I believe it's stopped."

"Am I going to die?" I blurted out.

"Everybody does, eventually," he said. "I feel confident your final day is not today. Hold that ice pack in place until your face becomes numb, then take it off for a short time."

"But all that blood," I said.

"Not as much as you might think," he said. He dabbed some gauze with rubbing alcohol where my finger was cut by Tommy's tooth. It stung, but I didn't show it. He moved the ice pack higher on my face. "I believe you will have quite the shiner."

"Shiner?"

"Black eye," he said. "Nothing serious, merely uncomfortable. They last a couple weeks and heal without complications. Are you injured anywhere else?" I shook my head. "Despite my cursory medical training, I believe I can diagnose your injuries as minor. Other than a few more bandages and a few days of rest, you require nothing else to

make a full recovery." He took another cotton ball and dabbed my face. Feelings rushed into me.

"Why aren't you going to write a referral?" I asked.

"Whatever for?" He sounded surprised.

"For fighting," I said. "You know I got into a fight."

"Perhaps you did, and perhaps you didn't," he said mysteriously. "As I explained to Mr. Hanley, there was no other participant when I arrived. Therefore, there is no evidence of any altercation, and therefore no need for an office referral. I trust this matter is clear." I wanted to argue. I wanted that referral. It would prove it happened. Like welts from a whipping.

"But I. . ."

"Mr. Welles," he interrupted. "Nothing would be served by involving the disciplinary authorities. If this alleged fight transpired, I feel as though I know you well enough by now to trust you had good reasons and no other choice but to engage in violence. While I'd never encourage such behavior, I fully understand in some situations the only option is to defend yourself." He leaned in close. "Besides, it's about time someone clobbered that bully."

I blinked.

"If you repeat that, I assure you the consequences will be severe."

I smiled. "Ok," I said.

"I'm glad we understand each other."

He turned around. "My parents are getting a divorce," I blurted out.

He turned back towards me. The gentle expression on his face was so different than his usual stern look. "I'm very sorry to hear that," he said softly. He wasn't just saying it, either. He meant it. "Does this impact your living arrangements in any way?"

I shook my head. "I'm still going to live with my uncle. My mom is moving to Denver with her new boyfriend and my dad lives in his office. Really, I don't care much if they get divorced."

"I disagree," he said. "It's clearly bothering you. Divorces are extremely disruptive. Many children of divorce can't help feeling as though the situation is somehow their fault despite all evidence to the contrary. They feel as though they've lost control of their lives, that big decisions are being made about them without taking their feelings into

account. Many children worry they'll become failures because their parents failed. Many children feel abandoned by their parents, especially when difficult custody arrangements need to be made."

It was like he was seeing right inside me, telling me things I didn't even realize until he said them. "How did you know?"

"These are common experiences for children experiencing divorce," he said. "Perhaps you can take some comfort that others in similar circumstances feel the same way as you, and nearly all learn to overcome it." He put his hand on my shoulder. "I repeat my offer from earlier today. If you ever feel you need someone to talk to, you can find me before, during, and after school. For now, I think it's best we get you on your way. I'd feel better releasing you to an adult. Can we call your uncle to pick you up?" I nodded. He motioned for me to follow him.

"Mr. Humber?" He turned. "Thanks."

"There's no need to thank me, Nick. This is what I do."

We were in the office waiting for Jeremy when I realized he didn't call me Mr. Welles.

I sat on the couch in the lobby with my legs curled up, propped up on all sides by pillows. The ice pack was thawing on a towel on the table. I stopped using it a while ago. Too many logs were used to build the fire, the room filled with dry heat and the smell of smoke. The windows rattled from the wind. The temperature was falling fast, on its way to negative numbers. Jeremy put another pitcher of cocoa on the table. It was gone in less than ten seconds. Simon filled my mug without asking, pressing it back into my hand. He hadn't left me alone since I saved him from Tommy. I hoped he wasn't going to act like my personal assistant at school. It would be embarrassing if he tried to carry my books around for me.

"I came around the corner," I said in an eerie voice. "There it was, an ogre at least ten feet high."

"More like fifteen feet," Parker said.

"Twenty," Chris joined in.

"Alright, fifty feet high," I said, stretching my arms out wide. "The stench was beyond imagination, so powerful it could drop an elephant a mile away. The stench of an ogre who never bothered to use a bathroom." The way they laughed made me smile. "Even though it was gigantic, it had a brain the size of a pea. I said to it: 'Unhand that peasant, you fiendish brute!'"

"Peasant?" Simon said.

"Sorry. 'Unhand that prince, you fiendish brute!'" Simon nodded his approval. "It stood there looking as stupid as possible while it figured out what to do. The ogre took so long I had to remind it I was there with a push."

"That's when it told the prince to stay there because it wasn't finished with him," Simon said.

"Right. The ogre breathed foul green gas onto me. When it opened its mouth I saw vampire bats hanging from its teeth. The gas was so powerful it knocked me on the ground, and before I could get up the ogre kicked me so hard I flew a hundred feet into the air. I charged at it with my trusty sword, but it swung this big spiked club with poison tips around and hit me in the stomach."

"If it had poison tips, why aren't you dead?" Chris asked.

"The poison barely missed me. I fought back, but it's hide was so tough my sword bounced off. I thought about running away, but I knew the prince and his kingdom were depending on me. So I let the club hit me in the face and then thrust my sword right up into its balls." Everyone cheered. "The ogre crashed to the ground and I hacked at it with my sword. I told it to never be seen in these parts again. It ran off and there was a huge celebration in my honor and the kingdom rained down gold and jewels on me."

"I would've killed the ogre," Chris said.

"You weren't there," I answered. "I was."

"Yeah, whatever," he said, getting up. "Let's play some more pool."

I watched him go. "Do you need anything?" Simon asked. I shook my head.

Andy went back to the stereo. He found a bunch of Jeremy's records from the band who sang the "we don't need no education" song a few years ago. I'd never listened to them before, but I wanted to hear more.

Parker, Daniel, and Jonathan were playing pool with Chris. Brian poked the fire, making it burn hotter and faster.

This morning felt like it was a million years ago. The need to be alone was gone. I wanted to be surrounded by as many friends as I could find. Daniel and Jonathan made Chris wait up for me after school. I didn't notice them watching Mr. Humber take me to the nurse's office. Simon told them the whole story. Everyone came home with me, and Jeremy made up a story about us studying for a big test so they could stay later. He was so convincing even Brian's dad bought it. He bought us pizzas and made hot chocolate until we ran out of milk.

I thought Chris would be angry because everyone would want to play at my house once they saw the pool table, the pinball machine, and the big screen TV. Chris was only angry I didn't tell him I had all those things. I was worried Jeremy would try to join in, but he left us alone. He made cocoa and joked around a little, but mostly he stayed in the kitchen or in his office. He smiled at me a few times. I smiled back at him.

We took everyone home at eight. I sat in the back, talking with everyone as we dropped them off one by one. The van felt empty when we dropped Simon off last. He triple-checked to make sure I had his phone number.

"I think you made a friend," Jeremy said as I moved to the front seat.

"More like someone's annoying little brother," I said.

"It's his way of saying thanks."

"I know," I said.

"How about some coffee and cheesecake from the diner?"

I shook my head. "I want to go home." He nodded. I picked up his hand and put it on my knee. He squeezed. I think he already understood I was moving back into the bedroom with him. I wanted him to hold me, touch me, and make love to me the way we did before everything got complicated. I didn't want to fight with him anymore. I didn't want to fight with anyone anymore. All that was left from the anger inside me was a bloodstain on the sidewalk behind the school.

"I'm so proud of you," Jeremy said.

So was I.

461

James Edison

Part 5

James Edison

Chapter 33

March 17, 2007

I stood in the middle of choreographed chaos.

To the casual observer, the narrow backstage halls were choked with kids randomly careening like pinballs. But there was purpose to every step, every glance, and every word. A perfect machine that could be appreciated but never fully understood. A symphony so discordant it became supremely tonal. I had an abundance of borrowed energy from these kids, forcing me to move, to act, to *do*. I wasn't exactly a part of the machine, but all machines need grease to keep them running.

"Nick!"

I turned towards the voice. Hannah charged me with the intensity of a half-ton bull intent on goring the matador. I was confident she could bowl me over even though she weighed ninety pounds soaking wet. "Oh my fucking god, you are not going to believe this." She grabbed my hand, peeled my fingers apart, and shoved a small cardboard box into my palm. "Empty!"

"Out of matches again?" I asked. I shook the box. She groaned with supreme annoyance at my obvious stupidity. "I'm sure someone has another book of matches. Half you guys smoke."

Hannah groaned again. "Do you seriously think I didn't ask?" I could never tell if she was an over-dramatic personality or hamming it up. "I can get a dozen brands of cigarettes and a hundred lighters, but no one has a single stinking match." She threw her hands up and yelled at the ceiling.

"Use one of the lighters," I said, to tease a little.

"You know the song, the one that talks about the last match?" She pinched my cheeks and forced me to nod. "What are we supposed to do, sing about the lighter running out of fluid? We need matches. Little sticks tipped with sulphur. Mat-ches. Go. Find."

I hunched up one shoulder. "Yes, master. I find matches."

"Good boy," she said. I watched her disappear into the crowds of actors, production managers, and musicians. I remembered how the moments before a school performance tingled with nervous excitement and wondered if the hallways backstage at a Broadway performance were as thick with static electricity. It would be a shame if those dressing rooms weren't as brilliantly alive as these. I had to think they were, because the Pinehurst theater department could hold their own against any professional company.

Matches were easy – I had a dozen books leftover from the last time this happened. Nothing like opening night's wardrobe malfunction, a pair of tight pants ripped open at the seat. I had raced to a dry cleaner at breakneck speed, intercepted the owner at the back door as he closed the shop, pushed a large wad of bills into his hands to encourage him to spend five minutes on a sewing machine, and raced back to the theater only moments before curtain. I got a standing ovation from the whole cast that night. They even presented me with a medal made from cardboard, aluminum foil, and a safety pin. Courage beyond the call of duty.

I didn't see him coming, the impact slamming me into the wall. I shook the dizziness from my head, staring into the embarrassed face of a young teenage boy. "Sorry," he mumbled.

"My bad, Rhys," I said. "I missed the whirling dancer crossing sign back there. When they say break a leg you're not supposed to take them literally."

"Funny," he said. The kids all rolled their eyes when I cracked lame dad jokes, but I had the feeling they liked them anyway. He smiled a little, penetratingly cute. My heart skipped a beat. "See you later," he mumbled.

I wanted to watch him whirl off into the crowd, but I had a mission. I snaked my way to the back door, acknowledging each "Hey, Nick,"

each nod of recognition, and each smile. A cast is a close family, and even if I wasn't on stage, building scenery, or working tech, I was a part of it. Every theater needed a gopher and I was happy to be theirs. Here, I wasn't Mr. Welles. I was Nick. I *belonged.*

Two imposing gentlemen with earpieces stopped me at the stage door. Clearly not normal rent-a-cops. I had to fish the radio tags out of my pockets, waiting patiently as one of them spelled my name into a hidden speaker while the other one never broke eye contact. Security was tighter than usual tonight due to the presence of several members of Congress. The Pinehurst theater had a reputation that could fill seats outside the school community, but the demand for our show was off the charts. The word got out thanks to a gushing review in the Sunday arts section of the Washington Post, calling our production "more professional than professional." Tickets were scarce. Enterprising students hawked their spares for a couple hundred bucks. I grabbed the matches from the car and went back through the security ringer, this time featuring a metal detector that didn't like my belt buckle.

I didn't have much time. Devin would be on stage from the moment the show began and he needed the matches. Still, when I saw Hunter leaning against the wall with his hands shoved in his pockets, I knew it couldn't wait. I put my hand on his shoulder. He didn't look up. "Have you heard from your parents?" I asked in a soft voice.

He shook his head. "They're not coming."

"Not even your mom?"

"She won't come without him," he said.

"Maybe she'll surprise you." He shrugged in a non-committal teenage way, his hands digging a few inches deeper into his pockets. "Give them some time, they'll come around eventually. Staying with us again tonight?"

"I feel like I'm in the way. Maybe I'll stay with Oliver, even though his parents are getting weird about it."

"Whatever you'd like to do is fine with me," I said. "You've got a place to stay no matter how long it takes to get this worked out. We won't get weird about it. You'd better get ready, it's almost curtain. See you at the party tonight?"

"Yeah," he said. He shuffled off, looking much older than sixteen. It was beyond my comprehension how parents could behave so poorly when their children came out as gay. The world barreled toward tolerance, but I suppose there'd always be some who chose their prejudices over their own kids. I worried parents like his might interpret my allowing him to stay with us as interfering in their private affairs, possibly engaging a legal system all too eager to destroy other people's lives. I refused to be intimidated. He needed someone to look after him, and I'd be there to support him no matter how long it took. I couldn't take a chance someone would take advantage of him. He was especially vulnerable now, easy to manipulate with a little warmth and sympathy. I knew all too well what that kind of vulnerability felt like.

I found Devin in his dressing room and pressed two books of matches into his hands. He was already in character, surly and angry at the world, picking at his guitar. He grunted his acknowledgment. He wasn't the best singer of the group, but as an actor he stood out from the others. No doubt in my mind I'd see him in movies someday. My next stop was two doors down from his.

"Hey, kiddo," I said.

Alex turned around and smiled. "Did you hear the rumor? There's supposed to be someone important hiding in the audience tonight, like a casting agent." I fought the urge to grin. His eyes narrowed and sparkled. "You know something, don't you? Tell me."

"I can neither confirm nor deny anything," I said.

"I knew it," he said triumphantly. "Just watch. I'm going to bring down the house tonight. Maybe I'll land a part in something big on Broadway, my name in lights. As long as I can get through my songs without my voice cracking." He sang a high clear note, holding it for a few seconds to make sure there were no squeaks.

"Your performance brings the house down every night."

"Thanks," he said. I toyed with the idea of giving him a hug. I didn't want to embarrass him, but he was Alex. The very idea of embarrassing him was an oxymoron. He hugged me first.

No one would admit exactly how the school secured the rights to perform Rent. The film version had just been released and a new national tour announced. Someone knew someone who knew

someone. A benefit of an obscenely expensive private school education. The administration not only allowed but encouraged the department to perform the complete, unedited show. A benefit of a more liberal private school education.

Alex knew from the beginning which role he wanted to play. "Mark isn't my character type. I'd make a better Roger, but I'm going out for Angel instead of the lead."

"Why not?" I asked. "You've got the talent."

"That's not how it works. Haven't paid my dues yet. Gotta be strategic."

He kept his audition number a complete secret. Something about bad luck. When I sat in the audience to watch at the open audition, I saw his act for the first time like everyone else. He came on stage wearing a full boy scout uniform, carrying a cardboard box of snack foods. He nodded to the pianist, tossing snacks into the audience as he started singing something unfamiliar about being eliminated from a competition.

> *You wanna know how? You wanna know why?*
> *My unfortunate erection. . .*

I had no idea what came after that because the entire crowd burst into raucous laughter. He kept belting out the song, not losing his outraged demeanor for a second.

> *I don't blame my brain, but I do blame my penis,*
> *My unfortunate protuberance*
> *Seems to have its own exuberance. . .*

After knowing him for several months, I didn't think he could still amaze me. Standing on that stage singing "erection" at the top of his lungs helped realize how wrong I was. I couldn't imagine singing about an erection at thirteen. I would've died of humiliation. I pounded my hands and whistled as best as I could as he took a deep bow and ran off stage at the end. He pretended to act surprised when he got the part. I knew better.

I let his hug linger a moment longer than necessary. "Alright kiddo, they've called ten minutes. I've got to find my seat or I'll be stuck back here watching the show. Knock 'em dead."

"Deader than Daisy Eagan's career," he quipped. As usual, his knowledge of theater bulldozed mine. "Won the Tony for the Secret Garden when she was twelve. It was all downhill for her from there. Lots of kids made it big too young. That's why I don't audition for something professional. I might get it and end my career prematurely."

"Others have built successful careers as adults," I told him.

"Not worth the chance," he said. "Patience, grasshopper."

I made my way to the front of the house. Pinehurst had a theater worthy of its reputation as one of the top private schools for the arts in the country. Built three years ago, it was huge for a school, capable of seating over a thousand people comfortably. I made my way up the aisle so I could see Jake in the tech booth behind the front orchestra section. The heavy headphones he was wearing looked like an anachronism from the seventies. He sunk his teeth into his tech class, managing to get a prime job working what had to be the most complex computer-controlled lighting and sound system known to man. It had at least a thousand knobs, sliders, switches, dials, buttons, and assorted gizmos packed around a dozen color LCD monitors. I compared it to the mixer board we'd used during my junior high productions – it had an on/off switch and four sliders (the third had a short so you had to jiggle it). I smiled and waved into the booth. He allowed me a quick nod back before getting back to whatever he was doing.

I put my suit jacket over the seat next to me, center fifth row. When I bought tickets, it didn't occur to me Julia wouldn't want to see every single show. She came on the two previous Saturday nights but otherwise the seat stayed vacant. I could've sold it even though it was a single, but I kept it in case she changed her mind. The reason I bothered was a mystery to me. We sat next to each other those two nights, but if anyone looked they would've assumed we were complete strangers. We only shared the typical pleasantries of casual acquaintances and we both scrupulously avoided the armrest in the middle. It was only a matter of time before the papers arrived. I told myself we were going in different directions and wanted different things. No hatred, no bitter words, and

no protracted fights. We simply drifted away from each other. A part of me wanted to fix things between us. I still loved her, in my own way. I didn't want her to leave. But to repair years of neglect, I'd have to invest time to keep her. My time was fully invested elsewhere. With my new theater tribe. With my gay teenage tribe. With my boys.

With my Alex.

My life was drastically improved thanks to him. "I need to pump some iron," he said one day out of the blue. "I'm a pathetic dancer and some muscle would help. The school has a nice gym, but since I'm staying with you guys most of the time it would be easier to get a membership at the gym near your house. Besides, they'll have more hot gym rats in the locker room." He made puppy dog eyes. "They won't let someone under eighteen sign up by themselves, some kind of stupid insurance thing. I was thinking you could get a membership and add me to it. Please?"

As though I could say no to him. I thought my job was done when I purchased the ultra-deluxe membership, but an early morning phone call corrected that misconception. As it turned out, kids under eighteen weren't even allowed to use the equipment without a responsible adult present. I threw on some clothes with the intention of finding a comfortable chair. It didn't take me long to realize he had no idea what he was doing. The machines worked him more than he was working them. He struggled with the weight, butt lifting off the seat, back contorting in all kinds of directions. He'd hurt himself if I didn't do something.

"You're lifting too much," I told him. I adjusted the weight down. "Keep your back straight, your chest puffed out, and your stomach tight. Pull it down slowly and don't let go at the bottom. Keep the weight under control. Breathe out on the way down, in on the way up." I helped him straighten his shoulders during his first rep.

"It's too light. I hardly feel anything."

"Do it the way I showed you fifteen times and then tell me it's too light." He figured out what I meant around rep twelve.

"How do you know so much about lifting?" he asked.

I didn't answer his question, just as surprised I remembered so much. I'd only lifted weights for a short time many years ago. Sitting next to

471

Alex dredged up memories of Coach Z, sitting next to me while I made the exact same mistakes, correcting me in the same way.

I followed Alex around for the rest of his workout, adjusting his form and giving him pointers. "You should finish up with something to get your heart pumping," I said, pointing to one of the elliptical contraptions. He got on and worked the controls.

"How about you, are you getting on?" he said as he started pedaling.

"Me? No way."

"Come on, it's easy," he said. "Try it." He made puppy dog eyes at me again. I groaned and somehow lumbered onto the machine, less than eager to endure the misery of exercise. I gave it one minute. He smiled at me when I stopped.

"You're doing great," he said.

I had no choice but to start again. Every time I stopped, he used that smile to start me back up. I wound up staying on for fifteen minutes, barely able to pedal fast enough to keep the machine powered up, a river of sweat soaking my shirt. A heart attack seemed inevitable and imminent.

"You did well," he said. I collapsed in a chair, no breath available to answer. "I'm going to the locker room, maybe catch some muscle jocks coming out of the shower for a few minutes. Are you going to be ok?" I nodded and waved him off. "I hope you keep coming here with me. Sometimes, I worry about your health. The exercise would help a lot." I stared at him as he headed to the locker room, unable to shake the feeling that he planned this from the moment he asked for the membership.

His display of tenderness coupled with incessant nagging encouraged me to dutifully report to the gym every day with him. The first week was miserable, but I was amazed how quickly it got easier. Four months later and fifty pounds lighter, I could get through an hour-long workout at a pace I would've thought impossible. I no longer woke up in the middle of the night with a pounding headache and a sweat-soaked pillow. The doctor took me off my blood pressure medication because he worried it was too low instead of too high. Alex didn't stop at exercise. He planned meals with more protein and less carbs. He made the junk food in the pantry mysteriously vanish. Every time we went

out to eat, he flashed me a withering look if I attempted to order something I shouldn't. I felt better than I had in a long time. I had energy again, even if it wasn't enough to keep up with him.

For the first time in a long time, I felt energized and eager to actively participate in life. My combination Christmas present and congratulations to Alex for winning the role in Rent was a perfect example. I was stunned when I found out that he'd never seen an actual Broadway show. Over break, I put my boys on a train to New York. We did the city in style – a room at the Plaza, dinner in trendy restaurants, and overpriced premium orchestra seats for all the hot shows. Every night over coffee and cheesecake I was enraptured with the way he talked a mile a minute.

"Did you hear about Billy Elliot?" he asked one night. "Elton John wrote a musical based on the movie about the boy who lives in a coal mining town and wants to dance ballet. It's playing in London."

That offhanded comment was all it took to put the wheels in motion. Two days and three emergency passports later, I dragged two very pleasantly shocked boys to the airport and put us on a plane across the ocean. Alex loved the show, especially the cross-dressing friend. We were sitting in the middle of a crowded pub after the show when Alex learned Equus would be opening soon with Daniel Radcliffe. "Harry Potter naked?' he shouted. "Oh my fucking god I'm going to shoot in my shorts. I would give my left nut to see that!" The next table over burst out laughing and bought him a beer.

The lights in the theater came down and the actors took their places for tonight's performance. I sat on the edge of my seat, as eager to watch as the first night I saw my tribe perform. Brandon showed us around the apartment on stage. I cheered with the audience as the lights went out. I wanted to hold on to each moment of their performance, but I always found myself impatient to get to Alex's big scene. I mouthed the lines like I was trying to speed them up. My heart skipped a beat when his intro music swelled. Alex made his grand entrance, dressed in tight colorful leggings, a very feminine Santa jacket, wig, and full makeup. He never failed to stop the show. For hours, he worked to perfect his flamboyant strut and stereotypically gay intonation. The audience cheered him on as he danced energetically around the stage. His one

and only solo ended too soon, the audience erupting as he held his pose, smiling. I knew he was looking at nothing because the lights were in his eyes, but I preferred to think he was looking directly at me.

I was so in love with him it hurt.

Alex was still revved up four hours after the show ended. He couldn't stop bouncing in his seat. "I'm stellar," he said to himself in a way that was meant to be overheard. The same nameless benefactors who secured the rights to perform the show also persuaded two of the original stars to come up on stage after the performance. The mystery guests remained a secret, so it was a complete surprise to the cast. One of them singled out Alex, telling the whole audience how his performance was stellar. Alex jumped up and down and hugged the guy.

The party was scheduled for tomorrow after the final performance, but most of the cast and crew showed up at my place for an informal get together. Many of them were regular visitors, so it wasn't different from any other night. My house had become an extension of the campus. I was stupid to think I needed to compete for their attention with a television, food, or video games. Normal parents don't want gangs of teenagers trashing their house and blasting music at two in the morning. The battle was over when I made it clear I welcomed their presence instead of merely tolerating them. I became part of the tribe instead of the village elder, invited and included. Even Jake got over having his father around. At least he stopped dropping hints I should get lost.

We sat in a circle made of couch cushions and folding chairs. I was happy to see Hunter and Oliver decided to stay, talking softly in the corner. It made me wonder what upset Hunter's parents more – the fact that he had a boyfriend, or the fact that he had a black boyfriend. Either way, they made a cute couple. Jake was passed out, snoozing in a ball by the roaring fireplace (as if a gas fireplace could roar). I was exhausted, but if Alex was awake I wasn't going anywhere.

"Sing another one," I said to him. "Something we haven't heard."

"I can't sing anymore," he complained. "My throat feels like a cat scratched it from the inside out."

"Come on, choke out one more," Hannah teased.

"I have one," he said, looking thoughtful. "Maybe I shouldn't. It's not the right time."

"You can't leave us hanging," I said playfully.

"I haven't sung it for anyone yet," he said, full of uncharacteristic doubt. "I'm not sure it's ready."

"If it's that terrible we'll boo you off stage," Devin said.

"Ok, but I warned you." He picked up his guitar and carefully tuned it. "This is the first song I've ever written. Sort of. I wrote the music, but I borrowed the lyrics from someone else. I hope the author won't be too mad at me."

"I didn't know you wrote your own music," I said.

He looked straight at me. "Just this once."

He cleared his throat and began to pick a soft, tender tune, somewhere between a ballad and a spiritual.

> *When I am happy, you are there to share it,*
> *When I am scared, you help me to be brave*

The smile drained from my face, a cold lump stuck in my throat. I felt one of my monster headaches coming on, the first one in weeks.

> *When I say I love you, it means forever,*
> *And when forever comes, I will be there,*
> *To comfort you, to hold you in my arms, to keep you safe,*
> *Because when is now, and forever.*

I was stunned, dumbfounded, frightened, angry, unable to move. I wanted to jump out of my seat, pull the guitar from his hands, and smash it into a thousand pieces. But the clarity and purity of his voice held me in place and demanded that I listen. At first, all I could hear was the corruption behind my childhood words to Jeremy. The reason I wrote the poem. What it really meant when I asked if he was ready and told him I was waiting. Alex's sweet alto changed it, washed the filth away,

transforming it into something innocent and pure. Maybe I wrote the poem to offer myself to Jeremy, but it was my childhood love for him that rang true. Nick from long ago reached out and reminded me when I felt like I could fly. How it felt to be held while I cried. By the last few wistful notes, I was breathless. My emotions were awake. I was touched. Moved.

"That was sweet," Hannah said in a soft voice. "I'd *so* be your girlfriend if you weren't such a raging queer." Alex didn't answer. He cleared his throat, eyes fixed on me. I had no words. Hannah picked up on the palpable tension in the room. She yawned loudly and stretched her hands over her head. "That's all folks. I'm going to crash." The rest of the group took the hint and filtered out, Jake stumbling upstairs half asleep. Alex and I remained fixed like rocks in a receding tide. Even when the room was empty and the house still, neither of us said anything. He looked at me nervously.

"Are you angry?" he said in a quavering voice.

"Where did you find it?" I croaked.

"In the box you gave to Jake," he said. "Not the one with the swords and armor. The *other* box. It was stuck in the middle of some papers." I had no memory of putting any papers in that box, let alone that poem. I thought it was one of the things from my childhood that was lost. Like so many other things. "The calligraphy was beautifully written. Too bad there was a big red mark on the edge of the paper."

"Sealing wax," I murmured. The original. I'd also forgotten Jeremy left it behind. For some reason it made me melancholy to realize he didn't have it.

"I have it in my room if you want it," he said. "I should've told you when I found it, but it made such a nice song. I wanted to write it for you as a present. For being so nice, helping out with the show, and letting me be a part of your family. Sorry, I'm getting all sappy."

"I like sappy," I said, putting my mask back on. "What you did with my poem was truly beautiful. If I had other poems I wrote as a kid, I'd insist you turned them all into songs."

He reached into his guitar case and pulled out a small Ziploc bag. "I've been saving this for a special occasion." He handed it to me. Small

rolled up papers, stuffed and wrapped carefully, a few small clips loose in the bag.

"Is this what I think it is?" I asked.

Alex winked. "The last of my brother's home-grown stuff, really good shit. Want to share?"

"You're asking me to smoke pot with you?"

"Sure," he said. "You're cool, right?"

"I guess I'm as cool as the next old fart," I said. "But it'd be wasted on me. I've never smoked pot before. I don't know how." I handed the bag back to him.

"Seriously? I thought everyone did at least once."

"Some of us listened to Nancy Reagan," I quipped.

"You're in for a treat. This stuff is much better than random junk off the street. You never know what's mixed in with that crap." He found a lighter in the guitar case and handed me one of the joints with a clip attached. "Put it in your mouth."

"I'm not so sure about this," I said, but I was powerless to resist him.

He flicked the lighter. "When it's lit, suck the smoke and hold it as long as you can. Easy." I tasted the first bit of smoke and launched into a massive coughing fit. He laughed as I yanked it out, holding it like it was an abnormally large insect. I handed it back and watched as he took a deep breath, holding it in for several seconds before blowing the smoke at my face. "Like that," he croaked. "Try again."

I managed to hold in a tiny amount of smoke for a few seconds before coughing it out. "I can't believe I'm doing this," I sputtered. "I could get in so much trouble."

"Nobody cares about smoking pot," he said.

"Not for smoking pot. For corrupting a minor."

His laugh sounded like a clear brook running over mossy stones after a spring rain. I nearly slapped myself for thinking of such a sophomoric metaphor.

"Too late, I'm already corrupted," he said. "Besides, who's corrupting who? You're the one who's never toked before."

I took another puff, holding it longer this time, managing to avoid a cough when I blew it out.

"You're a natural," he said.

We traded it back and forth until it was reduced to a miniscule stump. He took the last part of it. "Damn, that's good shit." He burst into giggles. "Why do they say that? There's nothing good about shit." He giggled for so long I wound up joining in. He lit another and handed it to me, then lit one for himself.

"What makes this enough of a special occasion to smoke the last of your brother's really good shit?" I asked.

"My performance was *stellar*," he said in a dreamy way. I watched him take a puff and imitated him expertly. "See? It's like you've been doing it your whole life." He stretched his arms. "I'm starting to feel it. How about you?"

"Yeah," I said, but in truth I didn't feel anything. My head felt a little light. Maybe. Smoke hung in the air as we finished our joints. He stared at me intently and burst into laughter. I joined in again. When I finished, he lit another joint and handed it to me.

"I am so fucking wasted," he said.

I took a long, deep pull. "Play it again, Sam," I heard myself say.

He picked up his guitar. The music felt like a soft blanket I could wrap around myself, protecting me from everything the world could throw at me. I hugged it, pulling it tighter. I realized it was becoming too tight but I couldn't stop it. It constricted like a snake, suffocating and strangling me. I shook myself free, rocketing out of my seat, wobbly on my feet until I collapsed back into the chair.

"Are you ok?" he asked, the music gone.

I felt a terrible emptiness I needed to fill.

"I wrote that poem such a long time ago," I said. "I was twelve. I meant every single fucking word of it."

"You must've had a massive crush on that girl. Did you give it to her?"

"I was drunk off my ass. My first time. I downed a whole bottle of wine. I didn't even know I was plastered. I ran off because I was too embarrassed to stay while he read it."

Alex's eyes went wide. "He?"

"Huh?"

"You said that you were too embarrassed to stay while *he* read it. Maybe you meant to say she."

I knew somewhere inside my muddled head I shouldn't tell him. Maybe I was just high. Maybe something else was driving this sudden, irrepressible need. The look on his face assured me he already knew. I focused on a small spot on the wall.

"It wasn't a mistake," I said. "I meant to say he."

"You gave that to a boy," he murmured.

"Not exactly," I said. "He was older than me. An adult. He was there for me when no one else was."

"The guy in the picture," he said, perceptive as always.

"Jeremy," I said. "I met him when I went out to shovel driveways. He offered me fifty bucks, a fortune back then. He was kind, generous, and paid unlimited attention to me. It didn't take long for me to fall in love. Soon, I was living with him and one thing led to another." I closed my eyes. "He took advantage of me."

"Oh," Alex said softly.

"I didn't mean to make you uncomfortable," I said. Maybe I did.

"I'm ok," he said. "Sex doesn't freak me out."

"I shouldn't be telling you this," I said to get him to ask me more.

"Did he force you?" Alex said in a surprisingly tender voice.

"I gave him that poem for his birthday," I said. "I was the birthday present. I knew he wanted me because he'd already explained he was attracted to boys. I needed him so badly and I was terrified of losing him. I was willing to do anything."

"So he took you," Alex said.

"He tied me up and raped me."

"Oh my god," he whispered. "I'm so sorry." He wrapped his arm around my shoulder. It sent a jolt through my body. "Did you tell someone?"

"I never wanted to tell anyone," I said. "He was everything to me. I loved him and he loved me too. It was the happiest time of my life." What was I doing? I had no business telling anyone I was happy while I was being molested. That kind of thing was impossible. No child could be happy while being abused. It was sacrilegious to even suggest such a thing. Sexual abuse did one thing and one thing only – screw you up irrevocably for the rest of your life. I'd settled this a long time ago. He arranged things the way he needed them to be. He was a virtuoso at

playing my emotions. He wound me up so tight I made myself believe what he wanted me to believe. I was manipulated by a master.

But in that moment with Alex, my carefully constructed narrative crumbled into dust, replaced by truth I'd never wanted to acknowledge.

"I was twelve years old, getting fucked twice a day by a guy twenty years older than me, and I was never happier." His body pressed against mine. I had to fight the urge to paw him. "You know what's strange? He fixed me. When I met him, I'd almost succeeded at hanging myself. He helped me find strength I never knew I had. I blossomed, I found I had talent, and I went from outcast to popular. He was never anything but kind and gentle to me. He was the kind of person who made sure I came first, even when it hurt him."

"How could someone like that rape you?" Alex asked.

"I didn't mean to make it sound that way," I said. "I asked him to tie me up. He never forced me to do anything, ever. I was into bondage before I met him. I tried for weeks to get him to have sex with me. He had a bad experience before he met me and was afraid it would ruin our relationship. He knew I had no interest in sex and was only offering to please him. He refused to take from me no matter how hard I pushed. I wore him down. I had him tie me up because I was afraid I wasn't going to be able to get through it. I couldn't let him find out how much the idea of sex terrified and disgusted me." I shook my head. "Saying it out loud makes it sound like bullshit. Like I'm making the typical justification most pedophiles use. 'He wanted it.'"

"It doesn't sound like bullshit," Alex said. "It sounds like you were in love with him and wanted to make him happy. We all do things for people we care about even if we don't want to." He smiled a little. "The stuff you gave Jake was from him, wasn't it? When you were a kid. Everything is too small to be for an adult."

I nodded slowly. "I asked him to torture me. I needed it, far more than just for sex. Somehow, it helped me to let go of all the emotions bottled up inside. He bought that bondage equipment to help. He locked me up for hours in the basement with my hands chained over my head. He whipped me so hard and for so long I couldn't scream by the end."

Alex tensed up. "Now you've officially freaked me out."

"I'm sorry," I said. "I didn't mean to upset you." Maybe I did.

"I don't understand how anyone could hurt someone they cared about. I could never hurt anybody even if they asked me to. I mean, I tried a couple of times with Jake, but I. . ." He turned bright red. "Oh shit. Shit shit shit shit shit shit. Forget I said that. I made it up."

"Jake wanted you to torture him?" I couldn't imagine the possibility. It had to be just bondage. That's the only part he could've inherited from me. The torture came from a very different place and for a very different reason. The need to be punished never came from my dick. Alex looked scared.

"It's ok," I said. "If Jake is going to experiment, I'm glad it's with someone he can trust. Someone I can trust."

He took a deep breath. "I wish I could help him. I'm worried about him. He showed me this sick story once about a kid who got sold by his parents to be tortured. I couldn't read it. I always thought that no idea should ever be censored, but that story was so bad it made me think I was wrong. That's what Jake wants. To get sold. To get taken away and never let go."

"Just like me," I said, more to myself. "I was the same way before I met Jeremy. Why is he like that? The torture came from a place of emotional distress, not a sexual fantasy. I hated myself. I thought I deserved to be punished. You don't think he'd actually act on his fantasies, do you?"

"No," Alex said. "At least I don't think so. But sometimes sex makes you do stupid things."

"You don't know how right you are," I murmured.

"Actually, I do," he said. "Since you're telling me your deep dark secrets, I'll tell you one of mine. I did something incredibly stupid once. Remember how I told you I played Toby for that summer stock production of Sweeney Todd? I got my first intense crush on the guy playing the lead. He was an amazing actor even though he was still in college. I learned so much from him. On top of that he was gay, and I mean flaming flamboyant fabulously gay. And on top of that, he was a hunk. We were in his dressing room talking and we smoked a couple of joints and it just happened. He didn't try anything, I came on to him. Not all the way, we just messed around. He didn't hurt me, he was

sweet and gentle the whole time. I liked it. He gave great head." He sighed. "I wish I didn't do it."

"It wasn't your fault," I said.

"It's not like I was some little kid who didn't know what he was doing. I've got a grown-up dick and I can make a baby, so I should be able to do what I want with my own body. It's just sex, why does everyone have to make such a big deal out of it? The next day he wouldn't talk to me. Three days later he quit the show. It hurt how he never said goodbye. I didn't understand at first, but now I understand he was scared because he could get in serious trouble. Having sex with a thirteen-year old is worse than murder. It's my fault he ran away."

I felt like he stabbed a knife right through me as deep as it could go. Everything that happened with Jeremy was my fault.

"Sweetie, you shouldn't think like that," I said gently. "He's the adult, not you. Whether you realize it or not, he abused you. Just like Jeremy abused me."

"He didn't make me do anything," Alex said.

"He knew what it meant to go ahead when you offered. He knew the consequences. It was his responsibility to be the adult. All he had to do was stop you and nothing would've happened. You might still be good friends, maybe something more when you were older. Sex screws everything up. I still care about Jeremy, but I can't and won't forgive him for it. Maybe I was happy and maybe I was willing, but in the end he put his needs first and that's not ok with a child. He gave me what I wanted instead of what I needed. If he managed to keep saying no, maybe things would've worked out very differently for me. Your guy and my Jeremy, they both had the responsibility of being the adult, and they blew it."

Alex looked at me for a second and then burst out laughing.

So did I when I realized what I said.

"That is *not* what I meant," I said when we stopped, which made us start laughing again.

"I've never told anybody any of this," I said quietly when we finally stopped. "I've barely told myself any of this before now.

"I won't tell, I promise," he said. "It makes me feel special to be the person you decided to tell. You talk to kids like they can think. I really like that about you."

"For years, all I felt was hatred towards him. Your song brought something out in me. You reminded me of things I made myself forget for a long time. You reminded me that I loved him. I want you to know that you're a very special person."

He leaned into my shoulder. "That's another thing I like about you. You give a shit."

I knew it was the wrong thing to do but I couldn't stop myself. I had to say it. Besides, he was Alex. At thirteen he was more perceptive than any adult I knew. I was only going to tell him what he already knew. He made that abundantly clear.

"I have an intense crush on someone," I said.

"Really?" He perked up. "Who?"

I gripped his hand. "You."

I felt like I was going to be sick when I saw the stunned look on his face. I was wrong. He had absolutely no idea. It was all gone. He would find my confession creepy. No doubt he would pick up his things and leave the house, even if it was the middle of the night. Maybe he'd wait until morning, barricaded in Jake's room, telling my son how his pervert father made a pass at him.

But he was Alex.

The stunned look melted away.

He held my hand tight.

"That's so sweet," he said.

Chapter 34

February 14, 1983

I t's scary how quickly everything can change. One minute you're going along doing normal things and then poof, something happens. It's like driving in a car with no brakes. The main road is blocked, so you swerve onto a side road you didn't know was there. It's too narrow to turn the car around so you keep speeding onward without any idea where you're going. Life is a one-way road. I didn't realize that before.

This wasn't the way I expected to spend Valentine's Day. The school dance was last week. Jeremy made reservations for a fancy dinner in the city on Saturday. None of my friends had anything remotely resembling a girlfriend, so there wasn't much left to celebrate on the actual day. I planned to go to school, hang out with my friends afterward, do my homework, and practice piano. A normal day. Maybe something special at night under the covers, but no matter how creative I tried to be, I couldn't think of anything that we hadn't done a million times before. I wasn't supposed to be standing in my best blue suit, freshly cleaned and pressed, with my hair neatly blow dried and brushed out until my scalp burned. I wasn't supposed to be looking out an unfamiliar window in an unfamiliar house at a street in an unfamiliar city. I wasn't supposed to be waiting nervously for someone to tell me it was time to go somewhere unfamiliar without any idea how to act, what to say, and most important, what not to say.

From the unfamiliar window, I watched the long, black limo pull up slowly in front of the house. It still seemed inappropriate to me. I used

to think limos were for celebrations. They were supposed to be fun. But I'd never look at a limo the same way again. In my mind, they'd forever be a symbol something terrible happened.

I didn't understand the truth about limos when I saw one parked outside our house last Saturday morning. I slept over Chris' house the night before and rode my bike home, so it was a surprise. I thought it was cool how the driver tipped his hat and said good morning to me. I figured Jeremy arranged it to take us to dinner tonight, which was seriously awesome. I wondered if it had a TV. Or a sunroof I could stick my head through. Or maybe it was one of those limos with a hot tub. We could be naked and no one in traffic would know.

When I went crashing inside shouting how cool the limo was, I wasn't ready for what I saw. Jeremy was sitting on the floor in the lobby, his knees pressed to his chest. An empty bottle and a full glass were on the coffee table next to him. I could tell his eyes were bloodshot all the way from the front door.

"Kiddo," he squeaked, and broke into a full-blown sob.

I knew that the right thing to do was sit down next to him, find out what was going on, and try to make him feel better. But I was certain whatever made him cry had something to do with me. Maybe my parents decided I couldn't live with Jeremy anymore. I stayed exactly where I was in the entryway with the door still open.

"What's going on?" I asked.

He struggled to get a hold of himself. "Do you remember when I told you about my Aunt Rachel? How I went to live with them when I was your age?" I nodded slowly. "My cousin Amy. . ." He crashed his fist into the table next to him so hard I thought he was going to break the glass. The empty bottle tipped over and rolled onto the floor. "Three days ago, she passed away."

At first, I was thrilled it had nothing to do with me. Then I felt terrible. Someone Jeremy cared about died and I was happy about it. What kind of a horrible, selfish person would feel that way? I ran up

and sat next to him on the floor, no idea what to say. Why couldn't they teach us what to say in school instead of all that other useless stuff?

"She had Hodgkin's disease, a kind of cancer. She was sick for two years and nobody told me." Jeremy slammed the table again and I jumped. His face softened. "I'm sorry, sweetie. I didn't mean to scare you."

"It's ok," I said softly. He touched my cheek.

"I'm going to the funeral in San Francisco," he said. "I'll be gone for a few days, but you're old enough to take care of yourself. I'll leave plenty of money so you can order pizzas for dinner. Maybe you can stay with Chris. I'm sure his mother won't mind."

"I want to go with you," I said.

"I want you with me too," he moaned. "But it's not that simple, nothing ever is. My whole family will be there. They'll ask all the difficult questions and never believe whatever story I tell them. I can't risk losing you if they decide to interfere."

"We'll figure something out," I said. "We'll keep it a secret. No one has to know I came with you. I could stay in the hotel room. I could hide. I could pretend to be someone else. Come on, let me go so I can miss a couple days of school." I waited for him to smile, but if he understood I made a joke he didn't show it. Joking was a stupid idea. "I'm coming with you."

"Kiddo. . ."

"No. I said I'm coming with you. I won't let you go by yourself."

He started bawling again. I felt like I wanted to cry too. I didn't understand why I felt sad, since I didn't know his cousin. My shoulder got wet when he hugged me. I patted him on the back.

"Ok," he said through his tears.

I blinked. It worked? I didn't think it would work. Was I sure I wanted it to work? Why couldn't I make up my mind?

"I should pack my stuff," I said.

He ran his fingers through my hair. "I already packed a bag for you," he said. I looked at him sideways. "I had trouble deciding what to do, so I thought, just in case."

Ten minutes later we were in the limo on our way to the airport. I wanted to stick my head through the sunroof. I wanted to turn on the

television. I wanted to chatter about flying on a plane for only the second time in my life. I didn't. I sat quietly, holding his hand. I didn't know if that was the right thing to do. Maybe it would've cheered him up if I acted silly and tried to make him laugh. Maybe it would've made him feel worse. The one person in the world I could ask what I should do was the one person I couldn't.

<div align="center">⌒⚊⟩✗⟨⚊⌒</div>

I heard a tap on the door. I opened it somberly, trying to look sympathetic.

"We're ready, dear," Aunt Rachel said. She wore a black dress, a thin veil hanging from her hat to cover her face. If she was crying before, her face didn't show it. "Please get Jeremy. Let him know it's time to leave."

I nodded, and she put her hand on my shoulder. The way she touched me seemed like it expressed exactly what should be expressed at a time like this. I wished I could learn how. I watched her go down the stairs, wondering what it was like to be her. I'd never known someone who died, especially someone so close to me. I tried to imagine what it would be like if my parents died, but that wasn't big enough. I tried to imagine Jeremy dying, but that was too big to wrap my head around. Then I tried to imagine what it would be like for Jeremy if I died. That was also too big.

I waited until she was downstairs before I knocked on Jeremy's door at the other end of the hall. "They're ready for us to go," I said. He didn't answer, so I went inside. He sat on the bed like he was in a trance, staring blankly at the wall. I closed the door softly, putting my hand on his shoulder the way Aunt Rachel did to me. It didn't feel like I did it the right way. He looked up at me with watery eyes, bloodshot, the same way his eyes had been for the last two days. His tie was lying on the bed. I draped it over his shoulder, kneeling behind him so I could tie it.

"Do you remember when I did this for you that first Christmas eve?" he asked. "You were so frustrated. Helping you made me feel like you were my own son."

"I remember," I said. Somehow, I managed to get the knot right.

"You're so good to me," he said. I used the handkerchief he gave me to wipe his face. I found his shoes under the bed, bent down to tie them for him, and helped him with his jacket. His breath smelled like alcohol, so I got him a cup of mouthwash from the bathroom and made him use it. It was nice to do things for him. Helping him made me feel like I had a purpose instead of being a useless kid.

"I love you," I said to him.

"I love you too," he said. "Let's get this over with before I lose what little courage I've got left."

Jeremy, Aunt Rachel, and I were alone in the limo to the church. They didn't talk much on the way and I didn't know if I should try to start a conversation. I wouldn't know what to talk about anyway. I watched the scenery go by, sitting as close to Jeremy as I dared without sitting so close that it looked wrong. The parking lot at the church was full of limos and fancy cars. I got out of the limo first, holding out my hand to help Aunt Rachel. She smiled and touched my shoulder again. I turned to Jeremy in the limo.

"Do you remember the story?" I asked in a low voice.

"I'm not going to be able to keep it straight," he said. "We'll have to do our best to avoid everyone. I don't want to see any of them, and I'm sure none of them want to see me." He let me help him out of the car. The three of us walked arm in arm to the church, me in the middle to help both of them. I never felt so grown up.

I had to remember that "I'm very sorry for your loss" was the right thing to say to people when someone died. That's what everyone said to Aunt Rachel when the service was over. Sometimes people would say other nice things, like how Amy's suffering was over, or how brave she was, or asking Aunt Rachel if she needed anything.

We stood next to Aunt Rachel while people walked by even though there were hundreds of people who knew her better than we did. I didn't think it was a good idea, in case Jeremy's family was there. No one said anything. Most of the people didn't even know who Jeremy

was. After everyone went by, I walked between them back to the car, keeping my face somber. Aunt Rachel called me a "perfect gentleman" when I helped her out of the car at the cemetery.

We'd just gotten out of the car when the priest walked up. "I wasn't able to place you until now, but I suspect you're the boy I used to see in my church many years ago," he said to Jeremy. "The boy who always found the piano in my rectory no matter how many locked doors were in his way."

"It's nice to see you, Father," Jeremy said quietly.

"I hope next time it'll be under better circumstances. Is this young man your son?"

I was about to speak, but Jeremy interrupted me. "Nick is like a son to me."

"God be with you," the priest said to me, shaking my hand.

"Umm, god be with you too," I said back. He smiled, so I figured I got it right.

"Jeremy, we're in need of one more pallbearer. I've come to ask you to serve."

"Please, no," Jeremy said, in a thick voice like his tongue was swollen.

"I'll do it," I said, even though I had no idea what a pallbearer was.

"While your eagerness is a blessing, we need someone who can help support the weight."

Support the weight, like carry something? What needed to be carried?

"The honor is yours," the priest said to Jeremy. "You were close with Amy years ago. Now is the time to put aside any strife and come together as a family. For Rachel's sake, and for Amy's." Jeremy looked down and nodded, walking away with the priest. I went to follow but Aunt Rachel held my hand.

"Stay with me," she said. "Keep an old woman company. Make everyone think a young man might still be interested in me." I couldn't believe she made a joke. She winked at me, and then her face went back to a blank expression. I watched Jeremy walking over towards the hearse, nervous for him. "He'll be fine," she said to me.

I didn't understand what Jeremy was supposed to do until he took one of the corners when they pulled the coffin from the back of the hearse. The idea of carrying a dead body gave me the shivers. It took six people to carry it, but if it was heavy they didn't let it show. The grave was a short walk from where we parked. The hole in the ground looked too small to fit the coffin. Jeremy helped put the coffin on a platform above the hole and then sat down with us in the front row. Nothing happened, so I guessed none of the other people carrying the coffin were his family.

People spoke about Amy – friends talking about how full of life she was, how she was always so kind to people who needed help, how she was talented at so many different things, and how bravely she faced her final days. They told stories. Some of them were funny, like the time she found a hurt squirrel when she was seven and brought it home. It got loose and destroyed Aunt Rachel's house. Some of them were sad, like how she volunteered to help little kids with cancer. Some of them died before she did. I wondered if Jeremy would get up and tell a story, but he didn't move when the priest asked if anyone else wanted to speak. I thought telling nice stories is what a funeral should be, remembering what the person was like when they were alive. I didn't like the parts afterwards – when they lowered the coffin into the hole, when the priest said something about ashes and dust, and when people lined up to throw a shovelful of dirt into the grave. I didn't understand how it was supposed to make everyone feel better. I helped Aunt Rachel throw in her shovelful of dirt. It was the first time she cried for real. It made me shiver when it was my turn. Burying the coffin made me feel responsible, like I had a part in killing her.

Jeremy stayed in his seat until everyone went by. I knew he didn't want to, but I thought it was important he did it along with everyone else. I stood in front of him with the shovel. "Don't make me do this," he said. He let me pull him to his feet. His hand squeezed mine hard enough to hurt. I didn't care. He could squeeze as hard as he wanted. The look on his face when he held the shovel nearly made me cry again. "It's not fair," he moaned. "This isn't the way I wanted to say goodbye." He took a shovelful of dirt and threw it in the hole.

"I didn't get to say goodbye!" he yelled.

"Then say goodbye now," I said.

He dropped the shovel and wrapped his arms around me. I knew it wasn't a good idea, but he needed a hug. Aunt Rachel told me that people needed hugs at times like this. I felt like everyone was staring at us.

It turned out only one person was staring.

"You've got a lot of nerve."

Jeremy let me go so fast it was like he spat me out. A tall man was standing behind us. The look on his face was cold enough to freeze the sun. If you took away the mustache, a few inches, and some of the hair, he looked a lot like Jeremy.

"We were just leaving," Jeremy muttered.

"You're not welcome here," the man said. "I thought you knew better than to show up at a family function. You don't belong out in public."

"Leave me alone, Robert," Jeremy said.

Robert? *The* Robert?

"No one invited you," Robert spat.

"Rachel did," Jeremy said. "I have just as much of a right to be here as anyone else. Amy was. . ."

"Showing up is one thing," Robert interrupted. "But you had the unmitigated gall to bring *that* along with you? What was the story I heard, your girlfriend's son?"

I realized "*that*" meant me.

"You don't even have the decency to concoct a reasonable lie. As though any woman would find you remotely interesting. As though *you'd* find any woman remotely interesting. No, we both know the truth. The only person you'd find interesting is her young son." Jeremy looked down. "You know the terms of our agreement, and here you are, flaunting your deviance in our faces. You know what you're capable of and the harm you've already done, but clearly you haven't learned your lesson. I should throw you to the wolves, let you rot in prison for the rest of your life. You disgust me."

I stepped in front of Jeremy. "Leave him alone," I growled.

Robert looked straight through me. I was reminded of taunts on the playground where kids would one-up each other on how low the other

one was. That look made me feel lower than the dirt underneath the dog shit on the chewing gum stuck to the bottom of a sneaker.

"Tell your little whore to shut his mouth," Robert sneered.

I watched it happen in slow motion. Jeremy charged, his face purple and his fists clenched tight. Robert didn't budge. Maybe he didn't think Jeremy would actually hit him. My head wanted to grab Jeremy, keep him from doing something stupid. But my heart screamed for him to kill Robert. Jeremy yelled and swung wide, his fist slamming into Robert's chin. They both staggered, and for a moment I thought they would fall into the hole with the coffin. Instead, they stumbled away, Robert falling on the mound of dirt and Jeremy falling on the chairs.

"Son of a bitch," Robert said as he got up, nowhere near as hurt as I wanted him to be. "Who puts a roof over your head and food on your table?" He sounded exactly like my father. "It's over. I'm cutting you off. No more protection and no more handouts. You're on your own. I want you out of my house by the end of the month. I don't give a shit where you go or what you do. I swear to God if I see your face or hear your voice I will personally feed you to the vultures."

Then he turned to me. "As for you, don't think your little scam is going to work. If you come looking for a dime in hush money, I will take great pleasure in making the rest of your life a living hell."

"I'll kill you," Jeremy growled. He picked up the shovel and raised it above his head. Robert's cold look melted off his face.

"Robert Stillwell!" Aunt Rachel snapped. Her voice was strong, like she was the general in charge of all the other generals. She touched my shoulder as she walked by me. "If my sister were alive, she'd be appalled by your behavior!"

"Rachel," Robert said, his tone all business. "I meant no disrespect."

"Disrespect is all you've shown and you most certainly meant it," she said, standing right in front of him. He was a lot taller, but somehow, she looked bigger than him. "Haven't you caused enough pain? All those messages, all those letters from Amy and myself. You never sent any of them to Jeremy." Robert brushed the dirt from his coat. He had a little smile on his face that reminded me of Chris. "Maryanne has provided for Jeremy. You have no control over him, no matter what

you might believe. She wanted you to look after your younger brother. Your own mother. You haven't a shred of decency in you."

"I don't have a brother," he said coldly.

"The whole lot of you Stillwell boys never learned how to behave like men." Aunt Rachel said. "Take a good look at this boy, Robert. He's more of a man than you'll ever be."

Robert laughed, cold and cruel.

"I think it's time you were on your way," Aunt Rachel said, leaving no room for him to argue.

"You're right, I've seen more than enough," Robert said. He straightened his coat. "I meant what I said," he spat at Jeremy. Then he turned to me. "I meant what I said to you as well." He mouthed the word. *Whore.*

Jeremy saw it and picked the shovel back up. I stood in front of him. "He's not worth it," I said softly. I took the shovel from him and threw it on the dirt pile. Then, I stared at Robert. I don't know what he saw in my face. Whatever it was, his little smile disappeared right before he turned and left.

"Don't worry about him," Aunt Rachel said, wrapping my arm around hers. "Life is too short and precious to waste it worrying about the Robert Stillwells of the world." She bent down to whisper in my ear. "I meant what I said about you as well."

"Thanks," I said, feeling even more grown up.

I didn't understand why everyone brought so much food to Aunt Rachel's house. Every counter and table that wasn't already covered with flowers was covered with casseroles and desserts because the fridge was stuffed. I watched carefully all day, but Aunt Rachel and Jeremy didn't eat anything. Food seemed to be the last thing they wanted. Maybe people should've brought something else. Extra tissues would've come in handy.

The house finally emptied sometime after eleven o'clock. I sat next to Jeremy, who was lying on the couch staring at the ceiling. Aunt Rachel sat on her legs in a big chair with her dress draped over them. I

thought it was a weird way to sit for someone as old as her. Was she fifty, sixty, maybe seventy? I had no idea. I was nibbling on a chocolate, hiding it from them because it felt wrong to be eating when they weren't. The silence felt nice after the constant noise. Not that it was loud in the house when everyone was there, because everyone talked softly. It was more of a buzzing in the background, like a fly that wouldn't leave you alone.

"For goodness sakes, eat the chocolate," Aunt Rachel said to me. I shrugged. "When you're through, come sit with me. I have something I want to show you." She pulled a big book from a long line of identical books on the shelf and sat back in her chair, patting a small spot on it. I'd be sitting on top of her if I tried to squeeze in. I looked at Jeremy for help, but he was too busy studying the ceiling. "I don't bite," she said. "Well, not usually."

The book was full of pictures, stuck to the pages with little triangle corners. "Here's the one I wanted to show you," she said. The picture showed a teenage girl with a friendly smile standing with her arm around a boy about the same age as me, his blond hair short from a buzz cut. He wasn't smiling and he wasn't frowning. He looked kind of deflated. Like someone found his little tube and let all the air out. "That's my Amy, when she was fifteen," she said softly. "Do you know who this is?"

I stared at him and burst into a fit of severely inappropriate giggles when I figured out it was Jeremy.

"Why are you doing this?" Jeremy said to Aunt Rachel. "You show him those photos and he's never going to let me live it down."

"Hush. I'm sure Nick wants to know all about you as a boy, don't you?" I nodded hard. "This picture was taken when Jeremy first came to live with us. He had wonderful cornsilk blond hair as a boy. It didn't turn dark until later. He lived with us for three years, from the time he was your age until he was fifteen."

"I look like the walking dead," Jeremy said, looking over our shoulders. "How did you put up with me?"

She smiled and turned the page. "I don't remember him," she said, pointing to a picture.

"Mr. Boll," Jeremy said in the voice grown-ups used when they were remembering things. "He was one of my tutors. The poor guy tried so hard. I was a brick wall, but he never lost his patience with me."

"You had tutors?" I asked.

"I didn't go to school when I first came here," Jeremy said.

"That's so cool," I said.

"I suppose," he said.

"You were in no state of mind to go to school," Aunt Rachel said quietly. I knew why. I remembered the story he told me about military school. Kid Jeremy's face was exactly the same in every single picture, as if the thing adults said about making faces came true. Aunt Rachel turned the page.

"At least you're smiling in this one," I said, pointing to one picture.

"I remember that day," he said. "Amy decided she was going to make me smile. She made faces, told stupid jokes, and tickled me for hours until I caved in. She always wanted to help people. You'd think a sixteen-year-old girl wouldn't be caught dead with her catatonic kid cousin, but she dragged me along everywhere. She gave up dates to take me bowling or to the movies. She made sure her friends always made me feel welcome. At first, I hated her for it. I wanted to shut the world out and never leave my room. She dragged me out of my funk. She saved me after that military school disaster." He put his finger on the photo. "I forgot how pretty she was."

"Maryanne knew you weren't the sort of boy who'd thrive in military school," Aunt Rachel said. "She fought hard with your father to keep you home. He wouldn't budge – family tradition and all that nonsense. She knew you were a sensitive artist, but there was no room for a sensitive artist in that household. Business, everything was always business. I'm sorry, but I'll never understand what your mother saw in that man. When you came home the second time, she put her foot down and sent you to me."

"Sending me here wasn't Father's idea?" Jeremy said, shocked. "I always thought he was dumping me because I wasn't of any use to him. I'd never seen Mother stand up to him."

"Your mother could be a force of nature when she chose," Aunt Rachel said. She flipped a few pages forward. "That's her," she said to

me, pointing at a picture of a woman standing with Jeremy, the Golden Gate bridge in the background. The look on her face told me she was a nice person. "It's still hard to believe she succumbed to something as trivial as a bump to the head."

"Mother slipped on a step in the house," Jeremy said to me. "Everyone thought she was fine. She went to lay down and never woke up. I miss her." I let him squeeze my hand for a second, shaking him off before Aunt Rachel noticed. "Too much tragedy."

"Life goes on, dear, and the living must keep living," Aunt Rachel said. "Our time in this world is too short to linger on tragedy." She turned the page.

"Where in the world did you get this picture?" Jeremy asked. It showed a sea of pianos in a warehouse, kid Jeremy sitting at one of them. Even though he was far away, I could tell how intense he looked.

"One of the clerks was kind of enough to mail it to me," she said. "They were all struck by the boy who spent eight hours in that store picking the right instrument."

"I remember," he said. "I could hear and feel the differences between them, but I didn't understand what those differences meant. I was terrified I'd pick the wrong one."

"Music brought you back to life," Aunt Rachel said. "Once you started playing, our job switched from getting you to talk to getting you to shut up." I giggled. "I loved listening to you play, even though there were times I had to escape the house. You made such rapid progress." She turned the page.

"Yimmy!" Jeremy said, excited, pointing at a picture. "His real name was Jukka-Pekka, but he wanted everyone to call him Jimmy. The funny thing was he didn't know how to make the 'j' sound so it came out sounding like Yimmy." The picture showed him playing cards with a younger boy around ten years old. "I was so upset when his family went back to Finland. I wonder what happened to him."

"He looks younger than you," I said.

"I guess," Jeremy said, turning the page. I burst out laughing when I saw a picture of him as a teenager, wearing a ridiculous shirt with all kinds of swirling colors, sunglasses, and a tie-dye headband. "Laugh it up," Jeremy said. "Everyone dressed like that."

"You look like hippies!" I said between my giggles.

"We *were* hippies," he said, sounding hurt. "At least, we pretended to be. Amy took me down to Haight-Ashbury on the weekends to ride the flower bus and listen to music."

"If I knew the two of you were going down there, I would've locked you in your rooms," Aunt Rachel said, but I could tell she didn't mean it.

"What's Haight-Ashbury?" I asked.

"It was the center of the hippie universe," Jeremy explained. "Everyone came together to create a different way of life. Free food, free music, free LSD while it was still legal, and free love." He raised his eyebrows and I giggled. "It was the first time I felt like I fit in somewhere. I learned to play guitar sitting on a street corner, soaking up everything I could from the musicians around me. It was a fantastic place until the word got out. Soon, every runaway, drug dealer, and low-life showed up. In a matter of weeks, the whole thing was ruined. Now it's a slum."

"Your father never forgave me for the way I sent you back to him," Aunt Rachel said with a smile. She flipped the page and showed me another picture of Jeremy, older, his hair darker and down to his shoulders.

"Father demanded I cut my hair the day I arrived," Jeremy said. "You should've seen his face when I called him 'the man' and told him to go to hell. Just like when I told him I wasn't going to his fancy prep school because I was going out for the school of the arts. It felt good to stand up to him. Scary, but good. I wouldn't have been able to do it without Amy. She taught me to take care of myself. She taught me not to take shit from anyone. She made me think I was worth something." He jerked to his feet. "Excuse me," he mumbled and headed for the door.

"Where are you going?" I asked. I heard the side door open and close. Aunt Rachel put her hand on my shoulder when I got up to go after him.

"Let him go," she said quietly.

"I have to go with him," I said.

"He'll be fine," she said. "Let him be. I'm sure he'll be back in a few minutes. Besides, it gives us a chance to get better acquainted." I looked at her, not sure what she meant. "I'm going to fix a pot of tea. Would you be so kind as to help me?"

I nodded and followed her to the kitchen. She turned on the stove to heat the kettle, putting some loose tea into a small pot. She turned and looked at me in a way that made me think she'd known me for years instead of just a few days.

"He cares for you very deeply," she said. "I've never seen him so happy. If you don't mind me being forward, I can see that you care for him the same way."

"I dunno, maybe. I mean, he's just my mom's boyfriend."

She shook her head. "A blind person could see how much you love each other," she said. "It's no secret in the family what makes Jeremy tick, and I've known longer than anyone else."

"I don't know what you're talking about," I said, my voice shaky.

"I think you do," she said. She hoisted herself onto the counter like she was a kid. "There's no need to worry. I've been watching the two of you – the way you hold hands, the way you hug, and the little looks you exchange when you think no one is watching. I see two souls that seem as though they were made for each other. Let me tell you something I believe right down to the core of my being. When two people love each other, it doesn't matter if they're the same race, have the same beliefs, or if they're the same sex." She paused for a moment. "Or how old they are."

"I don't. . ."

"I want to hear that you love him," she said. "I want to hear that he's taking good care of you, and that you're happy with him."

I wanted to look away. I wanted to run. I wanted to lie to her as easily as I lied to everyone else about Jeremy. But I couldn't look away, and I couldn't run. And I sure as hell didn't feel like I could lie to her. Even more, I didn't want to lie to her. I *wanted* to talk to her about it. I didn't realize until that moment just how much the truth wanted to come out.

"I love him a lot," I said in a small voice.

"I know, dear," she said. "How long have you known him?"

"A year and a half," I said. "I moved in with him last January because my parents are getting a divorce. They work all the time so they're never at home. He's teaching me how to play piano."

"He says you're more talented than he is, and that's saying something." She patted the counter next to her, and I climbed up. "What do you enjoy doing together?"

"All kinds of things. Movies, going out for dinner, riding bikes, and playing piano of course." I shrugged a little and she put her hand on my knee. "He helped me a lot. When I first met him, I was kind of messed up. He fixed me."

"I can see how special he is to you from the way you're so protective of him," she said. "The way you've looked after him tells me you're a remarkably mature young man who understands what matters." I smiled a little. "How did you find out he liked younger boys?"

"He told me the truth," I said. "A long time ago."

I couldn't tell her about our deepest secret, could I? But if it was going to come out, she was the right person to tell. I could feel it.

"When I was young, I was married for a short time to a man I thought was the most wonderful person on the face of the earth," she said. "I loved him so much that even though he hurt me, I never dreamed of leaving him. Eventually, I realized something. If he truly loved me as much as I loved him, he wouldn't be hurting me. I left him, even though it was the most painful thing I've ever done. It took a little while to get over my feelings for him, but once I did I never looked back." She squeezed my knee. "I need to know if he's hurting you, dear."

"Jeremy?" I said, upset she would say a thing like that. "He's the nicest, kindest person in the world. He'd never hurt me, ever."

"I'm glad to hear that," she said. "I thought it was important for me to ask. Sometimes people need somewhere to turn. I want you to know that even though we've only known each other for two days, you can always talk to me. Jeremy is a part of my family, and that makes you a part of my family too." I smiled. "Since you're family, I expect you'll visit me regularly. I know Jeremy will make promises he doesn't intend to keep. Both of you are welcome here, anytime, as often as you like. As yourselves, without any need to hide."

She held my hand. "You have to hold onto the people you love with both hands and never let go no matter how bumpy the ride gets. Time has a way of slipping by without being noticed. Don't take the people you love for granted. Make sure you make the most of the short time you have with them. Take it from someone who learned that lesson too late." A tear ran down her cheek. "Would you get me a tissue, dear?"

"Sure," I said, sliding off the counter. I turned around and held her hand. "I'm sorry," I said in a soft voice, and I really was. She didn't deserve this. She was too nice of a person for something this bad to happen to her. She nodded and smiled a little, holding back her tears.

The door opened while I was getting tissues out of the box. "It's freezing out there," Jeremy said. Aunt Rachel came out of the kitchen when she heard him. I handed her the tissues. "I'm feeling better now," he said to both of us. "Nothing like a brisk walk in the cold to clear your head."

"I think I've had enough for one day," Aunt Rachel said. She held her arms out, and I gave her a hug. A real one. Jeremy hugged her too. "Would you be a dear and shut down the house for me?" she said to Jeremy.

"I'll do it," I said. "You should go to bed too," I said to Jeremy.

He smiled. "It's been a long day. Are you going to be ok, kiddo?"

"Yeah," I said.

I wasn't going to get any sleep. I had heartburn of the brain.

I was lying in bed when I realized how close I was to a big disaster. When Aunt Rachel asked me if Jeremy was hurting me, I immediately thought of him hurting me like hitting or yelling at me. I said no because he'd never do something like that. But what she meant was sex. If she had asked more specifically, I might've said he was. I trusted her that much. Only luck kept us from being discovered. Liking someone and trusting someone had limits. It seemed horribly sad because it felt so fantastic to be honest with her.

I didn't want to wait until morning to talk to Jeremy, but I needed to wait until I was sure Aunt Rachel would be sound asleep. It was after

two in the morning when I crept silently down the hall to Jeremy's room. Without knocking, I turned the doorknob and pushed it open, making sure to keep it turned while I softly closed it.

"Can't sleep?" he asked softly.

"No," I whispered. I pulled my shirt off, dropping it on the floor.

"This isn't a good idea," he said. I slipped into bed next to him and pulled the covers up, slipping out of my underwear. "If Rachel catches us. . ."

"She already knows," I interrupted. He jerked up in bed. "Not that we do it. She knows we're more than friends."

"Exactly what did she say?" he whispered.

"She asked if you were hurting me," I said. "I told her you'd never do that. It's ok, she believed me."

"How do you know she believed you?"

"She said she's never seen you happier. She also said we should come back out whenever we want and act like our real selves. She wouldn't have said that if she didn't believe me." His face was covered with doubt. "Trust me. Come on, I'll give you a back rub."

He lay back down, sighing softly as I rubbed his shoulders.

"You know I love you," I said. "Even when it seems like I don't."

"Sweetie, of course I do," he said.

"I don't take you for granted."

He turned over. "What's wrong?"

"I was thinking about what it'd be like if you died. Amy was only a few years older than you."

"You don't need to worry," he said gently. "I'm not going anywhere."

"But what if you did? What if you got in a car crash or slipped on a step and hit your head? You know how last summer we said we were going to go to all those places and then we never did? What if that keeps happening? What if we keep saying we're going to do all those things but we never do them? I think we should stay in California for a while, just you and me. This is my first time out here and I don't want to go home without seeing anything. I remember you telling me all about the road by the ocean, the mountains, and the redwood trees. I want to see

it all. Not some other time that'll probably never happen. Right now. This time."

He didn't say anything.

"When we get home, I want you to tickle me. It's been ages since you did. I remember how I used to laugh so hard I couldn't breathe, and still you wouldn't stop. I want to roughhouse more. We used to have so much fun chasing each other around and wrestling on the floor. I want to make gross-out mixtures from the leftovers when we go out to eat. I want to have pillow fights, build couch forts, have squirt gun wars, and spray cans of whipped cream at each other. I want to have more picnics on the rock. I want to find out where that road goes. I want to sleep out under the stars with you." I took a deep breath. "I don't ever want to do anything to make you think I don't love you."

Before he could say something, I grabbed onto him. I let him cry on my shoulder and held on as hard as I could.

With both hands.

James Edison

Chapter 35

March 3, 1983

For the third time in less than a minute someone I didn't think I knew said "hi" to me in the hallway. A few days ago, Andy had finally explained why everyone acted differently towards me. "Don't you get it? You *mutilated* Tommy Walker. I heard his nose is permanently crooked and he had to have brain surgery because a piece of bone got wedged up in his head."

"So everyone thinks I'm a psycho?" I asked him nervously.

"No way!" he said. "You're a *celebrity.*"

At first, I couldn't figure out the difference between hitting Tommy over the head with a chair and beating him with fists. Eventually, I realized it wasn't what I did but the way I did it. The time with the chair I was out of control, crying and screaming like a crazy person. The time behind the school, I was calm. I teased him. That made all the difference.

"Nick!" A girl I recognized from class ran up to me. I knew that I knew her, but I couldn't remember her name. "I wanted to give this to you," she said, handing me a pink envelope. "It's an invitation to my party tomorrow night. My mom said I could invite more people so I thought you might want to come."

"You're inviting me to a party?" I said. I must've sounded like an idiot to her.

"Yeah, if you want. We're going to hang out and have music and pizza. I hope you can come." She stared at me and I realized I was supposed to say something.

"Ummm, yeah. Sure."

"Cool! See you tomorrow!"

"Bye." She bounced off. "Angela. Your name is Angela." Shit. I said that out loud. I hoped no one heard me.

I fought against the crowds going to lunch even though the bell was about to ring. The gym was empty. I knocked on the open door to the office.

"Shouldn't you be at lunch?" the gym teacher said, frowning at me.

"I wanted to drop this off," I said, handing him the green piece of paper.

"The deadline passed. Tryouts were last Tuesday."

"I know. I couldn't get to the doctor's office until yesterday because I was in California for a funeral."

"I'm sorry to hear that," he said. "Tell you what. Be here after school on Monday, dressed and ready. You've got one shot to show me what you can do."

"Ok, thanks," I said. My stomach dropped. Did I just sign up for a sport? Well, not a *real* sport like football or baseball. I'd be laughed off the field. I was only signing up for track. But me – a geek, a spaz, a dork – on a team? I had no business doing any kind of sport.

When the gym teacher announced track and field tryouts in class, it went in one ear and out the other. If we never went to California, I wouldn't have thought about it again. But I couldn't get the things Aunt Rachel told me out of my head. Life was short, and I didn't have time to waste. The gym teacher said running was all about conquering pain. I didn't know anything about sports, but I knew a lot about pain. I was good at conquering pain. I shouldn't miss this chance to do something I might be good at.

Jeremy and I wound up spending two whole weeks in California. Neither of us cared about missing school because we had more important things to do. We started with San Francisco, and when we ran out of things to do we rented a car. We drove up the northern coast where massive redwoods looked like skyscrapers. We drove down through the Sierras and Yosemite park covered with snow. We drove on Highway 1 chiseled into the side of the cliff above the ocean. We made it all the way to Los Angeles, finding stars on Hollywood

Boulevard and watching sunsets on the beach. When we decided we still weren't ready to head back, we drove through the desert to Las Vegas, gawking at the lights and feasting on 99-cent all you could eat pancakes at three in the morning.

We talked, and talked, and talked some more. Jeremy told me endless stories about the sixties and bought music I never heard like Janis Joplin and the Grateful Dead. He told me about protests and "be-ins" and drugs. He told me about the school of the arts in New York and what it was like at Eastman. He told me about his mother and how much he missed her. He told me things only I could hear, like what really happened with his friend Yimmy. How they played strip poker games and how they jerked off together to dirty pictures.

I told him about the school play. Even though he was nervous about Mr. Humber, he said he was happy I was doing it. I told him about wanting to join the track team. I told him about the things I wanted to do, the places I wanted to see, and my ideas about the future. I told him that I loved him all the time. In the car listening to music, in fancy restaurants, and in bed.

I managed to get from the gym to the cafeteria without being stopped by a teacher. "Where were you?" Chris said.

"I had something to do," I said. "Daniel could've played my character." I handed half my sandwich to Parker.

"Are we sleeping over at your house tomorrow?" Andy asked.

"I guess you guys will have to go to Chris' house," I said. "I can't come."

"What?" Chris exploded. "First you disappear for two weeks. No one knew what happened to you. Now we can't sleep over at your house?"

"I got invited to a party," I said like I was apologizing. I didn't know why. Wasn't it a good thing to be invited to a party?

"You're full of shit," Chris said.

"No, really," I said. I took the invitation out of the envelope. Andy grabbed it from me.

"You got invited to Angela Petersen's party? She's friends with all the popular girls. She's friends with the football players." He squinted at Chris. "She's friends with Cindy Davis."

"Shut up, I hate that airhead," he said. We all knew he was full of shit.

"You have to let me go with you," Andy said. "A lot of girls will be there. *Real* girls." I thought he was going to start drooling. "Who knows what games they'll play. Make-out city. Pleeeeease?"

I didn't know how parties worked. Was bringing friends allowed?

"Gentlemen." Mr. Humber stood behind one of the empty seats at the table. "May I borrow Mr. Welles for a few moments?"

"Am I in trouble?" I blurted out in front of everyone.

"None whatsoever," he said. I shrugged and followed him out of the cafeteria, my friends whispering and watching from the table. He took me down a side hallway no one ever used because the only thing there was the janitor's office. "Have you seen Brian today?" he said. He sounded worried. Mr. Humber never sounded worried. I realized he said Brian instead of Mr. Hanley.

"I think he's out sick again," I said. "I haven't seen him today."

"He came to see me after fourth period," Mr. Humber said. "Can you think of anyone else who might know where he is?"

"I don't think he has any other friends," I said. "Is Brian in trouble?"

"He's not in trouble, but I'm worried about him," Mr. Humber said. "Please, think carefully. Have you noticed something unusual in his behavior? Maybe he said something to you that didn't make sense? Anything, no matter how insignificant, could be a big help."

"I have no idea," I said. "I don't get it. He hasn't been in school for the last two days and I didn't see him in any of my classes today. How did you see him after fourth period?"

"I think he only came to school to see me," he said, leaning against the wall. "I'll have to try another route. I'm sorry for disturbing your lunch. I appreciate your help."

"Why are you worried about him?" I asked.

"We had a difficult conversation earlier," he said. "Before you ask, it would be a breach of his trust to share the topic." He took a small notepad from his pocket and scribbled something on it. "If you see him, please ask him to call me. The top number is for the school, and the bottom number is my home phone. Please keep my number confidential."

Mr. Humber giving me his home number scared the crap out of me. I went back to the cafeteria. "What was that all about?" Daniel asked.

"He was looking for Brian," I said. "I thought he was still out sick today."

"No, he isn't," Parker said. "I saw him right after English. He slammed into me as I was coming out of the room."

"I saw him there too," Daniel said. "I don't remember him being in class, though."

"He wasn't in any of his classes this morning," I said. "I'm going to ask anyone else if they saw him."

"What's the big deal?" Chris said, annoyed we were delaying his game. "It's not like he's your friend."

"He is too my friend!" I spat at Chris. "Why are you such an asshole?"

"What did I do?" he muttered as I stomped off.

I found a table of kids from our English class. "Did anyone see Brian Hanley today?" I interrupted.

"Yeah, I saw him cutting," Scott said. "Right after fourth period. I was at my locker and he went out the back door."

"That wimpy kid cut class?" Arthur said.

"Are you sure it was him?" I asked. Brian cut class? *Brian?*

"Yeah, I'm sure," Scott said.

"Thanks," I said. I went back to my table. Everyone stared at me. I didn't want to think about what I was planning to do. If I did, I'd realize how stupid I was.

"Someone saw Brian cutting class after fourth period," I said. "I'm going to find him."

"You're *what?*" Parker said. "You can't cut school!"

"Yes, I can," I said. "Right now. If I don't come back before the end of school, tell Mr. Humber I went to look for Brian."

"You want us to *tell* a teacher you cut?" Parker yelled. "Are you nuts? You'll get suspended! We'll all get suspended!" Everyone glared at him. He realized yelling about cutting school was a dumb thing to do.

"I don't care," I said.

"If you're cutting, I'm coming too," Chris said, standing up. I stared at him as hard as I could. He sat back down without saying a word.

"You should go out the back door near the science rooms," Daniel said. "It's closest to the woods and it's never locked. All the burnouts go that way." He picked up his books and stood up. "I'll be a lookout for you."

"Me too," Andy said, standing up with him. Jonathan nodded and joined them.

"You're fucking mental," Chris said, but then he stood up too.

"We're going to get in a shitload of trouble," Parker said. Still, he stood up with the rest of us.

They fell in behind me as we headed for the door.

I thought escaping school would be the hard part. We planned it like we were staging an assault in a D&D game. We figured out the best positions for everyone to take so we could intercept any teacher who came by at the wrong time and rehearsed what we would do if anyone tried to stop me. When the bell rang and the hallway flooded with people, I made a mad dash for the doors. I didn't stop or look back until I crossed the field and was safely hidden in the trees. It worked – no teachers stuck their head out the door yelling at me to come back. Way easier than I thought it would be.

The hard part was figuring out what to do next.

I wound up heading for his house first because I couldn't think of anywhere else to start. I knew Brian wouldn't be there because he wasn't allowed inside while his dad was sleeping. Maybe something would help me figure out where to look next. It took a while to get there because Brian's house was pretty far from the school and I kept off the roads, cutting through backyards and keeping an eye out for police cars. Brian's house had a small garage for one car, but it was full of stuff so his dad always parked outside. The driveway was empty. No big gold truck. That had to mean his dad wasn't home, which was weird. He was always home during the day. I crept around the back,

afraid to ring the doorbell. I imagined Brian was outside, reading or doing chores. I'd feel stupid. But the backyard was empty too.

Then I noticed the back door was hanging wide open.

I stared at it, paralyzed, expecting his dad to walk out any second and catch me. The door banged lightly against the house when the wind caught it. I don't know how long I stood there before I got the courage to peek inside.

"Hello?" I whispered. "Anybody home?"

Silence.

"Hello?" I said a little louder. "Brian?" Still no answer. I took a deep breath and went inside, walking into a small kitchen. I'd never been inside his house before. "The door's open," I called. Still no answer. I looked around, immediately noticing a giant rock covered in dirt sitting on the counter. Everything else was neat and clean so it looked even more out of place. I tiptoed over. Someone put it there to hold down a piece of folded notebook paper. I looked around to make sure no one was watching before I pulled the paper out. Dirt went everywhere. The note was in Brian's handwriting.

Dear Dick,

You're right. It's all my fault. I'm leaving and never coming back. I know you won't try to find me because everything will be better with Mom once I'm gone. I'm sorry I took your emergency money but I'll pay you back as soon as I can. I hope you have a better son than me some day. Goodbye.

Your ex-son, Brian

My throat felt like it had a big lump inside. I remembered the time he told me about running away, how he had nowhere to go and came home but his father locked him out all night. Brian sounded like he meant to run away for real this time. I was scared for him. This was too big for me. Jeremy would know what to do.

I put the note back and dashed out the back door, leaving it open. Like I was never there. The woods were a couple blocks away, the start of the two-mile path ending near my house. I started off at a walk, but I was running before I even got to the woods because I was so frightened. I imagined Brian begging for food at the side of the road. I imagined him going to New York because that's where runaways went. Bad people would force him to sell drugs. Or worse. Jeremy told me how runaways sometimes wound up in Times Square as boy hookers. He would get himself hurt. Or killed. He wasn't the kind of kid who knew what to do. Maybe he was already at the bus station. I thought about going directly to the bus station, but I had no idea where it was. I tore through the woods as fast as I could.

"Nick?" I heard someone say. I whipped my head around and slipped on some dead leaves, falling flat on my face.

"Are you ok?" the voice asked. Brian stared at me as I rolled over.

"I've been looking everywhere for you!" I said, pulling myself up.

"What are you doing here?" he asked. "School's not over yet."

"I cut so I could find you," I said. "Mr. Humber was worried and someone saw you cutting."

"Why would you care where I am?" he said.

"I'm your friend," I said, confused why he was angry at me.

"Not anymore," he said. "If you were my friend, you'd want to do things with me. All you do is play with that stupid asshole Chris kid. I don't need friends like you."

I wanted to scream at him. I wanted to tell him fine, I would leave. He could go get himself killed for all I cared. He was always such a baby about everything. But for some reason my anger fizzled when I looked him in the eyes. He didn't look angry. He looked frightened. I felt bad for him.

"I'm sorry," I said, looking down. "You're my best friend."

"Then act like a best friend!" he yelled.

"I thought that's what I was doing when I went looking for you," I said quietly. "I care about you. Mr. Humber was worried and I got scared."

He blinked and his shoulders slumped. "You cut school to look for me?" he said, softer.

"Yeah," I said.

"I don't know what to do," he moaned, sitting on the ground.

"I saw the note at your house," I said.

"You were in my house?"

"The back door was open," I explained.

"You can't tell anyone where I am," he said. "Promise!"

"I promise, I won't tell anyone," I said quickly. "But you should call Mr. Humber. He gave me his home phone number. He's really worried."

"I never want to talk to him again," Brian spat.

"I thought he was your friend," I said, confused.

He didn't answer, pulling two huge backpacks from a bush. "Here," he said, dropping one at my feet. "You can have my books. I can't carry them."

"I don't want your books," I said.

"Then leave them, or give them away, or throw them out, or burn them in the fireplace. I don't care what you do with them." He put the other backpack on. It reminded me of the time I met him, when his backpack looked so heavy I thought he'd fall on his back and be stuck like a turtle. "I have to go."

"Can I help?" I asked.

"I don't need help from anyone," he said.

"I could get you some food," I said. "You'll need money, too. I have a few hundred dollars at my house, you could have it if you want. I'll give you as much money as you need from my bank account." I pulled out my wallet. "Here's ten dollars. Take it. Just promise me that you won't go to New York. A lot of runaways go to New York and they get seriously messed up."

"I don't know where I'm going yet," he said softly.

"Come home with me," I said. "You don't have to stay long. I'll make a fire so you can warm up. I could make some soup or spaghetti if you're hungry. I'll help you figure out what to do."

"Sure," he said in a flat way. "Why not."

"Let me carry your backpack, it looks heavy," I said. He didn't stop me when I pulled the straps off his back. It was even heavier than it looked. I put the backpack with his books on my other shoulder so I

was carrying three backpacks including mine. If I fell, I'd be the one stuck like a turtle.

He followed me the whole way home without saying anything. I looked back to check on him a few times, but every time I did, he wouldn't look at me. "Is Jeremy home?" he asked when we got out of the woods. "He might call my dad."

"I'll check first," I said. I went inside and made sure the Porsche was gone. Brian was hiding in the bushes when I came back outside. "I think Jeremy went shopping, so we have an hour or two before he gets home." Brian followed me inside. "Are you hungry?"

"Yeah," he said, standing in the entryway.

He didn't move while I made a can of tomato soup and started a fire. I was pouring soup into a bowl when I noticed he was at the table, his head down on his arms. The teachers made us put our heads down like that in elementary school when we got too loud. He looked like a little kid. He swallowed the bowl of soup in five seconds and finished the whole bag of pretzels I gave him afterwards. "I guess you're hungry," I said.

"I haven't eaten since yesterday," he said. "There wasn't enough room for food in my backpack. I didn't want to buy anything because I was too afraid I'd get caught."

"You ran away yesterday?" I asked.

"Three days ago," he mumbled. "Do you have anything else to eat?"

"I'll make some spaghetti," I said. "If you ran away three days ago, how come the note was still there?"

"My dad's gone for a while," he said. "He's busy with something. He's so busy he doesn't care that I'm not answering the phone."

"Parents suck," I said. He didn't smile.

I put food in front of him until he finally couldn't eat anymore. He didn't want to talk while he ate. After he finished, we sat in front of the fireplace. He was so close to the flames I thought his clothes might catch. I kept feeling like I should say something, but nothing felt right and I didn't want to make things worse.

"I'm going to buy a tent and a bigger backpack, the kind that has a frame for camping," he said suddenly. "I'll find a nice spot deep in the woods and live there. It's almost spring, so it won't be as cold. I'll find

a creek so I have water and figure out something for food. I should get a fishing pole."

"I hate fishing so you can have mine," I said. "I could leave food in a secret place so you could get it whenever you wanted. I'll leave you money so you can buy other food because you'll probably get sick of fish."

"I hate fish," he said. It seemed like we should laugh, but we didn't.

Brian jumped up when the garage door started opening. "I gotta go," he whispered.

"No, wait," I whispered back. "Your dad doesn't know you're missing, right? So, you can stay here until he does. If your dad calls, you can sneak out." Brian looked panicked.

The door opened. "Nick, are you home?" Jeremy said.

"Yeah," I said. "Brian's here with me."

He came into the house with grocery bags. "Hey Brian, long time no see."

"Hi," Brian said, trying to look normal.

Jeremy looked at us sideways. "You two look like cats that swallowed the canary. What's going on?"

"Nothing," I said casually. He looked even more suspicious. "We're going to hang out upstairs. Can we get some pizza for dinner? Oh, and Brian's going to sleep over tonight."

"It's a school night," Jeremy said slowly. "Is your father ok with you staying?"

"His dad's not home," I said. "Brian's home alone for a couple of nights. I thought it'd be better if he stayed with us."

"Absolutely," Jeremy said, still suspicious. "Stay as long as you want. There's no need for you to stay alone. Why didn't you ask earlier?"

"I dunno," Brian mumbled.

"Let's go upstairs," I said to him. I had to tug on his arm to get him to follow me. We lugged the backpacks upstairs, Jeremy watching us the whole time.

I convinced Brian to call Mr. Humber after dinner. Brian wouldn't let me listen to the conversation, locking himself in the guest bedroom for over an hour. When he came out, his eyes were red. I didn't ask him what they talked about. I knew it was wrong, but I was jealous how Mr. Humber paid so much attention to Brian. I liked Mr. Humber and I wanted him to like me too.

"Do you think Jeremy could drive me home? I want to get some stuff," he said. I nodded, and a few minutes later we were in the van driving to his house. I followed Brian into the kitchen, his house dark and cold because the door was open.

"Can you help me?" he asked, pointing to the rock. I helped him take it outside to a big hole in the ground next to a small garden. It made me wonder how he got it inside by himself. We cleaned the dirt off the counter and washed it down the sink. He stuffed his note into his pocket, writing a new one on a piece of paper from a "To Do" pad stuck to the fridge with a magnet.

Dad,

I went to stay with Nick.

Brian

He put the note on the kitchen table and pulled a big bunch of money from his back pocket. "I gotta put this away," he said. I watched him go through the small living room into a door next to the stairs, putting the money into a dresser drawer. He went upstairs without looking at me, coming back a few minutes later wearing different clothes. "My clothes were smelly." I thought about asking if he changed his mind about running away, but it was obvious he did. If he didn't want me to know, he would've told me to wait in the van. I figured he was telling me without saying it out loud.

He didn't say anything on the way back, staring out the window. We went upstairs when we got home. "What do you want to do?" I asked.

"I'm tired," he yawned. "I didn't sleep much outside. It was too cold."

"You can have the bed," I said. "I'll get a sleeping bag for the floor."

"I'll have to go home when my dad gets back," he said.

"Where did he go? Is he on a business trip?"

"My dad doesn't go on business trips," Brian said. "He works at a candy factory." He went into the bathroom without explaining where his father was. I went to get the sleeping bag. He was sitting on the bed in his underwear when I got back. I sat next to him.

"My dad is staying at the hospital with my mom."

"Is your mom sick?" I asked, my stomach sinking.

"Sort of," he mumbled. "I was fighting with my dad. She got upset and had to go to the hospital. She'll probably be there for weeks, like the last time."

"Are you going to visit her?"

"My dad won't let me," he said. "He says I upset her."

"That's so unfair," I spat. "He won't let you see your own mom?" I couldn't find the right words to say how outraged I was. I punched the bed. "I'll bet it's him that upsets her, not you. He's the one who acts like a jerk."

"I feel like I'm in a cage," he said. "I hate my dad so much I want to run away, but I can't because I don't want to leave my mom alone with him. I have to do what he says even though he treats me like I'm stupid. Sometimes, I think about stabbing him with a kitchen knife. The idea of stabbing him makes me want to throw up, but I get such a vivid picture in my head I feel like I'm about to do it. I wish he'd have an accident at the factory or get in a car crash so it wouldn't be my fault. He's never going to let me do what I want. He says if he's paying for college, I have to follow his rules even if I'm not living at home. He'll make me pay him back afterwards when I'm working. I'll never get away from him." He squeezed the blanket with his fist so tight his fingers turned white.

I was furious with myself. I wasn't the kind of friend I should've been. He was my first true best friend. It made me miserable to see how unhappy he was. I learned in California that life was too short to spend

it being depressed. I wanted him to be happy. It was my responsibility to fix him. My mission. My quest.

I put my arm around his shoulder. "I'll help you," I said in a soft voice. His lower lip shook and his eyes overflowed with sadness. He seemed so small and helpless to me. I knew what to do. Maybe it wasn't the kind of thing you did with a friend, but I wanted to show him how much I cared.

I kissed him on the cheek.

He looked confused.

"Everything's going to be ok," I whispered and leaned in closer.

I couldn't stop shaking.

It was after midnight. My body ached from being held in the same position for hours. There was an annoying itch on my nose, but I didn't dare move. I would've stopped breathing if I could.

I couldn't tell if he was asleep. He was probably just as terrified to roll over as I was. He wouldn't want to see me and be reminded what we did.

What I did to him.

I never forced him to do anything and he never told me to stop. He let me kiss him on the lips. He let me suck on his neck. He didn't say anything when I took off my clothes. He looked away when I pulled off his underwear, but he didn't try to stop me. He didn't object when I started playing with him. He got hard right away. He gasped a little when I started to suck him. He only said something once.

"Wait. Stop. I'm going to. . ."

"That's the idea," I said.

He looked confused. "But I'll. . .in your mouth. . ."

I smiled. "That's the idea."

"Oh," he said.

I started again and he finished.

That didn't count as telling me to stop.

He didn't complain when I told him he didn't have to do anything. He rolled over onto his stomach when I asked. He didn't move while I

rubbed myself against his butt until I got off. When I was done, he rolled over and pulled the covers up without saying anything. He was still there, as naked as I was.

I could tell myself it wasn't that bad, but I knew the truth. I did a horrible thing to him. He didn't know anything about sex. He'd always know his first time wasn't with a girl. I *poisoned* him. The truth about why I did it wrapped its hands around my neck and choked me. Not to make him feel better. I did it because he turned me on. Jeremy's body never excited me. Brian's body, on the other hand. . .

I told him he was sexy.

Because he *was* sexy, even with his sunken chest and bony arms. I didn't know what made him seem sexy to me, only that he was. His dick was bigger than mine even though he was smaller and younger than me. He had a few hairs. He could make his own stuff even though I couldn't yet.

My heart skipped a beat when I heard the covers rustle. I heard him go into the bathroom, listened to the sound of his pee splashing in the toilet, heard the flush, and felt him get back into the bed. I held my breath.

"Nick," he whispered. "Are you awake?"

I didn't answer for a few seconds. "Yeah," I whispered back.

He was quiet for a minute.

"You could do it again if you wanted," he whispered.

I closed my eyes. I should apologize to him. I should tell him how horrible I felt. I should tell him I never meant to hurt him. I knew why he offered to let me do it again. He was afraid of losing his only friend. I couldn't do that to him.

My dick told my brain to shut the fuck up.

I rolled over and looked at him. "Are you sure?" I whispered. He nodded slightly.

I slid next to him, pushing my body against his.

"Best friends," he whispered.

Chapter 36

March 25, 1983

Jeremy parked in front of Brian's house. "Are you going to ring the doorbell?" he asked when I refused to budge.

"Just honk," I mumbled.

He rolled his eyes, imitating the same thing I did whenever he said something boneheaded. It made me annoyed. I wasn't the one being asinine right now. "I don't want to talk to that guy," he said. "If I honk, he might come outside. Go ring the doorbell."

I crossed my arms. "*You* ring it."

"Something wrong?" he asked gently. "You seem moody."

I relaxed a little. "If something was wrong I'd tell you," I said. I sighed and got out of the van, trudging to the front door. To certain death.

"My dad keeps a loaded shotgun under his bed," Brian told me one night after we did our thing. "I found it when I was seven. I knew what it was. I didn't touch it and I didn't play with it. I was so scared I didn't sleep all night. Somehow, he knew I found it. I don't know how he knows things like that, but he does. It was the only time I ever got spanked. We can't let my dad find out about the stuff we do. He'll kill us."

"Yeah," I said.

"You don't understand," he said. "He'll *really* kill us. He'll shoot us both in the head. He hates *fags*. He talks about it all the time."

"You mean he'd actually do it?" I said, shaking. Now I was the one who wasn't going to be able to sleep all night.

"Yes," he said. "I know he would. Promise me you'll never tell anyone about us. Ever."

I promised him as sincerely as I could, but I wasn't sure he believed me. I wanted to explain to him that he could trust me more than anyone else. It's not like I wanted anyone else to know I was doing it with my best friend. Besides, everything would be ruined if Jeremy found out I cheated on him. Besides that, I was an expert at keeping big secrets from everyone. And besides that, we weren't fags, we just fooled around with each other. But I couldn't tell him any of that, so the only thing I told him was that I swore to God, crossed my heart, and hoped to die some other way besides a shotgun.

I was about to push the bell when the door flew open. I almost peed in my pants, expecting the wrong end of a gun staring at me. Just his dad. Without his gun. "I thought I heard a car outside," he said so loud I winced. Brian's dad always talked too loudly. It made him sound stupid. "Brian's in his room getting his stuff together. You should give him a hand."

Not until later tonight.

Shit, why did I think something like that? I prayed he couldn't read my mind.

He clapped me on the shoulder hard enough to hurt and pushed me into the house. "How about a drink?" I pictured something brown, strong enough to strip paint from walls. After all, a drunk kid wouldn't be able to dodge if he was being used for target practice. I wondered if there was a certain prayer you were supposed to say before you died.

"I'm not thirsty," I mumbled. With or without permission I dashed for the stairs to Brian's room. He had the whole second floor to himself. It sounded impressive, but the second floor was only one small room. The stairs ended right in the middle so there wasn't much space for furniture. Brian didn't even have a door.

"Hey," Brian said. Clothes were tossed all over the place and his bed wasn't made. Brian's dad demanded everything in his house be perfectly clean. It was bad enough Brian made a mess, but his nose was buried in a book. Reading. *In the house.* He wasn't allowed to have books. If his father caught him with books, he'd throw them away. The empty bookshelf in the corner should've been proof, but it wasn't empty

anymore. The beat-up books from his backpack were mixed with new ones, filling the bookshelf until it was overflowing. Brian must've lost it. His twenty-sided die only went to nineteen.

"You got some new books?" I croaked.

"I used my birthday money," he said.

"I thought your dad took that away for college."

"He gave it back," he said. He'd probably explain later. He liked to talk afterwards. I wondered if it was something about being naked, like at the lake over the summer. I'd have to ask him, if I could ask something that embarrassing.

"We'd better go or we'll be late for the movie," I said.

I followed Brian down the stairs even though I thought it'd be safer to escape out the window. Brian's dad was watching sports on TV like he always did, holding a massive brick in one hand. He wasn't going to shoot us after all – he was going to bash in our heads. Something happened in the game that made him scream and throw the brick at the TV as hard as he could. I cringed, expecting the TV to explode, but the brick bounced off the screen. Like it was made of foam. Which it was. I started breathing again.

"Can you believe that idiot? It was a simple lay-up and that loser couldn't even scrape the rim. What kind of a moron coach puts in a third string player when they're only leading by five? I've got twenty bucks on these jokers, what was I thinking?" I was pretty sure he was talking about basketball, but in case I was wrong I just nodded. He put his beer on a folding table and retrieved his brick. "Maybe you boys should watch a while. You could learn something important."

"The movie starts soon," Brian said. "See you tomorrow."

"Don't forget, we have an appointment at two," his dad said, sitting back down. "I suppose you want some money."

"I have my own," Brian said sharply. "I don't need money from you." This was it. I was about to find out what it felt like to get shot. His father didn't turn around.

"Don't raise too much hell," he said.

"Let's go," Brian said to me. I didn't relax until we were safely in the van on our way to the movie theater. Somehow, everything had changed. His books were openly displayed on his shelf. He left his room

a mess. He had his birthday money back. His dad let him sleep over without a fight. He wasn't being treated like a baby any more. He had freedom. The whole week he stayed with us I told him he had to stand up to his dad. Maybe he did. Maybe they fought a battle and Brian won.

I felt like I had a part in making that happen, which made me glow inside.

<p style="text-align:center">～✕ ✕～</p>

"What a zoo," Jeremy muttered.

I made a noise that was supposed to sound like an elephant. It sounded more like one whose trunk was cut off and had a bad cold. "Are you saying that kids are animals?" I said.

"Absolutely," he said. "Dirty, messy, smelly animals."

Right then, Brian let out a huge fart to make sure we all knew exactly how smelly kids could be. Farts were the funniest thing back in second grade, but as I got older they became less funny. I laughed like I did when I was seven. "Geez!" Jeremy said, holding his nose. "Couldn't you wait until you got outside?"

Jeremy slammed on the gas, the van lurching forward into an opening in the traffic. It really was a zoo at the dollar theater. Teenagers drove crazily, couples kissed in the middle of the road, packs of girls floated around in large clumps, and boys skateboarded on the ledge doing insane tricks. The old Nick hated this kind of chaos. He would've taken one look and told Jeremy to find a nice quiet restaurant full of adults. But I wasn't the old Nick anymore. The wild party atmosphere looked like fun. I couldn't stop bouncing in my seat. I could tell Brian was uncomfortable because he was more like the old Nick. I wanted to show him that he didn't need to be scared. I wanted him to have fun like I did. I spotted two of my friends from drama club standing in front of the theater.

"We're getting out here," I said, opening the door before he slammed on the brakes. "Pick us up when the movie's over." I pulled Brian out of the van with me.

"Pick you up where?" he shouted. Too late, I was already closing the door. He'd figure it out. Brian followed as I weaved my way through the crowd.

"Hey guys," I said, coming up from the side. "What's up?"

"Piano man!" Sean said, holding up his hand for a high five, which I returned energetically.

"This is my friend Brian," I said, moving back a little until he was standing next to me.

"Cool, any friend of piano man is a friend of ours," Sean said, holding up his hand for another high five. Brian slapped Sean's hand weakly.

"Did you see Michelle tonight?" Leon said. "Oh. . .my. . .god, she's wearing this hot pink skirt that comes up so high you can nearly see everything, and she's got this black top, I think I saw it at Macy's, perfect for her shape, and she's got a great shape." I nodded. Leon fascinated me. He always went on about how some girl or other was hot, like everyone else did. At the same time, he knew everything there was to know about girl's clothes, he hung around with girls, he had girls for friends, he acted more like a girl than a boy, and he had a funny way of talking that screamed he was gay. I wanted to ask him, but I was worried what would happen if I was wrong. He'd be insulted, then he'd figure out what I was, and then he'd blab it all over school because he was the biggest gossip who ever existed.

I felt a tap on my shoulder. "Piano man," she said.

"Hi, Ana," I said. Was everyone going to call me that?

"You sounded fantastic in rehearsal today," she said. "I loved what you did with Suppertime."

"I made it jazzy," I said. Actually, Jeremy made it jazzy. He changed the chords and showed me different rhythms to make it interesting. "I thought you sang well on the doctor song too."

"Thanks," she said brightly. "You should play something for the talent show. You'd definitely win first prize."

"I only play classical stuff," I said with a shrug. "No one likes that."

"Doesn't matter. Everyone in drama club would vote for you. You're *sooo* much better than the girl we had last year." Another girl

called her name. "I'll save you a seat inside." I stood paralyzed while she gave me a quick girl hug and ran off.

"Damn, you're smooth," Sean laughed.

"What do you mean, me and her?" I said. No way. She was in eighth grade. Everyone knew eighth graders did *not* date seventh graders. It was one of those "universally acknowledged truths" from the first line of some book Mr. Humber talked about. On top of that, she was cool and popular. She had a line of bigger, older, and much cooler boys than me waiting. Not to mention I didn't have any business dating girls.

"You should totally ask her out," Leon added. "You'd make a cute couple." I shrugged to look like I didn't care.

"Nick!" Everyone seemed to want to talk to me today. Roger was barreling right for me from the parking lot. The captain of the track team didn't mix well with my drama club friends. Like milk and orange juice. Putting them in the same place caused a stomachache. "Did you hear about Kevin?"

"Yeah, he did something to his foot skateboarding," I said.

"Broke his ankle in two places," Roger said. "Out for the season. Matt flagged his math test, so he's benched until his grades come back up. That means you're it. Ready to run?"

"Me?" I'd only been on the team for two weeks. I wasn't supposed to *actually* run a race.

"Coach said you looked promising. We're training Monday before school. Be there at six-thirty. Later." I waited until Roger left to groan. Six-thirty? *In the morning?*

Sean laughed. "You're fucked. Let me know if the sun comes up that early."

By the time we got our tickets, popcorn, and drinks, at least ten other people called me piano man. Some of them weren't even in drama club. I imagined a secret bulletin board somewhere in the school that everyone knew about except me, with a note taped to it telling the whole world to call me piano man. At least it wasn't a bad nickname.

"Where should we sit?" I asked Brian.

"We should sit by that girl who likes you since she's saving a seat," he said.

526

"She does *not* like me," I fired back. "She's popular and I do stuff like play D&D."

"You're popular too, ever since you beat up Tommy Walker," he said. "I like sitting up front. The screen takes up your whole peripheral vision so it gives you the feeling like you're in the movie."

"Per what vision?"

"Besides, everyone in the back rows are necking," he said. He was right. I followed him to a couple of seats in the middle of the second row, balancing our popcorn buckets on our laps. The coming attractions were starting, but I was more interested to see who was at the movie and who wasn't. None of my other friends would be here because of Chris. He was grounded *again*, this time for throwing water balloons at moving cars. Everyone else was grounded too even though they didn't throw any, which wasn't fair but it was how parents worked. Chris told me his mom threatened to send him to military school, but she'd said that a million times so he didn't believe her. Even though he was my friend, part of me hoped his mother would send him away. Chris was good at getting everyone else in trouble. Besides, the only way I got Brian to come to the movie was to promise Chris wouldn't be here. I felt bad thinking things would be easier if Chris was gone.

"Is everyone going to be quiet when the movie starts?" Brian asked, slouching down in his seat.

"Probably not," I said.

"Why do people go if they're not going to watch the movie?"

"To hang out with friends," I explained.

"That makes no sense." He poked around inside the bucket on his lap. "The popcorn is stale. You have some in your hair."

I brushed my hair out with my fingers. "Is it gone?"

"Yeah." Popcorn sailed over his shoulder and landed on his leg. "Now they're throwing it at me, too."

I was going to tell whoever did it to knock it off, but then I figured out what was going on. "They're not throwing it just at you, they're throwing it at everyone." Popcorn was flying around the theater like little missiles. I grabbed a few from my bucket and threw them randomly.

"What are you doing?" Brian whispered harshly.

"Having fun," I said. Roger was sitting three rows back. I took aim and hit him right in the forehead. "Score!" I shouted.

"Hey!" he shouted. I waved at him and threw another piece. "You're so dead." He fired popcorn at me like a machine gun. His friends joined in. I had to spend all my time ducking behind my seat to keep from getting hit.

"Are you going to help me or not?" I said to Brian.

"We're going to get in trouble," he said with his arms crossed.

"It's fun," I said, picking up a piece and dropping it on his stomach.

"Now you're picking on me too?" he said.

"I'm not picking on you," I said. "Everyone's doing it. Besides, the stuff tastes like Styrofoam. I want you to have fun." I threw a handful in his face. He glared at me, furious. I went too far.

"Sorry," I said softly.

Without any warning, he dumped his entire bucket over my head. Roger and his friends cheered and clapped. I pulled the bucket off, trying to scrape the greasy bits out of my hair. Without thinking, I dumped my bucket over his head. More cheers and claps. Brian spit a few pieces out of his mouth. I was worried I went *way* too far now.

"You've got popcorn in your hair," he said, his eyes narrow.

"You too," I pointed out. "That was fun."

"Yeah, it was," he said back.

I smiled. He was going to be ok.

Jeremy offered to take us out for pizza and ice cream after the movie, but Brian said he wasn't hungry. Brian was always hungry enough to eat a whole pizza by himself. He was seriously upset about something, but I didn't understand what. I asked him when the movie was over if he liked it. He told me it was the best movie he'd ever seen, but he said it in a horribly depressed way.

We went straight upstairs when we got home. "Jeremy is going to take me to opening night of the new Star Wars movie," I said. "Do you want to come with us?"

"I guess," he said with a shrug.

"You still have a lot of popcorn in your hair," I said, picking it out.

"You smell like fake butter," he said.

"Gross. I'm going to take a shower. You should take one, too."

"Yeah," he said, looking away.

I pulled my shirt over my head. "Let's take one together so we can make sure to get all the popcorn out."

"Sure," he said, but he didn't move. I took off the rest of my clothes. He let me grab his hand and lead him to the bathroom. I looked in the mirror while he undressed.

"Fucking popcorn got everywhere," I said. "I just picked a piece out of my butt." I giggled but he didn't laugh. When the water was hot, I held his hand while we got in.

When Jeremy and I did it, we did a lot of stuff besides the actual sex. Stuff like kissing, cuddling, back rubs, tickling, touching, and just messing around. When I thought about it, the extra stuff took a lot longer than the actual sex. Jeremy told me all of it was sex, from the moment the first piece of clothing came off until one of us was snoozing. I didn't agree. The other stuff was about love, not sex.

That's why doing it with Brian took less than five minutes.

We were all business, none of that lovey-dovey side show. We didn't love each other. We were friends, that's all, so we went straight to the good part. Our routine was sort of like how things were at the beginning with Jeremy. I sucked him, and then I got myself off in a way that involved his body without making him do anything. I didn't want to go all the way because I knew it would hurt him and he wasn't ready for that. Brian asked me a couple times if I wanted him to suck me. I knew he wasn't into it the same way as me so I told him no. I let him do it once, but he was terrible at it.

I didn't want to wait. As soon as we were in the shower, I was on my knees with my hands on his butt. He finished quickly and silently like he always did. He leaned against the wall so I could rub myself against him. That didn't take long either. I smiled at him. He looked miserable.

"What's wrong?" I asked.

"If you were Elliott, would you go with ET?"

529

"I don't know," I said, picking popcorn from his hair. "Could I come back whenever I wanted?"

"No," he said. "If you went, you could never come back."

"Then I wouldn't go," I said.

"Why not?" he said.

"I'd miss my friends," I said. "What about you?"

"I would go," he said. "I wouldn't want to come back. I used to think about it a lot. I've wanted to go into space since I was a little kid. It's got to be better. In space, I think I'd belong. Would you miss me if I went?"

"Of course I'd miss you. You're my best friend."

"Before I met you, I wouldn't have missed anyone," he said. "But I'd miss you too, a lot. I don't understand why you want to be friends with me. I'm not fun to be around. I don't fit in with the other kids. I don't like having popcorn fights in movie theaters. I talk funny and I look funny and I act funny. I'm scared you're going to stop liking me. Then I won't have any friends at all."

"I'll never stop being your friend," I said. "Who else would run around with me in the woods yelling lines from Lord of the Rings? I don't care if you talk funny or act funny or look funny, none of those things matter. I don't care what other people think. You're my best friend and you'll always be my best friend because you know what it means to be a best friend. That's more important than anything else."

"You're the best Sam this Frodo could ever want," he whispered.

I didn't know why he was talking about our scenes. I hugged him anyway.

Chapter 37

April 5, 1983

Jeremy wouldn't stop shaking me. "Wakey, wakey, wakey!" I pulled my pillow over my head. "It's quarter to six. You're going to be late."

"I'm too tired," I moaned. He yanked the covers off, leaving me naked in the freezing air. "Hey!"

"You instructed me to make absolutely positively sure you got up in the morning to run with the track team. I'm only following orders." He spanked me, hard enough to sting. "Don't make me get the ice cubes."

"You wouldn't dare," I mumbled.

"Try me," he said, spanking me even harder. He pulled me over to the edge of the bed and sat me upright. "Let's get you dressed and get some food into you." I slumped over but he pulled me back up. "You stayed up too late last night."

"I had to do my. . ." I yawned. ". . .science project."

"You should've been in bed by nine. You're a growing boy, you need your sleep."

"That's what I'm trying to tell you," I said. I stuck my arms up like a little kid. He put my running shirt on for me. "I had rehearsal yesterday and a lot of homework so I couldn't get started until nine. I didn't have time to practice either."

"Lift up," he said. I stuck my legs out so he could slide my underwear on. "You haven't made any real progress on the Chopin or the Bach in a month because you haven't had enough time to practice. What little

time you get on the piano is taken up by the show." He slid my shorts on. "We've got to do something about this. You should be practicing at least two or three hours a day."

"I could skip school two days a week," I said. He laughed. "I'm serious. Every day I run out of time."

"Let's figure it out together," he said. "I know you like doing the play and I'm all for you being on the track team, but you're losing focus on your music. You've got to make it happen while you're young. If you're not in a conservatory by fifteen it's too late."

"I know, I know," I said.

"I'll get you one of those little pocket calendars," he said. I rolled my eyes at such a dorky idea. He put my socks on and motioned for me to get up so I could pull up my shorts and underwear. "Awake yet?"

"Yeah. Thanks for getting me up."

"I only wake you up for selfish reasons," he said. "It's fun, and whenever you go running in the morning I can expect an especially energetic roll in the hay at night." I punched him in the shoulder.

Breakfast was always the same when I went running – three packets of maple and brown sugar oatmeal with extra raisins and bananas mixed in. I drank only one big glass of water because I didn't want to get cramps. By the time I finished breakfast, I was itching to run. I was going to break a nine-minute mile today, I could feel it. Not that nine minutes was good – it was a guaranteed embarrassing last place finish. When I started running, I thought I was already good at it. I thought I could run fast for as long as I wanted. Ha ha ha. I could barely finish a mile back then at a pace that put me dead last on the team. Running was both harder and easier than I thought it was going to be. Harder because there was so much to keep track of, like correct form and breathing. Easier because it turned out to be less painful than I thought.

"I'll practice for two hours today after rehearsal, I promise," I said to him on the way to school. It would mean another late night because I had a lot of assignments due before spring break. He was right – it was important. I was going to be a concert pianist, so I had to practice.

Had to. I wasn't sure why I didn't *want* to.

Chris grabbed my arm in the hall before English class, yanking me so hard I almost fell over. "What gives?" I yelled, jerking away from him.

"You tell me what gives!" he spat. "Today's the first time I've been allowed to play in weeks. Daniel says you're not coming?"

"I can't. I've got rehearsal until 5:30, I have to practice piano, and I have to study." He stared at me like he didn't know what I meant. "You know, the social studies test? And science projects are due at the end of the week."

"Since when do you think I give two shits about a stupid social studies test or some dumb science project?" he growled. "Fine, since you're so *busy* you can skip today and come tomorrow."

"Roger is making us work out in the weight room after school. I won't get out until five." He folded his arms. "Before you ask, I can't come on Thursday because I have rehearsal again."

"Let me get this straight. You can't come over until the sleepover on Friday?"

"I can't sleep over. I have the track meet Saturday morning."

"That's not until later in the morning," he said like he scored a point.

"I'm not on the bench, I have to run," I said. "If I stay up all night playing, I'm going to suck."

"Fine," he said. "You know what? Don't bother coming again. I'll kill off your character. We don't need you."

"That's not fair! I like playing. It's not like I'm blowing you off. This stuff is important!"

"Sure, everything is more important than your friends. Except you don't have friends anymore. Go sit at a different lunch table from now on."

"You're such an asshole," I muttered.

"Fuck you," he said with his little annoying smile.

"Fuck you, too," I spat back. If we weren't in school, we'd probably be punching each other.

"Is there a problem, gentlemen?" Mr. Humber boomed. "Certainly, I did not catch a whiff of language unbecoming to students in honors level English class."

"No problem," Chris muttered. "See ya around." He knocked into my shoulder on his way into the room. I barely kept from giving him the finger.

"Mr. Welles, is everything alright?"

"Perfect," I muttered. "How am I supposed to be in two places at the same time?"

"I would suggest a very large axe," Mr. Humber said.

"I'm serious," I said, rolling my eyes.

"Well, as long as you are *serious*," he said. "I believe one of the most important lessons in life is to realize there will always be enough demands on your time to more than fill every moment of every day. The secret is to spend your time on the demands that matter and ignore the ones that don't."

"But how am I supposed to know what matters if everything's important?"

He was about to answer when the bell rang. "At this particular moment, your decision is simple. The demand on your time that matters the most is my class." I groaned.

"Ladies and gentlemen," he started, like he always did. "Yesterday, we frittered away far too much time discussing how your short story assignments will be evaluated. I would like to dedicate our time today to a review of the tools at your disposal to transform a mere story into a work of literary art. What better place to begin than at the beginning. Mr. Welles, if you would please read the sentence on the board aloud."

I knew he'd call on me after what happened in the hallway. "Call me Ishmael."

"As some of you may be aware, this is the first line of the classic revenge tale by Herman Melville, Moby Dick." Scott snickered for a tiny fraction of a second, but that was all it took. "Mr. Epstein, would you care to enlighten us as to the subject of Moby Dick? I'm sure you have an appropriate response which avoids any implication this novel is pornographic in nature." The entire class laughed.

"It's about a whale," he said, barely able to keep a straight face.

"What exactly is about a whale?" Mr. Humber asked.

"Moby Dick," Scott spat out. We all laughed.

"Thank you," Mr. Humber said. "While the story is ostensibly about the titular whale, on a more fundamental level the tale. . ." The door suddenly opened. "Mr. Richards, what a pleasant surprise. We were just discussing whales. Would you care to join us?"

"No thanks, maybe next time," he said. Mr. Richards was the kind of principal who believed the spelling rule about how your principal was your pal. He tried pretty hard to be friendly, but he always came off as dorky. "I'm sorry class, I need to borrow Mr. Humber. Mrs. Golecki will be your substitute for the time being."

For a moment, it seemed like Mr. Humber didn't know what to say. Mr. Humber *always* knew what to say. "Ladies and gentlemen, please afford Mrs. Golecki the same attention and respect I expect from you at all times." He left quickly.

Mrs. Golecki sat down at Mr. Humber's desk and looked through the papers for a moment. "Put your notebooks away, we're going to have an impromptu essay."

"Mr. Humber said we wouldn't have to do any more impromptus until we were done with our stories," Parker whined. We all murmured and nodded.

"I see," she said. "In that case, find some quiet work. . ."

The door flew open. "Ken, please," Mr. Richards said from outside the room. Mr. Humber came back in.

"Thank you, Mrs. Golecki, I'll take over from here," he said. Mrs. Golecki looked from Mr. Humber to Mr. Richards and back again before getting up from the desk. Mr. Humber didn't wait for her to leave. "Let's put this disruption aside so we can focus on the matter at hand. As I was saying, the opening line of Moby Dick establishes Ishmael as the narrator, but is that all it does? After all, how could it do more? It's a mere three words in length. But why those three words? Why not 'My name is Ishmael'? Listen to those three words again spoken differently. Call me. . .Ishmael. Do they suggest an alternate meaning? What do you think, Mr. Hanley?"

"Umm, I. . ." Brian stuttered. "You make it sound like he made up his name. Like he's lying."

"Precisely," Mr. Humber said, pacing in front of the room. I noticed Mr. Richards looking through the window in the door. "It's intriguing,

a narrator lying about his name. If he lies from the very first sentence, how can we trust anything he says for the rest of the novel? From that point on, it's up to the discerning reader to determine what is truth and what is fiction. As the novel unfolds with the story of Captain Ahab, of a life wasted in the hollow pursuit of revenge against the whale that took his leg, the reader will always have doubts about the truth. Through that doubt comes the understanding that life is very short and you have to make the most of every moment. . ."

He stopped. Right in the middle of a sentence. Like his brain left his body completely and wandered off somewhere else in the universe. He stood there for what felt like forever.

"Mr. Humber?" one of the girls asked.

He came back into his body. I could tell immediately that he wasn't the same Mr. Humber. "I apologize," he said in a very soft voice. "I find myself unable to continue. Please excuse me."

He turned toward the windows, stared for a moment, and turned around to walk slowly to the door. The unsure way he walked was nothing like his usual walk. He went into the hall, closing the door softly behind him. Everyone erupted into confused chatter, all of us looking at each other for an explanation. Nobody had one. My friends were no help. Brian looked like a robot whose switch was flipped off. Parker scribbled in his notebook. Chris put his feet up on his desk. I scowled when he threw a paper airplane that landed on Mr. Humber's desk. That would be ok in any other class under the same circumstances. Not Mr. Humber's.

One, two, three minutes ticked by without a word from Mr. Humber. I felt nervous in a classroom without a teacher. "Someone should find out what's going on," one of the girls said. Brian seemed like the best choice to me because he knew Mr. Humber from their lunches. But that was before he ran away. He meant it when he swore never to be friends with Mr. Humber again. I shuddered when I realized I was next. I was the piano man in drama club. I had no plan when I jerked up, walked to the door, and looked through the window. Mr. Humber was leaning against the lockers, his hands buried in his face.

The entire class crowded around me. "What's going on?" someone whispered.

"I don't know," I whispered back. "It looks like he's crying."

"Maybe you should call the office," someone else whispered, like I was in charge. It seemed like a good idea at first. Mrs. Golecki would come back and everything would go back to normal. Then I realized Mr. Humber would probably get in trouble for leaving us alone, maybe big trouble. No way I was going to get him in trouble.

"I'm going. . ." I realized it was silly to whisper. "I'm going to find out what's going on. Can you guys move back so I can open the door?" I didn't expect anyone to listen to me, but they cleared a path without resisting. I opened the door wide enough to slide through, closing it behind me. The hallway was empty besides the two of us.

"Mr. Humber?" I asked, taking a couple steps toward him.

"Please return to class, Mr. Welles," he said in a soft voice that didn't belong to Mr. Humber.

"Are you ok?" I asked without moving. I wanted to slap myself. Of course he wasn't ok, what a stupid question.

"I need a moment," he said in that same quiet voice.

"What's wrong?" I asked, taking a few steps towards him. Another dumb question. As though a teacher would tell me what going on. He looked up at me, blinking.

"Someone very important to me. . ." He trailed off, but he didn't need to finish because I already understood. I felt the same way I did at Amy's funeral. I didn't know who died and still I wanted to cry. Aunt Rachel explained it to me, that I was crying for Jeremy, not for Amy. This was different. Mr. Humber was my teacher, even if he was my favorite teacher ever.

"I'm sorry," I said, standing right in front of him. I worked so hard to learn the right thing to say was "I'm sorry for your loss" and I screwed it up. He looked like he was about to start bawling. I had to do something. Not because I knew him from class, drama club, and book club. Because of how nice he was to Brian. Because of how he told me he was glad I clobbered Tommy. Because he was the only teacher I ever knew who really *cared*. I hugged him before I could think about what I was doing.

He hugged me back. A real hug, tight enough to be almost uncomfortable and more than a little weird once I realized I was hugging a teacher. The whole class was probably watching us right now.

"I'm sorry," he said when he let go. "That was inappropriate."

"It's ok," I said. "I don't think it's inappropriate at all. People need hugs when this kind of thing happens."

"You're wise beyond your years, Mr. Welles." He blew his nose into a tissue. "I thought I'd be able to keep teaching, but Mr. Richards was right. Still, I think I'd rather be with my class. It's going to be a very difficult day. My friend who passed away was a teacher here until last November. News will spread quickly. My students are going to need me, and I'm going to need them. It was very kind of you to come looking for me."

"I was worried," I said. "We were all worried. Everyone likes you. You're the best teacher I ever had. Everyone else thinks so too."

"You're going to make me start crying again," he said with a smile. "I truly admire you for being so compassionate."

He admired *me*?

"I owe my students an explanation," he said, straightening up his shoulders. Everyone scrambled to get back in their seats when we went back into the classroom. "Would you kindly get my chair and put it in the middle by the blackboard?" he said to me. I nodded.

He faced the class. "I'd like to re-arrange the room into a circle," he said. Nobody moved. Putting desks in a circle was elementary school stuff. I put his chair in front and moved my desk. As soon as I started, everyone moved too. I wasn't sure I liked having everyone look at me to figure out what to do. He waited until we made a lopsided square, sitting backwards on his chair.

"No more lecture," he started. "No classroom, no teacher, no students. For the rest of the day, we're twenty-seven human beings. I apologize for leaving you. I found I was unable to hold myself together. When I was called out of class, I learned from Mr. Richards that a close friend of mine passed away. Some of you may know Mrs. Sheffield, she used to be a teacher here." A few kids gasped.

"How many of you have lost someone you cared for?" he asked. A lot of hands went up. "That many? You're so young. I count myself fortunate I've experienced loss only a few times in my life."

"What happened to her?" Jenny asked.

"Cancer," he said. "Cancer is an insidious disease. In her case, she showed no signs or symptoms until it had spread throughout her body."

"I thought only old people got cancer," Jason said.

"You're so stupid," Jenny spat. "My cousin died from leukemia when he was fourteen."

"Jenny, please," Mr. Humber said. We all noticed he called Jenny by her first name. "There's no need to put anyone down. Cancer can and does strike anyone, young and old, healthy and sick, boy and girl. I'm very sorry about your cousin."

"He was sick from the time he was a baby," Jenny said without her usual snootiness. "I didn't know him very well."

"My baby brother died of SIDS when I was five," Jonathan said.

"SIDS is when infants stop breathing for no apparent reason," Mr. Humber said, answering my question. "No one understands why. I'm very sorry, Jonathan. What about you, Scott? I saw your hand was raised."

"My grandpa," Scott said in a very serious voice that didn't belong to the class clown. "Last year."

"This is stupid," Chris burst out. Everyone stared at him. "Why do we have to talk about this? It's sick!"

"What's wrong with you?" Daniel said.

"Shut up!" Scott yelled at Chris.

"Who did you lose?" Mr. Humber asked Chris.

"Who cares?" Chris said. "I don't care if someone dies. They're dead, worm food, rotting corpses with bugs crawling in and out of their eye sockets."

Scott jumped out of his seat. Chris finally crossed the line and was about to become worm food with bugs crawling in and out of his eye sockets. Scott's best friend David jumped up too. I thought he was going to help Scott pummel Chris into the ground. Instead, David grabbed Scott, pinning his arms behind his back. Everyone screamed at Chris,

who leaned back in his chair with that patented annoying smile painted on his face.

"Everyone settle down!" Mr. Humber boomed. He shocked everyone into silence. "David, please accompany Scott to the restroom."

"Yeah," David said quietly. He let go and Scott ran out of the room. Mr. Humber squatted in front of Chris' desk, speaking very quietly in his ear. I watched the smile disappear from Chris' face. He turned away. Mr. Humber touched his shoulder. Chris jerked away so hard he almost tipped his whole desk over.

"You don't understand anything!" he screamed, taking off for the door, slamming it so hard I thought the glass would break. Mr. Humber stood up. He didn't look angry.

"What a jerk!" Jenny spat, her snootiness back to normal.

"People grieve in different ways," Mr. Humber said. "Some people like to talk. Others bury it deep down inside. Some pretend nothing happened. Some become angry. I think it's important to let people grieve in their own way, not the way we think they should. I hope you can find it in your hearts to forgive Chris for his outburst." I couldn't believe Chris pulled that kind of shit without getting trouble. Mr. Humber picked up the phone to the office. "I have a distraught student. . ." was all I heard before he went in the hall.

I went to Andy since he sat closest to Chris. "Did you hear what Mr. Humber told him?"

"I don't care what Mr. Humber said to that asshole," Daniel muttered before Andy could say anything. "He crossed the line. I don't want to talk to that shithead again for the rest of my life. David should've let Scott bash his head in. I would've helped." Andy shrugged. Parker was still scribbling in his notebook. I couldn't tell what Jonathan was thinking, nobody could. Brian was still shut down. Maybe he was reciting memorized lines from books – he told me he did that sometimes. Nobody else gave me any hint what I should think or how I should feel.

Mr. Humber came back into the room. "Mr. Richards intended to wait for lunch before making an announcement, but word is spreading quickly. Classes have been canceled for the rest of the day. You'll be

able to leave before the final bell provided an adult is available to sign you out. The guidance staff and teachers are. . ." He was interrupted by a loud buzzer followed by Mr. Richards asking all teachers to contact the office. Scott came back into the room with David. Mr. Humber put his arm around Scott's shoulders, talking softly to him.

I felt a powerful desire. I wanted to be the one talking to Scott. I wanted to make him feel better. I wanted to help him. I didn't care that I had no idea how. The feeling was overwhelming. Mr. Humber called me compassionate. It was the perfect word. I wanted to be compassionate. I *needed* to be compassionate.

Mr. Humber walked Scott back to his seat. I went to Scott's desk. He looked at me suspiciously.

"I'm very sorry about your grandpa," I said softly. I thought about hugging him, but boys didn't hug other boys. I touched his shoulder a little – that seemed like enough without going too far. Scott looked like he had no idea what to say or do.

"I'm sorry, too," David said, doing the same thing I did.

Before I knew what was happening, everyone in the class was standing around Scott, telling him they were sorry, boys shaking hands and girls giving him hugs. I couldn't have dreamed something like this was possible. Kids who didn't like each other came together to make someone feel better. I doubted I'd ever see something like it again. I looked over my shoulder at Mr. Humber, wondering if he thought I did the right thing. He was smiling and blinking hard to keep from crying.

"Come on, Daniel," I said, running after him.

"No way," he said without stopping.

"Everyone else is coming."

"Only because you talked them into it. That shithead's not worth it."

"He is too worth it," I said, grabbing him on the shoulder to slow him down. He shook me off. "You guys have been friends for almost

five years, right? Doesn't that mean anything? Aren't you supposed to stick by your friends?"

He stopped and turned around. "Only if they stick by you."

"I don't get it. How did he not stick by you?"

"I don't want to explain," he muttered. He stared at me. "Fine. I'll go. Just back off." I took a step back when he stared at me in a scary way. I decided it was better not to ask any more questions.

I was the new kid, the one who wasn't part of their group all through elementary school. Still, I was the one who had to talk them into going to Chris' house after school. They even wanted me to be the one who rang the doorbell. It shouldn't have been my job. Someone who knew him longer than me should be pulling his friends together. That's what I thought at first, but I realized I was probably Chris' closest friend. Maybe I was his only real friend. Maybe the rest of them had put up with him for so long it became a habit. Earlier today I hoped he would get sent away, but now I felt sad for him.

I rang the bell. Chris sneered at me when he opened the door. "What the hell do you think you're doing here?" he said.

"Aren't we going to play?" I asked.

"I thought you were too *busy* for your friends," he said.

"Everything got canceled," I explained.

"So, you only came because you've got nothing better to do," he spat. "We're the last thing on your list. Who said I'd even let you play anyway?"

Daniel pushed his way through and without any warning punched Chris in the chin. I wasn't surprised that Daniel and Chris would fight, but I thought there'd be more of a buildup. Chris shook it off and shoved Daniel hard in the chest. "What the fuck?" he shouted. "You want to fight?"

"I'm going to kick your ass," Daniel muttered, charging Chris again.

"Guys, stop," I said. They ignored me, throwing random punches at each other. After a few seconds, Chris grabbed Daniel and pulled him to the ground, turning it into a wrestling match. We stared at them while they grunted and rolled around the hallway. No name calling, no taunting, just a desire to murder. I thought I should stop it before one of them got hurt for real, but I felt paralyzed.

Until Andy started giggling.

I stared at him. We all stared at him. Andy broke into full out laughter so loud that Chris and Daniel noticed. They stopped fighting and stared at him. Andy held up one finger like he wanted us to wait until he caught his breath.

"You guys should get a room," he said, making kissing noises.

Everyone burst out laughing. I thought us laughing would make Daniel and Chris even more furious, but they started laughing too, pushing away from each other. Andy started chanting. "Daniel and Chrissy sitting in a tree, f-u-c-k-i-n-g." It took five minutes for us to calm down.

Parker was the first one to break the weird silence that comes after laughing. "Can we play now?"

"Yeah, let's play," Chris said. Daniel held out his hand and helped Chris stand up. Like nothing happened. Like someone erased that part of the tape and recorded normal stuff on it.

What happened at Chris' house that afternoon wasn't how I pictured it'd be like. I thought it would go more like it did at school. A lot of us stayed in Mr. Humber's class even though there was an assembly in the cafeteria. All the normal rules of school were thrown out the window. Kids were allowed to wander around the building, assignments were pushed off until after spring break, and tests were canceled. The lines between teachers and students didn't seem so clear anymore, everyone hugging and crying together. A lot of older kids came in and out of Mr. Humber's room, girls crying and boys looking somber. We did nothing but talk endlessly, but I didn't realize how time flew by until the bell rang.

Scott talked about his grandfather – how they used to go to baseball games, how they'd play practical jokes on his dad, and how he died without any warning from a heart attack. Other kids told stories about grandparents and great-grandparents, the favorite baby sitter who died in a car crash, and the uncle who committed suicide. I talked a little about Amy, but mostly I listened. Everyone listened, and for once, everyone cared. Mr. Humber told Scott he was sorry for starting the whole conversation, but Scott looked at him like he was crazy. "This was the best day of school I've ever had," he said.

I supposed talking was the grown-up way of doing it, and I supposed since I liked it that I must be growing up. At the same time, we were still kids. When the grown-ups weren't around, we did it our own way. There was a fight, we cracked up, and then we played the funniest, silliest, stupidest game of D&D that was ever played, complete with +9 farts and roomfuls of naked women with four boobs each (five if you counted the extra one in the back). We didn't talk. We wanted to have fun. That's what friends did.

Mr. Humber told me something that stuck in my head. "You asked me a question earlier about how to determine what's important. I believe there isn't one answer that works for everyone. Some people measure their lives in the things they accomplish, some in how much money they make, some in how many things they've collected, and some in how many friends they've made. I've chosen to measure my life in how many other lives I've touched. No one can say what's right or wrong. The only thing that matters is finding your own happiness. If something doesn't make you happy, then it's not important." He smiled. "Except homework."

Sitting at the table with my friends, I felt like I did something important.

<p style="text-align:center">～✕ ✕～</p>

"That was amazing," Jeremy purred, kissing me on the neck. "You've never done that before."

"It felt like the right time," I said. His fingertips brushed my chest. "How do you feel?"

"Me? I'm so in love I can't hold it all in."

"Well duh, I can see that. A whole bunch already leaked out." He laughed when I grabbed him down there. "Uh oh, seems like there's still more."

"Enough, enough," he said, but he didn't push my hand away.

"It's not healthy to hold it in. We have to get every last drop out. Doctor's orders."

"Can I at least have an intermission?" he said.

"Two minutes, but then we'd better get started. It's an *emergency.*" I tugged on his dick and then scooted off the bed to go to the bathroom. He pinched my butt.

"You've got the cutest little butt," he said.

"No, I don't," I said, trying to sound insulted. "I have a cute *ass.*"

"Your butt is cute," he said. "Your *ass* is hot."

"Then kiss it," I said, wiggling it at him. He gave it a big, wet sloppy kiss that made me giggle.

"What's gotten into you?" he said as I wiggled my way to the bathroom.

"I told you that I had a weird day at school."

"I can't imagine this level of weird," he said. "Not that I'm complaining."

I winked at him and closed the door. I rummaged around in the cabinet beneath the sink until I found the mouthwash. If Jeremy and Brian were two different kinds of cheese, Brian was the mild kind while Jeremy was the moldiest, stinkiest cheese ever. I let the mouthwash burn in my mouth before I spit it out and then did it again, just to make sure. Even with the horrible taste, I never regretted sucking him. I didn't regret any of the other things I did for the first time tonight. It felt like the right time to do the dirtiest, grossest, scuzziest sex things imaginable.

Adults loved to ask kids impossible questions. The one I used to hate the most was what I wanted to be when I grew up. When I was little, there were only a few choices – policeman, fireman, airplane pilot, and teacher (but that was just for girls). None of them sounded interesting. When I got older, I told people I wanted to be a lawyer or have my own business because that's what my parents did. They didn't sound interesting either. The question kept me up at night sometimes. I wondered why I didn't know what I wanted to be when so many other kids had it all figured out. Nothing fit for me. Every job I could imagine fell into two categories – things I didn't want to do, and things I wasn't good at. When concert pianist fell into my lap, it was an easy decision. Something I loved and something I was good at all rolled into one job.

I didn't want to stop playing the piano. I loved hearing music that I created. I never wanted to lose that feeling. Music would be a part of my life forever. But just a part, not my whole life. Jeremy was going to

545

tell me I was squandering my talent and that I owed it to music and to the world to develop into a true musician. But when I thought about the piano, I realized it wasn't that important to me. Today, I learned what was important. What made me truly happy. Being compassionate. Touching other people's lives. Making a difference. Like with Scott this afternoon. Like with Brian last month. Like Jeremy did for me. Like I wanted to do with the whole world starting as soon as I could.

I had no idea how I was going to tell Jeremy.

I set my face in a sexy smile and went back into the bedroom.

Chapter 38

April 25, 1983

M r. Humber picked up his briefcase. "Ready to depart?"

I threw my backpack on my shoulder. "Ready," I lied.

I wasn't ready, not for any of this. The idea of getting into a teacher's car and going somewhere outside school was disturbing enough. The few times I saw teachers in the grocery store or at a restaurant were always strange. Teachers didn't belong outside of school. Once the day ended, they shut down like robots. I assumed they got packed in mothballs for the summer. But that was nothing compared to the sense I was getting in way over my head. I had no business trying to help someone I'd never met. I felt the same way at my first track meet, like a total imposter. I had such bad butterflies, I tripped over my own feet on the first lap and lost the race before it really started. These butterflies were worse. Killer mutant zombie butterflies.

Simon waved me over on our way out of the cafeteria. He was volunteering to work on the set, probably because I was playing the piano. He still liked hanging around me at school even though I rescued him from Tommy Walker months ago. We never hung out after that day. "I wanted to tell you I can come to your party on Saturday," he said.

"Cool," I said. "It starts at seven."

"Ok, see ya," he said and left.

"Aha!" Mr. Humber said like a detective who just solved the mystery. "All the buzz about a legendary party leads to you."

"It's just a little birthday party with some of my friends," I said.

"Just a little party? From the rumors that have reached my ears, I'd hazard a guess you've invited everyone in Newton Falls between the ages of eleven and fifteen."

"It got a little bigger than I thought it would," I said. The truth was I wanted it to be big, like Jason Goldblatt's bar mitzvah. I'd never seen a party like his before. They rented out a whole restaurant, had a huge live band, a giant arch made of balloons, massive Styrofoam decorations on the tables, and a big sign-in board where everyone wrote funny things. His friends even filled a wine glass with all kinds of stuff and sealed it with candle wax as a souvenir to remember the party. "You can come if you want."

"Unless you've invited other adults, I respectfully decline. It would undoubtedly be a bizarre experience for all involved."

"Why? Everyone likes you. I think it'd be fun if you came."

"I'd be a disruptive presence," he said. "As a teacher, I have authority over my students. I decide on grades, can issue or deny hall passes, and ignore infractions or write a referral at my sole discretion. As a result, my presence would create an uncomfortable situation. No one would know what to do. Imagine if I were to start dancing." I giggled uncomfortably. "Now imagine if a game of spin the bottle were to break out." I giggled even more uncomfortably. "I sense a glimmer of understanding."

I followed him down a short hallway across from the office I'd never noticed before, and out to the parking lot, which I'd never noticed before either. I walked by that parking lot every day on my way to Chris' house and I'd never noticed it. How was that possible?

"I apologize in advance for the state of my vehicle," Mr. Humber said. "I rarely have the need to transport others. I assure you I'm a responsible driver. The majority of damage to my vehicle was caused by previous owners."

"Oh," I said. Wait, *majority?*

The car had to be older than me. Maybe it used to be the puke green color that seemed popular when I was a baby, but it was hard to tell because most of the paint had peeled off. There were a *lot* of dents. He had to jiggle his key to get the door unlocked. The sound the door made when he opened it was worse than nails on a chalkboard. "Give

me a moment to clear some space," he muttered. The front seat was covered with a messy pile of books and papers. It had a gash in the back that looked like it was about to vomit foam filling. I got in cautiously when he motioned he was finished.

"Where's the seat belt?" I asked.

"I believe the vehicle is old enough to have been manufactured before they were available," he said. The car made a sound like an old person coughing up a lung when he tried to start it. "Nothing unusual," he said, pumping the gas pedal. It sounded even sicker on the second try. "It has once again decided to be uncooperative. However, I've never lost this battle and I don't intend to lose today."

I nodded, trying to find a Mr. Humberish enough word to describe the situation. *Incongruous.* I'd never imagined what kind of car he drove, but if I had I would've pictured one of those little Japanese cars, neat and clean like his desk. Definitely not empty McDonald's boxes and dirty clothes in the back seat. Like there were two different Mr. Humbers. If the good one was in class, this one had to be the evil version. I jumped when the car made a sound like a gun going off. He raced the engine like he was showing off, but when he stopped it sputtered. "I have prevailed yet again," he said. We pulled slowly out of the space, the smell of exhaust so powerful I thought I was going to pass out.

"Can we listen to the radio?" I asked. I needed a distraction.

"If I had a functional radio, I'd be happy to oblige. May I suggest we engage in the lost art of conversation? Please feel free to select a topic."

Only one topic came to mind, but if I started talking about helping his friend, he might realize how nervous I was. I had a million questions, like what should I do, what I should I say, what shouldn't I say. Should I talk about his mom or not? I thought I should already know the answers. If I asked such basic questions he'd lose confidence in me.

Last Friday, he asked me to stay after class. "Earlier this week, you mentioned a desire, as you so eloquently put it, to touch lives and make a difference. To that end, I have a proposition for you. A young friend of mine needs assistance. The more I consider the issue, the more I believe you're the right person to offer this assistance. Before I discuss the matter, I'd like to impress upon you the need for the strictest

confidentiality. If you're going to help people, it's critical to understand the damage that can be caused by blabbing about their problems to friends or even family."

I wanted to tell him I was turning thirteen in four days, so I knew what confidentiality meant. And I sure as hell understood how to keep something confidential. I had *lots* of practice. Instead, I searched for a Mr. Humberish word. "I'm intrigued," I said.

"An excellent selection," he said, like I picked the special from a menu. "When my friend passed away, she left behind a son named Jeff. He's in sixth grade, and his father is looking for someone to tutor him until he's ready to return to school. I believe he needs a friend more than a tutor. Jeff has taken his mother's passing very hard, to the point where I'm concerned for his well-being. He's locked himself in his room and refuses to come out. The last time his father tried to talk to him, he became violent." I couldn't stop myself from picturing a mirror shattering when hit by a baseball bat. "His father chose to withhold the seriousness of his mother's condition from his son. While Jeff knew his mother was ill, he didn't understand her condition was terminal. Jeff believed his mother was recovering when she came home a month before she passed. His father couldn't find it in his heart to tell his son the truth."

"That's terrible!" I blurted out.

"It's easy to judge from the outside," he said. "We might disagree with his decision, but that doesn't give us the right to question him. We can never truly understand what a man losing his wife was experiencing. He was trying to protect his son, nothing more. Regardless of his decision, Jeff needs someone he can talk to." He took a deep breath. "Knowing all this, are you interested in helping?"

"Definitely," I said. This was exactly what I wanted. A chance to fix a kid messed up by his stupid parents.

Now that we were on our way to meet him for the first time, I felt as far from definite as possible.

"So," I said, still looking for something to talk about. Something that had nothing to do with fixing a messed-up kid. Or school, because talking to him about school when we were in his car was weird. "Are

you married?" I asked. It sounded all wrong after I said it. Asking a teacher about his life outside school felt off limits.

"I have yet to find a woman who'd put up with my work ethic or tolerate my slovenly vehicle," he said. "Relationships require work and commitment, and I find myself with little time to spare beyond my professional endeavors."

"School is only six and a half hours a day," I pointed out. "And what about summer break? There's lots of time."

"I beg to differ," he said like he was insulted. "While it may appear being a teacher is a cushy job, those six hours at school barely scratch the surface. Preparing lessons takes far longer than you might think, as does grading papers. Frequently, I find myself awake long after midnight reading essays and pondering how to convey the material I want to share with my students. Beyond that, I have several tutoring commitments to high school students on nights and weekends, and during the summer I teach at a program for aspiring authors. If I somehow find myself with a few free moments, I try to fill them with my own humble attempts to write something meaningful."

"You're a writer?" I asked, sounding more surprised than I should've.

"One day, I hope to craft the next great American novel, but so far my efforts have not borne fruit."

"If you want to be a writer, why are you a teacher?"

"Well, to put it bluntly and in appropriate junior high school language, I suck." Mr. Humber saying something sucked was *way* beyond incongruous. "While I aspired at one time to be a great author, teaching became my true passion. I can't imagine giving up the thrill of delivering a lesson and seeing a glimmer of understanding in my student's eyes. Too few people in this world have the drive and bravery to make their passion into their career, and it's a heartbreaking thing to spend a lifetime working in a profession that feels like a chore. For now, I will continue to be married to my job and I certainly have no shortage of children in my family. And with that, we've arrived at our destination."

The neighborhood was unfamiliar, full of houses old enough to have George Washington slept here signs. I figured we were somewhere near

the middle of town. The car died by itself when he shifted into park. "How convenient," he said. I followed him up the brick walkway, past a rusty iron bench, and up six steps to a long, wide porch. Mr. Humber rang the doorbell. We waited a long time before it was opened by a tall thin man with gray hair and round glasses like the ones Jeremy wore. I thought he looked like an asshole.

"Ken," the man said.

"How are you holding up?" Mr. Humber asked him.

"Fine," he said in a voice that said the opposite.

"Len, this is Nick, my student," Mr. Humber said, looking at me.

"Len Sheffield," he said, holding out his hand. I shook it without saying anything, unable to stop thinking how their names rhymed. "I've heard a lot about you. Thanks for coming."

"You're welcome," I mumbled. "I'm sorry for your loss."

"That's very kind," he mumbled back. "Please come inside, and for goodness sake have something to eat. I have enough cake, cookies, and pie to feed Napoleon's army." The house gave me the shivers when we got inside. The shades were closed, which made the dark red walls look like they were bleeding. The furniture looked as old as the house. Vases of dead flowers were everywhere. Mr. Humber and I sat down on an ancient couch while Mr. Sheffield (or Len or Mr. Dickfaceasshole, I wasn't sure what I should call him) got a plate of desserts from the kitchen. I was sure they'd be crawling with bugs.

Mr. Sheffield slouched in a chair across from us. "Ken tells me you're friendly with Chris O'Neill," he said to me. "How's he doing?"

"Ok, I guess," I said, frowning. How would he know about Chris?

"Chris' family used to live in the house two doors down," Mr. Humber explained. "Nancy, Mrs. Sheffield, used to babysit often for him. He was friends with Jeffrey until he moved away four years ago."

"After the divorce," Mr. Sheffield said. "I worry about that boy."

"I take it that Chris never mentioned he knew Nancy," Mr. Humber said. "Perhaps now you have a better understanding of his behavior in class the other week."

"Yeah," I said, even though it made his behavior even more inexplicable.

"Thanks for coming to tutor Jeffrey," Mr. Sheffield said. "Ken, did you and Nick work out a price? A dollar an hour seems fair to me."

"I thought I was doing this for free," I said. That was a stupid thing to say. If he wanted to give me money I was going to take it. "I guess you could pay me if you wanted."

"I'd feel better if I did," he said without explaining, his face going blank.

"I'll take Nick upstairs to meet Jeff," Mr. Humber said. Mr. Sheffield stared off into space while I jerked out of the chair. Mr. Humber picked up a pile of schoolbooks from the bottom of the stairs and gave them to me. I recognized some from last year. At the top of the stairs was a narrow hallway. The door at the far end had a homemade sign made of four pieces of orange construction paper taped together that said "GO AWAY!" in huge letters with thirty exclamation points. A plate of desserts sat outside the door, uneaten.

Mr. Humber knocked on the door. "Jeff? It's Ken Humber. I have someone who'd like to meet you." He nodded at me.

"Umm, hi," I said to the door. It didn't answer. "I'm Nick. I'm supposed to tutor you instead of going to school." The door still didn't answer. Mr. Humber tried the handle but it was locked.

"I'll leave the two of you to get acquainted," he said loudly enough to be heard. "Talk to him," he whispered to me. He gripped my shoulder for a second before disappearing down the stairs, leaving me alone with the silent door. I listened for any noises from the room, but other than the ghosts creaking and groaning all over the house I didn't hear anything.

"Mr. Humber told me you're in sixth grade. I'm in seventh."

Nothing.

"What's your favorite subject in school? Mine's vacation." I tried to laugh. "Do you play any instruments? I play piano. I'm on the track team too, do you play any sports? What kind of books do you like to read? What's your favorite television show? Isn't it cool that the new Star Wars movie is coming out next month?"

More nothing.

"I heard you used to be friends with Chris O'Neill. What was he like when he was younger? What kind of stuff did you do with him?"

Even more nothing. Maybe he wasn't in there. Maybe he'd snuck out the window hours ago and went to the arcade. I'd look stupid if I was talking to an empty room.

"I found some cookies out here. Can I have one? They look good, chocolate chip." I bit into one. "Yum. Want some?"

Still more nothing.

"I'm supposed to tutor you, but we don't have to do schoolwork if you don't want. We could hang out instead. I could get some Playboys and beer."

Absolutely nothing.

"I heard about your mom," I said, running out of ideas.

Something heavy crashed into the door. "G-g-g-go aw-w-w-w-w-way!" a kid's voice shouted.

At least I knew he was in there.

"Can-n-n-n-n't you r-r-r-r-read?" He had a bad stutter, the kind where it takes forever to get a sentence out because he repeated the same sound over and over.

"I didn't know you stuttered," I said. I knew it was a dumb thing to say while I said it. "I mean, it's cool."

"G-g-g-g-go away!" he screamed again. Something crashed into the door again, hard enough to make the house shake. I took a step back, no idea what I should do. Go for help before he destroyed his whole room? Tell him to stop? Break the door down and make him stop? Wait until he came out with a baseball bat to kill me? It only took me a few minutes to screw him up worse. I was terrible at this, and if I kept going I'd probably do even more damage.

"Sorry I bothered you," I said, running away. Mr. Humber was at the bottom of the stairs. I cringed at the obvious sound when something else smashed into the door.

"Everything all right up there?" Mr. Humber asked.

I was about to tell him everything. How Jeff screamed at me and threw stuff at the door, how this was way over my head, and how they should get someone else to help who knows what he's doing. But I took a deep breath and thought twice. Maybe I shouldn't give up so fast. Maybe I shouldn't rat Jeff out.

I asked myself what Jeremy would do. That was easy.

"Everything's cool," I said. "I wanted a glass of water."

He looked at me suspiciously for a moment. "I'd be pleased to get it for you," he said slowly. I sat down on the top of the stairs to wait. Mr. Humber climbed the stairs and handed me a glass of water. "If things are getting out of control, don't be afraid to call for help."

"Ok," I said. The more I thought about it, the more I realized calling for help was the last thing I wanted to do. Jeremy would never give up, so I wasn't going to give up either. I sat against the wall by his door. "Sorry," I started. "I said some dumb things. It's ok if you don't want to open the door. I'll read you the homework from out here." Nothing crashed into the door. I figured that was a good sign. I searched through the books. "For social studies, you're supposed to read chapters 34 through 37." No answer. "I'll read them to you. Ask questions if you want."

I started reading about what happened after the Civil War, stuff I remembered learning last year. I felt stupid reading to a closed door. He probably put headphones on to tune me out. But I didn't stop reading until I finished all four chapters. I stopped a few times to ask if he had any questions. I asked him if he thought this stuff was as boring as I thought it was. He never answered. I moved on to math, reading the problems out loud, talking through each step as I solved them. When I finished a page, I pushed it underneath the door. Every page I read and every problem I did made me want to win this battle even more. When the house got dark, I found a light switch and kept going. Mr. Humber came up a couple of times to check on me. I waved for him to go away. My throat got scratchy.

"You've got some science homework too," I said, drinking the last of my water. "Hold on, I'm going to get more water because I can't talk anymore." I stretched my stiff legs, my foot asleep for the fifth time. I was halfway down the hall to the bathroom when I heard the door click. I froze, expecting something deadly to fly at my head. When I looked, the door was cracked open, someone barely visible behind it.

"Hi," I said. He disappeared into the room. I forgot about the water. "Can I come in?" He didn't answer, but I figured it was ok since he left the door open. The only light in the room came from a little kid's nightlight. It didn't take a lot of light to see that the room was a total

disaster. The biggest dictionary I'd ever seen was lying face down in the middle of the doorway. That must've been what he threw against the door.

His bed was completely disassembled, the mattress propped up on the desk at an angle, blankets and sheets hanging from it to make a fort. A dresser was turned over to make a wall, making it impossible to get into the fort from the front. On the other side of the room was a five-foot high volcano of clothes, books, papers, toys, and who knows what else. The room smelled like pee. I couldn't see him anywhere, so I figured he was probably hiding in the bed fort. I wondered if I should clean up, but if he wanted his room a mess that was his right. It was *his* room. I brushed some socks off a bean bag in the corner so I could sit down. "I was going to read your science homework next," I said, opening the book on my lap. He peeked through the blankets in the fort.

"I d-d-d-don't c-c-care about hom-m-m-m-mework," he stammered.

"Me neither," I said, closing the book.

"You're a j-j-j-j-j-jerk," he spat.

"Why am I a jerk?" I said.

"Bec-c-c-c-cause y-y-y. . ."

I interrupted him as rudely as I could. "Because I won't go away?" He nodded violently. "Guess what? I'm not going to leave you alone. I'm going to sit here and read the rest of your homework no matter how long it takes. I'm going to come back tomorrow and the next day and the next day and every day until you go back to school. You're the jerk, not me. You made me sit in the hallway this whole time."

He disappeared into the fort. "F-f-f-f-f-fine, s-s-stay if y-y-y-y-you w-w-want. I d-d-d-d-d-don't c-c-c-care."

"Fine," I spat back at him.

I opened the science book and started reading.

When I heard him snoring, a big part of me wanted to invade the fort so I could kick him awake. Instead, I closed the book and tiptoed

out of his room. Mr. Sheffield was asleep in the living room chair. I found Mr. Humber at the kitchen table with a bunch of papers spread out.

"I take it things went well by the lengthy absence of communication," he said softly.

I shook my head. "I think he hates me. He called me a jerk after he finally let me into his room."

Mr. Humber blinked. "He let you into his room? I believe you were far more successful than you realize. While I'd like to hear more, it's imperative we get you home as soon as possible. It's after ten."

"That late?" I didn't realize I'd just spent over five hours reading his homework. I hadn't even started mine yet.

"We also need to discuss my conversation with your uncle."

"You talked to him?" I said, raising my voice a little. He put his finger on his lips and pointed to Mr. Sheffield. I watched him gather his papers and followed him to his car. "Why did you talk to him?" I asked when we were in the car.

"I think the relevant matter is why he was unaware of your activities tonight. You assured me you discussed this with your uncle and secured his approval. When I contacted him to request you remain later than expected, he was under the impression you were at an extended rehearsal. I don't know if you fully appreciate the awkward position in which you've placed me. I'm now responsible for transporting a student away from school without the permission of his guardian. This is a very serious issue. I could lose my job."

"You could get fired?" I got cold all over.

"I take comfort in the fact your uncle was remarkably understanding and supportive of your endeavors once I described the situation. I don't believe he's interested in making this an issue with the school. I trust you'll assist me to ensure it remains that way by accepting full responsibility for your actions."

I was silent as he battled with the car to get it started. I couldn't think of an apology big enough for what I did. I had good reasons for telling Jeremy I was at rehearsal instead of helping Jeff, but they weren't anywhere near good enough. I didn't imagine my little lie could have

such huge consequences. I couldn't let Mr. Humber get fired because of me.

"I'm really sorry," I said after he got the car started.

"You've breached my trust," he said. "If you recall, I specifically validated earlier today that you had permission, and you affirmed that you did."

"I know," I said. "I can explain."

"Explanations are unnecessary," he said. "I believe you didn't fully grasp the ramifications of your actions, and I feel certain you had no ill intent. Everyone is entitled to make a mistake, but I must emphasize that I cannot allow you to make this mistake again. I trust we understand each other."

"Yeah," I said. "I won't mess up again."

We didn't talk for the rest of the ride, except to tell him where to turn. "This one?" he asked as we pulled up. I nodded. "This is quite an impressive home. Your uncle must be very successful at his chosen profession."

"He doesn't work," I said. I didn't want to lie to Mr. Humber any more.

"That only serves to increase my envy."

"Thanks for driving me home," I said. "I'll see you tomorrow in school." I got my backpack from the back seat. I didn't expect him to get out of the car too. "What are you doing?"

"I intend to apologize personally to your uncle," he said.

"I'm sure you don't have to," I said too quickly. Having them meet could be bad. Like vinegar and baking soda. I had to learn a mixture that was actually explosive. He put his hand on my shoulder in a way that made me even more nervous.

"Is something bothering you?" he asked gently.

"No, nothing. Like what?"

"Anything you'd like to share," he said.

"No," I said.

"Then I'd prefer to convey my apology in person," he said. I shrugged and led him to the front door. The door opened by itself. Jeremy was standing in the doorway, his arms crossed. "Mr. Stillwell, it's good to see you again," Mr. Humber said. They shook hands.

"Good to see you again too, Ken," Jeremy said using his smooth voice.

"Unfortunately, we ran even later than I anticipated when we spoke on the phone," Mr. Humber said. "Please accept my apologies once again, and let me assure you I won't allow this to happen a second time."

Jeremy smiled and waved his hand. "There's no need to apologize. I think the only one who owes an apology is Nick." I sagged my shoulders to emphasize how sorry I was. "I hope the extra time was worth it."

"I believe so," Mr. Humber said. "Mr. Welles was successful beyond my expectations this evening. He should be commended. I'm grateful for your understanding and flexibility." I didn't feel much like being commended.

"Good for you," Jeremy said to me. He was doing an amazing job hiding how angry he was with me. "We'd better get you fed and into bed, you have school tomorrow." He motioned me into the house. "Thanks for bringing him home," he said to Mr. Humber.

"It's no trouble at all. Thank you for your understanding. You have a remarkable nephew." Jeremy smiled. "I'll see you tomorrow in class, Mr. Welles."

"Night," I said. Jeremy shut the door. I stood very still.

"I made dinner if you're hungry," he said softly, turning away.

"Thanks, I didn't eat anything," I said. He walked towards the kitchen. "I'm sorry. I should've told you. I thought it was an important thing to do."

"I'm proud of you," he said. He didn't sound proud. I followed him into the kitchen, the smell of meat heavy in the air. I watched him take a prime rib out of the oven. "I hope it's not too dried out."

"You made prime rib?" I said, feeling even worse.

"I wanted to make you something special," he said. "It's almost your birthday and you've been so busy. I was hoping we could have a nice dinner, just the two of us. A little surprise."

"I feel so bad," I said, hugging him from behind. "It was nice of you to make a special dinner. Maybe I could do something special for you later if you wanted."

"Something special," he repeated. His body got stiff and he pulled away from me. "Is that all you think about? I don't give a shit about the sex. I want to be part of your life. It's not just tonight. You haven't been telling me anything about school, what you're doing, your friends, nothing. You're entitled to a few secrets, but you don't have to lie to me. You're cutting me out of your life and it hurts. It really hurts."

"I don't mean to," I said.

"Are you sleeping with him?" he said suddenly.

"Am I what?"

"Your English teacher. Are you having sex with him?"

I stared at him like he was crazy.

"You go silent about everything that's going on. The next thing I know, you're being driven home at ten at night after being who knows where. I think it's a fair question."

"It's a ridiculous question!" I yelled.

"He's into boys like me!" Jeremy shouted, slamming the counter. "Why the hell do you think I warned you to stay away from him?"

"No, he isn't!" I yelled.

"Oh, yes he is," Jeremy said. "I can see it from a mile away. Between the stories you used to tell me and that conference we had, I am one hundred percent positive. He's stealing you from me!"

"I'm not having sex with Mr. Humber!" I yelled. "Are you going crazy or something?"

"Why did you lie to me?" he yelled.

"Because I thought it would make you freak out!" I shouted. "See, I was right! Are you jealous? Why are you jealous of him?"

He slid down to sit on the floor. "I want you back," he moaned. "Do you remember when you told me you never wanted to do anything to make me think you didn't love me? Well, you're doing it. You're never around. You're always off doing other things and I'm left behind. The only time you spend with me is in bed. That's not what I want. I want *you*, not your body. I want to go back to when it was just the two of us, when we did everything together. I'm scared I'm losing you. I'm scared you don't care anymore. I'm terrified I'm going to wake up one day and find you gone."

I couldn't understand why Jeremy was yelling at me. He never yelled at me, no matter how angry I made him. But now I understood. He wasn't angry. He was scared. Maybe that's why Jeff yelled at me too. I pushed my own anger down inside myself like I did with Jeff.

"How can you think that?" I said. "I never want to leave you."

"But you will," he said in shaky voice. "Boys don't stay boys forever. They have this infuriating habit of growing up. Even though you're not an adult, you're no longer a child. You're somewhere in between. It happened so fast. Before I know it, you'll have a girlfriend. Then you'll be off to conservatory. Then you'll get married and have a family of your own. We're not going to be together forever. I only have a few short years to be with you."

"I'm sorry," I said.

"Don't be sorry and please don't look so miserable. This is the way things are supposed to be. It's the curse of what I am. I miss what we used to have. I'm being torn apart by the thought our best times are already behind us."

I got on the floor and gave him a hug. "I'm still here," I said.

"Please don't shut me out," he whispered. "Please let me keep being a part of your life. There's not much time left."

"I think you owe me a pillow fight," I said. It was the only thing I could think of to show him I was a still a kid.

He looked up at me. "I think you're right about that."

I helped him up. I ran for the lobby, Jeremy right behind me.

The pillow fight didn't last long. A few smacks and a little wrestling, which turned into touching, which turned into kissing, which turned into what it always did. Of all nights for it to happen, it had to be this one. Jeremy acted all excited when I made my own stuff for the first time. I was relieved at first. I'd been getting worried enough to go to the doctor. But tonight, it was just another sign I was growing up.

He told me afterwards he was sorry about what he said. He told me he didn't mean it and that he was feeling lonely and didn't understand why I made up a story. I couldn't tell him the whole truth, not yet. I stuck to being nervous about him knowing I was with Mr. Humber. I left out the more important reason about doing something different with my life. About giving up the piano.

"If you're feeling lonely, you should tell me," I told him. "You tell me not to hold things inside so you shouldn't either. You don't have to be scared to tell me how you feel. I'm not going to leave. You're my home. Until forever comes."

He told me he would, but I wasn't so sure. I wondered what else was inside him wanting to burst out. I wondered when it would. When it did, it would be my turn. I would be there to comfort him, to hold him in my arms, and to keep him safe.

To fix him like he fixed me.

Chapter 39

May 19, 1983

I turned the page back to the beginning of the song. "From the top," I barked. "One, two, three, four. . ."

Jeremy taught me a "vamp" is a few bars of music that can be repeated until the actors are ready to start the song, usually because they have lines before singing. I played the vamp three times before Leon elbowed Allison to remind her she was supposed to start. She did her lines so fast I couldn't understand a word she said, even though I knew every single line in the show. When I started playing the verse, she sang so softly I couldn't hear her. So I played softer. She thought that meant she was singing too loud and got even worse. Then she stopped singing altogether, probably because she forgot her lines *again*. Leon and Sean did their parts, trying to prompt her. She stood there looking dumb until she got to a part she remembered. Everyone looked confused when the song ended.

"I can't hear you at all," I said. I decided not to remind her to learn her lines.

"I'll have a microphone when we do the show," she said.

"I'm standing right next to you and I can't hear you," Sean said.

"At least I sing on key," she said.

"As if!" he fired back. "Maybe in the key of I'm flat."

Allison ran off stage. Her friend Becky glared at Sean. "Nice, real nice," she spat.

"All I said was that she sang flat," Sean said.

"No, you said she *was* flat!" Becky hissed.

"I quit!" Allison shouted from backstage.

Everyone looked at me like I was supposed to do something. I tried to hide behind the piano. Mr. Humber had to pick these five minutes to disappear, and he had to tell everyone I was in charge. How was I supposed to be in charge? I was just a seventh grader. "Let's try something else," I said. "How about Happiness? We never work on it."

"We need to change the blocking," Leon said. "It's too complicated. We keep tripping over each other,"

"The performance is in two weeks," I mumbled. The show was going to be a complete disaster. Everyone forgot their lines, couldn't sing, didn't know where they were supposed to stand, and had no idea when to come on and off stage. We were going to look ridiculous in front of the entire school. Total humiliation.

Mr. Humber came back into the room, so I was done with being in charge, thank god. "That's a wrap for today, ladies and gentlemen," he said. "Kindly return your props to the prop closet. Remember, next week we have an extended rehearsal schedule so plan accordingly with those responsible for your transportation. Also, please take an additional three posters and place them conspicuously around the school tomorrow. It seems many of our advertisements have disappeared. Thank you."

I stuffed the music book into my backpack. "You wanna come to the mall?" Sean asked. "Jack and I are hitching a ride with his sister and her friend and getting some pizza."

"I can't," I said. "I've got too much stuff I have to do." I really wanted to go. I liked Jack's sister. She was a junior in high school. Even though she had a car and a job she was always nice to us lowly junior high school kids. Hanging out with them made me feel mature. Sean went on his way, leaving me alone with my responsibilities. I always had responsibilities.

"What is your assessment of our current state of preparedness?" Mr. Humber asked.

I looked around to make sure we were alone. "We suck," I said quietly. He laughed. "I'm serious! Nobody remembers their cues, I can't hear the singers no matter how softly I play, we don't know the closing number yet, and Allison just quit."

"Perhaps you will find this difficult to believe, but in my opinion we are ahead of schedule." I looked at him like he was nuts. "The theater is a great mystery. Disaster seems imminent, but at the very last moment everything will resolve itself. My faith is unshakeable in this matter. I've directed the school musical for seven years. Each year the show has pulled itself together, often from a far worse condition than what you witnessed today. They might look unprepared now, but during dress rehearsals you will witness a remarkable transformation." Bullshit. Cramming at the last minute wouldn't work. It wasn't like a test. "It appears the cast and crew have evaporated as always, leaving behind a dramatic mess. May I impose upon you to assist me?"

"Can't. I'm supposed to meet Jeff outside. We're playing basketball."

"How typical," he muttered. "The only student remaining has a valid excuse." I laughed.

I slipped off to the bathroom to change into gym clothes before heading behind the school to the basketball hoops. Right after school they were always crowded, but by now everyone had gone home. Jeff sat on a corner of the court with a basketball in his lap, his father squatting next to him. I took a deep breath. So far, everything I tried with Jeff ended in disaster. I always said and did the wrong thing. Every time we met, I left him more depressed than when I started. But I wasn't going to give up. My latest idea was stashed at the bottom of my backpack, waiting for the right moment.

Mentioning Chris to him was one of my mistakes. Jeff became furious because Chris stole a baseball Jeff's father bought at Yankee stadium. I asked Chris about it the next day at lunch.

"I didn't steal anything," Chris sneered. "He gave it to me as a going away present. Why are you hanging around with that dorky kid anyway?"

"Do you still have it? I want to give it back to him."

"No way," Chris said. "It's mine, he gave it to me. End of story."

"It's not like you care about baseball," I pointed out.

"Doesn't matter. Tell the little bed-wetter he's shit out of luck."

"Bed-wetter?" I asked, shivering a little.

"He used to piss the bed every single night," Chris said with delight. "He had to wear a diaper, I saw it. I'll bet he still does."

It clicked. That's why his room smelled like pee. If I told him I used to wet the bed too, it would give us something in common. I could hardly believe I was considering telling anyone that deep and dark of a secret, but I was actually excited to share it with someone who'd understand. I told him that night when I was helping him with homework. He wouldn't talk to me for three days afterwards. Another giant mistake in a long line of giant mistakes.

It took me a week to wear Chris down. He finally sold me the baseball for ten bucks, calling me the biggest sucker ever to walk the face of the earth. I didn't care if I was. I knew the baseball would turn everything around with Jeff. He'd be thankful I got it back, we'd talk, and things would be better. I smiled and made my shoulders straight as I walked up to them. "Hey," I said to Jeff. He looked past me like I wasn't even there.

"Remember what we talked about," his father said, standing up. "Good to see you again, Nick," he said. We shook hands quickly. "Jeffrey's bicycle is in the rack. I'll pick you boys up at the mall at eight."

"I thought we said nine," I said.

"Eight is late enough," he said. "Make sure to take the back roads to the mall, the highway isn't safe. I'd prefer you boys got burgers for dinner. Jeffrey needs some meat instead of pizza." He handed me a ten-dollar bill.

"Ok," I said, barely able to keep my eyes from rolling. Mr. Sheffield acted like I was a babysitter instead of his friend. No way I was going to take the backroads to the mall, and we *were* going to get pizza. Even if Jeff hated me, he still understood the code of kids. He wouldn't tell.

"Call me when you get to the mall, you have dimes for the payphone," he said to Jeff. "Have a good time." Jeff didn't answer, pretending that his father was already gone. As soon as his father was around the side of the school, Jeff threw the basketball at me as hard as he could.

"Hey!" I shouted, hitting it out of the way. "What was that for?"

"I d-d-don't kn-n-now," he muttered.

"Do you want to play or not?" He crossed his arms and shook his head. I went to get the ball. "Playing basketball was your idea. How

come you don't want to play now?" I took a shot, the ball bouncing off the rim. I still sucked at basketball.

"W-w-w-w-one on one is s-s-s-s-stupid," he said.

"Let's shoot baskets." I tried and missed again. "Isn't there some kind of game that's just shooting baskets?" He didn't answer. I took another shot from further away, missing the hoop entirely. I ran after the ball as it bounced off the court.

"You s-s-s-s-suck," he said. He was in an especially bad mood today.

"Oh yeah? Let's see who's better. First person to twenty wins." I moved into position and lined up my shot, finally managing to get one in. "That's two for me." I passed the ball to him, but he let it bounce off the court.

"Th-th-th-this is d-d-d-d-d-dumb t-t-t-too."

"You're only saying that because you're going to lose," I taunted him, running past him to get the ball. I dribbled it in and managed to surprise myself by scoring another basket. "Score! I'm going to kick your ass." I hoped being hard on him would get him playing, and it worked.

"N-n-n-n-no y-y-you w-won't." He grabbed the ball out of my hand and took his shot from the line. He missed. "W-w-wait, I m-m-messed up," he snarled, grabbing the ball and taking another shot right near the basket. It went in this time.

"Throw me the ball, you had two shots," I said. He ignored me and took three more shots before he managed to get one in. "Now you have four points too." He ignored me again, taking another shot. I ran in and grabbed the ball right before he could catch it.

"N-n-n-n-not f-f-f-air!" he protested. "You're t-t-taller than m-m-m-me!"

"You took like seven shots," I countered, throwing the ball up and managing to get it in. "Six to four."

"N-n-n-no it isn't, you ch-ch-ch-ch-cheated." He threw an easy one in. "Now I g-g-g-get one m-m-m-m-m-more." I frowned. He threw another easy one. "Eight for m-m-me to s-s-six f-f-for you."

"Fine," I said, standing in the same spot as him.

"N-n-n-n-no, you have t-t-t-to take a h-h-h-h-harder sh-shot."

"Ok," I growled, moving back a few feet. He waved his hand more, and I kept backing up until I was past the line. "This is far enough." I missed completely. He laughed.

"You r-really s-s-s-suck," he said again, then missed his next shot. "W-w-w-wait." He tried and missed *again*.

"My turn now," I barked, holding out my hands. I was running out of patience. He threw the ball in the other direction and crossed his arms defiantly. He liked being a deliberate jerk to make me mad, and it usually worked. I glared at him, considering ways I could force him to get the ball by using pain. But I let my anger go, like I usually did. I reminded myself I wasn't here to win at basketball. Instead, I imagined what Jeremy would do, like I always did. It never took me long to figure out the answer. I ran off the court and brought the ball back.

"Here, try again," I said. "You were really close that time. Go ahead, I'll bet you get it in this time." He grabbed the ball violently from me, dribbled it to the foul line, and threw it so hard it sailed over the backboard. "I'll get it!" I ran for the ball again. He watched me bring it back. "Try again." This time he didn't bother to throw it in the same direction as the net. The ball bounced around the corner of the school. I ran after it again.

I didn't hand it to him when I got back. "I'll do it this time," I said, throwing the ball as hard as I could into the open field. He looked at me without comprehension as I ran off. He was sitting on the blacktop when I got back. "Again?" I barked like a dog and let my tongue hang out.

He fought it, but I could see a smile trying to break through his scowl. I got down on all fours and pushed the ball towards him with my nose. Good thing no one was around to see me act this way, they'd never stop teasing me. "D-d-d-don't m-make me l-l-l-l-laugh," he muttered.

I barked until he decided to play along. "F-f-f-fetch, d-doggy," he said, throwing the ball. I leapt to my feet and ran after it, dropping the ball in his lap when I got back.

"W-w-w-wanna p-p-p-play the r-r-r-right w-way?" he said.

I held out my hand and helped him to his feet.

"They said the pizza would take another five minutes," I said. Jeff stared at the book I bought for him. I didn't understand how anyone could find lists of baseball statistics interesting. Still, if that's what he wanted, fine with me. I took out the new fantasy book Mr. Humber recommended and started reading.

"Piano man!" Sean yelled across the courtyard. Jeff glared at me.

"Hey!" I waved in a way that was meant to tell them to get lost, but they didn't take the hint. "We're just waiting for our pizza," I explained when the bunch of them came up to the table.

"We're getting one too, so let's sit together," Sean said. "I'm Sean," he said to Jeff, who ignored him.

"This is Jeff," I said awkwardly. "He's a friend of mine but he can't talk because I jinxed him. These are my friends from school, Sean, Jack, his sister Nicole, and her friend. Casey?" She nodded. "Ha. I remembered."

"I haven't played jinx in forever," Sean said.

"Let him out so he can say hi," Nicole said. Jeff pointed to his mouth and waved.

"You guys take your jinx too seriously," Jack said.

"If you break the jinx, it costs you five bucks," I added.

"Is it ok if we sit with you guys?" Nicole asked.

"Sure," I said. Jeff glared again. I knew once he got used to them, he'd see they were nice people. They wouldn't make fun of him for having a stutter. At least, I hoped they wouldn't.

"Do you go to Witherspoon?" Jack asked.

"No, he's in sixth grade," I answered quickly.

"Oh," he said. "I could've sworn you looked familiar."

"Weird, I was thinking the same thing," Casey said. "That's funky, maybe we knew each other in a former life."

"You'd have to have a life to get a former one," Sean joked. He covered his head with his arms as Casey smacked him with her purse. "Ow! What've you got in there, bricks?"

"I'm serious," she said. "What's your last name?"

"Sheffield," I said for him.

"Oh my god, I know who you are," Casey said. She looked like she was going to cry. Jeff grabbed his book and ran off into the mall.

"Wait!" I called after him. He disappeared around the corner.

"What's with the munchkin?" Jack asked.

Casey slugged him with her purse. "Don't call him that!" She looked at me. "He's Mrs. Sheffield's son, isn't he?"

"Yeah," I said.

"The teacher who died?" Nicole asked. "That's so sad! I didn't know you were friends with him. Maybe you should go after him."

"He'll come back," I said. I hoped.

"Is that why he didn't want to talk?" Jack said. "Because that jinx thing sounded like bullshit."

"He gets embarrassed because he has a bad stutter," I said.

"That was very sweet of you to make up a story," Nicole said. "We wouldn't make fun of him."

"I would," Sean said. "Th-th-th-th-that's all folks!" Nicole smacked him this time. "What? I was kidding!"

"You're not funny," Casey said.

"We should leave you guys alone," Nicole said, standing up.

"It'll be ok," I said. "You can stay."

She shook her head. "I don't think he wants anyone to know his mother died. Tell him we're sorry."

"What about the pizza?" Sean asked.

"Is food all you think about?" Casey asked.

"Mostly," he said. "I also think about really big boobs." He covered his head expecting to get hit again. The girls shook their heads in disgust.

"Why can't you be more like Nick?" Nicole said. "He knows how to behave like an adult."

"I don't want to act like an adult until I can buy my own porn," Sean said.

"Mature boys get the girls," Nicole teased. "You're a sweet guy, and pretty cute too," she said to me right before kissing my cheek. I think my heart stopped beating. It wasn't the first time I got kissed by a girl, but it was still exciting. And nice. And scary. Sean's jaw dropped.

"I'm mature too," Sean whined, puckering up his lips.

"Unlike Nick, you still act like a little boy," she said to him. "Make sure he's ok. For me?" I nodded.

"Me too," Casey said. "Tell him I'm sorry about his mom."

"Ok," I said, waving at them as they left.

I should have been more excited about being kissed by a girl, especially a seventeen-year-old one. But kissing on the cheek was like getting walked to first base and I scored home runs every day. She was nice, but I didn't feel it like I did with Molly. We had a connection. I still wanted a girlfriend who was exactly like Molly.

I found Jeff sitting on the benches in the middle of the mall with his knees pulled up to his chest. "Our pizza's ready," I said. "How come you ran away?"

"B-b-b-because," he said.

"They wouldn't make fun of you. They're my friends and they're really nice."

"I d-d-don't w-w-want to hang out w-w-w-with anyone," he muttered. "I w-w-w-want t-t-to be by m-m-m-m-m-myself."

"Oh," I said. "Do you want to meet up when your dad comes?"

He was silent for a moment. "N-n-no."

"Do you want to have pizza?"

He shook his head. "N-n-n-not hu-u-u-ungry."

I was stuck again. "Did Casey make you sad when she figured out who your mom was?" He looked away from me. "Do you feel like crying? It's ok if you do. I used to stop myself from crying all the time. Once I let myself, it helped me feel better."

"Sh-sh-sh-sh-sh-sh-shut up," he growled.

"I was just trying to help," I said helplessly.

"G-g-g-go away," he said, louder.

"What do you want me to do?" I asked.

"L-l-l-l-l-leave me alone!" he screamed at the top of his lungs. The entire mall went silent. Every single person stared at us. At *me*. Including the security guard heading straight for us.

"Great," I muttered. "You got us in trouble."

"Is there a problem?" the guard said, annoyed.

"No," I said.

"I wasn't asking you," he said. "I asked him if there was a problem."

"Why c–c–c–c–c–can't ev–v–v–veryone leave m–m–me alone?" Jeff screamed so loud it echoed around the mall. My stomach dropped. We were going to wind up getting arrested for something.

"He's upset about something," I said to the guard. Jeff threw his book at me, hitting me in the head.

The guard looked at me. "Who's responsible for you?"

"Umm, no one, we're here alone," I said.

He picked up his walkie-talkie and said something into it. "You'll have to come with me and call someone from the security office to pick you up."

"Please, he'll be ok. Our pizza is done."

"Now," the guard said forcefully. "Or I'll have to call the cops. He's making a disturbance."

"Come on, Jeff," I said, touching his arm. He looked at me with wild eyes. "Let's go home. We'll call your dad." He slumped over. I tugged on his arm harder and after a few tries he gave up, walking mechanically beside me as the guard led us to the security office. He made us sit in a couple of chairs across from his desk. Jeff crossed his arms and looked down at the floor.

"Phone number?" the guard barked.

I gave him mine, thinking it might be better if Jeremy came to get us instead of Mr. Sheffield. Jeremy would know how to cheer Jeff up, and then he could drop us back off in time so Mr. Sheffield would never know something happened. But Jeremy didn't pick up the phone. We couldn't just sit in the security office because Mr. Sheffield would be coming to pick us up in an hour. If we weren't at the meeting place, he'd probably freak out. I didn't have a choice. I gave the guard Jeff's number.

"Your father will be here in twenty minutes," the guard said when he hung up the phone. "Until then, you two sit there without moving. What've you got in those backpacks?"

"School books," I said.

He took my backpack from me, rummaging through it. "What's this?" he said, pulling out the new book I bought. "This isn't a school book. Looks brand new. Why are you lying?"

"I bought it at the bookstore today," I said.

"Do you have a receipt proving you bought it?" he said.

"I think I threw it out," I said, my stomach sinking even further. Jeff curled his legs back up and buried his head between his knees. The guard looked at him for a moment.

"You can go to jail for shoplifting," he said harshly.

"We didn't steal anything," I said, but I didn't sound very convincing.

"Don't move," he ordered, dialing the phone. "Yeah, this is Carl with mall security. I'm holding a couple of boys on suspicion of shoplifting. They have some of your merchandise and can't produce a receipt." He paused. "One is about twelve with red hair, the other younger, blond." He paused again. "A red paperback, science fiction, and a larger book, sports statistics." He looked disappointed. "Thanks," he said, slamming the phone down. "You're lucky they remembered you buying those books, or your father would be bailing you out of jail instead of picking you up here."

"I told you we didn't steal anything," I muttered.

"Watch your tone," he barked. "I don't want to see you in my mall again without an adult, understand? If I catch you here alone, you'll be banned and arrested for trespassing." I was about to tell him that wasn't fair, but he interrupted me before I could start. "No talking."

Jeff curled into an even tighter ball and lay down on his side. I glared at the guard and then turned to Jeff. "Your dad will be here soon, ok? Just hang in there a few more minutes."

"What's wrong with him?" the guard said harshly. "Is he sick?"

"He's upset," I snapped. "Leave him alone. You're scaring him. His mom died a few weeks ago. Can't you be a little nicer? Can't you see he's upset? Why do you have to be such a jerk?"

I went way too far. The guard looked furious. I braced myself, hoping he would stop at telling me to shut up. It seemed more likely he'd send me to jail or strip search me to make sure I didn't steal anything. I should've been scared or angry, but neither described how I felt. I searched for a Mr. Humberish word. *Indignant.* I scowled at him, my eyes locking with his. For a moment, we stared each other down. His look withered. He sank back into the chair, looking down

at his desk. He started writing something in a small notebook, but I thought it looked more like he was just scribbling.

I couldn't believe it. I won. Against an adult. Like the time I stared down Robert. I didn't know exactly how, but I did.

Jeff seemed to notice and sat back up.

A few days ago, I was helping Jeff with homework like I usually did. I couldn't concentrate because a pair of his underpants were hanging on a mobile of the planets. They were embarrassing, so I knocked them down to the floor. I couldn't stop staring at them on the floor, so I put them in the empty hamper hanging on his closet door. But cleaning up one pair of dirty underwear didn't make any difference because they were everywhere. I picked the rest of them up and put them in the hamper too. I didn't stop, cleaning up the rest of the dirty clothes and piling up dirty dishes. Jeff stopped doing his homework and helped. We put the books back on his bookshelf, put the toys in a box at the end of his bed, took the fort apart, put the mattress back on his bed, and put the dresser back against the wall. He tried to stop me when I took the sheets off his bed. I did it anyway, exposing the rubber pad. I told him I used to have one too. He pulled a trash bag from under the bed filled with wet and very smelly pajamas. We took them with the rest of the dirty clothes down to the basement and started a load of laundry. We dusted, vacuumed, and sprayed a whole can of Lysol. It took us almost two hours to get his room clean. I felt good about it afterwards, and I could tell he did too.

When we got back from the mall, his room was right back to where we started, bed fort and all. "What happened?" I moaned.

"I g-g-g-g-got m-m-m-mad," he said, kicking a plastic ball across the room. It knocked over an old plastic trophy on his dresser.

"I can help you clean it back up," I offered.

"N-n-n-n-no," he said. "I m-m-m-messed it up, I'll c-c-c-clean it." He picked up a baseball glove from the floor and put it on. That reminded me of the gift I had for him.

"I almost forgot," I said, digging down into my backpack. "I got this for you."

"Y-y-y-y-you g-g-got me a b-b-baseball?" he said, confused.

"No, I got *your* baseball," I said, handing it to him. He turned it over in his hands once or twice, looking at the initials he had written on it with magic marker when he was a little kid.

"W-w-w-w-where d-d-did. . ."

"From Chris," I said. "I made him give it back."

"W-w-w-w-why d-d-did you d-d-d-do th-that?" He sounded angry.

"You said you wanted it," I said.

"I d-d-d-didn't w-w-w-want this b-b-b-back. I g-g-g-gave it t-t-t-to him."

"You said he stole it," I said.

"N-n-n-no I d-d-d-didn't," he said.

"Great. I gave him ten bucks to get the baseball back and you don't even want it."

"W-w-w-why d-d-d-did y-y-you p-p-pay. . ."

"Because I'm your friend!" I interrupted. "I wanted to do something nice for you. I wanted to cheer you up a little."

"I d-d-d-don't need y-y-you t-t-to..."

"Yes, you do!" I said sharply. "You can't keep doing stuff like this. Look what happened at the mall. You almost got us in big trouble!"

"I c-c-c-can d-do what I w-w-w-want!" he shouted. "Y-y-y-you're n-n-n-not my d-d-d-dad!"

"I'm your friend! I'm your only friend!"

"Y-y-y-you're not my f-f-f-f-friend!" he yelled back. "Y-y-y-you only c-c-c-come b-b-because my d-d-dad g-gives you m-m-m-money!"

The anger melted away. I felt hollow inside. That was it. I was out of ideas. I failed.

"Fine," I said softly. "I never wanted the stupid money in the first place. I wanted to help, but I guess I messed things up worse. I'll leave you alone. It was nice knowing you. I'm really sorry about your mom and I'm sorry about what your dad did, and I hope one day you'll be ok."

He stared at the floor. I sighed and picked up my backpack. I didn't know what I was going to tell Mr. Humber. He was going to tell me how I tried my best and succeeded beyond his wildest dreams, which would only make me feel worse.

I opened the door. "Bye," I said quietly.

"W-w-w-wait," he said as I was leaving. "Y-y-y-you d-d-don't have to g-g-go."

He collapsed into the beanbag chair, pulling himself into a ball.

"Do you want me to stay?" I said.

"I'm u-u-u-used to you," he said.

I went back into the room and closed the door softly, sitting next to him on the beanbag. "Are you crying?" I asked. "It's ok if you want to cry. I'd cry if my mom died. Your dad shouldn't have lied to you."

"I kn-n-n-new she was going to d-d-d-die," he said softly. "She t-t-t-told m-m-m-me. I p-p-pretended I d-d-d-didn't know."

"Do you miss her?" I said, putting my arm around his shoulder.

He nodded.

"It'll be ok," I said quietly. I knew what to do. I did it before. I could fix him like I fixed Brian. I wanted him to make him feel better. I put my hand on his thigh. He didn't react. My breath quickened. He needed a true friend.

I kissed him on the cheek.

His whole body jerked away from me. "W-w-w-w-what are y-y-y-y-you d-d-d-d-doing?" He rolled off the bean bag chair and stood up, looking at me wildly.

"I didn't mean to scare you," I said. "Sorry, I didn't realize it would freak you out."

"D-d-d-d-don't ever d-d-do th-th-th-that again," he said.

"Promise," I said, holding up my hand, sounding as reassuring as I could. He looked at me suspiciously. I tried to think of something to say to explain why I just kissed him.

"Nick, your uncle is here," Mr. Sheffield called from downstairs.

"Coming!" I yelled. I pulled myself out of the beanbag.

"Still friends?" I asked him.

He nodded.

"See ya tomorrow," I said.

"S-s-s-see ya," he said. He watched me leave the room.

I didn't let myself start shaking until the door was closed behind me. I never considered he wouldn't want me to kiss him. I would've gone further, like I did with Brian. I almost made a huge mistake. Right then, right there, I swore to myself that I would never, ever, ever do something like that again.

I pushed the whole thing out of my mind before I could think about it.

Jeremy and I stood side by side, brushing our teeth. "What do you and Brian have planned for Saturday night this week?"

"Brian can't sleep over. He's going somewhere with his dad early on Sunday morning."

"That's too bad," Jeremy said.

"I was thinking about playing D&D, but we could do something together if you wanted," I offered.

"That would be nice," he said gently. "Did you have a good time with Jeff?"

I didn't want to think about what happened. "I got kissed by a girl."

"You what?" He grinned and slapped my back.

"She's seventeen," I said.

He whistled. "Is she hot?"

"Oh yeah," I winked. "Big tits."

"Nice," he said. I knew he was pretending. I knew better than everyone that he didn't care about girls being hot or big tits. "Is this going to be a steady thing?"

"Come on, she's *seventeen.* She's not going to date a seventh grader. We're not even friends, she's Jack's sister. Besides, it wasn't a real kiss, just on the cheek."

"Give her a week, she'll be madly in love with you."

"Puh-lease," I said.

"It's easy to fall in love with you," he said, kissing me on the head. I finished with my teeth and stood in the doorway to the bathroom, watching him reading in bed.

"What would happen if I got a girlfriend?" I asked.

"I would buy you all the condoms you needed," he said without looking up from his book.

"I'm serious," I said.

"I'll be happy for you when you get a girlfriend. No, I won't be jealous, and no, I won't think you're cheating on me. Besides, you'll be on your own at conservatory soon enough."

"You said you would get an apartment wherever I got in so we could live together."

"You'll be happier living with the other students, making friends and living your own life. I'd be in the way."

"What if I didn't get into a conservatory?" I asked. "What if I went to school here and then a regular college?"

"Don't be silly, you'll have no problem getting in."

I tried to look away, but he noticed.

"That's not what you mean, is it?" He patted the bed but I couldn't move. "I've been putting off this conversation for too long. I've noticed the change. You're still practicing diligently, but your heart isn't in it. You don't play like you used to play."

"I still love playing," I said.

"You don't think you can do it?"

"I don't think I want to," I said. He put down his book and looked at me with sad eyes. "Please don't be mad at me."

"I'm not mad," he said gently. "I want to understand."

"I never want to stop playing the piano," I said. "I love making music. But when I think about spending all my time practicing and performing, it doesn't feel right. I want to do something important with my life. Something that makes the world a better place. I want to help people who need help, other kids that have problems or need a friend. Help them like you helped me." He didn't say anything. "You're disappointed."

"I'd be lying if I said I wasn't," he said softly. "You have so much talent. It would be a shame if you didn't share it with the world and leave your mark on music. I think that's important." He came over to me, lifting my chin with his hand so I looked at him. "I want you to know something. What you do with your life isn't my choice. It's yours

and yours alone. Never let anyone tell you what to do, not even me. If this is what you want, I'm behind you one hundred percent. What happened to the boy who knocked on my door with his shovel? He turned into a confident, outgoing, and mature young man who has the brains and the balls to make his life whatever he wants it to be."

"I'm not like that," I said quietly.

"Like hell you're not," he said fiercely. "It's been hard for me to accept, but in my heart, I know what I have to do. I have to get out of your way. I will always love you and I'll always be here for you. I hope I'll always have a place in your life. The way things used to be, when it was just the two of us – it's never coming back. And that's the way it should be. What I need doesn't matter. You need the freedom and space to find your own way. Ever since that night you came home late and I said terrible things about your teacher, I've been coming to terms with something I've always known but couldn't admit. Loving you means I have to do the right thing for you. I want you to make me a promise, a very serious one. Don't look back and don't feel guilty. I'm going to be alright. I'm here to catch you if you need it, but don't feel like you ever need to miss out or hold yourself back because of me. That means you go with your friends when you want. That means you sign up for the play, you run on the track team, you help whoever you need to help, you get a girlfriend, and you go off to college. Live your life the way you want."

"I don't want to leave you," I said.

"I don't want you to leave either," he said. "You'll always have a home with me and can stay as long as you like. Just not as long as *I* like. Never do anything because you think it's what I want. That includes sleeping with me."

"What if I still want to sleep with you?" I whispered.

"Then you'll always be welcome," he whispered back. "Even when you're sixty-four."

"I love you," I said.

I did. And I would. Even when forever came.

James Edison

Part 6

James Edison

Chapter 40

April 1, 2007

I'm holding him close to me, our bodies pressed together, his back to my chest. I'm naked, and I know he is too. I can feel his stomach under my hands, taut and smooth. I can feel myself, hard like I haven't been in ten years, nestled into the cleft of his ass. I know he's hard too. I can hear it in his breath and feel it in his body. I know we've already made love. I explored every crevice of his beautiful body. I've been inside him and he's been inside me. I know he's ready for more, and I know I am too. I know that nothing has ever felt so perfect before. I kiss him on the neck. He turns over, his dark hair in his face, his eyes full of tenderness, welcoming me. My sweet Alex.

I woke up, sweating and shaking.

At first, I was convinced it was a memory, not a dream. My version of erotic dreams were usually terrifying nightmares, following a strict pattern of losing control, exposure, and humiliation. I knew nothing happened after I told him I had a crush on him. We snuggled on the couch for a while and went to bed. Separate beds. End of story. At three in the morning, alone in the darkness, it was hard to convince myself that my original memory was the real one. Maybe it was a lie I told myself to forget what really happened. Or maybe my memory was faulty because we smoked too much really good shit. It took me the rest of the night to convince myself nothing happened.

I should've felt relieved. Instead, I was disappointed.

Jeremy used to tell me the universe had a plan. It didn't whisper very often, but when it did you had to seize the opportunity or lose it forever. I remembered a time when Jake was a toddler. Julia dragged me to a Halloween party thrown by one of the moms from his Gymboree class. We didn't know them well and Julia didn't like them, but she wanted to make sure Jake had playdates. I slipped away from the conversations about sports and granite countertops to a home theater in the basement where six pre-teen boys had set up shop. They didn't mind an adult invading their space, and I certainly preferred their company. Before long, I joined in with one of them to heckle the movie. By our final count, the hero had fired sixty-one shots from a revolver without reloading. The others drifted off, but my new friend stayed until the end. He even followed me out of the theater when the movie was over. Julia found me, demanding that we leave because she couldn't stand to spend another moment with these people. I would've preferred to linger a while longer and get to know my new friend, but I couldn't say no to her. I shook his hand, told him I was disappointed we couldn't make fun of another movie, and asked his name.

"Jeremy," he told me.

The universe was whispering to me. We were meant to meet. Maybe more. I couldn't listen because it would've been too difficult to explain to Julia why I wanted to befriend a twelve-year-old boy. Ten years later, that encounter still nagged me. What would've, could've, and should've happened if I listened.

With Alex, the universe wasn't whispering. It was screaming.

And this time, I was going to listen.

My confession didn't drive Alex away. If anything, it made us closer. For the last couple of weeks, Alex and I had been constant companions. Jake had buried himself qualifying for an honors program at school, spending every free moment locked in a room studying with a group of friends. Most nights he didn't bother coming home, sleeping on floors and couches in the dorms. I thought Alex would make himself scarce since Jake wasn't around. Instead, he made himself scarce everywhere else.

I didn't think Alex would be up so early, but by the time I had a pot of coffee brewing I heard his door open. He stumbled downstairs in his

boxers, providing yet another opportunity for me to ogle his body. He found plenty of opportunities to show off. Including the holy grail of them all, the time I came out of my room to catch him in the hall going from the bathroom to his bedroom, wearing nothing at all. Except a towel. Around his neck. He knew how I felt about him, and he'd become even more of an exhibitionist.

It was a sign.

"Coffee," he mumbled. I filled a giant mug that held three full cups, adding a healthy dose of sugar substitute. He took a sip and shook comically all over.

"I thought you'd sleep in," I said.

"Nah, I'm awake," he said. "Especially after drinking this sludge, it's like Monster on crack. Want to see what I did last night?" He dragged me into the office and fired up the computer. Somehow, he captured the video I helped him make. His song, even if they were my lyrics.

"I put it up on YouTube," he grinned. "Look, I've already got three five-star reviews. Who cares if they're all from friends. This video is still going to make me an international celebrity. Practically everything is on YouTube these days. Check this out, it's from the first show I ever did. I had an amazing fourth grade teacher, Mrs. Sawyer. She found the theater group and drove me to rehearsals. I loved the experience even though we were bad, and I mean seriously terrible."

The sea is so full of a number of fish
If a fellow is patient, he might get his wish
And that's why I think that I'm not such a fool
When I sit here and fish in McGelligot's pool
It's possible, anything's possible

The kids forgot their cues, didn't know their lines, and sang so softly they couldn't be heard. It felt so familiar. Alex, on the other hand, belted out his song, loud and clear, impressive for a nine-year-old kid. At least he looked like he was having fun. The rest of them looked like they had stomachaches. I realized he chose to show me this particular video for a reason. If I was patient, I'd get my wish. I wasn't a fool for fishing in this pool. Anything's possible.

It was another sign.

I'd noticed at least a hundred signs over the last two weeks, all pointing at the same thing.

He gave me a particularly clear sign the time we spoke about Julia and I possibly separating a few days ago. "Are you going to start dating again?" Alex asked me.

"I don't think so, at least not for a while," I told him. "We haven't even talked about separating, but I know it's going to happen. My marriage is crumbling because I didn't put any time into our relationship, and I don't think I want to put any time into another relationship right now."

"You need to find the right guy," he said, winking.

"What?" I asked, stunned.

"You're gay, aren't you?" he asked. I stared at him, dumbfounded. "Sure, you're still in the closet, and that's cool, people should make up their own minds about coming out. But that doesn't mean you have to date women. When you're ready, let me know. I might know somebody."

"Look, just because I had some experiences as a child. . ."

"When you're interested, let me know," he said, winking again.

He made it patently obvious he meant himself.

I watched him spinning in my office chair after the video ended. "Let's work out," he said. "I've got tons of extra energy this morning. Besides, Sunday morning is prime viewing for mega-hot gym rats in the locker room." He stood up and fell backwards at me, forcing me to catch him. "If I don't see a naked man soon I'm going to explode."

Granted, I'd never be a mega-hot gym rat, but it was still another sign.

He was particularly well rewarded this morning, the locker room full of the kind of guys who didn't hesitate to show off. Alex enjoyed pointing out which guys were peacocks, strutting their stuff to prove their superior manliness, and which were probably cruising for quick sex. He called his ability to tell the difference "gaydar" and swore he'd never been wrong. I didn't want to explain to him how wrong he was about me. I was something very different from gay. We spent three hours working through the weights because his form was off this

morning. I took every opportunity to gently push parts of his body into the correct position. Another sign.

We were sore and exhausted by the time we made it back into the locker room. The crowd at the gym had dwindled to a few hard-core stragglers, leaving us alone in the locker room.

"Hey, the spa is empty," he said. "Let's go in."

I changed into my swimsuit while he used the bathroom. I thought about waiting so I could watch him change, but the opportunities to ogle him would be limited if he wasn't distracted looking at other guys. I staked out our spot in the spa in case someone else got the same idea. He came in a few minutes later, a towel wrapped around his waist. "Eek," he said when he touched the water with his toe.

"Feels great once you get in," I said.

"Sure, once you're roasting you can't feel it anymore," he said. "After fifteen minutes, we'll be like Bugs Bunny in the cannibal pot. Gaga-oombaga-eem. Alex and Nick soup." He let his towel drop.

Alex was naked. Stark. Raving. Naked.

I had a heart attack.

"Bonzai!" he yelled, sliding into the water. "Shit oh shit oh shit oh shit my balls are on fire!" He hopped around madly. I was speechless, unable to move, form a coherent thought, or do anything besides stare. After a minute he stopped hopping around, settled on the bench across from me, and hissed as he sank into the water.

I snapped back into myself, doubts creeping in. I wasn't sure if a fourteen-year-old boy was even allowed in the spa, let alone in the nude. I could be arrested for sitting in a hot tub with an underage boy. That had to be worth at least twenty years. No matter how much I wanted to stare at him for hours, I had to do something. "You should put on a suit," I said quietly.

"Why? It feels great like this. You should try it."

"What if someone comes in?" I whispered harshly.

"Everyone goes in naked. No one cares and it's not like we're jerking each other off."

Another sign.

He slid off the bench. "Come on, live on the edge. You should try it. Life is more fun when you're not scared to do what you want to do."

Another sign.

"What if I don't want to?" I whispered, even though I absolutely wanted to.

"You don't need to be embarrassed. No one else is watching. It's just me." His eyes sparkled. "If you don't get naked I'm going to pants you myself."

If this wasn't a sign, I didn't know what was. I didn't care where we were. I wanted to grab him, hold him, and press his body against mine. I wanted to let him see me the way I really was. I knew I should be an adult. I needed to get out and tell him to get dressed. If anyone came in I could be revealed, outed to the whole world.

But I didn't want to be an adult.

The universe wound up making sure I didn't do something stupid. Before anything happened, one of the gym attendants came in with a pile of towels. Alex immediately backed off, scooting to the side closest to the door to obscure his nudity. I pulled myself out of the tub and glared at him.

"I'm having problems getting my locker open, can you give me a hand?" I said to the attendant. I followed him out. By the time the attendant explained I was turning the handle the wrong way, Alex had extracted himself and slipped into a shower. The attendant did his thing and left, leaving me to sit on the bench to catch my breath. Alex came back a few minutes later, looking around furtively.

"That was a close one," he said. "Although I really don't know why it was close at all. It's not like guys aren't letting it all hang out in here all the time."

"How many of them are under eighteen?" I pointed out.

"You have a point, but it's unfair for kids to be held to a different standard." He dropped his towel. I had another heart attack. I couldn't bring myself to look away. He had to notice my intense stare, but he didn't acknowledge it. "I don't think people should be ashamed about their bodies."

"You have nothing to be ashamed about," I murmured.

Oh shit, I said that out loud.

"I mean, you're in good shape, not like me." In case he understood what I really meant.

"You're looking much better," he said. "Besides, I see guys in here way fatter and older than you who don't give a shit if anyone's looking. If I see something that doesn't turn me on, I look away. It's not like I'm going to start pointing and telling everyone to get a load of lard-butt in aisle three. This isn't high school. I've decided I'm going to help you get over being embarrassed."

"How are you going to do that?" I breathed.

"Make you believe in yourself," he said.

It was a sign.

I didn't need any more signs.

My decision was made.

"How do I look, apart from the pants falling off because they're too big?" Alex asked when he came out of the dressing room. "Blue is definitely my best color, don't you think? I can't believe I'm wearing a suit. I've never owned a suit in my entire life. I feel like a total sell-out."

"You look stunning," I said.

I waved the tailor over, who immediately got to work measuring and marking with soap. "You can have it done in an hour?" He shook his head, mumbling something about a big job. I knew how to deal with that. A few bills for him and a few more for the salesman. I'd managed to score last minute reservations at the fancy French place in Great Falls, the one that booked up weeks in advance. I wanted to take my Alex out for a nice meal, and I wanted him appropriately dressed before I showed him off to the rest of the world.

Next stop was the salon. Alex insisted on having his hair done by the most flamingly gay guy he could find. He said he wanted a little trim, but when he disappeared into the back of the shop for an hour, I assumed that little trim had morphed into a complete change of style. I expected him to appear with half his hair shaved off, the other half in bright blue spikes to match the suit. When he finally emerged, it took my breath away. The jet-black mop was gone, replaced with a neat, sandy blond conservative haircut. He was always attractive, but now he was cute too. I loved cute.

"Wow," was all I could say.

"I'll probably get all kinds of shit for such a preppy look. I thought since I was wearing a suit tonight, I should have the hair to go with it. Quick, line up a job interview before I put it back to normal."

"I think you look fantastic," I murmured.

"I knew you'd like it," he said.

He did it for me. Another sign.

We picked up his suit when it was ready and headed directly for the restaurant. Alex was unusually quiet on the ride. Maybe being dressed up so nicely made him feel uncomfortable. I couldn't help stealing a look as often as I could. "What are you thinking about?" I asked to break the silence.

"I was pondering how marvelous life can be," he said. "My dad used to tell me he'd disown me if he ever caught me wearing a suit. Not that it really means anything for him to say that since he doesn't own anything in the first place. He really meant if I sold out, became a corporate lawyer or investment banker. Still, he specifically said wearing a suit. Now here I am, wearing my first suit."

"Nothing says teenager like a little rebellion," I said.

"It's not rebellion," he said thoughtfully. "It's change. Like one of those native American coming-of-age rituals without the pain and starvation. Out with the child and in with the man. I felt it on my first day at Pinehurst, but nowhere near as strongly as I feel it right now. Today begins a new part of my life. I'm someone different."

"Who are you?" I asked.

"Alex Welles," he said simply.

"TMF," Alex moaned dramatically. "No more, not even a wafer-thin mint."

"Maybe you should've skipped that second dessert," I said. "Seriously, I can't figure out where you put it all."

"But everything was *soooooooo* yummy," he groaned. He sat up and flashed a wicked smile at me. I took his cue and slid my glass over to him. He drained what was left. "Ahh, nothing like a little champagne

to clear everything up." He made a show of unbuttoning his pants. "Bring on the appetizers, I'm ready to start over."

The waiter dropped off a plate of chocolates and a slip of paper I was afraid to look at. I pushed the chocolates over to him and put my credit card down, hoping it wouldn't melt. He moaned when he bit into it, handing me the half-eaten chocolate so I could taste. "See? That is so good. The only word I can think of is orgasmic." He ate another chocolate, moaning like he was in the throes of sex. I shook my head as an apology at the waiter when he picked up my card.

"I think you're a little drunk," I said.

"I'm buzzed, there's a difference," he pointed out. "Next time we should get wasted first. Can you imagine what this meal would've tasted like if we were high?" He picked up another chocolate, a longer one, pushing it slowly into his mouth with a little wink to me. As though I didn't get the hint. The waiter came back to drop off the check along with a second box of chocolates wrapped in a bow for Alex.

"I will treasure these always," Alex said dramatically to the waiter. "You're cute. Wanna get together when you get off work?"

"My wife might object, and since she could easily kick both our asses I think we'd better not."

Alex pouted. "Can I at least give you a hug?"

"Let's keep it to a handshake," the waiter said. "You're one fantastic kid. I wish I had the guts to say whatever was on my mind when I was a teenager. This is absolutely the most fun I've had waiting a table in ten years. It's been a true pleasure."

I gave him a huge tip.

"We've got to come back here for dinner every single day from now on," Alex purred. "Great food and cute waiters."

"Special meals aren't special if you have them every day," I said. Jeremy used to tell me that.

"Special people are even more special when you see them every day," he said back. I had no response, just like I had no response when he named himself as my son or when he made a toast to "my family" during dinner.

Alex pretended to stumble on the way out of the restaurant, hanging on to my arm for balance. "What's that?" he asked, pointing at an

archway lit with white Christmas lights. He leaned on me as we made our way down a brick pathway lined with carefully trimmed shrubs and low voltage landscape lights.

"A path, where does it go? Lions and tigers and bears, oh my." The noise from the restaurant faded away to the sound of wind in the trees and the music of crickets. Stairs led down to a large brick patio, the noise of rushing water from the river right below.

"I suppose they do weddings out here," I said.

"It's a nice place to get married," he said, leaning over the railing to look at the dark water below. "Maybe by the time I'm old enough I'll be able to marry the person I want. I wonder if I'll wear the tux or the dress." I leaned against the railing and put my arm around his shoulder. "You'll come, won't you? To walk me down the aisle?"

"Of course," I said, turning him towards me. "I'll be there."

Our eyes locked. The moment was perfect, even though we weren't in a private place.

A giant raindrop pelted him in the face. "It's raining," he said in a small voice, his eyes not leaving mine. Heavy drops stained the brick around us. "Oh shit, it's really raining."

Giggling, we ran for the steps, huge drops falling like grenades around us, more like a summer thunderstorm than a spring shower. "Woohoo!" Alex screamed, whirling around with his face up in the air. He could've easily left me behind but stayed near as I jogged up the path. We dashed across the parking lot, tumbling into the car, barely getting the doors closed before the skies completely opened up. Rain battered the car, demanding to get in. Water dripped down Alex's face, his careful hairdo flattened and scattered, his new suit clinging to his body. He shook his head like a dog, water flying everywhere. "You're all wet," he pointed out.

"You too," I answered.

I started the car. "Where to next? I guess we'd better go home, it's coming down pretty hard."

"Home sounds good," he said, stretching his arms. "I'm ready for bed."

A jolt of electricity ran through me.

"Alex," I murmured, turning towards him. His face was open and inviting, just like I remembered from my dream. I brushed a little hair from his face. I couldn't wait until we got home, the desire burning inside me so strong that everything else was shoved aside. I didn't care if the car was an awkward place or that someone might see through the windows. I leaned over, my hand on his cheek, turned his face a bit more to the right angle, and shifted myself to get over the center console, my lips inches from his. . .

He jerked away from me, pressing himself against the car door.

His smile vanished.

"Whoa," he said as a warning.

I listened to his rapid breathing, studied his wild eyes, and fought to comprehend the uncomfortable shock written on his face. I slammed myself back into my own seat, the sound of the rain deafening against the windshield.

"Did you just try to kiss me?" he said in a small voice.

I swore a long time ago I'd never make this mistake again.

"This isn't happening," I said to myself. "I really thought. . ." I slammed my fists into the steering wheel, screaming. He pushed himself harder against the car door, eyes full of panic. My insides were tearing themselves into ribbons.

"Why?" he asked in that same small voice.

"I was so sure it's what you wanted," I moaned. "I told you I have a crush on you."

"Shit," he said. "I thought you meant like a son. I love you as a dad, not a boyfriend."

"Then what the hell has been going on for the last two weeks?" I screamed. "You've been flirting with me constantly! Snuggling in front of movies, walking around in your underwear, getting into the hot tub naked. You said you knew someone I could date if I was interested and made it clear you meant yourself. What was I supposed to think? You were telling me to go ahead!"

"I thought I could help you loosen up a little because you're so repressed about being gay. Oh shit, ok, I was flirting with you a little, but I never thought you were interested that way. I didn't mean for anything to actually happen." He groaned.

I told myself for the last few months that my mind was clearing. I told myself the cloud hanging over me for twenty years was finally dissipating. I told myself it was ok to feel.

I should've known better.

The real cloud evaporated, the one that fogged my mind when I started down this road with Alex. I remembered why I decided not to feel, why I decided to shut myself away from the world. I remembered what nearly happened with my four-year old son in the bathtub. I remembered what nearly happened with Billy. I remembered what *did* happen with Brian. The trail of devastation I left behind me. The trail of devastation *within* me. I'd never get over what Jeremy did to me, what *he* turned me into. I foolishly allowed myself to care again. I nearly devastated the sweetest, smartest, most amazing boy I'd ever met. I almost doomed him to the same hell as me.

I knew what I had to do. I had to find the strength *he* couldn't find.

I threw the car into reverse and backed out.

"None of this is your fault," I said quietly. "I made myself see something that wasn't there, convinced myself of something that isn't possible. Of all people, I should know better. I don't want to hurt someone I care about so much. I know better than anyone how sex ruins everything. It leaves behind a trail of permanent devastation."

I looked straight ahead, gathering my strength.

"I'm taking you back to school," I said. "You can't stay at the house anymore. I'll send your things along tomorrow. I'm sorry."

"You're kicking me out?" he asked.

"I have no choice," I said as we pulled out of the parking lot. "It's the only way to keep you safe."

He made a strangled whimper, like a small animal being crushed in the jaws of a predator.

"I thought you loved me," he said, voice cracking.

"I'm doing this because I love you."

"I don't understand," he said. I made the mistake of glancing in his direction. The devastated look on his face tore my heart to shreds, even more than it was already torn apart. I couldn't let that stop me. I deserved far worse pain for the unforgivable crime of letting myself feel.

"If you stay, it's only a matter of time," I said. "Something will happen and I might not be strong enough to stop it. I care too much about you to take any chances."

He took a deep breath. "Ok," he said, more to himself than me. "Ok, so you tried to kiss me and I said no. No big deal, right? Now you know I wasn't trying to tell you I wanted to be your boyfriend, and now I know you thought I wanted to do it. It was a colossal fuck-up for both of us. Why can't we go back to normal?"

"Things can't go back to normal after something like this. Not for me, and certainly not for you." We turned onto the highway, making the left to head towards school instead of the right to head for home.

"Maybe things can't go back to normal, but we can act like it never happened. Can't we talk about it? I'll stay at the house one more night so we can talk in the morning when our heads are clear. If you still think I should leave, then I will, ok?" I didn't respond. "I'm not freaked out anymore. I shouldn't have gotten that freaked out in the first place. It was just a kiss, no big deal. I've kissed people before. I mean, if you wanted to kiss me then I guess it'd be ok. I guess we could go further. I mean, if you wanted we could go all the way. It's not like I haven't fooled around before."

"Stop," I said quietly. I was terrified he might change my mind.

"If you wanted, I could tie you up, since you like that kind of stuff. I guess if you wanted you could tie me up. . ."

"Stop!" I screamed. He cringed. "I've sat exactly where you're sitting right now. Trust me when I say this road leads to disaster. It's a deal with the devil. Listen carefully to your own words. Every time it comes out as 'if you want'. Tell me honestly if you're offering because you want to have sex with me."

"It's ok if. . ."

"I asked if it's what you want!"

"What am I supposed to say?" he whimpered. "You're kicking me out. I'm serious, I don't want to leave. I'll do anything you want if you let me stay. It's not like you're forcing me. I still love you."

"Sex will ruin your life," I said. "You mean too much to me and have too much ahead of you to sacrifice everything for a cheap thrill." I pulled into the left turn lane to head to school.

"Tell me what I'm supposed to do," he said quietly. "I don't understand why I can't stay. You're my family, don't you understand? I never had a real family before, not like this. I can't go back to not having a family again."

"If you stay, it'll happen," I said. "One day, you'll decide you'll be making me happy by offering yourself. You'll think it'll guarantee you'll never have to leave. Maybe I'll say no once, maybe twice, but eventually you'll wear me down. You'll catch me in a moment of weakness. What happened to me ruined my life. I had a bright future like yours. I was going to be someone, but I never recovered from being abused. You'd never recover from being abused either."

"I'll never recover from being abandoned," he said quietly.

The light turned green. We'd be there in less than five minutes. "You will," I said. "You're an amazing person. You have the brains and balls to make your life whatever you want it to be. I couldn't live with myself if you turned out like me. I'm so sorry I let this go on for so long. I shouldn't have let you get attached so deeply. I know it's going to hurt for a little while. But you'll see, the hurt will fade. After a few months, you'll forget all about me."

"No I won't," he said. "I won't forget what it was like to have a dad."

"Please don't make this harder than it already is," I said.

"I want to make it hard," he said, voice trembling. We reached the gatehouse, the guard taking one glance at my sticker and waving us in. "You can still change your mind. Pull over, we can talk about it." I passed the small lot, continuing up to the main loop so I could drop him off. "Please! What if I told you I'll kill myself if you kick me out?"

"Alex," I said quietly.

"I will," he said. "I'll overdose. I'll jump off the roof. I'll blow my brains out. I'll slit my wrists. I'll leave a note saying it's because you were abusing me so you'll go to jail." He tried to look fierce, but all I could see was terror.

"Alex," I said quietly again. I pulled up to the curb.

He whimpered. "Ok, so I'd never kill myself and I'd never hurt you. Please, just give me a second chance. I'll do everything right. I'll never flirt again. I'll always wear clothes in the house, I'll do all the chores, I'll

mow the lawn and pull the weeds and do the dishes. I'll even learn to cook." He grabbed my coat. "Don't make me leave. You're my dad. I'm your son. For real." I tried to loosen his hands but he wouldn't let go. "Please!" he screamed.

"It's time to go," I said.

"No," he said, shaking his head like a petulant three-year old. "I'm not getting out of the car."

"You need to get out," I said.

"No!" he shouted. "I'm not letting go!"

I didn't want to have to do it this way.

"Get out of the car!" I screamed. "Out!" Shell-shocked, he opened the door and scrambled out of the car, standing on the curb with the door still open. I reached across and yanked it shut. Even through the rain, I could see the desperate look on his face.

I looked away.

He didn't move as I screeched away from the curb, fighting hard not to look in the rear-view mirror. I knew this was the last time I'd ever see him and I didn't want to remember him as a young and fragile boy standing alone in the rain.

I got on the highway and went the wrong way on purpose, no idea where I was going. I told myself I should be proud. For once in my life I did the right thing. But I couldn't make myself feel proud. All I could feel was what it was like to be left behind, to have everything disappear in an instant. To be truly alone.

I drove off into oblivion.

James Edison

Chapter 41

May 25, 1984

I laced up my running sneakers, checking them carefully to make sure everything was snug and comfortable. The obscenely expensive sneakers Jeremy bought for me a few weeks ago were still in their box and that's where they'd stay until after this weekend. It wasn't a good time to make a change. I knew how these sneakers behaved. They were my lucky piece of clothing that saw me through the entire season. You could smell I was coming from a hundred feet away, but lucky sneakers had to smell better than lucky underwear.

I opened the front door to darkness even though it was nearly June. I liked how still everything was this early in the morning – cars still parked in their driveways and kids still asleep in their beds. The world belonged to me. The temperature was already warm and the air was thick with humidity, but a miserable day was never an excuse to skip a run. If anything, I saw it as a challenge. I couldn't imagine starting my day without a long run. I ran in the heat and the cold, through snow, rain, wind, and ice. When I ran, my mind was clear, I had energy, and my mood stayed cheerful no matter what life tried to throw at me. The harder I pushed myself and the more exhausted I was at the end, the better I felt. Last winter, I slipped on ice and twisted my ankle, forcing me to take two weeks off. Everyone noticed my foul mood.

The timer on my watch told me I beat my best time ever to the main road, but I hadn't scratched the surface of what I could do. I poured it on, breaking into a full-blown sprint, imagining the road buckling underneath me and the coyote left in the dust with a taunting "meep

meep." Not that I was much for sprinting – I got walloped every time
I tried. Distance was my skill and my passion. The two-mile was my
specialty, only because two miles was the longest competition for junior
high school kids. I was training to run the New York marathon in
November, and I wasn't just going to finish. I was planning on winning.
Not the whole thing, just my age category.

I kept up the sprint until my lungs burned and my legs ached, slowing
down to a normal run so I could recover. My first stop was coming up
soon. Starting here, I'd have to set a more reasonable pace because no
one could come close to keeping up with me on a distance run. Jonas
wasn't alone this morning, joined by Steven and one of the seventh
graders, Peter. I downshifted my gears without a second thought. This
run wasn't about me anymore. It was about the team. I nodded as they
fell in behind me. I downed half of the big paper cup of water Jonas
handed me and poured the rest over my head. Unlike our afternoon
runs following practice, nobody joked around. Morning runs were for
serious training.

Steven and Peter weren't the only ones to join my regular crew. By
the time the last mile to school rolled under our feet, every single
member of the team had shown up. Some of them struggled to keep
up, so I slowed my pace to an easy jog and ran with the stragglers.

"Doing ok?" I asked Timothy, one of the seventh graders.

"Tired," he said through clenched teeth.

"You'll get past it," I said. "Concentrate on your breathing and pick
up your feet, you're dragging." I put my hand on his shoulder. "You
can make it all the way to school. It's all in your mind. Do you want
it?"

"Yeah," he muttered without any determination.

"You can do better than that," I said, raising my voice. "Do you
want it?"

"Yeah," a few of them shouted.

"Come on!" I yelled. "Do you want it?"

"Yeah!" they shouted back at me. Timothy included.

"First one to the track gets a free garbage sundae!" I yelled. "And
I've got a brand new, never used centerfold for anyone who makes it
five miles around the track with me!" They cheered.

I watched some of them take off, staying behind with the stragglers, offering a word of encouragement every time one was ready to throw in the towel. I loved running, but this was my favorite part of being on the team. Kerry was the official captain but encouraging wasn't really his thing. "Push through, fast as you can!" I yelled as we turned the final corner.

The seventh graders collapsed when they made it to the fence around the track, but still they fought through to the end. I echoed the look of pride on each of their faces. "Let's hear it for Timothy, Raphael, Peter, Zach, and Chris!" I shouted, leading the entire team in a cheer. Kerry gave me a quick nod. He didn't mind that I did this part of the job for him.

"Five miles, who's with me?" I shouted. I knew very few of them would make it the whole five miles, but no one was going to miss the start. Not even the seventh graders, who looked at each other and peeled themselves off the ground. I made sure to give each one a clap on the back.

"Looking good!" Coach Z called from the bleachers as we ran around the track. He showed up early in the mornings to let us into the school so we could shower and change. Jeremy also showed up early to bring my clothes, books, and some breakfast. When he saw the whole team was there, he dashed off to get enough bagels and orange juice for everyone.

"What time today?" Jeremy asked.

I thought about my schedule. "Better make it five-thirty."

He tipped his imaginary hat. "Limo service at five-thirty. Have a good day."

I gave him a big hug. That kind of thing stopped embarrassing me a while ago. "You too."

Coach Z gathered us up in the locker room, holding up his hand until we quieted down. "Tomorrow, this team is going to lead John Witherspoon Junior High to its first ever state final for any sport in the history of this school!" Cheers. "You've all worked your asses off to get here, and I know every single one of you will give a hundred and ten percent tomorrow. No matter what happens, I'm proud of the finest team this school has ever assembled. You should be just as proud of

601

yourselves, whether we win or lose." He paused for a second. "But I already know we're going to win!" Everyone yelled, and we put our hands together for a team shout.

Coach Z sat down next to me, holding his nose. "Promise me you'll burn those sneakers after the meet." I laughed. He leaned in and spoke softly. "You're the reason we're going to the state finals."

"I'm not the only one winning events," I pointed out.

"Your leadership brought out their best. You inspired them in a way I never could. The school should hire you as coach. Feeling good?"

"Real good," I said.

"Ready to kick ass tomorrow?"

"Gold or bust," I said.

I spotted Timothy sitting on the bench on my way to the shower, still in his running clothes. "Aren't you going to take a shower?" I asked, sitting down next to him. He shrugged. "Are you embarrassed? It's no big deal if you are. Anyone who teases another guy in the shower has to do a hundred pushups." He didn't budge. "We're all boys, so there's nothing to be ashamed about."

"But. . ."

"You can tell me," I said softly.

He whispered in my ear. "I'm not. . .circumcised."

"Who cares?" I said. He blinked. "Want to know a secret? The more you look like you care, the more everyone gets interested. If you act like you don't care, no one else will either. Sometimes I get a hard-on right in front of everyone. Fucking embarrassing, right? But I don't pay any attention so no one bugs me about it."

"That's because you're you," he said. "No one makes fun of you."

"I remember you from elementary school when you were in fifth grade. Remember me? I was fat and got teased all the time. I figured out the more you let it bug you, the more they tease. All you have to do is believe in yourself. Ok?"

Timothy smiled, just a little.

He looked awfully cute when he smiled.

"Good morning, this is your eighth-grade student council president Nick Welles with the morning announcements. Today is May 25th, TGIF. The forecast is sunny, humid, and hot – but not hot enough to close school for the day so don't get excited. Miss Riccoli in the nurse's office wants to remind everyone to drink lots of water. As always, Mr. Richards asked me to remind everyone to walk in the stairwells – we don't want anyone breaking a leg. Also, jumping those last few stairs is forbidden and punishable by life in prison without parole, so keep those feet on the ground, people. Mr. Richards also wants me to remind you that smoking is forbidden at school, but since that only gets you suspended it's no surprise the bathrooms smell like ashtrays. Mrs. Kowalski has canceled choir practice this afternoon, so don't show up unless you like singing solo. Coach Zacarro wants me to remind everyone that tomorrow your track team will be competing in our school's first ever state final competition, including yours truly running the two-mile. We hope the whole school shows up in East Brunswick to cheer us on. Tickets go on sale for Snoopy the Musical today at lunch, directed by everyone's favorite English teacher Mr. Humber, with musical direction by guess who. It's like these announcements are all about me. Tickets are two dollars in advance, three at the door. Our performance is next Saturday at seven and it's going to be awesome, so don't miss it! As always, tutoring club will be in the back corner of the cafeteria during lunch, no sign-ups required. We're always looking for more tutors especially in math, so if you're one of those math people stop by and share your brain for a few minutes. Mentors, meet after the final bell in front of the office for a quick check in. If you're interested in helping one of your fellow students, please stop by or grab me in the hall. This weekend is Memorial Day, so have a great barbecue and take a moment to think about all those people who gave their lives to keep our country free and give us a day off school. You guys rock. One last thing. It's come to your announcer's attention that a certain English teacher who wishes to remain anonymous is celebrating his 33rd birthday today, so if you see him in the halls make sure to wish him a happy one. Remember, you decide what kind of day you're going to have, so make it a great one. All you have to do is believe in yourself. This is Nick, signing off. Later."

I pushed the button on the microphone. "Mr. Welles!" Mr. Humber's voice boomed across the office. I grinned broadly at him. "You and I are going to have a *very* lengthy conversation about the meaning of the word confidentiality."

I was working on a witty response when Mr. Richards poked his head out of his office. "I thought we talked about keeping the ad-libs to a minimum. Life imprisonment without parole?"

"Just making it fun for everyone," I said. "Besides, Mr. Humber isn't angry I told everyone about his birthday."

"Furious is more like it," he growled. "If I were capable, smoke would be curling from my ears."

"Come on you two, I only have a few minutes," Mr. Richards said. "Let's get Nick off to class on time for once." Mr. Humber's eyes drilled into my head as he followed me into Mr. Richards' office.

"You've done a commendable job on the tutoring and peer mentoring programs," Mr. Richards said to me as I sat down. "How many students do you have participating as tutors? Ten?"

"Thirty-seven," I said. "And we have twenty mentors so far."

He looked surprised. "You've done a fantastic job, well beyond anyone's expectations." He opened my proposal and paged through it. "I appreciate what you're trying to accomplish with this peer counseling proposal, but I have a couple of reservations about allowing a program like this."

"Like what?" I asked.

"The district believes counseling is best provided by trained professionals," he said. "We already have three guidance counselors, and it strikes me student counselors would likely interfere in their work. The idea of absolute confidentiality feels dangerous to me as well. If a student is being hurt or hurting themselves, it's critical they get the help they need. Besides that, I could only imagine what would happen if a student shared highly confidential information which then became public knowledge. Even well-meaning students have trouble keeping secrets. There's also the question of liability if something were to go wrong."

I smiled because Mr. Humber and I had gone over all those points before so I knew what my answers would be. "My proposal addresses

all those things," I said. "Peer counselors are very different from guidance counselors. We'll have a training program that helps peer counselors understand confidentiality and when to get outside help. Other peer counseling programs have worked through these problems. We can follow their model."

"I'd like you to think more deeply about the issues I've raised and polish this proposal a bit further before I take it to the superintendent. Ken, can you help Nick work these things through?"

"Of course," Mr. Humber said.

The bell rang. "You'd better get yourself to class," he said to me. Mr. Humber followed me out as I grabbed my books from the microphone desk.

"You've apparently ruffled more feathers than I expected," Mr. Humber said quietly to me. "I feel strongly Mr. Richards is supportive of your efforts, but he is rightfully concerned about resistance from the guidance office as well as the district's attorneys. My job will be to ascertain the full nature of his concerns so you can properly enhance your proposal to address them." He put his hand on my shoulder. "You've done a remarkable job putting that proposal together. Assembling sophisticated arguments and detailed facts would be a challenge for most experienced adults, let alone an eighth-grade student. I am, as always, impressed with your ability and perseverance."

"It was your idea," I said.

"Never be afraid to accept credit where credit is due," he said.

A bunch of girls shouted in the hallway. "Happy Birthday, Mr. Humber!"

He cringed. "But you will still answer for your actions this morning!"

"Happy birthday Mr. Humber!" I yelled. The whole hallway joined in. He shrieked like a girl and fled.

"I still don't get it," Carl said. "How can a number get smaller when you multiply it?"

"Because you're multiplying by a fraction," I explained. "When you multiply by a regular number, it means take this many of that number

and add them together. But when I multiply by a fraction, I'm saying I take only part of the number so it's smaller. What's a quarter of eight?"

"That's easy, it's two," he said, scratching his head.

"You just multiplied eight by one fourth," I said, pointing to the first problem on his worksheet.

"Really?" he said, staring at the sheet. "That's easy."

"Yup," I said. "You do the next one." He made a face and scratched at the sheet with his pencil, figuring out the answer to twenty-seven times a third in just a few seconds. "That's right. Now how about the one where you have to multiply by three fifths over here?"

"Wait, I think I get it. Do I figure out one fifth first and then multiply that by three?"

"You don't need my help anymore," I said. "Get lost."

He grabbed his worksheet, mumbling thanks before heading back to his lunch table. I sat back in my chair and took a bite of my sandwich before anyone else needed help. Lunch was open tutoring, so anyone could get help for a few minutes on anything they wanted. "Nick," Scott called from the other table. "What's the difference between xylem and phloem again?"

"Xylem carries the water up and phloem carries the sugars down."

"Oh yeah," he said, turning back to the girl he was helping. I never would've thought class clown Scott Epstein would turn out to be the most dedicated tutor in the club. He wasn't the smartest person in my classes, but he sure as hell was a genius at tutoring. Once he understood something, no matter how complicated it was, he had a way of explaining it so the most confused kid understood. I learned how to tutor by watching him. Whenever someone asked him why he spent so much time on the tutoring club, he said it was because he got to hang out with a lot of girls. But I knew the truth. He was addicted to helping people, just like me.

Ana slid into the chair next to me. "I watched what you did with that kid and the fractions. I don't think I could be that patient."

"I'll bet you'd be good if you gave it a try," I said.

"I have enough trouble with my own homework," she said. "Are you busy tonight? I was thinking about going to the dollar movies. Want to go?"

"I promised my uncle I'd hang out with him," I said. "How about going with me to see Andy's band? They're playing a garage concert Monday afternoon."

"What are they calling themselves now, Ubiquitous Sludge?" she asked. "What's that supposed to mean anyway? I heard they were terrible."

"They're getting better. Besides, they renamed it Bone Marrow Transplant." She laughed. "I know, but he's my friend. It'll be fun, at least until the neighbors call the cops because of the noise. Pick you up around noon?"

"As long as I'm back for dinner," she said. "I'll bring extra earplugs for you. Mr. Humber says we're starting in five minutes. I've got to get changed."

I watched her wind her way through the tables. Ana was as close as I'd come to having a "thing" with a girl, but in truth she was just a friend. I liked her and she liked me, nothing more. I supposed if I was going to have a girlfriend she'd be the one, but I didn't feel it with her. Not like I felt it with Molly Idontknowherlastname, with her frizzy hair and love of science fiction, holding hands by a pond under the stars at a fancy restaurant. Anastasia wasn't Molly. Not quite.

I went out of my way to a table off to the side where Brian and his two seventh-grade friends were playing chess. Brian had been bitten badly by the chess bug. The three of them ate, breathed, and crapped chess. He was playing a speed game where they only had a second to make a move, pieces flying around the board so fast I couldn't tell what was going on. I played sometimes when Brian and I hung out on Saturday nights and I always lost spectacularly. Brian and I were still friends, but I think we both knew we were going in different directions. I was happy he found these two kids. He deserved friends with more time than I had.

"Mate in three moves," Brian said flatly. The other one knocked over his king. "Good game," he said, and looked up at me. "Hey, Nick. Want to play?"

"I've got to do a thing for the musical," I said. "Pick you up at seven on Sunday since the meet is tomorrow?"

"Yeah. See you later." He turned back to his friend. "Another game."

The rest of my old friends hadn't changed a bit since I first met them. Sure, they were all taller, their voices had changed, Chris had a major problem with acne, and Jonathan was dating Ann Solomon, the girl he asked to dance at the seventh-grade Halloween party. Otherwise, it was like time left them behind. They still played D&D at lunch, carrying on about plus five swords and bags of holding. But they were my friends and would always be my friends. Maybe D&D wasn't quite as interesting as it used to be, but it was still fun, and I wanted to make sure I remembered who my friends were at a time when friends were a lot harder to come by. "Look who descended from his throne to join the commoners," Chris said. "You're not joining in the middle."

"I know. I wanted to make sure we're still playing Sunday morning."

"Only if you're bringing pizza," he said.

"Your face is enough pizza for all of us," Andy said to him.

"Yeah, I'll bring pizza," I said before Chris could flip his lid. "You supply the beer."

"That's my department," Daniel said. Being caught shoplifting tapes at the mall three months ago didn't slow him down. It only made him more careful.

"Whatever," Chris said. "Bring four this time, Parker can eat two by himself."

"I can't eat two pizzas," Parker whined. "One. Not two."

"I'll be there at ten," I said.

"Yeah," Chris said. "Ok, back to the giant flesh-eating maggots. . ."

I made my way to the front of the cafeteria, sitting down at the piano. Mr. Humber snuck up behind me, his hands menacingly on my shoulders. "I've not had a moment's peace since your impromptu announcement this morning," he muttered. "My third period class broke into song and my fourth period class presented me with a three-foot high handmade birthday card. Rest assured, I'll be certain to repay your kindness when the opportunity presents itself."

"What can I say?" I grinned. When he found out what we had planned he was really going to flip.

He jumped up on stage and stood in front of the microphone. "Ladies and gentlemen, if I may have your complete and undivided attention! For your dining pleasure, the cast and crew of Snoopy the Musical would like to present a small taste of what lies in store for the privileged few lucky enough to possess tickets to our performance next weekend. Maestro, if you please." I played my vamp while everyone took their places.

Normally, Snoopy was a musical for six actors. Mr. Humber and I (along with a lot of help from Jeremy) adapted it to add a chorus and move the singing parts around. Much better than the way we did Charlie Brown last year, when three or four kids played a single role, switching after each scene and using colored shirts to show what part they were playing. I spent a lot of time working with everyone on their singing. I didn't know much about how to sing well, but I *did* know how to make it sound like music. The song came off without a hitch, even though it was a disaster when we ran it a week ago. Just like last year, the show was coming together at the very last minute. The entire cast shouted Snoopy at the end, the cafeteria bursting into applause. I'd never get tired of the feeling of excitement I got from people clapping at me.

"Thank you!" Mr. Humber said into the microphone. "Tickets are a measly two dollars in advance and three dollars at the door, so we hope everyone joins us next Saturday night at seven! And don't forget to be everything you can be!" Ana grabbed the microphone from him and nodded to me. I played the final bar so that everyone knew what we were supposed to sing. Mr. Humber put his hand over his face while the entire school sang Happy Birthday to him. I ran up on stage when it was done to help give him his present.

"For our esteemed director!" Ana said, and the cast parted to reveal a director's chair and old-fashioned megaphone. Jeremy took me all the way to New York to buy them. Mr. Humber sat down, looking like he was going to say something when the bell rang.

"That's a wrap!" he yelled through the megaphone. "Five minutes until fifth period!"

Mr. Humber came up to me while I was getting my books from the piano. "This has your name written all over it," he grumbled.

"Although I must offer my compliments. The chair and megaphone are an inspired and unique gift. I've come to expect yet another complete copy of Shakespeare's work for every birthday and Christmas. It seems that being an English teacher immediately causes everyone to think of Shakespeare. I'm sure I'll achieve my ambition of having a full fifty copies before my fortieth birthday."

"Seriously, we almost bought one for you," I said, laughing.

"So maestro, what is your assessment of our state of preparedness this year?"

"Pretty darn good," I said. "I played as loud as I wanted without drowning anyone out, everyone knew their lines, and no one missed a cue."

"It's a miracle how a show comes together," he said. "I've never had a cast sound so polished and professional in all my years of directing at this school. Since I've not altered my methods, the only logical conclusion is the introduction of a new element has caused this exponential improvement. That element is you."

"I didn't do anything special," I said.

"Your dedication, willingness to offer yourself whenever a cast member needed help or there was a chore to be done, insistence that everyone give their best performance, and constant encouragement has inspired this cast to greatness it wouldn't have otherwise achieved. You have a quality that inspires those around you to care as much as you do." He bowed down in front of me. "I remain impressed and continue to expect great things from you. But I will not hesitate to write a referral if you are late for your fifth period class."

I felt like I was glowing as I pushed the doors open and joined the throngs of kids in the halls.

My halls.

My school.

"He shoots, and he. . .scores!" I yelled, giving Jeff a high five so hard my hand stung. He picked up the ball and bounced it to Eric.

"Twenty-eight, twenty-four," Eric yelled. "One more and you goin' down!" Jeff and I nodded slightly at each other. We'd make a good show of it, but we'd let Eric get this basket and win the game. We decided to lose on purpose, but only if we could do it so Eric couldn't tell. When I first met Jeff a year ago, he wouldn't have thrown a game if his life depended on it. People change.

Eric bounced the ball to Drew, who looked for an opening. Drew was probably the best mentor we had, so Mr. Humber and I both thought he was the best match for Eric. I'd never met a kid in foster care before. He moved in with Ana's family three months ago, which was the only reason I knew Eric was a foster kid. She told me some scary details. Both of his parents were in jail for selling drugs. They used to have him carry the drugs around in his backpack because the cops would never stop a kid. There was a rumor he might've seen a guy get shot in the head right in front of him. Eric fascinated me because he had real problems, not the usual inconveniences caused by parents, friends, and schoolwork. It wasn't our job to fix him – he had therapists, social workers, and some lady called a resource worker who followed him around school all day. Our job was to give him a taste of what it was like to be a normal kid.

I put my arms up and blocked Drew as best as I could, but basketball wasn't really my game. He easily dodged around me and passed the ball to Eric, who charged aggressively at Jeff and bowled him over. I figured that's how they played basketball in Jersey City. Eric threw the ball in the air, trying to do some kind of fancy move and completely botching it. At least he caught the ball on the rebound and put it in.

"Yeah!" he shouted. "Kick yo' ass!"

"Shit!" I shouted, for effect. It made him feel better if he thought we were mad about losing. "You wouldn't have gotten that basket if you didn't foul Jeff."

"Hey, I didn't do nothin' wrong," he said. "I didn't hear no whistle."

"Because there's n-n-no ref," Jeff said. "You'd already b-be benched."

"You mad cause you got torched," Eric said, giving Drew a high five.

"Next time," I growled. "We're going to wipe the floor with you."

"In yo' dreams!" he gloated.

Jeff and I left the two of them to shoot baskets, heading back into the school. "You didn't tell me how you did on that big math test." He made a sour face and dug into his backpack. "You faker. B plus! You didn't think you'd get better than a C on it."

"I r-r-remembered some of the things we s-s-studied," Jeff said.

"It'll be an A next time, you'll see," I said.

"The speech th-therapist says I'm g-getting better."

"Duh, anyone can tell that," I said, rolling my eyes. "You hardly stutter anymore. I don't care about this shit. I want to hear about Jodi Turner. Did you ask her out?"

"I can't tell if she l-l-likes me," he whined. "A-and my stuttering g-g-gets worse when I t-talk to her. It's g-going to be embarrassing."

"Come on, she definitely likes you," I said. "She's probably one of those girls who doesn't like to ask first, but I saw you guys talking at the mall. She's totally into you. Just ask her."

"She's going to say n-n-no," he muttered.

"All you have to do is believe in yourself," I said. "She won't be able to resist your charms. You'll take her to the dance and sweep her off her feet and probably get to second base if you play your cards right."

He turned red. Seventh graders always got so embarrassed by everything. Was I that bad when I was twelve?

"Who are you g-g-going with?" he said.

"Ana, duh," I said.

"But you t-told me she's not your g-girlfriend," he pointed out.

"Closest I've got right now," I said. "Why get tied down to one when you can have a dozen? I'm a popular guy."

"Did you get to s-s-second base before?" he asked.

"Oh yeah," I said. "Further."

"Wh-what was it l-like?"

"Scary at first," I said honestly. "Most guys are scared to do something with a girl the first couple of times, but the girls are even more scared. Then you get used to it and it's the most awesome thing ever."

"Who did you d-do it with?"

"That's a secret," I said. "The last thing you ever want to do is talk about what you did with a specific girl. Doing that makes you a huge jerk. I'm giving you some homework for tonight. When you get home, call Jodi and ask her to the dance. I won't be home so leave a message. If you don't ask her, you have to run five miles with me Monday morning."

"F-f-five miles?" he said. I think he actually gulped.

"So you'd better do it," I said, poking him in the chest. He nodded as though I was serious. "Still coming to the meet tomorrow?"

"My d-dad is driving me with Kyle and S-s-sam," he said. Kyle and Sam were his neighbors, twins in fifth grade. I hung out with them once, but it felt more like babysitting to me. I think Jeff liked it because he could have a little vacation from being a teenager. He still had his moments, shutting himself in his room and screaming at everyone. Not very often any more, especially since I made sure he wasn't bullied. A kid named Ivan was picking on Jeff at the beginning of the year. I cornered him in a hall and was about to tell him that if I ever caught him bullying anyone in my school, I'd wipe the sidewalk with his ass. Right before I opened my mouth, I realized I was about to *be* the bully. So instead, I told him I'd heard all about him and wanted him to join my new tutoring club because he was such a cool guy. I think that strategy worked out a lot better, because he turned out to be a decent kid. The same with Tommy Walker. Beating him up didn't stop him from being a bully. Getting him a mentor, which turned into a guidance counselor, which turned into a professional thing made a difference. He wound up going to a different school, but he actually apologized for being such a jerk to me before he left. I told him that meant a lot to me, and I think that meant a lot to him too.

"My dad's here," he said. "See ya t-tomorrow."

"Not if I see you first," I fired back.

"You don't stare at me like you used to," I said. The sunset made everything look pink.

"I don't remember staring at you," Jeremy answered.

I rolled over on the blanket. "All the time," I said. "I'd look up from a movie or doing homework or practicing and catch you staring at me. I used to like when you stared, and even had a name for it. I called it your love look."

"I suppose I'll try to stare at you more often," he said. "I don't remember deliberately staring at you, but I guess it makes sense. You're important to me."

"I know why you don't stare," I said. "You're not attracted to me anymore. Sometimes you stared at me out of love, other times because you thought I was hot."

"I don't think that has anything to do with. . ."

"It's true," I interrupted. "I don't look like a little boy anymore. I grew six inches last year. I have hair growing in my pits and a forest in my crotch. My voice dropped and my shoulders got broader. I've got pimples trying to pop out. I'm starting to look more like an adult than a kid. You're into younger boys, not teenagers."

"That doesn't change how I feel about you in the slightest," he said.

"You don't want my body the same way," I said. "My ass isn't as hot and it's not as much fun to suck my dick, is it? We're still screwing every night, but I can tell it's not the same and it's been that way for a while."

"I don't want things to change," he said.

"You can't change who you are," I said. "I don't mind. I like sleeping with you. I still love you and I know you still love me. I was thinking it's time for you to find another boy who needs you."

"I don't care how old you are or what you look like," he said. "I never want to split up with you."

"I didn't mean that we'd split up, only that you got involved with another boy." I leaned against his legs so he could wrap his arms around me. "A lot of boys need someone like you. Someone who really cares and makes them feel like they're someone worth loving. I got a lot of nice compliments at school today from people that count. Mr. Humber said he was impressed, twice. Mr. Richards said I did a great job on the tutoring and mentoring clubs. Coach Z said I was the reason we're going to the state championships. Even though I don't know everyone at school, they all know me. I have more friends than I can keep up

with, and I could probably get any girl in the school to go on a date with me. All because of you. You believed in me. You were there for me when no one else was."

"All I did was nudge you along," he said.

"It'd be a waste if you didn't do the same thing for other boys who need someone like I did."

"Come on, how am I going to find another boy?" he said. "The only reason we're together is because you rang my doorbell. How many other lonely eleven-year-old boys have you seen at the front door lately?"

"I can help you find younger boys who need someone."

"Nick," he said gently. "What we have is special, maybe even unique. A lot of things had to happen in just the right way for everything to work out the way it did. You were the right boy with the right parents and the right set of circumstances. The chances of everything coming together so perfectly were astronomical enough. Imagine the odds against winning the lottery twice. It's too likely things won't work out. The potential cost for me and that boy is just too high. I have you. That's enough for me."

"You're lying," I said. "It's not enough."

"Why do you say that?"

"Because I know you watch our sex video tapes when I'm not around," I said. "You probably didn't think I knew. The only reason I know you watch them is because I watch the torture video, when I'm in the right mood. Every time I look for it, the tapes are in a different order. It doesn't bother me that you watch them."

"Let me put it this way," he said. "It's going to have to be enough for me. I've got movies, pictures, and memories, and that's what I'm going to settle for because that's all I'm going to get. I'm never getting involved with another boy. I couldn't start over after what I've had with you. I'd want things too fast and I'd push too hard. You're right, I prefer younger boys and I miss that interaction. The emotional interaction, not just the sex. That doesn't mean I'm lying when I say I love you very deeply."

"I know," I said. "I can't imagine what it's going to be like waking up in the middle of the night without you snoring next to me. It's going

to suck when I go to college and have to sleep alone. I'll have to get a girlfriend who snores really fast."

He laughed and held me tighter.

"The reason I do things to help other kids is because you helped me. I got so much and I want to give some of that back. I want some other kid to get fixed the way you fixed me."

"Who knows what the future will bring," he said. "If the universe wants me to find another boy, it'll make it happen no matter how much I try to stand in its way. Promise me you're not going to play matchmaker. I don't want you getting sucked up into anything that could ruin your future."

"Ok," I said.

"Can I ask why you watch that particular tape?" he asked. "Do you think about asking me to do that to you again?"

"No," I said. "I mean, I still think about being tied up sometimes. I don't think that desire will ever go away completely. I don't ask you to tie me up because it feels like going backwards. I want sex to be about love, not pain. I watch that tape because I want to remember what it was like. I remember one time when you told me I was a really tough kid. I thought you were full of shit. When I watch myself getting tortured, I realize you were right. I look so young, but I survived it. I get strength from watching it. Whenever I feel like there's too much pressure from school, friends, and all the stuff I'm doing, I watch that movie and realize how tough I can be. It reminds me I can do better than survive. I can accomplish anything I want."

"If anyone told me you'd be saying this when I was doing it to you, I would've called him a lunatic." I laughed. "You're an amazing person, Nick Welles."

"Thanks," I said.

"Graffiti rock," I called out.

"Waterfall," he called out a minute later.

"River," I called out a few minutes later.

"And that's the white rock," he said, bringing the car to a stop. "This is as far as we've ever gone down this road. Are you ready to keep going?"

"Yeah," I said, but I wasn't very sure. He continued to drive slowly down the winding, narrow road. To our left, a rock wall rising about fifty feet. To the right, some trees blocked our view of the river even though it less than a hundred feet away. I could hear rushing water clearly through my open window.

I hung on to Jeremy's explanation why we turned around each time we reached a new landmark. "Whatever's down there can't possibly be as exciting as anything you can imagine. So why spoil it? It's more fun to keep imagining exotic, secret places where government agencies dissect aliens from crashed UFO's, or mysterious valleys where dinosaurs still roam. Don't let the mundane world crush your fantastic dreams."

He turned a corner. My breath caught in my throat, choking back a small scream. In front of us was a red traffic light. And two signs.

He read the yellow diamond one. "One lane road ahead."

I read the white rectangle one. "Five minute red light."

We both said "whoa" at the same time.

Life was a one lane road. No way to turn back.

We had five minutes to decide.

I was scared shitless.

"I have a bad feeling about this," he said.

"Turn the ship around," I said back.

"I think you're right," he said.

As he turned the car around on the narrow road, I somehow knew the road didn't go much further. We were almost at the end. Whatever secrets it held and whatever mysteries it promised to reveal, this was the final gate, a portal to the other side. We couldn't go through without being changed forever.

I decided this was as far as I'd ever go.

James Edison

Chapter 42

June 8, 1984

I was starting to think I got sucked into a Twilight Zone episode.
Jeremy sat up in bed when my alarm went off at four-thirty in the morning. He never woke up with me. "What are you doing?" I asked.

"Getting up," he yawned, stretching his arms.

"Pretty early for you," I said. "Do you feel ok?"

"Busy day, lots to do," he mumbled.

"Like what?"

"You know," he said. "I need coffee." He sleep-walked out of the room.

"Weird," I said to myself.

When I got downstairs, he'd already drank an entire pot of coffee and was making a second pot. "Want some?" he asked, bleary eyed.

"I can't drink coffee before a run," I said. "I have to leave. Are you going to be ok?"

"Ok as anyone can be at five in the morning. How do you get up this early?"

"Go back to sleep," I said, patting him on the head. "Leave getting up early to the grown-ups."

I laced up my sneakers and opened the front door, ready to do my stretches. Jonas, Kerry, and Seth were standing at the end of the driveway. I blinked, but they didn't disappear. Maybe I was having a bizarre dream. I pinched myself but nothing changed. "What's going on?" I asked.

"We thought we'd run with you this morning," Kerry said. "Seth's mom dropped us off. Are you ready?"

"You guys decided this at four in the morning?" I asked like he was full of shit.

They looked at each other. "Last night," Seth finally said.

"Why didn't anyone tell me?"

They looked at each other again. "Surprise," Kerry said.

"You guys are acting weird," I said.

"Hey, look who showed up," Jeremy said, poking his head out the door. "Aren't you leaving?"

"I have to do my stretches," I said.

"Well, hurry up. Clock's ticking." He ducked back inside before I could say anything. I caught him checking on me through the window while I went through my stretching routine, and I caught him checking again just as we were leaving. When we got to the top of the hill, I noticed headlights off to the right side and heard the distant roar of a truck engine.

"It's five in the morning," I muttered. "What the fuck is a truck doing here this early?"

"Let's go this way," Kerry said, turning in the opposite direction.

"Wait, I want to check it out," I said. "They might be robbing houses."

"Let's race," Jonas said. "Last one to the school has to wash everyone's jock straps."

"Has to what?" I asked, but the three of them took off without waiting for me. I groaned and ran after them, looking over my shoulder at a big truck slowly lumbering down the road. The three of them were really booking it. If I didn't pick up the pace, I'd lose sight of them. At this rate they'd be exhausted before we reached the halfway mark. They were going to be humiliated. None of them could come close to taking me in a distance race. Still, I sped up, determined not to let them get too far ahead.

They didn't let up for a second. I was running a real race just to keep up. When I turned the corner to the street where I usually picked up Jonas, I was more than thirty seconds behind them. The three of them

had collapsed, while three other guys had taken off at top speed. "What the hell is going on?" I yelled.

"Relay!" Jonas shouted.

"You gotta beat the whole team or you lose!" Kerry yelled. They grinned as I passed them by.

"It's the only way anyone can beat you!" Seth yelled while trying to catch his breath.

You want a race? You've got a race.

I poured it on.

<center>❧ ❧</center>

Mr. Humber was standing outside the locker room door when I walked out. "Mr. Welles," he boomed. "Just the man I was looking for."

"You're looking for me?" I asked, puzzled. School didn't start for another half hour. I was planning to get some studying done. "Do you need something?"

"I require some aid with a rather large but mundane task," he said. "I was hoping you'd volunteer your assistance so as not to require me to impress my students into slave labor."

"I guess," I said warily. "What do you want me to do?"

"Please accompany me to the office." I walked behind him. "Did you have a good run this morning?"

"Kind of," I said. "The guys organized a surprise race. They got to relay while I had to run the whole thing by myself."

"Were you victorious?"

"Not even close," I said. "I have no idea why they did it."

"I'm certain I have absolutely no idea either," he said in a way that made me think he absolutely had an idea but wasn't going to tell me. I followed him into a small room the guidance counselors used for meetings. Several large cardboard boxes filled with paper were on the table. "The school arranged for programs to be printed for this afternoon's award ceremony. However, said programs were inadvertently delivered unassembled. Each box contains a different page. Your task is to assemble them in the correct sequence, fold them

<center>621</center>

like so, and use the stapler to assemble the booklet." He handed a finished program to me.

"This is going to take hours," I moaned. I should've run away when he said he needed help. The last time he asked, I spent hours cleaning out the prop closets behind the stage.

"I will arrange for you to be excused from your classes this morning," he said. "I will also endeavor to find other volunteers to assist, but I am relying on you to complete this task before the ceremony commences at one o'clock."

Ana poked her head into the room. "Mr. Humber, you said you needed some help?"

"Ah, wonderful," he said. "Please assist Mr. Welles, he will explain the task."

"Mr. Humber, what if. . ." He waved briskly and left without waiting to hear my question. "You've got to be kidding me. We're supposed to put these booklets together. There's got to be a thousand of them. This is going to take all morning."

"Then we'd better get started," she said brightly.

"How come you're here so early?"

"Eric had an appointment, so Mom dropped me off early." She hummed to herself as she assembled and folded, so I did the same thing. When the bell for homeroom rang, I went into the office to do the announcements. Jeff was behind the desk, talking to Mr. Humber.

"Hey, Jeff," I said as I came into the main office. He stared at me like I was a zombie about to eat his brains for lunch.

"I g-g-gotta go," he said, ducking into the vice principal's office, slamming the door behind him.

Mr. Humber beckoned me to the microphone. "The announcements await your attention," he said.

"What was that all about?" I asked.

"If I intended to share the subject of my conversation with anyone other than Mr. Sheffield, they would've been invited to participate." The announcements were over quickly because everything was canceled today for the awards ceremony and school was ending the week after next. Mr. Humber walked me back to the guidance room

like he was a guard escorting a prisoner. Jonas was inside talking to Ana. They went silent the moment they saw me.

"What's going on?" I asked.

"Jonas was telling me about your race this morning," Ana said.

"Yeah, about that," I said to Jonas.

"Sorry, late for class," Jonas said, ducking out before I could say anything.

"What the fuck?" I asked, looking at Ana for an explanation. She didn't respond. "Ok, this is going to sound a little crazy, but all week I've had the strange feeling people are talking about me behind my back. Yesterday a group of girls were in the hall, and I know I heard one of them say to be quiet because I was coming. And another thing – no one will leave me alone for a second. A bunch of people swarm me between classes. I can't even go to the bathroom without two other guys suddenly needing to go at the same time."

Ana put the back of her hand on my forehead. "You're not running a fever, so it must be perfectly normal paranoia."

"I'm serious. Mr. Humber keeps pulling me out of class for random chores. I haven't done any tutoring all week and I haven't seen Jeff for mentoring in two weeks because he keeps changing the schedule on me. I swear, it's like everyone's coordinating with walkie-talkies. 'He's coming past the science rooms, your turn to keep him busy.'"

"Ooh, I love conspiracy theories," she said mysteriously. "Maybe I'm in on it too. Trust no one."

"I'm going to the bathroom," I muttered.

"I'll go with you," she said.

"See?" I pointed triumphantly.

"I'm joking," she said. "Go."

"I will. All by myself."

I went out into the office, surprised and not surprised to find Andy standing at the front desk. "Hey," he said to me. "What are you doing here?"

"Folding programs for Mr. Humber. Why are *you* here?"

"Mr. Humber sent me to pick up an envelope but it's not ready yet," he said quickly. Almost *too* quickly.

"Really." I folded my arms.

"Really," he said. "Right, Mrs. Connolly? I'm waiting for an envelope for Mr. Humber."

"That's right," she said. "It'll be a few more minutes."

I groaned and headed out. "Where are you going?" Andy asked.

"To the bathroom," I said.

"I've gotta go too," I stood my ground and tapped my foot. "What?" he said.

"You tell me," I said.

"Tell you what?" he asked.

I groaned again. "Nothing," I said. He followed me through the halls. I was sure the few kids we passed were staring at me. I stood next to him at the urinals. Maybe Ana was right about being paranoid. Or maybe not. I had an idea how to find out.

"I know what's going on," I whispered to Andy. "I'm only pretending I don't."

"What do you mean?" he said.

"I mean I *know*."

"Know about what?" he asked, sounding baffled.

"Nothing," I muttered.

I was washing my hands when two seventh graders came in. I couldn't hear what they were saying, but the moment they saw me they turned around and left in a big hurry.

"What the hell?" I said to no one.

Which is probably why no one answered.

"Boys and girls, please find a seat and settle down," Mr. Richards said into the microphone. "We have many awards to distribute this afternoon and a limited time in which to do it, so your cooperation is mandatory. Please observe the following rules. If your name is called, make your way to the table up front as quickly as possible to retrieve your award, and then take one of the empty seats to my left. While applauding and cheering your friends is encouraged, insults and other negative speech will be dealt with immediately. No second chances. Finally, please sit quietly and show respect for the students receiving

awards today, as they've all worked hard to earn this recognition. Now, we'd better get started or we'll still be here Monday morning." The room laughed.

I put the program under my seat, memorized after folding and stapling so many of them. Individual class awards, then clubs, then sports, and finally the big overall achievement awards, one for each grade. Those mattered because they came with a two-hundred-dollar scholarship. I knew the track and field award was mine, but I didn't expect to win anything else. I'd already made sure Scott would get the tutoring award and Drew would get the mentoring award. My job today was to clap for everybody, because the ceremony took forever and people got tired of cheering after a while.

When it was over, I wound up with three little wall plaques. I won the music class award which was a surprise, and Mr. Humber gave me the drama club award even though I told him to give it to someone else. When it came time to announce track and field, Coach Z went to the microphone and said, "Like I have to read the name on this one." I got a standing ovation. I was happy Ann Solomon won the eighth-grade achievement award so Jonathan wouldn't be stuck comforting her later. She was rabidly worried about winning awards.

"Ladies and gentlemen, I know it's been a long afternoon, but I beg your indulgence for a few moments longer," Mr. Humber said into the microphone. Mr. Richards had disappeared. "Please remain in your seats, we're not quite done yet." I knew there wasn't anything else on the program. The entire room started to murmur. "Please give your full respect and attention to Mr. Jeffrey Sheffield, who will be presenting this final award."

Jeff? He walked to the stage, dressed in a full suit and tie, clutching a piece of paper in his hand. The murmuring in the room got louder. "Ladies and gentlemen, your continued cooperation is appreciated." Mr. Humber said. He pointed to the back, where Mr. Richards was opening one of the doors.

Jeremy walked in, carrying the video camera.

Followed by my *mother.*

Followed by my *father.*

My stomach did a cartwheel. I really was crazy. Crazy enough to be hallucinating.

"Thank you, Mr. Humber," Jeff said into the microphone. I stared at him, my mind a complete blank. "As Mr. Humber said, my name is Jeffrey Sheffield. I'm a seventh grader here at John Witherspoon Junior High School, and I'll be presenting the final award today." He took a deep breath. More hallucinations. The kid on the podium didn't sound like Jeff. This kid's voice was strong and confident. He didn't stutter at all.

"The award I will be presenting is called the Nancy Sheffield Memorial Award. It's different from the other awards given to students today. It's not an award for getting good grades, or being accomplished at sports, or participating in clubs, or achieving a lot. Instead, this award is given to a student who has made an outstanding contribution to this school as a citizen. Let me explain what I mean. Nancy Sheffield believed a school is like a community, and all of us have a responsibility to contribute for it to be successful. This award is about making our school a better place.

"Nancy Sheffield was my mother. She was also an English teacher at this school. Some of you might remember her. Last year, she died of cancer." A murmur broke out across the room. Jeff stopped until it ended. When it did, there was absolute silence. No whispering. No chairs sliding. No coughing. "My father and I decided to create this award to honor her memory. It includes permanent recognition for the winner on a memorial plaque that will be dedicated this summer in the front lobby of the school, and a scholarship for one thousand dollars.

"At first, I didn't want to present this award. I still miss my mom and it's hard to talk about her, especially in front of a lot of people. I'm also not very good at giving speeches, and my friends know I sometimes stutter. But when my father told me who was getting the award, I knew I had to get up here, even if I had to give a speech." He looked out at the audience. "This is r-r-really scary."

The room clapped and cheered. Some kids didn't because they thought it was cool to be cruel. But there were a lot more of us in my school than them. Jeff waited until the room was quiet again.

"The winner's name won't stay secret for long because every single person in our school knows who he is. I'm going to tell you about him anyway. He's a scholar. He gets top grades in his classes even though grades aren't important to him. What he does care about is doing the best work he can even when he doesn't have to. I asked his teachers and heard stories about his projects and assignments which were some of the best they'd ever seen. He's a musician. I don't know a lot about music, but when he plays the piano he sounds like a professional to me. I asked students what they thought of the Chopin piece he played for the talent show, and a lot of them said they liked it. Think about that for a minute. Kids said they *liked* classical music. He also did an incredible job as musical director for the spring musical. I used to go to all the spring musicals because my mom was a teacher here, and I can tell you this year's show was the best I ever saw. He's an athlete. He led our track and field team to the first state final competition in the history of this school. Coach Z told me it was because of his leadership that we finished in fourth place overall. He came in second place for the two-mile but only by a fraction of a second. Think about that. One of the two fastest junior high school kids in the entire state goes to our school. He's popular. He's friends with everyone and he makes it easy to be his friend. That's why he won the student council election by a landslide. He's a comedian. I don't know about you, but I laugh out loud every morning during the announcements.

"But being a scholar, a musician, an athlete, popular, and a comedian is not what the Nancy Sheffield award is about. It's about making our school a better place. I want to tell you an embarrassing story about how I first met him. My mom had died only a few weeks earlier and I was so sad I didn't want to leave my room. He came over to tutor me. I wouldn't open the door. I screamed at him to get lost. But he wouldn't leave. He sat outside my door reading my homework to me for three hours. Three *hours*. I finally let him into my room. I told him he was a jerk. He told me he would keep reading as long as he had to, and that he'd come back tomorrow, and the next day, and the day after that. He wound up reading until I fell asleep. That's what he's like. He doesn't give up on anyone.

"He wanted to do more, so he started our tutoring club. Because of him, almost forty kids are volunteering their time. Think about that for a minute. Forty kids giving up their free time during lunch and after school to help other kids do better on their homework. I asked some of the kids in tutoring why they go. They said they went because it was a way to get help without looking uncool. I think this is the most amazing thing he's done. Who else could get kids to say doing homework wasn't uncool?

"The tutoring club wasn't enough for him, so he created the mentoring club. In mentoring, a student volunteer gets paired with another student who needs a friend. I talked to some of the kids in mentoring. Some of them were the kind of kids who got teased, picked on, laughed at, and bullied. Some of them were the kind of kids who did the bullying. Some of them were just lonely and sad. Every single one said mentoring helped them. The mentoring club changed our whole school. Look around you. When was the last time you saw someone getting bullied in our school?

"Everyone I asked had a story about him. They told me he's here early every morning and late at night giving everything he's got to make our school a better place. He helps at car washes and candy sales for clubs he doesn't belong to. When the mentoring club wanted to go to Great Adventure but didn't raise enough money, he contributed the rest from his own pocket. He even folds programs and cleans out stage closets when a teacher asks without complaining.

"People told me how he said something nice, gave them a word of encouragement, or made them laugh right when they needed it most. When I asked what word best described him, I heard cool and smart a lot. I also heard words like dedicated, caring, compassionate, kind, and inspiring. He tells everyone all they need to do is believe in themselves. But when he says it, he *makes* you believe in yourself because you know he believes in you. He made me believe in myself enough to stand in front of the whole school and give an embarrassing speech. He inspires me every day to be a better person. I called him a scholar, musician, athlete, popular, comedian, and inspiration to everyone around him. But more than any of those words, I'm p-p-proud. . ." He took a deep breath. "Proud, honored, and lucky to call him my friend."

I couldn't move.

"It's my privilege to present the first annual Nancy Sheffield award to my tutor, mentor, and good friend. . ."

He looked straight at me. The silence in the room stretched into an eternity.

"Nick Welles."

I knew the room erupted into deafening noise, but I couldn't hear it. I knew everyone was on their feet, but I was stuck to my chair. I knew hands were clapping me on the back, but I couldn't feel it. I knew it was me that finally got up and walked to the stage, but it didn't seem like it. And I knew this was actually happening, but I couldn't believe it.

Mr. Humber met me on the podium. It felt like this was something I should be watching on television instead of living. "N-n-now you know why I d-d-didn't want to talk to you for the l-last couple of weeks," Jeff said in my ear. He handed a huge plaque to me. I picked faces out from the audience. The cast from the musical. The track team. Tutors. Mentors. Chris, Andy, Daniel, Parker, and Jonathan. Kerry and Jonas. Sean. Ana. Brian. More faces than I could count.

I came back into myself. "Am I supposed to say something?" I asked Mr. Humber

"There's no obligation," he said. I stood in front of the microphone, waiting for the room to settle down.

"Ummm, wow," I said.

The room erupted again.

"I was right! Something weird *was* going on!"

Laughs.

"I don't know what I'm supposed to say. Even if I had time to write one, I could never give a speech as amazing as Jeff did."

Screams of approval.

"I can never find the right word for things like Mr. Humber does."

More screams.

"I don't do things because I want to win awards or get screamed at like I'm some kind of rock star."

More screams.

"Stop it already!"

Even more screaming.

"I'm probably supposed to thank a million people but that would take forever, so I'm just going to say thanks to the whole school all at once. This is Nick, signing off. Later."

More screaming, but I wasn't getting sick of it. Not by a long shot.

Mr. Humber stepped in to the microphone. "Ladies and gentlemen, this concludes our award ceremony. For those of you who are participating in this afternoon's festivities, please follow the instructions you were provided this morning. For those of you who are not, school is now officially dismissed. Have a great weekend and see you on Monday." Everyone scattered.

"Afternoon festivities?" I asked.

He winked. "We're not done with you quite yet."

The party showed no signs of stopping even though it was already dark outside. The band, a real band with fourteen people in it, was playing the shout song for the third time. A hundred kids packed onto the dance floor to scream "Shout!" loud enough to shake the windows in the house. The toy guy was handing out yet another party favor – this time a wand with strands of plastic that had tiny colored lights at the end. People were still lining up for food. The idea of eating made me queasy. Maybe I shouldn't have had three lobster tails. Or that second funnel cake. Or the extra scoop on my sundae from the do-it-yourself bar. Or the cotton candy. Or the kettle corn. Or those little appetizer things the waiters brought on trays. Or who knows how many helpings of freshly made donuts. I couldn't stop eating them, they were so, so good.

Jeremy pulled the party together right under my nose. Every single person in the school knew about it because every single person in the school was invited. Two weeks ago, Mr. Humber told Jeremy I was going to win a special award. Jeremy decided to throw a party to end all parties right in our backyard. He conspired with Mr. Humber and all my friends to make sure I was distracted enough not to notice. Once the party was announced at school, they made sure I was never alone,

because everyone knows kids can't keep a secret to save their lives. The run this morning was organized to make sure I was gone in time to start setting up. They almost got caught – the truck I saw this morning was delivering tents, tables, the dance floor, and cooking equipment. Mr. Humber even made sure the programs came disassembled to keep me busy. Everyone worked together to do this for me. For *me*.

"Awesome party," a couple of kids yelled to me. I gave them a big thumbs-up and slipped inside the house, domain of the adults. Instead of a band, a jazz quartet, and instead of milkshakes, bottles of wine. Inside was just as crowded as outside, wall to wall parents and teachers. "There's the man of the hour," one of them said. I think he was Timothy's dad. I shook his hand firmly, working my way through the crowd.

"Can I borrow my mother?" I said when I found her. I led her to a quiet corner in the dining room. "Sorry I didn't get a chance to talk to you until now," I said.

"Don't be sorry," she said. "This is your party. You should be enjoying yourself with your friends."

"I am," I said. "I still wanted to talk to you. How are you?"

"I'm doing well," she said. "Clearly, I don't need to ask you the same question. What you've been telling me is barely the tip of the iceberg. I've spent the last four hours getting an earful of the most incredible stories about you." When she reached up to brush something off my shoulder, I realized I was taller than her. "To say you've become a remarkable young man does not do you justice. I've been struggling to find the right words, and that's saying something for me. I can't begin to express how proud I am. You're still planning to spend some time with Allen and I over the summer?"

"For a week in July," I said. "Jeremy knows the date."

"A week," she said. "Hardly enough time to get to know you better. Isn't that sad? You're my son and I barely know who you are." She smiled but couldn't hide the sadness in her eyes. "I should let you get back to your party."

"It's ok, we can talk more if you want," I said.

"We'll talk during the week," she said. "I have to get going anyway. It's getting late, and I have an early flight in the morning. Have a good

time, be with your friends, and celebrate your accomplishments." I gave her a hug and watched her wind her way through the crowd. She was a different person since she started living with Allen. I knew she was sorry for the way everything happened when she lived with my father, even though we hadn't talked about it yet. It felt strange to be the only fourteen-year-old I knew who liked his mom.

"Have you seen my father?" I asked Jeremy quietly.

"He left hours ago," he answered.

"Good," I said. I still meant what I said about divorcing him.

"There you are," Ana said. "Everyone's looking for you." I flashed a helpless look at Jeremy when she grabbed my arm. He winked. She dragged me out of the house. "Ok, I'm the only one who was looking for you, but still. Want to dance?"

"Sure," I said. The band started a slow song right on cue. I put my hands on her waist and she put hers on my shoulder, standing just the right distance apart for a slow song – not so far that we looked like we didn't want to touch each other, and not so close that it seemed like I was trying to cop a feel.

"Are you having a good time?" I asked her.

"This is the most amazing party ever," she said. "Your uncle must've spent a fortune but it was totally worth it. Oh my god, did you try those doughnuts? They were incredible!" She shifted her hands a bit, and I knew right then and there she wanted me to ask her out. Ana wasn't the kind of girl who was shy about anything. But she wouldn't ask me. It wasn't the first time I'd realized, but I'd always let the opportunity slip by without saying anything. I told myself the same things I'd always said – how she was my friend and how I didn't feel it with her like I did with Molly. On that dance floor under the bright floodlights with all those people dancing around us, I decided maybe it wouldn't be so bad. Maybe I shouldn't keep making excuses why a popular guy like me didn't have a steady date. Maybe I shouldn't keep disappointing her. Maybe I could make the most severely abnormal part of my life just a little more normal. Maybe I'd feel something for her if I gave her a chance.

"You look pretty tonight," I said. I wasn't lying.

"No I don't," she said.

I kissed her on the cheek.

"Oh," she said in a choked-up voice.

I kissed her on the lips. Right there on the dance floor, in front of everyone. I didn't care. It was supposed to be a little kiss but turned into something more. I pulled her close as our faces locked together. I'd done this more times than I could ever count. It still felt completely new because we did it out in the open for everyone to see. I was barely aware of the cheers and "woo" noises around us as the kiss ended.

"Want to go out with me?" I asked her.

"Duh," she said back.

I kissed her again.

"Someone catch her, she's going to faint," the band leader said. "I think we've got our best kiss of the evening award right there." I didn't look away from her. "We're ready? Ok, we're ready. Come on up, lover boy. We need you on stage." Ana pushed me when I didn't react.

"Oh, they mean me," I mumbled. Everyone laughed. I stumbled when I hopped up on stage. When I looked out over the crowd, I realized I just kissed Ana in front of everyone – not just kids, but all the teachers and parents too. Including Ana's. They were smiling so I wasn't worried. Her parents were cool that way. Ana slipped off with a group of friends. I assumed my kissing technique was about to be critiqued.

Someone pushed a champagne glass into my hand. "Mr. Welles," Mr. Humber said into the microphone. "There's little I can add to Mr. Sheffield's impassioned and heartfelt speech. Perhaps to the list of scholar, athlete, musician, and comedian we should add the title of lover."

The entire crowed made the "woo" noise again. I gave him a look of death. "Consider that my repayment for the incident on my birthday," he said under his breath to me. "John Witherspoon Junior High School is fortunate to have as dedicated and inspiring a student as you. To Nick!" The crowd lifted their glasses and echoed him.

Jeff took the microphone from Mr. Humber. "On behalf of the Nancy Sheffield memorial fund, I'm proud to present you with this scholarship for one thousand dollars." The crowd applauded as Jeff handed me an envelope. The photographer blinded me with his flash.

"Speech!" someone shouted. The whole crowed started joining in. I tried to wave them off but that only made them shout louder, so I didn't have a choice. Jeff handed me the microphone.

"Come on, I didn't have time to write a speech," I complained even though I'd been thinking about what to say for hours. "Besides, I could never write a speech like Jeff did. Giving that speech was one of the bravest things I ever saw anyone do." I lifted my glass and drank to him.

"I don't know what to say other than thanks. I guess I should thank everyone, but I want to call out two very special people." I figured most people would think I was going to say my parents, but that's not where I was going. "First, I wouldn't have been able to accomplish much of anything without Mr. Humber. Where would I be today if I didn't look up at the footprints on the ceiling?"

He made a great "who me?" face that cracked everyone up.

"Without Mr. Humber's help as faculty advisor for the tutoring and mentoring clubs, neither of them would've ever happened. If he wasn't there to give me advice, I would've screwed it up. If he wasn't there to encourage me every step of the way, I would've given up. I'm going to borrow his words when I tell you John Witherspoon Junior High is fortunate to have such a dedicated and inspiring teacher." I lifted my glass to another round of applause.

"Second, I want to the thank the person who put together the most incredible party in the history of Newton Falls. Jeremy, where are you?" I spotted him in the crowd. I knew he didn't like having the spotlight on him, but he came up on stage anyway to cheers from the crowd. "How about this party?" I yelled, and the crowd screamed. "He should be the one getting awards. Without him, I wouldn't be the person I am today." I wanted to say a lot more, but that would have to be enough. I hugged him. In front of everyone. I didn't care.

"Everyone's been asking me the same two questions. I'm getting sick of answering them individually so I'm going to broadcast my answers right now. At the award ceremony, I said I don't do the things I do to get awards. So, everyone's been asking me why I do them. When I needed help, people were there for me, like Mr. Humber and Jeremy. I want to help other people the same way. Not because I feel like I have

a debt to pay or that it's my responsibility. Making someone's life better gives me such a fantastic feeling that I'm totally addicted.

"The second question is what I'm going to do with all that money." The crowd laughed. "Whenever someone asked, I asked what they think I should do with it. Responsible people told me I should save it for college. Less responsible people said I should buy a car, or go on a trip, or buy a fleet of dirt bikes, or a few other things that won't be legal until I'm eighteen." More laughter. "But I've got a better idea." I held the envelope above my head.

"I'm going to donate this money to cancer research. No kid should ever have to lose their mom."

The crowd was silent for a moment before applauding madly. Jeff started crying and his father hugged him. I teared up for him, just a little.

In front of everyone.

I didn't care.

<center>⌒⌒ ⌒⌒</center>

It had to be after midnight. The band had left, the food was being cleared away, and the tents were coming down. But the party was still going strong. Important people who meant something surrounded me. Lots of them.

Ana and I squeezed together into one of the big chairs in the lobby, our bodies intertwined. She was going to spend the night, and I intended to find out just how different it was to make out with a girl. So far, Ana had proved to be more than a willing companion on that adventure. Chris and his gang had set up shop around the pool table, staying overnight as well. Jeff and his father were in the kitchen, deep in conversation. Jeremy was at the piano playing songs from musicals while Mr. Humber and my friends from the play were singing along. Friends from the track team, the tutoring club, and the mentoring club were packed all over the lobby, basement, and den. Most were staying too (I had no idea where or how). Brian was even here, in a corner of the lobby on his own. I made sure to spend time with him, because I knew he felt lonely and out of place.

"I've got an idea," Ana said, extracting herself from the chair. I watched her whisper in Jeremy's ear. I knew the song from the first note. After all, I'd played it for the show. Jeremy started singing first.

> *If just one person believes in you*
> *Deep enough and strong enough, believes in you*

Ana joined in.

> *Making it two*
> *Two whole people who believe in you*

The room got quiet. Everyone was listening. Mr. Humber joined at the right time for the third person.

> *Making it three*
> *People you can say believe in me*

The rest of the cast joined.

> *And if three whole people, why not four*

Jeff and Mr. Sheffield joined from the kitchen door.

> *And if four whole people, why not more*

The whole room sang.

> *And when all those people believe in you*
> *Deep enough and strong enough believe in you*

All of them singing to me.

The moment came and went so quickly, slipping through my fingers like all moments do. I wanted it to linger inside me forever. I wanted to hold on to it, etch it in stone, capture the feeling like no picture or video could. The feeling of belonging. Mattering. The feeling that

everything up to now was just a warm-up lap. The real race was still ahead of me. I wasn't just going to win. I was going to set world records. I was going to change the way races were run. I could do anything.

Because I was Nick Welles.

Chapter 43

October 4, 1984

I didn't notice the curb until my foot banged into it. My body flew forward and I stumbled a few steps, recovering my balance right before I splatted on the sidewalk. I stopped, hands on my knees, cold waves of panic turning my legs to grape jelly. Only a millimeter away from disaster – a sprained ankle, broken leg, or maybe worse. The marathon was only a month away. I wouldn't have time to heal from an injury, let alone train. One misstep could shatter my entire life's plan.

I took a couple of minutes to calm down before I continued my run. I told myself to concentrate, watch for obstacles, remember to breathe, and let the rhythm of sneakers on concrete drive everything else out of mind.

But nothing could clear my mind right now.

I was in *love*.

I thought I knew what love felt like. I had Jeremy and Ana. But I'd never felt anything like this. My head, heart, and dick didn't belong to me anymore. It treated me like a four-year old treats his stuffed animals. It threw me down the stairs, chewed on me, left me out in the rain, and squeezed me until I couldn't breathe. I lost all control over my life. I didn't want this and I didn't need this. I had Jeremy. I had a girlfriend I truly cared about. I had the piano. I had homework and tests. I had tutoring, mentoring, and a peer counseling program to launch. I was running the New York marathon next month. I had a charity Christmas auction to plan. I had a million reasons why I needed this feeling to just go away.

At the same time, it felt incredible. Sincerely fucking *awesome*.

There's no such thing as love at first sight. Love takes time and effort. You need to know someone before you can love them.

Now lust, on the other hand. . .

"I've selected the perfect mentoring match for you," Mr. Humber told me a couple weeks ago. "Billy Foster is a seventh grader in my honors English class. He's recently moved into the area and I believe he's feeling displaced. While my observations are cursory, he's awkward around his peers in a way that should result in merciless treatment. However, he has a quality that makes taunting him unsatisfying."

"Is he shy?" I asked.

"Completely the opposite," Mr. Humber said. "If there's such a thing as being too friendly and accommodating, Billy would fit the mold. While I cannot further discuss my reasons why, I believe you possess the right skills and temperament to be an effective mentor for him. Call it a hunch."

He was right, but for all the wrong reasons.

Mr. Humber arranged for me to meet Billy the next day after school. I waited for him in the guidance room, the same one where I folded all those programs last year. Memories of paper cuts and perfectly normal paranoia felt like they came from ages ago. I was about to go looking for Billy when a round faced sandy haired boy wearing glasses poked his head in. He didn't look old enough to be in junior high. "Are you Nick?" he said with a distinct English accent. I felt the first pang right then. English accents were irresistibly cute.

"That's me," I said.

"I'm Billy," he said. "Billy Foster? Mr. Humber asked that I see you. About the mentoring."

"Yeah, right, sorry, come on in," I said, trying to snap back into myself. But I couldn't. He was too cute for words. The right shape and size, skin as white as piano keys, and the cutest set of crooked teeth. I was absolutely smitten.

"Mr. Humber didn't mention you were from England," I murmured.

"Derbyshire," he said. "In the midlands, near Nottingham."

"Nottingham is a real place? I thought it was made up for Robin Hood."

"It's quite real, as is Sherwood forest," he said brightly. "Although Nottingham has become economically depressed in recent times." He sounded more like a news announcer than a kid. It made me quiver all over.

"Did Mr. Humber explain mentoring? It's not much more than hanging out and having a good time. We can do whatever you want as long as it's legal. What kinds of things do you like to do?"

"I'm quite partial to magic tricks," he said. "Would you care to see one?"

"Sure," I said. He pulled a pack of cards from his pocket and spread them out. "Select one." *Partial. Select.* Unbearably cute. I pulled one from the middle. "Go on, look at it, make certain you remember it. Now replace it." I slid the card into the deck. "In this trick, there's no need for me to find your selection, as the card will exit the deck and replace itself. It will fly about the room and will be quite easy to discover. Watch closely." He slammed the deck on the table. "Did you see it?"

"Nope," I said. I was too busy watching him.

"Well, it never fails," he said. With a single fluid move he spread the cards on the table to reveal only one upside down. "Go on then," he said. The upside-down card was mine.

"How did you do that?" I said.

"A magician never reveals his mysteries," he said.

"Well, do it again." He shook his head. "Come on, one more time. Please?"

"Very well," he said reluctantly, placing the cards down on the table. He held up his hands as though he was spreading out the deck. "Select one." He sounded bored. I pantomimed pulling an imaginary card from an imaginary deck. "Not that one." I did it again. "Better. Make certain you'll remember it. Come on then, you have it backwards, how can you remember your selection?" I pretended to turn it around. "Good,

now replace it. Brilliant. Your card will exit the deck and replace itself." He slapped the table and pretended to spread the cards. "Oh dear. I'm afraid I can't see them. Perhaps you could tell me your selection?"

"Four of clubs," I said randomly.

"Four of clubs," he repeated. He pulled out another deck of cards from his pocket, going through them until he found a single card upside down. The four of clubs.

"Holy shit," I said. "That's impossible."

"Do you like it?" he said, putting the deck away.

"That was amazing, seriously."

"I know lots of tricks. I plan to become a professional magician, like David Copperfield. Billy the Magnificent."

"If you can do tricks like that, I think you could be a professional magician right now," I said. He flashed me a priceless crooked-toothed smile, standing up to put the other deck of cards in his pocket. They got caught, causing a small pile of change to spill on the floor.

"Sod it all," he said quickly, down on all fours to pick it up. I was going to help but wound up completely paralyzed by the site of an incomparably beautiful little butt staring up at me. His shorts rode up just enough to make sure I knew precisely how it looked.

It had started with Allen's son Josh – he was terribly cute too. After him, it kept getting worse all summer. I couldn't take my eyes off the younger boys. The mall, the arcade, the dollar movies – they were everywhere. Going to the swim club with Ana's family was unbearable. It was hard enough to look at her lying next to me in a bikini, but all those boys in bathing suits jumping around in the pool made my life pure torture. I had to keep a towel over my lap at all times. It was terrible. And wonderful. And confusing as hell.

"Sorry, I need to go the bathroom," I mumbled.

For the last couple of weeks, Billy and I had met at school. Today, I was invited to tea at his house. A chance to learn more about him and meet his parents.

My heart skipped a couple beats when I saw Billy waiting for me near the bike racks. Even though it was getting colder, he was wearing shorts. He told me it was an English thing for boys to wear shorts all year long. I thought the idea sounded wonderfully civilized. *Brilliant*, as Billy would say. I took a deep breath, trying to hide just how madly, head over heels, insanely, and irrevocably in love I was. I was certain I'd fail.

"Lots of homework today?" I asked as we started walking.

"The homework is quite manageable, much less than primary school in England," he said. "The only master, I mean teacher, we call them masters in England, who reminds me of an English school is Mr. Humber. He is quite demanding, strict, and unpopular with his students. Everyone received poor marks on their assignments earlier this week."

"It's October," I laughed. "By the end of the year Mr. Humber will be everyone's favorite teacher."

"I find that statement quite difficult to believe," he said.

"I got you something," I said, fishing the book out of my backpack. "You said you were interested in learning how to become an escape artist. I saw this in the bookstore and thought of you." It wasn't important to tell him Jeremy drove me to five different stores before I found it.

"The Secrets of Harry Houdini," he said. "Brilliant!"

"It has lots of pictures and illustrations of the tricks he did, but it doesn't say much about how he did them."

"Books that reveal the mysteries of magic are very dear and must be purchased in specialty shops," he said. "My da took me to one in London. They had a whole series costing fifty pounds each. If I had books like those, I could be a real magician." New plan. Jeremy takes me to New York, we find a magic store, and buy a fifty-pound set of books.

"Here we are," he said, turning into a pathway through a white picket fence. There was no yard in the front, just a large garden. "Hello mummy!" he called to a woman digging a hole in the ground.

"I'm Margaret," she said to me. "I'll have to meet you properly in a moment, I'm quite covered in dirt."

"Nick," I said, smiling. I followed Billy into the house.

"Hello, da," Billy called out. A man poked his head from the kitchen. "Nick has come for tea."

"Ah, the famous Nick at last," Billy's dad said, wiping his hands on a dirty white apron.

"It's a pleasure to meet you, Mr. Foster," I said, using my business voice. I held out my hand to shake.

"Gordon," he said without shaking my hand. "You'll forgive me, I'm afraid I'm quite sticky with jam."

"Jam? Something for tea?" Billy asked.

"Bakewell tarts," Mr. Foster said.

"Brilliant!" Billy said with a huge smile, his eyes lighting up. That did it. I melted. Like the witch, a pile of sludge on the floor. "Oh please, give us a taste?"

"I daresay they're nearly ready," Mr. Foster said. "Why don't you take Nick to your room? We'll call for tea."

"Bakewell tarts will make a proper tea," he said excitedly. "Come on then, I'll show you my magician's costume." He bounded up the stairs. I expected his room to be neat as a pin because of his accent, but it was a perfectly normal messy room. "Give us a moment," he said, rummaging around in his closet. I put my backpack down on his bed and looked around randomly until I homed in on a picture frame sitting on the dresser. The picture showed Billy at a beach somewhere, but he wasn't wearing a normal swim suit. It was more like a girl's bikini bottom. Skimpier. It couldn't have possibly covered half his butt. I wondered how I could steal the picture without him noticing.

"That's when we went to Cheddar last year," he said from the closet.

I looked over. He was in his *underwear.*

I pulled my shirt down.

"The other is in London," he said, facing away, but I wasn't interested in a picture from London.

He pulled on some dark clothes. "Ta da! I assembled it from cast-offs, but I did make some changes." He shook his arm and a coin appeared in his hand.

"Looks great," I said.

"Introducing Billy the Magnificent," he shouted, picking up a few metal rings from the floor and going through the routine of linking them together.

"You should do magic at my Christmas charity fundraiser," I said. "One trick for a dollar, or show them a simple one for five dollars. I'll bet we'd make a ton of money."

"Brilliant," he said.

"I don't get it," I said, opening the book. "You don't need so many chains to tie someone up. And how come he's practically naked?"

"The chains are for show," Billy explained. "He's wearing so little to prove he's not concealing any keys. I've been led to believe he hid them in his mouth if his escape required one."

"Ah," I said. I had to wonder if there was another reason he was undressed. One more familiar to me.

"Tea!" Billy's mother called.

"Sod it, I don't want to soil my costume," he said to himself, and quickly stripped off while I watched, my eyes glued to him. He set it carefully on a chair and opened the door, still in his underwear. "Coming?" he asked.

Actually, yes I am...

He bounded down the stairs. "William, you march right back upstairs and put on trousers," Mrs. Foster said. "This is no way to behave in front of a guest." He tore back up the stairs, brushing past me on the way to his room.

"I'm sorry if he embarrassed you," she said to me. "That boy would run around nude if permitted."

"Not at all," I squeaked.

Billy appeared an instant later, his shorts back on. He didn't bother with a shirt. I wasn't going to survive this. His parents set up a small plate of sandwiches with the crusts cut off and a platter of pastries in the living room. "Would you care for tea or chocolate?" his mother said.

"Oh chocolate, please," Billy said. He squeezed himself next to me on the couch.

"Of course you want chocolate," she said playfully. "I meant Nick."

"Tea is fine," I squeaked again. She poured some cream into a fancy cup, then some tea from an equally fancy pot, topped off with a rough brown sugar cube.

"I feel as though I already know you," Mr. Foster said to me. "You're all Billy speaks about these days. I've heard you're training to run a marathon."

"The New York," I said. "In about a month. I also want to do the Boston next year."

"Have a cucumber sandwich," Billy said, shoving one into my hand. "They're my favorite." His fingers brushed against mine.

"Good show," Mr. Foster said. "I was never much of a runner myself, just a spot of cricket years ago."

"Isn't cricket like baseball?" I asked.

"It may seem that way in that there's a ball and bat, but that's where the similarities end," Billy said. "We can play sometime if you like. I'm a competent bowler."

Sure, I'll play with you. . .

I *had* to make myself stop thinking these things.

"That'll be fun," I said. "When does the restaurant open? We want to come for opening night."

"Next week, I should think," Mr. Foster said. "A few more inspections. Which reminds me, I'm considering serving these as a dessert and I'd be interested to know your thoughts as an American. They're a bit of a local specialty back home." He put one of the pastries in a shallow bowl and poured cream around it.

"They look really good," I said.

"Give us some too," Billy said with a mouthful of cucumber sandwich.

"Mind your manners, Billy," Mrs. Foster said gently.

I took a spoonful. "That's lovely," I said with the best English accent I could manage. They laughed. "Seriously, this is good. I would order this. A lot."

"Flattery will get you everywhere," Mr. Foster said.

"Billy, before your tart, do us a favor and take care of the turtles?" Mrs. Foster said. "They need feeding and to have their enclosure cleaned."

"Come on then, I'll show you my turtles," Billy said, pulling on my arm.

"Let Nick finish his tea," Mr. Foster said. "Go on then, be a sport. You can show Nick after you've tidied up." I stopped chewing on the tart, alarm bells going off. They wanted to talk to me alone. I had no reason to think it would be something bad, besides my head full of dirty thoughts. Was it that obvious? I didn't think I could stand being cut off from Billy. He disappeared out the back door.

"We wanted you to know how appreciative we are of everything you're doing for Billy," Mr. Foster started. "He's felt lonely since the move and you've already made quite some difference in his attitude. We thought perhaps we could share some information about him. Confidentially, of course, you understand."

"Everything in mentoring is confidential," I said. "Whatever you tell me is kept a secret unless someone is in danger."

They looked at each other. "Perhaps you've noticed Billy tends to please others," his mother said.

"A little, I guess," I said.

"And perhaps you may have noticed Billy is rarely bothered by anything," his father joined in. "He's never perturbed when scolded or disciplined. Negative experiences with his mates have no effect either. Not that he's a deliberately disobedient child, he's as agreeable as they come."

"We were forced to withdraw Billy from his previous two schools when his mates took advantage of his nature," his mother said. "Children can be quite cruel, and they've put Billy up to doing the most horrible things to himself. Billy simply complied without complaint. By the time we became aware, Billy had done things as awful as licking dirty toilets clean."

"That's horrible," I said. "Kids can be mean."

"We're hoping you can keep a watchful eye," his father said. "In our experience, schools haven't treated this matter seriously. As he grows older, the danger grows as well. He could be put up to committing a crime or hurting someone and wind up on the wrong side of the law. Billy understands the danger, and we've spent a great deal of time speaking with him about it, but he still succumbs to his nature."

"Of course, I'll watch out for him," I said. "Wow, I've never heard of a kid quite like him."

"We inquired into your background as a prerequisite to Billy's participation," his mother said. "Not to be deceptive, of course. We've allowed Billy to participate because of your qualities, achievements, excellent references, and impeccable character. If your schoolmaster had not specifically recommended you, I daresay we would've declined. The wrong person in a position of responsibility with Billy would have extraordinary power over him. I'm sure you understand our concern."

Mr. Humber didn't tell me I was the only one they trusted. I would have to talk to him. "I'm honored you're placing that kind of trust in me," I said. "I won't disappoint you."

Billy came running back in. "Finished. Would you care to see the turtles now?"

"Sure," I said. I took another bite of the tart. "I'm serious, I'd order this every day."

"Perhaps you'd care to stay for supper? Nothing fancy, I've prepared some meat pies."

"Definitely," I said. If I stayed, I'd be late to pick up Ana. We were supposed to "study" together tonight at my house. My house was a better place to "study" because Jeremy understood "studying" required privacy. I wasn't worried – she was always flexible when it came to mentoring. Especially after what happened with Eric. She cried for a week when they sent him back to his parents. Nobody understood how or why.

Billy dragged me outside to look at his three turtles, chattering on about them. I didn't hear a word he was saying, because I was completely wrapped up in the battle going on in my head.

He'll do anything someone asks him to do.

And the other side.

You promised his parents you'd look after him.

You could never hurt another human being.

He's just a kid.

"Let's go back up to my room," he said, grabbing my arm again. I followed him up the stairs, trying to pull myself together. When I secretly hid both my pairs of handcuffs in my backpack this morning, I

swore to myself I had no intention of doing anything with them. They were supposed to sit undisturbed at the bottom of my bag, nothing more than a fantasy. But fantasy was growing dangerously close to reality right now. I wouldn't be hurting him, would I? I wouldn't be getting him to do anything he didn't want to do, right?

I closed the door to his room behind us. There was no lock, but his parents didn't seem like the type to disturb us. Besides, what I was doing wasn't exactly wrong, even if it wouldn't look exactly right.

"I almost forgot. Since you like doing escape tricks, I thought you might want to play with these."

"Brilliant!" he said, taking both pairs of handcuffs from me. "They seem quite sturdy."

"Real police issue." I handed him the key. "Go ahead, try them." He snapped them on his wrists and easily released them.

"With these, I could do a real escape," he said. "Just like Houdini."

"Just like Houdini," I echoed.

He wouldn't understand what I meant.

But he did.

I couldn't look away when he dropped his shorts to the ground. "Not quite right, is it?" he asked himself, rummaging through his drawers. He pulled out a small bit of fabric. The bathing suit from the photo. "This will do nicely." I gawked as he pulled his underwear down, standing in front of me in all his glory. Only for a moment, but it wasn't as if that bathing suit left anything to the imagination.

"I want a proper challenge," he said.

I pretended like I was thinking, even though I could only think about his body.

"How about a hogtie," I mumbled. He looked puzzled. "Hands behind your back with your ankles locked to your hands. Might be a difficult escape, though. Maybe we should try something easier."

"No, it sounds brilliant," he said. "Would you mind helping out a bit? I don't think I can do it on my own."

He lay face down on the floor, his hands behind his back. My heart pounded like I was running the last hundred yards of a race. I didn't spend much time thinking about tie-up stuff anymore, and I sure as hell never thought tying up another boy would be exciting. That's not why

I put the handcuffs in my backpack. Or was it? I didn't know anymore. My mind was in a fog as I snapped the cuffs on his wrists. "Too tight?"

"No, that's proper," he said, squirming a little. "Do my feet."

"Bend your legs," I said, pushing down on them to get his feet close enough to his hands. The handcuffs barely fit on his ankles, but somehow I managed to get them on with the chain threaded between his wrists. "Are you sure you're ok? You look pretty uncomfortable."

"No, it's brilliant," he said, his teeth clenched.

"It's more challenging if you can't see," I said, picking up a sock from his floor. He picked up his head and let me tie the sock around his eyes.

"Give us a proper amount of time to get free, would you?" he said.

"Ok, but the moment you tell me to let you out, I'll untie you right away."

I placed the key in his hand. I should've left him an escape route, but I put the handcuffs on with his palms out and keyhole facing away from his fingers. I knew from experience it was impossible to escape even with the key. I sat on the bed, watching him contort his body.

My hand slid down my pants.

"Are you ok?" Ana said, leaning against me.

"Huh?" I said, looking up from my book.

"You're quiet tonight."

"I'm doing my homework," I said.

"You haven't written anything in twenty minutes," she said gently.

"I guess I was daydreaming," I said.

"About what?"

About what? A couple hours ago I did a horrible thing to a sweet, gentle, defenseless little boy. I told myself I never suggested taking off his clothes. I told myself he was the one who suggested a proper challenge. But I was lying to myself. I packed the handcuffs this morning. I showed them to him. I suggested the hogtie. I cuffed him so he couldn't escape.

As soon as I finished (which took a whole minute because I held back as long as I could), I was instantly overwhelmed with horrible guilt. The sight of him writhing on the floor, nearly nude, in some pain, and completely vulnerable made me sick to my stomach. He complained I didn't give him enough time when I unlocked him. He argued I should give him another chance. I told him no, but I knew if the chance came again, I would take it. I might not be able to stop myself from going further. I knew without any doubt I would, because I was already figuring out how to create the next opportunity. I tried not to think about how weird it was that I was turned on by kids younger than me. When I did, I told myself it would go away when I was older. I was still a kid myself, after all. Nothing to worry about.

"Nothing," I said, closing my book. "Let's go upstairs."

"I have to finish my math homework," she said. I kissed her on the neck. "Come on, I have to do these last three problems."

"Do them afterwards," I said quietly nibbling on her earlobe.

"That's not fair," she sighed. "You know I like that."

"You can't resist me," I said, breathing in her ear.

"Stop it," she said, but her tone said the opposite. I kept going until she pushed me off. "I'm serious. Let me finish and then we can neck all you want."

I sat back up and pouted. Her pencil scratched on the paper.

"Do you ever wonder what it would be like to get married?" I asked.

"Married? Not really. I'm a modern woman. I want to be a doctor. I don't want to get married until I'm a lot older. Like around twenty-five."

"I think a lot about getting married," I said.

"Boys don't think about getting married," she pointed out.

"I do," I said. "I think about being with the right person for the rest of my life. I'd be happy to settle down with the right girl and have kids, a house, and all that stuff."

"Are you sure you're not a girl?" she asked.

"Want to check to make sure?" I said slyly.

"I've felt it through your pants enough times to know it's there," she said flippantly. I put my hand on her cheek and turned her face towards mine.

"You're nice, you're pretty, and you're smart," I said softly. "I don't need to keep looking. I don't care if we've only been going out for a few months. I already found the right girl to marry." Her eyes became soft. "I love you," I told her for the first time.

"Oh," she said in that choked up voice she used when I kissed her on the dance floor at my party. "I love you too." She slammed her book shut. "Forget the stupid homework."

"See, that's why I love you," I said. "You know what matters." We ran upstairs to the guest bedroom. I shut the door, locking it behind me.

"Are you sure your uncle won't bother us?"

"Nah," I said, slipping my shirt over my head and flopping on the bed beside her.

"Ooh, you're *soooo* hot," she said, wrapping her hand around my upper arm. "All that weight lifting is paying off. Like stone. God, you're making me so horny."

"I guess I'll have to do something about that," I said. "Your blouse looks tight. How can you breathe?"

"I can't," she said, lying back to let me unbutton her blouse. "That's much better."

"I'll bet it is," I said, pulling her toward me. Our faces locked together, tongues intertwined. She moaned. My hands went around her back, fumbling with the strap on her bra, trying to figure out how the stupid thing worked.

"What are you doing?' she said, pulling her face away from mine.

"Being a bad boy," I whispered in her ear.

We'd never gone that far before. Kissing, necking, and a little bit of touching above the waist was where we drew the line. She always kept her bra on, just like our pants always stayed zipped. I'd never pushed her limits, afraid of where it could lead. Afraid I would mess everything up.

But tonight, I was in a *mood.*

"I'll do it," she said. Her bra fell loose a moment later. I yanked it out of the way, kissing her like a wild man, unrestrained and beyond passionate. Before I realized what I was doing, my jeans were halfway

down to my knees, my mouth was fixed on her breast, and my fingers searched for the catch on her pants.

"Nick," she said.

I didn't, couldn't listen. I felt it give, tugging at her zipper.

"Nick, stop it."

I knew I should listen. I knew I was going too far, but I couldn't stop. I needed to keep going. I needed to prove to myself that I could do it. I needed to be turned on by her.

I was. . .but I wasn't.

In my imagination, it wasn't Ana beneath me.

It was a cute eleven-year-old boy with crooked teeth and an English accent.

My hand snaked into her panties, finding her most secret places.

"Stop!" she yelled, pushing me off. "What's gotten into you?"

I snapped back into myself, suddenly aware of what I'd just done.

"I don't want to go that far. I told you before that I'm not ready. I don't want to go all the way." She zipped her pants and put her blouse back on.

I sat up, a pit in my stomach like I'd swallowed molten lead.

"I didn't mean to," I moaned. "Oh shit, I'm sorry. I got carried away."

"It's ok," she said, her expression softening. "I understand. Guys get it worse than girls. I'm not ready yet." She touched my cheek. "But when I am, I want you to be the one."

"No, you don't," I said, shaking my head. "Not me."

"Yes, you," she said.

"I'm sorry. I'm so, so, so sorry." I felt a tear run down my cheek.

"Are you crying?" she said.

The dam broke. I cried like I hadn't cried since all that shit from the past was being cleaned out of me. I curled up on the bed, letting her rub my head as I sobbed like a baby. She never asked me why I was crying. If she had, I would've been helpless. I would've told her everything. Jeremy. Brian. Jeff. Billy. Secrets that could never be shared with anyone. But I wanted so desperately to tell her. She was the only person I could imagine telling. She was the only person besides Jeremy who I trusted enough to allow myself to cry like this.

I guess I really did love her, in my own way. Just not the way I was supposed to.

I hoped she could forgive me.

Chapter 44

October 12, 1984

I never understood why people paced. If a person wanted to think, it was easier to sit still. The only thing pointless walking back and forth accomplished was a worn line on the carpet. I wasn't pacing – I was wandering aimlessly around the house. Into the kitchen, out of the kitchen, up the stairs, down the stairs, around the piano and back again. I didn't snack or even open the fridge. I didn't play a single note. I didn't straighten the house. But I was thinking.

About Billy.

For the last week, I'd been spending every free moment I had with him. His parents wanted me to keep an eye out for him, and I intended to do just that. If I had to keep him away from anyone who could potentially hurt him, so be it. No cruel, heartless kid was going to take advantage of such a vulnerable and sweet boy. Not on my watch.

I was drifting through the dining room when I noticed the mail truck pulling away. Something to do. I ripped the mail out of the box, sifting through the envelopes. Bill, junk, junk, bill, another one of those letters for me. Philips Andover again. The letters started coming during the summer and wouldn't quit. Always the same thing, we'd like to invite you to apply, blah, blah, blah. Philips, Exeter, Peddie, Choate, Lawrenceville, Hotchkiss, Milton, Pinehurst, and a dozen others. Even one from Eton in England. I assumed they knew about me because of the award last year, but it seemed strange that some of the most prestigious private schools in the country would care about a little thing like that. Jeremy told me the application was a formality – I was clearly

already accepted. He told me to consider going to one very carefully. The best chance to meet the right people and have it made for life.

I considered it for about a millisecond.

My life was here. I had my school, friends, plans, and people who depended on me. I had Ana and Jeremy.

Now I had Billy.

Just thinking about his name sent a spasm through me. It took everything I had to force down an urge to dash upstairs and furiously get myself off. I hadn't gotten off for two days. Two whole *days*. The longest I'd voluntarily denied myself before was two minutes. I told Jeremy I was too tired last night, the first time we'd missed screwing for ages. He insisted on taking my temperature. I wanted to be as horny as possible for Billy tonight. I told myself I was doing it to make my time with him more exciting.

It was going to happen tonight.

I had a thousand different scenarios, like the way the WOPR played endless games which all led to the same conclusion. The strategy didn't matter. I had nuclear weapons against a defenseless adversary. Would I use the handcuffs again? Or would I suggest a shower together? Or show him dirty magazines? Didn't matter. Every version led to a naked Billy in bed with me. His mother told me he didn't care about being naked, but really, he *liked* it. One time, I was helping him with homework and his mom insisted he take a bath. He wanted me to sit in the bathroom with him. Another time we were wrestling and he was in his underwear like usual. I might've sort of helped them slip off. He thought it was hilarious. He tried to yank my pants off too, but I couldn't let him for obvious reasons. If he found naked wrestling fun, wait until he found out just how much fun other naked activities could be.

My head knew what I was doing was beyond wrong. It reminded me what happened with Jeff. It tried to explain that Billy wasn't ready for any of this. He was still a little kid. It tried shame. It tried guilt.

My dick laughed. It was completely in control. Maybe the reason I denied myself was to make sure my dick stayed in charge. Otherwise, I might've had a few minutes where my head took over and made sure none of this would happen.

If Ana was here tonight, I'd be safely making out with her. Billy would stay home and none of this would be happening. But she was somewhere in Connecticut with her family until tomorrow. I had a night to myself, Billy's parents wanted a night out, and Billy said "brilliant" a million times when I invited him to sleep over.

I didn't deserve Ana, and she sure as hell deserved someone better than me. No denying it and no lying about it. I cared about her. I meant it when I told her I wanted to marry her. I wanted to spend the rest of my life with her. Start over and do it right this time. I knew what marriage was because I'd already lived it. Sort of.

I loved Ana, and I wanted to fool around with Billy.

Those two things didn't go together very well.

Billy wasn't coming over for a few more hours. Every second dragged out into an eternity. Worse than watching the clock in the most boring class ever. Worse than counting the last few moments before your own execution. Dread and anticipation mixed together into a sludge with a life of its own. If it happened with Billy, things would be damaged forever with Ana, not to mention what it might do to him. If it didn't, I missed out on the perfect opportunity. No matter what happened, I was going to win and lose tonight.

I needed something to distract myself, stabbing the remote until the television came to life. A commercial. Perfect, even more mindless than a show. Right now, I wanted a channel full of commercials. Even if they were about feminine hygiene products and diapers.

"We're back," the host of the talk show said. I felt around for the channel button on the remote. *Anything* but this. "Today we're taking about the hidden victims, sexually abused boys."

I jerked my finger away.

"This should be a laugh," I said out loud.

"We've been talking with Dr. Simmons, a therapist specializing in the treatment of men sexually abused as boys. Dr. Simmons, you talked about the personality of the pedophile, but what about the boys themselves? How does a pedophile go about choosing a victim? Is there a particular type of boy he targets?"

"Most men attracted to boys prefer pre-pubescent or young teen children between the ages of ten and fourteen. While we've seen

documented cases of pedophiles attracted to much younger boys, even toddlers, the vast majority of victims are first abused as pre-teens."

Yup. I was eleven when we met.

"Like any predator in the wild, the pedophile seeks the easiest prey. They home in on boys who are lonely, withdrawn, and isolated. Often these boys have uninvolved or neglectful parents, few friends, and have been rejected by their peer group. Boys who've been starved of attention are more vulnerable to the pedophile. It's far easier for these men to insinuate themselves into a boy's life when he doesn't have a strong support structure. If you think about it, a normal boy with family connections and friends wouldn't give the time of day to a grown man. They prefer the company of children their own age."

My parents were uninvolved and I didn't have any friends.

"We spoke earlier about how many people imagine the typical child molester driving around with candy, looking to randomly snatch and assault an unwary child," the announcer said. "You've mentioned this isn't a typical scenario at all."

"While cases of random stranger abuse do occur, the vast majority of sexual abuse cases are perpetrated by someone the boy knows and trusts," Dr. Whateverhisnamewas said. "The man who preys on boys is more likely to be their coach, scout leader, favorite uncle, or friendly neighbor across the street."

Bingo.

"The common stereotype of the abductor with the candy is what helps pedophiles avoid detection. They become free to molest dozens of boys for decades under everyone's noses without being caught."

"Wait a minute," the announcer said, leaning forward. "Dozens of boys?"

"Absolutely. The research shows many molesters abuse dozens or even hundreds of victims before being apprehended. These men are masters of manipulation, adept at hiding what they are and what they do. They frequently have successful careers and might even be married with children of their own. Many parents don't suspect anything because they appear to be living perfectly ordinary lives."

Got that right.

"This seems impossible," the announcer said. "How can a child molester abuse dozens of boys over a period of years without any of those boys reporting it?"

"In our society, boys are taught to be tough, keep their feelings inside, and take it like a man. Our societal image of abuse always assumes a female victim, so law enforcement and the therapeutic community are structured to deal with girls. I've had men tell me many times how they reported their abuse as a child and were either ignored or told they were lying. Not only by parents, but by a teacher, a doctor, or even the police. Boys become the hidden victims, afraid and actively discouraged from coming forward. Many are rightfully frightened they'll be labeled as gay and subjected to ridicule if the abuse is ever discovered. The pressure on an abused boy is so intense that the pedophile rarely needs to threaten his victim into silence. The boy himself is motivated to go to great lengths to keep the abuse well hidden. You might find it surprising that many men come to believe they're responsible for being abused as a coping mechanism."

Some of my smile melted away.

"So how do we focus on identifying the boy who is being abused so we can get him the help he needs?" the announcer asked. "Should we look for specific behaviors or warning signs?"

"It's not as easy as you might think. Typical warning signs include sudden shifts in mood or school performance, changes in friendships, alcohol or drug abuse, or premature sexual activities with peers."

Like sucking your friend's dick or trying to fuck your girlfriend?

"Sounds like normal adolescent behavior to me," the host said.

"Precisely. In many cases, the boy goes to such lengths to disguise the abuse that no warning signs may be present. I've even seen school and social performance improve as a part of building that cover story."

This is feeling a little too familiar.

"If there are no warning signs, what should concerned adults do?" the announcer asked.

"I focus on spotting the abusive relationship instead of watching for vague warning signs. For example, the molester will often shower expensive gifts on his victim to create guilt and buy silence."

Jeremy bought me lots of expensive things.

"He will work to isolate the boy from his family. In many cases, the pedophile will find ways to make him completely dependent on the relationship. Not just for companionship, but even for basic needs such as food and shelter."

Jeremy had me move in with him.

"He will work to convince the boy that no one else in the world cares. Without the molester in his life, his victim will be hopelessly alone."

I remember how that felt.

"It's important to realize molesters will often groom their victims for months before pressuring the boy into a sexual relationship."

I lived with Jeremy for months before we started doing it.

"The molester manipulates the child with professions of love, coldly takes advantage of the child, and moves on to the next victim. There's no real love on the molester's part."

My smile was completely gone.

"I teach that we need to be constantly vigilant. If it doesn't feel right, it probably isn't. Parents should be asking themselves if it's normal for their son to receive private lessons from the coach. Or that their son's favorite scoutmaster has been inviting him to stay overnight. Or that their son is spending an awful lot of time with the neighbor down the street who has all the latest video games. Clearly, every man who interacts with a child is not a predator. Most are committed professionals and volunteers who would never dream of hurting a child. But I teach that it's better to err on the side of caution because the potential damage is so devastating."

Devastating?

"It's a long and hard road for the boy who's been molested. The psychological damage to a child victimized by sexual abuse is lifelong and permanent."

Permanent?

"Many men never seek therapy, afraid they'll be ridiculed or labeled as a homosexual. Many of those who seek therapy never learn to cope with their feelings of shame and guilt. Many are overcome by rage or depression. Often, these men find it difficult to hold down steady jobs and maintain long-term relationships. Mental illness and suicide are far

more prevalent amongst men sexually abused as children. It is also a well-established fact that many men who commit violent crimes were often victims of child abuse, and this phenomenon correlates to sexual abuse even more powerfully than physical abuse and neglect."

It was getting hard to breathe.

"It's also critical to keep in mind the research shows many child molesters were themselves molested as children. This is often called the cycle of abuse. Put simply, the abused boy often goes on to abuse others. For this reason alone, identifying victims before they become predators themselves has to be our priority."

I felt like the doctor was staring right at me.

"What can we do to prevent this cycle?" the announcer asked. "Can pedophiles be cured, or do we lock them up and throw away the key?"

"Cured is not a word I use when speaking about treatment for pedophiles."

I stopped breathing altogether.

"Some men respond well to therapy and take responsibility for their actions, but like the alcoholic they're prone to slip at any time in the presence of the right trigger. We teach these men how to cope with their behaviors and avoid situations that could cause them to abuse a child. They need a lifetime of therapy, monitoring, and a strong support structure. Because it's such a long and difficult road, the research shows the recidivism rate to be extremely high. And I'm only speaking about the men who recognize their guilt and are motivated to get help. To tell the truth, most pedophiles I've worked with don't believe they've done anything wrong. They firmly believe the boy was a willing participant and that he even enjoyed the abuse. They see themselves as the hero instead of the villain. This delusional pattern of thinking is nearly impossible to break. In my experience, these men don't respond to therapy. We have no choice but to remove pedophiles permanently from society through incarceration or civil commitment. If given the chance, they will never stop."

I smacked the remote until the television shut off. The room fell silent, and I felt like I was falling with it. My stomach churned. I raced to the bathroom, certain I was about to puke my guts out. I knelt in front of the toilet, heaving, but nothing came out. I wished something

did, because puking always made me feel better afterwards. I eventually gave up.

The kid in the mirror across from me looked like shit.

I imagined him in a doctor's office, stark naked. The doctor listens to his heart, tells him to take a deep breath, sticks a thermometer in his ass, and holds his balls while he turns and coughs.

"Well," the doctor says. "I have good news and bad news. The good news is you're not actually gay."

"What's the bad news?" he asks.

"You're a child molester. A pedophile. A predator."

"Can you give me a pill or shot and make me better?" he asks.

"Nope. It's hopeless. You're permanently devastated. You need to be removed from society." The police come in and handcuff him and drag him away naked to lock him in jail for the rest of his life.

The guy on TV described me *perfectly*.

I showered expensive gifts on Billy.

I was isolating him from other kids.

I'm getting him used to be naked around me.

What the hell am I doing?

Then there was Brian.

What the fuck have I done???

The garage door opened. Terror paralyzed me. I heard Jeremy come into the house.

"Nick?" he called. "Are you home?"

His voice sounded sweet like poison gas. Terror turned to rage. Rage like I'd never felt before. Every nerve in my body screamed.

The abused boy goes on to abuse others.

It was pretty fucking clear who I should blame.

I slammed the bathroom door open so hard the handle put a hole in the wall. Jeremy jumped. The grocery bag he was carrying spilled on the floor.

"You scared the crap out of me," he said, catching his breath. "What's wrong? You look terrible. Are you sick?"

"I'm not the sick one," I growled.

"Who's sick?"

"You are!" I shouted, unable to comprehend why he didn't understand what I was saying.

"What do you mean, I'm sick?" He stared at me. "You look pale. Do you have a fever?"

"You want to have sex with little boys," I hissed.

"There's a news flash," he muttered, picking up the groceries on the floor. "What gave me away?"

I stared at him, the steam inside me building. I was close to detonation.

"You're being serious," he said. "Something's wrong. You're not acting like yourself."

"I'm more myself right now than I've been for a long time," I said. "I finally figured it out. I can't believe I never saw it before. You manipulated me so you could fuck my ass. You don't love me. You never loved me."

I shouldn't have said it. I didn't mean it and I didn't truly believe it. But the fury had taken over and wouldn't let go.

He looked like I slapped him in the face. "Of course I love you," he said. "What happened? Something's got you really upset. Is there anything you want to talk about?"

"I'm done talking," I growled. "You bend and twist everything around until I believe whatever you want me to believe. I fell for it. All these years, you were just using me. You never cared about me. You never understood me. You told me whatever I wanted to hear."

"How can you say that?" he said, his voice trembling. "You know I love you more than anything. You're everything to me."

"Ha!" I shouted. I pointed my finger at him like I was accusing him of murder. "All you saw was a kid who didn't have any friends and parents who didn't care. You moved right in, gave me all those presents, and kept me all to yourself so you could guilt me into letting you screw me."

"I never wanted to make you do something you didn't want," he said gently. "The sex was never what mattered to me."

"What a load of bullshit!" I shouted. "You're still trying to manipulate me. It's over, get it? I understand now! No more cheap thrills for you!"

"I really thought you wanted. . ."

"Wanted what?" I interrupted. "To get fucked by some old hairy guy? Come on, what kid wants that? Kids want to be with their own friends. They don't want to hang around with some creepy adult! I still get grossed out every time I see you naked. I was twelve years old. Twelve! I was a little kid! What the hell did I know? I didn't understand what it meant! You made me think it was all my responsibility!"

He slid down the wall and sat on the floor. "Oh god," he said, holding his head in his hands. "Please, no. I knew this would happen someday, but no, please, not like this."

"Of course you knew," I spat. "You planned it all out like a chess game. Keep moving your pieces until the poor kid is checkmated."

"You have every right to hate me," he said softly. "I deserve it. All of it. But you have to know I love you. I've always loved you, even though I've done terrible things to you."

I shook my head. "I'm not your puppet anymore. You can't pull my strings."

"Please, talk to me," he said. "Something happened. I want to understand. Did you break up with Ana?"

"I'm done talking!" I shouted, storming off down the hall.

I knew I should tell him. I *wanted* to tell him. I knew he'd tell me the TV program was all a pack of lies and I shouldn't listen to that kind of crap. I wanted to believe him so badly because I wanted everything to go back to normal. To the life I was building and to the people I cared about.

But there was no going back. The only lie would be that everything I heard was a lie. That doctor guy nailed me, shot an arrow right through my heart. He knew me better than I knew myself. He could probably glance across a room and spot me in a crowd. He'd shout: "Him, he's the predator, get him!" I couldn't lie to myself. I knew what I was doing to Billy. I knew what I'd become. Because of Jeremy.

I whirled around when I heard him coming. "You'd love if I broke up with her, wouldn't you? Getting me all back to yourself again? Oh wait, I forgot, I'm not some little kid anymore. You don't get your kicks from staring at my ass. You'd rather jump in bed with Billy. He's

cute and small. His voice is still high and he doesn't have any ugly pubes."

I watched him realize. "Did something happen with Billy?"

"Shut up!" I screamed.

"Just take it easy," he said, taking a step towards me. "We need to talk about this."

"There's nothing to talk about!" I screamed. I wanted to get away, but he stood right in front of me, blocking me from getting out. "Get out of my way!"

"Kiddo." He grabbed my left arm.

I knew before it came out how wrong it was to say.

"Get away from me or I'll call the cops," I growled. He went white, like fresh snow waiting to be shoveled. "Wait until they get a load of what's on those tapes. They'll put you in jail for the rest of your life."

"Don't do this," he said, voice trembling, but he didn't move.

It was the anger. Not me.

My hand curled into a fist. It swung around and connected with his chin.

My hand exploded in agony.

His eyes went glassy.

I was only a kid, right? I couldn't really hurt a grown-up, right?

But I wasn't a kid anymore. I was only three inches shorter than him. I could bench press a shitload of weight. I was a marathon runner.

He slid down to the floor, limp.

"Jeremy?" I asked in a tiny voice.

"Please, no," he whispered.

I backed up. "I gotta go."

"Don't go," he pleaded. "Don't leave me. I need you."

I turned away.

"Don't leave me!" he screamed like a four-year-old.

I threw the front door open and ran without looking back.

Running always helped me straighten out tangled thoughts. But it couldn't wipe away the pain. My hand throbbed like it was broken. It

would serve me right if it was. My head throbbed and my heart ached. But there was something deeper, something more sickening, something that went right down to the core of my being. I once saw a cheesy movie where a guy got his soul ripped out of his body. It looked like a bunch of grapes. That's the part that hurt right now.

I couldn't remember hating myself this much in a long, long time.

I punched Jeremy. For real.

But that wasn't the worst part.

I made the most horrible threat I could possibly make.

I had a lot of things I needed to fix. I had to fix things with Billy first. I had to put an end to this before it went any further – before I permanently devastated him the way I was devastated. Then, I had to fix things with Jeremy. I said and did terrible things that deserved an eternity of punishment far more severe than anything I endured in the basement. And then I had to fix myself, even if the doctor on TV said it was impossible. Maybe I could get the therapy he talked about. Maybe I could get a support structure, whatever that meant. I couldn't give up all hope because people depended on me. I didn't want to let them down worse than I already had.

Billy's mother was in the garden like she always was. "Nick!" she called out. She was holding a long fork that looked like a claw, dangerous enough to rip my throat out. If she knew what I was, she'd probably do it. "This is unexpected. I believed we were to drop Billy at your house at half six this evening."

"Yeah, about that," I said. "I'm really sorry, but I messed up. I was supposed to do this thing with my mom tonight. I completely forgot about it and she's angry with me. I have to cancel." It was lame but it was the only thing I could think of.

She looked sympathetic. "That's a shame. Billy was looking forward to it."

"I know," I said. "I wanted to apologize to him in person."

I had a lot of things to apologize for.

"He's up in his room," she said, motioning towards the door. His father poked his head out of the kitchen.

"Your uncle rang twice," he said. "He sounded quite concerned. Is everything alright?"

"Yeah," I said. "I'll call him back. I owe you another night, I know you and Margaret were going out. I'll watch Billy whenever you want."

"No worries for us," he said. "Just mind Billy."

I climbed the stairs slowly. When I told him I couldn't be his mentor anymore without explaining why, it was going to destroy him. The hurt I was about to cause tore me to pieces. But I had to save him from devastation. That was worse.

He was sitting at his desk, headphones on his ears, throwing his head back and forth to the music so wildly I thought he would shake his brain loose. I tapped on his shoulder when he didn't notice me.

"You gave me quite the start," he said in that sweet voice of his. "Did I misunderstand, were we to sleep here tonight?"

"I came by because I can't do the sleepover tonight. I have something I have to do with my mom. I'm really sorry."

I noticed the disappointment in his eyes. "That's quite alright. Perhaps tomorrow?"

"Probably not," I said. He looked at me, full of trust that should never be given to someone like me. The only thing I did with trust was stomp all over it. I had to tell him.

But when I opened my mouth, I didn't. Couldn't.

"How about next weekend?" I mumbled.

"Brilliant," he said.

"Yeah, brilliant," I said. "Billy, I. . ."

"Yes?" he said when I didn't go on.

"I gotta go," I mumbled.

"See you Monday, then?" he said brightly.

I didn't answer. My eyes stung as I left his room.

It's a terrifying thing to realize you have no one to talk to.

Of all the days for Ana to go off with her family to some other state, it had to be the day I needed her so badly I couldn't put it into words. I ran by her house, but it was dark and empty. Just like I knew it would be. I needed to hold her. I needed to cry with her. I desperately needed to talk to her.

I was so used to having someone there for me when I needed them that I'd forgotten how scary it is to be alone. Maybe I didn't need Jeremy so much anymore, but knowing he was there always made me feel safe. This was different than any other time. I needed to talk about him instead of with him. Here I was, the most popular kid in the school, and when I really thought about it I didn't have a single friend I could lean on. Jeff? He leaned on me. I couldn't lean on him. Chris? That was a laugh. Parker, Daniel, Andy, Jonathan, Kerry, Jonas, and Sean? People I did things with, not people I was close to. Dozens of people in the tutoring club, mentoring club, the track team, and the musical? Nothing more than casual acquaintances. Mr. Humber? I couldn't tell him something like this. I'd learned enough from the counseling proposal to know what could happen if I shared any of this with him. How could someone be surrounded by so many people and be so alone?

Once upon a time, I had a special friend. Our bond went beyond being a playmate or companion. But we had drifted apart. I was going to visit him over the summer in Maine, but we never went. Our Saturday night promise didn't resume when school started. I'd been telling myself for a while that we were going in different directions. I told myself if he ever needed me, I'd be there for him. Now I understood the real truth. Every time we saw each other, we were both reminded of what I did to him. I'd permanently devastated him. I *molested* him. Brian didn't have parents who cared and friends he could lean on. I couldn't go to him. I could never go back to him again.

All I had was Ana.

It was getting dark and I had no idea where to go. I wanted to go home so badly, but I was terrified what I might say or do. Terrified the anger would take hold again and push me to do something that couldn't be undone. I knew what I was capable of doing. I punched Jeremy in the face. I swung a baseball bat at my mom's head. I kicked the chair out from under me. I might do something to him. I might bash in his head or slash his throat with a knife. I couldn't go back there, not until I was sure he was safe from the monster lurking inside me. There was only one place I could go. The place where I deserved to be.

I got the key from its hiding place in the backyard.

I went into my parent's house.

I climbed the stairs to the old Nick's room.
I stripped off my clothes.
I used my shoelace to tie a loop to the headboard.
I rolled over until it was tight around my hands.
I pissed in the bed on purpose.
I stayed that way for a long, long time.

Chapter 45

October 13, 1984

I woke up to the first real autumn morning of the year. Crisp and clean, the sun clear and bright with no summer haze to hide it. The leaves were beginning to rust on the trees, still a week away from the brilliant oranges, golds, and purples they would become, at least until they fell and were swept into bags to rot for eternity or get crushed into powder under unfeeling boots. It was a perfect morning for running. To feel the wind in my face. To listen to the sharp echo of my running shoes pounding on the pavement. To smell the lawns being mowed one last time and the curl of smoke from fireplaces that had sat unused for months. To listen to the sound of birds singing their last songs before winging away for better places. To watch kids enjoying their last days outside without coats, hats, and mittens. Beauty that couldn't be described in a poem or song, only in a feeling I wished I could capture and keep.

I hated it.

I wanted dreary gray clouds. Rain. Thunder. Misery. A perfect day was like the world telling me to go fuck myself, that it didn't care how miserable I felt. I wanted to destroy the sun and bring back the blackness forever.

The room was cold when I woke up. I had no blankets, the heater was off, I was still naked, and the bed was damp and smelly. I must've loosened the shoelace at some point, because it wasn't tight enough to snap my wrists. Just enough to keep my hands trapped. I let myself out and went through the old routine. Like riding a bicycle, I couldn't

forget how. But I kept being thrown off because things were different. My bed was smaller. Someone moved the cabinet with the detergent lower. The shower head was barely high enough to get my head underneath. I only knew it was the same tub where I used to read books, even though it was forbidden, because of the cracked tile fourth from the right on the ninth row.

I thought I knew who I was. Fourteen years old, in ninth grade. Popular and successful. Training to run a marathon. This house, no matter what had changed, made me feel like a fat, lonely eleven-year-old all over again, tying myself up and wetting the bed. It didn't matter if the old Nick was buried in the backyard with only a little twig to mark he'd existed. The house resurrected him as though he'd never died.

I had to get the hell out of there.

I didn't feel like I left the house behind until I started to run. The old Nick wouldn't be able to keep up with me. He couldn't run a hundred yards without collapsing. I left him panting on the first corner. I didn't hold back, running faster than I should've, spending my energy early without caring. I grunted, picking up the pace, already feeling the strain in my legs and the burn in my lungs. The grunts turned to shouts, outbursts that attracted annoyed stares by people mowing lawns or playing catch with their kids. Even if I cared, there was nothing I could do. It would be like trying to hold in a massive burp – it'd come out no matter what you did. I was running too fast and too hard, but I wanted to run even faster and harder. I wanted to be unable to catch my breath, my legs threatening to collapse if I took another step. I was going to wind up falling face down if I kept this up. Wasn't going to stop me.

I'd heard about runner's high before, but I always thought it was bullshit. I'd trained all summer and never once felt anything like that no matter how hard I pushed myself. Until now. A cool wave washed over me. My exhaustion disappeared. I could breathe and my legs felt strong. I shouted and took off even faster. I was on top of the world, like I felt when I walked up on stage to get the Sheffield award, like I did when I kissed Ana the first time.

It vanished as quickly as it appeared. My legs turned to quivering goo and my lungs screamed for air I couldn't suck in fast enough. I slowed

to a jog until I had enough energy to go back to a full run, my feet finding their own way through the streets.

I only realized my feet took me home when I was at the front door.

I thought the door should look more frightening than it did. Yesterday, my problems seemed big and hopeless. Maybe it was the run, maybe it was getting some sleep, or maybe it was just that high I felt, but when I stared at the door I felt like things weren't so big and hopeless. I didn't know what I was going to say and do to make it right, but I had to do something. I needed him. Why was it so difficult to imagine saying the things that needed to be said, the secrets I was keeping from him? I realized how ridiculous I was being. Of all people, he'd understand. He was an expert. He'd know what to do and how to make things better.

I opened the door. "Jeremy?" I said in a small voice.

The house was still and silent.

I went inside and closed the door.

"I'm sorry," I said. "I know you're mad at me and you should be. I said and did some horrible things but I didn't really mean them. I feel so terrible. I never want to hurt anyone, especially you. I promise I will never, ever do something like that again."

The house didn't answer.

"Please, I need to talk to you. I have to tell you something important."

Nothing.

"Jeremy?"

Maybe he was still asleep. Or drunk. I could understand if he got drunk.

I climbed the stairs. The bedroom door was half open, the bed unmade and empty. Drawers were hanging open, clothes sticking out randomly. Only his drawers. Mine were closed. Jeremy could be a slob sometimes, but this went beyond sloppiness. I glanced at the giant teddy bear in the corner of the room. The only witness to all the things that happened here, the good and the bad.

The bear looked desperate.

My heart stopped. I didn't know how I knew, but something was very wrong.

I poked my head in the closet. Clothes on the floor, off their hangers.

"Jeremy?" I heard myself saying.

The bathroom was empty. The toothbrush and razor he always left on the counter were missing.

"Jeremy?" I called out louder.

I ran down the hall and threw the door open to the guest bedroom, the blankets still messy from the last time Ana and I made out.

No Jeremy.

I checked the empty bedrooms. Nothing.

I tore down the stairs, two at a time. Holding my breath, I opened the door to the garage. The van was gone.

"He went for croissants," I said out loud.

Even I didn't believe myself.

The lobby was just as quiet as when I first came in.

I had to be dreaming. Any moment now I'd wake up and everything would go back to normal.

"Jeremy?" I yelled.

Nothing.

I opened the back door. "Jeremy?" I yelled at the lawn. Nothing.

I looked wildly around the kitchen. A few dishes in the sink. A dirty pot on the stove.

And a folded piece of paper on the table.

I crept up to it.

It said "Nick" on the outside.

I didn't want to touch it. It looked like a bomb about to explode.

"It says he went for croissants and he'll be right back," I said out loud. *I'm going to feel like an idiot when he gets back.*

I took a deep breath and unfolded it. The whole page was covered with writing. It didn't take a whole page to say he was going for croissants. Some of the words were blurry from spots of the paper that had gotten wet and dried.

My dearest Nick,

I suppose there's not much use apologizing. There's nothing I can say or do to change the past. I would give everything I

have to take back the mistakes I've made and the wrongs I've done to you. I would sell my soul in a heartbeat if it could erase my sins and save you. I knew this day would come. I think I've always known it would come from the moment I fell. The time always comes when the devil demands to be paid. And yet, it hurts more than I can bear. My heart is broken for you. I want you to know that none of this, not a single little shred of it, is your fault. You've done nothing wrong and you have no reason to feel guilty. This is my doing, and mine alone.

I am so sorry. I'm sorry I've put you through so much, sorry I've taken your innocence, sorry I've abused your faith and trust in me. Sorry I was too weak to be what you needed. Sorry I've hurt you in a way that is so hard to heal. Sorry that I've given you a terrible burden to bear, something that has destroyed me but which I know you will conquer. You know what I mean.

You were right about everything, except this one thing. You won't believe me now, but maybe one day you'll understand. I have loved you from the moment I met you and I will love you until the day I die. I will never love another person as much as I love you. There will never be a person in my life who could come close to meaning as much to me.

For once in my miserable excuse of a life, I'm going to do the right thing. You don't need me anymore. You haven't needed me for a long time. You are the strongest, bravest, and toughest person I've ever known. You give everything of yourself and expect nothing in return. You are a wonderful human being whose name will be known generations from now for the things you've done to make this world a better place. You deserve far better than me. I have to do what's best for you. I need to get out of your way, stop holding you back, and stop reminding you of what I've done. If I do, you'll have the chance to find your way through the horrors I've inflicted on you. The only way you can move on is for me to no longer be a part of your life.

You might decide to take or leave it, but the house, the car, the piano, everything is yours. The only things I took are clothes

and some reminders of our life together. Robert won't throw you out. He doesn't care what happens here. Tell him nothing and you'll be able to live here as long as you like. You're mature enough to live on your own. I added about forty thousand dollars to your bank account so you'll be able to buy whatever you need. When you go through the papers in the office, you'll find everything you need for the college fund I set up for you. I completely understand if you don't want anything from me, but I hope you take it anyway.

Maybe someday, years from now, when the hurt has had time to heal, you'll let me see you again and tell you how sorry I am in person. Until then, all I can say is that I love you, I will miss you terribly, and I wish you nothing but happiness and joy. You were a brilliant star in a dark life and for me you'll always shine the best and brightest.

I will love you until forever comes.

Jeremy

I collapsed on the floor. My head went between my knees.

This isn't happening. This can't be happening.

I screamed so loud my throat burned.

The room spun.

You stupid fucking idiot why didn't you come home last night???

I felt dizzy, the world shrinking around me to a little dot like a television set being turned off because the program was over.

I lurched to my feet, stumbling into the lobby. I needed to see his face and hear his voice. I needed to know he was real, that I didn't invent him or create him in a dream. I needed proof of everything that happened because my memories felt like they were melting ice on a scorching day.

The pictures around the lobby were missing. All of them.

I threw the cabinet door open.

It was empty. Every single video tape was gone. Decorating the Christmas tree. Swinging swords in Maine. Getting whipped in the

basement. As if they never happened. It really was all a dream. I finally woke up.

I screamed and ran out the front door, leaving it wide open.

I ran and ran and ran.

My body complained. I told it to go to hell.

I tripped and fell. My knee bled. My face felt raw. I kept running.

My whole life was nothing but a giant lie I told the world. The Nick who was funny during the announcements, who tutored and mentored, who everyone knew and liked – he didn't exist. It was nothing but a part in a play. I was stupid enough to believe it myself. To let myself do something as stupid as believe in myself. But the play was over. The only thing left was the actor. He was nothing more than a scared little kid. The man behind the curtain was gone. No more pretending. I knew who I really was.

I couldn't make myself think. I had to find him, but how was I supposed to do that? Report him missing to the police? Hire a private detective? He told me we'd disappear if we were ever discovered, how no one would be able to find us. That's what he was doing right now. Disappearing for real. He had to know I didn't really mean it, didn't he? Of all the things to say, why did I have to say the one thing that should never, ever, ever have been said? I tried to make myself angry at him for leaving, but that didn't work. The only anger I felt pointed straight at me.

The running wasn't helping. My thoughts were getting muddier. The pit in my stomach was growing. I had to figure out a plan. But the pictures in my head kept getting in the way. Each one more beautiful than the last.

Cooking dinners together in the kitchen.

Sunday morning breakfast with the New York Times.

Blasting classical music out the window on the highway.

Picnics on the rock.

Spilling hot chocolate all over the white rug only to have it ignored because he was worried I hurt myself.

These were the moments that defined what it meant to be part of a single person called Nick and Jeremy.

I realized there weren't going to be any more moments.

Tears mixed with the sweat on my face.

The sun was setting and Ana still wasn't home. I couldn't stop myself from thinking she was never coming back, just like Jeremy. I wanted to ride back to our house to check, but I'd already gone back twice. It was still empty. I left a note on top of his. That I was at Ana's. Not to leave, no matter what. That I was sorry. I wrote a hundred so's in front of my sorry. To come get me if he got back and I wasn't there. There was too much time in between Ana's and home – too many chances either of them would come back when I was halfway and not be able to find me. I'd miss my chance to make things right and it would be gone forever. I thought about taking the Porsche. Something as petty as a driver's license didn't matter at a time like this. I even got in the car. How hard could driving be? Push the gas, press the brakes, steer, and don't crash. I didn't know how the stick shift worked so that plan fizzled. My bicycle was the only choice.

I couldn't sit still, walking back and forth, riding around the street, barely able to keep from screaming at people doing ordinary things on a day like this. I was halfway down the street when their car turned the corner. I watched her wave at me from the window, pedaling furiously to get to her house at the same time they did. She was getting out of the car as I threw my bicycle down on the curb.

"Hey, you," she said. "Were you waiting for me?"

I threw my arms around her like I'd never let go.

"I've only been gone for a couple of days. Did you miss me that much?"

"I have to talk to you," I said.

"We're dropping off the suitcases and going out to dinner. Want to come? I can ask my parents."

"No. I have to talk to you. Alone. Right now."

"Something's wrong," she murmured. She touched my cheek. "You've been crying again, I can see it. Your face is all scratched up."

"It's important. It's really important."

Her father called over. "Ana, we can you bring you something back if you'd rather spend some time with Nick." He waved at me. I waved back weakly.

She hesitated. "Bring something for Nick too," she said to him.

I grabbed her hand. "Let's go to your room."

She let me drag her up the stairs. "You know the door doesn't lock."

"I don't want to make out," I said. I sat down on the frilly white blanket that covered her bed and grabbed a pink teddy bear with a heart, holding it tight. She sat down next to me.

"What's going on?" she said gently.

"Let's get married," I said.

"Married?"

"Yeah, married. For real. Man and wife."

"Wow, you really missed me," she joked.

"I'm not kidding," I said. "I want to marry you. I want to be together for the rest of our lives. I want to have kids, and a house, and get old with you."

"Come on," she said. "I'm fifteen and you're fourteen. We can't even get married until we're eighteen."

"Then run away with me," I said. "Come live with me."

"Run away? I don't want to run away. What's with you?"

"I love you," I said, sliding off the bed. I found a little plastic ring on her dresser, the kind you get as a favor from a kid's birthday party. I knelt in front of her. "Will you marry me?"

"Oh my god," she said.

"I'll get a better ring later. A diamond one if you want."

"This is getting a little weird," she said.

"Don't you love me?"

"Of course I love you," she said. "But we can't get married. We have to finish high school and college and get jobs. I don't want to run away. I love my family even if my parents can be a pain in the neck. Besides, what would we do for money?"

"I have almost fifty thousand dollars," I said.

Her face dropped. "Seriously?"

"It's enough until we can get jobs."

"You're scaring me," she said.

I grabbed her hand. "No, no, don't get scared. I'm going to take care of everything. I want to be together."

"Are you scared I'm going to break up with you or something?" My eyes went wide, her arrow too close to the target. "Aw, that's so sweet. I'm not going to break up with you. I love you. When it's the right time, I want to get married. I could never find someone better than you." She ran her hand through my hair in a way that reminded me of Jeremy. I shivered. "What's going on that made you think I'm going to break up with you?"

"Something happened today," I said. "Something bad. Really bad."

"Did someone get hurt?" she asked.

"Do you love me no matter what?"

"Of course I do," she said. I could see in her eyes that she really, really meant it. I had to convince her to come live with me. We wouldn't have to get married or run away. She'd take care of me. She'd look after me. I wouldn't have to be alone. "Nick, I love you," she said as I put my head down on her lap like I did a week ago.

"I want to make love to you," I said.

"We can make out if you want," she said.

"No, I want to make love. I want to go all the way. When you go all the way with someone you love, there's a feeling I can't describe. It's like being one person, like you can't tell whose arms or legs are whose. I want to feel that with you. I want you to feel that with me."

"I'm not ready to go all the way," she said nervously.

"No one's ever ready their first time," I said. "I want to be naked with you – not just my body but my feelings and my thoughts. I want you to know everything about me and I want to know everything about you. I want us to be so close other people can't tell us apart." I could tell she didn't understand. "Look, there's something I want to tell you. A secret, one you can't tell anyone ever."

"Ok," she said in the same way she said she wasn't ready.

"Jeremy left. He's gone and he's not coming back."

"What do you mean he's gone? How could he just leave?"

"He took some clothes and he's gone. Because of something I did."

"What the heck could you do to make him leave like that?"

"He's not my really my uncle. He's not even a part of my family. He's just a neighbor. We're not actually related."

"So you're not related," she said. "Why is that such a big secret?"

"I met him when I was eleven," I said. "I wanted to buy a video game so I went out to shovel driveways. He was the only person who hired me. We started out being friends, and soon I went over his house all the time. When my mother got the job in Denver, my parents wanted me to go to boarding school. I freaked out and wrecked my room so they let me live with Jeremy instead. He was nice and he was always around. He knew how to make everything better. I started to love him."

"That's beautiful," she said.

"I still love him. I really love him and he's gone and I don't know what to do."

"We'll figure it out," she said gently. "I'll help you."

"I mean, me and him, we're more than just friends."

"I can tell," she said. "I wish every kid with bad parents had someone who cared."

"I've been sleeping with him," I said.

She went stiff. "You what?"

"I mean, we. . ." I took a deep breath. "We do it."

"Oh my god," she said. Her eyes were huge. "He makes you do it?"

"No, no, nothing like that," I said. "He doesn't force me. We do it because we love each other. That's how I know. I know what it's like to be totally in love with someone. I know what it's like to make love. I know it's hard the first time but once you do you never want to go back and you never want it to end. I love you and I want to be with you forever."

"You're gay?" she said in a tiny voice.

"No, I'm not gay. I love him, that's different from being gay."

"You do it with a guy," she said. "How long have you been doing it with him?"

I closed my eyes. "Every day since I was twelve."

She didn't answer. I watched the look of shock on her face melt into anger. "Since you were twelve? You're telling me I'd make out with you and then you'd screw around with your whatever he is?"

"Yeah, but it's not. . ."

"You asshole!" she screamed, pushing me away.

"Wait, you don't understand."

"You lied to me!" she screamed. "You told me you loved me and you were two-timing with a grown-up man. Oh god, you're gay!"

"Let me explain." I couldn't catch my breath.

"I can't believe I kissed you!" she yelled. "I can't believe I kissed the same mouth that was probably giving him blow jobs!" She looked at me with such disgust it was like being stabbed. "You probably gave me AIDS!"

"He doesn't have. . ."

"You disgusting pervert!" She shot me right in the heart because it was truer than she knew. "You made me fall in love with you! It was all a lie, just a stupid lie. I hate you!"

"Ana, please," I said, desperate.

"Get away from me!" She kicked me as I tried to get closer to her. "Get out! It's over!"

"Don't do this to me!" I moaned. "I need you!"

She started throwing things at me. Books, the plastic ring, a brass paperweight heavy enough to kill me. I put my hands over my head to protect myself. "Get out of my room! Get out of my house and get out of my life! I never want to see you or talk to you ever again!"

"Please!" I screamed.

She screamed back so loud I thought my eardrums would burst.

I ran, down the stairs, out the door, down the walk, into the street, and out of her life, running and running forever.

I was alone. Really and truly alone.

Jeremy left me.

Ana dumped me.

The whole world hated me.

I couldn't live at home. Being in our house would remind me every day what things used to be like. I couldn't stay at my parent's house either. I'd be hanging from the ceiling in my old bedroom within a month. I couldn't show my face at school. By Monday, everyone would know Ana broke up with me and why. I would be an outcast, ridiculed behind my back. Faggot. Everything I had was gone.

There was nothing left for me here. I could run west – there was lots of room out west. Maybe I could find a small town with some nice people who always wanted a son, like the Bradbury story. Or I could run east – take a bus to New York. I could become one of those boy hookers in Times Square, getting guys to fuck me so I could pretend it was Jeremy. Or I could go out and hitchhike on the highway until someone kidnapped me, locking me away from the world, doing all the horrible things I deserved before putting me out of my misery.

I needed money and clothes.

I ran back home. My father's car was in the driveway. He was sitting in the lobby.

"What are you doing here?" I screamed.

He didn't look like himself. I wasn't even sure it was him. I think it was the first time I'd seen him not angry.

"He called me," my father said.

"He called you?" I screamed. "He called you but he didn't call me?"

My father didn't answer.

I ran up the stairs, kicking the bedroom door so hard it came off its hinges. I stomped over it. I tore open my drawers, clothes flying in a giant tornado. I didn't need much. A couple changes of underwear, socks, and a sweatshirt for when it got cold. Only what fit in my backpack. I grabbed my watch, my gold bracelet and necklace, and the ring he bought me. I could sell them. I shoved my bankbook into my pocket.

"What are you doing?" my father asked from the open doorway.

"None of your fucking business!" I screamed.

He didn't answer.

I zipped my backpack. He blocked the doorway. "Get out of my way," I growled.

"No," he said in an infuriating soft voice that didn't belong to him.

"What do you mean, no?" I said. "Get out of my fucking way!"

"I'm not going to let you go," he said.

"You? You never cared about anything but your stupid work and your stupid office and your stupid business! I'm not your employee and I'm not your son. I'm not anything to you! You can't tell me what to do!"

It only took one punch to knock down Jeremy. I wasn't going to stop at one with him. I was stronger, younger, and faster. He'd go down and I'd be free, out the door, gone forever. No more Nick from Newton Falls. I'd start a new life in a new place as a new person who didn't remember any of this happened.

I collided with him.

His arms encircled me. Somehow, I got turned around, my back against his chest. My arms were pinned to my side. He was much stronger than I expected. I writhed around, but I couldn't get free. "Let go of me!" I screamed. I stomped on his foot. I tried to kick the back of my heel into his balls. Anything.

He wouldn't let go.

He pushed me a step at a time back into the bedroom. I tried to dig my heels in. I was strong too. I gritted my teeth, twisting, using my weight to throw him around, trying to slam him into the wall. But his arms were still wrapped around me.

"I'm not letting you go," he said quietly.

"I'll fucking kill you," I growled.

I felt myself being lifted, feet off the floor. I didn't know how he did it. He stumbled into the bedroom while I kicked, swore, and spat. I managed to pull an arm free and tried to hit him in the face. All I did was scratch his cheek. He lost his balance and fell forward, the two of us slamming into the bed. He pinned me down, trapping my arm again.

"I hate you!" I screamed. He didn't let go.

"We're going to get help for you," he said gently.

"I don't need any help!" I screamed. I kicked, lashed, shouted, bit, cried, tore at his hair, tore at his clothes, elbowed him in the side. He still didn't let go.

I didn't know how long he held me. I became weaker and weaker. My energy was gone. I curled up into a ball. My thumb wound up in

my mouth. I felt myself wet my pants. I cried and cried and cried and cried.

"We're going to get you some help," he said again.

But nothing could help me.

Darkness closed in.

I hoped my eyes would never open again.

Forever had come.

Part 7

James Edison

Chapter 46

April 5, 2007

The cell phone started ringing twenty minutes after I drove away from the school. I didn't have any intention of picking it up, but I checked the screen each time it rang. Alex cell. Alex cell. Alex cell. Alex dorm. Alex cell. Jake cell. Jake cell. Alex cell. Jake cell. Julia cell. Alex cell. Jake cell. Alex cell. And so on. I finally tossed the phone into the back seat. It vibrated until the battery died.

I drove onto the beltway and back off again, north into Maryland and up to I-70. West to nowhere. I continued all night with the radio off, letting the yellow lines on the road relentlessly hypnotize me into a blank-minded stupor only occasionally disrupted by the squeaking of windshield wipers.

In days long past, I drove aimlessly to clear my mind, taking endless all-night trips down back-country roads in Loudoun and Fauquier counties, careening around sharp turns faster than I should and tearing down highways at a hundred miles an hour. Driving was an expression of freedom back then. At some point driving became a chore like any other, and I stopped my nocturnal wanderings.

What I was doing wasn't wandering – it was running away. As far as possible.

I pulled off the road around five in the morning at a rest stop in western Ohio with a cheap chain motel and an all-day breakfast place. I ate to make up for the last six months. I ordered three full breakfasts. I ate my butter and syrup with pancakes on the side. I ordered the omelet with triple the cheese and the bacon with as much fat as possible.

I had a job to do and I wanted to get it done as fast as possible. I needed that weight back doing what it was supposed to be doing. Insulating me from everyone and everything.

I wound up in bed with horrible indigestion, sleeping in fits, waking up drenched from nightmares too frightening for me to dare remember. I got back on the road after a massive dinner, west again, no idea where I was going or when I would stop. The cell phone stayed dead in the back seat.

I was in the middle of Kansas at two in the morning when I spotted one of those signs that said how far it was to each city. Denver, 462 miles. I slammed on the brakes and pulled over to the side of the road, heart pounding. There was no way I'd let myself get any closer to Denver. My mother was in Denver. The bitch that abandoned me, that left me with *him*.

I plugged in the phone and called Julia even though it was the middle of the night. "Nick, thank god," she said. "Everyone's worried sick about you! I called the police and the hospitals. Jake is going out of his mind. Where are you?"

"Kansas," I said flatly. "462 miles from Denver."

"Kansas? What in god's name are you doing in Kansas?"

"I don't know," I said. "That's where the road went."

"Nick," she said in a very tender voice. "Come home."

"I don't think I can," I said. "Not for a while."

"Please talk to me," she said. "Whatever it is, let me help you. You've been a different person lately. You've been coming back to life, more like the person I fell in love with. I know we've grown apart, but I don't want that. I don't want to lose you again. Please."

I wanted to tell her the truth about Alex and about myself, but I'd made that colossal mistake once before.

"I'll call again tomorrow," I said.

"Don't go," she said.

I hung up the phone.

The icon said I had forty-seven messages. A message from Alex. "Please, please pick up your phone, call me back in my dorm room or on my cell. I just want to talk to you."

A message from Jake. "Dad, what the hell? Alex is hysterical. He said you threw him out of the house but he won't tell me why."

A message from Julia. "Nick, Jake is upset. Something about throwing his friend out of the house. Please call me when you get this."

And then one that didn't belong. "Mr. Velles, this is Jochen Hartmann with UBS bank in Zurich. There is a matter of some urgency we need to discuss. Please contact me at your earliest convenience." He left an impossibly long phone number and email address.

Hang up messages from Alex. A scorcher from Jake calling me a fucking asshole. Julia pleading with me to call her. And message after message after message from Jochen Hartmann with UBS bank in Zurich. A matter of some urgency to discuss. I was on the wrong list if they thought I was this big of a prospect. I called him so I could yell at someone.

"Hartmann," he said with typical German efficiency.

"This is Nick *Velles*," I imitated. "Whatever list I'm on get me off it right now."

"I've been trying to reach you for days. There is a matter. . ."

"Of some urgency to discuss," I snapped. "I get it. Don't you guys know when to quit?"

"I've been instructed to turn over a safe deposit box to you. It is imperative you receive the contents of this box as quickly as possible."

"For crying out loud, just drop it in the mail."

"You are required to appear in person to accept the contents. I would be pleased to make arrangements to fly you to Zurich on the next available flight."

"Uh huh," I said. "I suppose you want my credit card number first. Is there a Nigerian prince involved or did I win a sweepstakes?"

"Nothing is required. The flight is being provided courtesy of the bank. I see a flight from Dulles airport leaving this afternoon which could have you in Zurich the following morning. Can I make these arrangements for you?"

"I'm somewhere in Kansas right now," I said.

"I would be pleased to make arrangements from the closest airport in Kansas," he said. "I understand this is highly irregular, but I can assure you the circumstances are entirely legitimate. Time is short."

If I was in a normal state of mind, I would've told him to get lost. It had to be a scam, even if I couldn't figure out how it worked. Swiss bankers didn't fly people for free to Europe to turn over the contents of a safe deposit box. That kind of thing only happened in James Bond movies. I could think of no other possible explanation.

But I wasn't in a normal state of mind. I was in the middle of nowhere Kansas at two in the morning after running away from the hardest thing I've ever done in my life. So, what the hell, I thought. What more could I lose? I drove to Wichita, got on a plane to Chicago, switched to another plane in New York, and before you could say bag of peanuts I was in a cushy business class seat courtesy of Jochen Hartmann with UBS Bank, listening to an announcement in three languages that we'd be landing shortly in Zurich. I had no luggage and no clothes other the ones I'd been wearing since I started running, decorated with various breakfast food stains.

I didn't have anything else, but by remarkable coincidence I had my passport. I found it in the small folder hidden under the emergency kit in the trunk. I had so much fun when I whisked Alex and Jake off to London over Christmas that I thought we might do it again. I kept our passports handy in case the urge struck me to fly off to Japan or India on a whim.

I didn't honestly care that I was halfway around the world without knowing why. The Swiss were good at food. I was going to switch from American breakfasts to expensive cheese and chocolate until I broke out in a rash or collapsed into a diabetic coma. No way I was going to pay back Jochen Hartmann from UBS Bank for the flight and hotel when he figured out I wasn't the Nick Welles they were looking for. My plan was to go to whatever hotel room they arranged, take a nap and a shower, buy some overpriced clothes, stuff my face, and then figure out what was going on. I sailed through customs, spotting the man dressed in the impeccably neat black uniform with a Welles sign. He led me to a stretch limo parked out front.

"Take me to the hotel," I said as we drove away.

"I'm sorry, sir," he said. "My instructions are to take you to the bank."

Instructions, requirements. That's all these people thought about.

I should've been fascinated by the scenery – an exotic city in an exotic country I'd never visited before. But I found myself unable to pay attention. Not only because I was dirty, sweaty, exhausted, and famished. As the limo wound its way to the city, a nagging urge in the back of my mind grew. Something was wrong. I knew I should go back to the airport and get out of there as fast as I could. I decided I would. After I stuffed my face with cheese and chocolate, all courtesy of you know who, Jochen Hartmann with UBS bank.

The limo pulled up in front of a large stone building with white columns that screamed money. I must've looked ridiculous in my stained shirt and wrinkled slacks, but none of the people wearing thousand-dollar suits paid any attention. A sharply dressed Germanic man with equally sharp features stepped up to me inside the lobby. "Mr. Velles, I am Jochen Hartmann," he said.

"With UBS bank in Zurich," I continued in a tired voice.

"Please," he said, escorting me to an elevator. We rode up to a posh floor, all wood and plush carpeting. He led me to an office that spoke of status, decorated with expensive furniture and windows overlooking the street. "Please, make yourself comfortable."

I collapsed into an overstuffed chair. "Ok, you got me. Thousands of miles from home with no idea why."

"I understand your frustration," he said, opening a folder on his desk. "I assure you, we do not typically operate in this manner. However, we are obligated to observe the wishes of our clients." He pushed the folder across the desk. "Please sign these papers to take possession of the deposit box and account. May I please see your passport?"

I handed my passport over before it registered. "Account?"

"Yes, an account being transferred to you," he said.

"Enough!" I snapped, pushing the folder away. "I'm not signing anything until someone tells me what the hell is going on here."

"I understand your concern," he said. "I've been instructed to inform you that the answers you seek are contained within the deposit box itself. Unfortunately, a requirement of transferring possession of the box is to also take possession of the account."

"How convenient," I said.

693

"You'll see the papers are all in order," he said, pushing it back to me. They were in English, a simple transfer of ownership document without indicating who the previous owner was. Secret Swiss bank stuff.

"Fine," I said, throwing the pen down after I was done signing. "I've got to be out of my mind. How much money is in the account? Or do I owe someone a small fortune?"

He studied my signature, handing back my passport when he was satisfied. "Everything is in order," he said, punching some keys on the computer. "As of this moment, the account is valued at ten million, one hundred seventy-two thousand, three hundred fourteen."

"How much is that in dollars?" I asked.

"That is in dollars," he said.

I jerked to my feet. "You handed me an account worth ten million dollars? That's not possible. You made a mistake."

"I assure you, everything is in order," he said.

I grabbed my head. "Ten million?"

"You speak of this as though it were a bad thing."

"Holy shit," I said. What the hell was this, some kind of setup? Drug money? What could I possibly have done? I grabbed at the paperwork, ready to tear it into ten million little pieces.

"Before you make that decision, allow me to escort you to a private location where you can view the contents of the deposit box. Afterwards, I'll be happy to dispose of the funds in the account in any way you see fit. Please."

"I don't understand," I insisted.

He led me to a small meeting room. A well-dressed woman brought in a long metal box, the same kind any bank might have. They left me alone, closing the door. I stared at the box, desperate to know what the hell was going on, and too afraid to find out what the hell was going on. I finally used a single finger to flip it open, expecting the box to bite. I was sure it would contain wads of cash from five countries, a dozen passports, drugs, guns, and microfilm (as though I knew what microfilm looked like). Something that forced me to remember all that secret agent training conditioned into me. Bourne Identity bullshit.

The box was mostly empty. A booklet for DVD's and an unmarked envelope with the flap open. No spy stuff. Nothing that would self-destruct once I read it. I opened the envelope.

The blood drained from my face as I read the note inside.

This wasn't spy stuff. It was much, much worse. The handwriting was shaky, but I recognized it instantly.

My dearest Nick,

I never expected you to come this far, but here you are. Not fourteen any more, but I'm no spring chicken either. It's been too many years.

I'm sorry for all the secrecy, but I was terrified you'd run away again if you knew it was me. I couldn't bear the thought you wouldn't take the one thing I could give you. I know money can never make up for what I've done, but please take it. Make a better life for your family. Do something more with it than I have.

After all these years, I'd like to tell you in person how sorry I am for everything I've done. I know it won't change anything, and I have no right to ask anything of you, but please, please, just one last chance to make my amends. I'm at University Hospital here in Zurich. Room 268.

I've never stopped loving you.

Jeremy

The air was sucked out of the room. I gasped and heaved, desperately trying to breathe.

Son of a bitch.

I tore the DVD book open so violently a handful of zipper tines scattered around the room. The first disc was labeled in the same handwriting.

Christmas 1981.

Son of a bitch!!

I stumbled out of the room. "Do you require anything?" Jochen Hartmann with UBS bank asked.

"Yes," I said, seething. "A ride to University Hospital."

"The driver is at your disposal," he said.

"Go to hell, you son of a bitch," I said out loud.

I could do better than that.

"Rot in hell, you fucking son of a bitch."

Better. I'd need something to throw in his face. A cup of water, a food tray, or maybe some kind of medical instrument. No, a bedpan. A full one.

My rage felt sharper than it had for years. He manipulated me into getting on a plane halfway around the world to take his stinking filthy money, the same money he used to seduce me when I was a defenseless young boy. All these years and he's still manipulating me. He even did it right when the wound from Alex was fresh. Jeremy burdened me with this curse. Jeremy was responsible for hurting Alex. Jeremy ruined my life. I let myself think that I missed him, that I still cared about him, and that there was some good mixed in with the horror. I was a fool. Never again would I let my belief falter or give in to weakness. I was going to throw his money in his face. I was going to tell him I'd never forgive him for the lifetime of pain he caused me. A lifetime of shame, hiding, lies, and the worst kind of loneliness.

"Room 268?" I asked at the front desk.

"Elevators behind you to the second floor, first doors on your left. The name of the patient you are visiting?"

"Stillwell," I spat as I walked away. The elevator was waiting when I pushed the button. The woman at the desk was calling out to me, but I ignored her.

"Rot in hell, you fucking son of a bitch," I rehearsed.

The elevator doors opened. First doors on the left, the title in German. A psych ward? Prison ward would be more appropriate. I pushed the button to open the doors, walking along the hall. Room 268 was on the right side. Two nurses ran down the hall, calling out to

me. I didn't listen. I threw the door open so hard it quivered when it hit the doorstop.

The room had one bed, neatly made and empty.

"Please, sir," one of the nurses said.

"Where's the patient?" I demanded. "Stillwell, where is he?"

"I will get someone to help you, please, right in here," she said, pointing to a small conference room across the hall. I got a strange pang in my stomach. I held my ground, trying to recover my composure.

"I only want to know where you've moved Jeremy Stillwell. Someone punch a few keys and I'll be on my way. There won't be a need for a disturbance."

Another woman in a white coat appeared. "I am responsible for Mr. Stillwell's care."

"Finally. Where is he?"

"Please," she said, motioning to the conference room. I groaned and threw up my hands, but followed her in. I sat down on one of the couches, hardly surprised that hospital furniture looked like it was made by the same company no matter where it was in the world. She sat down next to me.

"I'm very sorry to be the one to inform you, but Mr. Stillwell has passed away."

My mind went blank.

"How?" I heard myself croak.

"He suffered from stage four liver cancer aggravated by cirrhosis. By the time he sought treatment, it had spread throughout his body. There was very little we could do for him."

"When?" I croaked again.

"Just last night," she said. "Is there anything I can do for you?"

I came back into myself.

"There's nothing to be done," I said, shaking my head. The son of a bitch slunk away before I could let him have it. He was always good at running away. I didn't have to tell him to rot in hell because he was already busy rotting away. I didn't have to see his face. I didn't have to hear his voice. I didn't have to bring up all those memories I didn't want to remember.

The room began to swim. I heard someone asking me if I felt alright as I collapsed onto the couch. Another nurse ran in, her mouth moving with no sound coming out. The room swirled and faded away. I left myself. I found myself in another time and place, feeling the same thing I felt back then.

I waited too long. Again.

"Sir!" the nurse yelled into my face, shocking me back.

"What?" I shouted back, annoyed.

"Are you feeling alright? Please, let us make sure you are ok."

"I'm fine," I spat, brushing her away. "Just a little dizzy, leave me alone." They backed off and left me in the conference room to stare at the blank walls. Time stopped. The world shrank. I couldn't move.

I wanted to cling to my rage, letting it protect me from everything.

Instead, I felt like I had a giant hole blasted right through the middle of me. A hole that could never be closed and never be filled. Permanent devastation. A part of me I didn't know was there was gone forever. I would never hear him call me kiddo again. I would never feel his hand in my hair again. I would never get the chance to tell him how sorry I was about that horrible day, how I never meant the things I said. No chance to get his help, confess my problems and fears, and hear the solution only he would know.

I'm supposed to hate him. I'm supposed to tell him to rot in hell. I'm supposed to throw a bedpan in his face. But I only felt emptiness. I wanted another chance to see him. I realized that's all I ever wanted. And that chance was gone forever.

I cried like I was twelve again.

Someone came up to me while I was crying. "You must be Nick," he murmured. "Jeremy told me all about you. We have a lot in common."

I didn't look up.

"He couldn't hold on any longer. He knew you were on your way and that you'd be here this morning. Knowing you were coming made him happier than you could imagine."

He put a business card in my hand.

"You don't know me, but when you're up to it, I'd like to talk to you. I'm staying at the Park Hyatt, suite 601. I'll wait for you."

He touched my shoulder. By the time I looked around, he was gone. The card fell onto the floor.

I felt so empty and so alone. I needed to go to my hotel and sleep. I was halfway there when I remembered the mystery guy and his card. I didn't really want to talk to whoever it was, but I had no choice. He might know things about me that he shouldn't know.

I found the card under the couch in the conference room.

Dr. Colin Amory, MD, PhD
Psychotherapy
Children, Adolescents, and Families

It included an address in Seattle. Shit. Jeremy was talking to a shrink.

I instructed the driver to take me to the Park Hyatt. I knew things you told your shrink were like things you told your lawyer, but there were exceptions for child abuse. They could be investigating me right now. They could be talking to Alex and Jake. They could be digging up other things from the past. I had to find out what he knew.

I flipped the card over and over again in my hand. Why was he talking to a shrink in Seattle if he was hospitalized in Switzerland? Dr. Amory. Dr. Colin Amory. The name had a strange familiar ring to it, like something I read in a book or saw in a movie. Maybe he was a celebrity therapist who did the talk show circuit. I might've watched him without remembering. Children, Adolescents, and Families. Dr. Amory. Dr. Colin Amory. Colin.

An old memory surfaced. My whole body felt cold.

I tore through the lobby, stabbing the button to the elevator until it opened. Suite 601 was at the end of the hall. I pounded on the door. The lock pulled back and the door opened.

"I'm glad you came," he said softly. Without hesitating, he reached out and threw his arms around me. I pulled back quickly.

"I'm sorry," he said, backing off. "I feel as though I know you, even though you don't know me."

"I know who you are," I spat.

"Who am I?" he asked.

"You're Colin. The other boy. The first boy."

"I suppose I am," he said softly. "Why don't you come in? This probably isn't the kind of conversation we should have in the hallway."

"I don't know if I want to talk to you," I said without moving. "I don't know if I want to give you a high five or a kick in the balls."

"Let's talk first, then you decide. I won't stop you either way." I refused to budge. "I have a lot of things to tell you. Come inside. Just talk, nothing else."

"For about fifty minutes, right?" I said.

"This is as far from a therapy session as I'll ever get," he said. "I had them re-stock the minibar. How about a drink? Usually I'm not much of a drinker, and I'll probably swear off the stuff tomorrow for good. Today, I think I'm entitled to get rip-roaring plastered."

I took a step into the room. "One drink. Something strong."

"Scotch?" I felt like I wanted to be sick. "No, vodka then." He poured it and handed me the glass, closing the door gently behind me.

"I'm glad you came," he said. "Sorry about all the cloak and dagger bullshit, but Jeremy was sure you wouldn't come if you knew it was him."

"I don't know if he was right about that," I said.

"You came to the hospital looking for him," he said.

"Only to tell him off," I said. "The exact words I planned to use were 'Rot in hell you fucking son of a bitch.' I planned to throw a full bedpan in his face. He left before I got the chance. But hey, that's Jeremy. He always knew the right time to run away."

"You're very angry with him," he said.

"Now you sound like a therapist," I said. "I've talked to enough to know what your type sounds like. Of course I'm angry with him! I have every right to be angry. He ruined my life. From what he told me, he ruined yours as well."

"It's not what you think," he said softly. "The real story is far more complicated."

"It's not complicated for me," I said. "I can't believe I'm about to say this, but what the hell. He molested me, more times than I can

count. He took advantage of me, exploited me, and ran off at the first sign of trouble. At least you had the guts to turn him in."

He drained his glass. "I need a drink every time I hear that." He poured another small bottle and drank the whole thing straight.

"He told me about you," I said. "The story stuck with me over the years. You were in the hospital because you swallowed a bunch of pills. He stayed with you all night, and when he went home to change you turned him in."

"That's *not* what happened," he said. "I'm going to tell you something I don't tell a lot of people. I'm a survivor of real abuse, but not from Jeremy. What happened between us wasn't right, but I choose not to see it as abusive."

"He had sex with you, right? He told me. Or are you denying it?"

"No, we did," he said softly.

"Oh, I get it," I said coldly. "The cycle of abuse. The abused boy goes on to abuse other boys. He molested you and now you want to molest other boys. He turned you into a pedophile like him, making excuses, convincing yourself that your victim wants it."

He snorted. "Cycle of abuse, what a load of horseshit. No one serious in the field has believed that crap since the eighties and yet there's still self-proclaimed experts out there shoveling it. The literature has repeatedly proven beyond any shadow of doubt there's no simple correlation or direct causation between abusers and being abused as a child. Just like those debunked statistics that one in six boys have been abused by the time they're eighteen. Repeat a lie often enough and it becomes the truth. You did exactly what everyone has been programmed to do. Anyone who doesn't toe the line must be a predator themselves. Don't you just love that word? Predator. Says everything they want you to believe. No shades of gray with someone like a predator.

"Have you heard of the Rind Report? Of course you haven't. Nobody outside the field has. The only piece of peer reviewed, valid psychological literature that had APA support withdrawn due to congressional pressure. It wasn't even a study – it only assembled other studies to look at them as a whole. I'm simplifying a bit, but it looked at boys that had a sexual relationship with an older male. In the majority,

not all, but a majority of the cases, the boy not only viewed the relationship as neutral or positive as a child, but also as an adult. Science, proven science. That report changed everything for me. It told me I wasn't alone. It let me admit to myself that Jeremy was the best thing that happened to me after my father ran off. The sex, well, I wish it never happened. It made everything more complicated than it needed to be, and at thirteen I wasn't even close to being ready for that kind of relationship. But Jeremy, he loved me. I knew he loved me. He might've been a weak, damaged person, but he wasn't a predator. The sex was never what really mattered to him. I mattered to him. I was important."

"You turned him in," I stammered.

"I did no such thing," he snapped. "When he explained he thought that's what happened, I became sick to my stomach." He took a deep breath and drained his glass again. "I'll go back to the beginning. He told you how my father ran off one day and never came back? I was working in a comic shop for scraps because I loved being around them. I had a fantasy of writing and illustrating my own someday, even though I could barely draw a stick figure. He came in, we had a nice conversation, he left, and I didn't give it a second thought. A week later he came back and gave me his entire comic collection. There were books in there worth hundreds even back then, and I knew it."

"Expensive gifts," I murmured.

"You could look at it that way," he said. "The child molester's manual, right? Give the kid expensive gifts so he feels guilty and gives it up. Maybe Jeremy was consciously manipulating me. Maybe he wanted to give them to someone who'd appreciate them. Maybe he had no expectations other than making someone else happy. A guy buying a woman dinner could be seen through a sinister lens, too. You knew him. What do you think was going through his head?"

I didn't answer.

"When Helen Underwood saw those comic books, she went crazy," he said. "Jeremy didn't know much about her. She was some kind of social worker, or at least that's what my mom thought. She stuck her nose into our lives after my father took off. My mother rubbed her the wrong way from the beginning. She wanted us to go to church with

her and find comfort in Jesus. My mother told her the last thing we needed was God when God made it very clear we were the last people he needed. Helen Underwood was mortally offended. From that point on, she made it her mission to make us as miserable as possible. Sometimes I'd come home from school to find my mother in tears from whatever Helen Underwood did to her that day. I hoped my mother would stand up to her, but she felt too helpless back then to fight.

"Helen couldn't stand anyone interfering with her project to turn us into good Christians. She hated Jeremy from the start. The more I defended him, the more she attacked. At some point, she called him a homosexual. She was grasping at straws and even as a kid I knew she was, but I guess I stumbled. I didn't even know what I did wrong. She latched on and went to work on me when my mother refused to listen to her accusations. She tried being sympathetic, how I was the poor defenseless boy that Jeremy was abusing. She tried frightening me, telling me about the tortures awaiting me in hell. She threatened to send my mother to prison for failing to do anything about it. She told terrifying stories about what happened to homosexuals in the orphanage. Even though she was relentless, I didn't give in. I cared about him. I never would've turned him in, no matter what she told me. Things were different then. I guess she needed something more than suspicion to put wheels in motion.

"I worked as hard as I could to insulate Jeremy from what was going on. I was convinced if he knew she suspected him that he'd leave me. If there's one thing I wished I did differently, that was it. If I'd only told him, he would've used his family influence to squash her like the insect she was. Keeping that secret tore me to pieces, divided between two terrors. Either he'd leave me or he'd be hauled off by the police. I started skipping school. I dropped out of everything. I did drugs. Nothing numbed my terror. He responded by spending even more time with me. I tried to push him away. I told him I hated him, but at the same time I was clinging to him like a toddler. I didn't know what to do, so I swallowed a bottle of pills. Not to kill myself. I was crying for help.

"I woke Jeremy up and told him what I did. He carried me into the hospital like I was a little kid, screaming at everyone until they paid attention. After everything that's happened, I still can't get that image

out of my mind. They took care of me, but Jeremy was beside himself. He stayed with me all night even when they told him to leave. He told me he'd do anything to make things better, even if he was the problem. Once the doctors knew I'd be fine, I told him to go home so I could sleep. I made up my mind to tell him everything when he got back.

"Helen Underwood was waiting," he said. He poured another drink. "The moment he left, she came into the room. She didn't say a word to me, directing the orderlies to hold me down. They flipped me over, pulled up my gown, and took the evidence they needed by force. By that time in my life, I had intercourse with Jeremy more times than I could count. But until that moment, I didn't understand what it meant to be raped."

I couldn't speak.

"She had Jeremy arrested, took me away from my mother, and confined me in a handpicked foster home. They were psychotic. Their mission was to get me to renounce homosexuality and accept Jesus Christ as my lord and savior, amen. They would stop at nothing to achieve that mission. I had no contact with the outside world. I was never allowed to leave the house, not even to go to school. They wouldn't give me food unless I prayed out loud for them. They sat me in a chair and took turns reading endless bible passages to me until I thought I'd go insane. They gave me hours to reflect on my sins in a dark closet. I tried to run away, so they made sure I couldn't by taking all my clothes from me every night and making me beg for them the next day. They burned the few comic books I was allowed to take right in front of me. I cracked – anyone would crack under that kind of treatment. I told them what they wanted to hear in grisly detail and became a good Christian. They told me my confession sent Jeremy to prison for fifty years. I actually thanked Helen Underwood. I told her I was happy he wouldn't be able to abuse any more children.

"I finally got out of there, went to college on the state's dime as a foster kid, and threw myself into education. After being stifled with everything Christian, college was a wonderland of ideas. I never wanted to leave, which is why I chose medicine and went back afterwards for my doctorate. Being analyzed is part of becoming a therapist. I had a fantastic professor who worked with me through the program, helping

me understand why I had such strong feelings for Jeremy even though I was convinced those feelings were wrong. I tried to look for Jeremy on and off, but I always hit a dead end. His family wouldn't help and even when the internet came around he was completely off the grid. I'd given up hope when he called me, out of the blue, two weeks ago.

"I dropped everything to get on a plane. I needed to be at his side just like he was for me. He was so weak and frail I hardly recognized him. He wanted to talk but a lot of the time he was either too doped up to be coherent or in too much pain to concentrate. I stayed with him to make sure we had the chance to talk during his lucid moments. It felt wonderful to set the record straight. We relived old memories and we learned about each other. And he talked about you – god how he talked about you. He loved you. He told me how he watched you turn from a withdrawn, depressed kid into a truly remarkable young man. Whatever you think of him, he was hopelessly in love with you until the day he passed. He wouldn't tell me why the two of you fell apart, but the pain of losing you wrecked him. He never recovered. He was sure you didn't want to talk to him, but I helped him reach out. He was happy you were coming. He wanted so badly to undo whatever hurt he did to you."

"He ruined my life," I moaned.

"It didn't sound like it," he said. "It sounded like he saved you."

"He abandoned me," I said. "There one day and gone the next. I said some horrible things to him, called him a liar, told him I was going to turn him in, and even punched him. But I never wanted to hurt him. I was struggling with my own attraction to boys. Some stupid talk show fed me all that stuff about abused boys becoming abusers. The belief that I was ruining lives forever made me so terrified I couldn't think straight. I ran away and didn't come home until the next day. He was gone."

"He regretted leaving for the rest of his life," Colin said gently.

"He didn't have to leave!" I screamed. "He drank himself to death, didn't he? It's my fault, it's all my fault!"

He sat down next to me and hugged me.

"Oh god, I miss him so much!" I burst into tears like the little boy I still was.

"Hello, Julia," I said when she picked up the phone.

"Nick, thank god," she said. "Where are you?"

"Zurich," I said. "Switzerland."

"Switzerland? The Switzerland?"

"Alps and yodelers, that kind of thing."

"What in the name of sanity are you doing in Switzerland?"

"There was something I needed to do," I said. "I'm coming home tomorrow on the first flight I can get. I'd really like if you were there when I got home. We have a lot of things we need to talk about."

"I'll be here," she said gently. "You just get yourself home in one piece."

"Why do you still care about me?" I asked in a small voice. "I've been distant and cold for so long. I'm an unfeeling lump who eats too much and pushes everyone away as hard as I can."

"I've loved you since the day we met," she said. "There's another Nick underneath your shell, one I used to see a lot more. He was coming back to life. I want him back."

"I'm going to try," I said. "I'll explain everything when I see you. I'm going to need you. I can't do this without you. Both you and Jake."

"I don't understand," she said.

"It's a long story. I promise you I will explain everything, and I mean everything." I paused. "I'm lucky to have you. I love you."

"You haven't said that in a long time," she said. "I'll be here, I promise. Get yourself home."

"I will," I said.

"Did you reach her?" Colin asked when I came out of the bedroom. I nodded. "Ready to watch?"

At first, I wasn't sure I wanted to let him see the home movies Jeremy had saved. They were from my life, not his. They might include memories I wasn't ready to share. But it wasn't fair to keep Jeremy all to myself. Colin had no pictures or videos to help him remember. And I had another terrifying feeling I couldn't shake. If there ever was a fellow traveler in this world, it was him. Would it be so terrible to trust him?

My breath caught in my throat as I appeared on screen, in the lobby, a Christmas tree in the background. "Was I ever that young?"

Jeremy appeared next to me, and we both gasped together. "It's so nice to see him the way I remember him," he murmured. I put my arm around his shoulder. We watched as Jeremy put that young boy on his shoulders to decorate the top of the tree, applauding when it was done.

The camera focused on the giant bear. "He bought that at FAO Schwartz on Christmas Eve," I said, choked up. "He somehow had it delivered to the house before we got home that night."

It was all new and yet so familiar at the same time. We were laughing at something silly I was doing for the camera when the scene changed. The camera focused in on two young boys decked out in armor and swords. "Ok, good, here we go. Do something," Jeremy said behind the camera. The metal clanged as the two of them fought. I couldn't smile anymore.

"That's fantastic," Colin said. "Buying outfits for you and your friend seems like something Jeremy would do. Where are you guys right now?"

"My friend's grandfather had a cabin in Maine," I mumbled. Brian looked so determined as he swung his sword, finally running it under my arm so I could die a horrible death. "I stayed with him that summer for three weeks."

"You guys look like great friends," Colin said.

"He was my best friend," I said. "I miss him a lot."

I didn't explain, and he didn't press. After the short battle, we watched the scenes Brian and I so carefully executed. The video switched to our campsite, in all its messy glory, carefully narrated by Brian. And then it moved on to other places and other times. Just a few short minutes – not enough for me to recapture those three perfect weeks. Brian gave me a whole childhood in those three weeks. Where was I when he needed me?

"What do you think this one is all about?" he said, handing me a DVD. "The others have dates, but this one just says special."

I turned it over in my hands. "If this is what I think it is, it's a little private and definitely illegal."

"Ah," he said. "Say no more."

A wild idea took hold. "Let's watch it," I said.

"I wouldn't want to intrude on something so personal," he said.

"I think I'd like if you watched them with me," I said. "We shared someone, and this was a big part of what we shared. Besides, I'm going to have to destroy it before I head back. There's no way I'm taking something like this through customs."

I started the video. Blackness for a few seconds, and then the camera focused on my very animated twelve-year old face. "Welcome to the Nick and Jeremy show," he/I said, humming something I guessed was meant to be a theme song. His/my head bobbed to the beat. "On today's show, Nick and Jeremy make a porno film!"

"Oh my god, I remember doing this," I groaned playfully. The camera panned out, and him/me sat down next to Jeremy on the bed.

"Do you want me to stop it?" Colin asked.

"No. Let it run."

"So, what do you want to do today?" Jeremy asked, very self-conscious.

"I know," he/I said. "Let's make a porno movie!"

"Ok," Jeremy said.

He/I looked at the camera. "See, porno movies don't need a plot." Colin and I burst out laughing.

Clothes came off and flew around the room. He/I did a silly and very childlike dance naked in front of the camera, making sure to get close-ups on various body parts, including a full moon that made Colin and I crack up and cringe at the same time.

"That boy doesn't seem very unhappy," Colin said gently.

"He wasn't," I said.

He wanted me to stay, and I found I didn't want to leave. We ordered dinner, late night snacks, and watched the sun come up. I only left when I had to catch my flight. We talked and talked. I could hardly believe I was talking to him the way I was. I'd just met the guy earlier that day, and we were sharing the most intimate parts of our lives with each other as though we'd always been best friends. I talked to him

about my life with Jeremy. I told him about the basement, and at two in the morning we watched the video together. I told him about Billy and about Brian. I told him about Alex. Even though I could get in serious trouble.

It was scary. And fantastic.

He helped me understand what I didn't realize I already knew, as true for him as it was for me. I couldn't place the blame for everything entirely on the sex, even though it made things a lot harder than they needed to be. It put a burden of secrecy on me, confused the development of my own identity, set me up for a lifetime of doubts, and made me too comfortable with sex at an age when I didn't possess the right tools to control my impulses with others. Like Colin, no matter what I thought when I was twelve, I wasn't ready. But the sex itself wasn't the real culprit. Being abandoned turned my life into the disaster it became. And I'd just repeated the same mistake over again. Alex wasn't answering his phone, but this kind of thing had to be done in person. I needed to go home. I needed to find him. Too much time had already past, time where anything could go wrong. I couldn't let myself be too late again.

Colin helped me admit I wasn't wrong when I set the old Nick free.

This is what he told me:

"I've seen a lot of survivors in my practice, kids and adults who've been truly abused, forced into sex and prostitution, threatened and beaten into silence. The abuse leaves behind lifelong scars, but you know what damages them more than the abuse? Being told they're damaged for life. People can recover from trauma. They can move past it to build a happy life."

And this is what he told me:

"You can spend your time focusing on the bad things that have happened to you, pining away about the mistakes you've made and the wrongs you've suffered. You can spend your life wondering what would've happened if things were different. Or you can let it go, stop wondering, and make the best out of what you've got. If you care about Alex and he cares about you, then go with it and do what feels right. He's still the child and you're still the adult. Behave like one. Be responsible and strong for him. Look out for him, nurture him, and

guide him. You're not doomed to repeat the past. You're free to find your own way and make your life the way you want. Do for Alex what Jeremy did for both of us on an emotional level. Because that's all you've ever really wanted to repeat."

I did. And I would.

For Jeremy.

Chapter 47

April 16, 2007

Julia met me at the airport when I got back from Switzerland. I had her take me straight to the school. "Do you have to do this right now?" she asked. "You just got back. I still don't understand what's going on."

"It has to be right now," I said. "I did a terrible thing and need to fix it before it's too late. I might already be too late. I promise, I'll explain everything, but I can't let another moment go by. This might take a while. You don't have to wait."

"I'm not going anywhere," she said.

The school was abandoned for spring break. Even with our parent pass and car sticker, we had to fight with the security guard just to let us in. After that, I was able to walk right into the dorm without any trouble. The lights flickered on for me because no one else was there. Except Alex. He hated the dorm, even though he was a social animal. When he told me how kids took great joy blocking the light sensor and pulling the fire alarms at three in the morning so they could watch everyone scatter in the dark, I understood why he didn't want to stay there. He was past that kind of thing when most kids were just becoming ready for it.

His door was closed, light and music seeping out from inside. He was playing the guitar, singing something melancholy and wistful that I couldn't make out. I hoped it was our song, but I knew it wouldn't be.

Just like I knew why all his things were still at the house. He abandoned them the same way I abandoned most of what Jeremy left for me. I wrapped the Porsche around a tree three days after I got my license so I wouldn't have to look at it anymore.

I knocked on his door, terrified.

"I'm not here," he said. "Leave a message."

I knocked again.

He played a sour chord. "Can't you take a hint?" The door flew open. His eyes registered surprise for a moment, then turned sullen. "Why are you here?" he said, his words full of ice.

"Can I come in?" I asked gently.

"No," he said. "This is *my* home. Say whatever you want to say from the doorway and leave."

"I did a terrible thing."

"Yeah, you did," he said, crossing his arms.

"I'm here because I want you to come home. I want to make things right between us."

"Oh really? Well, I'm not here right now. Leave a message at one-eight-hundred-I-don't-give-a-fuck. Or you can email me at Alex at I-don't-give-a-fuck-dot-com. That might be easier for you."

"I deserve that," I said. "I hurt you. You have every right to be angry, and even though you won't believe me, I know exactly how you feel. I'm asking for a second chance. Come home with me."

"I *am* home," he spat. "My ten by ten little slice of heaven, communal bathroom with piss on the floor included at no additional charge. So, did you decide you wanted to get into my pants after all?"

"Alex," I said.

"You left me. In the rain. You wouldn't pick up your phone. I didn't have my pass, my key, or a change of clothes. Why the fuck am I even talking to you?" He pushed the door closed, but I blocked it with my foot.

"I love you," I said. Saying those words made him look even more fierce. "No matter what you think right now, I do. I'm past any thought of getting into your pants, that's over. I thought I was doing the right thing. I thought I was protecting you. While I was gone, I finally realized I was doing the same thing to you that happened to me."

"Shove it. You sound like a bad movie." He pushed the door until I moved my foot.

"I didn't get a second chance," I said through the door. "I said the worst things to the most important person in the world to me. He ran away before I got the chance to apologize. You know who I'm talking about. He died before I got the chance to talk to him one last time. I understood it wasn't the things we did that hurt so much — it was how he left me behind. I just did the same thing to you. I'm not going to let things end this way. I'm taking you home."

"I'm not going anywhere," he shouted.

"Neither am I." I sat down and leaned against the door. "I'm pretty good at waiting people out. I've done it before. I'm not giving up on you."

"I'm giving up on you," he shouted. "Go ahead, wait there all night if you want. I'm calling security. Maybe they'll show up in a week to haul you away."

"I'm not going anywhere," I said.

"You're such an asshole!" he shouted.

"I am," I said. "But I'm still not going anywhere."

"Why are you being such an asshole?"

"Because I care about you," I said.

"Why should I believe you?" he said. His voice cracked.

"You're my son," I said.

He opened the door. "Asshole," he said.

"Alex," I said gently as I moved closer. He tried to slap me, pushing me away. I grabbed him, hugging him tightly. He struggled for a couple of seconds before going limp, leaning into me.

"How do I know you won't do it again?" he moaned. "How do I know you mean it this time?"

"I'll have to earn your trust back," I said. "One day at a time. I'll do whatever it takes to convince you I mean it." I held him close. "Let's go home."

"Ok," he said softly. I let him go, but he didn't let go of me.

"That wasn't as hard as I thought it was going to be," I said.

"You had me at hello," he said. "Now I sound like a bad movie."

"There's my Alex," I said.

I knew he meant it. I would've felt exactly the same way.

<center>⌒⋉ ⋊⌒</center>

"You never told me you grew up in such a cute town," Julia said. "I would've made you bring me here years ago."

"When you're a twelve-year-old boy, cute equals boring," I said.

Julia sat at the mirror, doing whatever women do in front of mirrors. I watched her, leaning on the door frame. We found a cute little B&B right near the center of Newton Falls, much better than the chain hotel by the mall. Being in a house felt a little more like I was connecting with the boy I once was.

"I'd like a little time to explore, maybe do some shopping," she said. "If you're still a little boy who thinks it's boring, take the boys with you. Do something boy-like."

"I'll take them tomorrow. Why don't we go to New York for a couple of days? No wait, I've got an even better idea. Let's go to Paris."

"Paris, as in France? We're not prepared to go to Europe."

"Who cares if we're prepared? Let's just go. I'm sure Paris has better shopping than Newton Falls."

"You're crazy," she said.

"And you're beautiful," I said back. I put my arms over her shoulders. "You remind me of someone. Let me see, who was it? I remember a woman I used to like. I thought maybe I might've married her."

"Are you flirting with me?" she asked.

"Maybe," I said. "What if I am?"

"You should keep doing it," she said. "Are you ok?"

"I'm fine," I said. "But I could think of something that would make me feel much better."

"What would that be?" she asked. I kissed her cheek. "What do you think you're doing, sir?"

"Being a bad boy," I whispered in her ear.

"Well, bad boys always get the girls."

"I don't need any other girls," I said. "I've already got the best one. I'm not flirting. That's the truth."

<center>714</center>

"It's getting awfully mushy in here." Her eyes told me everything I wanted to know. "Now shoo. I'm not finished yet, and if you think you're getting me back in bed you'd better take a cold shower."

I didn't deserve someone as amazing as Julia.

We went straight home after picking up Alex from school. I'd spent the last day wondering what her reaction would be if I told her everything. Not just what happened to me as a child, but what happened with Alex. I needed her to stay by my side, but I found it impossible to believe she would once she knew what I was. She'd react with horror and disgust. I'd get hurt again just like I'd been hurt when I confessed the truth to another girl so long ago.

But I couldn't stop short. If I was going to be with her, she had a right to know everything. I wanted her to know. I wanted to be naked in front of her. I didn't want to have to hide for the rest of my life. My head told me she would throw me out, banish me from her life and Jake's life forever. My head told me not to trust her.

But my heart was in charge now.

When we got home, I took her to the bedroom. She sat in the chair in the corner while I sat on the floor leaning up against the bed. "When I was a child, I had an intimate sexual relationship with a man. I met him when I was eleven and lived with him for three years. I need to tell you what happened. All the good he did for me. I wouldn't be here if it wasn't for him. And the bad."

I told her the whole story, starting from the snow shovel. Sometimes she covered her mouth, sometimes she wiped her eyes, and sometimes she gasped out loud. But she didn't stop me, not once. Not when I told her about the basement. Not when I told her about Brian. Not when I told her about Billy. I talked until I was hoarse, until the sun was coming up.

I told her about Alex. "I still have these feelings," I told her. "I still look at a boy like Alex and I want to have the same kind of relationship I had as a child. I used to think I was doomed to repeat what happened to me. I don't think so anymore. I think it's up to me. I don't want to hurt him. I never want to put that burden on anyone. Maybe I shouldn't have let him get close, but if I hadn't, I wouldn't have woken back up. I would've stayed in my shell and slowly eaten myself to death. I don't

want to go back to being that person. I want to change. I can't do it without you. I need your help."

I couldn't imagine what was going through her head.

"I'll understand if you never want to see me again," I said.

"That's not what I want," she said. "I've stuck with you through all these years when you shut yourself away from everyone because I care about you. I'm not about to stop now. Nothing you've said changes how I feel about you. I've always known you weren't completely straight. I've noticed when your eyes wandered in directions I didn't expect. I still feel betrayed and I can't help questioning your commitment. But I married you because I loved everything about you, the good and the bad. I'll be there for you, as long as you promise me you'll keep being honest. You have to come to me if you feel like you're slipping. You have to promise me you'll stay strong and never do anything to hurt a child, especially if Alex is going to be a part of our family."

"I don't want to hurt anyone," I said.

"I saw the boy who cared deeply about others inside when I married you. Promise me you'll never bury him again. I want him back."

"Ok," I said softly.

"I love you," she said.

"I love you too," I said. "Oh god, I love you."

We went to bed and I made love to her for real for the first time.

We were holding each other afterwards when I told her. "I want you to quit your job."

"I can't quit," she said. "Not that I want to be gone all the time – I'm done with that part of my life. We have to be practical. You've been out of work for months, our savings are dwindling, and we're starting to eat into the house. Your father can't support us forever and it's not like my parents have anything. We have bills to pay."

"Jeremy left me ten million dollars," I said. "It's stashed in one of those secret numbered Swiss bank accounts. That's why I was in Zurich."

"Ten million?"

"Ten million and some extra," I repeated. "Are you angry I didn't say anything earlier?"

"A little," she said. She rolled over and kissed me. "I think I'll get over it. Now you'd better cover your ears because I'm going to scream like a schoolgirl."

<p style="text-align:center">━❮ ❯━</p>

"This doesn't look right," I said.

"Maybe you should drive," Julia said. "We're going around in circles."

"I was never the one driving," I said stubbornly. "I only know the roads from the passenger seat." I looked around, all the buildings and roads unfamiliar. We'd gone by the school twice already without finding our way to the road. The one that led to our rock.

"Are we there yet?" Alex and Jake said simultaneously.

"Not far now, my little Smurfs," I answered.

"What kind of Smurf are you, Jake?" Alex asked. "I'm Smurfette." They snickered. "Seriously, I'm getting leg cramps, are we. . ."

"Turn!" I shouted. "There! Left!"

Julia strangled her cry and slammed on the brakes, managing to turn onto the steep, twisting road without flipping the car over.

"This is it. I know this has to be it." I was practically bouncing in my seat.

"Now what?" she asked, the car leveling out at the top of the hill.

"Don't turn, don't do anything. Keep going straight down this road. I'm sure we found it." I didn't feel so sure because the road didn't look quite right. I remembered it being empty and abandoned, but it was lined with homes that were clearly old enough to have been here when I was fourteen. The houses finally thinned out and we drove into the woods.

"We're in the middle of nowhere," Julia said.

"That's the idea," I said. "No one knows about this road. I don't think we ever saw another car pass by when we used to come up here. Look at the potholes. No one maintains this road because no one uses it."

"I noticed," she said, gritting her teeth when we hit a big one.

The road climbed gently, winding its way through the trees. It still wasn't as empty and desolate as I remembered. We passed the occasional mailbox, a car parked here and there, several cars going in the opposite direction, and even a small gas station that looked like it had been there for fifty years. Was my memory defective, or was it clouded by the younger me doing what kids are so good at doing? Seeing only what they wanted to see, ignoring the rest.

The road crested. "Stop here!" I shouted, pointing at the side of the road. I was out before the car stopped. "That's the rock, right over there. Come on guys, let's grab the stuff."

Jake, Alex, and I pulled the basket, chairs, blankets, food, and drinks from the trunk. Everything we needed for a picnic. I could hardly believe Gunther's shop was still there after all these years, but what really floored me was finding him standing behind the counter, *exactly* the way I remembered him. It turned out "Gunther" was Gunther's son, but they looked so alike I couldn't stop calling him Gunther. He even did the same thing with his eyebrow. The croissants were better than I remembered. We bought a pile of them along with cheese, pâté, foie gras, salamis, jam, fruit, wine, and French fizzy water. Everything Jeremy brought whenever we had a picnic on our rock.

"You don't seriously expect me to climb up there," Julia said.

"The back way is easier," I said, leading her through a patch of ferns. I watched the boys scramble up the rocks like I used to. It looked like a broken ankle waiting to happen. We made our way around the gentle slope on the other side.

"What do you think?" I said, sweeping my arm across the view when we reached the top.

"It's beautiful," she said. "Is that the Delaware down there?"

"I think so," I said. "We never went all the way down to find out."

"Come on, I'm starving," Alex said dramatically.

"Go ahead," I called to him. Julia followed me as I walked over to the far side of the rock. I hardly believed the monster tree was still there. Not as big as I remembered, but nothing was. "Take a look at this," I said softly to her.

"NW and JS," she said. "One of your girlfriends?"

"No," I said, tracing my fingers across the letters, soft and rounded from time and weather, not sharp and clean the way I remembered. "Jeremy Stillwell. We used to come up here for picnics. This was kind of a private place where we could be ourselves."

"You carved his initials into a heart with yours," she said.

"I was twelve when I did this. I loved him. I still do."

She put her arm around my shoulder. "Are you ok?"

I closed my eyes so I could feel the power of this place, but no matter how hard I tried the feeling eluded me. At first, I didn't understand why I brought my boys here. This was a place for boys, but I realized it wouldn't mean anything to them. They had to find their own magical places. But as I watched them laughing and joking with each other, I understood. Bringing them here was closing a circle, like Gunther passing his shop down to his son. I was passing on the responsibility of being boys to them, because I wasn't a boy anymore. As strange as it might seem for a thirty-seven-year-old man to think, I'd never truly felt like an adult until that moment. I supposed that was why I couldn't feel the power in this place anymore.

And that was ok.

"Let's eat," I said to her, walking arm in arm to the blanket.

When we were done, we loaded back into the car. "It's time to find out where this road goes," I said. We slowly made our way down the hill, past landmarks I called out as we reached them. The graffiti rock was gone, but the waterfall was still there. I recognized the moment we started running parallel to the river. We reached the white rock and kept going, which meant it wasn't far to the. . .

"Traffic light," I said out loud.

It was still there. Red. Like it had been for twenty-five years.

"One lane road ahead," Julia read.

"Five minute red light," Alex read.

"What do you think is down there?" Jake asked.

"I have no idea," I said, shaking.

On cue, the light turned green.

The car rolled down a narrow road cut into the side of the rock, a short drop to the river on our right side, winding back and forth as it followed the contour of the hill. My heart pounded madly. I didn't

know how long it would take. A minute, an hour, a mile, a hundred? I was going to find out, once and for all. No more wondering, no more waiting.

We passed through another stoplight.

The road made one more turn, and right then, right there, the secret I'd wondered about since I was a boy revealed itself to us.

"I-80 west, right turn. I-80 east, straight," I read. The Delaware bridge loomed over us. The only choice was to get on the highway.

"That's it?" Jake said. "That's the big deal at the end of the road?"

"I guess so," I said.

"Wow, that was *amazing*," Alex drawled. "Can you believe it was a highway entrance? But hey, it's a cool bridge. Well, kind of. Nah, it's a pretty lame bridge."

My fourteen-year-old self was right. I should never have gone through that portal.

Jeremy was right, too. Dreams were better than reality.

<center>∽≺ ≻∾</center>

Julia turned the car into the parking lot for John Witherspoon Middle School.

"You've *got* to be kidding me," Jake said for the fourth time.

"A school is *exactly* where I want to be on break," Alex joined in.

"I know I'm torturing you guys. I want to see a few more things, then I promise you we can do something fun."

"Something fun?" Alex asked brightly. "Can we go to the play land at McDonald's? I want to go on the swings. Pleeeeeeease?"

"Of course," I said just as brightly. "As soon as we get you kiddies out of your car seats. Who needs a diaper change? Anyone want a juice box?"

"Burn," Jake said.

"It used to be a junior high," I said to Julia as we walked up. "I guess they changed it."

Jake opened the door. "Ugh. It smells like school."

"What do you mean, it smells like school?" I took a whiff. It did. That was the school smell. I had no other way to describe it or equate

<center>720</center>

it to anything else. No way to break it down into its components. It smelled like school, and that was that.

"All schools love to show off their trophies and plaques," Alex said, wandering over to the large glass case across from the office. "This must be the most important one around here. The Nancy Sheffield Memorial Award. Wait a minute, seriously?"

"What?" Jake said, peering over his shoulder. "Whoa."

Julia read the plaque out loud. "For outstanding service to our school. 1983-1984, Nicholas Welles." She snapped a picture with her pocket camera.

"No fucking way," Jake said. "1984 New Jersey State Championship, two-mile, second place. You were a track star? I can't even imagine you running to the fridge."

"Thanks a lot," I said, sounding hurt. "I'll have you know I lost by a fraction of a second, and I was training to run the New York marathon that fall."

"Did you run it?" Alex asked.

"I had to drop out," I said. "We'd better check in before they have us arrested."

The office was smaller than I remembered, but otherwise it hadn't changed one little bit. Like it was stuck in a time loop. Kids carrying notes back and forth, going in and out of guidance counselor's offices, and waiting outside the vice principal's office to get chewed out. School stuff. The microphone for the announcements was newer, but it was still in the same place on the desk to the side.

"Would it be ok for us to look around?" Julia asked. "My husband was a student here a while ago."

"Of course," the woman behind the desk said. "After the students leave, I'd be happy to show you around. What years were you here?"

"82 through 84," I said quietly.

"Long before my time," she said. "I think a few teachers are still here from that far back."

"Mr. Huang." His voice boomed across the office. I'd never forget that voice, or how it boomed. "I trust your presence here has been authorized by your classroom teacher." He put a hand on a boy's shoulder, listening to a complicated explanation, but I wasn't interested.

His hair was gray, he had a bit of a paunch, he was wearing glasses, and his face was lined and careworn, but there he was, unchanged. Still wearing the same tweed jacket with patches on the elbows.

"Here's someone you might know," the woman behind the desk said to me. "Ken, we have a former student from the eighties here to look around."

He pushed his glasses higher on his face. "Always glad to welcome an alumnus. . ." He stared at me.

"Hi, Mr. Humber," I stammered.

"Mr. Welles," he said with wonder.

"Afraid so," I said.

"Oh good, you know each other," the woman behind the desk said.

He threw the papers he was carrying on the desk next to him, not caring when they spilled on the floor. His eyes were fixed on me as though he expected me to vanish like a mirage. Until he threw his arms around me.

"Nick Welles!" he said. "Jenny, you haven't brought me any old alumni, you've brought me *the* alumni! This is Nick Welles!" He sounded as excited as a twelve-year-old kid.

"The one from the Sheffield award?" she asked.

"The very one! I can't believe you're here! It's been such a long time! I haven't seen you since. . ." He put his hands on my shoulders. "I trust that you've. . .ah, to heck with it." He threw his arms back around me.

"It's good to see you too, Mr. Humber. I mean Ken. I mean I have no idea what I'm supposed to call you."

"I think we're past formalities at our advanced ages," he said.

"This is my wife, Julia, and my boys, Alex and Jake," I said. "This is Mr. Humber, my mentor when I went to school here, and by far the best teacher I've ever had."

"You have no idea how ancient you make me feel having sons old enough to be my students," Mr. Humber said. "What brings you back here? What have you been doing with yourself? I want to hear everything!"

"You two need to catch up," Julia said. She shook her head when I was about to protest. "Hush. I'm taking the boys to the mall. Call me when you want me to pick you up."

"Thank you," I said, kissing her on the cheek.

"Come on," Mr. Humber said, leading me down the hall.

"Not that room," I groaned. "The programs. I still have nightmares about the programs."

"For the award ceremony," he said, nostalgia written on his face. "It was quite the task to keep you occupied at all times, let me tell you."

We sat at the beaten table, the same one I remembered. I ran my finger across it, feeling very connected to the boy who sat here feeling paranoid many years ago. I could almost see Ana sitting across from me, warning me to trust no one.

"You have a wonderful family," he said.

"Thanks," I said. "How about you? I remember you telling me no woman would ever put up with that disaster of a car you drove around."

"Disaster of a car, I beg your pardon," he said. "I don't quite remember that particular conversation, but then again, I feel fortunate if I wake up and remember my name these days. I believe I told you I was married to my work and had no shortage of children to care for. On that subject, nothing has changed."

"I wish the world had more like you," I said.

"I'm beginning to suspect you're angling for a better grade," he said with narrowed eyes. "How is your uncle? I'm having trouble. . .Mr. Stillwell. . .Jeremy, wasn't it? How is he?"

"He passed away. A couple weeks ago."

Mr. Humber put his hand on mine. "I'm so sorry. I remember the two of you were close."

"Losing him made me think about that part of my life, so I came back to look around. I didn't expect to run into you. I thought everyone I knew would've left Newton Falls a long time ago. But I can't tell you how glad I am to see you. It gives me the chance to apologize."

"Apologize?" he asked. "If you're referring to the incident when you revealed my birthday to the entire school, please be aware I will carry a grudge until the day I die." I laughed. "If you are not, I have absolutely no idea what would give you cause to apologize."

"I let you down," I said. "I disappeared without so much as a phone call, a goodbye, or anything. There were so many people depending on me, especially you, and I walked away without looking back."

He looked at me with so much care my eyes stung. "I've been teaching for nearly thirty-five years," he said. "In all that time, I've never seen a student come through these doors like you. I want to show you something." I followed him back into the office to a bulletin board hanging on the wall outside the front desk.

"Tutoring club sign ups," I read softly.

"The same club you created," he said. "It's been continuously operating ever since. Not quite as well-staffed as when you were in charge, but it has a life of its own. And here."

"Mentor training," I read just as softly.

"And here," he pointed.

"You made it happen," I said. "You got them to start a peer counseling program."

"Your proposal made it possible. I merely shepherded it along. The very notion you let anyone down is simply ludicrous. The collective consciousness you started here was so powerful it never died out. Others stepped in to pick up where you left off. I've played a role keeping it alive, but I'm barely a caretaker. You provided the inspiration."

"I'm still sorry," I said. "I had a responsibility to do great things, and I never did. I've wasted my life. All that time you spent with me for nothing."

"Something happened to you, something traumatic. But if you go around beating yourself up about what could've been, *that* is a waste of a life. You're still here and have years ahead of you. The person you were then is somewhere inside. A bright flame like him can only be suppressed, never extinguished."

"I'm thirty-seven years old, and you're still my teacher," I said.

"And I always will be, if you allow me," he said. The bell rang. "Except for the next couple of hours. Would you be surprised to hear I have rehearsal? I would invite you to assist, but I have a better use for you." He scribbled something on a piece of paper. "I'm not the only one who's still in Newton Falls. When you've completed this task, you will meet me downtown at six sharp and it will be my pleasure to buy

you a beer, since I am permitted to do so. Failure to appear on time will result in an office referral."

"Oh boy, that's big trouble," I said. "But I'm buying."

"You test my patience," he said.

I watched him go. The question planted by Jeremy in a fit of jealousy stayed on the tip of my tongue. I thought I needed to know if Mr. Humber suffered the same curse I did. In that moment, I understood it wasn't important. If he did, he'd found the best way to deal with it anyone could ever find. Using it to make lives better. In the end, that's all that really mattered. Not whether you had it. What you did with it.

<center>⁓⋊ ⋉⁓</center>

Mr. Humber gave me an address without telling me who lived there. The office helped with directions, and since it wasn't too far, I decided to walk instead of calling Julia with the car. It felt good to have familiar sidewalks rolling underneath me, reminding me of days when I never walked. In those days, I ran.

I realized where I was when I turned onto the street. I knew this house. I knew who lived there. Still lived there, after all these years. The house where I sat outside a bedroom for three hours reading homework.

I walked up familiar steps and pushed the doorbell, familiar chimes echoing. The door opened but no one was there.

"Nick!" a small voice shouted.

I stared at a little boy barely two years old. "How did you know my name?"

"Nicholas!" a woman's voice called from inside the house. She appeared from around the corner, cradling an infant. "You know you're not supposed to open the door without mommy."

"Nick!" he said, toddling off into the house.

"I'm so sorry," she said, coming up to the door. "Can I help you with something?"

"I'm looking for Jeff Sheffield," I said. She looked at me suspiciously. "I'm sorry, this must seem pretty strange. I went to school with Jeff a long time ago and happened to be in town. My name is Nick."

"Nick!" the little boy shouted inside the house.

"You went to Penn with Jeff?" she asked.

"No, nothing like that," I said. "We went to junior high school together."

She stared at me like I was more than a little deranged, but then her suspicious look evaporated. "You're *that* Nick, aren't you?"

"Nick!" the little boy shouted again, grabbing her leg.

"Shush," she said to him.

"That Nick?" I said. "I'm not sure what you mean."

"Come in, sit down, and close the door or Nicholas will go wandering around outside," she ordered. "I'm Kelly, nice to meet you." I closed the door behind me.

"Nick!" the boy said again.

"We seem to have the same name," I said. "I'm Nick too."

The living room had changed since I'd been in this house. The red walls were gone, replaced with a brighter neutral color. The ancient furniture was nowhere to be seen. It didn't feel dark and gloomy like it once did. It was bright, colorful, and full of life. The way a house is supposed to be.

Kelly left the baby in a swing and returned with a large picture frame. It contained a picture of twelve-year-old Jeff in his suit standing on the podium at school, two pieces of notebook paper with the original speech he gave written in a child's handwriting, and a picture of him handing me the envelope at the party. The small brass plaque on the bottom read "1st Nancy Sheffield Award. My very good friend Nick Welles."

"Yeah," I said softly. "I'm that Nick."

"Wait until he finds out you're here," she said, juggling the now crying baby and her phone. "Jeffrey, it's me. I want you to come right now. . .No, the kids are fine, just come home. . .I don't care if you have a meeting with the Queen of England! When your wife says come home you do it. . .Just come home *now*. Bye." She looked at me. "He's in his office downtown so it'll only take a couple of minutes. Can I get you something to drink? I need a vodka tonic, but a cup of tea will have to do."

"Tea sounds great," I said. "Please, let me help you." Little Nick was clinging to her leg.

"It's a relief talking to an adult," she said, dragging little Nick along to the kitchen. "I feel like I'm going bonkers in here."

"I know what you mean," I said. "I only have one, but he's thirteen now. Two was easier."

"Just what I needed to hear," she muttered as she started the kettle. "It must have been a while since you saw Jeff, isn't it? I know we haven't met before."

"Twenty years at least," I said.

"He's going to be a kid in the candy shop when he sees you," she said. "Tea is in the corner cabinet, not that one, over there. You know, he still talks about you. You're his inspiration."

The front door opened. "Where's my Nick?" I heard Jeff say.

"Dada!" little Nick squealed, running for the door

"So he *can* say something besides his name," she said, rolling her eyes.

"There's my big boy!" he said. "Kelly, what's the emergency?" I followed her into the living room. He looked great, fit and trim, handsome enough to be a magazine model. On top of the world.

"Nick!" little Nick shouted, pointing at me.

"I'm sorry, I didn't realize we had guests," he said. Then he cocked his head sideways and stared.

"I'm having that effect on people today," I said.

"Is that really you?" he asked, sounding very childlike.

"Afraid so," I said.

"Nick!" little Nick said, just to make sure we understood.

"We named him after you," Jeff mumbled. He put his boy down, taking a single step toward me as though he didn't believe I was there, just like Mr. Humber. I did the rest. I pushed his outstretched hand aside and hugged him. He wrapped his arms around me and squeezed with so much force I thought his arms would slice through me. "It really is you. I can't believe it. It's so good to see you."

"You're looking fantastic," I said. "Unlike me."

"Come on," he said gently. "What are you doing here? The last time I saw you, you swore you'd never set foot in Newton Falls again. I'm

sorry, I didn't want to bring that up, I just can't believe it's actually you. I've missed you."

"Things change," I said. We sat down, his wife quietly taking the children into the other room and closing the door. "You really do look great. What have you been doing with yourself?"

"You won't believe me," he said, excited. "S-s-s-stuttering Jeff talks for a living! If anyone asked when I was twelve what I'd be doing as an adult, attorney would be the farthest career from anything I thought possible. I did some courtroom work, but it didn't suit me. Lately I've been speaking at conferences and seminars. Because of you. I never would've had the guts to chase down something like this if it wasn't for you inspiring me. You know, I've been wanting to say that to you for a very long time."

"I don't know what to say," I said. "Look, the last time we saw each other, I said some things. . ."

"Stop right there," he said. "They were forgiven the moment they were said. Don't tell me you came here to apologize for some harsh words you never meant twenty years ago."

"No," I said. "For disappearing. For letting everyone down."

The warmth in his eyes overwhelmed me. "Whenever I think of you, I remember that infuriating kid who sat outside my door for three hours reading my homework. You were there for me, over and over again. I know I'm speaking for every one of your friends when I tell you no one thought you were abandoning us. We were worried sick about you."

"You were there for me when Brian died," I said. "I wish I realized what kind of friends I had when I was fourteen. I disappeared because I didn't think I had friends I could lean on. Everyone leaned on me, not the other way around. Things might've been very different."

"We became close, after Brian," he said. "We're still in touch. We still talk about you." I found myself unable to speak. "You don't need to say anything," he said, holding my hand tight. "But now I'm going to blow your mind. Would you believe Chris is an engineer? He works on nuclear power plants."

"Chris? We're all going to die."

"Scary, right? Andy's in the city managing small bands. I've heard a couple of them and they're as terrible as the ones he kept putting together in school. He's barely scraping by, but he's having the time of his life. Makes you think about priorities. Jonathan and Ann are married, junior high school sweethearts. They're both college professors – he's at MIT and she's at Brandeis. They have three kids. But wait, you won't believe what Daniel's up to."

"Either he's retired with a fortune, or in prison," I said.

"Not even close. He's FBI." I burst out laughing. "How's that for ironic? He's living in DC and getting married in a few months. Jonas lives in Florida where he made a fortune in real estate. He's got five kids and a sixth on the way. He's got to be out of his mind. Sean's living in Seattle with his partner. They have a cute little B&B. We thought about staying there, but it's not really for our demographic. If you take my meaning."

"Sean? Partner?" I stared at him, incredulous.

"Yup," he said.

"Big boobs Sean? You're putting me on."

"Never judge a book," he said with a wink.

"Of all the people I knew, I never would've guessed," I said. "What about Parker?"

"Not everything is sunshine and lollipops," he said. "No one knows where Parker is. He dropped out of school his junior year and rode off into the sunset. I've tried to find him a couple of times but I'm not sure he wants to be found. Kerry was working with his brother at Cantor Fitzgerald. In the tower. His parents still haven't recovered from their loss."

I looked at the floor silently, letting myself remember the quiet leader who never felt intimidated by my popularity with the team.

"Do you know where Ana is?" I asked softly.

"Last I heard, she was married to a marine biologist and living somewhere in Australia," he said. "We don't keep in touch. She wasn't a part of our group. Whatever happened was too much for her."

"I said some terrible things the last time I saw her," I said.

Kelly poked her head in. "Have you invited Nick for dinner?"

"The boss wants you over for dinner," he said. "Better do what she says. I've learned never to mess with her."

"I'd love to, but I already promised Mr. Humber – I mean Ken – I mean I'm not going to get used to this. I promised that guy I'd meet him for a beer later. You should come with me."

"With Ken? Not on your life. He won't leave me alone. He's possessed by the crazy idea I should run for Congress."

"You look the part," I joked. "I'm sure he'll go to work on me if he can't convince you. If he manages to get me on board, I'll sit outside your room until you give in."

"Don't you start, I'm no politician," he said. "Besides, I thought you'd be the one to run for President."

"Me? I've got so many skeletons in the closet, I wouldn't dare run for president of the homeowner's association." We laughed together. "I promised you know who a beer, I've got my family with me, and I've got a few more stops to make. I'm not sure dinner is going to work out."

"Make it a late dinner, then," he said. "Kelly won't take no for an answer. After dinner, you and I are going to make some calls. A lot of people will be excited to talk to you."

"This one," I said to Julia. She parked the car along the curb.

"Nice," Alex said. "At least it's not all Brady Bunch like the rest of the neighborhood."

"There's a for sale sign," Julia said. "I'll see if we can get a tour."

"No, don't do that," I stammered.

She ignored me, getting out of the car.

"It doesn't look like anyone's lived here for a while," Alex said. He came around and opened the door for me when I wouldn't move. "I haven't gotten the chance to talk to you all day. Are you ok?"

"Don't worry about me," I said. "I'm a little freaked out. This house is freaking me out."

"I thought you said you wanted to remember everything," he said.

"You're right, I did say that." I took a deep breath and climbed out of the car. "But I'm still freaked out."

"The realtor is on his way," Julia called to me. "He sounded desperate."

"I can't see anything inside," Jake said. "Watch out, there's dog crap everywhere."

The lawn was a disaster, half-dead and overgrown with weeds. The shrubs were out of control, growing in every direction. Someone had spray painted on the brick. The house looked and felt sad. It felt lonely. It wasn't the place I remembered. Warm and cheerful, the lights always on, the piano echoing off the windows, and the smell of cocoa drifting from the kitchen.

The realtor screeched up three minutes later. "It's a bit of a handyman special, but at the price we've listed it's a steal in this market," he said. "The previous owners had some legal issues, but they're finally able to sell. I'm sure they'll be very flexible." He opened the front door, Julia and Jake following. I was rooted to the sidewalk.

"Let's go," Alex said. He grabbed my hand and pulled. I gave in, walked up the front walk, weeds and grass sticking up through the brick. I closed my eyes when we got close, opening them when we got inside.

"It looks exactly the same," I murmured. "Smaller than I remembered, but it's the same. Just empty."

"I guess you were smaller too," Alex said.

"We used to call this room the lobby because it reminded me more of a lobby in a fancy hotel. We had a big grand piano off to the side there, some couches and chairs on that side, and those bookcases were filled with music books and records. And pictures of us, everywhere."

Jake joined us, but I didn't mind. "The den was through there. We had a big sectional couch, a pool table, and one of those projection TV's that didn't work very well. We had a pinball machine too, but that was downstairs."

"Grandma and grandpa had a pinball machine?" Jake asked.

"This wasn't their house," I said before I realized what I was doing.

"You said you lived here," Jake said. "I don't get it."

"Chill," Alex said.

"Chill what? Is there some kind of secret?"

731

"Alex, it's ok," I said. "When I was around your age, grandma and grandpa worked all the time. I lived here with a friend from the time I was eleven until I was fourteen. That's when I went with Grandpa to Virginia."

"You stayed with a friend for three years?" Jake asked. "Pretty cool friend. You never told me that before."

"I want to show you something," I said to Jake. "Alex, give us a couple minutes, ok?" Alex looked like it was the last thing he wanted to do, but he nodded anyway. I led Jake through the doorway to the basement, down into the darkness. The lights didn't work. I had to feel my way across to the spare bedroom, opening the door to let the light from the small window spill in. It wasn't enough to dispel the gloominess.

"Right over here," I said to him. "This is the room I want to show you."

He peered in. "It's just an empty room." It hadn't changed, unfinished, still a storage room after all these years.

"A lot of things happened in this room," I said. It was too dim to see much, but I didn't need to see. "I want to tell you some things, if it's ok with you. Some of them might be a little difficult to hear, so if it starts to upset you, tell me to stop."

"You're acting weird," he said.

"I was ten years old when I first tied myself up," I said. "I didn't understand what I was doing. The things I used to think about scared me half to death. I imagined being kidnapped and tortured. I thought there was something wrong with me. When I was eleven, I met the friend who lived in this house. He was an adult, not a child. We became very close with each other, and he helped me explore my interest in being tied up."

"Oh shit," Jake said. He took a step back.

"When we started out it was a game, but before long it became a lot more serious. I can't really describe what it was for me, but it went well beyond a sexual desire. I needed to be punished, and even though it was hard for him, he gave me what I needed. He bought the equipment I gave you when I was twelve. We used it, down here, in this room. He chained me up and left me for hours. When I yelled for him to let me

out, he put the gag in my mouth and the clips on my chest. He whipped me hard enough to make me bleed. The strange part is that the punishment helped me let go of all the misery and self-hatred I had bottled up inside. He did it to me four times, each time worse than the last."

"Shit," Jake said in a strangled voice.

"I'm not telling you this to upset you," I said. "I'm telling you this because I want you to know I understand. I want to help you understand yourself. Honestly, I'm not sure I understand it myself. Once I let go of all that stuff I had inside, my need to be punished disappeared. I don't know if it's the same for you or not. It makes me really wonder if there's something more to this for both of us. I should've talked to you after I gave you the equipment, but I wasn't able to have that conversation yet. Heck, I probably shouldn't have given you that equipment in the first place. I'm sorry about that. I want you to know I'm here and you can talk to me."

I listened to Jake's heavy breathing. "He chained you up?" he asked.

"With my hands above my head, like this." I demonstrated.

"And he left you by yourself?"

"For hours," I said. "Overnight."

"What do you mean by clips?"

"Those little things on the chain," I said.

"Clamps," he said in a little voice. "They're called clamps."

"Ok, clamps," I said. "They hurt like hell. Even more when he took them off. He left them on for hours."

"Everything he did is dangerous," Jake said softly. "You're never supposed to leave someone tied up alone, ever. Especially with your hands above your head, there's something with the heart and blood flow, you can pass out. And leaving clamps on too long can cause gangrene."

"You know a lot about this," I said. "More than I do."

"I read on the internet," he said, turning away. "I don't like to talk about it."

"I understand. When I was a kid, I thought I was the only one who had these kinds of desires."

"Lots of people are into it," he said.

"I know this is a lot for you to process," I said. "I just wanted you to know I'm here. I'm your dad, and by definition that makes me clueless. But I might be able to offer you a different perspective on this one topic. Tomorrow, next week, or next year, it doesn't matter. I'll be there when you decide you need me. When *you* decide, not when I do."

"I don't think you're clueless all the time," he said. "*Almost* all the time."

I accepted that as a small victory in the long struggle ahead.

"I found it," I said quietly.

My family stood at my side. Somber and quiet. Julia handed me the flowers.

"He was the one from the book?" Alex asked quietly.

"Yes," I said.

The shrubs were tended, flowers beginning to bloom, and the grass carefully trimmed. I placed our flowers next to the headstone and the small, golden ring on top. We found it attached to a Gollum bookmark in the mall bookstore. It looked like the real ring with elvish inscriptions around the band. Brian would've liked it.

Alex read the inscription out loud.

"Brian Hanley. Beloved son. Born July 5th, 1970. Died July 5th, 1989." Alex shuddered. "He was only nineteen. He died on his birthday?"

"Yes," I said again.

"How did he die?"

I couldn't answer. I didn't want to think about it. I didn't want to think about everything else that happened the last time I was in Newton Falls. The last time I saw my old friends.

"I'm sorry," I whispered.

He wasn't there to tell me it was ok.

Chapter 48

July 8, 1989

When I was a stupid kid, running helped me think clearly, keeping things straight and sorting things out. But I wasn't a stupid kid anymore. I preferred to let my mind go blank. Driving helped empty my thoughts.

Driving was better than running for so many reasons. Running didn't let you wander very far. Eventually, you'd run out of steam and discover you'd gotten nowhere. Driving allowed you to find new roads, make random turns, wandering until you had no idea how to retrace your steps. The best part about driving is no one could strike up a conversation or run along with you. At most, you got the "thanks for letting me go first" wave when you did, or the finger when you didn't. I usually got fingers. Like I cared. The car was my suit of armor, protecting me from the outside world. No one could bother me when I was safely cocooned inside.

When I drove on country roads through Loudoun and Fauquier counties in the middle of the night, I liked cranking down the windows so I could blast noise at the farmhouses. Not music – the angry pounding bass and screaming lyrics dominating this crap didn't qualify as music. *Noise.* That night it was too hot and humid, so I had the windows rolled up tight and the air conditioning at maximum. I woke up around noon, didn't bother to take a shower, put on the same clothes as the day before, and left without grunting at my father. He didn't need to know where I was going or what I was doing. Not that I knew where I was going or what I was doing. I had nowhere to go. I had nothing to do.

I had no one to do it with. I had my car and enough money to buy gas and food for a week. A couple hours ago, I decided my own bed sounded better than some skanky cheap motel, so I headed home. The streets were deader than dead in boring old suburbia, where the sidewalks rolled up at nine and people's idea of a good time was watching the brats play at the fast food hellhole.

My street was just as dead, but not abandoned. Cars occupied all the open spots on the road. Someone *had* to have a party. I didn't give a fuck – people could have a party as long as I didn't get invited and didn't have to hear it. But they went way too far when they parked in my own fucking space in my own fucking driveway. "Fuck!" I yelled in the car. I had to drive halfway down the street to find a parking spot. When I found the offending house, I planned to pound on their door and tell them to move their fucking car before I fucking had it towed out to fucking oblivion, thank you very fucking much.

The only house that wasn't quiet and dark was mine.

I saw lights in our front window. My father never had people over at two in the morning. He never had people over at all. And he sure as hell didn't leave the lights on by mistake – he was a Nazi about the electric bill. I stomped up to the house. The curtains moved when I got close, like someone was watching. I stopped at the bottom of the walkway. The front door opened by itself.

"You're home," my father said.

"You didn't have to wait up for me. I'm not a kid."

"Come inside," he said, sounding exhausted.

"I've got to get this asshole out of the driveway," I said.

"Some people are here," he said.

"Like who? They could've parked on the street." I scowled as I headed inside. "Tell whoever it is to move their car so I can park. Whatever you've got going on, I'm not shaking hands or any of that bullshit. I'm going to bed so you can. . ."

The living room was full of people. People that sure as fucking hell didn't belong there. People that were from another lifetime. People I left behind five years ago. They hardly looked like the people I remembered, but I was still able to tell who each one was.

The muscle bound, crew cut, military type had to be Chris.

The shorter pudgy one had to be Parker.

The tall, thin Japanese guy had to be Daniel.

The one with the long hair and the Aerosmith t-shirt had to be Andy.

The one with the MIT book bag had to be Jonathan.

The two standing in the corner looking like frat boys had to be Kerry and Jonas.

The guy with the earring and the Les Mis t-shirt had to be Sean.

The tall, pretty boy had to be Jeff.

The last person required no guesswork. He looked exactly the same, dressed in a tweed jacket with patches on the elbows.

"Hello, Mr. Welles," Mr. Humber said in a very soft voice.

"You should sit down," my father said. Jeff and Chris slid over on the couch to make space between them.

"What the hell are you guys doing here," I said, standing my ground.

"Sit with us," Jeff said. I rolled my eyes and gave into their bullshit. Sitting between them felt like I was in the back of a car between two big Italian guys being taken to my execution. Everyone looked around the room at each other silently.

"Not much of a family reunion," I said. No one laughed.

"We've come with some difficult news," Mr. Humber said. "Two days ago. . ." He broke down, and I mean he really broke down. Full blown sobbing his eyes out. Jeff put his arm around Mr. Humber's shoulders. I frowned.

Chris sat on the coffee table in front of me. "Nick," he said gently. The soft tone of his voice and pained look on his face didn't seem like something Chris was capable of doing. "Two days ago, Brian Hanley took his own life."

"He what?" I said.

"He committed suicide," Chris said.

"If this is some kind of practical joke, it's not funny," I said.

"It's not a joke," Chris said in that same tone of voice. "I wish it was."

"Come on," I said. "Brian would never kill himself. Besides, his birthday was two days ago. Who would kill themselves on their birthday? You guys are fucking with me. How about telling me why

you're really here? How about if you tell me how you found me in the first place?"

Chris put his hand on my shoulder in a comforting way that I didn't like. "He took his father's shotgun, put it in his mouth, and used his feet and a stick to pull the trigger."

"Why did you have to say that?" Jonathan wailed, starting to cry. *Jonathan.* He was Spock. He never showed any kind of emotion. I was shocked into complete silence.

I would've expected the Chris I knew to fire off a snide remark, but he didn't. "Sorry. You're right. I shouldn't have said that." He stood against the wall, putting his forehead on his arm. "Dammit," he said softly.

"I don't understand," I said.

"Brian's dead, alright?" Jonathan said in a raised voice. "How can you not understand?"

"It's ok man, it's ok," Andy said, hugging him. *Andy.* The kid who was deathly afraid of showing any kind of affection to another boy in case he got labeled as gay.

"It's not ok," Jonathan moaned.

"You guys came all the way down here to tell me this," I said, fury building. "Why? He's not my friend anymore. None of you are my friends anymore. Get the fuck out of my house." They looked at each other. "I said, get the fuck out of my house! Leave!"

"I know it's hard to understand," Chris said.

"What do you know about understanding anything?" I screamed. "Get out! Don't ever come looking for me again! I don't want to see any of you again for the rest of my life!"

Chris grabbed me in a bear hug. *Chris.* He was *crying.* An awful feeling flooded over me. Brian couldn't be dead. He couldn't have done what they said he did. He had to be ok. Because if he wasn't ok, I knew only one possible reason why.

I'd be just as responsible if I pulled the trigger myself.

Chris let me fall back into the couch. "This isn't happening," I murmured.

Jeff sat next to me. "I wish I could tell you he wasn't gone. But it's the truth, no matter how hard it is to accept or believe. Brian passed away two days ago. There's nothing we can do now to change that."

"Why?" was all I could ask.

"We don't know," Mr. Humber said. "We need your help. Brian left a note, but no one can read it. I think it's meant for you."

"For me?" I said woodenly. "I haven't seen him in five years."

Mr. Humber pulled the red book from his bag. The one I gave Brian for his birthday. I felt like I was going to throw up. He handed it to Jeff. A thick ribbon tied around it held a piece of folded parchment with an H imprinted into a small piece of broken red wax. Jeff opened the parchment and handed it to me, the golden paper thick and stiff in my hands. It was covered with small and precise calligraphy, the neat black lettering familiar and alien at the same time.

"You're right," I said. "I'm the only person who can read this."

Why would Brian do this to me? Did he want to torture me for the things I did to him? Running through the woods and writing secret messages to each other was so long ago. He had to be telling me it was my fault. I felt a terrible feeling bubbling up inside, the same one I felt five years ago on a day I wished I could forget.

"Please," Mr. Humber said. "I need to know what it says."

"It's going to take me a little while," I said. "I can't read it without the cheat sheet."

"However long it takes," Mr. Humber said. "If you want to wait until morning, I understand."

"I'll do it now," I said woodenly. "I need my box of papers."

"I'll get it," Dad said.

"Would you like some company?" Chris asked.

"I'd rather be alone," I muttered.

I took the papers to my bedroom, locking the door behind me. Words echoed in my head, words I thought I'd forgotten years ago.

"But I am going to Mordor."
"I know that well enough, Mr. Frodo. Of course you are. And I'm coming with you."

Brian went to Mordor without me.

The cheat sheet was old and worn, smeared from use and being outdoors, but Brian's neat and concise handwriting was clear enough. I focused on the letters, avoiding the words, covering what I'd written with another sheet to keep myself from getting distracted. With each letter, I got faster. Halfway through, I didn't need the cheat sheet anymore. Like I re-learned to ride a bike.

The cover sheet fell away from the finished translation when I picked it up.

To my best friend Nick,

It's been a long time since I talked to you. You probably don't know this, but I tried to find you a couple of years ago. No one knew where you went, and I gave up quickly. I wish I'd tried harder. I need to talk to you so badly. I don't know why. I suppose we don't know each other anymore. I guess we're not the same people we once were. But you were always my best friend and you always will be. I have no idea if this note will ever find you. If it doesn't, everyone will have to wonder what it means.

If you're reading this, I'm dead. It's hard enough to describe how I feel to myself, let alone to you. I can't imagine going on anymore. This isn't a new feeling for me. I've tried to end it a few times before, but I didn't have the guts. I think I will this time. I'm so lonely and I know it's never going to get better.

I don't want you to feel sorry for me. I'm somewhere better now. I didn't do this to get attention, or cry for help, or punish anyone, especially you. I don't want you to feel responsible in any way. None of this is your fault and I won't let you blame yourself. The only reason I got this far in life is because of your friendship. I remember how you saved my life the day we became friends. I remember those three perfect weeks we had together in Maine living like animals, running around wearing armor and swinging swords too heavy for us to lift. I remember how you went along with my strange ideas about the woods. I

remember how you tried to get me to play D&D with your friends over and over again. I remember how you tried to make me have a popcorn fight in a movie theater. I remember how you cut school to look for me when I ran away. I remember what happened that night, and the nights after. I didn't understand it back then, but now I know it was your way to show me how much you cared. Because of those nights, I knew when you told me you'd always be my best friend that you truly meant it.

When you left, I told myself if I had one best friend, I could get another. But it never happened. I had acquaintances – people I could eat lunch or play chess with – but I never found someone like you. Someone I could talk to who would really listen to me. Now, even those acquaintances are gone, scattered to different colleges. No one's left. I have no hope. I know you left for your own reasons. I guessed a long time ago what was going on between you and Jeremy. I'm sorry he hurt you. I wish I could've been there for you when you needed help.

You became someone amazing, popular, smart, and more dedicated than anyone I've ever met. And still, you were my friend. Still, you stopped by my lunch table every day. Still, you hung out with me on Saturday nights when you had your choice of parties. I wish I could've told you back then how much you meant to me.

I have a couple of favors I'd like to ask of you. Please tell my father I want to be buried in Maine, next to the lake. I want to be buried in the clothes and armor. I know they won't fit anymore so just lay them on top of me. I want you to be there. I hope you can say a few words for me. You were always good with words. The red book is yours now. Please keep it safe.

I wish we could have it all back. I wish we could be children running through the woods. Why can't we live in that time forever? I hope you find the happiness I never did. But don't dwell on me. I've crossed the sea on a white ship. You cannot always be torn in two. You will have to be one and whole, for

many years. You have so much to enjoy and to be, and to do.
Your part in the story will go on.
You're the best Sam this Frodo could ever want.
Your best friend in this age and the next,

Brian

I crumpled the translation and threw it in the trash.

We left for New Jersey early in the morning. No one slept the night before, but no one said they felt tired. We stopped frequently to get gas, coffee, use the bathroom, take a break, and exchange hushed conversations. I switched cars each time we stopped. No one would let me drive after the way I came downstairs when I finished translating Brian's note. They only saw fury. They couldn't see the big empty space inside me.

"I was so mean to him," Chris said. "Remember that time we were playing and I accused him of looking at my notes? Paul told me he wanted to go home. You and Jonathan brought him back down. He never came to play with us again. Maybe if he did, we would've become better friends. Maybe things would've been different."

"I saw him," Jonathan said. "In the mall, a week before he did it. I'm sure he was writing that note because he had a calligraphy pen. I was with Ann and we were late to a movie, so I passed him by without saying hello. I should've said something. Maybe we would've talked. Maybe he would've changed his mind. Maybe I could've stopped him."

"Do you remember the day he ran off from school?" Mr. Humber said. "I knew he was getting attached to me in a way that wasn't appropriate, but I didn't take the steps I should've to reset boundaries. He had a personal crisis that morning. I never truly understood what happened. He came to me and asked if he could live with me instead of his father. I explained I couldn't do that. I was his teacher and there were rules. He became angry and ran off. He never spoke to me again on a personal level. I should've pressed more. I made a mistake waiting

for him to come to me on his own. Maybe if I hadn't, I could've helped him. Maybe I could've found out enough to get him out of that house to a place where he could've been appreciated. If I'd done what I should've done, maybe this didn't have to happen."

Everyone had a story, but they were all wrong. Each of them blamed themselves. They had no idea I was the one to blame. I didn't give them a translation of the whole note. How could I? He mentioned what we did and he mentioned Jeremy. I told everyone it was a private note, but I gave them enough information to satisfy their need to know. I told them he wanted to be buried in Maine with the clothes. I told them he didn't want anyone to feel sorry for him. And I told them he blamed his father. I knew it was big lie with bigger implications, but I was terrified someone would look deeper. They might discover just how responsible I was.

I watched the streets roll by as though they were part of a distant dream. These were streets I used to run. Streets I grew up on. Streets I once felt like I owned. Streets I'd worked hard to forget. Streets I never wanted to see again. I was in Newton Falls for Brian and for Brian alone. I had a responsibility to bring the adventure clothes and to pass on the message that he wanted to be buried in Maine. I didn't want to be here. I didn't want to be reminded of that day when my life fell apart.

When Jeremy left, my father tried to take me back to his house. I told him I wouldn't live there. So he got us a hotel room. He tried to drive me to school on Monday. I told him I wasn't going to school there anymore. So he withdrew me and I never set foot in that building again. He told me everyone was calling, trying to find out what happened. I told him I never wanted to talk to any of them ever again. So he disconnected the phone number. He tried to get me to leave the room just to have dinner. I told him I never wanted to see Newton Falls again. So he sold his business and we moved to Virginia. I wound up staying with him even though my mother kept trying to get me to move out to Denver. Living with him was easier because he let me do what I wanted.

"It was Mr. Humber," Andy explained when I asked how they found me. "Brian's dad found the note and started calling his old friends. One of them suggested he call Mr. Humber. Mr. Humber recognized the

writing, so he called all of us to find you. No one knew where you were. He pulled your file at school and found out where they transferred your records. Don't tell anyone – he could get in a lot of trouble."

"Why did he do it? Why did everyone come along?"

"We're your friends," he said.

We stopped at Jeff's house to change into suits and ties. When Jeff came out, I couldn't look at him. It reminded me too much of the award ceremony. Mr. Sheffield was sympathetic, offering to do anything he could for me. But there was nothing to be done. I didn't want his sympathy and I didn't want his help. We squeezed into two cars to drive over to the funeral home. We didn't speak unless we had to.

The funeral home was a place I must've passed a thousand times without noticing. A gold truck, *the* gold truck, was parked out in front. Brian's dad had already decided to bury him in a nearby cemetery, another place I'd probably passed a thousand times without noticing. "I'll talk to him," Mr. Humber said. "Stopping the service would be insensitive to everyone who came to pay their respects. Maybe we can make arrangements to do the burial according to Brian's wishes."

"I'll go with you," I said.

"Why don't you hang out with us?" Chris said. "We're going to see the casket. You should come too." I shook my head but he didn't take no for an answer. He wrapped his arm around mine like he was an escort and led me into the funeral home, the rest of the group following behind.

I'd only been in one other funeral home – the time I was in San Francisco for Amy's service. Everything here was on a reduced scale. Less space, fewer seats, and smaller flowers. Like Brian was less important. The casket itself was on top of a small pedestal below a stage with a microphone. It was closed. Brian's dad, Dick, the asshole himself, was in the back of the room wearing sunglasses. I found that offensive. Mr. Humber was talking to him, but he wasn't moving. Sitting next to him was a frail woman wearing a black shawl and a veil. Even from the front of the room I could see Brian's face in hers. She had to be his mysterious mother who I'd never met in all the years I knew him. I looked away, unable to stand the sight.

OK.

"Ok, alright, let me go," I spat, glaring until they did. They watched me warily, ready to pounce the moment I did something. I brushed something imaginary off my jacket.

"I know how you feel," Chris said gently. "I was angry when Mrs. Sheffield died. It isn't anyone's fault."

"You don't know how I feel," I muttered. "Where do you even come off saying something like that? You don't know anything about me."

"I'm your friend," he said. "We're all your friends."

"You're not my friend," I said coldly. "You never were. None of you."

Chris looked like he was about to say something when Kerry grabbed his arm. "Let it go," he said to Chris. "He needs some space."

I kicked at a flower bed and stomped across the grass around the side of the funeral home, feeling their eyes on me the whole way. All I could see were those sunglasses and the furious eyes behind them. Faggot, they said. You turned my son into a faggot.

I stewed, alone. Mr. Humber found me ten minutes later, leaning against the side of the building next to me. "I tried," he said. "Mr. Hanley would prefer to bury his son locally, not hundreds of miles away where he would be difficult to visit."

"Like he cares." I snorted. "He never cared about Brian before. Funny time to start."

"People grieve in different ways," he said.

"I've heard that bullshit before," I said. "And the clothes?"

"He'd prefer to leave Brian as he is," Mr. Humber said.

"I'll bet he dressed Brian in a football uniform," I spat. "Did you know we used to lie to his dad all the time? We told him we were playing football. It was the only way he'd let Brian out of the house."

"I didn't know that," Mr. Humber said. "I understand you're upset."

"Upset? I'm not upset. Brian asked for a couple of things, and his father acts like a complete asshole. Why would I be upset?"

"He is Brian's father and we need to respect his wishes. I can't imagine what he's going through right now, losing his only son." I snorted, kicking the side of the building. "People are arriving. Please join me inside."

"I don't want to be in there," I said.

"Don't miss this chance to say goodbye," he said gently.

"This isn't the way I want to say goodbye, so it doesn't matter," I said. "I'll go to Maine myself. I'll bring the clothes there and bury them without him."

"I'd like to accompany you," he said. "I'm sure the rest of your friends would as well. We want to be there for you. We all care a great deal about you."

"Sure, right," I muttered.

"I'll make sure a seat is reserved when you change your mind," he said. He tried to put his hand on my shoulder but I shrugged it off. He left me alone. I made myself invisible behind some bushes, listening to the cars pulling up and hushed voices drifting across the lawn. None of them deserved to be here. Where were they when he needed someone?

"There you are," Jeff said. "They're going to start in a few minutes. Mr. Humber said you didn't want to come inside."

"Did he send you out here to change my mind?"

"No," Jeff said. "I came to see if you wanted to talk."

I shook my head. "What's there to talk about?"

"Whenever I was having trouble with my mom, you were always there to talk to me," he said. "I thought I could. . ."

"Help me the same way I helped you?" I interrupted. "I don't need any help. Besides, why would you want to help me anyway? It's not like I'm your friend anymore. I don't know why you guys are bothering. I haven't spoken to any of you for five years. If Mr. Humber didn't steal my school records you wouldn't have even found me."

"I'll never forget how you sat outside my door reading my homework for three hours, even when I screamed at you to go away," he said passionately. "I'll never forget you helping me clean my room, and when I messed it back up you helped me clean it again. I'll never forget how I tried to make you mad that one time with the basketball, but you made me laugh by acting like a puppy dog. I tried as hard as I could to push you away, and still you stuck by me. I don't care how long it's been or whatever happened to make you leave. You're still my friend and you'll always be my friend."

"I only did it because your father paid me."

"What happened to you?" he asked gently. "You're not the Nick I know."

"People change," I spat.

He walked away.

That's right, stay away from me. It's better that way.

The voices died down. I had no intention of going inside, but I didn't want to be stuck in the bushes either. I decided to take a walk. Maybe I could find a convenience store and buy some snacks. I slipped out of the bushes and walked onto the front lawn, glancing at a woman sitting on the steps. I went cold when I recognized her.

"Nick," Ana said.

I let her run up to me, looking at her with all the ice I could muster. "What are you doing here?"

"I'm sorry," she said. "Jonas called me. I heard you were going to be here and I wanted to see you."

"Why? Come to see the freak show?"

"It's not like that," she said.

"Then what is it like?" I crossed my arms. She was silent. "Uh huh, that's what I thought."

"I haven't forgiven myself for what I said to you that day," she said. "I didn't know what to do. I was fifteen years old. You were talking about getting married and running away, and I didn't know how to handle any of it. I never should've reacted the way I did. I've wanted to apologize to you for a long time."

"Yeah," I spat. "You're *so* sorry. I gave you my heart. You stepped on it and mashed it in the ground. Not that it matters anymore. I don't give a shit if you're sorry or not."

"It matters to me," she said. "I loved you too."

"You did? You loved a two-timing faggot? Wasn't that what you called me? You probably spread it all over the school."

"I never told anyone," she said quietly. "Never."

"It doesn't change how I feel about you," I said.

"I've never felt the way I did about you with anyone else," she said. "I would've married you. I would've been happy to spend the rest of my life with you. I'm sorry I hurt you. Every single day, I wake up and I wish I could take it all back. I'll regret it for the rest of my life."

"Forget it," I snapped. "You don't mean any of it. I don't care about your guilt. I was stupid to care about you in the first place. You're a shallow cunt who doesn't give a shit about anyone but herself. I don't have time for someone like you." She had no hatred in her eyes as she walked off. "That's right!" I yelled after her. "Walk away! Get away from me! I never want to see you or talk to you ever again!"

She turned around, tears in her eyes, and left.

It was harder than I thought it would be to keep myself from crying.

I never went into the service and didn't go to the burial. I waited outside the funeral home for Mr. Humber to pick me up. I told him I didn't want to go to Maine anymore. He drove me back to Virginia. We didn't speak for the entire ride.

"Something happened to you," he said when we pulled into my driveway. "Something terrible. Something that's left you angry and bitter. You've been hurt so badly you've forgotten who you are and the person you were intended to be. I don't know what happened, and if you wanted me to know you'd tell me. But you need to know something. You have friends who care about you. No matter how angry you are or how hard you try to push us away, we're not going anywhere. You touched a lot of lives more deeply than you can imagine. When you're ready, we'll be waiting for you. No matter how long it takes."

I got out of the car without saying a word to him. He'd never understand. Everyone needed to stay far away from me. I hurt people who got close to me. I left a wake of permanent devastation behind. I had no business ever trying to help another person. My legacy was a string of ruined lives. I wanted them to stop wasting their time on me. I wanted them to go on as if I'd never existed.

Most of all, I wanted to never feel anything ever again.

Chapter 49

June 10, 2008

I bring the car to a stop. "Everybody out!" I look in the rear-view mirror, the rest of the caravan slowly finding spots behind, in front, and all around. I hear car doors opening and closing, chatter and children's laughter echoing across the valley. The sun is an hour from setting, low in the sky, blazing yellow. It shines through the leaves of the trees, green and verdant, the forest alive with smells and sounds. It lends its life to me. It lets us in.

"Up we go," I say to my boys. They prefer racing up the rocks, honor and glory awaiting the first to the top. Jeff accompanies them – he likes a good rock climb every now and then, and he has the strength and skill to give two teenagers a run for their money. The rest of us take the easier way around the back, tramping through the ferns.

My mother shrieks harmlessly when she nearly slips on a rock. "I should've worn better shoes," she says as an apology, even though she's wearing brand new hiking boots purchased expressly for this occasion. Her idea of being outdoors involves a plush suite at the lodge inside the national park. I think of escorting her up the hill, but Allen steps in to take her hand. I like Allen. He's kind and generous, and he takes good care of her. I see them as two halves of the same person. They were made for each other.

My father pulls a branch out of the way to make it easier for her to get by. It's nice to see my parents cordial with each other, even if they'll never be friends. It took him a long time to acknowledge the pain of losing her to another man, but I think he's learned to accept his

responsibility for their divorce. He's not the type who's ever going to learn how to express much of anything no matter how much is going on inside him, but we've come to an understanding. I know he regrets a lot, and it eats him up inside. I know how terrified he was when he learned I had my own money, certain I would cut him off as completely as I'd cut off my mother. That's not what I want. We're not friends, but we get along. Maybe someday we'll have the kind of father to son talk we should. Until then, the occasional holiday and Sunday night dinner will be enough.

I enjoy spending time with my mother. It was difficult to call her the first time, hearing her voice on the phone after ten years of silence. She made it as easy as she could for me. We get along, maybe not quite on a deep emotional level, but as friends. When I'm in the mood for an intellectual conversation, I turn to her. We spend hours arguing about the economy, politics, history, or whatever new crisis was in the news that day. She tries to apologize for her mistakes, but I don't let her. The only thing that matters is now. I only met her step-son Josh once when we were kids, so we didn't discover what it felt like to have a brother until we were in our thirties. We went skiing in Aspen last winter with his three kids, and even though mine are older by a few years the half-cousins get along famously. We're going to make a tradition of it.

"Doing ok?" I ask Ken, holding up my hand to help him up a ledge. He has trouble with his knees, but he glares at me and refuses my help. In my mind, he is and always will be Mr. Humber, even if I've learned to call him Ken. When I need advice, I turn to him. He will always be my teacher and I will always let him. He has a knack of knowing what to say and how to guide me without ever telling me what to do. One night, I went to sleep at home and sat bolt upright in bed at eleven. I drove all the way to New Jersey, ringing his doorbell at three in the morning. He listened to me in his bathrobe over a pot of coffee while I explained what happened to me. At the end, he nodded without judgement and told me:

"It's nice to have you back, Mr. Welles."

I told him it was nice to be back.

Jeff stays at our house several times a month on his frequent trips to DC. He's given up on his practice and spends his time coaching young

lawyers how to do something better with their skills than chasing ambulances or leeching off large corporations. He's still not interested in politics. He has a conscience, and in politics these days that's more of a liability than an asset. I think he'll change his mind someday, and when he does I'll be there to back his campaign. He brings his children, little Nick and Samantha, giving poor (and pregnant again) Kelly a break from diapers and baby talk. Julia and I love having little ones around the house. It's exhausting, but at the same time it makes our home come alive. Jeff defines what it means to be a super-dad. If his kids don't come out perfect, it will be in spite of him.

I reach the top. Colin is engaged with my boys in a heated debate about some Japanese cartoon. Excuse me – *anime* – he'd be mortally offended if he heard me call it a cartoon. Colin looks like a boy himself, throwing his hands up dramatically while he tries to shake some sense into them. I don't get to see him as often as I'd like. He has his own family on the other side of the country and refuses to alter his practice one bit, even though Jeremy set him up just as comfortably as me. In him, I have the best friend I haven't had since I was twelve years old. We have fun being boys together at the bowling alley, driving range, or amusement park. Our conversations range from innocuous gossip to sharing intimate memories. When I slip back into self-hatred, or when I find myself captivated by a young man I saw somewhere in my travels, he's the one I call. He gets me back where I belong.

Jake notices me watching and gives me a little nod before calling Colin a few choice names. It's a long, slow road with him, three steps forward and two steps back. Somewhere along the way we've forged a quirky relationship uniquely our own. I'm incredibly proud of him. He's a dedicated young man, constantly earning the title of bulldog that Alex bestowed upon him. He's excelling in class, has taken up soccer and lacrosse, and has become a fixture on the technical crew in the theater department. His artwork continues to mature, and I'm looking forward to seeing just how far he can go. I see a lot of the person I was becoming at his age in him, and I see a lot that differentiates him. He's still a teenager. He can go from surly to jubilant and back again in a matter of seconds. We have our share of squabbles and slammed doors, but without those our relationship would be too plastic to be real.

He talks to me about his dreams and he vents his frustrations. Nothing unusual for a healthy father and son relationship I suppose, excepting the frankness of our sexual discussions. He's fascinated by the emotional component of my experiences. While he tells me he wants to go through the same thing one day, he also understands enough about himself to know he's not ready without me needing to tell him. We talk about the differences between fantasy and reality, and the dangers of trusting the wrong person. I'm supportive without encouraging him, because it's not my place to interfere. I'm proud to create a household where he feels free to be a sexual person without fear of recrimination. Not because it excites me in a voyeuristic way, but because sex doesn't deserve all the attention it gets.

"It's a nice crowd," Julia says, standing beside me.

Julia is my rock. When I'm in a storm, I can cling to her and know I'm safe. It would be dishonest to call her my best friend, and I can't say she's the first person I turn to when I need help. We don't share the same interests and we think very differently about many things. But without her, I wouldn't be able to truly experience happiness and joy. It's as though her presence unfetters and amplifies all my good emotions while beating back the bad. Without her behind me, I would fold up like a deck chair. I love her with all my heart and soul, and I know she feels the same way about me. I count myself lucky the universe chose such a perfect person to travel with me as my wife and gave her the strength to stand by me when anyone else would've given up. Her love still baffles me. I can't find other words. The way I feel for her doesn't fit well into language.

Throngs of people are already here and more are still filtering up. I told Jeff I wanted a small and intimate ceremony, but I should've known he wouldn't listen to me. I pick faces out of the crowd, people I've reconnected with over the last year. Chris is here with his wife and young son. He gives me a friendly wave when he notices me looking. I'm still trying to reconcile the grounded, mature, and unexpectedly sensitive guy he's become with the angry boy I knew and liked as a child. Daniel and his new wife make a nice couple. He still has a mischievous streak inside even if he's become a responsible super cop. Jonathan is here with Ann and their three daughters. He wasn't the same

kid I remembered at all. When I visited him up in Boston he didn't stop talking for hours. Andy came alone. He's going through his second divorce and taking it pretty hard, but he's laughing and joking with everyone just the same. He's gone to work on me to support his favorite bands even harder than he used to work on me to play in them. I already agreed. Jonas made it up from Florida without the family. He's having a tough time with the whole mortgage thing falling apart. If he needs me, I'll be there for him like he was there for me on the team. Sean winks at me and gives his partner a kiss. Big boobs Sean. I haven't had the chance to sit down with him yet, but it's going to be one heck of a conversation when I do. Kids are everywhere. Their screams and laughter are appropriate and welcome. A few faces are missing, but I wasn't going to give up on finding them. Parker. Ana. I found my own moment of silence to remember Kerry.

I close my eyes and imagine another face. I can't have him here with me, so I'll have to settle for the small gold ring on a chain around my neck. I carry it around with me all the time. I never take it off. I'm the ring-bearer now.

"When should we start?" Julia asks.

"Sunset," I say. "Just a few more minutes."

My eyes settle on my sweet Alex.

He's grown so tall. His voice broke into a gorgeous tenor, finally ending our fears his singing career would come to a premature end. He's been winning progressively larger roles in school productions, his crowning achievement being Thenardier in the big spring production of Les Miserables. It's only a matter of time before he gives in to the pressure to chase real roles with real companies. I'm looking forward to a new career as his full-time manager, chauffeur, and accompanist. I'm a long way from playing the way I once did, but it wasn't as hard to pick the piano up as I thought it would be. I find I love playing almost as much as I did as a child, even if I don't have the patience to practice as diligently.

I love Alex deeply. We're as close as two people can be without being intimate. My relationship with him is parental, brotherly, and friendly at the same time. We can't deny the sexual undertones. We hug, we snuggle, and we touch, but neither of us allows it to cross into

shadowy territory. It's not always easy. I succumb to letting my eyes linger longer than they should, snuggling a little closer, or placing my hand close to where it doesn't belong. He succumbs to teasing, reveling in his power to turn me on, and pushing the boundaries of how little he can wear before we both know it's gone too far. We're both cops and robbers at the same time. Sometimes we steal a little, sometimes we step in to enforce the law. I never let it get to the point where it's dangerous, and he's made it clear he wouldn't hesitate to stop things if he ever thought it was. That's our covenant. Without it, we wouldn't be a "we." At first, I wondered if I was living a giant what-if with him, tempted to think I'm exploring what would've been if Jeremy and I had never crossed the line. But we're different people in a different time. And I don't like thinking about what-ifs, because I am where I am today because of the whole package. The good and the bad.

There's someone else here. A spirit maybe, nothing as crass as a ghost. I can feel him sometimes when I come up here on my own. I sit on the edge and look out over the river, feeling the wind in my face and hearing the leaves in the trees. I close my eyes and reach back to touch the boy inside me. When I do, I feel him at my side. He smiles. He calls me kiddo. He runs his fingers through my hair. He tells me I'm doing fine and to get the hell out of here, because there's too much going on to linger in the past. He tells me forever isn't here yet.

"I think it's time," Colin says. I nod. The group quiets down and gathers around on its own, standing in a big semi-circle around us. I open the box at my feet and take out the urn and a heavy granite marker. I feel the warmth around me, the caring, and the love. I know whenever I'm struggling, and I will always struggle, this will be a moment that can bring me back to myself.

"I don't have a lot to say that I haven't already said," I say. "This is a holy place to me, like a temple or a shrine, but neither of those words do it justice. When I was a child, I'd come up here with Jeremy and everything would be ok. Some of the most important moments of my life either happened here or happened because of something that started here. I can think of no better place to end his journey." I pick up the granite marker. "When I wrote these words, I was twelve years old. A young boy, a child. But when I listen to them now, I hear wisdom that

transcends his age. I think we should all listen to the twelve-year-old inside us more often. He or she speaks with a clarity that gets muddied as we get older. Or maybe I'm way too impressed with myself."

They laugh.

"Alex, if you please," I say. He strums his guitar and sings.

> *When I am happy, you are there to share it,*
> *When I am scared, you help me to be brave*

I open the urn and pour out the ashes.

> *When I am in trouble, you protect me*
> *When I am mad, you calm me down*

The ashes fall into the ferns, filling crevices between the rocks.

> *And when it hurts more than I can bear*
> *You are there, to comfort me*
> *To hold me in your arms, to keep me safe*

I give some to Colin. He lets them fly in the wind.

> *When we are apart, you are in my mind*
> *When we are together, I feel like I can fly*

The urn is empty. He'll always be here. Forever.
We sing together.

> *When you are ready, I am waiting*
> *With all my heart, with all my love*
> *Because when is now*
> *And forever*

I will love him until forever comes.

Acknowledgments

I'd like to express my humble thanks to Mac, whose fantastic hand-painted watercolor graces my cover. I'd also like to thank Laura, Colin, Jeff, and Dutch, whose feedback on early versions helped me focus on what mattered. And finally, to Travis, whose support throughout this project made it possible.

Quotations

JUST ONE PERSON (from the musical "Snoopy")
Lyrics by HAL HACKADY
Music by LARRY GROSSMAN
Copyright © 1976 (Renewed) UNICHAPPELL MUSIC, INC.
All Rights Reserved
Used By Permission of ALFRED MUSIC

IT'S POSSIBLE (IN MCELLIGOT'S POOL) (from "Seussical the Musical")
Lyrics by LYNN AHRENS and DR. SEUSS
Music by STEPHEN FLAHERTY
Copyright © 2001 WB MUSIC CORP., PEN AND PERSEVERANCE and HILLSDALE MUSIC, INC.
All Rights Administered by WB MUSIC CORP.
All Rights Reserved
Used By Permission of ALFRED MUSIC

MY UNFORTUNATE ERECTION (CHIP'S LAMENT) (from "The 25th Annual Putnam County Spelling Bee")
Words and Music by WILLIAM FINN
Copyright © 2005 WB MUSIC CORP. and IPSY PIPSY MUSIC
All Rights Administered by WB MUSIC CORP.
All Rights Reserved
Used By Permission of ALFRED MUSIC

SIX STRING ORCHESTRA
Words and Music by HARRY CHAPIN
Copyright © 1974 STORY SONGS, LTD.
All Rights Administered by WB MUSIC CORP.
All Rights Reserved
Used By Permission of ALFRED MUSIC